PORTALS TO WHYLAND

COMPLETE SERIES

DAY LEITAO

- STEP INTO MAGIC
- KISSING MAGIC
- WITHIN MAGIC

Print ISBN: 978-1-9992427-6-3

CONTENTS

Get a Free Ebook and Learn How it All Started!   vii
Foreword   ix

About Portals to Whyland   1

STEP INTO MAGIC

1. On foot and shoes   5
2. Visits   13
3. Getting Real   19
4. Where?   28
5. Communication   42
6. One More   55
7. The Imaginary Pursuers   70
8. Fingers   82
9. The Meaning of Yellow   91
10. A Plea for Help   106
11. Night Revelations   121
12. A Long Way to the Top   137
13. Looking Ahead   144
14. About the Rebels   154
15. Backstabbing   167
16. Time to Turn Around   180
17. Truths and Lies   189
18. Going Separate Ways   201
19. About Sian   210
20. The Final Battles   223
21. Darian and Cayla   236
22. After the End   248

KISSING MAGIC

Prologue 251

1. Thirst for adventure 257
2. An invitation 263
3. The Garden 274
4. A guy where? 284
5. Decisions 288
6. Kyons 300
7. The Tower 310
8. The Village 320
9. Siphoria 329
10. The Junction 342
11. Lights 350
12. Nightmare 362
13. Travel 372
14. The Castle 380
15. Darian and Cayla 391
16. The Ball 405
17. Floating Stars 415
18. Unwrapping Secrets 428
19. The Well 437
20. The Lake 448
21. Understanding 466
22. The Other Castle 478
23. Out 491
24. Resist 508
25. Storm 523
26. The Lost People 530
27. Memories 543
28. Magic 552
29. Light Gardens 565
30. Let's Talk 575
31. Odd Request 591
32. Brothers 611
33. Towers 622
34. Sian 634
35. After the Fall 646
Epilogue 657

WITHIN MAGIC

1. Ice and Dreams 661
2. Challenges 677
3. Luminous 691
4. Breach 705
5. Visions and Gardens 718
6. New Lives 728
7. Gap 736
8. Light Gardens 753
9. Images 764
10. Plans 779
11. Crown 795
12. Secrets 812
13. A Forestglare Ball 828
14. Unmasking 840
15. Complications 853
16. New Plans 865
17. A Note 878
18. Illusions 893
19. Embracing Magic 902
20. Settling Down 914

About the Author 929

FOREWORD

This collection has three books: Step Into Magic, Kissing Magic, and Within Magic.

Step Into Magic is a fun adventure with a 14-year-old protagonist. For more romance and intrigue, you can go straight to Kissing Magic, in which the characters are a bit older and the protagonist is 16.

This is a coming-of-age series, so the characters evolve and grow. Hope you enjoy their journey!

ABOUT PORTALS TO WHYLAND

*N*ever *accept invitations to other worlds from strangers.* When Karina realizes that, she's already in Whyland, a kingdom in another dimension, running for her life, with no idea who to trust.

She came to help a princess defeat a witch, but when both rebels and the king are after them, Karina's only way out might be by using the magic in her power, which she barely understands. To make matters worse, the princess' boyfriend, almost-boyfriend, or whatever, has dubious alliances, and it might be their doom.

Then there's the mysterious Sian, who's intent on conquering the kingdom. He's greedy, cunning, and selfish—and fascinating. And that's the part that complicates it all.

Alternate dimensions, mysterious magic, strange castles, complicated romances, friendships between girls, first kisses, and teen angst. You can find all that and more in Portals to Whyland, a YA portal fantasy series for readers 13 and older.

. . .

This collection contains the following books:

STEP INTO MAGIC (SLIGHTLY ABRIDGED VERSION)

Special, scary shoes become Karina's ticket to Whyland, a kingdom in another dimension, where she agrees to help princess Cayla defeat a witch. But what should be a simple quest gets complicated after a tumultuous meeting between the princess and the guy she loves. To make matters worse, the girls are betrayed and face unforeseen enemies. With no idea who to trust, Karina has to figure out magic she doesn't understand and find a way to save herself, her friends, and even the kingdom.

KISSING MAGIC (YOU CAN START WITH THIS
BOOK, TOO)

Greedy, cunning, and selfish, Sian is not someone to be trusted. Still, when Karina is called to Whyland to break his spell with a kiss, she accepts. But when dark magic creatures from a mysterious castle chase her, she'll have to turn to him for answers and protection. Sian, the guy who says he's no hero. What could go wrong?

WITHIN MAGIC

Troubled by nightmares and trying to reach her beloved, Karina opens a new portal, but ends up trapped and helpless in a sinister ethereal city, where even her mind is not safe. How will she find her way out?

STEP INTO MAGIC

PORTALS TO WHYLAND BOOK I

1

ON FOOT AND SHOES

More than anything, Karina hated to be wrong.

Wait. There was something worse: admitting she was wrong.

But there she was, giving herself a firm reminder: *never accept invitations to alternate worlds from strangers.*

Quite useless advice, considering the odds of this experience ever being repeated. How could thoughtful, logical Karina have fallen for that? How did it even start? Ah, yes… she was looking for something. Something impressive. Something great. Something meaningful. She found something all right, but she was far from sure it was any of those.

As with any journey, it started with a walk.

~

Karina loathed questions without clear answers. Why couldn't everything be simple, like math? Either the answer's wrong or it's right. No *maybes* or *almosts*. That meant she hated history, especially that last stupid test and the embarrassing grade that came with it.

But did it even matter? She wanted to believe that life could be greater than just projects and school and family and classmates and all that day-to-day sameness. Karina stopped. Her feet had carried her some fifteen blocks from her apartment, and she found herself in a busy commercial street with nice shops, cafes, and restaurants. People passed by and the world moved around her while she tried to figure out where she fit in —and where she didn't, unable to find where that emptiness in her chest had come from. It wasn't just her low social studies grades.

Glittery letters on a cardboard spelled "Yard Sale," without any translation. This was an English neighborhood in a French-speaking city. Curious and having no real direction, she followed the sign.

Junk lay over brown, overgrown grass in front of an ancient, decrepit wooden house. There were coats, small objects, boots, and too many shoes to count. Karina wondered who would want other people's smells. Most shoes were somber: brown or black and slightly worn. One pair stood out, though, as the shoes almost looked like they were made of steel, not really for wearing, just decorative objects shaped like silver flats. Out of curiosity, Karina touched them. The feeling surprised her—they were as soft as fleece.

An old woman with a grey ponytail sat on a rocking chair, behind all the stuff. Karina asked her, "Excuse me, what material is this?"

The woman didn't raise her eyes from a brown leather-bound book she was gripping. "I have no idea."

Karina pretended to take a closer look at the shoes just to check if they had any unwanted smell without being rude or obvious. Thankfully there was none.

"They're ten dollars," the woman said, this time standing next to Karina as if implying she should either buy them or stop touching.

Karina put the shoes back on the chair where she'd found them.

The woman stared at her. "Size seven."

That was Karina's size, but she hadn't asked that question and wasn't planning on buying any of that crap. She turned around and walked away.

As she was getting home, she kept thinking how those silver shoes were curious objects. They felt so different from how they looked, and ten dollars was not a lot of money. But used shoes were a bad idea. Those didn't seem used, but who knew? Ten dollars could go for something more important, like… chocolate—perhaps not *that* important. When would she ever see shoes like those again? A disturbing thought crossed her mind. What if someone else bought them? Those precious shoes were a bargain. Someone would probably notice them. This could not be. Karina ran back as fast as she could.

The silver shoes were still there, shiny as ever, reflecting the sunlight. Panting, she gave the money to the woman and grabbed them. "I wanna take these."

They were Karina's now.

Cayla closed her book. She had memorized all the maps of Whyland; every river, every mountain, every major city, and yet, they remained two-dimensional: paintings on paper, still images without much meaning. Beyond the walls of the castle was a world she had yet to see with her own eyes. There was also someone she hadn't seen in over a year. Her chest tightened. She closed her eyes and tried to forget those memories and the pain they brought with them.

Inside, there was still something she wanted to learn. If she pressed her old teacher, sometimes he taught her a little, but only sometimes.

Master Odell raised his eyes. "I see you're finished. We'll pick more books from the library. Any subject you're interested in?"

He seemed to be in a good mood. Cayla's younger sister Ayanna was not in the room, so perhaps that was her chance. "It's not in books. At least not in any we'd find in the main library here. You know much more than you've taught us."

A flash of understanding crossed Odell's face but he sighed. "Some things need to be buried. Forgotten. Or at least that's what your father wants."

"He doesn't need to know."

Odell shook his head. "I serve your father, Cayla."

Cayla gave up and stared at her book. Odell was in a bad mood.

Karina stared at the shoes in her hands. Shoes. Right. Hardly an answer to some great question she was yet to ask. But the shoes were pretty—and different from any she'd ever seen. Despite their shiny finish, they were thin and flexible, almost like real ballet flats, but the sole was thicker, like normal shoes. Mysterious and fascinating, they'd become her special secret, a secret she didn't want to share with anyone, not even her friends.

A knock on the door startled her. Karina barely had time to shove her glistening shoes in the closet before Zoe walked in pulling a trolley suitcase. Overkill for a sleepover, but hey, to each their own quirks. For the first time since they'd become friends, Zoe was early, and Karina's mom must have welcomed her in through the front door.

Zoe spread the outfits onto the bed. "I brought clothes. For you and me. You'll look so good you won't even recognize yourself."

Karina glared at her friend. Zoe was pretty and all, and

Karina didn't usually mind her enthusiasm for fashion, but sometimes she went too far. Plus, Karina was perfectly comfortable with her own non-supermodel looks, wavy brown hair and eyes, thank you.

Zoe cleared her throat. "I meant… you usually look great. You're cute. It's just, sometimes, it's a matter of mixing and matching, trying different things. Not that you have to lend me anything—"

Karina shrugged. "You can have anything you want."

Zoe smiled. "Thanks."

The idea of Zoe borrowing anything from Karina was rather preposterous, as her clothes were so much plainer than her friend's, but at least she didn't want to make her feel bad about it.

Zoe started picking outfits. "We'll look amazing at the dance."

So that was what it was about. Karina had stopped caring about school dances long ago, but there was something sweet in Zoe's endless enthusiasm for them. At least her friend didn't bring her special eyeshadow for brown eyes or come up with a ridiculous suggestion to tame Karina's hair. But it was worse: she started talking about her crush. Karina had always felt like the least qualified person to give love advice, until she figured out that it wasn't so much about advice as it was about listening and nodding. Karina, for her part, didn't have a crush and was glad not to suffer from any of the illogical behaviors associated with the affliction.

Even with an overflowing suitcase, Zoe had somehow forgotten her pajamas. Karina prepared a bed on the floor and told her friend to get a pair from the top drawer in the closet. Not hearing any sound, she turned around to check on Zoe. "Did you find it?"

The girl stood in silence with her eyes fixated on something in the bottom of the closet. Oh, no. Not only had she seen the silver shoes, she stared at them with the greediest eyes. Karina's heart sped up, without any idea where that fear came from. All she felt was that by no means should her friend even touch those shoes.

She tried to divert her attention. "I'll get you the pajamas. We need to sleep."

Without moving her eyes, Zoe asked, "Where did you get those?"

Perhaps Karina could undervalue the shoes and make her friend lose interest in them. "They're yard sale shoes. Too small."

"Can I try them?"

"No!" Ouch. That sounded desperate. Karina tried to change her tone. "I mean… they won't fit you."

"My feet are smaller than yours."

"Yeah, they'll be too big for you."

Zoe bent to pick up the shoes. "I'll see if they fit."

Karina was faster, sweeping them up in her hands "You can't. They… are not mine. They're a cousin's, and she's going to wear them for a wedding."

Zoe rolled her eyes. "I'm sure *your cousin* won't mind if I just put them on for a second."

Karina sat far on the bed and put the shoes behind her back. "No."

Zoe sat next to her. "Karina, you're being ridiculous. Let me try your shoes. I just want to see how they look. Don't give me this fake cousin talk."

"Fine." Lying was pointless. "I'm sorry. These shoes, they're special to me. I don't know how to explain."

"Are you four or fourteen? Still haven't learned to share?"

"I just like them very much."

Zoe sighed. "You said I could have anything I liked from your closet."

"And you said I didn't need to lend you anything if I didn't want to."

Zoe sat down again, looked away for a moment, and then looked back at Karina. "So you're not lending me the shoes."

Well, no, and it sounded terrible when her friend put it like that, but before Karina could come up with anything to say, Zoe seemed to change her mind.

"Fine, you're right." Her voice was calm and understanding. "You don't have to lend me anything if you don't want to. There's no point arguing." She had a big smile. "You'll see."

By Friday the girls' argument had become little more than a distant memory. Karina walked into the school with her friend Tori. With lights down, doors shut, and only the gym illuminated, the school didn't feel like the place she went almost every day. Karina had on a black dress and a small purse, both weighed down by the discomfort she felt in most social situations. But something else was making her feel uneasy. Zoe would be coming around later, but that was normal. The girls found a corner near the entrance stairs and watched people coming in as if on a strange fashion runway surrounded by a handrail.

Karina was debating with herself whether she should nod to people she didn't usually say hi to when a familiar face at the top of the stairs cheered her up.

Zoe.

Karina was about to smile when she noticed what was on her friend's feet: the silver shoes. Zoe saw her surprised look and replied not with shame or embarrassment, but with a smirk. Karina felt hurt, betrayed. More than that, and beyond the feeling of not wanting to share something, she felt as if a part of her had been taken and was being used. A feeling almost as if someone had used her toothbrush or underwear, but this was much stronger.

Karina's first thought was to take back the shoes by force. Zoe would fall from her pride. Those thoughts formed an image in Karina's mind. As the image got clearer, her anger disappeared, replaced by worry. In her mental image, there was blood surrounding Zoe's head, as if Karina's desire had escaped her control and had become an independent monster. The awful image looked real, felt so real it was disturbing.

Zoe was about to descend the stairs. They were just stairs—surrounded by a steel handrail. But the impression remained. Karina ran as fast as she could towards her friend. The image in her head had almost become true; Zoe slipped. Had it not been for Karina holding her mid-fall, the girl would have landed face down from the top of the stairs. Not only had she slipped, the steel handrail had cracked.

2

VISITS

The day was so dark that Karina took longer than normal to wake up. But no. Her oversleeping had nothing to do with the grey clouds covering the horizon. It was exhaustion from the previous night. Zoe walking in the gym was the last clear image in Karina's mind. After that, all memories were a jumbled blur. Lights being turned on, an ambulance coming in, hoards of people surrounding them, the shoes flying off Zoe's feet, the shoes folded inside Karina's purse. The shoes—and what they seemed capable of doing—sent shivers down her spine.

In the kitchen, her mother blamed the poor maintenance of the school but was thankful that everything ended up well and added, "It was nice of you to go with Zoe to the hospital."

Karina recalled that part then. Just a broken leg. It could have been worse. Everyone said it, but she was the only one who understood the full extent of how worse it could have been. She felt guilty, certain that the shoes had played a part in Zoe's fall, although she had no idea how.

She ate quickly, helped her dad with the dishes, and ran back to her room. The shoes were still in her purse, rolled into a small size. Unbelievable that amidst all the confusion there had been time to hide the shoes and nobody— not even Tori— had noticed them. For everyone, it seemed that Zoe had come to the dance barefoot, because she'd never answered anything when asked about her shoes, claiming she didn't remember them, as if a near-death experience could make Zoe forget what kind of footwear she had on.

Enough from the previous night. The cracked handrail gave Karina chills. The shoes were evil, pure evil; succeeded in breaking a leg and nearly breaking up a friendship. Perhaps they should be returned or thrown away. But no, they were too precious for that. Karina would keep them, hide them, and never wear them or let anyone see them again. She placed the purse on a high shelf in her closet.

Despite the wet and gray weather, Karina's parents went out in the late afternoon, after inquiring a thousand times if she was okay, which was dumb since she wasn't the one who'd fallen. As a result, she found herself alone with her thoughts and decided to take a walk for the sake of sanity. A walk. She knew where she had to go.

Karina came to the same street where she'd found the sign. Of course there'd be no yard sale in this weather, but she could at least find the old house. But it wasn't in the street she thought it was—or in any street around it. Wasn't she able to recognize the house without the junk in front of it? Or maybe someone had renovated or demolished it. But there were neither demolished nor recently renovated houses anywhere. Maybe she was mistaken about the street. Maybe her memory was just bad. Maybe—she had no other explanation. The grey clouds were now coming down in minuscule droplets of rain, almost like a thick fog. She felt as if the dampness reached her bones, despite knowing well that it was a scientific impossibility. And she had definitely forgotten where the house was. Bad memory was not any type of impossibility.

~

There was something odd about opening the door and getting home by herself. How strange that not so long before, her parents needed someone to look after her, as if she would set the house on fire, run away, or starve to death. Now, a couple of years later, everything was different. That night, however, she felt lonely and slightly scared. Her mom had left dinner in the fridge, ready to be heated, but Karina decided to make toast instead. While cutting some moldy pieces from the old bread, she noticed that the lights in her room were on. And they changed as if something had moved near them. Karina told her stomach to chill. It could be Zoe. With a broken leg? Karina took a deep breath. What was the point in wondering, if she could walk there and find out? She felt stupid for that, but she actually had to gather her courage, get up, and go to her bedroom.

Indeed someone sat on her armchair: a beautiful woman wearing a long white dress that contrasted with her long, very shiny black hair. Her eyes were black too, deep, like old eyes that had seen many things, which was odd because the woman didn't look older than 35, 40 at most. Karina no longer felt scared or surprised. She had almost been expecting someone like that, not that she thought her parents had changed their minds and hired a cool-looking babysitter, but more that she had a feeling someone would come looking for the silver shoes, and the woman's looks fit the part. Karina's first thought was to run to her closet and check, but that didn't make sense because if the woman had been a thief, she wouldn't be hanging around. Karina wanted to say something but had no idea what.

The woman broke the silence. "You know why I'm here."

Karina thought she did, but thinking and saying are different things, and plus she didn't want to mention the shoes. "Uh, not really…"

The woman stared at Karina for a few long seconds, then said, "The silver shoes you have, I need them."

Karina closed her eyes, heaviness in her chest.

"Don't worry," the woman said. "I won't take them from you. In fact, that's something you should know already. The shoes cannot be stolen."

Or even borrowed. That explained what happened to Zoe.

The woman continued without moving her stare, "Those shoes were created by me, and they are magical, as I believe you noticed. Now you see, you might think magical shoes are a good thing to have, but that's not true unless you know how to use them. I am the only person who can take full advantage of the power of the silver shoes. Sure, other people have worn them and thought a tiny fraction of their power was good enough. But the problem lies in all the power they don't know how to control."

Karina didn't like where the conversation was going. She didn't plan on wearing the shoes again or letting anyone see them, but she still wanted to keep them, just to know that she had something rare and special. "So you're saying I should give you the shoes?"

The woman shook her head. "By no means. I want you to sell me the shoes. In exchange for them, I'll grant you a wish."

Karina almost scoffed but held herself back. The woman looked otherworldly and all, but she didn't look like a genie or anything. "And how can you do that?"

"Well, if I don't grant your wish, I'll be stealing the shoes. As I explained before, and as you witnessed yourself, the shoes cannot be stolen."

"But they're yours. Doesn't that have, like, a different rule?"

"They belong to you now. Now tell me: what is it that you want?"

Did she think Karina was that stupid? But on the other hand, the woman had said it with such conviction and power that it was almost contagious. It was hard not to trust the woman's voice and calm eyes. The idea was fair enough, even if a little crazy. No harm in trying. "World peace."

The woman looked confused and stared down for the first time. She was barefoot. "No, no, no, you have to wish for something for yourself."

"Why? That's a good wish."

"It is. But you see, you cannot mess with other people's free will."

Oh well, that meant there would be no new era on Earth thanks to her. Still, she had to protest. "But you said I could wish anything."

"I said you could make a wish, and I forgot you people in this world don't know how to make wishes. Now wish something for you."

That meant ending poverty and pollution were out of the question. Karina had an idea. She almost hated herself for the stupid, silly thing she was about to ask, but it was the only thing she could think that would not affect other people, and her conscience was clear that she had tried to wish for something more important. "I… I would like to be popular. Not necessarily in school, but be recognized, I guess."

The woman sighed. "You see, that's still about other people, because you want to change their perception of you."

Karina didn't agree. "No, people will perceive me as popular if I'm different, so the change is in me."

Again the woman thought for a moment before answering. "Yes and no. Right now what you want is only to change their perception of you. Think of something else, quickly, because my time's running out."

Karina waved her hands. "What can I wish? Everything I come up with you say doesn't work."

"I can't tell you what to wish, or I'd be wishing for you. Listen, I don't have any more time here. Let's do this: I'll come back tomorrow evening. I'll think of another way to buy the shoes from you. Ah, the shoes—try not to wear them. Keep them safe. There are other creatures in many worlds who want them, and not all of them are good. They can't steal the shoes from you or take them by force. But that doesn't mean they won't try."

Karina gulped at the thought of evil creatures looking for her and the shoes.

The woman continued, "I'll be back tomorrow. I have to go now."

Instead of disappearing in a cloud of smoke or flying out of the window, the woman simply walked to the front door and left. Perhaps she was just a great actress playing a trick, but then Karina noticed there was some sparkly dust floating on the place the woman had been seated. The woman—she had forgotten to ask her name.

3

GETTING REAL

Slowly, the sense of reality came back to Karina. Sparkly dust. Yeah, that was from blinking or whatever. Grant a wish. Was Karina still at the age of believing in fairy tales? She was a normal, logical person. Most fairy tales she knew were from a time when she had no word on the kind of entertainment assigned to her.

I want to be popular. Really? No. Really? That was the cherry on top of her stupidity. How could she have fallen for such crap? Thankfully she didn't sell the shoes for an empty promise. Wait. Did the woman have the nerve to steal the shoes right under her nose? Karina hurried to the closet and picked up her purse. The shoes were still there. What had this visit been all about then? Maybe Karina was just tired and seeing things, but what troubled her most was not having visions, but believing what they said. She went back to the kitchen, finished her toast, then returned to the bedroom, put on her pajamas, turned off all the lights, and lay on her bed. If she was going to believe in fairy tales, she'd better sleep before nine.

While midway on her journey between being awake and asleep, Karina heard what seemed to be something heavy falling in her bedroom. The sound would have startled her, had she not had enough of weird stuff and decided just to convince herself she was dreaming. Then she heard girls' voices.

"Ouch."

"It's all dark in here. I didn't think it'd be like that."

"Ayanna, you weren't even supposed to come. We need lights."

"We can try to find them."

"No, I'll take care of that."

"Cayla, you're not supposed to!"

"Shhh. Nobody will know about it."

"That's so cool."

At this point, Karina had the notion that she was awake and the voices were in fact in her bedroom. Her eyes were still closed in the hopes the voices would fade away on their own, but instead, they only got clearer and more real, to a point she could no longer hold her curiosity and had to look. She opened her eyes just enough to see without being noticed. A strange, orange glow illuminated the room. Two teenage girls stood near the window, reminding her of the woman she had previously seen, but dressed in simple green and orange summer dresses. Karina's study lamp lay broken on the floor.

This was getting to be too much. Arguing in her room was one thing, but starting to break things? No. Karina sat up. "Hey, what are you doing here?"

The girls looked surprised and scared. The oldest composed herself quickly, then walked to Karina and bowed.

"Our apologies for disturbing your sleep and breaking your, um, *thing.*"

The younger girl hesitated at first, then also bowed. Their formality was artificial and almost comical. Still, Karina was so puzzled at having more strange visitors that she just kept listening.

The oldest girl continued, "My name is Cayla. I'm a Whyland Princess. This is my little sister Ayanna."

Ayanna rolled her eyes. "Little sister?" She then turned to Karina and said, "Whyland princess as well. And your name is?"

Cayla pushed her sister back. "I ask." She turned to Karina. "Who are you?"

Karina just stared in amazement. After the phony genie, now it was time for two princesses. Special shoes can really make one feel important. In the dim glow, all she could see was their shapes, their dresses, and their dark hair. The situation was too strange to be real but too real to be a dream. She didn't know what to make of this visit and had no idea where that light was coming from.

Karina looked around puzzled. "What's with the orange glow?"

The room fell dark.

"What orange glow?" a voice asked in the darkness.

Some nerve these girls had. The light from the window would have been enough to make shapes distinguishable in the dark, but not right after a light had been turned off. Still, Karina knew her room well enough to walk up to the switch on the wall.

Now clearly visible for the first time, the girls were simply two normal looking teenagers. They both had dark hair but looked different. The older girl, Cayla, seemed about fifteen or sixteen, wore a beige dress and had sharp facial features. In a plain blue dress, not green, Ayanna had a pleasant round face with bright eyes. She seemed around twelve.

"What are you doing here?" Karina asked.

Ayanna jumped ahead and talked fast. "We're really sorry. We didn't mean to disturb you. It's important. We need your help. It's the sh—" She noticed her sister's stare and looked down.

"Continue," Karina said.

"Right." Ayanna looked at her sister, who nodded, then took a deep breath and started, "Sometime ago, a day or two, Lylah, the witch, came here." She almost stumbled over her own words as she went without pausing to catch air. "We think she came here, to this room, and talked to you. We think she wanted her shoes. We think you still have them. And if she gets them, it is bad, like, really bad—the end of the world." Then she breathed again.

End of the world? A day before? That wasn't making much sense. The girl's fear and urgency were probably contagious, because Karina felt a chill in her stomach as she sat on her bed.

Cayla crouched in front of Karina, looking right in her eyes. "Do you still have the shoes?"

"Yes." It was no occasion for lies. "But, no. I mean, the only visit I received was tonight, and she didn't seem to be a witch. I mean, I don't know. But still, it was a little less than an hour ago, not yesterday."

Cayla's eyes widened. "The time difference. It's greater... So you're saying she came tonight?"

"Yes. But, I'm not sure she's this witch you are talking about. She seemed nice."

Ayanna rolled her eyes. "She had to seem nice! She's cunning."

"We followed her path to get here, so we know it was her," Cayla said. "Was she really convincing?"

Spot on. Karina nodded. She remembered with embarrassment her delight at the opportunity of making a wish. But one thing bewildered her. "If she's evil, why didn't she take the shoes?"

Cayla snorted. "Whatever protection she placed on them is backfiring."

That made sense. "She said she's coming back tomorrow evening."

"She'll have a plan by then," Ayanna said, sounding scared.

Cayla paced back and forth as she ran her hands through her long black hair. "Yes, but that will give us plenty of time to act. If she's coming one day from now, and if one hour here is a day and a half back home, that should give us—"

"Over a month, in whatever you are thinking." Karina had no idea of which time difference they were talking about, but she was sure that if one hour equaled one and a half days, one day minus one hour equaled 34 and a half days.

"Right," Cayla said, apparently not pleased at the interruption.

"It can't be that much," her sister said.

Cayla scratched her chin and looked down, addressing no one. "It seems right, I think. We'll have to ask when we get back, but if we have at least one month, we'll be able to beat Lylah."

Things were getting clearer now. Karina got up and asked the dreaded question, "Is it the shoes you want?"

Ayanna shook her hands in front of her. "We don't want the shoes! They're evil."

Well, yeah. Karina knew that, but then she was confused as to the reason the girls were there. "What is it that you want, then?"

Cayla took a deep breath. "I'm gonna try to explain this from the beginning. That's why we came here." She tucked a strand of hair behind her ear. "Lylah is very powerful—"

"I get it," Karina interrupted. "She wants the shoes. You're saying she can't have them, so I won't give them to her. Does that solve your problem?"

Ayanna shook her head. "She'll find a way to get them. You'll be in danger, and us too."

"She can find you," Cayla added. "Then she'll steal them from you, or worse, make you give them to her. Next time she might not be nice about it."

Karina sat on her armchair and rested her head on her hand, with a slightly sick feeling in her stomach. Something didn't sound right in this story. The girls seemed fine, maybe a little annoying, but certainly not any of the so-called evil creatures that would come looking for the shoes—if it was true that evil creatures would come looking for the shoes. Unknowingly Karina still believed in what the woman had told her, and she was getting confused.

"Listen," Cayla said. "You don't want to keep those shoes; they'll only bring disaster into your life." She knelt and took one of Karina's hands in hers. "Lylah wants to take control of my father's kingdom. She is already gathering followers, but without the shoes, her plans can't go very far. My father has a strong army and can defend our people. But with the shoes, she'll be invincible. And there's more; with the shoes, she'll be able to cross over to different worlds easily, and that'll allow her to expand her dominion all over the universe. That means even the very world you live in might fall under her dark reign."

That sounded scary, but perhaps over-the-top, exaggerated scary. And something didn't make sense. "She just came. I mean, she just crossed over, didn't she?"

"Uh, yes," Cayla squinted. "But I think it would be different then. She would have power."

Fair enough. "And what do you want me to do?"

"Help us destroy the shoes," Cayla answered.

As Karina feared.

"You need to come to our father's castle," Cayla continued. "From there we'll set off. I'll help you, don't worry."

"Me too," Ayanna said.

Cayla scowled.

Did Karina hear right? "So, you mean, I have to go to your, uh, kingdom, place or whatever?"

Cayla blinked slowly and nodded. "Yes, you need to go to our kingdom. It's in a different vibrational frequency, so you can call it another world or dimension, for lack of a better definition."

Karina had a big smile. The idea of different parallel worlds was not that impossible in scientific terms, and if she could see it, she could perhaps try to understand the logic behind it. Why hadn't the girls mentioned this earlier?

Cayla returned her smile. "So, do you agree to come and help us?"

Karina shrugged. "Yeah, I think I could make, you know, the effort."

The right thing to say would have been "of course!" but Karina didn't want to sound too eager. The girls looked at each other, seeming hopeful and relaxed for the first time. Karina was also happy and excited, but suddenly, the thought of leaving her room in the middle of the night bothered her. "Wait... do you mean, now?"

"We can't waste time," Cayla replied.

"How long is it going to take?"

The girls looked at each other, and Cayla answered, "In our world, about a week or two, we think."

"Are the shoes that complicated to destroy?"

Ayanna opened her mouth to speak, but closed it when she noticed her sister's look.

Cayla answered, "Yes, a little complicated, but nothing we can't manage. But if she came yesterday, it means that a few days in our world will be just a few hours here."

That was true. What if not? Maybe the whole time difference talk was a way to convince Karina to go. Still, curiosity itched to the point of being unbearable.

Cayla insisted, "You'll be back in a few hours. We need to hurry."

"How will we get there?"

"Through the portal."

Karina was puzzled, and Cayla added, "It's hard to explain, you have to experience it."

Curiosity won in Karina's heart. A few hours could never

hurt her. It would be like dreaming. Some cushions under the blankets would hopefully fool her parents in case they opened the door. All she had to do was get dressed and pack. From her wardrobe, she pulled her backpack, threw the books and notebooks on the floor, then realized it could be almost a week. "Can I bring a suitcase?"

"What for?"

"Clothes."

"We'll lend you some. Bring only what's absolutely necessary."

Karina packed socks and underwear and the small purse with the shoes. She ran to the bathroom for her toothbrush, face wash, moisturizer. Should she take shampoo, conditioner?

"Hurry, we can't take long." Cayla's voice came from the bedroom.

Fine, no shampoo then. Back in the bedroom, Karina changed into jeans, a t-shirt, and tennis shoes. A good thing Karina was not Zoe, because for her, the strictly necessary would never fit into one small backpack. It was better this way; she felt light and free. Very light indeed—she felt as if she had no abdomen and if the floor below her was about to collapse. Was she being brave or insane? Well, she could always justify her decision with a perfectly logical desire for scientific inquiry. No one could argue against that.

Karina took a deep breath. "I'm ready."

She realized she had no idea how they would "travel" and wondered if a door would open in her room, if her mirror or window would become a portal, or if a spaceship would appear outside.

Cayla smiled, looked at Karina and asked, "What about the shoes?"

"They're here, do you want to see them?"

"No!" Both girls said at the same time, as if the shoes were made of some kind of infectious material.

"Fine." Karina felt a little offended and thought they were exaggerating, but at the same time regretted having ever touched them.

Cayla walked to the window and put one of her hands on it, holding her sister's hand with the other. Ayanna extended her free hand to Karina, who turned off the light then walked carefully to where the girls were and took the younger girl's hand.

"Close your eyes and hold tight," Cayla told her.

Both girls had their eyes closed, but Karina kept them slightly open, just enough to try to see what was happening in spite of the darkness. But nothing was happening yet. Again she wondered if it was a big scam, but what would be the goal of it if they didn't even want the shoes?

"Now close your eyes and relax," Cayla said.

Karina closed her eyes a little more so that even her short eyelashes clouded the small horizontal slit from which she tried to see something incredible.

"Can you close your eyes please?" Cayla insisted, this time sounding annoyed.

Karina looked at Cayla, figuring she would be staring at her, but no, her head was down. Since the girl insisted and nothing was happening anyways, Karina shut her eyes.

Immediately she lost balance and almost fell. She would have let go of Ayanna's hand if it weren't for the girl's firm grip. Through her eyelids, she felt strong flashes of light and didn't dare open her eyes. Her body felt no movement other than her first loss of balance. Maybe the older girl was pulling the light trick again, but a lot stronger, like daylight at noon, except that it flashed. After a few seconds, the flashes stopped, and just the feeling of being under direct sunlight remained.

4

WHERE?

Karina heard footsteps and, for the first time, started to believe she had actually traveled. Ayanna let go of Karina's hand and she assumed it was safe to look. In spite of the daylight, they were indoors, in a very tall but not very large, circular empty room with dark blue walls. Blue, not like painted blue, more like marble or rather some opaque blue stone she didn't know the name. The walls were smooth, with no apparent division between blocks. Sunlight came through a whitish, semi-translucent ceiling.

A blonde woman came running in from what seemed to be a hallway. "My girls!" She hugged Ayanna and Cayla, each with one arm. "What took you so long?"

"We were there for just a few minutes," Cayla answered. "The time gap is bigger than we thought."

"I see. I was so worried."

The woman didn't seem very happy to see Karina. She wore a loose dress that was not loose enough to hide her big baby bump. She looked too young to be the girls' mother, but then, perhaps people in this world aged differently with all the time difference and stuff.

A tall, thin, bald man with a long gray braided beard, wearing a long robe, came into the room. He had wrinkles, so people aged, and yet, there was something youthful about him. Odd.

He turned to Karina and the girls. "Follow me."

They walked through a hallway with green walls and that same whitish translucent ceiling. The floor seemed to be made of wood, but it was greenish instead of the usual brown tone Karina was used to. Ugly abstract paintings with colored lines and circles decorated one wall. Karina's poor understanding of art seemed to be universal. When they got to a big, green wooden door, the bald man led them into a room.

When the girl's mother was about to enter, the man blocked her—"Not you."—and closed the door.

"Nia's pregnant," Cayla whispered, as if it wasn't obvious and as if it explained why she was left outside.

Karina shrugged.

Cayla continued, "She can't have strong emotions."

Karina nodded, not sure if she understood. She looked around to make sure she was really in a room, not a roller coaster. Fine, it was a room in another dimension, which was super awesome. For her, not for the pregnant woman left out.

They all sat at the table. The bald man asked them, "Do you have the shoes?"

Karina took a second to realize that the question was for her, and then she nodded while a shiver ran down her spine.

"Can I see them?" he asked.

Karina took a deep breath. She hadn't really given much thought to the fact that destroying the shoes was the price for her otherworldly visit. She opened her backpack, took out the small purse, and opened it.

As she was about to take out the shoes, the bald man interrupted. "That's fine. They are real." He looked at the girls. "Well done."

Awesome. Karina was the one giving up unique shoes and the opportunity to make a weird wish, and the girls were the ones getting the credit.

The bald man with the long braid coming out of his chin then turned to her. "What's your name?"

Some attention at least. "Karina."

"I am Odell. I teach Ayanna and Cayla. You are a very brave girl to come all the way from your world to help us. We appreciate this very much."

That was getting better. She smiled. "Thank you."

"No need to thank us. Now, you'll need to rest. You'll set on your journey tomorrow."

Did Karina hear right? "Journey?"

"To destroy the shoes."

That sounded exaggerated, but she didn't want to protest because going on a journey sounded cool.

Odell looked at all girls attentively. "You'll travel at night, and you'll go on foot, it'll draw less attention."

Cayla squinted. "That'll take days."

As much as Karina didn't want to ask, she had to, because she wasn't following the conversation. "Where exactly are we going?"

Odell looked at Cayla. "You didn't explain to her?"

"You told me to bring her as fast as possible. That's what I did."

"You took hours," he said.

"It's the time difference. We were there for about fifteen minutes only."

Odell raised his eyebrows. "Really?"

His surprise seemed somewhat fake, to the point Karina again started to think that they were all actors fooling her. But if that was the case, at least the production was first class.

"That's even better then," Odell continued. "I'll redo my calculations."

They seemed to have forgotten Karina's question, so she had to repeat it, "And… Where are we going?"

"Of course. You haven't been told." Odell turned to Karina. "Those shoes were made by Lylah, and only her magic can destroy them. You'll have to go to her dwelling."

"So we'll need to bring the shoes to the scary witch who seems nice—the one who can't have the shoes?"

"Yes," Odell replied, a weird smile on his face. "But all you'll have to do is throw the shoes in her fire, and that can be done very quickly."

Karina thought she had heard something like that somewhere. "Fire? You mean like the crater of an active volcano in her land?"

Odell stared at her as if she was crazy. "That would be very hot—and dangerous. But no, it's nothing like that; it's her fireplace. That's where her magic is."

Karina almost face-palmed herself. Of course a volcano crater would be incredibly hot. Now, where was she getting those ideas? The real plan made a lot more sense.

"We can't waste time," Odell continued. "You'll leave tomorrow afternoon. I'll provide you with supplies."

"Who's coming with us?" asked Cayla.

"We cannot compromise this mission. Nobody can know about it," Odell replied.

Cayla asked, "So I'm going alone with Karina?"

"I'm going to go too," Ayanna said.

Odell nodded. "Yes, you three are going."

Cayla exhaled. "I'll have to take care of her?"

Ayanna frowned. "I'm not a baby."

Odell got up. "We'll meet again tomorrow. For now, rest."

Karina followed the older girl to the end of the hallway and stairs. On the upper floor, she had the impression she was above the hallway where she had just walked. But how could that be, if downstairs sunlight came from the ceiling? On this floor too, the ceilings looked the same translucent white from which light came through. She figured she was tired and mixing directions. Well, of course. She needed to sleep—too much weird stuff for a single evening, even though it was no longer evening. Cayla led her to a room with a normal double bed, complete with pillows and covers, which was a relief, because one could never guess how people slept in other dimensions.

Cayla stood at the entrance. "I'm right next door. Call me if you need anything." She closed the door and left.

Karina was left in that room with no idea how to call the girl or anyone else if she needed, as there was no phone by her bed, which made sense since she was not in a hotel, and they probably didn't have phones anyway. And how was she supposed to sleep when she was in a whole new dimension? She looked around. There was a narrow door in the room. She opened it, and it led to a bathroom. A pleasant surprise, even though the toilet bowl was a hole in the floor, and didn't seem to have any flushing mechanism. A small egg-shaped bathtub stood in one corner. She would ask about the bath later. Karina opened her backpack and realized she hadn't brought any pajamas. She remembered Cayla telling her to bring only what was strictly necessary. Right. Her mental grumbling stopped when she noticed a shelf with some nightgowns made of silk or something like it. They smelled clean and Karina slipped one on.

Once under the covers, she closed her eyes. The sheets or whatever were soft, but she had no idea what they were made of. Well, to be fair, she had no idea what her normal covers were made of, except maybe for cotton or fleece. Here she had many thin layers that were like a mix of those two kinds of fabric. Cozy. That ceiling was very bright, though. She wondered if she would be able to have a decent sleep. But despite the light, her eyes closed, and she started to doze off, until a sudden fear woke her. She had to check the shoes. As she got out of bed, the room was much darker than before. Had she slept that much?

She opened her backpack and took the purse. The shoes were still there. She lay down again, this time with the purse by her side and the straps around her wrists.

Karina woke when it was still dark. She turned sideways to look at the clock, but there was none. On the other side, no light came from the window, in fact, no window, only a faint glimmer coming from the ceiling. Of course, she was not in her room. There was a shadow on one of the chairs. Karina grabbed her purse tight and almost screamed, thinking Lylah was visiting her again, but then she saw a glimmer on long blonde hair.

"Did I scare you?" It was the blond woman from before.

Obviously. Was sitting in people's bedroom a local thing? "No. I mean, not you. I… I thought it was Lylah."

It was probably dawn because the room was getting lighter. The woman narrowed her eyes. "I'm Nia. Didn't you see her?"

Meaning that confusing the two of them was really stupid. Fine. But it was dark. "Yes, I saw her. Wasn't that the reason you sent the girls?"

Nia's expression darkened. "I didn't send them anywhere."

Of course. Anyway, Karina hadn't meant "you" as *you,* but still.

The woman sighed and continued, "I think they are too young to be risking their lives." She looked at Karina from head to toes. "And so are you."

Karina gulped at first, but then realized that the woman was probably just scared because she didn't know how simple the plan was. "I'm not risking my life," Karina explained. "They have it all planned; we just need to throw the shoes in her—"

Nia's horrified expression meant she had said too much. Way too much.

The woman got up. "Throw the shoes? Where? In Lylah's

fire, I suppose." She put her hand in her heart and took short deep breaths. "Do you by any chance have the slightest idea of the danger of going into her dwelling?"

"No," Karina mumbled.

"And yet, you think it's a good idea to give it a try. You think it's a good idea to put my girls in such danger."

"I… I don't know anything, I just came to… I'm just trying to help your daughters."

Nia stepped back. "They're not my daughters. But that doesn't mean I would ever agree to send them on a suicide mission."

"Suicide?"

Nia raised her eyebrows. "Well, do you think you can just sneak into her fortress?"

"No. I mean… Fortress?"

Nia put her hands on her waist. "Where do you think she lives? A little house in the woods, without any protection?"

As silly as it sounded, that was exactly what Karina had imagined. "I…"

Nia got closer to Karina and stared at her. "It's a fortress, better protected than any castle on Earth."

"We're still on Earth?"

"Don't change the subject."

Karina waved her hands. "It's not my fault. I didn't plan anything. I was sleeping, the girls woke me up, they asked for help, and I came. That's it."

Nia pointed her index finger towards Karina. "That's exactly it. They are only going because you are going."

"And what do you want me to do?"

"Go home."

"How?"

"The same way you came: through the flowing tower. I'll take you there, and you'll go. That's the best thing to do."

That was a little unfair because Karina still hadn't had the chance to see anything outside the castle. She was also afraid of going back home and being visited by some kind of evil creature, but at that moment what Karina was most scared of was the evil or perhaps not evil creature standing in front of her. Broad daylight came from the ceiling. Karina closed her eyes. "Fine. I'll come with you."

She took her backpack, put her clothes inside it and didn't bother changing because she figured a nightgown was a fair exchange for bothered sleep and a frustrated visit to an alternate world. The saddest part was saying goodbye to any hope of brave Karina saving the world. But if brave Karina could not even confront a pregnant woman, what chance did she have against a powerful witch? As they walked to the door, it opened, or rather, Cayla opened it. She was yawning, rubbing her eyes and squinting.

"Did you call me? I thought I heard something." She noticed Nia. "What are you doing here? Why are you two awake?"

"We were talking," Nia answered, sounding a lot less furious than a couple seconds before.

Karina bit her lip, torn between asking Cayla to help her get away from that crazy woman or acting like a good abductee and staying quiet.

Cayla looked at Karina and squinted as if to check if she was seeing well. "Why are you holding your backpack?"

Karina opened her mouth, but no sound came.

Nia answered instead, "I was going to take her for a walk."

"Oh. You don't need to carry all your stuff," Cayla said.

Karina again wondered if she should tell the girl what was going on, but Nia settled the matter. "To the flowing tower. Back where she came from."

"But you can't!" Cayla protested. "That's our only chance."

"According to whom?" asked Nia.

"My father and Odell."

Nia shook her head. "I don't like Odell, and I don't trust him."

"I do. And this is my chance to prove what I can do."

"You shouldn't have to prove yourself!"

Cayla was very serious. "If I am going to rule Whyland, I need to prove I'm capable."

Nia snorted. "Stop wasting your time. You're not going to rule anything."

"Who's going to rule then?"

Nia pointed to her belly.

Cayla stepped back. "You want to keep me from doing my duty in order to make way for your son instead?"

"You are accusing the wrong person. I'm only thinking about your safety. You don't need to go on a dangerous mission just to prove yourself. Let Karina go back home and take the shoes with her."

"But then Lylah's going to get them!"

"What's the difference? Do you prefer to deliver them in person?"

"At least then we'll have a chance."

Nia crossed her arms. "Oh, you want a chance to get killed?"

Karina wondered when they would ask for her opinion, not that she had any yet, but being ignored on a matter that concerned her was not very pleasant.

Cayla looked down, as if thinking, then stepped closer to Nia and took her hand. "Nia, please. Don't try to stop us. You know you can't. I'll tell my father. I'll tell Odell. You'll only get in trouble, and we'll go anyways."

Nia pulled her hand and resumed her menacing stance, this time directed at Cayla. "You think I can't stop you?"

The girl seemed more concerned than intimidated. "Even if you can, please, let me go. Let me destroy these shoes. I know we can do this, and that it's for the best."

Nia turned to Karina. "You. What do you think? Do you

think it's worth risking your life for a crazy plan that doesn't even concern you? That you know nothing about?"

Karina wished she had made up her mind earlier, because she wasn't sure what to say. Brave and craven Karina battled in her head. In the end, neither won. There was another, stronger contender: curious Karina. "I think we can at least try."

Nia looked shocked as if she had never expected Karina to decide to stay. Ha! Got that wrong.

"You want to get killed? Get killed then," Nia said.

Karina wondered how to answer, but Cayla beat her to it. "No, we're trying to do the right thing. Nia, if you are doing this because of us, because of our safety, please stop. Let us do it. It's my life, I have the right to do what I want with it."

"You're both too young to decide. This is wrong. Odell is a liar. You'll only see it when it's too late."

Cayla hugged her. "Thank you for letting us go."

That was the opposite of what Karina had understood, but whatever.

Nia didn't respond to the hug, but she let the girl finish, then said, "As for Ayanna, by no means will I let her go."

Cayla shrugged. "I don't want her to go either. It's Odell that insists."

Nia took a deep breath then said, "I'll deal with that." She then narrowed her eyes and looked at both girls. "I might not see you before you go. And probably not after. Just remember I warned you." She walked away while her words hovered in the air.

Cayla didn't seem bothered by her confrontation. Or was it a conversation? She asked, "You didn't take her seriously, did you?"

Well, in a way, yes. Karina had no idea who she was supposed to listen to anymore. But the girl was so cool about it, Karina thought she could be just as nonchalant. She shrugged. "Nah."

"I knew you'd never believe such nonsense."

Karina cleared her throat. "Of course not."

Cayla yawned. "I'm glad you woke me up. We need to get used to staying up at night."

Night? But sunlight came from the ceiling. Perhaps it was summer and nights were quite short. "Isn't it morning already?"

"I guess it depends if you count four o'clock as morning."

Before Karina pointed the ceiling, she realized this light had gone off and on too quickly to be the sun, so it had to be something else; something she didn't quite understand, and she felt really dumb for her assumption. At least she could still hide her dumbness. "I... just... I think I'm getting the hours mixed up."

Cayla laughed. "No wonder. Do you want to eat something?"

Food? Since the sleep had been interrupted anyway, that was a great idea. "Sure."

"Let's go to the kitchen then."

Cayla walked toward the door and Karina followed, but then she remembered the reason she was there to begin with and quietly returned to pick up her purse with the shoes. Again she looked inside to check if no one had stolen them, because who knew what kind of evil creature could be lurking in her bedroom. Oh no, that was a terrible thought—she wouldn't be able to sleep there anymore. Then she remembered it was Lylah who told her about the evil creatures, so she was probably lying. But then, if Lylah was the evil creature, Karina had proof that they could indeed sneak into her bedroom. Terrible thought again. The woman's words about the danger of the shoes echoed in her head, now mixed with Nia's words telling Karina she would get killed.

"So? Are you coming or not?" Cayla asked, snapping Karina out of her dreadful train of thought.

After many dimly lit corridors, a large hall with high ceilings and a smaller corridor, they came to a very bright room, so bright that Karina's eyes took a while to adjust. It was a huge room with some small round tables in a corner, and a couple of counters and large cupboards in the other. Everything was made of some kind of stone Karina would describe as marble, but although it was white it was not really marble, because it was shinier, kind of sparkly. All that whiteness gave the place a dream-like quality, which contrasted with the relative normality in the rest of the castle. Was that a castle? Did it have walls around it? Would it be considered a fortress? Some silliness.

The dining room had real windows, tall and large, but because it was night, all Karina could see was blackness and a few stars in the sky. An old woman who seemed to be a cook or servant attended them, offering food options that Karina had never heard of and didn't even catch the names, so she relied on the princess to choose something for her. The woman set to work on one of the counters. The "food" was a green gooey thing. Karina almost didn't eat it, but then she remembered that it was a good idea to try things first before deciding she didn't like them. That logic had some big flaws, as there were things some people should never try, but she did take a spoon. It tasted kind of like broccoli soup, but with different spices. It was actually quite good, and perhaps that logic was generally applicable to food. Cayla had told Karina not to talk about their journey in common areas, so the questions that popped in her head remained unanswered, moved over to a 'later' file in her brain that soon got too crowded.

She finally decided to ask Cayla a question that had been bugging her and was not forbidden: "Your lights, they are different from the ones I know, how do they work?"

"Lights?" Cayla seemed surprised at the question, then pointed to the ceiling. "You mean that?"

"Yes."

Cayla shrugged. "Well, it's sunlight."

"But it's night now."

"It's saved sunlight."

Saved sunlight. Wouldn't that be wonderful? To put sunlight in a little can, then open it later, quite useful in an electricity outage. "Of course not."

Cayla squinted. "Well, what is this light then?"

"That's my question."

The girl just shrugged. Karina looked down, thinking. At least her assumption that she saw sunlight was not so dumb after all. But it didn't make any sense. She tried to rephrase her question. "I see. So you use solar energy to produce light. Is that it?"

Cayla seemed to be making an effort to understand the question. "Uh… well, yes, light is energy."

No kidding. "But how does it work?"

The girl looked up as if thinking. "There might be something on the roof. I'm not really sure."

It was funny how the girl just took it for granted. Would Karina be able to explain her own lights? In general terms yes: electricity, wires, and stuff. But now she was in a completely different place. Then a thought hit her, and Karina almost laughed at her silliness. "Is it magic?"

"What?" The girl looked surprised, offended, or a mix of both. "No. That's really evil."

"Oh, sorry." Karina looked away. The girl's distaste of magic seemed strange and didn't match with the idea Karina had about her. Had she simply assumed she was in a magical place? Well, maybe being in a castle in a parallel dimension or whatever explained her impression. But there was something else. Karina remembered. "What about the light you cast in my room? Was that m—"

Cayla didn't let her finish. "No, no." Alarm and fear showed on her face, as she gesticulated frantically. "There was no light. It was dark. It was dark."

One would think the girl had been caught stealing or something. "Yeah, yeah, it was dark. I'm tired, confused, and imagining things." *Yeah, right.*

"You are," Cayla said as if to put an end to the subject.

The girl had cast a light in her room and they both knew it, but Karina didn't want to press it any further, so she just nodded and returned to her soup. But then, if magic was something forbidden like it seemed, how come they traveled through dimensions? Or was there a scientific explanation? Now, that would be a really interesting thing to learn. Maybe she should ask Odell if he was the know-it-all. A pity he didn't seem to be the teach-it-all.

5

COMMUNICATION

Darian looked at the panel in front of him. The lights represented the army's lifts. He had a good idea about who was in each one and knew how many people were on their side for sure. Some of them were maybes. Those were the most dangerous and could be their downfall. Still, their numbers were enough. He counted again, in disbelief, and then again, as if counting could change the numbers. They were enough. Enough. Darian swallowed. He should have been thrilled. He should have been glad. He should have been relieved that his dreams were about to become true, but he didn't feel any of that. His own reaction surprised him. And now it was time to tell the council, so they'd plan the next move. That was his duty. He knew it. After a long, deep breath, he put on a cloak and walked to the river waterfront, feeling the drumming of his heart. A war drum?

Perhaps he didn't have to say anything. Having played both sides for so long, lying had become as easy as breathing. He tried to understand what he'd been thinking. His thoughts turned to the castle and to who lived in it. A knot formed in his chest. He'd been wrong. Lying was much easier than breathing.

~

In the end, it was just Karina and Cayla who were going. Ayanna had gotten mysteriously or perhaps not-so-mysteriously sick. Nia had been intent on keeping her, and it worked. After some explanation from Odell, Cayla and Karina put the supplies in their backpacks, hooded robes over their dresses and walked to the corridor, while Odell stayed in the room. Karina wanted to laugh at how ridiculous Cayla looked in that ugly brown cloak, but then she remembered she was wearing the same thing and it was no longer funny. They would leave the castle through a small door by the kitchen.

Before stepping out, Karina asked to go to the washroom, and almost asked again when she saw the door, but she knew it was just jitters. How long could she delay her departure by peeing? On the door, Cayla turned a sort of combination lock, which opened it. They stepped out. Karina was about to discover a whole new world, but in spite of all her goosebumps, it only felt like stepping outside a door. There were no drums or trumpets. Nobody wished them good luck or farewell.

The afternoon smelled fresh, the smell of woods and water. They were at the foot of a mountain range, on a plateau high enough to allow a vast view. There was a river not far below, and even though Karina had seen it on the map, seeing it as a real river, much wider than she had thought at first, felt different. The sun was lowering on their left side, hiding beneath mountains, reflected on the river and painting the sky orange. Karina looked back to see the place where she'd been. The castle looked rather small. A large part of it must have been embedded in the mountain, which explained the lack of windows. The walls seemed to be made of a dark brown stone, or else the late afternoon light gave that impression. In front of the building stood a platform, with some silver round things, like giant umbrellas or air bags.

Cayla asked,. "Also wishing we'd take one of those?"

Karina was startled. "Uh?"

"We'd go much faster."

"Do you travel in those things?"

Cayla shrugged. "Well, I haven't traveled much, but people do."

Karina still couldn't make out what they were. "Are they pulled by horses?"

Cayla was puzzled. "Horses?"

"I mean, how do they move?"

"They fly."

"Oh."

How silly, where did she get the idea of horses? The things did look a little like zeppelins, except they were less oval and rounder, and didn't seem to have a basket beneath them. Karina would describe them as roundish things (it was a little dark) with airbags on top.

"Do you ride horses?" Cayla asked.

"What? Me? No, I—"

"Why did you ask about horses?"

Because it was a castle, there was a witch and yada, yada, yada. But that was not a good explanation. "I thought I saw a horse."

Cayla looked back and squinted.

"I think I'm a little confused." The confusion was indeed true.

Cayla sighed. "I know. Walking all the way just seems so…" She put her hand over her chest, as if thinking, then shook her head. "Well, that's what Odell told us, so he might have his reasons. Let's go. We have to find the path before it gets dark." She pointed up. "It's in that plateau."

That "plateau" looked like the base of the mountain, but

perhaps that was what it was. The girls walked upwards while moving away from the castle, in a diagonal direction. The trees were close together and had broad leaves. The trunks were brown, and Karina was somewhat surprised, because with all the green wood furniture she'd thought the tree trunks would be that color. Of course, that idea was really silly. In fact, the forest looked rather normal, with tall trees with broad trunks and moss on the ground. Her scientific mind would classify it as a tropical or semi tropical forest. Nature wasn't much different from the nature she knew, which made sense, if they were on Earth, wherever they were, whenever they were or whatever.

The sun was setting, but instead of cooler, the day was getting warmer, unless the walking made her warm. And the ugly robe. But it was true that the dress underneath seemed to cool her. The girls kept walking while the sky turned pink then purple then dark and darker blue. A quarter moon brightened the forest. There were sounds in the distance, like some insects or birds. Karina had a strange feeling she was being followed or watched, and even though she thought the feeling was pointless, it still bothered her. Then another thought bothered her. "How are we going to know we're in the right place?"

"I think we'll notice. Come."

Karina walked, and she felt hot from walking and the temperature. But her head was not cool, she heard strange sounds, and heard their steps as being extremely loud and bound to attract something or someone, but she had no idea what or who. After some time, the girls came to an area that was flatter, and they stopped going up, which was a relief. The wind stopped, and the air felt stuffy. All Karina could hear were their own footsteps; the forest had grown quiet. There were fewer trees in this area, and Karina could see the black sky full of stars. *Stars.* They could tell her where she was. Or not. She didn't know those stars. Maybe this was Earth, but in the Southern Hemisphere. Maybe it was something else. She decided to focus on where she was walking, not where she was geographically. What difference would it make? The ground was bare, without grass or moss, only covered here and there with fallen trunks. So much stillness and silence, and, strangely, that silence bothered Karina more than the noises she had heard earlier. Had she not seen trees around her, she would have believed she was in a desert. That place felt gloomy even though the moonlight illuminated their path. Oh, that was what it was.

Karina asked in her softest whisper, "Is this the path?"

"I think so," Cayla replied, also with a whisper.

The girl removed her cloak, and Karina did the same. She felt cooler, but not more comfortable. That place was weird. She told herself no animals or people would get near, so, in spite of the awful stillness, at least the path was safe. But then, if even animals avoided that place, there was a reason. She debated whether or not to ask what the reason was, but the girl probably didn't know it, and perhaps it was better not to know.

"The princess did what?" Sian had heard it right, but he wanted to double check that the boy in front of him hadn't gotten his words mixed up.

"She left the castle."

"You mean like that?" He snapped his fingers. "Puff? And nobody noticed it?"

The boy lowered his eyes. "My sister saw her coming out of the kitchen door."

Sian looked around to the alley where they were. Nobody paid attention to them, and yet, he knew people could be listening. He gestured for the boy to follow him in silence. Sian ran his hands through his long brown hair and tried to think. Had the princess run away or been captured, the king would have raised an alarm. Word would have gone out—unless the King wanted to keep it quiet. But then he would probably trust his closest general and advisor. That was Sian's father, and Sian would hear something about it. Perhaps they were just taking long to realize she left, or, more likely, the king knew about it. But for what purpose? Another option was that the boy was mistaken. Still, there had to be some truth in this information. They walked to one of his meeting points, a room in the basement of a market. Sian sat down.

"Who was with her?"

"Another girl. Not her sister."

Surprised, he rose. "That's it?"

The boy cowered. "Yes, yes, that's what my sister saw."

Sian was stunned to realize that the boy was afraid of him. At around twelve or thirteen, the boy was no more than five years younger than Sian himself. But then, standing up, Sian towered him. He sat down and smiled, trying to speak more softly.

"I'm happy you came and told me that. I'm really glad. Thank you." He winked. "Maybe you could be a good candidate for the military academy."

The boy looked down. "Maybe."

That meant no. Anyway, all Sian wanted was the information. "And who's this other girl?"

"Nobody knows. My sister didn't see her, but she heard that an unknown girl spent the night in the castle."

Sian nodded, as if it was the most natural piece of news ever. He thanked and paid the boy. Years of training had taught Sian how to tell when people lied, and the boy had been telling the truth—or at least believing he was.

What Cayla did or didn't do was the least of Sian's concerns, except if meant that something was out of order. Cayla walking out alone or almost alone didn't make sense. For him. Because he was probably missing a vital piece of information. There was something happening, and he had no idea what it was. Not knowing something, that was dangerous and could spoil all his plans.

He commed Jason, one of his trusted officers. "News on my brother?"

"Yes, sir, and there's something quite interesting. He disappears from the radar from time to time."

More unexpected news. "And you couldn't have told me this before?"

"I found that out yesterday and I was waiting for you to contact me. Sir. I fear maybe he could be helping with the insurgency."

Sian didn't trust Jason that much. "Keep your fears for yourself then, before my father hears any of that."

"I didn't mean—"

"It's fine. But report when he shows up again. And don't get any ideas. My brother knows what he's doing."

He closed the channel. Of course Darian knew what he was doing. Nothing good. But it was too early for anyone to know that. To rush and expose him now would be foolish. Everything in its time.

After some three hours of walking, Karina's feet hurt, but she didn't want to complain. Eventually they stopped to set camp even though in theory they should be walking at night. Cayla set up the tent in a matter of seconds. Inside it, the girl had a little light, from a clear crystal looking thing. This time Karina didn't want to sound like a primitive person and assume it was a magic crystal. Of course not. It was just science that she didn't understand. And probably neither did the girl, though she took it for granted. They ate some of the food they carried, which was like cake and dried fruit. Karina worried about crumbs on the bed, but maybe it was better than going outside. Sitting and relaxing,

Cayla looked like a regular girl, someone that could even be her friend.

Karina tried to start a conversation. "Are you excited? For doing this?"

The girl smiled. "Yes."

They fell silent again. Karina still had a question concerning Nia. "And you are sure, uh, the queen won't try to stop us?"

Cayla looked thoughtful for a moment, then replied, "As long as she doesn't know what we are doing, we're safe."

That made sense. No, wait, it didn't. "But she knows what we are doing."

Cayla seemed troubled. "What? But how could she know? How come you didn't tell us?"

"I thought… it was obvious, since she wanted to stop me from coming, no?"

"Of course not. Seriously, we could be in danger."

Karina stared at the girl, wondering if she had been hit in the head. "Fine. Now you are telling me Nia is dangerous."

"What? No. I was talking about Lylah."

That clarified things, a little. But then the girl had clearly misunderstood her. "I was talking about the queen."

"That's who I was talking about."

"Isn't Nia the queen?"

"Of course not."

Karina was more and more confused. "Who's the queen then?"

"Lylah. She calls herself the queen. Some of her followers call her that as well. When you said queen, that's what came to mind."

"I see. So Nia is—"

"Nia. My stepmother."

Karina nodded, almost laughing at the misunderstanding. But there was something she wanted to know. "You mention she's dangerous, Lylah. What has she done?"

"Lots of bad things."

"Like?"

Cayla lowered her head. "She tried to overthrow my father, and she'll try again if given the chance." The girl took a deep breath, exhaling slowly. "People died. Like… my mother."

Karina felt bad for asking. "I'm sorry, I had no idea."

"You couldn't know." She looked at Karina. "Do you understand now, how important this is for me?"

Karina nodded.

Cayla then added, "And yes, perhaps I don't know much, but Odell does. He says this is what needs to be done and I trust him."

They remained in silence for a while, until Cayla broke it. "What do you think of all this walking?"

Karina was so surprised at the change of subject that she blurted out the truth. "It's a little tiring."

"And we didn't even walk that much tonight."

"How many days are we going to go like this?"

Cayla shrugged. "Six, eight. I don't know. It depends on how far we get each day."

"But I thought," Karina was unsure, "I thought you didn't mind walking for days."

Cayla squinted. "It's not about minding or not. Do you think it makes sense?"

Karina shrugged. "Is there another way?"

Cayla had half a smile and a glimmer in her eye that could be seen even in the dim glow. "See, we're not in enemy's territory until after we go to the other side of the river. I understand why we must be careful there, I really do. But, you know, our mission is not to walk, what we need to do is get those shoes to her castle, and get rid of them. That's what we need to do."

Karina wondered where the girl wanted to lead this conversation. "Sure. But I don't know what the alternative is."

"I'm just explaining why I'm considering this… uh, option,

so you don't think I want to disobey Odell for no reason, or, uh…"

"Well," Karina almost rolled her eyes but refrained in time, "he's not my teacher. I don't care."

Cayla seemed relieved and surprised. "You don't care?" She looked around and smiled. "So, you don't mind if we go to the end of the path, like, in a different way?"

Karina stared at the girl and almost answered, "Of course I do. I really, really want to get tired and spend an entire week in a silent, gloomy and eerie forest, doing nothing interesting", but then she decided against it. She didn't know the girl that well.

Cayla noticed Karina's hesitation and became serious. "Do you mind?"

Karina laughed. "Of course I don't. I just don't understand what you're planning, that's all."

Cayla smiled, then quickly became serious again. "First thing, I can only consider this option if you promise never to tell anyone about this. I mean, not even Nia, Ayanna, or Odell. Nobody can know about it."

It wasn't as if she was best buddies with any of them. "I won't tell anyone."

Cayla stared at Karina. "Can you promise?"

"I promise."

The girl sighed. "I have a friend. He's just a friend. He pilots a lift. I think he could take us to the end of the path, if he can, of course. I've thought about it. We don't need to tell him anything. We say we're going camping, walking… He doesn't need to know, and nobody needs to know, and we won't necessarily be disobeying Odell, you see? And it's not that I can't walk or that I need his help, or that I want to see him. It's just that it makes sense. Right?"

Karina assumed a lift was one of those flying things. She would love to know how they worked. "Why didn't you mention this earlier?"

Cayla looked at Karina. "I... I don't know. I thought you wouldn't agree."

Karina laughed at how funny it was that the girl seemed almost afraid of her, as if she was going to judge her or something.

Cayla got serious. "Why are you laughing?"

Karina kept laughing. "I'm also afraid to say what I think to you, because I don't know you well. But, you know, we're in this together, we should trust each other."

"Yes," Cayla answered, seeming thoughtful. Then she laughed. "You're right."

They laughed together. Maybe Karina could start considering Cayla her friend.

"I'll contact him tonight, then," Cayla said. "You understand why I'm doing this, right?"

"Sure."

Actually, not really. If it was just getting a ride and going faster she wouldn't need to give all these explanations. Anyways, Karina didn't really care. She just hoped she would have the chance to get on one of those flying things. Another question was how exactly her new friend would contact anyone, considering they were in the middle of nowhere and didn't have a phone, but she was ready to be surprised, so she just waited to see what the girl would do.

Cayla looked down and hesitated. "You're sure you're not going to tell anyone in the castle about any of this?"

That was getting annoying, but then, maybe there was a good reason Cayla was so afraid. Karina tried to reassure her. "Don't worry."

Cayla looked down and smiled, her face soft. She pulled a necklace from under her dress. It had a silver chain and an orange clear stone. Karina realized both dresses her companion wore had the same high collar, and that it was perhaps on purpose. It also explained why she brought her hand to her chest. It wasn't her heart, but the necklace she was touching. Cayla glanced at Karina and a flicker of embarrassment crossed her face. The stone turned a little brighter, as if it had a light of its own. Karina had seen enough weird stuff to accept that it was a communication device. Lovely idea in fact. After some seconds, the girl pulled the pendant close to her mouth and spoke to it. Of course, the thing was indeed a communication device.

"Darian," Cayla said softly, as if waking someone who is asleep. "Darian?"

No answer came from the stone, assuming, of course, the thing was supposed to answer. She sighed and tried again, this time a little louder.

"Darian? Are you there?"

Cayla kept staring attentively at her stone and repeated the question a few more times, sounding more and more impatient at each time. She looked worried and disappointed. Finally, Cayla took off the necklace and tossed it. "It's useless."

So that was the answer on how they would contact anyone in the middle of nowhere: they wouldn't. But Karina tried to be cheerful. "We can still walk. That was the plan anyways."

Cayla waved her arms. "I don't mind walking! That's not the point. I mean, why wouldn't he…" She took a deep breath and looked down.

Karina didn't know what to say. She wondered whether Cayla's friend had a stone identical to hers and if, by any chance, it had caller ID. It obviously didn't have voicemail.

Cayla then lay down and turned to the other side. Karina decided to do the same, even though it was still early. After checking the shoes every ten minutes, she finally tied them around her waist, as they were flexible.

Still, she felt uncomfortable and it was not the shoes, but the discomfort one has when going to bed and not wanting to sleep. Karina stared at the top of the tent, trying to cheer herself with the thought that she was on an adventure, even though that moment didn't feel like one. Perhaps that was what real adventures were like: they felt ordinary and mundane when one was in the middle of them. Only later, when looking back, people would realize what it had been, which was sad because it meant nobody ever truly lived an adventure, only remembered it as one.

6

ONE MORE

Cayla tried to close her eyes and in an attempt to stop herself from thinking. After more than one year away from Darian, should it be any surprise that he would be too busy to talk to her? She'd been holding on to a faint hope against the fear that time had changed everything. That he'd forget her. But it shouldn't matter. What should matter was getting to Lylah and defeating her. By destroying shoes. There was something silly in the idea, but Odell had to be right. His hope had worked so far, as it had brought a friend willing to help her without asking for anything in return. It felt good to remember that there were still people in the world who would go far to do what was right.

Cayla had to stop thinking about Darian. She shouldn't even have contacted him. Maybe it was for the best. She looked at her bright necklace stone, casting a glow around it. Beneath it, her heart was dark with fear.

Cayla was snapped out of her sleep by a soft sound of someone —or something—scratching the tent. Karina also shot up in surprise. The sound had come from outside. No point wondering what it was. She pulled the knife from her bag, lit her crystal, and stepped out, ready to fight whatever it was.

"Who's there?"

Before she had time to illuminate the person's face, she heard the voice.

"It's me."

Knife and crystal fell on the floor. The light from the moon and stars allowed her to see the brown-eyed young man in front of her. She would have gasped for air anyways, because he was so good looking, but her surprise was double, because this was Darian, not as she remembered him, but older, different.

"What's happening?" he sounded worried.

"How did you find me?"

"Find you? I've been trying to find you for over an hour. Do you realize where you are?"

His angry tone surprised her, but there was something even more puzzling. "I never told you where I was."

He took a deep breath. "It's the necklace. I think... I didn't know it did that, but I can feel where you are." He then sounded angry. "What are you doing here?"

He was snapping. She could snap as well. "I'm confused. Could you or couldn't you find me?"

"Well it's not a tracker on a map. What are you doing here?"

He sounded as if she owed him an explanation, and she didn't. She shrugged. "I'm camping."

He frowned.

Cayla pointed. "Here's the tent."

"And you decided to camp on your own. In the hidden path."

"I'm with a friend."

He crossed his arms. "Friend?"

As much as his shoulders and arms were not as she remembered, what bothered her most was his bad attitude. He'd never been like that before.

At this point, Karina got out of the tent and waved. "Hey."

Darian frowned and stared at Karina, as if looking for something wrong.

Karina was probably super uncomfortable, because she added, "Cayla was showing me the forest. I… I study plants."

He raised an eyebrow and turned to Cayla. "Is that right? How come they let you out?"

As if Cayla were a prisoner or something. "Why wouldn't they?"

Darian snorted. "Well…" He changed his tone, and again sounded concerned. "Are you sure everything is all right?"

Cayla rolled her eyes. "Yes. We're fine."

"I see." He turned to Karina. "Hello, I'm Darian. Sorry, I should have introduced myself. It's just, such a strange place and all." He shook his head. "Sorry."

"No problem." Karina shrugged.

He turned back to Cayla. "I was worried about you."

"Really? Why didn't you talk then?"

"It's, it's complicated. I can't even start to… But you shouldn't be out by yourselves, this is dangerous."

Dangerous bla bla bla. As if Cayla were some helpless child. "We're fine. We've come all this way, and nobody's seen us."

"Well, look where you are!" he said. "I couldn't even find you."

"You just did, didn't you?"

He sounded nervous. "We should go. This place is not safe."

Karina asked, "Why?"

"This path isn't for anything alive," he said.

"Well, why did you come then?" Cayla asked.

He looked down for a while before saying, "My lift is near. Come."

Come? Yeah, it was Darian and all, but he wasn't going to order her around. "Who said I wanted to go anywhere?"

Darian looked down again and bit his lip. "I'll take you back, or wherever you want to go. Please don't stay here, not by yourselves."

"At least now you're saying please."

He stepped back. "What? I have to beg now?"

Perhaps it wasn't only his arms that had gotten thick. "Not beg. Ask."

"Well, I'm asking."

"And it makes a difference." Cayla smiled and turned to Karina. "Let's pack."

She shoved the covers in her bag in a matter of seconds, and even helped Karina with her stuff. Cayla then pulled a few strings to fold the tent, the structure spiraling and twisting the fabric in a cylinder the size of a thick bottle. Darian only looked, waiting.

Cayla looked up. "Where's your lift?"

"I told you, nothing comes here."

"Even in the air?"

He nodded. Cayla picked up her light and followed him as they went to the edge of the path. Karina was right behind her. As they descended a slope, he turned around and extended his hand. That was sweet, but Cayla was perfectly capable of descending without any help, and he wouldn't be able to walk backwards anyways.

She shook her head. "I'm fine."

He puffed, as if annoyed or offended, and then turned around. What had she done?

Karina followed as they went to the edge of the path and this time they really descended a slope in the dark. She wished she had a light, but then, that would mean one less hand to hold onto bushes and trunks. Thankfully there were lots of trees. Or perhaps not, because that also meant there were lots of roots one could trip over and fall. Cayla walked close to Darian. He looked back to check on her, and offered his hand a couple times, but she refused. Oh, she could at least turn around and offer her hand, if she was so sure of herself. But Karina didn't say anything. Slowly the forest came alive again with sounds. How glad she felt. It was as if her ears had been blocked and now they started working again.

She wondered where his lift would be parked, considering there were no clearings. Or would they walk outside the forest? Soon the moonlight illuminated what looked like a thin white pole. Actually, it seemed to be moving. As it turned, it revealed another pole, and beams between them. It was a ladder, a rope ladder, but made from what looked like silver or white ribbon. Karina looked up and saw the oval bottom of lift above them. Had she not known better, she would have thought that was a flying saucer, but of course it wasn't, it was a floating flying machine in a different dimension, something a lot more logical.

"You two can go first, I'll go last," Darian said.

Cayla gestured for Karina to go first. She felt nervous, because once she set foot on the ladder it became a lot more dangling than she had predicted. She then heard or imagined a voice saying, "Don't. Don't go!" It sounded like Cayla but when she glanced back the girl was silent, so it was only Karina's own fear. Still, she went up a few steps, but all the shaking made her even more nervous. The lift was high above, twice the height of the tallest tree, and she couldn't picture herself going all the way up on that dangling thing, especially with that dreadful voice echoing on her head. Well, but wasn't adventure and great things that she'd wanted? She was about to achieve new heights. She ignored the voice in her head and her own fear, and went step by step on that shaking, dangling thing, ignoring how high she was going.

$\sim$

Cayla watched as Karina went up and grabbed the ladder. She felt a hand over hers and her entire body trembled. Perhaps she'd avoided holding his hand because she wasn't sure how she'd react. It had been smart to avoid it on a dark slope. She turned and looked up at Darian. Looking up to see him was new and weird.

"What's happening?" he whispered.

That tone again. Demanding, ordering, so unlike the boy she remembered. She pulled her hand and went up the ladder.

When Karina entered the lift, she noticed it was much bigger than she'd imagined, with green windowless smooth walls, made of some kind of metal. There was a large empty area in the middle, a large bench on each side and a little table near the back. The place was illuminated the same way as the rooms in the castle. A small wall with a door separated what would be the cockpit or the equivalent of it, since there were no controls where they sat. Cayla came up, and then Darian. Karina took a better look at him. He was a regular looking teenager, the same age or maybe a little older than Cayla and a little taller, with brown eyes and brown straight hair down to his chin. He wore dark blue long-sleeved shirt and pants in some kind of synthetic material.

Cayla sat down. "Well, we're here now."

"And... were you even planning on going anywhere?" he asked as he closed the hatch from where they had come and rolled the ladder into a small compartment

"Yes," Cayla replied. "We were going to continue on the path, down until, uh, the mouth of the Black River, and I thought you—"

"Are you out of your mind?"

"Put me down if you have a problem with it," Cayla said.

Darian rested his forehead on his hand, as if thinking. "Just… tell me what's happening. Does your father even know you're out?"

"Well of course," Cayla replied. "Or else I suppose everyone would be looking for me, wouldn't they?"

Darian nodded. "I guess. But why do you want to go so far? Why the mouth of the Black River?"

"That's where we're going. But I can still walk. We were going to walk there anyways."

He laughed. "Really? You mean to tell me you were planning on walking for at least five days?"

Cayla shrugged. "Why not?"

He took a deep breath. "Maybe. But I'll tell you what, we could go somewhere else, I could take you somewhere safe, and, if you're running away, maybe—"

"I'm not running away!"

"What's happening then?"

"I told you. I'm camping."

He snorted. "You're not going to tell me?"

Cayla just stared.

Darian crossed his arms. "Maybe I'll take you back to the castle."

Cayla also crossed her arms. "My father will love to see you bringing me."

Darian looked down and sideways. Was that guy the trustworthy friend who would give them a ride? He and Cayla stood silent.

Karina thought it was her turn to say something. "It's the plants. Rare plants. Only near the, uh, Black River, and we need them."

He raised an eyebrow. "Which plants?"

"*Falucata stonensis*," Karina said, hoping the made-up Latin sounding name would be convincing enough. Now wait, were their plants named in Latin? Did they even know Latin? Why did they even speak English? But perhaps this was not the right time for those questions. Darian and even Cayla had puzzled expressions, so Karina tried to explain some more. "That's, uh, the scientific name. It doesn't have a real name, because people just call it... grass, because... that's what it looks like."

Karina actually enjoyed pretending she was a scientist, even if not a very precise one.

Darian looked at Karina as if seeing her for the first time. "Who are you? Where are you from?"

Yikes. She hadn't considered how to answer those questions.

Cayla replied, "She's Odell's newest apprentice. His niece. She came to live with us a couple months ago."

"How come you never mentioned her?"

Cayla looked down. "We... haven't talked much lately, have we?"

"I know." He sighed. "I'm so sorry, it's just, and so many things, and you disappeared."

Cayla stepped closer to him. "I'm sorry. I... couldn't contact you, or else I would. You should know it."

He sighed. "I know. I just... missed you."

Cayla looked down and away. "I missed you too."

"This is Odell's doing then?" Darian asked, his voice much calmer and softer than before. "Why would he send you out to study plants on the brink of an uprising?"

Cayla squinted. "Uprising?"

"I mean, it's just, the military thing, the generals think there's always the possibility of some kind of conflict, or uprising, and you'd be in great danger. Also, don't forget who supposedly dwells on the upper Black River."

"I know," Cayla said.

Darian raised his eyebrows. "And you still want to go there?"

"I'm not asking you to take me to the upper Black River, just the mouth."

Darian passed his hands through his hair and looked at

Cayla. "I'm telling you this is dangerous and you should trust me."

"I trust you, but I'll walk there if I have to."

"Fine," said Darian. "I'll take you there. Tomorrow, during daylight. And I'll come down with you to pick the plants."

"No, no. We need to be alone, and it takes at least a day, uh, to spot the plants."

Darian was about to answer when the door to the other part of the lift opened, revealing a teenage girl. She wore pants and a shirt similar to Darian's. She had a pleasant, pretty face. "Can we move now?" she asked.

"Sure," answered Darian, "I'm coming in a moment."

The door closed. Cayla stared at it as if she had just seen a three-headed monster. "Who is she?"

"Oh, Zayra. She's my partner."

Cayla looked livid.

Darian continued, "In the ship. She flies with me. We are supposed to fly two by two. I'm sure you know it."

Cayla stepped back and crossed her arms, squinting as in an effort to make sense of a blurred image. "Is that why you wouldn't talk to me?"

He frowned. "What? No."

There was fury in her eyes. "Why would you come with someone else?"

"I had no choice," he said. "We were on a patrolling assignment. But she's my friend, I trust her. You don't suppose I could leave the ship floating by itself, do you?"

Cayla shook her head in disbelief. "Nobody was supposed to know about us being here." She lowered her voice. "And she's heard everything we said."

"She didn't hear it; the door was closed. And she won't tell anyone about you. Besides," he lowered his voice, "she doesn't even know who you are."

"How can she not know?"

"I told her you work in the castle, and, uh, she thinks you're my girlfriend."

Cayla made a disgusted face. "What?"

Darian stepped back. He looked even more bothered than when he was on the path. "I had to explain why I wanted to help you." He put his hands in front of him, as if to distance himself from Cayla. "No pretension here."

He then turned around, entered the other part of the ship and shut the door behind him. Cayla sat quietly, looking sour and shaking her head. She covered her eyes with her hands. "We're doomed."

Karina thought that was an exaggeration and that her friend was jealous, but she didn't say anything. After a while the door opened. Darian's flying partner came in their compartment, or room. She seemed friendly, and was indeed very pretty, with large blue eyes and perfect brown curls.

The girl stepped in front of them and smiled, turning to the princess. "Hello, I'm Zayra. I'm really happy to meet you, Cayla." She sounded as if she really meant it. She then turned to Karina. "And what's your name again?"

"Karina."

"Kayna?"

"No. Karina."

"Oh, right." She sounded as if she still had not understood, then turned to both girls. "I just wanted to tell you we're going to spend the night in a small island in the lower Silver River. It's empty and we can all sleep in the lift. Tomorrow we'll take you to the crossing banks."

"Thank you," Karina replied.

Zayra seemed pleased and had an even bigger smile. "Oh, it's my pleasure." The girl then turned to Cayla. "You have the same name as the princess. How's that?"

Cayla, who had been staring straight in front of her, barely moved her eyes and shrugged. "How am I supposed to know? I never had another name."

Zayra laughed. "You're right. Do you know her?"

"Who?"

"The princess."

Cayla grimaced. "I live in the castle."

Zayra smiled. "Yes, of course. But, doesn't it cause confusion?"

For the first time Cayla looked at the girl. She stared as if examining her before answering. "People in the castle are not like you."

Zayra seemed confused. "What do you mean?"

Cayla had a half smile. "They are not dumb."

The girl stared at Cayla, as if trying to understand. After a few seconds, she laughed. "Oh. Right. Well, I have to get back." She opened the door and disappeared in the compartment.

Cayla looked sour. "Did you see?" She mimicked the other girl. "It's my pleasure. As if she's the one who's doing us a favor."

Did she change her mind about people hearing them? Cayla had been a little rude for no reason. Still, Karina tried to calm her down. "Don't worry, everything will be fine." She winked. "We'll collect all the plants we need."

Cayla sighed. "I really hope so."

Later that night, the lift landed on what was supposed to be an island in a river. Only Darian went outside to bring drinking water. The lift had a small bathroom, like a bus bathroom, inside the other compartment, which Karina had mentally named the cockpit, so she had to go there to use it. The most exciting part was of course being alone in the cockpit or control room, even if for a short period. Further inspection, however, revealed that it was not very impressive; it had three chairs, a window in the front (a windshield actually) and a black panel without any button, joystick or steering wheel. Karina wondered if that black panel worked like a smartphone screen, or if the pilot just conjured some magic, but then she reminded herself to stop being primitive and assume people used magic. She would need to catch them piloting or controlling the thing to learn how it worked. Or perhaps ask. She looked out the windshield. Since it was evening, she saw only a night sky and what seemed to be some water in front of her.

Karina went back to the main compartment. The table that had seemed somewhat small at first was actually bigger than she'd first thought and could easily sit eight or ten people. But only three people sat by the table. Four when Karina joined them. They didn't have a proper dinner, but rather snacked on bars and dried fruit, which seemed to be their staple travel food. Darian and Cayla were quiet and gloom. Zayra tried to make some conversation, but didn't insist much. One time Karina caught Zayra looking at Cayla like a scientist examining a rare specimen, but other times Darian's flying partner looked relaxed and almost happy, oblivious to the heavy mood around her.

Later, two large beds were pulled from beneath the side seats. Each of them was as big as a king sized mattress. The three girls lay on one bed, and Darian on the other. Karina had to sleep between Cayla and Zayra, because she assumed the princess would not want to spend the night near the other girl. Thankfully each had their own cover, but the middle position was not the most comfortable, as Karina couldn't move much to either side or she would bump onto one of the girls. Still, this was nicer than the silent tent in the middle of nowhere, and if she remembered that she was skipping a lot of walking, she could ignore the bad mood that still hung around the place.

Karina's eyes were open even after the lights had faded and everyone's breath had become smooth and steady. Cayla was now deep asleep and spreading her arms, squeezing Karina against Zayra. Was it that even asleep she felt entitled to a princess space? Not really because in truth Darian was the one with the biggest space, just because he was the only guy there. Karina sat up and looked at him. How old would he be? Sixteen, seventeen, not much more. Zayra also seemed to be the same age. Karina felt a sick feeling in her stomach when she realized she'd been flying in the hands of teenagers. Well, maybe people there aged differently, maybe lifts were really easy to fly or maybe she should just stop being paranoid and remember the tougher challenges ahead of her. Actually, perhaps it was better not think about future challenges and just try to sleep and enjoy the comfortable bed. Cayla had gotten what she wanted; they would fly a big chunk of their way, but somehow, she was really upset about being there. If she was jealous, why wasn't she simply nicer to the guy who had brought her here? Oh, mysteries of the Universe.

Karina woke up alarmed, fearing someone was stealing her shoes. She sat up but then realized she could still feel them around her waist. She then turned around, because she heard someone. Zayra was near their bags, and for a second seemed to be looking into them. But the girl smiled when she saw Karina, without any sign of alarm, surprise, or fear.

"It's good you woke up, we're almost there," Zayra said, as she folded a blanket.

Karina felt confused. She was still debating whether she saw or not the girl looking into their things.

"You'd better get ready," Zayra added, then looked at Cayla's direction. "Both of you."

The girl put the blanket in a compartment near the side seat then walked back to the controlling room. Karina decided she had confused the girl's blanket with their bags. Regardless, they didn't have anything important in their bags, not even a map or anything that could identify them, so it was no big deal. Karina got up and tried to see where they were, but quickly realized that was pointless, first, because there were no windows, and second, because she would not know where she was anyways, although it would be nice to admire such a different view. Cayla was still asleep. Karina knelt and shook her friend's shoulder. The girl jumped up scared, until she looked around, probably realizing they were not in the middle of any emergency, and sat down.

After a couple minutes, Darian walked in, addressing Cayla. "Are you sure you want to do this? There are dangers… you are not aware of."

Cayla shook her head. "I'm well aware of the dangers."

Darian looked down and bit his lip. "I could come down with you, stay close, just as a precaution."

"Don't you need to be patrolling?"

"I could leave Zayra by herself."

"Oh, now you can leave her. How interesting."

Darian looked at Cayla attentively, as if trying to understand something, before asking, "Why does she bother you?"

"Because nobody was supposed to know about us."

"I see. You're ashamed."

Cayla squinted. "No. It's just, it had to be secret."

"Well, you don't want me to come with you, I won't. I'll pick you up in the afternoon."

Cayla shook her head. "No, no, it's fine. We're going to take a boat home. From the Last Town."

Darian raised his eyebrows. "It's dangerous."

"Everything for you is dangerous. I suppose you consider breathing dangerous."

He nodded. "In these days, out there on your own, yes."

"You want me to suffocate then."

"No. I could protect you."

"Ah, you want to suffocate me personally. No, thanks."

He stared at her for a long while, then to the floor, then to her again. Cayla had a defiant look.

He stepped back, fists clenched, arms trembling. His voice came out soft and smooth, "That's it then? Don't you worry, Princess Cayla," he spoke slowly, emphasizing every word, "you will never run the slightest risk of me suffocating you."

He then turned around and got into the other compartment. The lift shook as he slammed the door. Cayla stared at the door with a confused expression, and then sat and looked down. Karina didn't know whether she should say something or not, and either way she didn't even know what to say.

Because the lift had no windows, she had no idea whether it was moving or not, until it slowed down and descended. Zayra came out and opened a back door. Had the door not been opened, Karina would never have realized it was there. She felt relieved that this time they were on the ground, in a clearing, so she would not have to jump, or worse, descend a loose dangling rope ladder. Better than jumping, actually.

Zayra stood by the door. "Bye, good luck."

"Thanks," Karina replied softly, because someone had to say something.

Cayla didn't look back or say anything. Karina watched as the flying machine went up and then far away.

Only then did Cayla look, and shook her head. "This could ruin our mission."

"We just skipped a five-day walk."

Cayla sighed. "I'm not sure it was worth it."

Karina was about to point out that it had been Cayla's idea, but then decided to stay quiet and just be glad they didn't have to walk all the way.

7

THE IMAGINARY PURSUERS

The mountains were low at this part, lowering to what was probably the place where the two rivers met. That much Karina remembered from the map. Cayla looked at that direction, then to the other side, as if trying to decide something. Karina didn't understand what the girl was thinking, because even she knew to which direction they were supposed to go.

Karina pointed. "Isn't the mouth of the river that way?"

"That's what worries me," Cayla replied.

"Why?"

"That girl knows where we are going."

Oh, no, Karina was hoping any annoyance against Zayra would have stopped once they stepped out of the lift. "So?" she asked, refraining from rolling her eyes.

Cayla frowned. "I don't like it."

That much Karina was aware, but she still tried to calm her friend. "Well, she doesn't really know where we are going and what we are planning to do. And if she's your friend's friend, maybe you should trust her."

"I'm not even sure I trust him." She said this as if acknowledging a painful truth.

Perhaps... it was too late to think that? But Karina asked something else. "Is there anything we can do about it?"

"Well, they think we're going to the mouth of the river, there, or perhaps that we'll stay in the woods near or between the two rivers. What we can do instead is walk to the other direction, and cross to the Black river through the mountains."

That mention reminded Karina of the bit of Odell's explanation she liked the least. "Don't jaguars live there?"

"Not there, they live further up, protected by real mountains. This part here," she pointed to the low mountains beside them, "they are not even mountains, just hills. Very little difference from walking close to the river. It just takes a little longer, but we're ahead anyways."

Karina looked up. Indeed the hills didn't have rocks that seemed difficult to climb, just trees wide apart. It would not be much harder than when they went up the plateau to the path. But that was not her problem with the plan. "What's the point in changing our itinerary?"

"If anyone follows us, they won't find us."

As much as Karina hated to argue, she had to point out something. "Right, but they have fast flying uh, things—lifts. If anyone wanted to find us, I don't think we'd be able to walk far enough from the last spot they saw us."

Cayla looked seriously at Karina. "You're right. But the mountains will be the last place they'll look. Let's hurry then." She turned around and walked fast towards the mountain

Karina regretted having said anything. She calculated that they would walk at most five kilometers in an hour, probably even less, considering they were going up. That meant that even if they walked eight hours straight they would only make forty kilometers. Karina had no idea how fast those things went, but she was sure that whoever was inside would have enough time to look for them in a forty kilometer range, regardless of the direction they went. She debated whether or not to mention those numbers to Cayla, but then decided against it, afraid that the girl would come up with an even crazier idea. Indeed, her pace started to get hard to follow. Karina then considered that at least the hills had some trees, meaning they would not be easily spotted by air, but then she told herself to stop calculating the odds that they would be found, because nobody was following them.

The pace was so tough that soon Karina stopped wondering about the reason they were going up and concentrated on her walking, breathing fast. The walk was rather smooth; few spots were steep or had rocks. After some two or three hours, when Karina's legs had already started to hurt, Cayla stopped. "Maybe we should rest now."

For a split second Karina almost reminded her friend that if they wanted to run from imaginary pursuers they should keep going, but then realized that if the pursuers were imaginary there was no need to hurry. What a brilliant conclusion. In fact, she should be glad that they would get a well-deserved break. For the first time since they'd started going up the hill, Karina had time to turn around and really look down where she'd come from. Through the trees she caught a glimpse of the valley below, the river, and low hills on the other side. There were many constructions here and there, especially near the river, in bright colors: green, yellow, red, blue, purple and others. She wondered what material they were made of, whether they were houses and if the colors meant anything.

When Karina turned around, she noticed the tent had been set up. That was fast—and silent. She was surprised, because she had assumed "resting" meant only stopping and perhaps sitting a little.

Cayla seemed to notice her surprised look. "We sleep during the day, walk at night, remember?"

Karina nodded. Of course she remembered the instructions, but what was the point in keeping to the rules if they were off course anyways? Still, a tent meant they could relax much better than sitting on rocks or branches. Cayla sat on the entrance of the tent, and started drinking water. Karina did the same and also ate one of her bars. Even though they could not see the buildings from where they were, Karina tried to start a conversation. "What are those buildings down there?"

"That's the Last Town."

Karina had heard this name mentioned as the city from where they would supposedly return by boat. That made sense and explained why Cayla thought they would not look for them in the mountains, or hills. "Last because it's the last by the river?"

"Ah, no, not really. The rivers continues. With a different name. 'Last' has to do with a war or revolt, it was the last city standing or something."

"I see."

Before getting frustrated that her friend knew so little, Karina reminded herself that she too was awful in history, so at least they had something in common. Unfortunately, common lack of knowledge didn't make a good conversation topic. Cayla sat down. Her black hair shone so much in the sun that it almost looked silver, in a way that was shampoo-commercial unnatural. But her eyes were sad, lost in the distance, as she touched the orange stone in her necklace that was no longer hidden under her dress. Karina debated whether to respect her friend's silence, or ask a question she was itching to ask. To favor the decision of asking, she weighed that since they were in such a difficult journey they should trust each other. "What's with you and Darian?"

Cayla let go of the stone quickly and widened her eyes. "What do you mean?"

Oh, did that need explaining? Karina tried to rephrase it. "How long have you known each other?"

"Ah, a couple years. He's, uh, almost like a brother." Cayla lowered her head. "Or was. I really trusted him."

Brother? Karina felt her lunch spinning in her stomach. Still, she thought Cayla shouldn't be so gloomy.

"But he came, he brought us here, exactly like you wanted."

Cayla shook her head. "No. I didn't want a random girl knowing about us. Who knows what she'll do with that information? This is just... wrong."

"But she's far away now, she doesn't know where we are, and has no idea what we're doing."

Cayla nodded slowly. "That's what I'm hoping. But still, she knows about me and Darian."

That wasn't making much sense. "But... aren't you, uh, like siblings? Surely everyone knows you are friends."

"They know we were friends, not that we still are."

"Why so much secret?"

Cayla sighed, bit her lip and looked down. "Well, he used to live in the castle, until my father, uh, he thought... Well, my father has forbidden me to ever see Darian again. But, it's not that I am really disobeying my father, because he imagined something that was not true. I thought my father would come around when he understood that me and Darian, we're just friends. That's what I thought, but I'm not sure about anything anymore."

Karina could well understand why her father would "imagine" something more than friendship. People are really creative. Then she remembered her friend was a princess and understood the problem. "I suppose you'll have to marry a prince or something."

Cayla squinted. "What?"

"I mean in the future." Karina was not sure if she was talking nonsense but she remembered something she had heard somewhere. "For an alliance with another kingdom or something."

Cayla shook her head. "No. I don't think he wants me to marry anyone. And I'm too young to even think about that."

"That's true. Is that the problem? That you're too young?"

Cayla agitated her hands. "I don't know. I don't know why my father won't let me… And this is not about Darian. I'm just answering the question you asked. You brought it up." She went inside the tent. "I'll try to lie down a little and rest. Close the tent if you come inside."

Cayla was a textbook example on how love made people illogical. Anyways, she didn't want to sit by herself. "I'll lie down as well."

With that, they entered and Cayla closed the tent. Karina was surprised that the tent felt cool inside, and was darker than she had imagined. It was a good place to rest during the day, even when it was hot outside, perhaps especially then. She lay down and put her legs up, over her backpack, so as to rest them. Cayla had her eyes closed even though she didn't sound like she was asleep. Karina's waist hurt a little from the sweat caused by the shoes, so she removed them quietly and put them beneath her legs, so that she could still feel them. But instead of relaxed, she felt worried. She heard a voice somewhat like Cayla's saying, "Karina, get up and run. Run, quickly." She looked at the girl, thinking that the princess' earlier paranoia had gotten contagious.

Cayla opened her eyes. "What?"

The question surprised Karina. "Oh, nothing."

Cayla closed her eyes again. Now, if she was calm, why was Karina feeling so edgy, as if they were on the brink of some disaster? Was it that they had deviated from the plan? Maybe Odell's words had impressed her more than she admitted. Maybe it was just that she needed to rest the mind more than the body, but that was nonsense, because it had gotten plenty of rest during that tough walk. Karina tried to think about something different, but fear and worry started to bother her so much that she made up her mind to convince Cayla to get up and keep moving. But before Karina said anything, Cayla opened her eyes and sat up. "Did you hear that?"

"What?"

Cayla gestured for silence. Suddenly, she opened her eyes wide. "Someone's coming. We need to hide."

She got up and got out of the tent. Karina still hadn't heard anything, but she thought perhaps her companion was suffering from the same anxiety that had gotten her. Karina started to put the shoes around her waist, but before she finished, Cayla came back and pulled her hand. "Come."

One of the shoes fell as they walked outside the tent. "My shoe!"

Cayla was strong and had already pulled Karina away from the spot. "We'll get it back later. Come." She headed to a tree and started climbing it.

Karina followed with a lot of difficulty, while the princess looked down in desperation, trying to hurry her. When Karina was a few branches below her travel companion, the girl gestured for her to stop and be silent. Cayla lay on top of her thick branch, so that she was partially hidden from whoever was below, and Karina tried to do the same. She looked down, trying to find the fallen shoe, but she couldn't see it. She felt the remaining shoe on her waist, and wondered whether she could lift the other one using magic, but perhaps she needed to wear the shoes for them to have an effect, or have someone else wear them. Or something. Or perhaps this was some big nonsense. She wished the shoes had come with an instruction manual.

Karina couldn't hear anything other than leaves, the wind, and small insects. Perhaps their fear had been just paranoia. Grabbing a branch was uncomfortable, not only the physical discomfort, but also that uncomfortable feeling of expecting something not to happen. How long does one wait for nothing? Not long, as she saw a group of five or six people, walking silently and yet fast towards their tent. No wonder she hadn't heard them. Someone walked to the tent and looked inside.

"Empty," a young woman said softly but loud enough to be heard from the tree. "They can't be far. You two stay here. The rest, come, we'll find them."

At that moment Karina's heart started to race, because the woman's words meant they were looking for someone. She rested her face against the branch, hoping it would hide her. Below them, people were moving around. After a few minutes, everyone seemed to have gone somewhere else. Karina wanted to look down to see what was happening, but her body refused to move. That proved a good thing, because seconds afterward she heard a woman's voice.

"I don't know. I still think this is a trap."

A man replied, "You think our commander's sister would set us up?"

"Not her. The boy she hangs out with."

"Wow, now, some respect," the man replied. "He's done more for us than anyone."

"I know, but I won't forget that he's General Keen's son. And has that brother. How do you suppose she knows the sisters are here?"

"He's certainly well connected," the man replied.

"Too well connected, that's what I think," the woman said. "Now tell, me, what would two princesses be doing down here, all by themselves? Isn't it, just… too easy?"

There was some silence before the man replied, "Well, it is odd. Still, if they are here, it's our great chance."

"And yet, if it's a trap, it might be our end."

"Why did you come then?"

"I'm not a coward."

The man didn't reply and the woman didn't say anything anymore. The mention of two princesses meant that they were really looking for them, perhaps thinking Karina was Ayanna. But nobody knew they would go to these hills. On the other hand, two people knew they had been dropped off near the foot of those mountains. A guy and a girl, just like "the traitor" and "the sister" in the conversation. And who were those people anyways?

After a while, the man said, "They're still searching, no sign of them."

"Hum," the woman replied, "whoever walked up the hills and set this tent must still be close, or else they would've left tracks. They can't have disappeared by magic."

"Well, technically, what if…"

"What, magic?"

"Why not?"

The woman laughed. "Some hypocrisy from our adorable king. But I still doubt it. Trust me, they're close. I'm going to climb the trees and look."

At that moment Karina didn't know if her heart stopped or sped or jumped. She certainly stopped breathing for a few seconds.

The man asked, "Didn't you think this was a trap?"

"The sooner we find the bait, the sooner we find out. Whistle if you see anyone, even if they're friends. I'll whistle as well."

The woman's voice sounded farther away from before, as if she had already made her way to another tree, thankfully not theirs. Still, she would eventually find Karina and Cayla, unless she missed their tree, gave up, or someone called her somewhere else. Poor odds there. The feeling of patiently waiting to be caught was anything but pleasant, and yet, it felt unreal, as if Karina had to disconnect herself from the reality awaiting her.

But before she disconnected too much, Cayla brought her back. "Two against one. It's our chance. Let's go."

Go? Seriously?

Cayla had already climbed down from her branch and she pulled Karina. "Down, quickly. We can run."

Karina started climbing down, unsure if that was really a good idea. Cayla was already further down. Karina then heard the sound of a loud bird. Or was that the man whistling?

"Jump and run!" Cayla yelled before doing what she had suggested.

A jump from that height could result in a broken leg, but Karina didn't want to wait by herself on the tree, so she jumped, falling on soft ground, without any broken leg or sprained ankle, realizing the jump hadn't been as high as she'd thought. She saw the back of a man running after something: Cayla. Before Karina weighed her options, someone pushed her to the ground and sat on her, then pulled her arms with one hand and pushed her face down with the other. The coarse ground scraped her cheek. Then the person above her—the woman—grunted and got up.

Cayla yelled, "Get up, fight!"

This time it was really Cayla, not some weird voice. Karina got up and saw Cayla against the woman, who was younger and smaller than she had imagined, and wore clothes similar to Darian's and Zayra's. Then another girl came, and she went for Cayla. The princess kept both of them away mainly by moving fast, turning and kicking. Karina looked around, searching for something to throw at them, but soon realized that they were moving too fast and she would miss, or worse, she might hit Cayla. She decided then to kick the girl and see if, together with Cayla, they could defeat both her and the woman. But out of the corner of her eye something glimmered in the sunlight: her shoe. It was far from the tent, farther than their equipment, which had been spread on the floor, and far from the fight. Karina ran to the shoe, grabbed it and started running, but she soon tripped and fell. The shoe flew far ahead of her. She felt some rope around her feet, meaning that she had not fallen from sheer incompetence.

"Get up and come with me," the man told her.

Karina obeyed, but with a lot of difficulty because her feet were tied, and jumping with feet together in an uneven slope was not the easiest thing to do. The man pushed her forward, back to where, from the grunts and yells, the fight was still going on. The woman now had a little knife in her hand, but Cayla kicked it then picked it up. The other girl mainly circled Cayla, and backed up, afraid.

Strangely, the man clapped. It didn't sound mocking or sarcastic, but a regular clap. "Great effort girl, now that's enough."

Cayla either didn't hear or pretended not to, as she kept advancing towards the woman.

"Enough, girl!" the man repeated.

The princess still ignored him. The man ran towards Cayla, and as the girl and the woman distracted her, he pushed the princess. As she fell to the ground, the woman quickly sat on her and immobilized her, the same way she had done to Karina. The man tied the princess's hand and feet. Being ignored, Karina accomplished a couple jumps, distancing herself from them, but she soon realized she would go nowhere tied like that. She sat and tried to untie herself, but found it difficult because she had strips of a jagged cloth tangled and adhered to each other everywhere, not a rope with a simple knot or opening. She fumbled through the strips, then heard people near her. Cayla was sweaty and red, and had hands and feet tied. The man and woman tied Karina's hands and tied both girls to a tree. The girl went somewhere else. Cayla whispered to Karina, "Did you see the advantage of two against one? Thank you for your help."

In a way, Karina understood that she hadn't helped, but, on the other hand, it had not been her fault. "I don't know how to fight."

"Seriously? All I needed was a little help."

"I tried. It was fast, confusing, and that thing that got my feet."

"Your feet got caught? I jumped. See? You have to think."

Karina didn't like the accusation, and plus, she was not even sure fighting or resisting would have helped. "They have people all around the hill. How far would we have gone?"

"Farther than we did, that's for sure."

8

FINGERS

The woman approached them and looked attentively at Karina. "What's your name, girl?"

"Don't answer anything," Cayla whispered.

The woman didn't insist on an answer and instead turned to the man. "That's not Ayanna."

"How do you know?" he asked.

"She's too old to be the younger princess."

Cayla then said, "You know I'm not a princess either, right? Why would I be here without guards? This is a trap, and you should let me go and save yourselves while you still have time."

"You fight too well, girl," the woman replied. "Lots of free time. You're the real thing."

Cayla squinted and stared at the woman, then, after a while, said, "Maybe I was sent here because I can fight, so that I can take all of you at the right moment."

The woman laughed. "Well, for one, if you were an impostor, you wouldn't say so. And two, if you were here to fight, why would you have a partner who can't defeat a flower?"

Ouch, that hurt Karina's feelings.

Cayla laughed. "Sure, trust that. You'll see. You're all alone and soon you'll be caught."

The woman looked at Cayla. "Is that supposed to be funny or scary?"

"Funny," Cayla replied. "For me. I'm going to be laughing soon."

The woman nodded. "Oh, I see." She turned to the man. "Lionel, I don't think she's the princess. I think she's the fool."

They both laughed. Cayla spit on the woman's face. Karina was impressed with the precision, speed, and distance, wondering if spit contest was a royal sport in those parts.

The man became serious but the woman only cleaned her face with the back of her hand and kept laughing. "Great aim. You really have some misused talent, girl." Then she became serious. "Little advice: don't do this to Rose."

"I don't need advice," Cayla replied.

The woman turned to Lionel. "See? Any doubt who's the princess here?"

"Nope."

Cayla yelled, "I might not be a fool but I can fool you."

The woman raised her eyebrow. "Of course. You're an expert impostor and I'm sure a swarm of lifts is coming to catch us."

"I'm glad you're aware." Cayla smiled.

The man and woman stepped away and talked quietly to each other. Even with effort, Karina couldn't hear what was being said. Cayla wiggled and struggled trying to untie herself. Karina didn't see the point in it but she moved a little, pretending she was also trying to free herself, just so that her friend didn't get mad. Karina was anxious to get this situation solved soon, wondering if they would be taken to Lylah's castle and if throwing only one shoe would do the trick, even though she had no idea what the trick was. Or maybe everything was going wrong, but then she remembered Odell telling them that they would be rescued, that everything would be all right. Those thoughts put her at ease, she only wished Cayla would also remember what she was told. But perhaps Karina had to remind her.

She whispered as close as Cayla's ear as she could, "Remember what he told us? Before we came?"

Cayla looked as if she had not understood, until she finally seemed to remember. "No, no. This is different…"

The woman approached them. "Different from what?"

That was Karina's question as well.

Cayla replied, "From the way *you* are going to be captured."

The woman sighed. "I know. Unfortunately, not everyone is as nice as we are."

Cayla looked away. At least she didn't try to come up with a smart reply, because it would have been awkward at that moment. Karina heard steps approaching the clearing, and soon three people joined the man and woman who had been watching them, but two of them soon went away. The person who remained was a young woman with short hair, and, unlike the others, wearing a dress. Karina made an effort to hear their conversation even though they were not very close.

The short-haired woman who had just come said, "Sonja, Lionel, good job. Did you confirm their identity?"

The woman, Sonja, replied, "The oldest girl is princess Cayla. I have no idea who the other one is."

"We haven't questioned them," Lionel added. "We identified the princess because of her behavior. I suppose one princess is enough."

The short-haired woman approached the girls. Karina noticed she had thick black lines painted on her cheeks, like some war painting, or perhaps meaning that she was their leader. Strangely, the paint looked good on her, in a menacing way, but still good.

The woman crouched, pulled a short knife then addressed

Cayla and Karina. "I'm going to do this once. Who are you and what are you doing here?"

Karina trembled with a dreadful sense of danger, noticing that the woman's eyes were pure hatred. And to think Karina had been afraid of Nia. The woman held the knife as if she meant to use it, and if this had been a game, it would have stopped being any fun. But since Karina could not quit, she started blurting the truth. "My name's Karina, I'm not from here—"

"We're not saying anything! We're not saying anything!" Cayla continued to shout until Karina stopped trying to tell where she was from and what she was doing.

"Just take us to Lylah," Karina pleaded.

At this point, all Karina wanted was to find the woman, witch or not, give her the freaking shoes, and go home.

The woman laughed. "Sure, Lylah, our savior, the one we wait and wait and wait. Or else, Lylah, the enemy, the faceless threat hanging upon us." She faced Karina. "I'm not taking you to where Lylah is, and do you know why? One, it would be bloody. Two, I don't want to lose a hostage. Lylah is dead, girl, dead."

Karina swallowed. Somehow, the news distressed her a lot, especially now that she was starting to consider the so-called evil witch a very nice woman. It also made their journey useless. Why were they out facing dangers to defeat a dead woman? Also, if Lylah was dead, who were those people, and why were they after them?

A teenage boy came panting and spoke to the shorthaired woman, "Nothing. They're alone."

He turned around, as if to walk away again, when something caught his eye. He knelt in front of Cayla, pointing to her necklace. "What is that?"

Cayla looked elsewhere and remained silent.

The boy got up and addressed the woman with the face

paint. "Rose, that's Darian's twin, I'm pretty sure. I told your sister his necklace must have had a twin, she never believed me." He glanced at Cayla. "They must be… you know. Does he know she's here?"

Rose rolled her eyes. "Of course he knows. How do you think we found her? Now, I need a big favor from you, very important. I need you to check the Black River bank, see if anyone's coming from that side."

"You want me to go alone?"

"I'm sure you can handle it. Go."

The boy nodded and departed. Rose, Lionel and Sonja exchanged glances. Rose crouched in front of Cayla and looked at her necklace, then got up and whispered to the others, but this time Karina could still hear them. "He's right, it is a twin necklace, and it's just like Darian's."

Sonja turned to Lionel. "I told you he was too well connected."

Lionel was serious. "Speaking of which, does Darian know about this?"

Rose stared at him. "You too? Take your guess."

The man looked down.

Sonja put her hand on his shoulder. "Sometimes we got to do what we got to do."

Rose glanced again at Cayla then turned to the others. "We'll figure Darian later. I just want to deal with the girl." She crouched in front of Cayla, and touched her necklace. "So you are the mysterious girl."

The woman grabbed the orange stone on her hand and pulled the necklace, but it didn't come out.

"Don't," Cayla pleaded.

Rose kept trying until she succeeded in pulling the necklace. She threw it on the floor and stepped on it, making a crashing sound. Tears ran down Cayla's eyes. The princess then spat on

Rose's face. The woman wiped it, and some of the paint on her cheek came out, revealing a thick red scar.

She knelt in front of Cayla and put her knife on the girl's face. "Do you want one like this?" she asked, touching her own scar.

Cayla remained silent, staring at her.

"Do you?" the woman repeated, and her knife was pierced the girl's face, revealing a little blood. Sonja and Lionel stepped closer, watching Rose.

"No," Cayla answered, the voice just loud enough to be barely heard from such a close distance.

The woman pulled back her knife, but not before cutting Cayla's face some more, but just a superficial cut, with a little blood, hopefully nothing that would scar the girl forever.

Rose turned to her companions. "I say we cut a hand from each and send to the king. That way he knows we have the girls and mean to harm them. If he doesn't back of his army in one day, we send him the other hands."

This time Karina really got scared. All she wanted was to disappear, teleport, or for an earthquake or some other natural disaster to save her. This adventure had definitely stopped being fun. Lionel and Sonja stared at Rose as if in shock.

"I thought we would only keep them as hostages," the man said.

Rose shook her head. "Then we won't pressure the king. We can't fight brutality with mercy."

Sonja and Lionel still stared at her, both wide-eyed.

"Oh, please!" Rose added. "We can make this fast and pain-less. I'm not evil, I know they're just girls." She turned to Lionel. "If you were in the army you'd have to obey."

He shook his head. "I deserted. I can desert again."

Rose shrugged. "Nobody's tying you."

"Wait," Sonja intervened. "You can't do that without

consulting the rest of the group. I for one agree with Lionel. I'm here to fight violence, not support it."

Rose sighed. "What about cutting the girls' nails? Would we need to consult the rest then?"

Lionel scratched his head. "I'm not sure the king would be able to identify the nails. I mean, perhaps, but…"

"I was joking," Rose said. "Now, really, I know what we stand for, but I also know what we're up against, and who we're up against. We have a unique opportunity. We can't show weakness."

"Fingers then," Sonja said. "Starting with the little ones."

Lionel stared at her.

Sonja raised her shoulders. "I don't like it either, but Rose does have a point."

"Little fingers then it is," Rose said. She turned to Lionel. "Do you still want to desert?"

He looked away. "Not yet."

Sonja took a deep breath. "I'll prepare the equipment."

Now where was the promised rescue mission if it all went wrong? Karina felt betrayed. Her mouth was dry, and she felt a knot closing down her throat. She looked sideways, and her eyes met Cayla's. The girl had been strangely quiet, and her eyes showed fear as well.

Karina then remembered Zoe. Zoe, falling from the stairs. Now, why was that image coming into her mind then? Of course! The shoes. If the shoes could break a handrail, they could certainly cut some rope, even weird, sticky, tangled rope. But had it really been the shoes? Still, even if it had been, Karina didn't have both shoes now. But the shoes were not with her when Zoe had fallen either. She closed her eyes, trying to concentrate, trying to think, trying to make something happen, even though she had no idea what. She opened her eyes and saw another young woman coming to their direction. She had something in her hand, and walked towards Rose, who was standing far from the girls.

"What is this?" the young woman asked. She had the missing shoe in her hand. "Is this some kind of magical—"

The girl didn't finish. She tripped on something on the floor, and the shoe flew away from her. Karina got up and grabbed it, without noticing she had ripped the ropes that tied her as if they had been made of paper. Rose and Lionel saw Karina and ran towards her. Rose had the knife on her hand and the menacing look of someone who decided not to mind losing a hostage. Karina froze for a split second, before realizing she'd better run. After that, she could not understand what happened and in which order. There was black smoke around her, but no smell of anything burned. The floor trembled. Rose fell. Karina found herself beside Cayla, but away from the tree, not sure how they had gotten there with all that smoke and earthquake. Was it an earthquake? She held Cayla's hand, also not knowing how the girl got untied. More black smoke, nothingness, a feeling of falling, then a thud on hard floor. Somehow, the strongest image in Karina's mind was Rose falling. Who said she couldn't defeat a flower?

Karina coughed. She had difficulty breathing, and no idea where she was. People approached her and she feared that she would be captured again, until she realized she was in the place where she had arrived at the castle: the circular tall blue room. She had teleported, or been teleported. She was safe. Tears of joy and relief came out of her eyes. This time she would just find Nia and go back home. She didn't want to go on any more journeys, and she couldn't care less who took the shoes and controlled the world.

Some four or five people encircled her. Because of her tears, she had trouble recognizing them. Why were they surrounding her? They seemed to carry something in their hands, pointing at Karina, but that could not be. She wiped her tears and took a better look. Indeed, they seemed to be some kind of guards and had something pointy, like spears. Perhaps it was just precaution until they checked her identity. Now, where was Cayla? The men had menacing looks. Why were they doing that?

"Take her. Before she escapes," a man said.

Two men grabbed Karina by the arms while someone put a hood on her. She was gagged before her scream came out.

9

THE MEANING OF YELLOW

Darian stared at the panel and the position of the lifts in the surrounding areas. There was no army and no rebels around the meeting of the rivers. And yet he felt uneasy. He touched his necklace. Should he contact Cayla? Or *suffocate her*. Right. Let her breathe. But at what price? No price. There was nobody in the area, no danger, and nobody knew she was there. He'd repeated these words some twenty times by now. And yet... he was the one suffocating with worry. Worry. For a girl who wouldn't even take his hand. Over one year waiting, and she treated him like an acquaintance. Maybe the fault had been his. Perhaps he'd been mistaken about whatever they had. It was not her fault. The alternative would be to be angry. Next thing he'd be smirking and saying stupid things like "love is poison" and become like his brother. His brother. Wonderful reverse role model. He was probably in Siphoria, partying and enjoying his sense of importance, oblivious to what was going on in the kingdom.

Zayra walked in. "We should be going, shouldn't we?"

He wasn't in a mood to talk. "No."

She looked down. "I mean… there are lots of things we need to do. You especially. You can't remain here all day."

"Can't I?"

"You can. Sure. When we're so close, you're going to ignore everything we fought for so long. You're going to forget all the people who need us, who support us, who support you, and stay here moping for a girl who's not worth it."

He leaned back. "Opinion taken."

Zayra slammed her hand on one of the seats. "That's it? You don't have anything to say for yourself?"

"I outrank you, Zayra. I don't need to explain anything." He hated the stupid army ranking system, but it could be convenient sometimes.

"Fine. Why don't you go and run after her? Maybe if you beg she'll look at you. Meanwhile, ignore everyone who loves you and cares about the cause you were supposed to fight for. Ignore everything."

She slammed the door and left him alone. Her accusations were pointless and her anger was puzzling, but he didn't want to bother trying to understand his pilot. He didn't feel guilty. A few hours wouldn't make a difference for anyone. And he felt responsible for Cayla. His necklace still shone. He'd always thought that the light was proof that she loved him. He'd likely misunderstood the type of love.

A light blinked in his personal communicator. Odd channel. He picked it up.

"Is this Darian?"

"Yes."

"This is Zee, I'm in Rose's group."

The name was familiar, but not much. Some new recruit, not from the army. He kept his eyes on the panel, hoping whatever Zee had to say was short.

Zee continued. "I didn't mean to disturb you, I just wanted to make sure that you ordered the princess to be captured."

He felt as if the seat below him had disappeared. "What?"

~

Karina woke on a strange bed with a splitting headache. Daylight, or whatever, came from a ceiling far above her. The room was circular, with yellow walls made of some kind of stone, but without any division between the blocks. Besides the bed, the room had two chairs, a small table, and a curtain. She got up and saw what the curtain had been hiding; a hole in the ground, a sink, and a small tub. Karina looked at the walls around her and saw no door. She felt something on her waist and noticed she still had one shoe tied around her. The other one was on the ground, near her bed, as if it were one of her slippers. The room looked a lot like the blue room from where she had come, but without doors.

Was she a prisoner? Indeed, the last time she recalled being conscious someone seemed to have captured her. But still, she had the clear impression she had arrived at the castle, the very place she had come to help. Could it be that she had gone to an identical castle? Perhaps Lylah's? Maybe. Could it be that the castle had been taken while she was away? Maybe. She realized with despair that she didn't understand anything about that place. Who were those crazy finger cutting people who had tied them? They were not with Lylah and not with the king, and that just mushed everything, because Karina had signed up to help on a battle of good against evil, and for that to work two parts were needed: good and evil.

She was feeling lonely and anxious, not knowing what was happening, and why she was being held on that place. She decided to yell to see if anyone would come. "Hello! Someone! Help! Helloooo! Helloooo!"

Even though the room was empty, with smooth walls and a high ceiling, there was no echo, which was odd. Karina sat at the table. Nice touch to give her a table, but it was missing the most important thing: food. Oh, how she wanted some real food. Actually, at that point, even fake food or weird bars would be welcome. She felt thirsty as well, and at least the sink was a real sink, with water, so she drank with her hands. Then she decided to yell some more: "Helooo! Food! I'm hungry! Hungry!"

Was there anyone near her room? She tried to touch the walls, seeing if she could find a door, a handle, something. Perhaps she was not a prisoner and was just being silly. But all she felt was a smooth, circular wall. She lay down again, trying to prevent herself from wondering whether she had been left there to die. Oops, too late.

She sat on the bed, then saw the shoe on the floor and picked it up, meaning to tie it around her waist with the other, but then decided to hold them both and look at them. She could hardly believe those were the same shoes she'd found at that yard sale. That past reality seemed so distant now. As for the shoes, they were so much more, and, at the same time, in comparison to the reality they brought her, almost ordinary. Unless… Karina tried to recall what had happened at the hill. She had meant to use the shoes to escape, and she did escape, but she wasn't sure if it had been the shoes, or if someone had captured or rescued them. Floor trembling and black smoke, all of that was quite weird for shoes to do, even magical ones. But what if they had done it? What if the shoes had saved Karina, regardless of the hostile reception where she arrived? There was one way to find out, and she almost laughed at her stupidity for not having tried them earlier. She felt like a prisoner in a cell who has a key and yet never tries it on the lock. Now, what could she try to do with the shoes? Blow up the walls? Reckless, and dangerous. Try to teleport, find Cayla? Now, wait, teleport: that was the magic word. If she had teleported away from the hill, perhaps she could teleport to the place she most wanted to be: her room, away from all those people and all this mess she didn't understand. And if any creature came looking for the shoes, this time, she would gladly give them away.

But… how was she supposed to teleport? Hold the shoes and close her eyes? Say a magic word? When they had come none of the girls had said anything, so she probably didn't need any magic word. But there had been a portal, whatever that was. Perhaps it would be easier just to forgo any logic, because magical shoes were not logical anyways, and give it a try. Karina put on the shoes, closed her eyes and imagined walking into her bedroom. Nothing happened, but she took a few steps, as if walking could make a difference. Or should she touch a wall? Before she tried anything different, she felt as if she were falling.

When the feeling subsided, she opened her eyes. She caught her breath. *Home.* She was in her room, and felt a little scared and even skeptical that it was really her room, shocked at how easy it had been. Even though it was dark, she could see well, as if her eyes had adjusted in the seconds they had been closed. The lump under the covers was there, and so were the books on the floor, which she had removed from her backpack. Her pajamas were also on the floor. Now that was really stupid if she wanted to fool anyone that she was sleeping. On the clock by the bed she saw 12:16. She had no idea at what time she had left, but it couldn't have been much more than three hours earlier than that. The time difference was indeed real. She could get in bed, and nobody would even notice she had been gone. Even better, she could go to the kitchen and make herself a sandwich and a hot chocolate.

But something didn't feel right, and perhaps it was just that "too good to be true" feeling. Or not? Was she guilty that she had left? No, it could not be, because she had been given no choice. Karina decided she needed to forget what had happened in the last hours of her life, just be glad that she was back home and appreciate it. She crouched to pick up her pajamas, but, again, something was not right. She could not see her knees or feet or shoes. She could not see her hands or arms either, or any part of her body for that matter. A few hours before, she would have loved being invisible, and finally accomplishing one of her childhood dreams. But no, this was something else. That explained why coming there had felt too easy, maybe too light. She had not really come; it was if she had been dreaming. She then felt something pulling her as if she had been tied to the tip of an elastic ribbon whose force was now pulling her back. She saw blackness around her and felt as if she was floating mid-air. What could have been awesome in different circumstances was terrifying at that moment.

"Close your eyes and let go. Let go," a man with a familiar voice said.

She closed her eyes, even though it made no difference, as everything was black, but she had no idea what she had to let go, because she was not holding anything. Unless it was her thought. The thought of home, her room, escape, safety. But how could she give up those things?

"Let go. Come back."

The voice, she recognized now, was Odell's. His voice meant she was about to be rescued, and that thought encouraged her to return to the reality of the yellow room with no doors. Karina opened her eyes and realized she was lying on the floor. She looked up and saw Odell standing beside her. Never before had she been so glad to see an acquaintance she had known for two days. But something was wrong. His face was grave and stern. Was he a prisoner as well? Karina sat and looked around. She saw an open window some two meters above the ground. In fact, that was not a window, but a door, and probably the reason Karina had only found smooth walls when looking for an opening near the floor. Cayla stood at the high door, and Karina felt relieved to know that she was alive and well. But then again, no. Something was wrong; she looked distressed. Was she a prisoner as well? Karina felt disappointed that they were not there to help her, but still a little relieved that at least she would have company in her adversity.

"What's going on?" Karina asked.

"It's useless," Odell answered, sounding cold and menacing.

"What?"

He seemed angry. "Trying to escape. Your shoes don't work here. The most you'll accomplish is to hang between two worlds, never settling anywhere. Never living, never dying."

She rubbed her eyes. Fine, perhaps trying to teleport home had been dangerous, but what was she supposed to do? "I was hungry, I… I yelled, nobody came, I, I was trying to go home."

He laughed, not a nice laugh, but, for some weird reason, a mocking laugh, then stared at her. "Home? Nice try. We know what you want."

Why was he being so weird? Could he have figured something even Karina could not? "Really? You need to tell me cause I'm curious. Unless you mean food."

Odell pointed to the table. "Come, you can eat now."

Karina saw that the table was no longer empty, and didn't hesitate to accept the invitation, ignoring his weirdness. She glanced at Cayla, who still stood at the door, looking distressed. Or was she hungry as well? She should come down if that was the case. Karina filled a plate with weird rice and vegetables. At least she was finally getting real food and for that she could forget and forgive the strange behavior around her.

After she took a couple bites, Odell said, "So, you were planning to keep the shoes all along."

Karina almost choked. She forgot her good manners and answered before swallowing, "I cou 'ave tay 'ome."

Not very intelligible. Odell only stared.

She swallowed quickly and tried again, "I could have stayed home. I didn't need to come here and I wouldn't have come if I wanted to keep the shoes. I had them." She noticed her feet with some surprise. "In fact, I still have them. I'm wearing them."

He nodded. "Exactly. You just proved that you knew how to use the shoes and meant to use them."

"What?"

Karina took off the shoes and kicked them away, then she took another bite of her food, because she was really hungry. She was starting to think that he didn't look or act like a prisoner, so she hoped he would come up with a long explanation that would clear up everything—and give her time to chew and swallow.

"You came here to seize the power," he said. "Or worse, to help Lylah seize the power."

Perhaps this was one of those awful nightmares in which everything goes wrong and nothing makes sense. But it couldn't be a nightmare because food still tasted like food. The problem was that she didn't even know how to start arguing against absurdity. "I... no. Uh... If I wanted to help Lylah I could have given her the shoes when she visited me."

He raised an eyebrow. "Except you couldn't."

"Uh, no, but..."

"And you admit you met her before coming. And that you thought she was nice."

Where was he going with that? "Well, yes. In truth, she was nice. Very different from you."

He nodded. "And that's why you betrayed us."

"No. I mean now, now you're being mean. You seemed nice before." She looked at the door—where Cayla was—and hoped to get some support. "Cayla, help me, tell him what happened. That we were close to the meeting of the rivers, then we went to the hill, then we were captured, and they wanted to cut off our hands, then our fingers."

Cayla remained silent.

"Help me," Karina pleaded to the princess. "I saved your life, or at least your fingers. C'mon, we were in this together."

Her plea caused no reaction from the girl at the door, who kept staring at some random point on the wall.

Odell looked at the princess then addressed Karina, "That means you did use the shoes to get here."

What was that now? "No. I mean, I don't know."

"How, then," Odell asked, "can you claim you saved her life?"

Karina shrugged. "I don't know what happened. Fine, maybe I used the shoes to save her life. But maybe not. Regardless, she should speak up for me." She turned to the girl. "Cayla!"

Again the girl answered only with her silence. Karina felt betrayed, and she didn't understand why she was being accused like a criminal.

Odell continued his interrogation, "You're saying you were close to the meeting of the rivers. How could you have gotten so far?"

Cayla's silence got to her nerves.

"Why don't you ask her?" Karina pointed to the princess standing at the high door. "Ask her why she had to get a ride from her boyfriend, ex-boyfriend, almost boyfriend, almost brother, whatever."

Cayla looked pale but still stoic, except for a slight movement in her head, as to say no.

"We can see through your lies," Odell said. "The only reason you need to slander the princess is because you're desperate."

If there was one thing Karina didn't like was being called a liar. She got really angry with those people who were turning against her, especially the girl she had considered her friend. "It's true. Every word."

Odell looked seriously at her. "Your lies won't help you. Or anyone for that matter."

"I'm telling the truth. Cayla even has his twin necklace, the one with the orange stone, and she talks to him using it."

Odell laughed. "What nonsense. She never had a twin necklace, and even if she had, twin necklaces can't do that. Do you know why magic doesn't work in this room?"

Karina shook her head.

"It's yellow," he said. "Yellow blocks magic. No magical artifact would be yellow—or even yellowish."

"I'm saying what I saw."

He shook his head. "You're making up lies."

As he said this, she noticed he had a ring with a yellow stone similar to the one in Cayla's necklace.

He noticed it caught her eye and waved it. "This, for example, is to protect a person from magic, which must be the case with her necklace. If she had one. Your lies won't help you."

Karina was about to ask what would help her, when she heard yells coming from behind the door where Cayla stood. Cayla turned towards the noise. Odell looked at the door and seemed worried.

"Just a moment," he told Karina before moving towards the door.

He sounded strangely normal when saying this, as if he had paused his evil-mode button. Karina heard some voices amidst the confusion.

"Go away, you're forbidden here," a man said.

"Odell's the one who should be imprisoned, he's a traitor!" a woman yelled. It sounded like Nia.

Meanwhile, Odell reached the door, pulled a ladder, climbed it quickly, then closed the door behind him, blocking all sound. Karina was again left alone in a yellow room with smooth walls, hearing nothing of what happened behind them. At least now she would be able to eat. She tried to think. Perhaps Nia was right: Odell was a traitor who had turned against Karina, but the problem was that he was not acting alone. Since Karina had no idea about what happened behind closed walls, she had to try to make assumptions based on what she saw. Odell, and whoever was backing him up, seemed to fear Karina would use the shoes and take the power. What nonsense. She would certainly not be able to handle a kingdom of crazy people. And she didn't even want it. But the weirdest thing was that if they were so afraid of the shoes, how come they left them with her? It made no sense. But then, if they were so afraid they didn't even want to look at the shoes, maybe they didn't want to touch them or something.

The idea that Odell was the traitor made sense, especially given how concerned he seemed when he heard Nia accusing him. But why was Cayla silent? Unless... what if someone was standing behind her? Actually, Karina had heard voices; someone had in fact been standing behind her. Perhaps she shouldn't have said anything about Darian. But then, he did seem involved with the finger cutting crazy people. Another weird thing was that Odell seemed to defend Cayla or perhaps Darian, even using chromo magic science to back up his arguments. Oh, Karina should stop trying to understand anything or she would go crazy. But maybe that was the explanation: everyone was crazy. Crazy, crazy. The worst part was that she would have to deal with them and try to find a way to save herself, but she had no idea who to trust anymore or even what to do. If only she had returned home when she had the opportunity. Or better, stayed home. She made a mental note never to accept invitations for other dimensions from strangers again. Hey, why hadn't anyone ever told her that? But it was too late now. And what was the point in learning with an experience that would never be repeated? Anyways, this is where Karina was, and from where she would need to find a solution and a way out.

Sian rushed through the narrow passageways leading to the yellow tower, the highest security cell in the entire kingdom, built at a time when superstition and outdated beliefs overcame reason. Six guards stood by a translucent door. Behind it was the one loose piece that didn't fit anywhere. Of course, the prisoner was innocent and completely harmless. Sian would have been astonished if Odell had actually imprisoned a dangerous criminal. Now that he thought about it, he could hardly say that these times were any less guided by superstition and old beliefs. But that should change soon.

He took a closer look. The girl was sitting on a bed, muttering to herself and counting with her fingers, as if trying to figure a solution to a complex problem. He smiled. Maybe he had the answer to her problem, and she had the answer to his. Not that he would be able to discuss much of it with six guards watching them, but he could at least try to get an idea. The last he'd heard about her was that she'd been caught by his brother's criminal buddies. Then she was in the castle. The timing didn't make sense. But then, Cayla out alone with her didn't make sense either.

Sian turned to the guards. "Open the door. I'm coming in."

"I'm sorry, sir," one of the guards said, "So sorry." He looked down. "Nobody is allowed to enter."

Annoying. And surprising. Sian almost asked, "Not even me?" but they obviously knew who he was. The guard who told him he couldn't enter seemed uncomfortable having to say no. He looked at the six guards. All about seventeen or eighteen, which was young to be serving in the castle. Beginning of their careers. Eager to please. Changing their minds would be as easy as snapping his fingers. Assuring they didn't tell anyone about it would be a different thing, though. But he had to know who she was and where she fit. He heard steps behind him and turned. Odell. Sian hated the charlatan.

"What brings your illustrious visit here?" the bald man asked.

Sian snorted. "Isn't it obvious?"

Odell just raised his eyebrows.

Sian smiled. "There's a pretty girl down there."

The old man shook his head. "Aren't there enough for you in Siphoria?"

Sian shrugged. "Too many. It gets boring."

"Well, she's too young for you."

The freak either didn't know basic math or he'd forgotten Sian's age, but that was beside the point. "Too young to be executed then."

The old man grimaced, in what looked like disgust. "Nobody's getting executed."

Sian exhaled, relieved. That meant all he needed was time. He refrained from laughing as he realized he'd managed to get information from the bald man.

Odell continued, "But, again, with all due respect, I need to ask you to leave."

"The guards are here."

"Royal guards. They can remain in a Royal-only area. I do appreciate your visit and your concern, but your advice is not needed."

With Odell there and aware about Sian, talking to the girl would be impossible. Next time he wouldn't even be allowed in the corridors. But then, if she was there, perhaps whatever she knew or whatever she meant wouldn't affect the coming events. Maybe. He took one last look then turned to leave, but decided to have one last jab and turned back to Odell. "Tell her I said hi."

"She's never heard of you."

Sian frowned. "What an empty, meaningless life." He sighed and shook his head while laughing inside. The old freak had just given him another piece of information.

～

Alone for a long time, Karina feared being forgotten, realizing that she preferred to have someone accusing and questioning her and not having time to eat than being alone without any clue about what was happening, even though the accusations didn't really shed any clue. When the high door finally opened, she was happy to see Odell. Cayla wasn't there this time. He looked so distraught Karina would have pitied him if he hadn't been acting so evil.

She decided she was tired and didn't want to argue or answer any more questions. "Listen, just take the shoes, I don't care. I just want to go home."

He raised an eyebrow. "You know it doesn't work like that."

Karina looked down, but then she remembered something. "Actually, it does. Lylah told me I could sell the shoes. I can sell them for a ticket home. How's that? Then you deal with them. I don't care."

"It doesn't work like that."

Karina waved her arms in despair. "How does it work then? What do you want?"

"First, I want you to talk about, uh, the person you said betrayed Cayla. Tell me what you know about him."

Karina felt guilty that he pressed on this point, not knowing whether Cayla was still on her side or not.

"I… I made that up."

He raised his eyebrows in surprise and seemed pleased. "I see. So now you are confessing you were lying."

Karina shrugged. "If that's helpful, yes."

"I want the truth here."

Karina sighed. "What happens if I tell the truth? Can I go? And if you don't believe me? And if I lie? Seriously, just tell me what you want."

"Just answer the questions. How did you get to the place where you claim you were captured?"

"The place I *claim* we were captured? Does it make a difference? I just want to go home. I can even take these shoes if you really don't want them. I'll hide them really well."

He shook his head. "We know that if we let you go, you'll help Lylah."

"Wasn't I going to take the power? And wasn't she dead?"

"Now you want to convince me she's dead?" Odell asked.

"Uh? No. The people there, the ones who wanted to cut our fingers, they said she was dead."

Odell laughed. "And you believe everything you hear?"

Karina scratched her head. "I really have to stop that, like when two girls came to my room and told me I needed to help them save the world and defeat an evil woman. Believing what people tell me, what nonsense."

For a second Odell had half a smile, not an evil smile, but the smile of someone really amused, then he became serious again. "Well, you're confessing then. You'll have to stay here for now. Don't try anything silly; it won't work."

He walked towards the door. She was glad he didn't insist on his questions because she would have to tell the truth, and that seemed to upset him even more. But there was something she wanted to know. "Wait!" Karina yelled. "How long are you going to keep me here?"

Odell turned around. "As long as it's necessary."

"And how long is that?"

He started going up the ladder.

She repeated the question: "How long is that? How long?"

Odell ignored her.

Karina yelled, "Hey, it's not fair, you told me I'd be taken home, you told me it was safe. I only came to help. Hey—"

The door was closed.

A PLEA FOR HELP

Karina woke up with a hand on her mouth, and she felt terrified thinking perhaps she would be killed. The lights on the ceiling were dim. Karina looked around and saw long blond hair. Nia. Karina wanted to jump and hug her, so happy she felt, but the hand on her mouth kept her from moving.

"Try not to make any noise," the woman whispered.

Karina was even happier then, because that could only mean this was a rescue mission. How great it was to finally see a friendly face.

Nia looked around and asked, "Where are the shoes?"

Karina tried to mumble something with difficulty, then Nia lifted her hand and allowed Karina to speak.

"They're on me. On my waist. Do you want to see them?"

"No, no, it's fine. I can get you out of here, but I need you to promise me a favor."

Karina wondered if the woman wanted the shoes. "What favor?"

"I want you to get my son, then get us out of the castle."

Karina stared at the woman's belly, which was still large. "Son?"

"He was born two days ago."

"How am I supposed to get him?"

"Your shoes. You can use them to teleport."

This felt like a nicer version of Odell's accusations.

"They're not my shoes. Even if they were, I'm not sure I can—"

"They brought you and Cayla here."

"Really?"

Nia was serious. "Don't tell me you didn't know. I can't take you out of this tower if you can't get my son and me out of the castle. You know I tried to save you before without asking anything in return, but now I need your help. Do you want to come or not?"

Karina had promised herself she would follow whoever suggested taking her home, so she didn't want to refuse Nia's invitation, but she was still unsure about her ability to help anyone. Karina remembered Zoe, then she remembered Rose and the hill, and how she had done something with the shoes. She had even almost teleported home, although "almost" was a problem.

"I tried to use the shoes. To go home." Karina looked down, somewhat embarrassed. "And blow up the walls. They didn't work."

"It's this tower. It blocks magic. It'll be different outside. Now, time's running. If you want to come, then promise to help me, and come."

"I want to come. I'll help you. I promise."

Nia then gestured for Karina to follow her, and climbed a knotted rope leading to the high door, which was open. Now, the ladder would have been much nicer, but Karina didn't complain. The door was much higher than she had thought, but she put her best effort and climbed that rope, until she got close enough that Nia pulled her by the hands. At the hallway, two men were sitting, looking straight ahead. Karina gasped. For a second she feared they were dead, until she noticed they were breathing, so they were sleeping with their eyes open. Weird. The only reason she didn't ask Nia about them was that she had a stern face and gestured for silence. The woman closed the door from where they had come from, which was translucent from that side, meaning that Karina had indeed been watched.

Nia walked down the hallway and Karina followed. Further down, there were a few more men who seemed to be in that open-eyed sleeping state like the others, but Karina didn't get close to them. Instead of continuing, Nia touched one of the walls, as if looking for something. While she looked, part of the wall moved and a door opened by itself. Nia was startled and stepped back. Odell stepped out of the door and gasped in surprise. He noticed Karina, then looked at the men on both sides, as if grasping the situation. He gestured for silence. Nia took a knife and was about to stab him, but he pushed it away from her hand and took it.

"You're smarter than that," he said. "Follow me. I can help you."

Nia stepped back as much as she could. "I don't trust you. Never did."

Odell loosened the grip on Nia's arm and returned the knife to her. "Who do you trust then? The king? At least you know on whose side I'm not."

Sounds of steps were heard coming from the end of the corridor. Nia looked.

Odell continued, "You're out of options." He pleaded, "They'll arrest you. Please, come."

Nia sighed then followed him through the door, and so did Karina. Was that what she was supposed to do? The man closed the door, then walked fast through small corridors.

When they were in a long corridor, soldiers came from both

sides and surrounded Odell, Nia and Karina. Leading them, a man with a silver overcoat. It was General Keen. He laughed. "Who would guess? The two traitors together."

"You should thank me I stopped them," Odell said.

Keen laughed. "Nice try Odell, but I meant you and the woman. You helped her escape."

"Preposterous!" Nia said. "I can escape by myself."

Nia shouldn't be so offended. At least the general still counted her as a person.

"Are you that much of an idiot?" Odell asked Keen.

While he spoke, Nia whispered in Karina's ear, "Hold your breath."

Karina did as she was told, but she didn't fill her lungs with air for fear of being noticed.

Odell continued, "How do you suppose I can imprison them if they don't believe I'm on their side? Now they'll escape and the king will know about this."

The general had an unpleasant smirk. "I have twelve soldiers with me. I don't think anyone will escape. But the king will know what you are doing."

Odell was calm. "Let's bring our accusations to the king, then. But if they escape, the fault is yours."

Karina started to feel out of breath.

Keen laughed. "Except they won't." He turned to the soldiers. "Seize them!"

Odell raised his arms as if surrendering. Karina did the same. She didn't know for how much longer she would be able to hold her breath, and even if it mattered. A soldier approached her and held her wrists. General Keen himself approached Odell while four soldiers walked towards Nia. Karina figured it was all over, and she almost caught some air, but she made one last effort, trusting Nia's words. She wondered whether her face was turning purple. Instead of tying her, the soldier let go of her arms. In front of her, Keen lost balance and fell. All the soldiers collapsed on the floor, and Odell and Nia ran. Karina followed, and after some seconds finally caught some air.

They ran through narrow corridors until they reached a door that hadn't seemed to be there before. Karina wondered why she was following the man who had come up with weird accusations and kept her locked. She considered turning around and running, but she preferred not to distance herself from Nia. The secret door led to a small circular room, where he opened another secret door, leading to what looked like a cave, with rocks for walls. As the door to the cave was closed, darkness engulfed them, and Karina realized she had nowhere to escape, and how problematic that was. Odell lit what looked like a type of candle, which made things slightly better. The room, cave, cave room, whatever, had a table on a corner where Odell put the candle.

Odell turned to Nia. "Thank you for that. What did you do?"

"Thank you? I have no proof you weren't telling Keen the truth."

"Unfortunately, I can provide none. But you'll have to agree I had no choice."

"Choice? You should have fainted with them."

"I noticed you held your breath," Odell said. "Unlike General Keen. But you need to go quickly. If that was a gas bomb, as I suspect, they'll wake up in a few minutes and the castle will be on lockdown."

"I'm not leaving my son," Nia said.

"He's the best-protected person in the entire kingdom. But you have to go," Odell pleaded. "They'll be twice as careful next time. You don't suppose they had more than ten soldiers for Karina."

Nia laughed. "You're joking, right? Keen will be after you too."

"No. I'll be right there, fainted with him. And the King still trusts me. If anything, General Keen will be the one who'll have to explain your escape. If you don't leave now, I don't think I'll be able to get you out of the castle. Keen might have someone follow me. All the hallways will be watched. Either you go now or you stay and… I don't want to think about it."

"I know how to protect myself," Nia said.

"Yes. And you also know how to protect the girls. Nia, please, I know you've never trusted me, but you're an intelligent woman. You know I'm the enemy of your enemy."

Nia raised her eyebrows. "You mean to say I was always right about you?"

"Just trust that I am on your side. And the girls' side."

Nia frowned. "The girls? Why?"

"I… I've been taking care of them since they were little. Way before you, in fact."

"But you said it as if protecting them was a task assigned to you."

"It is a task…" Odell glanced at Karina then continued, "I assigned myself." He said this last part quickly, as if wanting to end the subject.

Nia still had narrowed eyebrows. "And how do you propose to help me?"

"This room leads to a way out. It's secret. I'm the only one who knows about it. Cayla and Ayanna are there already. They need to be taken away from the castle. Cayla is in trouble, she might still be safe for some time, but I can't predict how long. As for Ayanna, she's her sister, she's worried, and she's been asking questions. I can't vouch for her safety either."

Nia frowned and looked down, thinking. Karina felt a little guilty for the things she had said about Cayla, wondering if she had caused any trouble. Odell seemed to notice and turned to her. "It's not your fault. Although, why didn't you just do as I said? Why did you contact anyone outside the castle?"

Karina felt defensive. "It was Cayla, she—"

"I know," Odell interrupted. "Like I said, not your fault."

Because he no longer sounded evil, Karina had the courage to ask a question that had been bothering her. "You're not afraid I'll use the shoes?"

"Not in the way you think. But they're dangerous, and you can't control them, so don't try anything." He turned to Nia. "Now, please, trust me. Your son will be safe. You'll be reunited."

Nia snorted. "Sure. Like Cayla's mother? Or Ayanna's?"

Odell closed his eyes as if in pain. "That's why I have to save you."

"I don't want to be saved. Now, are you going to let me pass, or do I have to get rid of you?"

This time Nia sounded scary. Even Odell looked intimidated. Or was it something else? She wondered what she would do to him, perhaps immobilize him like the guards in that corridor?

Odell took a deep breath then said, "You'll just leave the girls?"

"Why don't you go with them?"

Odell shook his head. "I can't."

Nia scowled. "Is this some kind of trap?"

"You don't know me. Or you'd never ask that question. There are other ways to protect them."

Nia's eyes were misty. "I can't try to save my son, because I have to help the King's daughters and their friend? It's not a fair choice, you know?"

"Choice is a privilege we can't always afford."

"And what do you want me to do?"

"Ayanna will tell you. You'd better leave now."

She looked down for a moment, thinking, then turned to him. "If anything happens to Leo, I swear, I'll make sure you remain alive. You'll regret having been born."

He nodded. "I will, for sure. And if anything happens to any of the girls, I'll understand it's not your fault and you did your best."

Nia grimaced, as if annoyed.

Odell opened a trapdoor on the junction of the floor and the wall. It had a ladder leading to an underground tunnel. He turned to Karina and Nia. "You need to go down here. The girls know what to do. They are waiting for you."

A voice came from the tunnel. "We're here!" It was Ayanna.

Karina trusted the girl and felt relieved that it wasn't a trapdoor leading to her doom. Okay, maybe it would lead her to her doom, but at least she'd have company. Odell looked worried and urged her to go quickly. She went down the ladder, realizing she had no equipment or supplies, and that they would be three girls and a young woman with an army after them. Still, she felt relieved when she got down and saw Cayla and Ayanna.

Nia followed, her face somber, as the trapdoor was closed above them. She stared at Karina. "You. Take me to my son."

Cayla stared at them in alarm. While Karina was thinking what to say, the woman pulled a knife and put it against her throat. "Teleport. Now."

Cayla stared at her. "What are you doing?"

The cold blade still touched Karina's throat. Nia said, "An emotional spike. She needs an emotional spike to teleport."

That made some sense, and then Karina wondered how come she had the nerve to be interested in teleporting logic.

Cayla pleaded, "You can't expect her to… she doesn't know any magic!"

"The shoes!" Nia was breathing fast. "She promised. The shoes will bind her to her word."

Cayla moved fast towards them. Karina closed her eyes, fearing something would happen to her, but as she opened them Cayla kicked the knife far.

"The shoes are dangerous!" Cayla said. "What if they teleported you, her, or even your son somewhere else? What if the shoes killed you all?"

Nia sighed.

Cayla stepped closer to her. "He's my brother. I also care about him."

Nia looked away, gave Karina one last scary stare, then asked the sisters, "What are you planning?"

Ayanna replied, "We need to get to a tunnel that will take us to the Apex. From there we'll get to the Black River and go to Lylah's place."

Nia shook her head as if in disbelief. "Lylah? What madness is this?"

"All this problem is because our father thinks we want to take his power," Cayla explained. "But once we destroy the shoes, he'll understand we are on his side. Everything will be brought back to normal."

Karina was astonished at the idea that they should escape only to do the bidding of the people who had imprisoned them.

Nia rolled her eyes. "Is that Odell's plan? He's trying to fool you all. And things will never go back to normal."

"Can we please discuss later?" Ayanna pleaded. "We need to hurry before they find this tunnel."

The girl started walking towards the darkness. She had a blue crystal in her hand, and, as she lifted it, it illuminated a long straight tunnel, going downwards.

Cayla looked at it. "I'd never heard about this tunnel before. How come you know it?"

"Odell taught me last night," the younger girl replied.

"Why you?" Cayla asked.

Ayanna shrugged. "He said they were watching you."

"Still… He should have told us about it before…"

"Them," Ayanna said. "There are many tunnels. He said they were secret. We have to take the third door on the right."

"There are no doors," Cayla said.

Karina agreed that she didn't see any doors, but maybe they were further down.

"We're gonna have to find them," Ayanna said as she touched the rough wall.

"I can see them," Nia said.

Karina only saw rough, rocky walls, and she made a mental note to go to an optometrist when she got home, hoping of course that she would eventually get home.

Ayanna was surprised. "You do? That's so great, because I'm still not very good at finding those doors."

Nia walked a few steps, then showed a part of the wall. "This is the third door."

"Now I can also see it," Cayla said.

"Do you want to open it?" Nia asked.

Cayla shook her head. "Odell said you would be our guide."

"I don't want to hear about him," the woman said as she touched the wall. She then pressed a spot that didn't look different from any other spot, and part of the wall moved forward. The door was not square, but roundish and irregular, accompanying the shape of the rocks, which explained a little why it was so hard to be seen.

The girls and the woman entered. Ayanna lifted her crystal. She turned to Nia, "Are you sure this is the third door?"

"If you want, we can go back and I'll show you."

Ayanna looked at the tunnel. "I believe you, but I thought it should go up."

"Didn't you learn about these tunnels?" Cayla asked.

"Yes," the girl replied, "and this one should lead us to the top of the highest mountain."

Karina looked at the straight tunnel and came to her conclusion. "But if the tunnel is secret, it has to have some distance from the castle before going up."

Ayanna nodded. "Yes, that makes sense."

"Hopefully," Cayla said.

"Yes, let's go," the younger girl said. She started walking, then stopped. "No. Wait. Can you help me carry these things?"

She dropped a large bag on the floor, then took out two bags from inside it and put some things in them. She gave one to Cayla and the other to Karina, who was relieved that someone had thought about bringing supplies. But a question bugged her, "Why only two bags?"

"I picked them up in a hurry," Ayanna replied, then started walking.

Cayla walked fast, passed her sister then took the lead. Karina took a deep breath, then followed. She was finally on the way to her freedom, something she'd been dreaming and wishing for the past two days. She should be jumping up and down with happiness, but the tunnel felt oppressive and gloomy, and she wasn't sure where this path would take her and when she'd be able to go home.

The group kept walking, and, as they moved, the tunnel became slightly sloped. So it was going up. A little at least. Cayla asked her sister a few questions about the tunnels, and Ayanna again confirmed that they would go to the top of a mountain. Now that Karina thought about it, it didn't make any sense. "If it's a tunnel, why not go straight to the other side?"

Ayanna shrugged. "I don't know."

Karina left it at that, now used to questions without answers. The group kept walking.

After a few minutes, Nia addressed Karina in a soft voice. "You're assuming whoever built this wanted to cross the mountains. Perhaps that was not the case."

Karina nodded, then felt bad that she agreed with Nia, and bad again for having failed to rescue her son, even though she wasn't sure if she would have been able to. "I'm sorry."

Nia didn't reply. She only looked at Karina as if taking in the information. The woman walked slowly, increasing her distance from the girls in front of them. Somehow, instead of taking the opportunity to distance herself from her, Karina matched her pace, perhaps curious to hear if she had anything more to say.

Nia gestured for silence and replied in a whisper. "I know. This must be hard for you. I should have understood you were afraid. But I'm afraid as well."

The idea surprised Karina, because she thought Nia was powerful and confident. Ayanna turned around to look at them, and Nia addressed the whole group. "Don't you think we should stop and sleep?"

Cayla frowned. "We're still close to the castle."

"We'll never be far enough," Nia replied. "We have to hope they won't find this tunnel. If they do, they'll catch us regardless of our distance. Either this is secret and we're safe, or it doesn't matter."

Was that Nia's lullaby? With such thoughts, Karina would sure sleep like an angel. And the worst was that Karina agreed with Nia's logic.

"Well, it's true that I'm tired," Ayanna said.

"We stop then," Nia said.

Cayla looked displeased. A good thing that Ayanna had come prepared, because she took some blankets from her bag for them to sleep on. The downside was that the floor was rough, so sleeping there would still be uncomfortable even with the blankets, but on the upside, that was better than the comfortable bed in Karina's prison. Ayanna grimaced when she realized there were only three blankets.

"I know. Two of us will have to share. I can share."

"I can share as well," Nia said.

Karina was relieved. It wasn't that she didn't want to share a blanket, even though she didn't want to share it, but she didn't want to sleep by Nia. She then wondered why only three blankets, and if one of them had not been originally supposed to be there. Nia? Herself? But this time she didn't ask.

The group sat, and they all ate some dried fruit bar things and drank very little from the only water skin they had. Cayla touched what looked like her necklace, no longer hidden under her dress. The stone was red, however, unless it was the light, or lack of light, in the tunnel. Now, was that really her twin necklace? How did she even get it back, and in one piece? Karina didn't ask anything, because when Cayla realized Karina was looking, she seemed embarrassed then quickly hid the crystal under her dress. Karina looked elsewhere, pretending she hadn't noticed it even though it was obvious she had.

Later, Karina lay down because that was what everyone else did, but she was afraid of what could happen if she slept. The bluish light from the light crystal illuminated the side of the tunnel: brown rock, slightly shiny from dampness.

Sian walked through the hallways of the castle. More soldiers than usual had been deployed there, and he had on good sources that some people had escaped. All the hush hush and mystery just confirmed that the girl from the yellow tower had escaped. He couldn't fathom how anyone could escape such a high security cell, but there was certainly more to the story. He wasn't upset, though. If she was free, it meant he had a chance to learn what was happening, and adjust his course of action. And better than anything, he didn't even have to chase information. His own father had called him there.

General Keen was sitting on his usual armchair, hands steepled.

Sian walked in and kneeled. "My father."

"Get up and stop this nonsense. You're my son, not some worthless nobody. You should never kneel. Sit down."

Annoying his father was always satisfying. Sian got up and grabbed an armchair.

The General asked, "Do you know who escaped?"

"Odell's high-security prisoner."

A corner of his father's mouth lifted. "Well informed, as always. And do you know who was with her?"

Sian didn't know, and it annoyed him. His thoughts turned to Nia and Cayla, but that didn't make much sense. "I assume that information has been kept secret."

"It has, it has. The thing is: I don't think she was Odell's prisoner. Not in reality. He refused to have her executed, and I know that he helped her escape. Not only her, but our King's traitorous ex-wife, as well as his annoying daughters. I told the King, I told him that they were plotting against him, but I can't break Odell's hold on him. He wants the girls back alive."

Sian was surprised at how much, for once, he didn't know. He raised an eyebrow. "And what are they plotting?"

"Magic, Sian, magic. They'll take over the kingdom again. Those girls wield magic, and they are dangerous."

Sian refrained from scoffing, but it took some effort despite the years of experience in keeping a straight face when his father started his nonsensical rants against magic. "I assume you brought me here to deal with this matter, then?"

General Keen had a satisfied smile. "Yes, my son. I have a task for you. I'll trust nobody else. The girls and that woman must be killed."

Whatever opinion Sian had about it, he buried them. "And you want me to order this?"

"Yes, yes, my son. But nobody can know about it."

"Where are the girls?"

"They escaped. We're combing the castle and the surroundings, and nothing."

"They must be far away then. Let me just confirm: you want me to have Nia, Cayla, and the other girl killed."

"There's also the younger sister, Ayanna."

Sian nodded. But there was something Sian had to say. "As you know, my brother, Darian, fancies the older sister. It could be a good chance for our family—"

"He'll thank us for it, my son, he'll thank us. Less suffering. Think about your brother when you spill her blood. Spare his pain of a broken heart. And he doesn't need to know who did it."

Sian nodded in acknowledgement. "I will deal with this—as soon as I find them. I just have one request, my father."

Keen had mocking laugh. "A request?"

Sian didn't lose his beat. "Let me deal with this. Personally. Anyone else involved, and the chances of the information being leaked will increase."

"I trust no one else."

Sian bowed and left. Child murderer. So this was his father's opinion of him. He wondered what he'd done to rise so much in General Keen's esteem.

NIGHT REVELATIONS

A hand touched Karina's shoulder. She opened her eyes, surprised that she should be awoken when she shouldn't have fallen asleep in the first place. It was Nia, who covered Karina's mouth even though the girl had not meant to scream. Should she?

"Don't worry," Nia whispered. "I just want to talk." She looked at the two other blankets on the floor where Ayanna and Cayla slept. "Away from the girls."

The woman took her hand from Karina's mouth. Karina was more curious than afraid, so she got up, careful not to make any sound, and followed the woman some steps away from the blankets.

Nia sighed. "What do you think of all this?"

That was a huge question, and Karina was not sure where to start. "You mean, me being here, and—"

"I mean why do you think he wants us to go to Lylah?"

"To destroy the shoes?"

"Do you believe the story the girls told us?"

Karina was not sure where the woman wanted to take this conversation. "You think they are lying?"

"Not them. Odell. I think he wants to help Lylah, not defeat her."

The idea made sense, and yet it didn't. "Why would he want the shoes destroyed then?"

Nia rolled her eyes. "That's what he says. Now, think with me. Those tunnels are attached to the castle. Why does Odell know them and the king doesn't?"

Karina remembered what Cayla had said. "He's all wise and learned, isn't he?"

"I disagree, but it doesn't matter. You don't need learning or wisdom to know secret passages, or else Ayanna couldn't have led us here. You need only to know people who know the passages. Do you know who lived here before the king?"

Karina shrugged, surprised that anyone would expect her to know any history let alone history about an alternate world.

"Lylah," Nia answered.

"The Queen," Karina muttered. "What happened then?"

"Well, she was the queen, before the king. But then, they said she turned evil and was defeated. That's the story they tell. But what matters for us is that Odell might know these tunnels because he knows the previous owner of the castle."

"You think he's evil?" Karina asked.

"I'm not even sure Lylah is evil. You saw her. What do you think?"

Karina tried to remember the dark-haired woman who had visited her in her now distant room. "She seemed nice. But I don't know. Cayla says she killed her mother or was involved in it. And everyone seemed nice in the beginning."

"I know," the woman had a sad smile. "But regardless, I think Odell wants us to take the shoes to Lylah. Well, that's I thought before, but now I am more certain."

"So you think we shouldn't go there?" Karina asked.

"What? No. Let her have her shoes. But… I need to protect

the girls. And my son. I think... I think they're being sent as hostages."

Karina remembered being tied by people who wanted to cut her fingers, and imagined how Lylah could do something similar. "We should tell them."

"No. We all have to go. You know who's after us, and Lylah might be the only person who can defeat him. We'll have to side with her, but make sure she doesn't harm the girls. And Odell or the king don't harm my son."

That was a bold change for Nia. Karina took in the information, thinking. She then said, "And you're not going to tell Ayanna or Cayla about this?"

Nia shook her head. "They're stubborn. Especially Cayla. She wouldn't believe it. Or worse, she could want to protect her father and do something stupid. It's best to let them think they will erase all evil from the world by destroying a pair of shoes."

Karina almost laughed at the stupidity of that idea, until she remembered she had kind of believed in it not long before. She cringed. But something didn't make sense. "But how can the girls be hostages if Odell said they were in danger? That the king was after then?"

"You have your answer in your question."

Karina didn't understand. "What?"

"Who said it?" Nia asked.

Odell. Of course. "Oh."

"But," Nia added, "there's another possibility. Maybe the king does know about these tunnels, maybe Odell is not betraying him, and they are waiting to ambush us and prove that we are traitors."

"Why send the girls then?"

"Maybe the King is after them."

"But," how weird that this thought only now occurred to Karina. "They are his own daughters."

Nia shrugged and shook her head. "I don't doubt anything anymore."

Karina still didn't understand. "But why? And why are *you* running away?"

"A somewhat similar reason you were put in that tower. He thinks I'm plotting against him, that I want to take his power. I was being watched, and things got worse after Leo was born."

Karina nodded, partly understanding, but she still had a question. "And where does Odell fit in all this?"

Nia shrugged. "Maybe he's protecting us. Maybe he's pretending."

Karina didn't like that second option. "What then?"

"If we get ambushed, we'll have to fight."

She liked that even less.

Nia then said, "Go, sleep, you'll need your rest. Don't mention this to the girls."

"I won't."

Karina started to walk back to her place and figured that at least she learned that Nia didn't plan to slit her throat. Karina lay down feeling calmer than before, because she had one less person to fear. That floor was really uncomfortable, and yet, she dozed off.

"Karina, Karina," someone called her. This time it was Ayanna.

Karina mumbled, "You too? Does it have to be now?"

"It's time to move," Ayanna said.

Karina covered her head. Getting up and continuing the walk was even worse than a secret conversation. And plus, it was still dark. "Let me sleep, just a little more."

"We're running away, remember?" This time it was Cayla who spoke.

Karina uncovered her head and sat, realizing it was obviously still dark because they were underground. And that was another reason not to get up.

"But this is a secret tunnel. It doesn't make any difference."

"We let you sleep for a while," Cayla said, "but we have to go. We're out of water." She turned down an empty water skin.

Even Nia was standing, as if waiting. Karina rubbed her eyes and stretched. "You drank it all?"

"There were just a couple sips anyways," Ayanna said. "Water's supposed to run on the walls of the tunnels, but I think it's further up."

"What if it doesn't?" Karina asked.

"Then we'll have to find a stream outside," Cayla said.

"That's a thirsty walk up."

"It'll only get thirstier the longer we wait," Cayla replied.

Karina got up, put her things in her bag, and was ready to walk with the group. They kept walking in that dark place, lit only by the dim crystal Cayla now carried. After a lot of walking, Karina felt insanely thirsty. She hoped to reach the running water soon, hoped it was clean, and also hoped they would not be ambushed somewhere. At least she was still full of hope.

Suddenly, Cayla stopped. "This is wrong."

"What?" Her sister asked.

"We're going down." She stretched her hand forward to make the crystal illuminate ahead, but not a lot could be seen.

Karina looked around, thinking that the tunnel was flat rather than sloped down, although, yes, flat was still a problem. Ayanna turned to Nia, "Are you really sure this was the third door?"

"Yes," Nia said. "Perhaps your teacher was mistaken?"

Ayanna thought for a moment, then answered, "He sounded sure."

Nia rolled her eyes. "We all know that he's good at sounding sure."

Ayanna asked, "Do you want to go back?"

Karina only imagined walking some three or four hours without water, and didn't like it. She said, "Maybe we should keep going and see where it takes us."

"Yes," Cayla replied, "but there's no way this tunnel will lead us to the top of the mountain."

Top of a mountain. That reminded Karina of something, something unpleasant. "Wait. Aren't there jaguars in the mountains?"

"Not on the top. Around the lakes, in the valley." Cayla replied.

"Lakes and a valley explain going down," Karina blurted out.

"And water dripping," Nia added. "Perhaps we are in the right tunnel, but even if we aren't, I don't see any option other than going forward."

After an hour or so they found water dripping running along the walls. Karina finally drank. The tunnel didn't slope up, but apparently, everyone was satisfied in getting to its end to find out where it would lead them. So much walking was tiring and the continuous darkness was oppressive.

They walked the whole day. Karina felt exhausted, but somehow her curiosity to find out where they were kept her feet moving and her body standing. A couple times she considered asking for the others to stop, but she didn't want to show that she was more tired than everyone. Finally, Ayanna asked to stop.

Nia refused. "Look," she pointed to the ceiling and walls, "the tunnel is getting wider and higher. I think we're getting somewhere."

Karina was sure they were getting somewhere: somewhere meaning further down the tunnel.

Nia continued, "We walk just a little more, to find out where we are. Then we stop for the night."

Cayla nodded and got going, and somehow her sister followed. Karina didn't protest because she noticed that the tunnel was in fact a little different. Did it mean they were near its exit? But then, wouldn't it be safer to sleep inside? On the other hand, a few more minutes walking wouldn't kill her. A few more minutes. After that she would put her blanket on the floor and lie down, regardless of what the others decided. But the tunnel got wider and wider, and the only reason they could not see much ahead was that it was curved. After a sharp curve, they reached a wide opening, more like a large cave, some five meters wide in each direction and high enough that the light from the crystal didn't reach the ceiling. Nia's idea had been good, as this would be a more pleasant place to sleep than in the narrow tunnel. Karina didn't wait for the others and spread her blanket on the floor. Ayanna did the same.

Cayla, for her part, seemed restless and illuminated all the walls, with Nia beside her. "Do you see a door?"

"Let's keep looking," Nia replied.

That conversation made Karina realize that there was something wrong with that cave: only one entrance, or exit. Her eyes met Ayanna's, who seemed to have realized the same thing at the same time. But maybe that fear was pointless. After all, Nia knew how to find secret doors. They had come through one, and this place would sure have another. Perhaps that was why Odell said the girls needed Nia to guide them. Karina watched as Cayla and Nia examined the walls. This looked like a very difficult door, as they circled the place twice, going slower the second time, and also illuminating the higher parts of the walls. This didn't look right, because the other time Nia had found a secret door she had acted as if they were quite obvious. The duo circled the place for a third time, and even walked back a little in the tunnel.

Nia was the one who decided to stop. "We need to rest. We'll look again tomorrow."

They all sat and ate. After that, Karina lay down and tried to forget everything around her, while the others started to discuss their situation. Cayla accused Nia of having lead them through the wrong door, and Ayanna of not having heard well the instructions. Nia thought perhaps this was a trap, Odell had made a mistake, or Ayanna had been mistaken. Ayanna thought Nia could have been mistaken and even started doubting her own certainty about the directions.

In the end, despite what each of them thought, they were all tired and had to sleep. Karina remembered that the time difference was not as much as she had first calculated, and it would be already two or three in the morning. If she didn't find a way back soon, her parents would notice her absence. Still, at this point, upset parents was the least of her worries. She had to stay alive first, and then make sure she found a way back.

Cayla opened her eyes. She shouldn't have fallen asleep. Her travel companions' chests moved up and down, peacefully. Sleeping. She walked away from them, back to the tunnel, and took her necklace.

"Darian?"

The previous night it hadn't worked. She didn't have much hope that it'd be different this time. The stone was still red. It had never done that, and it wasn't because that woman had stepped on it, as she'd picked it up in one piece. Darian was trying to reach her, and had been trying for the last couple days. But Nia and Ayanna couldn't know about the necklace. Now, in the middle of the night, she wasn't sure he'd reply. But before she expected, his voice came out of the stone.

"Cayla? Where are you?" he sounded sleepy and sad.

She'd still been a little mad at him, but hearing his voice made it all go away.

"Can't you find me?"

"It doesn't make sense. It's as if you're trapped somewhere, but you're in the mountains."

"I'm in a tunnel underneath the mountains," she said.

"That makes sense. You're beneath the Apex."

If he was right, there was an entire mountain above them.

He continued, "I'm so sorry. I trusted the wrong people. I was betrayed."

She'd imagined this conversation, and she thought she would yell at him, tell him he'd put her life in danger, but she didn't feel like doing any of that. The pain in his voice showed he knew what he'd done. And it hadn't been his fault. "It happens." She had a question, though. "But are you with them? With those people?"

"There's a lot that I need to tell you, but it needs to be in person. Just be assured that I serve the kingdom."

These words put her at ease. She trusted him.

He continued, "And you? What's happening? How are you?" His tone was soft and sweet like she remembered.

"Fine, I guess. Escaping the castle. I need to finish a mission for my father, or he'll still be upset at me."

"That can't be fine. I'll come and meet you. Take you somewhere safe." He sounded sad and pleading.

"You know how meeting me worked last time…"

"I'll be alone."

"I'm supposed to go to the Apex. You can go there. But I'm not sure I'll reach it. These tunnels didn't go up."

"I'll dig until I find you."

Cayla smiled.

He continued, "Also, I understand you want to be just friends—"

The words hit her like a boulder. "What?"

"It's what you told me."

That didn't make sense. "I never did."

"You never…" he paused.

Her heart was about to explode, unsure why he was saying that. Was it an excuse? Had he changed his mind?

He continued, "You mean... to say... you want to be... more than friends?"

That was a question? "What do you think?"

"I'm asking."

"Since when do you have to ask?"

"We never... I mean, usually people ask, right? I guess I should have asked, but I never had the chance. But... when I told you Zayra thought you were my girlfriend, you weren't happy about it."

"You do realize my father will kill you if he learns that, right?"

"Sure. But we weren't near your father. It was people I... trusted. I guess you have a point. Was that the reason you wouldn't take my hand?"

"What do you think?"

"I don't know. What about the suffocating and stuff?"

"You were all weird, questioning me, giving me orders." She made a thick voice. "What are you doing? I'll take you back to the castle."

There was a pause before he started speaking again. "I was worried. Maybe I was angry. I thought you didn't..."

"You were thinking it just now, and you were nice."

"I had made peace with the idea."

"Next thing you'll tell me the sky is yellow."

He spent some time silent, then said, "I'll meet you at the Apex then."

"Again, I'm not sure I'll make it."

"I told you I'll dig and find you. Or I'll move the mountain. Or something."

Cayla's cheeks got warm. The way he said these words, it reminded her why she liked him so much. And she did. She was sure of that. But there was something she had to tell him. "Darian. I'll be with Nia, Karina, and my sister. They can't know about us. I won't take your hand."

He was silent for some seconds, then asked, "But would you like to?"

Her face got hotter. "You shouldn't have to ask."

Darian spent an even longer time in silence. Cayla thought she'd have to say something, when she heard his voice again. "I guess you won't let me kiss you either. Would you like me to, though?"

The only reason her face didn't get any hotter was because it would catch fire. "What do you think?"

"I want to hear it. Make sure there's no misunderstanding."

Cayla took a deep breath. She thought the answer was obvious, but, from the way he said it, it wasn't. Why were these words so difficult? She forced herself to blurt them out. "Yes, Darian, I want you to kiss me. I've wanted it for a long time. But please don't."

"I'll get this all solved then I'll kiss you a thousand times."

She smiled. "That's not a lot."

"A billion. Trillion. Infinite."

Cayla laughed. "Now you're being reasonable." They were both silent for a few seconds. She then said, "I have to sleep."

"I have to prepare. Make sure nobody follows me. Sleep well. Cayla. I luh… look forward to seeing you at the Apex."

For a second she thought he'd say something else. But it didn't matter. She laughed. "Or in a hole somewhere."

"I'll find you. Goodnight."

Cayla walked back to her blanket feeling giddy and light. Maybe he'd been right, and nothing between then had been obvious. But now it was. She would fall asleep thinking about kissing him, knowing someday it would be true, knowing for sure that he liked her. He was her steady rock among all the things that had been shaken recently. All those things she'd rather not think about, otherwise she'd be consumed with fear that her father would not accept her back, that everything would change. No. The shoes would be destroyed and everything would be turned back to normal. This hope kept her moving forward.

~

Karina woke up while the others were still sleeping. The big cave was quite different from the small tunnels. The dim light from the crystal had been multiplied in many tiny rays, lining the cave with thin light streams. She looked up and noticed that she could see part of the ceiling high above them, and its texture. But the tiny rays didn't reach the ceiling: they rather came from it. Karina recognized a fraction of something she had not seen in days: sunlight! There was something up there, like an opening of sorts. She decided to touch Cayla's shoulder softly, just to check if she was really sleeping. The girl sat up quickly and looked around. "What?"

"Sorry, I, I just wanted to know if you were awake."

Cayla looked around, squinted, then laughed. "Then I wouldn't be sleeping."

"Indeed. But I have good news." She pointed at the ceiling. "Can you see it? There's light coming from there, so there must be an opening."

Cayla looked but didn't seem convinced. "That's impossible."

"But we can see the ceiling. We couldn't last night. And it's not the crystal."

Cayla looked for a longer period. "I see what you're saying, but there can't be any opening, because we're under a huge mountain."

She was grinning, which was a bizarre reaction if she thought they had no way out. And that certainty about their location was strange. "How do you know where we are?"

Cayla looked down. "I… have ways to find out."

"Why didn't you do that before?"

She pointed to her necklace. "You know... But it didn't work before. The thing is, we're at the right place, but I think Odell misread a map. He saw a line stopping at the middle of the mountain and assumed it went to the top."

Incredible. "So you think Odell made a mistake?"

"I guess." Cayla looked down, then took a deep breath. "We'll find a way to fix it, but I wanted to talk to you. Can you come with me?"

Karina nodded. The girls walked back to the narrower part of the tunnel.

Cayla spoke softly, "When you were in the tower, I couldn't help you. Neither could Odell. I'm sorry. He told me to stay quiet and that he had to play along."

"Who was he playing along with?"

The girl looked down. "I'm sorry for my father. I think... he's under a lot of stress. Maybe he's receiving bad advice, maybe... He'd never harm you, and... I'm sure it's the shoes that are messing with his head. He'll be back to normal once they're gone."

Karina stared at the girl, almost asking "Are you out of your mind?" but thankfully her thought was silent. Instead, she said, "No problem. We'll get to Lylah's and make things right—once we find a way out of here, of course."

"We will." Cayla then became serious and thoughtful. "But you shouldn't have mentioned Darian. I'm glad you didn't say his name, though. It could've cost his life."

Karina felt bad for that, but then... "What would you have done in my place?"

"I would have kept the secret. I trusted you. You are the only one who knows about it."

That was not true. "And Zayra, that angry girl Rose, and that man..."

"I mean here. Nobody else knows. Not even Odell. I had to

make up a story, and it was a lot of trouble to convince my father."

Karina wasn't sure she had to apologize, but she did it anyways. "I didn't know what to do, Odell was accusing me, I… I'm sorry. But later I said I had lied, so you see, I made up for that."

Cayla waved a hand. "Don't worry. It's past. Just please don't mention this anymore."

"I won't." Karina noticed the necklace again. This time it looked orange. She pointed at it. "Is it the same one? How did you get it back?"

Cayla shrugged. "I grabbed it. But I have no idea how we got back to the castle. Do you know what happened?"

Karina was about to say that she thought she had used the shoes to teleport, but then she decided it was best not to sound confident about that. "I… no. I have no idea."

"That's what I thought. But," she looked down, "there's something else I wanted to tell you."

"Yes?" Karina was even more curious.

"Darian." She sighed. "I was mad at him, but… we spoke. He apologized. It wasn't his fault. That girl, Zayra, it was her. I knew it. I told you. But Darian, he's on our side, just in case we, uh, by chance, happen to meet him or something."

Karina face palmed. "Again? That was what got us the first time."

"Because of the girl."

"Wasn't he on the side of those people who imprisoned us?"

"Not him."

Karina started to search her memory, because she thought she'd heard something different, but she decided to leave it at that. There was another problem, though.

"If by chance we meet him," Karina hoped it wouldn't come to that, "won't Nia and your sister notice?"

Cayla shrugged. "They'll think we're just friends."

Wait. Was that a confession? "Aren't you just friends?"

Cayla squinted. "Of course! But they won't know we're close friends and have been talking. Nobody can know about this."

"But they saw your necklace."

"But they don't know what it does."

So that was what Cayla was worried about? Karina made an effort to sound serious. "Don't worry. Your secrets are safe with me."

How could Cayla be worried about such trivial matters when she was running away from her own father, who had turned evil or at least weird, when they had an army looking for them and when they were in a tunnel without exit? Oh, a "close friendship" really messed with one's mind.

Cayla started walking back to their sleeping place when she turned. "What do you think of Nia?"

The question surprised Karina. "She's... nice?" She was starting to hate that word.

Cayla looked down then looked around. "Yes, it's just... It's not that I don't trust her. Odell trusts her, but he doesn't know that she tried to prevent us from destroying the shoes, and he doesn't know what she did to Ayanna."

"And that you helped," Karina added, before thinking whether it was a good idea to mention that.

Cayla opened her eyes wide. "Yes. But that was for her own good." Cayla then squinted and continued. "As I was saying, yes, he trusts her. But he says our father locked her for conspiring against him, and we know that it's not far from the truth."

Karina felt she had to defend Nia. "She was only worried."

"Yes, but... I know she has at least some magical knowledge, and Odell doesn't know that."

"I'm sure he knows," Karina corrected her friend.

"Fine then. Still. He trusts her blindly. Sometimes, sometimes I think she might have done something to him. Like, I don't know. Anyways, I like Nia, and I want to help her, but...

there's something odd about her. I'm not saying I don't trust her, but just—keep an eye on her. And don't listen to what she says."

Karina just nodded. "I'll pay attention." She felt bad because she knew Nia was planning on siding with Lylah, and she didn't tell Cayla any of this. She tried to change the subject. "Should we go back and look for an exit?"

"I guess."

They walked back. Ayanna and Nia were still sleeping.

Karina still thought there was an opening and asked Cayla, "What if you're wrong about our location?"

"I'm absolutely sure."

At this point Nia asked, "Sure of what?"

Cayla looked embarrassed. "Nothing, I mean," she pointed, "look, we can see the ceiling."

The woman looked and smiled. "There's the exit we were looking for."

A LONG WAY TO THE TOP

N ia sounded hopeful and relieved, and made Karina feel the same way.

Cayla didn't seem to agree. "But there's no opening."

"The opening is never obvious," Nia said. "I think it's either a secret door, or perhaps there are vines of some sort, I can't see much from down here."

"Can you go up there?" Karina asked, hoping the answer would be yes.

Nia looked up. "There must be a way, but we have to find that out."

Ayanna still slept, and Nia started again to look around the walls, but this time she was looking for a place to climb, rather than an opening. Karina also looked, thinking that the room was a puzzle to be solved, and how she liked puzzles. But she didn't like them when she couldn't find the answer, so trying to find a way up soon stopped being any fun. Still, she was proud of herself for having been the first to see the opening for what it was. She was getting good at recognizing otherworldly logic.

After a while, they sat to eat, realizing they were running out of food. Ayanna woke up and was happy to hear they had found a door.

Nia then got up and looked at the walls over and over. She finally sat again. "I don't see anything." She sighed. "We would need to go straight to the ceiling. A rope with a hook or something similar would work. But I can't think of what we can use instead. I… I don't know." She shook her head and looked down.

Ayanna asked, "You want a rope with a hook?" She got up and picked up her bag. "I have one." She pulled out something white and shiny from inside it and gave it to Nia, who looked surprised.

Cayla stared at her sister. "You had a rope all the time? And didn't tell us?"

The girl stepped back and raised her shoulders. "Nobody asked!"

Cayla rolled her eyes. "We were looking for a way up."

"How was I supposed to know?" The girl replied.

"You're right. I should have asked," Nia told Ayanna, then turned to everyone. "But at least we found the door and we know we're in the right place, or else she wouldn't have brought this rope. I'll climb to the ceiling."

She said this as if the climb was quite simple, even though it looked nothing like it, at least for Karina. In fact, Nia tried to throw the rope some eight times before she started reaching the ceiling, and even then, it took a couple more tries to get the hook safely placed. The girls only looked. Nia then jumped, grabbed the rope and started climbing it without any difficulty.

When she got to the ceiling, she touched it then yelled to the others, "They're vines. I need to cut them."

She held herself with one hand and legs while fumbling through her clothes, then came back down, looking distraught. "My dagger. I lost it. Does anybody have a dagger? A knife? Ayanna?"

Ayanna looked through her backpack, searched, then shook her head.

Cayla frowned, then took something from her bag. "Is it this one?"

Nia at first seemed surprised, then upset the girl had kept her prized object. She took it without saying a word, then climbed again and started cutting the vines as if they were made out of paper. Karina realized the blade was sharper than she'd imagined, and shivered thinking that it had been near her throat. The cuts on the vines revealed more dim light and an apparent opening.

Nia said, "I can see stairs." She moved up through the opening and disappeared in that dark ceiling. Only her voice could be heard. "Come on up."

The girls looked at each other. Karina thought the sisters were also wondering how in the world they would climb that thing. But no, apparently it was just indecision. Ayanna jumped, grabbed the rope, then climbed up, even if a lot more slowly than Nia. Cayla held the light, so she gestured to Karina to go first. The rope was straight, with no knots, unlike the one she had used to climb out of her yellow prison in the castle, and even then, close to a wall, she'd had a lot of difficulty.

Karina looked at her friend then whispered, as if speaking softly diminished the truth she was about to admit, "I don't think I can do it."

Cayla sighed, impatient. "There's no other way. Do you want to go back?"

Nia put her face in the opening. "What's going on?"

Cayla replied. "She says she can't climb it."

Nia didn't seem upset. "I'm sure she can. Cayla, climb first, that way she sees you and can do the same."

The girl nodded and climbed, holding the light between two fingers. She was fast and precise, almost like a circus artist, and Karina realized that she had seen circus and gymnastics stunts many times, and that they'd never increased her chances of being capable of performing them. But soon Cayla disappeared through the hole, keeping only the light pointing down. It barely reached Karina.

"Take your time. We're waiting," Nia said, in a tone that implied the opposite.

Karina tried as best as she could. She managed to grab the rope, but she was never capable of pulling herself up only with her arms. A few more tries yielded only exhaustion and pain. Karina sat on the ground, feeling defeated. She then tried to think, seeing if she could find a logical solution to make up for her lack of physical skills. She wondered if she could teleport, but more and more she felt it was impossible, and that perhaps she had not been responsible for their escape from the finger-cutting people on the hill. A loud thud snapped her out of her thoughts.

Cayla had just jumped down, and was beside her, looking annoyed. "Is that your plan? To spend the day sitting? How's that going to bring you up?"

"I was trying to think."

"You won't go up by thinking. Let alone trying."

Karina only stared, wondering if the girl had really gone through the trouble of jumping down just to scold her. Cayla was right beneath the rope, and pointed up, then pointed to her shoulders. "Here."

Karina crossed her arms because she was well aware she had to go up and she had to use her arms. "I tried, okay? I'm trying."

Cayla laughed. "No, no. I want to help you. Climb on my shoulders." She then crouched.

Karina climbed on the girl's back, then on her shoulders. She held the rope and stood up on Cayla's shoulders, careful not to fall. This time, she could touch the rope with both hands and feet, making her way up easier. With a lot of effort, she got close to the opening, and Nia pulled her up. She found herself on a metal grid, surrounded by a tube made of a sparkly white stone. There was a transparent spiral staircase, made of glass, or something similar. Dim light came from the steps above. Those were some huge stairs. A tunnel upward.

Cayla soon came up. "Well, at least we'll finally move. I was afraid we wouldn't reach the top by day."

Nia took a deep breath. "Let's just hope nobody's waiting for us outside."

Cayla shook her head. "No. I think this time everything will go well. I know it."

"Good for you," Nia said.

Karina feared they would start arguing, but they didn't. There was no point in trying to predict the rest of their journey when it stood above them. Karina then wondered how high that mountain was. From what she had seen from the castle it was an old mountain range. The highest peak couldn't be taller than some two kilometers, which meant that they could get to the top in no more than a couple hours.

After a few minutes climbing, Karina realized that she had greatly underestimated the effort and time to get to the top. After just a few turns, everyone's pace was reduced, and soon they all sat to rest. Nobody talked, because they were panting, even Nia and Cayla. They just passed the water around. Karina felt a little dizzy from all the turning and her legs hurt. They spent their next hours either climbing slowly or sitting and resting. At least the more they climbed the more light reached them, and it felt good to be moving away from darkness. The downside was that the more they climbed the taller the steps felt. They were the same size, but the strength in their legs wasn't.

Karina would never again complain about going up four, ten or even twenty floors. Not after she'd climbed the equivalent of some six hundred. Assuming her estimate was right, of course.

As interminable as the staircase had first looked, after many hours of slow climbing and resting they reached a place where they could see a small opening and patches of blue sky above them. The stairs finished, and they reached a smaller tube, some six meters high. A metal ladder led to the top. Cayla climbed first, and Karina last. She hated being last again, but at least she knew her arms and feet could take her out of that place. Actually, it wasn't as easy as it seemed. Trembling tired legs are not very efficient climbers. When Karina finally put her head outside, among branches, she saw that the tube from where they had just come out looked like a tree from the outside. That was a neat way to hide a huge staircase from anyone who went to that mountain.

Exhausted, Karina reached the ground, which was covered with grass. There were other trees around them. Karina realized how much she had missed the sky. The few clouds above them looked orange and pink. How magnificent it was to be out in the open.

"We need to find a place to spend the night," Nia said.

Cayla looked at her sister. "What did Odell say? I mean, what are we supposed to do now?"

Ayanna seemed to think for a moment. "Other than going to Lylah's castle, I don't think he had any more advice." She looked down, thinking. "No, he didn't. But I think it should be easy from here, right? I mean, because he didn't say much about it."

Nia narrowed her eyes as if thinking. "As far as I know this is an impossible place to reach—except by air. So we just have to make sure we're not spotted from above. Other than that, perhaps we're safe—hopefully."

They walked to a place where the trees were closer together, so that no lifts could spot them from above. They spread their blankets and sat. Karina felt exhausted, but she was curious to see the path ahead. She got up. "I just want to take a look there."

"I'm coming with you," Cayla said, and also got up.

Nia narrowed her eyebrows, then said, "Careful. It's getting dark. And don't go far."

The girls nodded, then walked about one hundred meters, until the forest, and the ground, stopped suddenly. There were mountains further away, in a crooked horizon. Beneath them, an ocean of thin clouds, covering a valley and a dark river. So that explained "black" river. Somehow Karina had imagined a more eerie meaning to the name. Amidst the clouds, in the middle of the river, she could see something white and shiny, similar to the stone surrounding the long spiral staircase. Karina took a better look, and realized it was a white castle on a small island, contrasting to the waters around it. It looked like a toy in the distance, or better, an icing cake decoration, and yet, that little thing was their final destination.

Karina then realized she had been so caught up in the tunnel and stairs she had completely forgotten the purpose of her journey. Her task was so much more than getting out of a tunnel. The darkness and enclosing had made her forget the great beautiful sky outside, and that this world was just part of some great bigger something.

13

LOOKING AHEAD

"I'm glad we're out. This is beautiful, isn't it?" Karina said. Cayla, who stood beside her, smiled. "It's amazing. And we're near her castle, so we are finally back on track."

"Back on track with everyone after us."

Cayla didn't seem worried. "We'll make it right."

Karina then thought about her change of mind about Lylah, her change of mind about the king, and how the mission seemed completely different now. She wondered if Cayla was at least open to feeling something different from the way she felt before. "And what if the reason we're here is different from what you expected?"

Cayla had a puzzled look. "Like?"

Karina shrugged. "I don't know. And you think we'll go in, throw the shoes, then puff, Lylah disappears?"

She had made an effort to sound serious, but she wasn't sure if it had been successful.

Cayla laughed. "You make it sound silly. I don't know, all I know is that Odell wouldn't tell us to do something dangerous or that didn't make sense."

Karina looked down. "It has been dangerous."

"I know, but if we hadn't had any problem on our first journey, we could be down there, on the other side of the river, on this same day, waiting for nightfall, without anyone following us."

Getting to the mouth of the Black River should have taken five or six days, so Karina corrected her friend. "Actually, we would still be near the meeting of the rivers."

"See? I was right. We did speed up our journey."

Karina laughed. In reality, she thought that a long and boring camping and hiking expedition around the mountains would have been better than all the trouble and danger they'd been through the last few days. But, would it really? She would still believe that the tyrant and crazy king was representing the good guys. She would still believe she would save the world by destroying the shoes. Of course, Karina wasn't thankful that she had been imprisoned and threatened. But still... like Cayla said, they had even sped up their journey.

Cayla noticed that she was thinking, but probably imagined something else, and said, "I know. Maybe we should have done as Odell told us, we should've walked all the way, I know. But I can't change that now."

Karina nodded, accepting what she thought was the closest to an apology her friend could muster. Another thought, unrelated to their conversation, hit Karina. "It doesn't have walls around it."

"What?"

"The castle. You said it had walls."

Cayla seemed to remember. "It's true. But it doesn't look like a fortress either."

"It doesn't."

Karina was no expert in fortifications or castles, but that delicate, white, shiny thing certainly didn't look like a fortress. She then tried to imagine what it would look like from the inside but the thought gave her a knot in the stomach. Even though the castle looked like a little toy, it was there, it was reachable, it existed. So different from the theory of Odell's explanation which now seemed to have happened an eternity before.

"Let's see the way down," Cayla said.

The girl walked closer to the edge, and Karina followed. She knew the descent was steep, but when she looked, her heart almost stopped. "Steep slope" was a huge understatement. What she saw was a humongous cliff, tall and wide, extending almost as far as they could see. Karina finally understood why, on their first journey, they would have to walk around it. There was no way they would go down that thing. Cayla also looked worried, so no, this wasn't supposed to be easy, not even for the people there. Cayla turned around. "We have to tell them."

The girls raced back, then told the others what they'd seen. Ayanna was surprised, but Nia not so much. "I told you this was an impossible place to reach by land. Didn't you ever see a picture of the divide between rivers?"

"I saw a map," Cayla replied. "It doesn't show the height." She then turned to her sister. "Did you bring any more climbing equipment?"

"Just that rope."

"And what did Odell say?" Cayla asked. "He must have said something."

Ayanna looked down and shrugged. "He told me what I told you, to reach the top of the mountain then go down to the river and the castle. He didn't say anything else. Is the mountain that bad?"

Cayla had a grimace. "Yes. And it's all smooth. And even if it was easy, we don't have the equipment."

Nia looked distant and strangely silent.

Cayla asked her, "What do you think?"

She shrugged. "Well, Odell sent us here. He either wants us to reach Lylah's castle, or he wants us to be caught."

"No. No way," Cayla said.

Nia raised an eyebrow, as if annoyed, then continued, "Well, if he wants us to reach the castle, and if he didn't send us any equipment, there's a way down. If he wants us captured, someone will show up and we won't be able to do much."

Cayla seemed upset. "I'm absolutely sure Odell didn't send us here to be captured. He'd never do anything like that. Never."

"We'll find a way down tomorrow then," Nia said. "Nothing to worry about."

Karina remembered the possibility of being ambushed. More and more this possibility seemed likely. And this mountain looked like the perfect place for that. She wondered why Nia seemed so cool about it. "Aren't you worried?"

Nia sighed. "I'm tired. But perhaps we could keep watch." She looked at Cayla, who didn't seem to like the idea. "Just in case. We're close to Lylah's land, we have the king after us, it would be safer. I can go first, then you two." She pointed at Karina and Cayla.

Cayla pointed at her sister. "Why not her?"

Before Nia replied, Ayanna said, "I can watch. I want to. Please."

"Fine, all four of us will rotate," Nia said.

Karina envisioned another poor sleeping night, but she thought it would be better than risking being caught sleeping. Well, they would be caught awake then. She didn't want to think what the difference was. They sat and shared the last food they had, which wasn't enough to appease their hunger, at least not Karina's. For the first time in this world she felt a cool breeze, instead of the stuffy hot weather or the stagnant air from the tunnels.

Cayla looked around and seemed alarmed. "Wait."

"What's wrong?" Nia asked.

"Silence," Cayla said. "I can hear something."

Karina couldn't hear anything, but by this time she was so used to being incompetent in her senses that she wasn't surprised.

Nia looked around. "It's just the wind."

"No," Cayla whispered. "Someone's coming. We have to get back in the tunnel."

They all got up, but Nia held Cayla back. "Bad idea. If someone sees us getting in, we'll be trapped there."

Cayla closed her eyes, gestured for silence, pointed up and started climbing a tree.

At this point Karina had the impression that she did hear something, but it could be that she was being influenced by Cayla. Nia didn't climb, but gestured to the others to move among some bushes. At least this was easier than going up the tree, and, since it was almost dark, perhaps they wouldn't be seen—if it was true that someone was coming.

Cayla closed her eyes and heard the world around her. There was wind, Nia, Ayanna's and Karina's breathing in the distance, lifts far away, the ocean at a great distance, jaguars in the valley —and someone walking carefully towards them. There was something familiar about those steps. Darian. It had to be him. But then, maybe not. The steps were heavier. She'd been wondering so much where he was that perhaps she was imagining she heard him. Only one person. It wasn't an ambush then, but it could be a scout. There could be people looking for them in all exits of the tunnels, and perhaps this person was one of them—and she wouldn't let them get away. She was lucky because the steps came in her direction. As the person walked below her, Cayla saw her chance and jumped, pinning the person to the ground face down. It was a man, back of his head covered by a hood, muscular back and arms, stronger than her. No way she could hold him down by force. But she still had skill.

She pulled his arm behind his back. "Move and I'll snap it."

He mumbled something, and she loosened the pressure over his head, just to hear what he'd say.

"It's me."

The voice she knew so well. But it didn't make sense. She had hugged him before. He should have been soft like his voice, the way he'd always been. Cayla moved away from him and got up. He got up and removed a hood that covered his hair and half his face.

"What's wrong?" Darian asked.

Cayla was still trying to match the person she'd held down to Darian. Even if she'd seen him two days before, somehow her memory was still of the boy she'd met almost two years before. "Sorry. I didn't know it was you."

"Do you, now? Cause you don't look like you recognize me."

"Well, you are different."

"Not at all."

As he said this, he wrapped his arms around her and pulled her close to him, hugging her really tight. He felt her head against his shoulder and wrapped her arms around his neck. She'd been longing for this hug for what felt like an eternity. It was Darian as she'd known.

He whispered, "Do you recognize me now?"

She squeezed him tighter and looked at him. "Uh-huh."

Their eyes met. Their faces were so close. Cayla didn't care what anyone would think—she wanted to kiss him.

But he let go of her and stepped back. "Sorry, I..." He shook his head. "I almost forgot."

He meant what she'd asked him. Not to kiss her. She almost regretted it now, but she could never forget the day she heard they wanted to kill him, and she'd never want to be responsible for that again. At least he had some sense, because she had none. "It's fine."

He smiled, then looked at the tree and back at her. "Wow, you had me there. How did you get so good at this?"

Cayla shrugged. "I don't know. Practice?"

"I thought you stopped wrestling." He raised an eyebrow. "Who have you been practicing with?"

"Nobody. Just… doing exercises on my own."

She felt a light in her direction. It was Nia, looking stern, staring at both of them. Karina was right behind her. Nia stepped closer to them, held up a light crystal and illuminated his face. "What's this? Cayla, how can you do this to us?"

Darian raised his hands, showing the palms. "I came here on my own. I'm not representing anyone. I know the king's after you, and I came to help."

He sounded so concerned, so honest, but Nia narrowed her eyes. "The king? Only the king? Aren't you going to mention General Keen? Protecting your family?"

Cayla wanted to protest, but Darian was faster, "This has nothing to do with my father." His voice was calm and soft. "I know I'm his son and I can't change that. But he knows nothing about this. I'm just here to help Cayla."

Nia hadn't changed her expression. "And pray, tell me, how did you find us?"

He pointed at Cayla. "She told me. Like I said, I came cause she asked."

The woman still didn't look convinced. "How could she have told you?"

He pulled his necklace. "This. Because we're friends."

Cayla had to catch some breath. She couldn't believe he'd just revealed one of their biggest secrets. Like that. And she couldn't even make a face, kick him, or tell him anything, or it would only make everything worse.

Nia turned to her. "Is that true?"

All Cayla could do was look down and mumble, "Yes."

Nia was still angry. "But he's in the army. Who knows who could've followed him?"

Again Darian showed the palms of his hands and shook them. "I came alone, by boat, nobody knows where I am." He looked at Cayla. "My flying partner has been dismissed from the army." Cayla couldn't repress a little smile. Darian continued, "I had nobody checking where I was."

Nia stared at Cayla. "You should have told us." She turned to Darian. "I hope this doesn't cause us problems."

He shook his head. "No. I'd never—"

Nia sighed. "I hope so."

Cayla wanted to change the subject, and asked him, "How did you get here?"

"Very tough climb. I don't understand where you plan to go from here."

"Isn't there a way down?"

"As far as I know only lifts come here. Or very experienced climbers."

Cayla laughed. "Since when you're an experienced climber?"

"Since you asked me to meet you at this almost impossible to reach peak."

Right. *I'll find you.* He'd meant it. Cayla looked down, thought for a moment, then said, "But if you could do it, I can do it as well."

"No doubt," he said. "But I came up. I'm not sure I can climb down."

"Are we trapped up here then?" Nia asked.

He shook his head. "I don't know. Maybe we can come up with a solution. But the good thing about this summit is that nobody will come looking for you."

Ayanna came out of the bushes where she was hiding.

Darian seemed surprised. "I didn't know your sister was also here." He turned to Ayanna. "Hello, I'm Darian, Cayla's friend."

Her sister just stared at him.

He also noticed Karina. "Good to see you again too. I'm sorry for what happened. I made a mistake and I would like to apologize."

Karina shrugged. "It's fine." It didn't sound as if she meant it.

"Thank you," he said, then looked at everyone. "How are you doing with supplies? I brought some food."

Cayla smiled. "How did you know we'd be out of food?"

"I didn't." He then returned the smile. "But I thought, why not?"

Ayanna had a big smile. "Thank you. I was starving."

Nia stared at her. "You said you had enough."

The girl looked down. "Cause I wanted to leave some for you."

Darian laughed. "Good thing I came then."

They went to their camping site and sat on their blankets. Cayla tried to avoid looking at him too much, but she couldn't help sitting beside him. The few times their eyes met all she felt was calm complicity and security. They understood each other now, and it made all the difference. It was just a matter of time for their infinite kisses.

Karina chewed the same bland tasteless dry things, but hunger had improved their taste. Pleasant night sky, nature, all they needed was a fire, except they obviously couldn't have one without drawing attention, which reminded Karina that this wasn't a camping expedition. Nia asked Darian how he'd kept in touch with Cayla. The girl looked down and seemed embarrassed. From their conversation, Karina gathered that he had left the castle over a year before, when he gave Cayla the necklace. He also said he knew the kingdom was under rebel threat but that he had no idea people so close to him would be involved. This last explanation didn't convince Karina very much, but, hey, he'd brought food, and for that she was willing to accept lame excuses.

At least he looked happy and relaxed, unlike the last time she'd seen him. Cayla was also at ease around him. Karina was usually terrible at noticing lovey-dovey stuff, but these two, with their bright eyes, had a virtual billboard saying, "we're in love and we know it." She smiled, happy that they'd solved whatever problem they had before.

Nia and the girls were tired, and soon they got ready to sleep. Darian had a tent, but Nia thought it would be better for them all to sleep outside, so as not to split the group. Nia still insisted they should keep watch and volunteered to be first. Darian volunteered as well, but Nia insisted it should be her.

This place had grass! It felt so soft and comfortable that Karina soon fell asleep. She woke up with a voice, "You're in danger."

14

ABOUT THE REBELS

Karina sat up and saw only Ayanna and Cayla sleeping. She didn't see Nia or Darian, but she heard soft voices a little further down, and went in that direction, where she saw them.

Nia seemed angry, and spoke to Darian, "You are going to tell me everything, because I didn't believe half the stories you told. I want the truth."

"Fine," he then noticed Karina, "but I'm not gonna talk in front of her."

Nia turned to Karina. "It's great you're here." She turned to Darian. "You. You owe her an explanation, remember? I doubt she believed your lousy excuses, because you're a terrible liar. Are you going to explain yourself, or do you want her to discuss her worries with Cayla?"

Karina almost defended herself, explaining she had no intention to discuss anything with anyone when she understood Nia was only arguing for Karina's inclusion in their conversation.

Darian looked upset. "I don't even know who she is. You can't expect me to—"

"Hey," Karina cut him off, "thanks to you I was captured,

tied, imprisoned. I would appreciate an explanation. And I didn't really believe what you told us."

Nia added, "She's Cayla's friend; I think you'll want her on your side."

Darian took a deep breath. "Fine. She might as well listen." He stared at Karina. "But I'll talk to Cayla personally. If she hears any of this from anyone but me, I'll—"

"Hey," Nia interrupted. "You're not in a position to be threatening anyone. Now, if you want us to help you and keep your secret, you'll want to explain yourself first."

He looked down, stroked an imaginary beard, looked away, then finally faced Nia. "So, unlike I said earlier, I knew people close to me were part of the insurgent movement, and... I'm also part of that movement."

Karina had guessed something like that, but maybe not that much. Nia took a step back.

Darian continued, "I know it sounds bad. But you need to know that I grew up in a village that was threatened by the king. I was sent to the castle, to my father, and all it did was confirm everything I suspected. And I got in the army and, remember I was sent far South," he pointed to Nia, "where you came from. Well, once you're there, you start to see things, and... They are doing everything they can to wipe out anyone who might oppose the king, or any community that appears to have the slightest chance of opposing him. Or anyone who yields magic. Or seems to do so. The definition of magic is quite fuzzy, though. Anyways, the first thing I did was to bring this up to my father." He looked down and closed his eyes, as if in pain, then snorted. "But guess who's responsible for all that repression? Guess who wants to enforce these laws with violence?" He shook his head. "My father. I realized I would never change his mind. I considered deserting, at the risk of being executed, unless my father intervened, which would put me in a very uncomfortable position. Then I thought there should be another way, and I found it. Other people also found it. The insurgents stopped deserting the army only to be found and killed. Instead, we became the army, or at least a good part of it."

"You've been conspiring against the king," Nia said.

Darian looked down and nodded. "Cayla's father. I had no way to tell her. I never had the occasion to see her or talk to her. But," he looked at Nia, "I know that the king's after you. I thought perhaps you'd side with me, you'd understand."

"We're all running from him," Nia said.

"I know. I'm in the army, remember?" He laughed. "By the way, they think you're highly dangerous, Nia. But for the others, the order is to return them to the castle alive." He looked down. "But Cayla didn't seem very concerned about her own safety. She said she had some problems with her father, that all she had to do was finish her interrupted mission and everything would be fine. That her father was upset that she failed or something."

Nia rolled her eyes.

The mention of their failed expedition made Karina ask a question. "Who were those people who imprisoned us and wanted to cut our hands?"

Darian raised his eyebrows. "Hands? No, they said something about fingers, but that it was just a threat."

"They later decided on fingers, but it wasn't a threat. They were even preparing the equipment."

His face paled. "I'm sorry. Really sorry. Well, Rose's group, they are not in the army. There are many scattered independent groups, and hers is one of them. I was good friends with her sister, Zayra." He looked at Karina. "You met her. Like me, she supports the insurgency, but I would never think she would backstab me like that. Also, Rose's group, they were not supposed to make decisions on their own. Still, I'm sorry for my part in it. But I did tell Cayla it wasn't safe to go wandering on her own. I offered to go with her, but no."

"There were six or eight people," Karina said, "I don't think you would have made much difference."

He looked down. "I didn't mean like that. Anyways, I left her and I thought no harm would come to her, or you, because if anything happened I'd be the first to know."

Nia raised an eyebrow. "The first?"

He looked down and around. "I, I deal with communication. And since I dropped her off, I was paying attention to that area."

"Wow, lots of attention," Karina said. "Thank you so much."

He raised his shoulders. "They never reported, never contacted anyone. They did it on purpose. They betrayed me."

"Fair enough," Nia said as if to end the subject. "And what does this insurgence of yours plan to do?"

"We have to depose the king."

Nia narrowed her eyes and stared at him as if trying to see something. "Then Cayla would no longer be a princess."

Darian shrugged. "I don't mind. In fact—"

"She does," Nia interrupted. "The thing she most wants is to succeed her father."

He stroked his imaginary beard. "Well, I could make her queen."

Nia's eyes widened. "What?"

"I mean, there's a lot of discussion on who should take power in case we succeed. It could, uh, somehow, eventually be her."

"I think she would love the idea," Nia said, "until the other people who also want to take the power start showing up with part of the army. It would be chaos."

He shook his head. "If you knew what was happening, you wouldn't fear chaos. But yes, her life could be in danger. That's why I'm not a supporter of Cayla as a ruler, at least not until everything is stable."

"Who would rule then?"

"We'll decide among the leaders."

Nia snorted. "Sure, whoever gets the biggest chunk of the army is king."

"No, not like that. We'll establish a council. That's what we do anyways, no single leadership."

Nia rolled her eyes. "That's cute and sweet and idealistic." She became serious. "Until there's power to be split. And what about Lylah?"

He took a deep breath. "We haven't seen or heard from her in years. Nobody can enter that castle of hers. I don't even know if she's alive and if she is willing and capable of governing anything."

Karina had to correct him. "I saw her. She's alive, or at least she was, until, uh, a few days ago."

"She's very much alive, and that's where we are going," Nia added with a strange certainty.

Darian grimaced. "Even if she is alive, you'll never get there. Not from here."

"Odell sent us here," Nia said, "and I think he wants us to go there for some reason."

"But that could be dangerous," Darian said.

"Do you have another alternative?" Nia asked.

Again he took a deep breath. "That's part of what I meant to tell you. Since you're all safe here, and we have a good part of the army… we could take the castle. Then—"

"No. My son's there."

Darian looked down and bit his lip.

Nia stared at him. "You can't. You can't attack the castle. Cayla would never forgive you. There's my son, there's her father, there's your father."

Darian closed his eyes. "I was willing to make this sacrifice."

Nia became the furious scary woman Karina had seen once. "Sacrifice? You want power!"

Darian was still calm but shook his head. "No, no way."

Nia was definitely furious. "Is that why you're all over Cayla? To be king?"

He squinted and answered in a calm but dry voice. "Both your suggestions are offensive."

"We'll see. Now, has this attack been planned? How much influence do you have?"

He raised his arms, showing the palms of his hands. "No, no. Nothing's been planned. It was just something that came up to me now, seeing all of you here and safe. Sorry if I forgot about Cayla's little brother. I was just going to say it was safe now. Other people, not me, have planned an attack before. We've been having a good part of the army for some time, but I always told them it wasn't safe to take the castle. I can access top information, through my father, so I get a say on that. But I've been lying. We do have enough power to take down the castle, and I thought now I could tell them the truth."

Nia pointed her index finger to him. "If there's an attack planned, you have to halt it."

"Nothing's been planned." He spoke in a soft voice, as if to soothe her. "Nothing. It was something I wanted to suggest. If your son's there, we'll think of something else. We'll find another solution. We'll—"

He stopped suddenly and looked behind Nia. Karina also looked. Cayla was walking towards them. She stepped closer, rubbing her eyes.

"What attack? What's happening?" She then looked up, and opened her eyes wide, looking scared. "Why didn't you wake me up?"

They all looked where she looked. A roundish silver thing stood almost above them. It definitely looked like a flying saucer from below. But, in their context, it was scarier: a lift.

Darian said, "Hide. I'll deal with them."

Nia shook her head. "I think they saw us."

"Now. Hide," the boy repeated.

He sounded so insistent that Karina turned around and ran to the place where Ayanna was, to wake her up. She noticed Cayla and Nia were beside her. In fact, Nia was the first to reach the younger sister and pull her up. "Get up. Come."

Ayanna seemed sleepy and confused, but she did as she was told. They moved to the bushes where they had first hidden.

Nia then pulled Cayla's hand, as if to prevent her from climbing or running farther away. "We have to stay together."

Cayla grimaced, but she also hid in the same place.

"What's happening?" Ayanna asked.

"They're coming for us," Nia replied.

"Who's coming?" the girl asked.

"I don't know. Let's be quiet."

They could not see what was happening beyond the bushes and closest trees, but they saw the gleam of a bright light.

A man or boy spoke loud enough to be heard from that distance. "You know what we're here for."

"Well, hello, Jax," Darian replied. "It's good to see you. I don't actually know. Sorry. Why don't you tell me?" He sounded calm and friendly.

"I think you're the one who has something to tell," Jax said. "Do you have an explanation for this?" His tone of voice was a sharp contrast to Darian's, as he sounded anything but friendly.

"I'm pretty sure I can explain anything you want, as long as you ask. I can't read thoughts, though, unfortunately. Let's sit and talk." His voice was soft and smooth.

"Darian, we're not against you," a girl said, "just let us take the princesses. I'm sure you know it's for the best. We won't harm them, I'll make sure of that this time. And we know they're here."

"Zayra, I thought we had agreed on this…"

At the mention of this name, Cayla got up, but Nia held her. "No. Wait."

"We can fight," Cayla replied.

"Try to listen," Nia whispered.

Cayla sat down, looking cross. Karina could only hear the last part of what Darian was saying.

"…understand my position."

"Diplomatic ties," Jax replied. "I'm willing to accept that. Now, make use of them and help our cause. We can win this."

"We can," Darian replied. "But the princesses won't help us. They are running away from the king. Why do you think they are here? They'd be useless as hostages. Trying to use them for bargain would only expose us."

"We'd rather take our chances," Jax said. "Unless you care to convince us."

Nia looked worried. "They're trying to gain time. I think there are more people coming from behind us. We need to move." She then turned to Karina. "Please. You have to try."

Teleporting, she meant. Karina had a fraction of a second to weigh the possibilities in front of her. Her conclusion was terrible, but it was better than wasting time trying to do the impossible. "I can't. I won't be able to do it. I have no idea how. Even if I did, we're four people, and I can't guarantee we'd all go."

That was an uncomfortable confession, not only because it meant they were in real trouble, but also because she felt bad to have to admit she didn't know something. Nia shook her head.

Cayla didn't seem upset. "We can still fight and take their lift. Before the others come."

Nia closed her eyes, as if thinking. "Assuming your friend is on our side."

"It's our only chance," Cayla pleaded.

Nia sighed, then looked at Karina and Ayanna. "You two, stay here. When we yell, make a run for the lift. Understood?"

Karina nodded. Nia turned to Cayla. "On the count of three. One, two—"

Cayla started running and Nia followed. The girl grabbed a twig, and the woman held her dagger. Karina wondered if her two companions would be able to win their fight, and what would happen if they lost. From beyond the bushes, she heard grunts and yells, and much sooner than expected, Nia's voice; "Girls, come."

Karina was startled, but she got up and ran, until she felt someone pushing her. She fell. She tried to get up, but then someone held her and put a hood on her. She tried to get away from the person holding her, or at least remove the hood, but she was being held so tight she could barely move. Soon she heard steps and grunts, felt that the person let her go, and found her opportunity to remove the hood. Cayla was trying to fight two people at once. Nia stood close, beside someone on the ground. Ayanna was getting up, her face dirty. Nia walked closer to one of the people Cayla was fighting. Nia tried to stab them. The person fell to the ground as if hit by something. Nia then stabbed the air close to Cayla's second opponent, who also fell. Her dagger seemed capable of affecting a person from a close distance, which was really weird.

"Run," Nia yelled, as she moved towards the lift.

Karina ran as fast as she could, then she heard a loud sound like an explosion, and the floor a few meters in front of her caught fire. She considered jumping or skirting it, but she heard more explosions and more places catching fire between them and the lift.

"They're throwing fireballs," Cayla said.

"We keep going," Nia replied.

The woman ran in the front and fanned the fire with her dagger, which only caused more smoke to rise. Meanwhile, Cayla turned around and threw a few stones. The smoke was so thick that the fire no longer could be seen.

"Come," Nia yelled. "They won't hit us."

Cayla and her sister ran towards that smoke, so Karina did the same, hearing more sounds of explosions behind them, and seeing fire all around them except in the place with the high smoke, where Nia had fanned the fire. Karina crossed the smoke and saw the lift, its back door open, bright light coming from the inside, illuminating the grass and bushes. Four people lay on the floor. One of them started sitting up. It was Darian, with a cut on his temple, looking confused.

"Get up," Nia told him. "You have to come with us."

"No!" Cayla yelled. "He's a traitor."

"But we need him," Nia said.

"We don't," the girl insisted, stepping inside the lift.

Karina assumed the girl knew how to pilot the ship, so she also ran inside, eager to get away from that summit and those people.

"Cayla, wait," Darian murmured, still sitting, his voice weak.

Nia was the last one to step inside, and stared at Cayla. "Can you fly this thing?"

"It can't be hard," she replied as she pushed something by the door that made it close.

More sounds of explosions were heard from outside, and when the door was almost shut, someone put a hand, as if trying to prevent it from closing. Cayla kicked it, and the door continued its movement until it was shut. Karina moved to the cockpit and tried to guess what was necessary to make that thing fly, but she had no idea. She turned to Cayla. "How does this work?"

The girl passed her hands through the panel. "I'm looking. Wait."

Nia seemed angry. "You're looking? Now it's too late to let him in."

"That's the idea," Cayla replied, still looking at the panel.

"You know? They might hurt him," Nia said.

"That's the idea."

"He's your friend!" Nia said.

Cayla turned and faced Nia. "No. He's with them. He defended her. And it's his fault these people are after us."

"Your fault," Nia corrected. "You're the one who contacted him. And either way, what are we going to do with a lift we can't fly? I thought you knew at least a little."

Cayla only stared at the panel. More and more sounds of explosions were heard. Karina stopped trying to figure out the panel and looked outside. The fire surrounding them was getting higher and higher. She imagined that thing exploding with them inside.

"What material is this lift made out of?" Karina asked.

"Oh. It won't catch fire, if that's what you're worried," Nia said. "But if we don't take off it might get hot. Too hot for us. Soon."

"And won't it explode?" Karina asked, wondering if the top had a combustible gas.

Nia had a puzzled face. "Explode? No."

Karina figured that despite the similar appearance the lifts were not anything like balloons or zeppelins. She would be really curious as to how exactly they worked, if she weren't more worried about her own life.

"Shouldn't we get out?" Ayanna asked. They all stared at her. The girl tried again. "Surrender?"

Nia shook her head. "No. We have to figure a way out."

"The only way out is through the door," Ayanna replied.

Karina thought they could still try to escape. "Maybe we could still get out and bring in someone who can guide this ship."

"No," Cayla replied, seeming horrified.

"I agree with you," Nia said to Karina, "I really do. But they're too many. No way we'll get out and back in again. If only," she stared at Cayla, "we had brought in a pilot when we could."

"Who knows where he'd take us!" Cayla defended herself. "You heard it. He's with them."

"Yes," Nia replied. "We're so much better without him."

The place indeed started to get warmer, and Karina hoped it was just an impression, fear, and increased heart rate, although, by its looks, the lift was becoming a pan.

"Who are they?" Ayanna asked.

"Insurgents. It's a long story," Nia said.

"Why are they after us?" Ayanna asked.

"Probably to take us as hostages."

Ayanna looked down, then asked, "They wouldn't kill me, would they?"

"They could harm you," Nia warned.

"I'm getting out," the girl said, walking to the door.

Karina admired the resolution in the little girl, and apparently so did Nia and her sister, who stared wide-eyed.

"Wait," Nia stepped in front of her. "Perhaps you're right. But we need a plan. Maybe try to capture and bring someone in, force them—"

"We're gonna get burned," Ayanna said.

Nia sighed. "I can't go back to the castle now."

Karina had a similar feeling, but she couldn't think of any other alternative, and she was feeling hot. "Maybe we can talk to them."

Nia took a deep breath. "Let's go out and hope for the best."

"I'm not going out," Cayla protested. "I'll fight until the end."

"The end doesn't need to be now," Nia said. "Sometimes it takes courage to quit. We'll have another opportunity." She looked down. "Hopefully." This last part was barely audible.

Cayla had tears in her eyes. "I don't want to face them. I don't want to see him."

"It's starting to burn my feet," Ayanna complained. She walked to the door, but she didn't know how to open it.

Cayla dried her tears and asked, "Does it look like I cried?"

Karina shook her head, lying, "No. Not at all."

Cayla touched a button near the door, which started to descend slowly. Granted, perhaps she couldn't take that thing out of the ground, but at least she knew how to get them out of that thing. Karina expected someone would come in as the door started to open, that they'd jump in and grab them, but nobody did. When the door was low enough, she saw that there were about fifteen people in a semi-circle around the door, some ten meters from them, pointing what looked like some kind of guns. The three girls and Nia stepped out. In the middle, a person who sent shivers down Karina's spine.

15

BACKSTABBING

"Drop the knife and raise your hands," Rose said. "Drop the knife."

See? Karina wasn't the only one who called it a knife. Nia threw her prized object—dagger—on the floor. Nobody took it, which was odd. Perhaps their fear of Nia's weapon explained their distance. Karina looked around for Darian, wondering on which side he really was, and if he would perhaps help them, but she didn't see him. She recognized some faces from when they had been first captured. Rose continued, "I don't want to see any fighting, I don't want to see any magic, and most of all, no attempt to escape."

"Or what?" Cayla provoked.

Rose smiled. "Jax, show them."

The boy, who had been behind Rose, stepped forward, holding a person with hands and feet tied and mouth covered; Darian. His head was down, and he didn't seem the least curious to glance up.

Rose continued, looking at Cayla, "Try anything, and you'll never see him again."

Cayla was pale, transfixed, staring at the scene in front of her. After a short while, she seemed to realize Rose had addressed her, and chuckled. "Why should I care?" She sounded sincere.

For the first time, Darian glanced at her, but he looked relieved rather than hurt. Rose stepped beside him, holding a circular blade with a handle near his neck. "Oh, really?"

Karina thought it looked like a pizza wheel, and perhaps out of nervousness, she burst out laughing. When she stopped, she realized everyone stared at her as if she were an alien, which in a way she was, and she burst out laughing again. Rose now ran towards Karina, brandishing her pizza cutter. "What's so funny?"

The possibility of being cut into slices was definitely not funny. Rose advanced with fury, and Karina was about to run, when the strange circular weapon flew from Rose's hand. Nia then grabbed her, pointing her dagger to the woman's heart.

"Try anything and she dies," Nia said to the group, with a much more menacing voice than even Rose.

Karina covered her head in fear, because she thought someone would shoot them or at least try to fight them, but nothing happened, so perhaps Nia's trick worked.

"What for?" Jax asked, then gestured towards Darian. "Then he dies. We'll both run out of hostages. The difference is that we have more people. And more weapons."

"But you don't have a hostage!" Cayla said. "We're not on his side."

"And he is useful to you," Nia added. "Not a good deal."

"But he's our friend," Ayanna protested, for which she only received hard glances from her companions.

Nia pressed the knife on Rose's neck. "We're not your enemies. All we'll do is take her with us, and only because we need someone to pilot the lift."

Jax laughed. "Rose cannot pilot these either."

"Oh, but her sister can," Cayla said, then stared at Zayra. "So, will you have the pleasure of giving us a ride this time?"

Zayra looked down and didn't answer. She seemed to be crying.

"No!" Jax said, as if scared, addressing everyone, not just Zayra. "The lift is pulsing. Stay away."

Karina looked back and realized that indeed it was covered in flames. It reminded her of a marshmallow on a campfire. This time she didn't want to laugh. It wasn't funny to see what she thought was her way out as melted candy. And it seemed to be shaking or something, which explained the boy's fear.

"Everyone, run back," Jax ordered his companions.

Their agitation, together with the fear of an explosion, made Karina run faster than ever. Ayanna and Cayla also ran. Karina then heard the loudest noise behind her, and ducked to the ground, even though she wasn't sure if that was the right thing to do. Looking back, she saw that the lift had been blown into pieces. Nia was far behind them, standing, apparently unharmed, still holding Rose, who was in that weird open-eyed sleeping state.

"You said it didn't explode!" Karina yelled at her, upset.

"It never does. Never did. Until now at least," Nia said.

The rebels now ran back and encircled them. Karina ran towards Nia because the woman seemed capable of protecting them. Indeed she yelled, "Not one more step."

Her words produced the desired effect, as the people encircling them obeyed. She continued, "I'm warning you. I'll hurt her, unless you take us where we want to go."

"And where is that?" Jax asked.

"The valley below," she replied. "You won't gain anything by holding us."

"Can we stop this nonsense?" A voice was heard from beyond the circle. Darian stepped in, untied. "Why don't we just sit and talk?"

"You?" Jax was surprised. "You were our hostage. And we can't talk forever."

"We can't fight forever either," Darian replied. "Let's solve this."

"Fine," Jax replied. "Let's try it your way. For now." He stepped closer. The others watched from a distance.

Karina was surprised not only that Darian had freed himself, but that somehow, they listened to him.

Cayla was probably thinking something else, and yelled at her ex-friend or whatever, "You. False. Deceiving. Liar."

"I didn't mean to discuss your opinion of me," he replied, unfazed.

He didn't look or sound anything like the guy who had brought them food and sounded concerned on how to tell Cayla about his role in the rebellion. Karina wasn't sure where he stood. He'd been held as a hostage, so he couldn't have been responsible for their ambush, although they could all have pretended.

Darian addressed the other rebels, "I say the princesses come with us. As to the other two, they are no threat; we can let them go."

"You have to propose something I agree," Nia said.

"I'm not coming with you," Cayla told Darian.

"It's for your own good," Darian replied, addressing Cayla in a formal and cold way that was meant to be heard by everyone else. "We mean you no harm. Just comply, and we won't even touch a finger of yours."

Yikes. That finger part brought Karina bad memories. He must have said that on purpose.

"I'll never comply, so that's a terrible deal for me," Cayla said.

"That's the best we can propose," Darian replied. "You are outnumbered."

"I have her," Nia said, holding Rose.

"And while you hold her—or hurt her—you won't be able to fight," Darian replied.

"All I need is someone to take us to the valley," Nia said, still sounding menacing. "Then I'll let her go. And I want you to promise you won't harm any of us."

"As long as you don't oppose us we won't harm you," Darian said.

Now Jax intervened. "Wait. We didn't agree on that." He pointed at Nia. "She's dangerous."

"But she's not on the king's side," Darian replied.

"But she's with his daughters," Jax insisted.

Darian shook his head. "She's the former wife of the king. She had to flee. He's accusing her of being a witch."

Jax raised an eyebrow. "Wonder why."

"So what?" Nia yelled. "Lots of people have magical objects."

"What about the other one?" Jax pointed at Karina.

"Also running away. Same grounds. Harmless," Darian replied.

"Fine, then. We take only the princesses. And take these two to the valley." Jax then turned to Nia. "But you have to free Rose."

"No," Cayla yelled. "I'm not going with them."

"Cayla, please," Nia pleaded, then whispered. "I think he wants to keep you safe."

"I don't want to be kept by anyone," Cayla replied.

"I'll give you one minute to decide," Darian said.

Karina also thought that was a good proposal, but on the other hand knew that those people were capable of violence and cruelty, and she didn't really trust Darian. But she saw no other way. And plus, if Cayla didn't come with them, it would be much easier to negotiate with Lylah. She was about to plead with Cayla to accept their proposal when she heard a voice inside her head. "She has to come. It won't work without her." Karina then remembered that Cayla had the key to enter the castle, so they wouldn't be able to enter without her, unless, as they were going to negotiate, perhaps they could knock on the door? Or gate? But all she thought was that Cayla had to come with them.

"We have to stay together," Karina said. "I'm not leaving Cayla."

Nia stared at her, surprised.

"That means I'll take you three?" Darian asked.

"I'm not going," Cayla protested.

Darian ignored her and turned to Jax. "Well, we could leave her here. You know, there's no way out."

"How did they get here then?" Jax asked.

Darian only looked puzzled and shrugged.

"Take us four, then," Nia said. "But we have to go with him," she pointed to Darian, "because he was the one who promised we'd be safe."

"No way," Jax protested. "She'll go all evil on us with that dagger and free the princesses."

"That's not a bad proposal," Darian said.

"For a traitor," Jax replied. "You want to protect them, that's what you want. We should tie you again."

Darian offered his hands close together and shrugged. "If you think I'll be useful as a hostage, I don't mind."

Jax just crossed his arms.

Darian lowered his hands and said, "Look, your initial plan was to take the four of them. Here we go. We can take them. Without a fight."

Jax thought for a moment, then replied, "I guess you're right." He then turned to Nia. "Let Rose go."

"I'm not coming with you," Cayla protested, grabbing a twig from the floor. "You want me; you'll have to fight."

The girl didn't stand up, though, but rather fell on the floor. Nia had "air stabbed" her. Everyone looked surprised. Darian was still unfazed.

"Oh, she'll be up and fine in ten minutes," Nia said. "Let's go."

The rebels walked to the edge of the mountain, on the opposite side of where they had been, where three lifts were waiting for them. They agreed on having Karina and her friends on a lift with Darian, Jax, two other guys, two other girls Karina didn't know, and Zayra. At least Cayla was passed out and didn't know that she would have her as a travel companion. Travel. Where? This lift was even bigger than the previous one Karina had seen. Zayra went to the front, with the other girl. Karina and her friends were on the back with four people watching them. Or five, if one were to count Darian. Nia held Cayla, who leaned on her shoulder. None of their bags had been brought with them, as someone had decided to confiscate their things. A good thing the shoes were safe on Karina's waist. The lift took off.

Nia addressed everyone, "Listen, we are not on the king's side. You won't benefit from keeping us. Just leave us at the valley. We might even be able to help you."

"Why don't you two go," Darian said looking at Karina and Nia, "and leave them here?" He gestured towards Cayla and Ayanna.

"Are we going to change plans again?" Jax asked.

"If it's for the best, yes," Darian replied.

Nia whispered to Karina, "Why not?"

"Cayla needs to go too," Karina replied.

"Yes, it might be safer. But I thought you had a plan," Nia said, then looked at Darian's direction. "Or that he had a plan."

"I think his plan is to keep Cayla close by," Karina replied.

Nia looked down. "While they might take the castle." She then addressed Jax, "You're smart, you know?"

The comment was odd. He seemed surprised and was about to reply when Nia got up, pulled her dagger and air stabbed everyone except Darian, who looked astonished.

"What are you doing?"

"Going all evil with my dagger." She pointed to Jax. "It was his idea."

Darian seemed upset. "Stop it. You know I don't mean to hurt you. I'm even willing to help you go where you want to go. You know that."

Nia ignored him and banged on the door to the front. The noise called the girls' attention. Zayra opened the door and looked back. In less than a second, she and the other girl lay motionless.

"Great," Darian said. "Now I have to go to the front."

He carefully pushed Zayra out of her seat and sat there. Nia also went inside and sat in the middle. Karina and Ayanna stood at the door.

Nia turned to the younger girl. "Go back and hold your sister."

Ayanna looked disappointed but went to the back and sat by Cayla's side. Nia looked at Darian. "Now, will you take us to Lylah?"

The boy was exasperated. "Nia, I told you, that is reckless and useless, there's no point."

Nia pointed her dagger at him.

"That's stupid," he said. "Who's going to control this if I pass out?"

"I could just hurt you," Nia replied.

Darian didn't look upset. "I know you won't."

"Fine," Nia said, now holding her dagger close to Zayra, the way she had done to Rose. "What if I hurt her?"

"You wouldn't do that."

"I would. For my son," Nia replied.

"I'll do my best to make sure your son is unharmed," he said. "What's better than to check on me in person?"

"I still want to go to Lylah."

"As I said before, I'll take you there, or close to there."

Karina had to press her point. "Cayla needs to go too."

"No, she doesn't," he replied. "Why would she need to go on a pointless and dangerous mission?"

Nia pressed again her dagger on Zayra, who was unconscious. "I don't care about your opinion. I'll hurt her."

"Knock it off," he said. "You're not that kind of person."

"Let's see, then. And there are five more, in case I go too far."

She pressed her dagger on the girl's arm. A drop of blood dripped.

Darian looked upset. "Stop it."

"So she *is* important," Nia said.

"Just because I don't want her to be hurt?"

"And why did you defend her when we were fighting?"

"You just don't hit someone when they're already down," he said. "I understand Cayla was mad, but still."

"You know, you really have to make up your mind."

"What?" Darian seemed confused, then his eyes widened. "Stop it."

Nia narrowed her eyes. "Let's try something different. Cayla is about to wake up. Since you like to pretend to care about her—"

"Not pretend. We've been friends for a long time."

Nia sighed. "Well, since you care about her, why don't you try to take her side, and take her where she wants to go? This is your chance to redeem yourself."

"She's going to be upset either way. What's the difference? At least she won't be in danger." He looked down. "Like last time."

Karina was annoyed that the conversation wasn't leading anywhere, at least not anywhere near Lylah. But the mention of "last time" gave her an idea. She turned to Darian. "If you're only worried about Cayla's safety, why don't you come with us? That way you can protect her."

He listened.

Karina felt encouraged to continue. "So even if Cayla is upset at you, she'll know you never meant to betray her. And you'll get to spend time with her." Somehow that last part seemed to matter.

He looked down, thinking, then replied, "But they'll see we're straying from our regular path. We might bring attention to us. It could be someone still loyal to the king."

Karina thought that was just an excuse, and argued, "Perhaps you could leave your lift far away, or something, not to draw attention."

He stroked his non-existent beard, then looked back. "But then they'll know I protected her."

Nia rolled her eyes. "As if nobody noticed. But I'm sure you can come up with something. I take back what I said; you're an excellent liar."

He looked down, embarrassed, thinking, or both. The silence was the perfect opportunity for Karina to ask Nia a non-related question she was too curious to hold, "How do you know how long they'll sleep? Do you have a timer or something?"

Nia was surprised at the question. She thought for a moment, then answered, "No. I just, when I stab them, from a distance, I know. If I have to do it too fast, I only knock them out for a couple minutes, though."

Darian snorted. "Some magical object you have there. To bring down all the people you did, in a matter of seconds. Of course, it must take a lot of practice."

Nia looked down, which was odd for her. "No. I had never used it before. I didn't even know it could do this."

Karina was astonished. "What about the guards?"

Nia shook her head. "That was different."

Darian was also astonished. "You're saying you had no practice? Can you imagine what you could do if you did?"

Nia snorted. "Maybe I don't want to imagine that." She faced Darian. "Now, will you take us to Lylah's castle?"

He sighed. "If that's what she wants..." He looked at his sleeping companions. "I'll leave them at the mountain, then we'll go. But I'm coming with you." He looked back where Cayla was. "Regardless of what she says."

Karina smiled. "Thank you."

The lift indeed changed course. Karina felt relieved, and happy that her idea had worked. Karina looked back and noticed that Cayla slept on the side couch, and so did Ayanna, who must have been tired, since they hadn't slept much.

Nia looked back, then turned to Darian. "She's going to wake up soon, and I have to ask you something." She then narrowed her eyes and observed him. "Why did you come to the mountain last night?"

"To help Cayla. And you all."

She still looked at him attentively. "It wasn't to lead the rebels then?"

"Why would I climb? I could have gotten there much faster."

"I have no proof you climbed," Nia said. "I don't mean to judge you, I understand this, uh, cause, means a lot to you. And that you think you can keep us all safe."

"No," he sounded offended. "I have no idea how they came, or how they knew where you were. I didn't tell anyone, and I took a lot of care not to be followed."

"How did they find us then?"

"I don't know." He stopped for a moment, then continued, "Unless, either someone heard me, but, I took a lot of care, or they put something on my things, to locate me. But again, I checked everything. Or else they knew how to locate you. I wasn't involved in any of this. Didn't you see I was tied? That Rose threatened to hurt me?"

Nia laughed. "That was fake, wasn't it?"

He shook his head. "It wasn't. Rose was furious."

"How did you escape then?"

He looked down, then glanced towards Zayra. "She untied me."

Nia narrowed her eyes looking at the girl, then at him.

Darian continued, "She was afraid they'd hurt me." As Nia kept her probing expression, he looked defensive. "It's not at all what you're thinking."

She looked puzzled. "You don't even know what I'm thinking. But let me ask, then. So she freed you, then you just walked out telling everyone what to do?"

"You took down Rose. She was the problem. And I didn't tell anyone what to do, I just tried to mediate things, and luckily it worked out."

Nia rolled her eyes. "Listen, I can see you care and worry about Cayla. But, see, she's like a daughter to me—"

"I know, that's why I talked to you."

"Well, what if you're such a good friend to her, you know, just because of who she is?"

"Of course it's because of who she is."

Nia stared at him, jaw dropped.

He seemed puzzled for a second, then looked disgusted. "Oh, Nia please. You mean because she's her father's daughter? I didn't mean that, I meant the person she is. That has nothing to do with where she lives or who her parents are. You know, you're sounding just like her father. What are you going to do? Forbid me to ever see her?"

"No, but I can talk to her." Nia sat sideways, winked at Karina then said, "Still… Cayla, I love her, but she can be a little, uh, fierce, and, somewhat rough on the edges, if you know what I mean. And I don't see her treating you very well. So, well, I wonder why you care about her."

The boy seemed furious, and Karina wondered if, so close to landing, it was a good time to annoy him.

But Darian kept looking straight ahead as he replied, "Do you even know her? Really? If you did, you'd know her rough edges, as you're saying, are just on the outside. And what's wrong if she's fierce? What's the problem? I can deal with that.

And you have no right to judge how she treats me, because you don't even know it."

Nia chuckled, which was weird.

Darian frowned. "I don't think I said anything funny."

Nia became serious. "No. Sorry. Just get us on the ground, then you can look behind you."

"What?" he said, then turned back.

Karina also looked. Cayla stood near the door, strangely silent, almost beside Karina. Darian was paralyzed for a moment.

"Watch out!" Nia yelled.

The lift hit the ground with a loud noise and tilted. Karina lost balance and almost fell. Why did Nia upset him right when they were about to reach the ground? Why?

Nia turned to Darian, "I told you not to look."

Sian turned off the comm. Found him—his brother. Quite confusing account, frankly. Still, the girls were with his brother, on their way to the insurgents not-so-secret hideout. Trying to take the girls from the insurgents would be foolish—and needless. There were bigger pieces about to be moved. It was time to prepare for the final strike. His curiosity would have to wait.

16

TIME TO TURN AROUND

Cayla felt dizzy. From the crash, from having passed out, from so much information she didn't quite understand. Darian walked to the back to open the door and passed her without meeting her eyes.

Ayanna came to the front, rubbing her eyes. "What happened? Did we crash?"

"No. Just a bad landing," Nia replied.

Cayla asked Nia, "Where are we going?"

"To Lylah's castle," Nia replied.

Cayla exhaled in relief while looking at the sleeping bodies of the people who'd wanted to imprison them. Maybe she'd been wrong, and Darian had been on her side, but he seemed to be on their side as well.

She turned to Nia. "He'll drop us off?"

"He's coming with us."

Coming with us? No. That had not been the plan. Nia got up and went to the back, where Darian and Karina were carrying some people out. Cayla noticed a person on the pilot seat and all her anger against Darian boiled up again. Still, she helped them carry a couple people outside, landing them carefully on the grass, even if they didn't deserve any decent treatment.

Without any enemies on the lift, they were ready to take off.

Nia put her hand on her shoulder. "Cayla, go to the front, so you can learn a little how to pilot this. It could be useful."

Still somewhat dizzy and confused, Cayla found herself in the front compartment. Alone with Darian. The first time in such a long time. Her heart was racing and she had trouble breathing, but she tried not to think about it. He'd been with those people—on their side—and her stupid heart would have to shut up.

He looked at her as if waiting for a reaction. Afraid? Curious? Unsure?

She stepped away from him. "For the record, I changed my mind about what I told you last night." She looked away. "No infinite nothing."

He sighed. "I figured."

"I just wanted to make sure, you know? No misunderstanding."

He shook his head. "None."

So that was it? It wasn't as if he cared.

He said, "You need a hand."

"What?"

He pressed his hand on the right top corner of the panel. "For the lift to fly. You need someone authorized."

The panel lit up. It annoyed her to know that they would never have taken off without him.

He continued, "The person needs to be alive, but could be sleeping, and not everyone is authorized for every lift."

"How can you turn this one on?"

"I have authorization for every lift in the army." He looked down. "My father."

She sighed. "Darian, I need to know. Whose side are you on?"

"Your side."

"Are you saying you support my father? That you were just pretending?"

He looked away, sighed, then looked directly at her. "It's more complicated than that. I have to play both sides. But I always consider you. I do think about the wellbeing of the kingdom, Cayla, and your wellbeing as well. Always." His eyes had been locked in hers, open. He then stared ahead, while the lift took off, distancing itself from the summit.

His words and the way he'd said them put her at ease. She trusted him. But there was one thing still bothering her. "Why did you defend her?"

"Zayra? You were going to kick her face. She was already down."

"I wasn't. What do you think I am? And we were fighting."

"You're a better fighter, Cayla."

"So you had to protect her precious pretty face. Nice."

He glanced at her, then back ahead. He had a little smile on his face. A smile? Cayla wanted to punch him.

He glanced at her again. "Are you…" A pause. Another smile. "…jealous?"

Cayla looked away. "What a stupid question."

"Was that the problem that night?" Darian scoffed. "Were you jealous of Zayra?"

Laughing. He was laughing! A pity he was piloting because she really did want to punch him. "You're so hilarious."

Darian shook his head. "No, you are. That's the most ridiculous thing I've ever heard."

"You're the one who said it! No wonder it's ridiculous."

"Ridiculous and absurd."

"Absurd, right? It's not as if I had been locked in the castle, while you were flying around and living wonderful adventures with your pretty partner."

He frowned. "She's not pretty. What about you? Going to

balls in the castle. Having a prince after you. I never, ever, ever thought anything about it. Ever."

"Well, the Arlenia prince is creepy and old, that's easy."

"He's nineteen. That's not old!"

"He's not like…" What was she even going to say? She lost her thought. And she was wasting time with stupid things when the most important mission in her life was ahead of her. "You're going to drop me off and let me do what I have to do, right?"

"Yes, but I'm coming with you."

That was terrible. He'd mess up everything. "Then I'll just ask Nia to make you sleep."

"I made a deal with her. She won't go back on her word."

"Make a deal with me then." Cayla pleaded. "If you care about what I think."

"I care more about your safety than your opinion." That tone again.

"Right. So you can tell me what to do."

"I'm not telling you what to do," he said. "I'm deciding what *I'm* going to do. It's different, you know?"

"But that's not what I want. I need to do this alone."

"Your sister, Nia, and the random girl there can go. What's the difference?"

Cayla was starting to feel impatient. "I can't explain it. You have to trust me. Don't you also have important stuff to do? For the kingdom? Well, me too!"

He stared at her, looked down, then looked away, as if thinking. "I can't let anything happen to you."

"You know I can defend myself, right?"

"That depends against how many."

She sighed. "It's not like you can take an army all by yourself either."

He shook his head. "Fighting, no. But I can talk to them."

Cayla rolled her eyes. "Impressive."

She looked away, decided to remain silent and distant. Maybe he'd get a clue. And then maybe not.

After some time, he said, "Lots of people are looking for you, rebel and loyal. That's why I can't just leave you."

"They want me as a hostage, Darian. If you're so good at talking, come and talk to them if I'm caught. You can't force your company when I don't want it."

He had a grimace. "I'm not *forcing…*"

Cayla stared.

He looked away, then back at her. "You'll need to promise you'll hide. And you'll contact me after you do whatever you want to do. And if it doesn't work, you'll hide in the woods."

"I don't need to promise anything, Darian. Stop doing that. I don't like it you when you try to tell me what to do. I trust you and you need to trust me—"

"But last time—"

"Was your fault. You exposed me to these insurgents, and you didn't tell me anything about them. You trusted someone you knew was conspiring against my father. You trusted her. Think about it. Let me take care of what I have to do, and take care of what you have to do."

"I should. You have no idea what I've…" He closed his eyes as if in pain. "You're right. There are things I put off for too long. Too long, Cayla. I need to fix this. But please—I'm asking— please contact me if you have any problem. And hide."

He sounded sweet again, and she felt bad for the way she'd spoken to him. She put her hand on his shoulder. "I know you worry because you care, but you can't cage me to protect me. Let me live my destiny, whatever it is."

He held her hand and closed his eyes, then opened them and looked at her. Her heart beat faster.

"I'll drop you off at the river." His tone was resigned and unhappy. He kissed her wrist, then let it go, and looked ahead.

Shivers ran down her spine as if his kiss had electricity. But the important thing was her task again. Cayla just smiled. "Thank you."

He smiled back, then looked ahead and focused, as if thoughtful. Other than glancing at her from time to time, it was as if he was concentrating before doing something difficult.

The lift stopped moving. Darian turned to her. "Please be safe."

He then opened the middle door and addressed everyone. "We're floating above the river. You'll all have to jump. Quickly, before anyone notices where I am."

Darian opened the hatch.

Jump? Karina hadn't been prepared for that. She wondered how he had changed his mind. Or how Cayla had changed his mind. Although, now that she thought about it, perhaps she knew how. And indeed this was a lot safer than leaving the lift and walking near it.

Nia went first, then Ayanna. At least Karina wasn't afraid of falling since she was supposed to jump anyways. She made sure the shoes where well tied, gathered her courage, and jumped. The river was warm, but just warm enough that the water was still refreshing. The moon was now less than a semicircle down in the sky, about to hide behind mountains. Cayla jumped a few seconds afterwards, splashing Karina. The island with the castle was further up, and they started swimming. Hopefully Lylah would have some kind of expressway to take Karina back home, assuming of course that she would help her go home, assuming that they'd be able to get into her castle, that she would be alive and that she would even be helpful. But none of those thoughts made Karina ever question her need to go forward, for the simple reason that she had no other choice.

Even in the dark, they could see that the island had white

sand, not the color of sand, but rather white like salt or sugar, even shiny like them, very much like the castle itself. There were indeed no walls around it, and in fact no fortification of any kind. There was something strange about it. Even from such a close distance it didn't look real. Perhaps it was just a detail that Karina took a while to catch: it had no windows, and from the side they looked, no doors. Cayla swam ahead, and dove from time to time.

"What is she doing?" Nia asked Karina.

Only then she remembered that Nia didn't know everything about their plan. "There's an underwater passage," she explained.

Nia dove and came out. "It's too dark."

Beyond the farthest mountain the sky started to become blue, meaning that the sun would soon be up, and they'd soon be able to find what they were meant to find. But no. Karina remembered what Odell told them. "We were supposed to come to the river at night."

"Night?" Nia asked, thinking. "It must have some kind of light. We'll have to find the passage before the sun rises."

Karina looked at that beach and realized they were wasting time. "It's not here, but over there," she said, pointing to the other side of the island.

"Why are you saying that?" Cayla asked.

"The river is too shallow here. A passage would need a steeper slope."

"I'll look over there," Cayla said. She then started to swim around the island.

Nia and Ayanna followed her. Karina lagged behind because she was a lousy swimmer. When she reached the other side of the island, the others were diving. This side was indeed better suited for a passage as there were rocks instead of a beach.

"Nia, come here," Cayla said.

The woman swam in her direction and dove with her. As they came out of the water, Nia said, "She found it."

Time to face Lylah. Karina felt a knot in her stomach. Or was it hunger?

"Karina!" Cayla yelled, as if to hurry her.

Oh, she'd better hurry, or they'd leave her behind. Actually no, she still had the shoes, so they wouldn't go in without her. One thing she would certainly miss was the sense of importance.

When Karina reached the others, Cayla turned to Nia and Ayanna. "You wait here. I'll go in with Karina. She'll throw the shoes, and we'll be back."

Karina feared she would be forced to throw the shoes, and that wasn't exactly what she had been planning. Not that she had been planning much.

"No," Nia said. "You don't know what's waiting for us. We all go in." She glanced at Karina. "Then we'll see what wc'll do."

"But—" Cayla started to protest.

Nia interrupted her. "If things go wrong, you may need me. Also, if I was supposed to guide you, I'll do it till the end."

Nia then dove as if meaning to enter the passage.

"Wait," Cayla said, then quickly turned to the others. "Follow me."

She dove fast, followed by her sister, then Karina. In those dark waters, she saw Ayanna entering a circle near the bottom which had a faint glimmer around it. It looked like it went down, not up, and that wasn't how she expected an underwater tunnel to go. She wondered how long it was and if she would be able to hold her breath for all its length, but she didn't have the opportunity to voice any of these concerns, because the girls had disappeared inside it and she didn't want to be left behind. The tunnel was circular, made out of that same shiny white material she'd seen around the stairs. It went down then curved and started going up, like a sink siphon. Karina almost ran out of air, but not quite, as she came out in a small artificial pond in a circular tall room in that same white stone. The others were already out of the water, and Karina followed. There was a fireplace lit at the back of the room. Now it would be time for the truth, as the girls would know she was siding with Lylah if she did not throw the shoes. The only piece of furniture was a very large square table with places for eight people. There was food at the table; fruit, some kind of bread and even scrambled eggs, or at least something that looked like it. Breakfast. At that moment, Karina thought she really liked Lylah.

Cayla approached Karina and whispered, "We need to find the fire."

"I know," she replied, because that was the only thing she could reply.

But that didn't make any sense. The fire was right in front of them. Could it be that Karina was the only one to see it? She wondered if anyone else would mention it. She turned back to glance at the water and didn't see anything. No pool, no opening of any kind. Was their exit blocked?

17

TRUTHS AND LIES

Would there be a door somewhere? Perhaps the food at the table meant they were prisoners. Not that again. Who would save them this time? But then, perhaps they could just go out the way they'd come, even though it wasn't visible.

"I'm hungry," Ayanna said.

Karina agreed, but she wasn't sure what to do.

Nia smiled. "Let's eat then."

Cayla stepped in front of her sister and squinted. "Are you crazy?"

"No. Hungry."

"It must be poisoned," Cayla protested.

Nia glanced at the table. "Too much trouble. There are much easier ways to kill someone. Trust me."

Her "trust me" was rather scary.

"Still, it has to be a trap," Cayla insisted.

"We're in her castle, with no way out."

"No." Cayla said, then turned around and pointed to the place where the little pool was. "Where is it?"

Nia shook her head. "It is gone. Now, if she wants us dead, there isn't much we can do. I'm eating with your sister."

She sat and so did Ayanna, who looked at her sister as if feeling guilty. Karina almost sat as well, but she didn't want to upset Cayla. The girl walked around as if searching for something before turning to Karina. "We have to do something."

The smell of food made Karina even hungrier. She looked around, seeing only smooth walls—and a fireplace. But she didn't want to think about that. "Do you see any door?"

Cayla shook her head, then said, "You might be able to do something. You have the key."

That didn't make sense. "No. You have the key."

"No," Cayla replied. "It was destroyed when the door opened. And I meant something different."

The girl glanced at Karina's waist. Of course. The shoes. But what could she do? Did the girl see the fire? It could not be, as she would have mentioned it. Nia and Ayanna were eating now, and none of them had dropped dead on the floor. All Karina could think was sitting with them and doing the same. Could it be dangerous? But that smell… And Nia seemed to know what she was talking about. Karina sighed. "I'm going to eat."

Cayla tried to hold her. "You can't. No. That's what she wants."

"I'm sorry."

Karina sat with Nia and Ayanna and filled a plate with bread and fruit. There was a jug with tea, but it was cold, and Karina filled a cup, because she was thirsty. When she drank it, she spat it out; it was water.

"It's from the river," Nia said. "It's brown but it's clean. It's just the plants."

Karina drank the water. Black River. Right.

Cayla still walked around touching the walls as if to look for a secret passage.

Nia noticed, then said, "Come eat. Forget it, there are no doors."

"I'm not eating. Who knows what's in this food? Maybe it'll make us obey her, turn against against each other, sleep, or, who knows?"

"You should trust me. If I'm saying this food is safe, it's because it is."

Cayla sat at the table. "Why then? Why this? Why would she want us to eat?"

Nia shrugged. "Maybe she wants to be friendly?"

"Exactly," Cayla replied. "Then she'll convince us to give her whatever she wants from us. She's going to try to take... you know."

"And if we don't eat, she won't try to take anything back," Nia said.

Ayanna pointed at the food. "This is good. You should try it."

Cayla just looked sullen and glanced at the fruit from time to time. When the others were about finished, the girl plucked a few weird-looking grapes and ate them. Karina looked around and realized that the place looked like her previous prison, except that it was white instead of yellow. She then thought that eating hadn't been the brightest idea, but that was easier said with a full belly.

"What now?" Cayla asked, plucking some pieces of bread without looking at them.

"We wait," Nia replied.

For what? Was Nia still considering siding with Lylah? Karina wondered if it had been a good idea not to tell the girls anything. Cayla never took a plate, she just plucked pieces of food and put in her mouth as if not looking at them could prevent any poisoning. At least, if there was something wrong with the food, they would be all doomed together. Having company in disgrace, that was a good consolation.

After they all ate, they remained sitting in silence for a

short while, when they heard a voice coming from the direction where the little pool had been. "I hope it was to your taste."

They turned to look. There was Lylah, walking in their direction, as if she'd always been there. She looked as impressive as she had looked in Karina's room, with very shiny black hair, dressed in white. A shiver ran down Karina's spine, as she felt certain that the woman would ask for her shoes.

Cayla got up, but Nia held her by her arms. "You cannot fight her."

Cayla pulled her arm but sat down.

Lylah also sat down and looked at Nia. "Thank you." Then she addressed everyone. "I understand you had a tough journey here, and I congratulate you on your determination," she turned to Nia and Karina, "and sacrifices."

The woman's behavior was weird, as she seemed happy they were there. Perhaps this was indeed a trap. The question was for what.

The woman looked at them all. "I apologize if some of you had to be..." she paused and looked sideways before continuing. "Deceived. I had no other way to bring you here."

Cayla squinted. "Bring us here?"

"Listen," Nia whispered to her.

Karina was also wondering the same thing. Was it for the shoes? But then, why so much trouble? Was there a rule that they needed to be home-delivered or something? Again she feared giving up her unique objects.

She hoped nobody else interrupted Lylah again, because she took a long time to continue talking. "You might be wondering then... why Odell sent you. Look at this place. This is not a castle, not a home."

Karina did look around, and then the woman confirmed her impression. "It's a prison. And a very strong one."

Great, so they were in fact all locked up.

Lylah continued, "Only two people can open it. Or their descendants."

"What do you want from us?" Cayla interrupted.

Lylah sat back in silence.

Cayla was impatient, and added, "You want something from us. I get that. Just tell us what it is." Then she whispered to Karina, "We can pretend to help her, then find a way to do it."

By "it" she probably meant destroy the shoes. Lylah stared at them for a long time. Maybe she wanted to annoy them.

The woman turned to the older princess. "Cayla, what do you know about your mother?"

"Less than you, I suppose."

Lylah nodded. "Very true. Do you understand that mothers sometimes have to make sacrifices? Look at Nia. You don't suppose she doesn't love her son, do you?"

"What do you care about my little brother?"

Cayla was fearless and provoking, and Karina wondered if that was a good way to address a witch in her own castle. Or prison, but still. The others were quiet. Ayanna seemed to pay a lot of attention to what was said.

Lylah sat back and closed her eyes. "I also have a little brother. I saw him grow up. I even took care of him. I love him almost like a son."

Cayla shrugged. "Why should I care about your brother?"

"Because you care."

Cayla seemed surprised at first, then thoughtful. "Do you mean... Darian?"

Lylah shook her head. "Not him."

"Then I don't know, and I don't care."

Lylah glanced at Nia, then said, "Your stepmother knows. "

Nia shook her head. "I'm not her stepmother. At least not anymore."

Cayla turned to Nia. "Who's her brother?"

Nia shrugged. "I don't know. It... it can't be."

"It's exactly who you're thinking," Lylah said.

Everyone looked at Nia. She looked unsure. "He's too old."

Lylah shook her head. "It's make-up. He pretends. He was a teenager when he joined the king."

"As a wise man?" Nia asked, incredulous.

Lylah nodded.

"Who is it?" Cayla asked.

"Odell," Nia replied.

Karina was stunned. She hadn't expected that, as much as she sometimes thought the bald man had been pretending.

"How come you never told us?" Cayla asked.

"I had no idea they were siblings," Nia said. "It occurred to me now. But I always told you he was working with her."

Cayla had tears in her eyes, and asked Nia, "Why did you come then? Why did you follow his directions?"

"Did I have a choice?"

Cayla looked down.

Lylah addressed Nia, "I know why you came, and I will do everything I can to protect your son. I'm grateful to you."

"We'd better move then," Nia said. "There is talk of an attack on the castle."

"Nia!" Cayla protested. "Are you going to turn against us?"

"I'm not against you," Nia replied. "One day you'll understand."

"I was hoping this would be the day," Lylah said, then turned to Cayla. "Have you ever considered that most of what you heard in your life were lies?"

"Now I'm hearing lies," Cayla said. "You're saying Odell's your brother, but that can't be. He's always helped us. I trust him. He'd never be against us."

"But he's not," Lylah said. "Why do you think he disguised himself for sixteen years?"

"It doesn't make any sense," Cayla replied.

"To protect you," Lylah said.

"You are lying."

Lylah was still calm. "Don't you trust Nia?"

"She's paranoid."

"Paranoid against your father, you mean," Lylah replied. "Could it be because he's threatened her with death? Have you ever wondered what happened to your sister's mother? Or your mother?"

Cayla got up and pointed her finger towards Lylah. "Don't you dare mention my mother."

Karina remembered what the girl had told her and felt guilty and sad.

Lylah closed her eyes and sighed. "Nia's right. Time's running out. I'll tell you what I want from you; then I'll explain why."

"We'll never help you!" Cayla said.

Nia grabbed the girl's arm, and sounded stern, "First you listen, then you say whatever you want to say."

Cayla pulled back her arm but remained quiet.

Lylah continued, "As you noticed, this is a prison, and the tunnel from where you came is gone. I need you to free me and free yourselves. There are two people who can free me. Either the person who built this castle, or the last person who locked it, and left me here, thinking he defeated me." Lylah looked down, took a deep breath, then continued, "I happen to be the one who built it, but I cannot free myself; I could only open the passage to other dimensions." She turned to Karina. "And that's how I came to your world." She then turned to everyone else, "And how I didn't die. The other person who can free me is the king. He locked me here. Unlike you might have heard, I have no army, and no assistants, except my brother. All I want is freedom, to be reunited with my family, and to help restore peace to the kingdom."

Cayla slammed her hand on the table. "You do want to take power!"

"Not necessarily. There are other people already fighting this war. I had to wait until you were old enough so that you'd come on your own free will." That last part seemed to be addressed at Cayla. "But now I can help them."

"You tricked us," Cayla protested. "You and Odell."

Lylah stared attentively at the girl. "Not really. You came to bring peace to your kingdom. That's what I plan to do."

"By force!"

"Listen," Lylah's voice was lower pitched, "I need either my daughter, or the daughter of the king, to open a door behind me. If you walk close to the wall, you will see it. This way we'll all be free."

Karina didn't see any door, but on the other hand, she was the only one to see the fire, so perhaps that prison offered a custom view for each of them.

"You're lying," Cayla said. "And I won't free you. I'd rather spend the rest of my life here."

Karina began to wonder how the rest of her life would be then. She hoped at least that Lylah would bring them some nice food from time to time. Not that it made up for losing her freedom, her life, her youth. Ugh, Karina didn't want to consider staying in that place.

But it was Nia who protested, "Cayla, my son!"

"Don't you see?" Cayla insisted. "He's safer if she's locked."

"You are the one who's not seeing it," Nia said. "Can't you see who she is? Because I can. Perhaps it's just that you can't look at yourself."

Cayla squinted. "What?"

To be fair, Karina had a similar mental reaction. Nia wasn't usually that enigmatic.

Lylah waited for a while, then continued to address Cayla. "In time, I'll tell you everything. For now, I need you to trust me. Cayla…" The woman paused mid-sentence, open mouthed, as if considering how to say something important. "Odell, you know how much he cares about you. I hope you trust him, and you should, because of all he's done for you."

"He's a liar." Cayla sounded sad.

Lylah shook her head. "He only did what he did to protect you. Odell…" Lylah looked down and took a deep breath, then faced Cayla, "…is your uncle."

That was underwhelming. With all that suspense and emotion, Karina was expecting some big revelation, expecting perhaps Odell to be the girl's father or something more dramatic.

Cayla for her part laughed. "You just said he was your brother. Your lies don't even make sense anymore."

Lylah fell silent. Nia also looked down. How could Odell be Lylah's brother and Cayla's uncle at the same time? Then it hit her. Oh, it was obvious. The first time Karina saw Cayla, she'd reminded her of Lylah, and, now that the two were together, the similarity was there, although not obvious.

Lylah continued, "Cayla, all these years, I've been waiting to see you. I could not come to you, and I could not let you know anything that could endanger you, but I never forgot—"

"Forgot what? How you killed my mother?"

Karina covered her face with her hands. Lylah stared at the girl in silence.

Nia held Cayla's hand and said softly, "Cayla, dear." She pointed to Lylah. "She *is* your mother."

Karina had guessed as much. But still, to hear it like that was somewhat shocking.

Cayla was still upset, looking incredulous and hurt. Tears ran from her eyes and she said, "Even if it's true. You don't expect me to come here and simply free you. Now. After an entire life."

Lylah just looked in silence.

Nia addressed Cayla, "She couldn't. Don't you understand?"

Lylah looked nowhere while tears ran down her cheeks.

Ayanna walked close to her and asked, "And do you know what happened to my mother?"

More and more tears ran down Lylah's eyes. "I'm so sorry. I tried. Odell really tried. He could not save her. He was too late."

"What happened? I'd rather hear it," Ayanna said.

"She tried to run away. With you. But the king caught her. I'm sorry, I'm so sorry. My brother could never forgive himself. At least he tried to give you the love your mother couldn't give. I know it's not the same."

Ayanna shook her head. "I'm sure he did his best. He's always been there for us."

Lylah had a half smile.

The younger princess then asked, "You need the king's daughter to free you? Can that be me?"

Lylah seemed surprised, then nodded. "Yes, it could."

Ayanna pointed behind Lylah. "And all I have to do is open that door?"

Again Lylah nodded.

"Ayanna, don't!" Cayla pleaded.

Ayanna turned to her sister. "Sorry, but I'm not going to spend the rest of my life here."

Karina, who was following their conversation, still didn't see any door. And the shoes hadn't been mentioned yet. Karina felt safe to assume they had been forgotten, and she was thrilled. Somehow, she'd never felt comfortable about giving or destroying them.

Ayanna walked to the back of the room, right beside the fire. "This?"

"I can't see it," Lylah said. "But if you see a door, that must be it."

Cayla watched in silence. Her sister moved her arms, as if opening an invisible door, but no real door appeared. In fact, nothing happened.

Ayanna turned to Lylah. "And what now?"

Lylah looked puzzled. "It should… Unless…" She looked at Ayanna. "But you saw the door, right?"

"It was here," the girl replied, then pointed and looked. "But… not anymore."

Could it be that Lylah had made a mistake? That was what it seemed. Apparently, something should have happened when Ayanna "opened" the door, but it didn't. The woman's expression worried Karina more than anything. This time she feared they would be locked there forever. A thunderous rumbling put an end to her worries. Lylah looked relieved, but just for a second. Her expression became grim. The floor and walls trembled. At first, Karina feared the whole place would collapse on them, but since she didn't see anything falling, she decided to look. The place wasn't collapsing, but instead closing on them. Walls were getting closer together, the ceiling was coming down, and the floor was coming up. If that movement didn't stop, they would all be crushed in a minute. Maybe much less, but Karina didn't want to calculate that.

Lylah yelled something, but, with all the noise, Karina couldn't hear it. The woman had her arms spread out and gestured for the others to come under, as if she were to protect them, but she still looked troubled and afraid. Karina had known Lylah for a short while, but long enough to realize that she wouldn't be scared of something silly. Karina was about to run to the woman when she saw the fire. Instead of bigger, it got smaller and smaller even though the wall moved forward. It was about to disappear.

Nia came close to Karina and yelled, "The shoes, use them! Or give them to Lylah!"

Karina realized all their lives were in her hands. Or waist. Karina had to think faster than she had ever thought in her life. Did the shoes contain Lylah's power? If they did, why would their destruction harm her? If the shoes had any power, it would, in fact, be released. If Karina's logic made any sense.

Karina then remembered Zoe's strange accident, and her own infatuation with the shoes. She also remembered Nia saying that the shoes would bind her. Karina had been bound for a long time. Too long. Lylah gestured for Karina. She wanted the shoes. The shoes. The power was in the shoes. Lylah's power. In a fraction of a second Karina made her decision. She untied the shoes from her waist, and instead of giving them to Lylah or trying to use them, she tossed them on the dwindling flame.

18

GOING SEPARATE WAYS

Something happened all right, because the noise increased, and the floor trembled even more. Karina fell down. The walls started to crack, and she thought they were about to crumble upon them for real this time. More than ever she regretted having left her bedroom and having to make decisions about things she didn't understand. What a terrible way to die: for a stupid mistake.

But soon Karina realized that although the ceiling was collapsing, no piece hit her. In fact, no part of the ceiling or wall reached the ground, as they disappeared mid-fall. As the ceiling opened, Karina could see the blue sky with a few clouds. After much trembling and noise, the castle, or rather, prison, disappeared. They all sat on muddy sand. Regular, beige sand, on the island in the river. The rest of the food lay on the floor, likely meaning that it had been real. Good to know that she hadn't eaten disappearing magical stuff. Everyone was alive, as they were moving, getting up from having fallen on the trembling floor.

Lylah walked to Karina and put a hand on her shoulder.

"How did you know? How did you know you had to throw the shoes?"

Karina was flushed. "It's just... I guess shoes should never be that important."

Lylah smiled. Karina was glad to have made the right decision. She was trembling, perhaps because she learned that the danger had in fact been real.

Cayla was getting up, when she said, "Something's coming."

Nia looked around, not seeming to have heard anything. "Should we hide?"

"No time," Lylah said, "but I doubt we'll see more than four lifts at once. I can handle them."

Either she was indeed all-powerful or she was quite presumptuous. Karina hoped for the first possibility.

"There are two lifts," Cayla said. "Maybe they are friends?"

A few seconds after, a lift appeared in the sky, above the mountains, then a second one. Something like a cannon pointed at them from the top of the first lift. Karina didn't remember lifts having weapons, or perhaps she simply didn't know. A huge ball of blue fire came in their direction. Her guess was that they weren't friendly. Karina considered jumping to the ground or the river, but before she did anything, the ball turned around, split in two, and hit both lifts, which fell on the valley.

"They'll survive," Lylah said.

One thing Karina noticed was that the lifts fell but didn't explode.

"More of them are coming," Lylah said. "We have to teleport somewhere away from here. I can do it, but only one at a time."

She turned to Ayanna, held her hand, then disappeared. In a matter of seconds Lylah was back alone. She then grabbed Karina's hand. The girl felt a now familiar feeling of falling, then found herself beside Ayanna, near the summit from the previous night, but beneath some trees. Lylah soon came with Nia, then disappeared. Some more time then passed, something like one or two minutes, before Lylah showed up with Cayla, who then sat on a rock and looked down. Lylah closed her eyes and kept them closed for a long time.

Karina didn't feel comfortable at that place, although it was unlikely that anyone would do anything to them with Nia and Lylah there. She felt a little sad and empty without the shoes, knowing that her mission was over and that she would no longer be important. At least she was still alive, so no regrets there.

Lylah looked down, thinking, then looked distraught, as if in pain. She looked at one of her bracelets. A red stone shone brightly.

"What's wrong?" Ayanna asked.

"Odell," Lylah replied. "He's in danger."

Nia grabbed the woman's hands. "My son. We have to go. Please take me there."

"It's not as simple," Lylah said.

"Please, just teleport me there. I know you can. Let me do something for my son. I've done a lot for Cayla."

Lylah closed her eyes for a moment, then said, "I'll come with you." She then turned to the girls. "Stay here and wait. I'll come back."

Nia looked worried. "Isn't it dangerous to leave them here?"

"No," Lylah replied. "And they can teleport if they are only two."

Karina didn't understand that, but maybe it had something to do with Cayla being her daughter.

"Actually, I'll take Ayanna as well," Lylah said. "I know a safe place for her. Come."

The dark-haired woman soon disappeared with Ayanna, then came back and disappeared with Nia, who still looked worried but did not protest. Karina wasn't upset at being left behind because she figured going to the castle would have been dangerous. Plus, that way she could keep Cayla company.

The girl sat down on the floor and plucked leaves of grass, looking sad.

Karina crouched beside her. "I know this may be difficult for you, but maybe you should give Lylah a chance. Just hear what she has to say. Maybe… talk to Odell. Perhaps, you know, you might see things differently."

Cayla shook her head. "It's not even that. I mean, it is, but… Either way you look at it, it's disturbing. Even if it's true that she's my mother, and that Odell is my uncle, it means I've been lied to my whole life. My whole life. It means there isn't a single person who hasn't been lying to me."

Karina looked down, then tried to come up with something to cheer her up. "I don't think Ayanna ever lied to you."

Cayla got up and gesticulated her arms. "Cause she's just a child! In the same situation as me. Or slightly better. You know, cause there's no chance her mother might be evil and take the kingdom. Because of me! It's all my fault. Trust me; I sure hope she isn't evil." She looked down. "But then, my father…"

Karina put her hand on her friend's shoulder. She had no idea what to say.

Cayla looked around. "I think we can see the castle from the other side. Let's look."

They walked to the other side of the summit. They could see an ocean of clouds, a valley with lakes, some hills, and, far away, a river. Karina couldn't see the castle, and it made sense, because it was so close to the hills by the river. But there was something she saw: fire near the river, like the fireballs and the fire that had consumed the lift the previous night. Karina remembered the attack Darian had mentioned. She felt sad that he hadn't kept his word, but on the other hand, she didn't know how much he could do.

Cayla looked shocked. "How is that? How can Lylah be doing that already?"

"Lylah has just teleported," Karina said. "I doubt she's responsible for the attack."

"Who is it then?"

Well, the rebels, of course. Karina looked at Cayla. "You know who's doing that."

"We have to do something. My father! Even if he's guilty, I don't want him to be killed."

Karina didn't think that was necessary. "Nobody said—"

"I need to make sure."

"And what do you want to do?"

"Go to the castle!" Cayla said as if it was rather obvious.

Karina didn't want to remind her that they'd been told to wait. By now, she understood Cayla was not good at following orders. For her part, she would much rather sit on the mountain and wait for all the trouble to stop. Either way, they were far from the castle. "How?"

Cayla pulled her necklace. "Darian. Darian." She sounded angry. Karina wondered how much she knew.

The stone, or rather, Darian, replied, "Cayla, are you alright?"

"I am."

"I see where you are. Please stay there and hide. I'll come for you as soon as I can. Right now, I can't… I'll explain everything when I see you again. Just stay safe now."

"Don't worry. I will." She sounded calm and complying.

"Really?" Karina asked.

Cayla grimaced. "Are you kidding me? Of course not! We're going to the castle. I mean, I'm going. You don't have to go."

Karina exhaled, relieved.

Cayla continued, "But I need to find a way to get there."

That sounded like a terrible idea. "Why don't you wait? It's dangerous going there. Especially alone."

Cayla shook her head. "It isn't. My father's army wouldn't

harm me. I don't think these insurgents would harm me either. I mean, at least I'm sure they won't kill me."

Maybe she had a point. Karina then remembered what Lylah had told them. "Can't you teleport?"

"What? No."

"How come you came to my place then, and brought me?"

"There was a portal already opened. And I didn't do anything. Odell had it all set up. I mean," she snorted, "now that I know who actually did it, it makes a lot more sense."

"But Lylah just said we could teleport if we were just in two."

Cayla shrugged. "I have no idea what she meant. Maybe she forgot you threw the shoes or something."

It could be. Or maybe not. "But don't you, I mean, don't you have some power, considering who you are?"

"That's not something you're born with."

"But you know magic, right? I mean, you cast a light in my room—"

"Well, that… Fine, it was magic. Odell taught me a little. Just a little. The thing is, whenever you go to another dimension, you're more powerful, so I was testing."

"And what was the result?"

Cayla shrugged and snorted. "Some light. Not very useful." Cayla looked down at the horizon far away. "I think I know how to get there. Come, follow me."

She ran to the place where they had fought at night.

"What do you want to do?" Karina asked.

"They might have dropped something." She looked down to the floor. "Something we could use to communicate. Help me find it."

"What should it look like?"

"It's usually silver. But it could be different. If you find anything unusual, let me know."

Her tone was urgent. Cayla really believed she would find

something. Karina tried to look. She wasn't sure if she wanted to find anything, though. The whole idea sounded dangerous.

Cayla looked behind Karina and smiled. "You can stop looking."

Karina looked at that direction and saw a lift coming in their direction. Great. "You think this is good?"

"Well, if it's the rebels, they'll take us to the castle. If it's the army, they'll take us to the castle. Easy, right?"

"Take you maybe. I'd rather hide."

"But you want to go home, right? You can only teleport from the blue tower, and you know where it is."

Karina shrugged. "I can wait."

"Fine. Wait then, but if it takes a month, don't blame me." Cayla crossed her arms, but then she got calmer. "There's something else you can do. Hide. See what happens. If they are friendly, you come with me. How's that?"

"And if they aren't?"

"You find a way to ask for help." Cayla sighed. "And, if by any chance, we don't see each other again, I want to—"

"Stop it." Karina was not ready for any goodbye. "Everything will be fine. I'm sure they are friendly and I'll come with you."

At least that was what Karina hoped. Cayla smiled. Still, Karina went to the middle of the bushes, while Cayla stood out in the open, waiting. Karina sat on the floor, and waited for some two or three minutes, until she heard the sound of a door opening. She ran to Cayla because she decided she didn't want to leave her alone, especially if the people were not friendly. There was a lift in front of Cayla. Two young men stepped out of it. One was very tall and thin, with wavy dark hair, and the other had average height and blond hair. The blond boy wore a similar uniform to the one he'd seen Darian and Zayra wearing. The tall boy wore civilian blown clothes, with leather-looking pants and a black shirt.

The taller boy glanced at Karina before turning to Cayla. "Hey, sis!"

Cayla crossed her arms. "Don't call me that."

"Fine, Princess Cayla." He gesticulated in an exaggerated way, while smirking. "I had no idea we were back to such formalities."

"Knock it off, Sian," Cayla said.

Sian seemed to know Cayla well, so it was safe to assume that they were not planning on imprisoning her or anything. He was a little weird, though.

"Hey, I came to help you," Sian said. He noticed Karina. "And may I have the pleasure of your name?"

"Karina. I'm Cayla's friend."

He stepped closer to her. "I'm Sian." He spread out his arms, then bowed. "At your service."

He was more than a little weird.

Sian then pointed to the blond boy. "This is Lee."

"Hey." Lee waved his hand.

Sian turned to Cayla, smug smirk on his face, "And to what do I owe the pleasure of coming to your rescue?"

"The castle. I need to go there."

He laughed. "You're kidding, right?" Sian stared at Cayla. "Nope, not kidding. That's too bad. As much as I'd love the honor of escorting you back to the castle, the place is, let's say, kind of messy right now. We wouldn't make it past the siege. Nobody could take you there, except... Have you tried my sweet little brother?"

Cayla stared at him in silence.

Sian frowned. "Oh, not even he'll take you. That's too bad. What's the problem, your beloved's too busy betraying your father?"

Cayla stepped close to Sian. "I asked you to knock it off. I did it nicely."

She raised her knee toward his groin. He blocked her and

stepped back. Cayla tried to punch him and he blocked. At the same time, Lee stepped behind her and put a cloth on her face. This was all too fast, so Karina had no time to warn her friend. Cayla fainted. Maybe the boys weren't friendly after all. Lee advanced towards Karina, but Sian said, "Leave her. She's harmless."

Karina was somewhat relieved and wondered when and how tales of her lack of bravery had reached him.

Sian looked at Cayla on the floor. "Brat." He turned to Karina while pointing at Cayla. "What she did was attempted murder. She might have killed my future children." He shook his head. "No love for her future nephews and nieces."

Karina wasn't sure if he was serious or not, so she refrained from laughing.

Lee said, "More lifts might come. We need to take them somewhere safe."

"Of course," Sian said. He then got close to Lee and put a cloth in front of his nose and mouth. Lee fainted. Sian held him careful so that the boy would not fall on the floor, then said, "But I make the decisions."

19

ABOUT SIAN

Sian had just betrayed his companion. Karina's heart raced. She had no idea what to expect from him. He noticed and waved the gray cloth on his hand. "You want to take a nap too?"

Karina didn't reply.

"I wasn't serious," he said. "You should've laughed. Are my jokes that bad?"

Well, yes, but Karina wasn't going to say that. She just stared.

"You don't talk much, do you?" He smiled. "I like it! My favorite type of conversation partner. I can hear more of myself."

This was annoying. "What are you going to do to us?"

"Am I supposed to answer? Do you want to hear all my evil plans?"

"Yes, of course."

He grimaced. "This one doesn't work when you reply. There's no evil plan. I'll take you somewhere safe. Lee here has connections with the rebels. I don't trust him, that's why I had to do this."

That meant Sian was not with the rebels. Karina wondered why he'd make Cayla faint then. Was it because she'd tried to kick him?

"Let's go," Sian continued. "More lifts could come, although most of the rebels are around the castle now."

Sian then dragged Lee and Cayla to the lift. Karina followed, because she didn't want to leave her friend. This lift was entirely different from the other ones. It had no division, and it had what looked like one weapon on each side, like cannons or something. Karina sat by Cayla, on the back, where there were two rows of seats.

Sian went to the front, then turned back, "Hey, why don't you come sit by me? The view is great."

Karina preferred to stay in the back with Cayla. "Thanks, I'm good here."

She looked down at Cayla sleeping, wondering where they would be taken, and unsure on which side and for whom Sian was fighting. Karina then heard a sound and looked up to see Sian crouching in front of her.

"You don't understand, do you?" Sian said. "I'm only keeping you alive cause it's boring to make sarcastic remarks when there's nobody to hear them." He smiled as he said that.

Karina could also smirk when she wanted to. "Maybe I'd rather die."

He tilted his head, curious. "Some people would agree with you. You owe me your life, you know?"

"Really? How so?"

He shrugged and said matter-of-factly, "I didn't kill you."

Karina snorted. "Wow, am I supposed to be flattered or something?"

He became serious and looked down. "No." For the first time, he looked anything like Darian. "I'm sorry. I didn't mean that. I just want to talk to you."

His eyes were hazel with long eyelashes, and from that distance they were really beautiful, but Karina shouldn't be noticing that. She asked, "For what?"

His smirk was back, which was good, because then he looked more annoying than anything. "We can exchange some information. How's that?"

Karina did want to learn where she was going and also wanted to figure out the mess she'd gotten into. She also wanted to check how those things moved. After a deep breath, she got up and sat in the front. His hands with long, thin fingers passed over the panel, and it became light blue, with black lines over it. Sian slid his hand over a strip of green light and the lift took off. They moved in a direction opposite of the meeting of the rivers. Karina saw lakes, the Black River, and even the ocean beyond the castle and the silver river. The view was indeed great.

Sian asked, "You've met my little brother Darian, haven't you?"

Karina remained silent, wondering where he wanted to take this conversation.

Sian laughed, "Oh, don't worry, I know you met him. I don't really need that kind of information from you. I know who the insurgents are, I know what they are planning, and I'm aware they are trying to take the castle right now."

"Good for you." She turned her face away from him and looked at the window.

"So, back to my sweet brother. I bet he never mentioned me, did he?"

Karina didn't reply.

"See? That's how much he cares about his family. But that's not my point. He thinks he got part of the army to follow him. I've been tracking all his steps. His rebellion will go nowhere."

Karina wasn't supposed to say anything, but she felt she had to. "He's not their leader."

"He convinced you of that? What did he say? No single leadership? People coming up with ideas on their own? He doesn't pose as their leader, but he gets them to do what he wants."

"He's too young."

"But that's the thing: young, idealistic. Quite catchy, you know?"

Karina wasn't sure if what he was saying was true or not, or even if he believed it.

Sian pointed to Cayla. "And that's why she's the perfect hostage. We'll ambush the insurgents once they are tired, but, if things go wrong, she might be useful. With her, we can get the king, and we can get Darian. It's just perfect. So you know why I'm doing this."

Karina felt a chill down her spine. She thought about Lylah. Cayla was too perfect as a hostage. But something he said didn't make sense. "The king? I thought you were protecting him."

Sian laughed. "The king is bonkers. That's another reason the rebels haven't been caught until now: they are doing the dirty work for my father. I, unlike my brother, care about family."

"You're doing this so that your father takes the kingdom?"

"No. Maybe I'm doing this because I think it's right. Whyland needs a better ruler." He smiled. "One with a charming older son. Who's better than Keen?"

Karina remembered escaping him, and then remembered what she'd heard from Darian and the rebels. "But he's cruel."

Sian waved his finger in the air. "You have to consider who told you this."

Maybe he had a point. But then maybe he didn't. Karina thought about Lylah and Nia. And how Sian didn't know about them. Lylah. Sian had no idea about her, and that could be the factor that changed everything. "Are you leading this ambush?" Karina asked.

"What do you want to hear? That no, I have nothing to do with it? Sorry but I'm not humble like my brother."

"Surrender then. Get your people to surrender, strike a deal, something. You can't win this."

He smiled. "Of course. I'll surrender just because you're telling me so. You'll need a lot more than a sweet smile if you want to tell me what to do."

Karina thought it was better to be honest. "Lylah. We freed her. And Nia. They're powerful. You won't beat them."

"I think I can deal with two ladies. So Lylah was freed? And she was alive?" He laughed. "Thanks for the info, by the way."

"Use the information then. Cancel this attack, ambush, whatever."

He shook his head. "I don't think Lylah can make any difference."

"She brought down two lifts. I saw it."

He raised his eyebrows, puzzled or incredulous, then laughed. "If she does," he pointed at the back, "I still have the perfect hostage. Unlike my pathetic brother, I happen to know who Cayla's mother is."

Bummer. Karina tried to argue, "I don't think you're a bad person. Why are you doing this?"

He smiled and his eyes brightened. "You don't think I'm a bad person? That's a great start." He got serious again. "Now, you want to know why? For order, peace. This insurgence could lead us into chaos."

"You're doing this for power."

Sian smirked. "Same thing as my brother."

"He means well."

"I mean well too. I know you're not from here. I have no idea where you're from, but let me ask you something: how much do you know about Whyland?"

Uh, close to nothing? The question caught her. Maybe he

had a point. But Karina remembered the rebels on the hill, and how they said that they were fighting brutality, she remembered what Darian had said, what Lylah had said. She knew that Sian was on the wrong side. She wasn't sure how much he knew, though, and whether his talk of taking power was real or some kind of joke.

Karina said, "I got to know people here, people who believe in what they are doing, and I believe in them."

"I also believe in what I'm doing! Get to know me! Did they give you a guide or anything? A book?"

"Well, no, but—"

"How sad. I'll get you a book. And you should believe me."

"Why do you care what I think?"

"Well isn't it obvious?"

"No."

"I'm just a guy trying to impress a pretty girl."

Karina hadn't expected that, but she tried not to show she was surprised, and looked around. "Where? I don't see any."

He looked at her intently. "Cause there's no mirror here."

Her face got hot. Was it some kind of joke? Anyways, he was just teasing and trying to get her confused. Maybe he thought she would get wobbly knees, feel out of air and stop thinking. Karina rolled her eyes. "I haven't brushed or washed my hair for five days."

"That explains the wild look."

She looked out the window.

He changed his tone. "I'll give you a better explanation, then." He pointed at Cayla. "She's a brat. I don't know how my brother can stand her. But somehow she trusts you. I don't know what's gonna happen, but of course I'll want a deal with my brother. Of course I want him by my side. That's where Cayla comes in. You might be able to help me."

"Strike a deal now. That's what I told you."

"See? We're coming to an understanding. If you knew me, you'd know I never fight when I can negotiate. But I need the upper hand."

"What do you want from me? Should I tell her that you mean well? That you're nice? You expect she'll listen? She doesn't listen to anyone."

He looked down. "I know."

"Why then?"

"I already told you, and now it's your turn to find an alternate explanation. Go on."

Karina didn't understand what he hoped to accomplish by treating her like that. She looked out the window.

He said, "So, I've told you all my secrets. What about you? What brings you to Whyland?"

Karina's story was so absurd she decided to tell it. "I came to bring a pair of shoes." He looked at her with an eyebrow raised. That was entertaining. She suppressed a smile and continued, "To Lylah." He looked at her in disbelief so she continued because she thought it was funny. "It was a pair of magical shoes. I thought they'd destroy Lylah, but they freed her."

If he lifted his right eyebrow any higher it would touch his hair. "Magical?"

"You guys are weird. You have interdimensional teleporting, but get all skeptical about magic?"

He frowned. "What do you mean interdimensional teleporting?"

"See? Weird."

"Tell me." All his smirking and attitude was gone. There was only curiosity and even some pleading. "I need to understand."

Guess who had the upper hand now? She smirked. "Halt the attack and I will."

He looked away, then looked at her, thoughtful. "Odell set it up. I mean, not the magic and everything, but having Cayla free Lylah."

Karina shrugged. "Maybe. If you want more information we'll have to strike a deal."

He shook his head. "It's fine. You don't have to tell me anything if you don't want to."

There was something soft and soothing about his voice. For a moment she wanted to tell him everything, for a moment she wished that all his talk about trying to impress her were real, she wished he really thought she was pretty, and then she wanted to slap herself to wake up and stop being stupid. He was obviously trying to manipulate her. She looked away and focused on her breathing. Air in, air out. The lift was descending into what looked like the crater of an inactive volcano. There were a bunch of lifts there. Probably ready to attack. Her heart beat faster and the whole breathing technique was gone. Some twenty or thirty. And they would take the castle by surprise. Maybe Lylah and Nia wouldn't make a differ-ence after all. Karina worried about her friends. Darian and Lylah needed to know about this attack. She looked back at Cayla. Her necklace! The question was when she'd have an opportunity to use it. And plus, she didn't know how it worked. The lift landed.

Sian got up and said, "Listen, I would love to take you to the most beautiful place in Whyland, but that won't be now. You'll go to a prison with Cayla. Are you going to resist, or can you just walk by my side?"

That was a stupid question because even if Karina had a black belt in martial arts, she wouldn't be able to leave that place on her own. "I can walk."

He nodded, opened the door and got out. Karina followed. Sian made a gesture and four men entered their lift and carried Lee away.

Karina was worried. "Is he gonna get hurt?"

"For real?" Sian asked. "I talk to you all the way up here, tell you all my secrets, and you're worried about him?"

His tone and gesticulation were exaggerated. But Karina didn't think it was funny. "Is he gonna get hurt?"

"I wouldn't tell you, would I? But don't worry. He's one of us. It's just that right now he needs to be detained." He made a sad face. "Of course, it still breaks my heart to see you only care about him."

Karina didn't know when he was being serious or ironic and was getting annoyed. Two young men carried Cayla and they all walked in a direction opposite to the one Lee was carried.

Sian turned to Karina. "I was joking. That was sweet."

More weirdness. "What?"

"Lee. You've met him for what? Twenty seconds? For all you know he would've attacked you if it wasn't for me. And yet you worry about him."

Karina shrugged. "I just don't want anyone to get hurt."

"Not even me I suppose."

Almost, cause now she thought Cayla's kick could have been deserved. But no more than that. "That's why I told you to surrender."

"Did you take a look around you? Still think we need to surrender?"

"Even if you don't need to, you can still strike a deal." Karina had no idea why she was pleading, but there she was. "Make peace. Assure nobody gets hurt."

"That's my plan. You should trust me."

They came to a prison cell, with a door made of iron bars.

Sian grimaced. "This place is ugly. I'm sorry, but Cayla needs to be kept somewhere safe. Hopefully you won't be here long. Do you want anything before I take the kingdom?"

Karina wasn't sure if he really meant that, but she decided to ask for something. "I don't want to be alone." Sian had a smile and his eyes brightened. Karina continued, "Could you... wake up Cayla? So she keeps me company?"

He looked down, making an exaggerated sad face. "I thought you meant me."

"Well, stay here then. Much more interesting than leading a stupid attack."

Sian laughed. "A lot more interesting!" He made a sad face again. "But what can I do? Duty calls me." He turned to the men carrying Cayla, and spoke in a neutral, serious tone, "Wake her up when she's inside. But careful. She's dangerous. Don't hurt either of them." He turned to Karina, "We'll catch up later." He turned around and left.

As Karina entered the cell watched as he walked away in sure steps, hair and overcoat flowing. He puzzled her. The guards entered and gave Cayla a shot. Her eyes opened. Karina wondered if the breathing cloth and the shot had any risk, and kind of regretted having asked for Cayla to be woken up.

The princess looked around. "Where are we?"

"We're in a military base, no idea where, while they are planning to attack the castle."

Cayla squinted. "Isn't the castle already being attacked?"

"By the rebels. These people are with General Keen."

"They're with my father then." Cayla squinted again. "Why are we in a prison?"

"Apparently Keen plans on betraying your father."

Cayla squinted even harder and tilted her head. "He's with the insurgents?" She sounded incredulous.

"No. He's with himself, I think. His plan is to let the rebels depose your father and then take power."

"How do you know all that?"

Karina looked down, embarrassed for some reason. "Sian told me."

Cayla had a puzzled face.

"I think he likes to talk," Karina added.

"He talks too much, that's what I think," Cayla said. She then looked around. "We have to get back to the castle."

Thanks, captain obvious. "No kidding, right? But there's something else you can do." She pointed to Cayla's necklace.

The princess raised her hands in despair. "How am I even supposed to know on which side he is?"

"He's with the rebels."

Cayla sighed, looked down, and closed her eyes. Yikes. Perhaps she shouldn't have received this information so suddenly. "You can't be sure."

"I can," Karina said. "Sian told me."

"It sounds like you guys became buddies or something. What else did he tell you?"

"Nothing." Karina looked down. "He wanted to explain why you were being held, that's all."

"How thoughtful of him."

Karina then pointed again at the necklace. "Are you going to try it?"

Cayla pointed at the guards. She didn't seem to want to contact him in front of them.

Karina then heard sounds of people moving. "What's happening?" she took a chance and asked one of the guards.

"The lifts are taking off."

Oh, no, they would attack now. The one upside was that at least Sian was kind of nice, so if they took the castle, they would hopefully allow her to go there, use the blue tower, and go home. But then, what about Nia, Lylah, Cayla, Ayanna? On the other hand, Lylah could maybe defeat them. Maybe.

"I can't believe we're here," Cayla said.

"Well, you're the one who thought they'd give us a ride to the castle."

"Come up with a better idea, then."

"Let's teleport!" Karina said, half joking.

"I told you. I can't do it."

Karina shrugged, "Well neither can—" An idea hit her, but

she was not sure about it. "Wait. What did you say about magic?"

Cayla glanced at the guards. "That it's really evil and only witches use it?"

"Right. You also said that, uh, evil witches, when they go to another dimension, they get stronger. Does that work for anybody? Or do you have to have training?"

Cayla looked at Karina and seemed to understand. She whispered, "You. It was you. In the hill with the insurgents."

Karina wasn't sure. She still thought it could have been the shoes.

"You have to try it," Cayla said softly.

"How?"

One of the guards banged on the door. "Hey, no whispering."

Cayla held Karina's hand. "Close your eyes and see yourself there. In the blue tower."

Could it be that easy? Nia had said she needed an emotional spike. Karina thought about home, and how her way there would be through the blue tower, she thought about the friends she'd made, about Sian. The ground below her felt as if it was moving. She lost balance. She knew what it was, and it felt great.

Karina fell on the floor in a tall circular room surrounded by blue walls… The blue tower! She'd done it! She got up and looked around, almost waiting for some hostile soldiers to attack them, but nobody came. The emptiness and silence were more disturbing than some sound or movement, though. There were cracks in the wall that hadn't been there before. Or maybe she hadn't noticed them. And too late she realized that she'd brought them right to the middle of a conflict, like the eye of a storm, knowing nothing of what was really going on. But hey, getting entangled in stuff she knew nothing about was becoming Karina's specialty. The prison would have been safer, except that it would be annoying to stay there waiting for Sian to come back with a superior smirk.

"I know where we need to go," Cayla said. "Come."

They got out and Karina ran after her friend through a long corridor. The light from the ceiling was so obviously artificial now that she knew about it. They turned a corner—and were ambushed. Two soldiers appeared in front of them, with guns, whatever they were and whatever they did. The girls turned around to see two more behind them. Karina raised her hands, and Cayla did that as well.

20

THE FINAL BATTLES

"I'm princess Cayla." Her voice was calm and steady, and she was probably calm, if she didn't fear the insurgents or the royal guards. "I'm the king's daughter. Darian's friend as well."

A male voice came from behind them, "Friends don't let friends be sentenced to death, my darling." General Keen stepped from behind two soldiers, looking at Cayla. "I wanted you dead, but I guess you'll be useful alive—for now at least." He turned to the soldiers. "Shoot the younger girl."

What happened next felt unreal for Karina, as if it wasn't really happening to her. It was like seeing herself in a dream, facing the soldiers pointing their weapons, pressing their trigger, blue energy coming in her direction. She never made a decision to do anything, because there was no time to think. All she felt was the ground moving, and found herself alone in the blue tower. She felt bad for leaving Cayla, but there had been no time to reach for her hand. There had been no time for anything. And still there was no time to digest the shock of having almost been killed. The walls seemed to have even bigger cracks now, as if the tower was breaking. Karina was shaking in fear, but got out and ran in the opposite direction she'd run before, hoping she'd find someone friendly, someone who could help them, who could lead her to Lylah or Nia or someone who could free Cayla and stop the general. After many meters, she almost stopped and laughed. She could have gone home! And yet she didn't. She wanted to help clean the mess she'd gotten herself into, even if she wasn't really sure what the mess was. And she wouldn't leave Cayla. But where should she go? Those corridors were like an interminable maze, confusing her.

"Halt!"

Karina trembled. It was a woman's voice. She turned around and raised her hands, hoping it wasn't anyone planning on killing her. It was just a young woman with brown hair and eyes —pointing a gun. And wearing the army's uniform. This could turn out badly.

"Who are you?" The woman asked.

Karina chose to say a name that could work either way. "I'm a friend of Darian's."

"From which side?"

Right. Of course the woman also knew that Darian's name meant nothing. Karina risked the truth. "Not General Keen's." She held her breath, afraid of what would happen.

The woman lowered her weapon slightly. "With whom them? Cause you clearly don't know our code."

Of course. The rebels had a secret code Karina had no idea about and Darian never bothered informing them. But this was not the time to think about that. She decided to say the truth. "I need to talk to whoever is leading you. It's urgent and important."

The woman looked at Karina up and down. Her hesitation was annoying. At each second that passed Sian's lifts were getting closer to the castle, and who knows what was happening to Cayla?

Karina said, "You do realize I'm unarmed, right? And it's urgent."

The woman lowered her weapon. "Come."

Karina followed, uneasy because she feared meeting General Keen or someone loyal to him. They came to a wide auditorium. Lylah and Nia were there, as well as Darian, Jax and Zayra, and some twenty other people. That meant that the insurgents had won, and had help from Lylah. They were probably discussing the fate of the kingdom, unaware of the danger inside and outside the castle.

"Hey!" Karina yelled without waiting for an introduction or anything. "You're about to be attacked. Some twenty lifts are coming this way, for an ambush. They are armed. They are under General Keen, and he plans to take power."

Some murmur was heard in the room.

Darian said, "The army doesn't have that many more lifts."

"I saw them." Karina lowered her voice. "Your brother's there by the way." She hoped that would ensure they didn't hurt Sian.

Darian frowned, and many people spoke at the same time. Lylah's voice rose above the others. "I can hold them back."

And now it was time to give the other, more important news. "There's more," Karina yelled. The room fell silent. Her voice trembled as she looked at Lylah. "General Keen has Cayla. He wants to use her as a hostage."

Lylah fell back on her seat, but her voice was still calm. "Where is she?"

"I don't know." Karina looked down. "He wanted to kill me."

"I can find her," Darian yelled. "I'll deal with this."

Lylah got up, "I can—"

"With all due respect, miss," Darian said, "Cayla's none of your business."

Karina face palmed, but the situation was too intense for any clarification.

Lylah turned to Karina. "Was Keen alone?"

"No. He had four guards."

"What does it matter?" Darian asked. "She's a hostage. We can't confront them. The fewer people the better. I'm still his son. I can talk to him." His voice became soft, smooth, almost relaxing. "I'm good at talking and I can solve this. Alone."

Lylah squinted. "You're Bianca's son." She said it as if she'd just recognized him, which was odd.

Darian raised his eyebrows. "So?"

"Go," Lylah said. She closed her eyes as if in pain. "I have an attack to halt."

Darian left.

Lylah turned to Karina. "Do you know where they are coming from?"

That was a tough question for Karina since she didn't know anything about the geography there, but she tried her best. "The place is near this river, but not in the direction where it meets with the Black River. The other. They were all gathered in a large place that looked like the crater of an inactive volcano."

Lylah nodded, then turned to Nia. "Help her go. Now. While the blue tower still stands."

Karina shuddered when she realized that it meant her. That it meant she would go home without knowing how everything ended. That she would go home without saying goodbye. Nia pulled her and Karina followed automatically, feeling sad and empty. But then, she wouldn't want to be stuck in this place that she still knew so little about.

They got to the tall blue room. Some pieces of the wall were falling, and the cracks were bigger. So it wasn't an impression. That tower was collapsing.

Nia held her hand. "Now close your eyes."

Karina figured closed eyes were necessary for interdimensional teleporting, wondering how many rules about it she would never have the opportunity to learn. The feeling of teleporting was in fact quite distinct from falling, and this time, she saw flashes of light through her closed eyelids. The lights didn't stop and Karina eventually opened her eyes, realizing that nobody held her hand anymore. It was day and she was in her room. This time she felt that she was in her room. So everything was back to normal. Sort of. How can anyone be normal after all that? She considered all the assumptions she'd had when she went to Whyland, and how each of them had been shattered. She even wondered whether Lylah and Darian were really on the good side, and if Sian was completely wrong. Well, he was. His father was indeed cruel and had almost killed Karina. But then maybe he was also under false impressions, and false assumptions. She wondered what made a person choose a side. Was it ideology, values, or just circumstance? Anyways, why was she thinking that? Was it about making excuses for the cheap flirter? Or was it just her mind going back and trying to understand how come nothing went as expected, and in the end it did? Karina had helped save a kingdom—depending on one's definition of saving, of course. If the kingdom had been saved, because everything could still go wrong. But then, she remembered Sian saying he always negotiated when he could, and that thought put her mind at ease.

Darian let his necklace guide him. He was shaking in anger. If only he'd answered when she called him. If only he'd turned around for her. If only. He only didn't punch himself because it wouldn't help. He needed to stay calm. Concentrate. And remain calm. He could do it. He had a gift for speaking, and this was his time to use it. Focused on his necklace, and where it guided him, he descended stairs he had never before been at. He came to an abandoned dungeon. The floor was wet and moldy, and mice scurried on the corners. Cayla was sitting on a chair. A large granite block hung above her, with a rope on a pulley and tied to a hook on the floor.

Keen had a hatchet, and said, "One step more and I'll cut the rope."

There were two guards with fireguns by his side. Darian wondered where the other two had gone. Cayla didn't seem scared. If anything, she looked annoyed or concentrated, maybe thinking about a way to escape. That would be foolish.

"It's me, father."

Cayla noticed him, and for the first time her eyes showed a hint of fear.

General Keen stood where he was. "Don't call me that. Is that how you pay me? After all I've done for you? After I've received you here and given you everything?"

Darian tried to calm himself down. He had to muster his calmest voice. "I was trying to be a good son. You wanted our family to stay in power, didn't you? That's how I infiltrated the insurgents. I have a good influence over them and no matter what happens our family will stay in power."

"Liar!"

His father moved his arm and Darian feared he'd cut the rope. Darian stepped forward, and the guards pointed their guns toward him.

But the general then stepped forward, away from the rope. "You conspired with them."

"I had to gain their trust."

General Keen looked at Darian as if he could see inside him. Darian looked at his father and didn't break eye contact. He knew he looked relaxed, calm, and truthful, and he hoped his father could be swayed.

Darian said, "Let's stop this. We can go to the main auditorium. They are revolting against the King. You can say you had nothing to do with this. I will support you. They listen to me, father."

General Keen laughed. "You know what's wrong in all that you're saying?"

Darian had no idea what his father meant.

"You never called me father. Not like that. You're like your mother. Never cared. You should pay for your treason, Darian, by watching the girl die." He stepped closer to the rope and touched it with the hatchet.

Darian had to remain calm. "I've never been the most loving son, no, but that doesn't change the fact that you won't gain anything by hurting the princess."

"Princess? She's no princess. Don't you know? The king is no more. It's going to be me. My true son is coming to take the power for those who really deserve it. Your silly plan to become king didn't work. It didn't work."

Darian glanced at Cayla. Their eyes met. She wasn't angry at him. She didn't believe the lies Keen was saying. Darian concentrated. Funny how sometimes he could do his convincing voice, but now it felt as if he was failing. "Let her go then. She's worthless as a hostage."

Keen laughed. "Oh, my innocent, stupid, ignorant, little son."

Cayla looked away. Darian had no idea what the laugh was about and he feared that it didn't matter because his father was losing his mind.

Darian tried to change his tactic. "Let her go, and I'll help you escape. In case your plans don't work."

"No."

"I told you I have good relations with the insurgents. Sian has good relations in the army. Our family can stay in power, no matter what happens. Let her go, and if the insurgents and Lylah win, I'll guarantee you'll still be general."

"And you think you can do that?"

"I'm good at convincing people."

"You're like your mother! Your unnatural magic, making people do what they don't want."

Darian had no idea that his father knew about his mother's special skill, and that he knew that it was considered a type of magic. Darian himself knew little about it. It was called spell-speaking, or whispering, depending on where you lived in Whyland. Darian once heard that he had that skill as well, but sometimes he doubted it. It didn't seem to affect his father, though. And the worst was that he feared his father's mental state. Darian's heart beat faster as his confidence melted away. Still, he had to remain calm and try to negotiate.

"Yes, I'm good at convincing people. And I can convince them you can still be a general. It would be good. We could re-unify the army. Let her go and I give you my word, a binding word, like we say in my village, that I'll do everything I can to make sure you'll keep command of the army."

"Everything you can is not good enough. I'm going to be king, or else she dies."

Darian sighed. He was getting frustrated. Why Cayla? Was his father trying to hurt him because he'd betrayed him?

Keen stepped forward. "Do you want to help me? Get that witch here. I'll negotiate with her."

A loud shot startled Darian. His father fell forward. The two guards had their eyes closed, as if sleeping, and yet, they'd shot General Keen.

"I'm sorry." A woman's voice came from behind Darian.

Darian turned around and saw Lylah.

"I'm sorry for your father. There was no way to reach him," she said.

Darian looked at the guards. They had now fallen on the ground, as if sleeping, the same way Nia did with her dagger, except that Lylah had no magical object or weapon whatsoever. Darian didn't know how to feel about his father, but he knew how he felt about Cayla. He ran towards her and removed the gag around her mouth. She had red marks on her cheeks.

"How are you?" he asked.

"Fine." Cayla was stiff, and looked at Lylah's direction.

Darian looked at the woman as well. "Thank you for saving her."

Lylah shook her head. "I still wish I could have avoided his death. I wish, and I'm sorry, but I couldn't take chances. One day you'll understand. Well, I have an attack to halt." She turned around and left.

Darian had a lot of work untying Cayla's hands and feet. Darian glanced at his father's body. He wished his father had been different, he wished he didn't have to die, he wished they could have been a family. Now all that was left was his brother, and he didn't have great expectations from that side either. Cayla got up and looked around, at the guards, and at General Keen.

"You tried," she said. "It wasn't your fault."

"Let's get out of here. I'll send someone for the body and the guards."

He reached his hand for her.

Cayla shook her head. "Lylah."

Lylah had left, but for some reason she made Cayla nervous. Either way, this wasn't the time to argue why she wouldn't take his hand. With all that had happened, he wouldn't be surprised if Cayla refused to hold his hand for a long time. He left the room, and she followed him. Darian wanted to ask her how she'd gotten in the castle, why she didn't stay where she was, why she hadn't listened to him, but he knew he'd sound angry. Angry at Cayla. And he was angry with himself.

He asked something different, "Weren't you afraid?"

"If it had been my time to die, I'd accept it. I only hoped the block was heavy enough that it would be quick. But then I was afraid for you. Cause you'd be sad."

"Sad? I think I'd die." He wished he could hug her, but she was still distant. "I'm sorry," he said. "You called me, and I didn't..." he looked down. "I'm sorry."

Cayla sighed. "It's how things had to be. The only upside is that we learned about your brother's plans. From what I see Karina managed to tell Lylah about it."

Darian closed his eyes. "My brother."

"He was defending your father."

"He probably didn't know it all. He's not like my father, he isn't. I have to—"

"Go. I'll be fine."

Darian didn't want to leave her, but he didn't want to risk seeing his brother killed, even if he hadn't spoken to Sian in over a year, even with everything. He ran to the dock outside, decided to find a way at least to communicate with his brother.

Gone, they'd said. Gone. Sian tried to make sense of the message from Mouth Mountain. Nobody simply disappears from a cell. Maybe the guards had betrayed him, or had been bribed, and had let the girls go. But then, maybe they were telling the truth. And if that was the case, it changed everything. She'd said it. Apart from the glimmer in her eyes, she seemed to be telling the truth. Sian knew when people were lying, he knew it. Teleporting. Interdimensional teleporting. Magical shoes. And if all that was true, then his plans were based on a flawed logic. He couldn't win a game if he didn't know all the rules. It meant that his father's fear of magic wasn't nonsense, as Sian had always believed. Magic. It was real.

Sian took a deep breath and considered. He looked outside the window and saw a few lifts in the distance, flying towards the castle. Would their surprise be gone as well? He considered cancelling the attack. Maybe he'd need to rethink. He should have known, though. And what hurt more was that, in a way, he did know. From the moment he heard about Cayla stepping out of the castle on her own, with an unknown girl, he knew that something didn't add up. Even then, perhaps he hadn't understood how much.

A red light popped on his panel. Written communication this time, no sender, one of his sources within the insurgents: *Girl warned about your attack. Cayla taken by general Keen. Magic woman with us. Powerful. Lylah?*

Sian didn't have to read it twice. The girls had indeed teleported. And yes, the woman was Lylah. Karina had told him everything, and had warned him. *Cancel the attack, negotiate. Strike a deal.* Her plea was not for her friends, it was for him, as in "please don't attempt something you can't win, or please don't risk getting hurt," as if she cared. And yet she'd told the insurgents about his plans. His own fault. The first time in his entire life he'd done something stupid. Of course, had he taken into consideration teleporting to the castle, he'd have done everything different. So many things he hadn't taken into consideration.

What about Cayla taken by his father? He felt uneasy, since General Keen had wanted to kill her. Sian hated Cayla, but still… Then again, his father must have known by now that she was a valuable hostage. He'd use the annoying princess to find a safe way to escape. That's what Sian himself would have done.

Sian's mind went back to the war strategy classes. He liked those, and liked to wrap his head around all logical outcomes. The history of war wasn't as elaborate as it should have been, though. Most battles were quite straightforward. But one thing he learned, even if he had never imagined he'd need it; fighting is not only about knowing when to advance, but when to retreat. Her words came to his mind. *I saw her take down two lifts.* That hadn't made sense then. He'd thought it was a bluff. Again, it was a warning. *Strike a deal.* Sian had to make his decision. He always won, but that was because he knew when to act. This wasn't the time.

He opened the channel for all his troops. "Operation retreat.

Spread out. Back up everyone, but don't return to Mouth Mountain."

He turned it off, and could almost hear the incredulous murmurs over the silence. A light came up. Liam.

"What's going on?" As Sian predicted, his friend sounded puzzled.

"I miscalculated. We'll have to surrender and negotiate. We need to blend in and support whatever new government they decide."

"What about your father?"

"He'll find a way to escape. His loyal soldiers in the castle have been imprisoned. Loyal troops are too far away to help us now. We'd plunge into a war we can't win. Not worth it. Our surprise element is gone as well."

"What's your new plan?"

Sian smiled. Liam knew that there was more to it than just surrendering. "I can't say right now. I'll be gone for a while. Could you lead the negotiations?"

"Wouldn't you—"

"Trust me. Contact my brother. He'll know how to get you to the insurgent chain of command. Tell them we were not supporting anyone, that it was just army's regular procedure, that we were an extra emergency force, answering a call from the castle."

"They won't believe me."

"No. But they'll be happy to pretend they do. They have the forces to take Whyland. The question is not whether they can win, but how easily. They'll take all the help they can."

"Why don't you stay then?"

"My precious ego can't stand bruises."

Liam laughed. "What about mine?"

"You didn't come up with the plan. No, I need time. I need to leave. I'll be in touch, though."

"Peace it is, then."

And like that, Sian dismantled one year of planning. Planning based on false premises, missing key points. He'd never again try to do anything before understanding more about magic. He'd have to understand what he'd always thought was nonsense, the nothingness his father fought against. But then, forbidding people to talk about something or pretending it doesn't exist didn't make it any less real. It was even worse, because it made people unprepared. Denial was stupid. The key was understanding. Sian was ready to revamp all his assumptions and beliefs. That was the only way he could ever reach his goals.

DARIAN AND CAYLA

Darian looked from the window in his temporary room in the Army tower in Siphoria. He could see a good part of the city, illuminated in its night-lights. Across the river stood the castle. He wondered what kind of place it would be. The leaders would meet the next day, and he wondered what would happen. Strange how he'd planned to depose the king and yet hadn't really planned about what would come after. It wasn't as he'd expected. Not at all. Not only he'd underestimated the forces loyal to his father, he had absolutely no idea about Lylah. He had always thought that he'd grown up surrounded by magic, or people who practiced so-called magic, but he had no idea that there was a type of magic that could manipulate elements, that could control people, that could help a single person take a castle in a matter of minutes. All of this was new, and all of this was something he had to think about and digest.

He hadn't been able to find his brother, but his brother had found him, for a weird goodbye with a book and a request, before disappearing, who knows where. At least he was alive.

Darian didn't dare tell him how his father had died. The thought consumed him with guilt.

But his biggest worry was Cayla, as she was in the castle that was no longer her father's. Nia had been nominated guardian of the castle, but still… And he couldn't talk to her since her necklace didn't work there. He wondered how she was taking everything, and what would happen to her, now that her father was imprisoned. He also wondered how she felt about his part in deposing her father. He'd left a note for her, but wasn't sure whether she'd got it.

Staying in the tower and worrying wouldn't accomplish anything. He decided to go to the castle. It wasn't the safest place for Cayla right now. There was always the possibility of an offense by some remaining forces loyal to the deposed King. True that Lylah was in the castle, which should dissuade anyone from attacking it. She'd probably be nominated queen. That was what many people wanted. Darian had always thought that there could be a different way to rule Whyland, but then again, his plans hadn't included a transition to a different type of government, and hadn't taken Lylah into consideration. He'd spend so long thinking he had to depose the king that he'd forgotten to think what would come after. Maybe restoring the queen would be a good idea. Lylah. She'd killed his father, but saved Cayla.

The night was warm but not hot, and he felt a cool breeze as he crossed the bridge over the Silver River, book in his hand. In the castle, the guards at the door knew who Darian was, and allowed him to get in. He had no problems getting anywhere. In the maze of corridors, he was still able to sense the direction where Cayla was. Maybe the necklace did work a little in the castle. Or maybe he could feel where she was. Darian didn't doubt anything anymore. He came to her hallway. His heart started racing. Of course he was afraid. He was coming to her bedroom. He'd never knocked on her door before, and he wondered if it was too intrusive, too…

"Hello." A woman's voice startled him.

Lylah was there. What was she doing in that area of the castle? Right. Royal quarters. Perhaps she would have more right to a room in that area than Cayla, but that was a day too early.

"Hello," he replied.

"Are you looking for someone?"

"I need to check how Cayla is."

She squinted. "At this time?"

Maybe Lylah could make someone shoot the person they were supposed to defend. Maybe, like some people said, she could even bring down lifts. She wasn't his enemy and didn't intimidate him.

"It was a long day." He pulled his necklace and held the now yellow stone. "You do know what this is, right?" Lylah had a look of recognition. Of course she knew. "Cayla has the other twin. So you know what we are."

She took a long deep look at him. "You're welcome to come back tomorrow."

"Cayla had a hard day and I need to talk to her. Tell me, do you plan on preventing me from seeing her?"

"I need to understand what you want."

Darian asked, "In her bedroom? I could name a couple things. None of them forbidden, based on everything people claim you believe. Or are they wrong? I'm just asking to check if you're like the previous king. Curiosity." Maybe he'd gone too far, but he had to know where this new, maybe-queen, stood. He had to. He hadn't gone through all this trouble to be forbidden to see Cayla again.

Lylah stared at him. Her eyes were calm, deep—and piercing, as if she could see his soul.

She spoke after a few long seconds. "I'm not forbidding

anything. Her door is the third on the left."

"I know."

Lylah had a half smile then turned around and walked away. The interaction had been odd. Why was she asking those questions? Darian walked to Cayla's door and took a deep breath before knocking. Perhaps she would be angry, surprised, or annoyed. But he had to see her.

The door opened sooner than he'd expected. From surprise her face changed to worry. She pulled him inside and shut the door. "What are you doing here?"

"I needed to see you."

"Here? What if someone catches you?"

Darian looked down. How could he say it in a way that wouldn't be rude to her father? He tried, "I don't think anyone minds." This didn't sound good. "Anymore. Meaning someone who can make decisions." She didn't look happy. He added, "I'm sorry for your father."

"Don't lie," she snapped, then changed her tone. "How did you get in? Didn't anyone stop you?"

He didn't want to mention Lylah and didn't think it mattered. "Not really. I just had to see how you were. I'll leave. Or we can go somewhere else."

She looked at him and took a moment as if considering. "Isn't it dangerous out there?"

He took a deep breath. "Well…"

Cayla snorted, then pointed to a table and chairs. "Sit."

Darian sat down.

Cayla sat across him. "Talk. Wasn't that why you came?"

"I also wanted to know how you're feeling."

Cayla raised her arms in a grand gesture. "Amazing. Didn't you know? Every single person I trusted lied to me. Every single one. Including you."

"I didn't lie. I just… I never had the chance to explain."

"You could have explained it when you met me, before

joining your traitor friend. You could have explained at the Apex. You could have told me when I asked you on which side you were. I asked you."

"I didn't think it was the right time. That was all, Cayla. I was waiting for the right time."

"The right time would be after my father was deposed, of course, because otherwise perhaps I'd ruin your plans. Tell me it isn't true."

That made sense, actually. Revealing his plans to Cayla could have been dangerous. Darian nodded. "It's part of the truth, yes."

Cayla closed her eyes. "At least you're getting better now. What about before you even left the castle? Before everything? You were never a great supporter of the king, were you? You didn't even support your father. You never mentioned any of that."

"Well, when we first met you didn't even mention you were the King's daughter!"

"I never denied it!"

He stared at her in silence for a moment. "I didn't want you to…"

"You know what the problem is? You never trusted me. You never bothered to share your plans with me, your thoughts, your hopes, your wishes. Why? Wasn't I worthy of knowing what you thought? Or was it that my opinion didn't matter? Tell me."

Darian looked down thinking, then looked in her eyes. "Maybe if I had more time, if I saw you more often, I would have told you, Cayla. I would have explained everything. But I only saw you briefly, when everything was already in motion. I'm sorry your father had to be deposed and imprisoned. I can take all the time in the world to explain the reasons why I was part of a movement against him. If you'll listen to me, I'll explain. But I didn't have all this time before."

Cayla shrugged. "That's something I have to come to terms

on my own. Maybe I was blind to certain things. What hurts is not so much the truth, but the fact that nobody bothered telling me."

He did see her point. "I understand. I was wrong. If I tell you that from now on, I'll always trust you, and I'll never hide anything from you, would that make things better?"

"You're assuming that there will be a *from now on*."

Darian bit his lip. "I don't mean… it can be as friends. If you want. Other than that, I can't turn back time."

Cayla looked away, then looked at his book. "What's that?"

This was hardly the time to ask for a favor, and he felt awkward. "I… I was going to ask you to give this to someone. But it's fine, I'll figure another way."

"No, I can give it. Who is it for?"

"Your friend. Uh, Odell's niece."

Her eyes widened. "Who do you mean?"

"That girl. What was her name again? Ka…"

Cayla squinted. "Why do you want to give Karina a book?"

"My brother. He said he'd promised."

"You found Sian?"

Darian felt uneasy. "He disappeared again."

Cayla rolled her eyes. "Awesome. And now he wants me to do him an almost impossible favor."

"No. I mean, if you know how I can find her… Maybe it was foolish, but I promised him."

Cayla snorted. "Your brother played a trick on you. He's probably having a good laugh right now. Karina lives…" she paused. "Far. Very, very, far. I also have things to explain to you, once I can understand them myself. I don't even know who I am anymore. But you can leave the book with me."

Her confusion was understandable. Darian pushed the book across the table. He had something more serious to ask her.

"What are you going to do now? I mean, I know you're living in the castle but…"

"I'll see what happens tomorrow."

"If Lylah is proclaimed queen... I don't know if you are going to live here."

Cayla had an odd expression.

Darian continued, "If you want, and it can be, you know, as friends, or acquaintances, we could move up North. I could find my village—"

Cayla shook her head. "Acquaintances don't move together. And we're a little too young for that." She looked in his eyes and her expression softened. "I appreciate the offer, I do." She looked away. "But you don't need to worry about me."

"I'll always worry. And I'm here, if you need anything. I think it must be hard for you now that you're not princess anymore. Trust me, I thought about it a million times, and I'm sorry for my part in that."

She stared at him. "Are you really sorry, though? Doesn't a small part of you feel happy that I'm no longer princess? That you feel you have more power than I do? Tell me."

"I won't lie. I'm glad that I'm allowed to see you now. The rest doesn't matter."

She sighed. "Fair enough. Maybe you'd better go. Now that you can see me you can come back another time."

Darian got up. "You won't be upset if I come see you again?"

Cayla walked toward the door. "It depends. Come asking another impossible favor and I might snap."

He followed her. "I don't mind you snapping."

She smiled. Her first genuine smile since her father had been deposed. It illuminated all her face. Darian was partly glad she was finally smiling, and partly struck, because even though she was very beautiful, she looked ethereal when she smiled. It was hard to believe that she was even real.

Of course, it didn't last long. Cayla squinted. "What are you staring at?"

"I like your smile."

She rolled her eyes. "Right. You're going to start flattering me now."

"I promised I'd be honest, what can I do? By the way, I also like it when you squint. Or roll your eyes."

She stared at him. "You like it when I frown as well?"

"Love it. I also like it when you stare at me as if you meant to kill me."

Cayla laughed and then smiled. Again. "That's good to know. Cause, you know, I plan on doing that a lot."

Their eyes locked. There was something different about her. The coldness and distance were gone. Her expression was open, eager, as she stood close to him. So close. He was looking at her eyes one moment, the next he had his eyes closed and lips locked on hers, arms wrapped around her. Cayla was soft, loving, and willing, holding him tight. He'd always wondered when it would be the right time to kiss her, but the truth is that he didn't even notice how they started it, and wasn't even sure who'd initiated it. Probably both.

She kept hugging him but moved her face and whispered in his ear, "For the record, I'm still upset you didn't trust me."

Darian held her even tighter and kissed her forehead. "I'm upset at myself." But he had something else to say. He kept one hand on her waist, but took a step back and showed the stone of his necklace. "Do you see this?" Cayla nodded. He continued, "It was black before. Do you know why it's bright now? These are twin necklaces. They'll shine when the two people wearing them love each other. So every time you look at it—"

"Hold on." She broke away from his grip and put her hands on her hips. He didn't understand why she'd be upset that he was telling he loved her. She continued, "You mean to say you've known I loved you for more than one year? And never bothered telling me what it meant? While I was here, alone, wondering if you'd forgotten me, you never needed to have any doubts, because you had a freaking stone telling you so. Really?"

"I... I..." He was puzzled, surprised, and unsure what to say. "I thought it was obvious."

"Cause you told me how many times again?"

"You are the most beautiful girl in Whyland. Anyone who sees you—"

Cayla grimaced. "The most beautiful blablabla. Maybe you need your eyes checked."

He sighed. "I've waited for you for more than one year and a half. I never even looked at anyone else. And the stone doesn't lie."

She snorted. "Yeah, and I only know about it now. At least now I understand your presumption. Sometimes I thought you were full of yourself."

"I'm not. At some point I thought that I was mistaken, that maybe the stone was about a different kind of love—friendship or something."

Cayla rolled her eyes. "Friendship? You can't be serious. Now, other than this stone, what about the rest? All the other things you hid from me? Are you going to tell me?"

"Let's sit. Unless you want me to come tomorrow or another day."

Cayla shook her head. "I want to know now. Now. Everything. Tell me everything."

Darian sat. He told her about his childhood and his mother, how he had grown up in a village in the North, and how they were being threatened by the King's forces. He told her about how he hadn't known he had a brother until he got to the castle, how his brother seemed to hate him for that, and how his father had always been cold and distant. He spoke about his days away from the castle, when he started seeing the King's forces committing unjust violence against defenseless villagers. He told her how he'd protected some of them, how he formed alliances, and how he helped connect everyone who was in the army and didn't agree with what was happening. Cayla listened.

Sometimes she asked questions for clarification, but she mostly heard. Her expression was one of understanding and complicity. Talking to her and telling him all the truths that had been hidden for so long felt as if a part of himself was healing, and he was becoming whole again.

"There's one last thing," he said. She listened. He continued, "My mother was great at speaking. When she spoke, it was as if a hypnotic energy took over. There was something almost magical about it. I've also seen how my brother charms people."

Cayla grimaced. "That depends on opinion, I guess."

"Fine, then, forget my brother. Sometimes I've noticed I have this skill, that I can talk to people, and convince them. Not always, though. Once I heard that I was called a whisperer, in the South, or spell speaker, in the North. As it's some kind of magic. But I've never again heard or learned anything about it."

Her eyes were calm. "There's a hidden library in the castle. We could look into it."

Darian nodded. "Thanks. But I have one fear. That perhaps, because of this skill, or power, maybe I made you fall in love with me."

Cayla laughed. "I'll ignore the presumption, now that I know about the ratting stone. Why would you think you bewitched me or something?"

Darian shrugged. "I was just a kid when we met. Scrawny even."

"You were sweet, though."

"Maybe. Still, sometimes I wonder."

"Let me test. Look at me and remain quiet for a second." He looked. Cayla tilted her head, looked at him up and down and examined his face. "You know what I think, it's your good looks. How dare you hypnotize me into liking you?"

He laughed. "At least we both need our eyes checked."

"Not me. Now seriously. You have the answer in your stone. I know a little about magic. Making someone fall in love with you would be evil and quite dangerous. Amplifying one's love or attraction is already dangerous enough that it could drive someone mad. Our twin necklaces would tell us that something was wrong."

Darian was puzzled. "How come you know about magic?"

"I have a lot to tell you. A lot. And I want to tell you, but let me come to terms with all of it first. Also… it's late. I don't want to sound like a prude, but I fear it might look, you know, if you spend that long in my bedroom."

"I understand." He was ready to leave, when he remembered his encounter with Lylah. *There are a couple things he could want in her bedroom.* In hindsight, that was inappropriate and disrespectful. He'd better tell Cayla. "I crossed Lylah when I was coming here—"

"Lylah?" She asked it as if he'd just told her the castle was about to explode. Maybe the woman still intimidated her.

Things were about to get worse, but he had to tell her the truth. "She asked me what I wanted with you, at this time. And maybe, I," his voice was trailing off and his throat was dry, but he made an effort to keep speaking, "didn't really prevent her from, uh, making assumptions."

The color faded from Cayla's face. She shook her head as if in horror. "You didn't. You didn't. Do you know who she is?"

"Probably the future queen."

Cayla took a deep breath, as if trying to calm herself down. "Sit down. Now it's my turn to tell you a few things."

Cayla woke up and realized she'd overslept. The sun was up. Memories of the previous night came to her. All the truths she'd finally shared with Darian, all their barriers melting away. She realized he was the person she most liked to talk to, and most liked to confide in. Not only was he the boy she loved, he was her best friend. His lies and the hidden truths had been an odd anomaly that had been solved in one night. Their talk had eased the difficult time she was going through. She felt closer to him than anyone else in the world. She got up and found him lying on the floor, over a blanket. Cayla wasn't sure how they'd made that sleeping arrangement or if she'd just had fallen asleep and he stayed. Cayla knelt beside him and brushed a strand of his hair away from his face.

He opened his eyes. "I'm sorry."

Cayla didn't understand what he meant.

He continued, "About your mother. That she thinks…"

Cayla laughed. "…we totally did it. If there was any doubt, now she'll be sure."

"I'm sorry."

"Look at the bright side. At least when the time comes, we know she won't mind."

His eyes brightened. "When the time comes?"

"I never said it was anytime soon."

"Neither did I. If it takes forever, it means I'll be forever with you."

"Haha, so sweet and romantic. Meanwhile, I'm sure you're thinking about… when the time comes."

Darian closed his eyes, held her hand and pulled it over his chest. "Uhm, I won't lie, the thought will give me some sleepless nights."

"Me too."

He opened his eyes and squeezed her hand. "You want to kill me from sleep deprivation."

"Maybe not. But first we have some kissing to catch up. For two years!"

Cayla leaned over and kissed him.

AFTER THE END

A good part of Karina's following morning was spent in the shower, using half a bottle of conditioner to untangle her hair. How come nobody had told her she looked like a cavewoman? Wait, Sian had told her. Yikes. She wondered if he was okay, if Cayla, Ayanna, Darian, Nia and Lylah were okay, and if everyone had gotten out of the castle.

Other than questioning her long shower, her parents didn't notice anything wrong or strange. It was as if she'd never gone anywhere. Karina then visited Zoe. It was good to see her again and remember that she also had good friends in her own dimension. Zoe would be shocked if she'd seen Karina wearing the same clothes for days and going without a proper shower, though. Some different priorities. Karina was itching to tell her all about her adventure, but she never knew how to start. Every sentence she imagined, like "so, I went to a different dimension," or "I was visited by a nice woman, who then I learned was an evil which, then I learned was a nice woman," sounded crazy. Unlike Karina thought, Zoe had no clue that the shoes had any special power. In fact, the girl had completely forgotten them. Karina didn't miss them or regret having destroyed them, which was a little odd. Perhaps it was if they'd never existed.

As for her adventure, Karina regretted not having learned more about the different science, or how to travel to different dimensions. Her adventure seemed unreal, especially because she couldn't share it with anyone, but she knew it had been real, because of the amount of time that passed, and because she ate, and unlike in dreams, food tasted like food. True that most of it had been a little bland, but still. The only thing she still wanted to know was how everyone was doing.

Her doubts were answered one day, when she came home from school and found a visitor in her bedroom; Lylah. Karina felt so happy she would have hugged the woman had she felt more at ease around her.

Lylah stared at Karina and said, "You have questions for me."

"How's everyone? How did the attack end?"

Lylah smiled. "Everyone is fine."

Karina was itching with curiosity. "But what happened?"

"We won. The ambush you told us about never happened. They made a deal with us. There was still some conflict in distant areas of the kingdom, but soon it was all settled. We took prisoners, but in time many of them were released. They were just following orders."

Karina sighed in relief to learn that everyone had survived, even Lylah's enemies, because she didn't wish Sian any harm. And she was happy to hear that in the end he did what she'd asked, even if it obviously wasn't because she asked.

Lylah continued, "There were good people on all sides. We've been working on reuniting everyone, reuniting the king-dom." The woman then smiled, "If you hadn't warned us, they would have taken us by surprise. Perhaps we could still have won, but it would take longer. And people might have gotten hurt."

"But you said they struck a deal."

"The fact that they no longer had surprise on their side might have helped."

That was good news. At least Karina had helped, somehow.

"But you have more questions, don't you?" Lylah asked.

Well, yes. "The shoes. What were they? Did they have any power?"

"Well… They were magical objects. When people go to other dimensions, they have more power. It works for magical objects as well. That is why the shoes were so fascinating for you here, and you almost forgot about them when you got to our world. In my world, they worked differently. I used them to communicate with you. Don't you remember I spoke to you sometimes?"

Karina forced her memory, but nothing came. "Uh, no."

The woman nodded. "I see. That explains a lot. But at least I knew what was happening to you, and I was able to inform and make plans with my brother."

"So… you could hear us?"

"I had access to your thoughts."

Awkward. Karina had never felt her privacy so abused in her entire life.

Lylah then added, "Only in what concerned my daughter."

Still, that was a lot. Karina would never, ever, call her mom nosy again. "Wouldn't it be easier then for Cayla to carry the shoes?"

"No. They were too connected with me, and I was in a powerful prison. If Cayla touched them, she could be taken to the white castle, with no means to get out. Her sister would've had no problem, but that wasn't something that could be easily explained."

"I see." But there was something else Karina had to ask. She still couldn't really believe it. "But if the shoes had no power… Was it really me? I could teleport?"

"Everyone has some power. Not only did you teleport, you

almost teleported from the yellow tower. That was impressive, although dangerous. You also made a lift explode."

"What?" That didn't make sense, unless… "Wait. Do you mean the lift that we were going to use to escape? You are saying I did it?"

"Yes. Lifts don't explode by themselves."

"No, no, no. You are saying I had some kind of superpower, and I used it to blow the vehicle that could have helped me escape?"

Lylah stared for a moment. "I also thought the choice was odd."

Karina covered her face with her hands. "That's the worst misuse of talent ever!"

"I wouldn't say that. You are still young."

Was that some kind of encouragement? Karina shrugged. "Well, I won't ever have any magical power again, so I'm sure I won't misuse it."

"That depends on how you define magic. Or power."

Perhaps the woman meant scientific knowledge or something? Karina didn't want to waste that either, and didn't want to think about that. She then wondered what happened to Cayla and Darian. She was about to ask when she remembered the woman was the girl's mother, and Karina would be mortified if anyone talked to her mom about boys. She asked another question, "How's Cayla doing?"

"She is slowly accepting things… as they are. She told me to say hello, and to tell you that she is doing well. Darian's also fine."

Of course, if Lylah had accessed Karina's thoughts, she knew it all.

Karina then changed the subject. "Can you really grant wishes?"

The woman sat back, smiled, looked at Karina for a while, then said, "I don't think you could have asked anything you could not achieve for yourself anyways. So I wasn't lying. But, no, I wasn't planning on buying the shoes, if that's what you want to know."

Of course, Karina knew that, but it was still nice to know she had been right, although she felt a little silly remembering her enthusiasm about making a wish.

The woman then smiled and said, "Don't dismiss what you did. You helped my family, my kingdom and me. A lot. Someone had to carry the shoes. You never quit, never gave up, never returned."

That was not really true because the only reason Karina had not returned was that she hadn't been able to.

Lylah stared at her. "No, Karina, you could have returned, but you didn't try it. At least not enough. You were not really trying to get back home. With the exception of a few difficult moments, the rest of the time you were focused on going forward, on finishing your task."

Had she just read her thought? Better not think about it too much. Karina had a more important question. "Why me?"

"Why did you buy the shoes? Why did you agree to come? It could have been anyone, but it happened to be you."

"Oh, I..." Karina didn't finish the sentence, because she was embarrassed to admit she thought she had been some kind of "chosen one."

"You don't understand," the woman said. "There are many things anyone could do. Each person is faced with infinite possibilities. It doesn't matter why you choose one or the other, or why life draws you one way or another. What matters is not why, or what exactly, but your choices along the way. Perhaps any girl could have done it. But not all of them would have done it."

"But I mean... there was no special reason then?"

"Maybe. Have you considered that perhaps the shoes called you? Or that you sought them? You can either think that everything happens for a reason or that everything is random. Both conclusions are identical."

That didn't make sense. "No. They are complete opposites."

Lylah laughed a normal, happy laugh. "You can see it any way you want." When she stopped laughing she became serious and thoughtful, then said, "I have something for you." She had a large bag, from where she took a large book and gave it to Karina.

It had a green cover in leather, and some maps and pictures inside it. Karina opened it, and recognized a map. It was Whyland. Everything in images. "Is it so that I remember my adventure?"

"I think so. Darian sent it to you. He says it's from his brother."

Karina was surprised to hear that. Sian remembered her? Her stupid heart beat faster. But maybe it was just that she was glad for the brothers. "So they're getting along now?"

Lylah shook her head "I'm afraid not. Sian has disappeared." She looked at Karina. "He wouldn't have faced any serious accusations. But now he's gone."

Karina hoped he was all right. But something didn't make sense. "How could he send the book then?"

"To be honest, I didn't ask. He must have met his brother before leaving."

Karina looked down. "Now I can know more about Whyland, but..." She looked at Lylah, as a sadness suddenly filled her chest. "Am I ever going to visit it again?"

"It would be hard."

As Karina feared. She felt sad.

Lylah continued, "The time difference is changing, and soon it will be reversed. The flowing tower was destroyed because it was connected to the white castle. But at least you won't forget the places you visited and the friends you made."

At least that was something. Karina had a sad smile. "I won't."

"I have to go now," Lylah said.

"Wait," Karina said. She wanted to change her mood, so she asked one last silly question, "How come you speak English?"

"Tu préfères français?"

That was odd. "No. I mean…"

Karina could not really word it. She was sure they would speak a different language in a different world. Or almost sure. Whatever.

"You understand things the way you understand them," Lylah said. "That doesn't mean that's what they are. Interdimensional travel warps the logic you know. Thank you for helping me save my kingdom. Goodbye Karina."

Lylah then disappeared, leaving only sparkly dust behind her. Karina was sure the dust wasn't from blinking. It was real. She opened the book. Maybe it would be a good idea to learn about the place she'd visited. On the other hand, maybe it would be an even better idea to learn more about her own dimension. Whyland didn't have to be her last adventure. There were so many places, so many countries she didn't know. Of course, she wouldn't be a hero again, but maybe all she needed was to do the little she could, and to make good choices along the way. True that the one problem with going to different places was missing the people she met. She held the book against her chest. It was better than not meeting them. At least their memory would be with her forever.

KISSING MAGIC

PORTALS TO WHYLAND BOOK II

Darian tasted victory all right, except that he could never before have imagined what its real taste was. There was something bitter and sour, perhaps incomplete. Yes, his insurgency had won. A new era was about to start in Whyland. And yet, his father... Gone forever. Gone was the chance to find any reconciliation, anything human in him. His brother had disappeared. Cayla... He'd have to talk to her.

Darian opened his bag and arranged his belongings. His future was uncertain, but this would be his new home for now; a room in Siphoria's military complex, close to Whyland's castle.

A sound at the window interrupted his thoughts. This room was on the seventh floor of the complex tower, so there shouldn't be anyone or anything at the window, but it would be unwise to dismiss the disruption as wind. It had to be an intruder, and a very skilled one, to have climbed to that height.

Darian could rush to the window, but the intruder probably expected that. Instead, he hid behind the bed and listened. As expected, someone entered his room. Before the intruder did anything, Darian jumped on the person and dropped him or her on the floor. It was a guy, based on his height and build, but before Darian could immobilize him, the intruder pulled Darian's arm and rolled on top of him. It was Darian who ended up pinned on the floor. With his foot, Darian reached for a knife but soon realized that it wouldn't be necessary, as he noticed familiar gleaming brown eyes in a face framed with wavy dark hair.

It was his older brother Sian, grinning. "Little brother, I'm happy you're finally showing me some love."

One would think Sian was on top of the world and had just won a war, not that all his plans had failed and that he was on the run. But at that moment, Darian was simply glad to see his brother alive and well. "You disappeared. I was worried."

Sian raised an eyebrow. "Worried you couldn't arrest me?"

"Worried about you. Can you let me go now?"

Sian tilted his head. "You don't like your brother's hug? Not surprising." He laughed and got up.

Darian also got up. "Stop being funny. Or trying to. Do you know how many people are looking for you?"

"Well, that's the point, isn't it? Not being caught. But I'm here because I wanted to talk to you."

Relief took over Darian's chest. "Listen, I'm sure the insurgents will forgive you. I know them well. I could—"

"No chance, brother," Sian interrupted. "Too long I've lived by my father's shadow. I'm not gonna live under yours."

"That's not at all what I was saying. What I mean is—" Darian sighed. "You don't need to run away."

Sian glared at him. "I don't run away. I retreat. Regroup. Rethink." He pointed at his head, then looked down, a bitter grin on his face. "I would have beaten you. I would have conquered the kingdom. But I didn't expect magic to make such a difference. My mistake, I recognize." He stared at Darian with fiery fierce eyes. "But I learn from my mistakes."

"And you hope me to just let you go?"

"I don't hope. I'm sure you will. There's certainly a bit of love buried deep within that chest." Behind his brother's impenetrable grin there was something soft, real.

"It's not buried. You'd do much better by my side, Sian. Think about it. With your knowledge, and your leadership—"

"By your side is the part where it all sours." Sian grimaced. "Not interested. Thank you, though. I guess." He smirked then became serious. "But if you want to help me, there's something you can do. You're close to the princess, Cayla."

Darian was taken aback. He couldn't imagine what his brother would want with her.

Before Darian said anything, Sian continued, "She traveled with a girl, Karina. I promised I'd give her a book, and I'm counting on your fraternal love to fulfill my promise." He took a large green book from a bag he had tied to his back.

That was an odd request. "Why don't you give it in person?"

"Not possible. I have to go." Sian then spoke with an overly dramatic and hurt tone: "Are you going to refuse your brother's last wish?"

"You're not dying."

Sian shrugged. "You don't know if you'll ever see me alive again."

"What's this about?"

"A promise. I keep my word." He smiled and looked up with an exaggerated dreamy expression. "Especially to pretty girls, you know? If you can, send it with all my love."

Darian rolled his eyes. "If you didn't flirt with every girl you meet, you'd have a girlfriend by now."

"You assume too much, little brother. I'm just a loving person with a broad definition of love. Maybe one day, if I ever decide to get a girlfriend, I'll do like you and obey her like a puppy while she ignores me."

Darian clenched his fists. But no. Sian had meant to offend him. That's what he wanted. He wouldn't give his brother that pleasure. Darian shrugged and put up his best smug smile. "Well, what can I say? At least it works."

Sian laughed. "Works wonders. I bet even you still haven't realized how lucky you got. Well done." He patted Darian's back, then became serious and distant. "But that's not what I want right now. I still keep my word, though. My broad definition of love has nothing to do with it."

Darian took the book. He could ask Cayla, he didn't see much into it. In fact, that would be an excellent excuse to talk to her.

Sian stared in his eyes. "Can you give me your word? That you'll make sure Cayla's friend gets the book?"

Darian scoffed. "Sure. You come here, offend me, while you're on the run, and I'm supposed to arrest you. Now I have to give you my word. Why again?"

"I didn't offend you. But I apologize if you felt that way. I just want to make sure the book reaches its destination."

It wasn't a big deal, really. "I also keep my word. I said I'd give it; I will. The book. Not the empty words that come with it."

Sian waved a hand. "Oh, please, I sure don't want you sending anyone any love."

Darian still wished he could convince his brother to stay. "Where are you going?"

Sian raised his eyebrows and smiled. "I'm on the run, right? Why should I tell you?"

"You can't go anywhere from here. You'll need to go downstairs, and—"

Sian walked to the window. Of course, he wasn't going to walk out the door.

"By the time you climb down, I'll have you surrounded." He didn't want to threaten his brother, but he would have to do something if given no choice.

Sian laughed. "Your guards are lighting fast, then. I'll be impressed." He climbed on the windowsill.

"Wait," Darian pleaded.

Sian stood up on the window and let his body fall. Cold emptiness was what was left in Darian's chest. He ran and looked down.

Instead of the body of his injured brother, he saw a flying machine, a lift, coming up, with his brother on top of it, climbing down to enter. Sian had planned to jump and to escape. How a private lift had gotten so close to the military tower, he had no idea. Darian wished his brother could have stayed, that they could have become friends, allies, but it wouldn't be this time.

He looked at the book. At least one bit of brotherly trust. There was still something there that could be salvaged between them. As much as it was no big deal, it meant a step towards reconciliation with his brother.

1

THIRST FOR ADVENTURE

Zoe laughed. "Who is the weirdo who would send their kids to learn forest survival with you? I mean, had it been real, chances are high you'd all die."

Karina rolled her eyes at her friend. "I'm just going to be a volunteer. I'm helping. And learning."

"You, nature, and forest. Doesn't go together. You want to volunteer on a camp, why not science and technology camp or something?"

"I work on my weaknesses." Karina shrugged. "Plus, you never know."

Zoe narrowed her dark blue eyes. "Of course you do. You'll never need to survive in a forest unless you go there in the first place."

"It's also for adventure."

Zoe laughed and shook her head. "Fascinating. Can't wait to see Karina the outdoor adventurer." She stopped laughing and stared at Karina. "And what about the science project? What do we need to do?"

"It's almost done. It's for Monday."

"That's why I'm here."

Karina took a closer look at her friend. She was dressed up, with her hair done, and wore a lot of smoky eye shadow. With her dyed black hair contrasting with her eyes, she looked like a model ready for a photo shoot for a makeup company, not someone who came to study. Well, of course! It was Saturday, and Zoe was one of those normal human beings for whom Saturday evening meant something more special than books, streaming, or science projects.

"And where are you going afterward?" Karina asked.

Zoe smiled. "Samy. We're going out."

"That's why you're dressed up?"

Zoe had a cheeky smile. "Uh, kind of. You see, Samy said he prefers when I look natural: no makeup. But he needs to know who gets to make decisions about my face."

"So you are putting makeup for a guy."

Zoe glared. "Don't be so insufferable."

"I don't even know what that means."

Zoe laughed. "You could come with us. Maybe not tonight, but some other day. Josh asked about you."

Samy's friend. Boring jock. Not ugly, not good looking. Not smart, not dumb. Not interesting, not annoying, not, not... Karina's stomach knotted.

Zoe noticed. "What's this face? Lot's of girls are into him, you know?"

"That's great," Karina said. "He should pick one of them."

"I'm not asking you to date him." Zoe tossed her hair. Perhaps she was so used to doing the hair thing to be convincing that sometimes she forgot Karina was a girl. She then stared directly at Karina. "Or even to make out with him" She smiled. "Unless you want to. Just, you know, give it a try. No guy is perfect."

"You're saying this just cause you want Josh to leave you and Samy alone."

"No, I'm saying it cause he's nice, you're nice, and, I don't know, you could be nice together."

Karina snorted. "When you put it that way, it's hard to resist."

Zoe laughed. "C'mon, he's cute."

Karina rolled her eyes. Zoe thought every guy who seemed to be slightly interested in Karina was cute.

Zoe continued, "You could come with us to Samy's cabin next weekend. It would be so much fun." She winked. "Just think about it."

Karina shivered with dread, then said, "You know, since you're going out with Samy, you don't need to stay and work on the project. I can take care of it."

"But it's still early."

"You helped me a lot with English and French this year. I can take care of the project. Maybe you can meet Samy earlier."

"Well, I trust you. You're a genius. But are you sure?"

Karina laughed. "Positive. Go." She hoped it didn't sound like she was sending her friend away.

Zoe grinned. "Well, thanks!" She then cast a guilty look. "Next time we can plan and go all together."

That meant going with Josh. Karina wanted to say *nah, I'm good*, but instead, she said, "We'll see."

Karina sat down and looked at her tentative robot. The thing just rolled around and was useless. Well, they would get a decent bonus grade for physics. Not that she needed it.

She took a deep breath. Maybe there was a tiny part of her that would have liked to go with Zoe, except that going with Josh wasn't anything she'd ever wanted. And she had the suspicion that he wasn't even interested in her, so it would make her even sadder to know that they were getting together just to please their friends. Getting together. *Don't get ahead of yourself, Karina.* But she wasn't getting ahead. The prospect was dreadful. She would be interested if it had been a guy more… more… She didn't know.

But it was true that she had just turned sixteen and still had never been kissed. Awkward. It was as if she'd couldn't get a basic achievement on a game. But then, did she really want to kiss a guy just to get "achievement unlocked"?

Maybe she was a little sad that her friends were moving to another phase in life while she was stuck home alone with science and reading efforts. More and more her friends slipped away from her, mind and time busy with their boyfriends. Tori had completely disappeared. It was almost as if they were crossing some barrier Karina couldn't follow.

As for Karina, she'd had some of these "opportunities" before. One would think that hanging out with the prettiest girl in school would be a liability, but it was the opposite. Some spillover attention went to Karina. But yeah, that was the problem: spillover. Was it even about her? Karina thought she looked pretty decent, not gorgeous, granted, but nice enough in her regular brown hair and eyes. But she wanted more than someone interested in her just because she looked nice enough.

Unable to concentrate, she decided to leave the robot as it was. A stupid rolling machine that did nothing. Well, a 10-dollar remote control car would have been similar. She didn't even need the grade. Her mind turned to summer, nature, survival. Maybe it was there that something exciting would happen. While it was true that kissing someone would be nice, what she most craved was adventure, discovery, new experiences. She wanted to swallow the world all at once but knew it was impossible. She would go on with tiny drops, taking a bit here and there, swallowing, absorbing and becoming someone new.

She decided to read a book. *Work on your weaknesses.* Her reading had gotten much better. She walked to her bookshelf and passed her hands through the spines. A huge book with a green leather cover caught her attention. A knot formed in her stomach. Adventure. Discovery. Bravery. The book contained maps and pictures of a land that was lost to her forever, a place where she had made a difference, a place where she had magic. No point thinking about it. She had promised herself she would forget it. But lately, more and more her thoughts returned to that land long gone. But longing was useless. Karina didn't want to spend her time in thoughts on her past when she could focus on the present and the future. She looked at the spine of her other books. She could maybe pick up a difficult one. *Work on your weaknesses.*

Or maybe she should just forget about it all and relax. She lay down across her bed, with feet on the floor, staring at the ceiling. As much as she tried to deny it, she was anxious that maybe she would never find anyone special for her. But she dreaded finding a jerk. Imagine Karina with a jerk? And then she dreaded even more finding someone who would break her heart. Or someone who would make her forget who she was. Not that she really knew that yet. But she didn't want to stop asking.

A noise startled her. It sounded like water boiling or strong wind. Fair enough, these sounds are not similar, but it was something in the middle. It wasn't outside, it wasn't in the kitchen, but in her own bedroom. Karina tried to look, but there was such an intense light, even though it was still day outside, that she feared for her eyes and turned away. When she finally peeked, she didn't see anything. Great, imagining things again. True that last time she thought she had imagined something it had turned out to be real. Real. How real? When it was all far away, in a land or dimension that she could no longer reach, stuck in her memories without anyone to share, it was hard to feel that way.

Whyland. The memory of an adventure now long gone. A whole new world she never again found. Why was she thinking about it again? Well, a sound in her bedroom, a strong light. Maybe those things rang a bell?

That sound again. And the light. When the light stopped, Karina looked. Her heart almost stopped.

Was it real? Two teenagers stood in her bedroom. Cayla and Darian! Karina was so happy to see them that she was going to ignore the fact that a guy just came into her room without being announced. At least Karina wasn't getting dressed. Last time she'd seen them, Cayla was the princess of Whyland, while Darian was her... Uh, Karina hoped they had stopped with any silliness and sorted out their feelings for each other by now. Whyland wasn't lost after all.

2

———

AN INVITATION

The two intruders, or visitors, seemed a bit confused and had their eyes closed. They were surrounded by white fog. A rock star entrance. Of course, had they been rock stars they would have stepped in the room with eyes open, oozing confidence. Cayla held Darian's hand. Holding hands was necessary for teleporting. But still, they looked cute and warmed Karina's heart.

Karina wanted to help them out of their confusion. "You're here. You can open your eyes."

Cayla opened her eyes, looked around, then walked towards Karina and hugged her. "Good to see you."

Only then, when she touched Cayla, did Karina believe that it was real, that they were actually there. It had all been so sudden. It was also good to see Cayla and know that she was all right. "Past time you made a visit!"

Cayla laughed. "If I could I would have dropped by earlier."

Darian looked dizzy, but slowly he opened his eyes, looked around, and acknowledged Karina. "Hi."

They hadn't aged more than Karina had, which either meant that there was no significant time difference between the two dimensions, or that people there didn't age as fast. Cayla wore dark green pants and a jacket in what looked like suede. Her marvelous shiny black hair was tied in a loose ponytail hanging over a shoulder. Darian had his same brown hair to the chin and wore brown pants and a jacket. His brown eyes reminded Karina of his older brother. In fact, Darian did look a little like him, with the difference that Darian had more delicate facial features and wasn't as tall. For the first time, she noticed that Darian was actually quite good looking. With all the craziness last time and with him being Cayla's whatever, Karina hadn't registered his attractiveness level, but now she realized that he and Cayla were quite a stunning couple. Each of them had a necklace with a clear orange stone, and Karina remembered with amusement how she'd been surprised that they could use the stones to communicate with each other. Her surprise hadn't been silly, as communicating necklaces were rare even in Whyland.

Darian looked at Cayla as if expecting something, and Cayla bit her lip and looked down.

Karina considered their expressions and came to a conclusion. "You want something from me."

Darian and Cayla looked at each other. Karina was right. She felt giddy because she thought they would ask her to go to Whyland, and she had wanted to go back there for a long time.

Cayla sighed. "It's a huge favor, and it's not easy, but Darian believes you can help him."

Darian? Karina couldn't imagine what he'd want with her, as she barely knew him. "What is it?"

"My brother," he said.

The name came as a whisper from Karina's lips, "Sian."

Karina's heart raced. She hadn't known him well, other than spending some 20 or 30 minutes with him because he wanted to keep Cayla hostage and take the kingdom for himself and his evil father. Despite these small nasty details, Sian had been polite to Karina. She remembered with embarrassment that she felt flustered and speechless because he kept flirting with her. Life had taught her to ignore those types, but, being her first time, she felt confused. Sian did send her a book—Cayla's mother had brought it to Karina—but all she could picture was a superiority smirk on his face while he told her that she needed to know more about Whyland.

Darian continued, "I know you didn't get to know each other much, and—"

"What is it? Just tell me." Karina hated long, unnecessary explanations, and was too anxious to hear them.

He looked at Cayla, who nodded, then said, "He's under a spell. There's a way to get him back, and you might be able to help."

Of course, having magical or even non-magical objects from other dimensions kind of did some trick. "Does it have something to do with the book?"

Darian shook his head. "Not directly. It's… I think you can break the spell."

"Me?" It sounded strange, but maybe not so much. Karina remembered that, at least in theory, she had magical power in Whyland because people have more power when they go to different dimensions. The only issue was that she had no clue on the nature of her power or any idea how to use it. "Because of my magic?"

Darian looked down. "I guess you could call it that."

Cayla turned to him and squinted. "Just tell her."

He cleared his throat and spoke fast. "That spell can be broken with a kiss."

Karina had heard that somewhere. "Like in fairy tales?"

"You mean stories?" He shrugged. "They gotta be based on something."

Karina was used to enough weird stuff not to argue with

that logic. But hang on. What she'd need to do dawned on her. "What do I have to do with a kiss?"

Cayla said, "A kiss, uh, usually involves—you know—two people." She put her two hands together, mimicking two mouths connecting.

"I know what a kiss is. But why me?"

Darian sighed, then said, "It's a kiss of true love."

Karina felt a hollowness in her stomach. "You don't expect me to—"

"It's not that," Cayla said. "It can work both ways. Of course you'd never love or feel anything for Sian. We know that. But it can work the other way around as well. Receiving a kiss from someone you love does the trick."

Karina didn't know how to feel. The guy was weird and maybe a little annoying. But love her? "That doesn't make any sense. I saw him for what? Half an hour at most. He just said I was pretty, but I'm sure he says that to every girl he meets, doesn't he?"

Darian and Cayla replied at the same time. "Of course not," he said, while she said, "Well, yes."

Darian and Cayla glared at each other. She said, "You don't want to lie to her."

"I'm not lying. We don't know it."

Cayla shook her head in annoyance and turned to Karina. "Sian is not somebody you could trust, and not somebody I'd trust to be in love with anyone but himself."

Darian said, "But he told me to send the book with all his love. Fair enough, he said he had a broad definition of love, whatever that is. But as far as I know, it counts. He went to great lengths to make sure you got a book. So there's something there."

Cayla looked up as if thinking. "That's true. My mother was freaking out." She made a shrill voice. "You can't bring objects across dimensions." She laughed. "But she agreed in the end."

Karina was happy to hear Cayla talking about her mother like that.

Cayla continued, "I know in theory it's a kiss of true love, but I think it's just because if they called it a kiss of superficial attraction it wouldn't have the same ring."

Darian shook his head. "Not necessarily."

"They barely know each other," Cayla said.

"So what?" He shrugged. "Never heard of love at first sight?"

"You mean superficial attraction? That's what I was saying."

"Fair enough," Karina interrupted. These two would never reach a conclusion. "Can't you find any of the other girls comprised in his…" Karina looked up and grimaced. "…broad definition of love, superficial attraction, love at first sight, or whatever?" She didn't want to upset anyone by using inappropriate terminology. And as much as she obviously wanted to go to Whyland, she also wanted to understand what was going on.

Darian shrugged. "I don't know him that well. We, we didn't get along."

That was an understatement. These were two brothers who had been in opposite sides of an armed conflict.

Darian continued, "I know we had our problems, but he's the only family I have. I don't know who else to ask. His friend came to me. Since Sian sent you a book, you're the only girl anyone has a clear clue, a clear lead."

"This time it will be quicker," Cayla added. "We'll go to where he is, you kiss the statue, and you can come back."

"Statue?"

"Yeah," Darian said. "That's what the spell is. He's been petrified."

A knot formed in her stomach as the image of a motionless Sian crossed her mind. Karina took a deep breath. "How long is it gonna take?"

"Some two, three hours," Cayla replied.

"In your time?"

Cayla shook her head. "The time difference is gone. But it's just two hours or so. We can't teleport straight to where he is."

Two hours. That would be fine. Karina wouldn't let a person remain transformed into a statue, of course. And she liked the idea of going to Whyland again. But still, one thing irked her. "You know, I have friends who ask for favors, but they also drop by sometimes, or do me favors, or, you know, act like friends."

Cayla said, "You have no idea how difficult it's been to teleport after the blue tower was destroyed. We took days trying to figure it out. And my mother can't know about it."

Of course. Dropping by and acting like friends wasn't easy when they lived in a different dimension. Karina should just be glad that they even came back. "Are you sure it's just two hours?"

"It could be even less," Cayla said.

"What if it doesn't work?"

"At least we'll have tried," Darian said. "I'll try something else, then."

Something else. Or someone else?

The whole plan sounded ludicrous, and it wasn't that Karina didn't believe Sian had had some kind of—very superficial—feelings for her, it was just that she wasn't sure that the nature of those feelings would warrant breaking a spell.

Breaking a spell. Fairytale land again. She had learned to accept quite a few things. But maybe she shouldn't be that accepting. "And what if there's a catch? I mean, if it's some bad guy's plan, or if he's actually been imprisoned by the good guys, or…" She ran out of ideas.

Darian said, "We don't really know what happened. I know my brother's not perfect. He can be selfish and greedy, but I don't think he is a bad person. It won't really matter for you. All you'll need to do is kiss him and go home."

Right. What a first kiss. Karina swallowed. They probably didn't know it would be her first. Go to a parallel dimension, break a spell, and then come back home, having to forget that somewhere, someone kind of loved her, maybe in a very superficial way, but still. The danger Karina felt was not physical, but something else she couldn't quite point out. But hey, adventure, knowledge. Drink up the world. She wanted all that. And she trusted her head over her shoulders that it would not go over her heels. Or at least she hoped. Sian wasn't that good looking anyway. Not ugly either. Far from ugly. Better not think about it.

Karina felt she had to bargain, and turned to Cayla. "I'll do this, of course, but please, promise you'll invite me to spend some time in Whyland. Later, when everything is sorted out."

Cayla shrugged. "You could stay longer now. I just thought… I don't know, you'd want to get home quickly."

"I do. I have a test and a project on Monday. But some other day."

"We can try to set something up when things are calmer," Cayla said. "It hasn't been easy lately."

Maybe things would never be calm. Karina felt a chill in her stomach. She could be wasting an opportunity to stay longer. But at least she was going. "Let's go," Karina said.

Cayla looked at Karina's clothes. "You should wear something warmer. It's kind of cold where we're going."

Indeed Darian and Cayla were not dressed for summer. Karina, who was wearing yoga pants and a tank top, grabbed a hoodie and tied it on her waist. She doubted it would be that cold. For a second she wanted to put at least some mascara and blush on, but she didn't want them to think she was trying to… She didn't even know what she didn't want them to think or why she felt like looking better, but whatever. It was just a quick kiss to break a spell; meaningless. She'd better remember that. Meaningless. Meaningless.

Cayla got up and held Darian's hand. Karina was about to hold Cayla's hand when she remembered something.

"Wait," she said.

Karina texted Zoe. She needed an excuse in case her mother wondered about her, and in case she took longer than expected. Karina put her phone on the desk, then held Cayla's hand. The girl stared at Karina's phone but didn't say anything. Karina closed her eyes. Nothing happened. And some more time passed. And nothing happened.

"It's not working," Cayla said.

Karina had a guess. "Could it be that we're too many people? Maybe we'll have to do two by two?"

"It could be," Cayla replied. "The tower we used to open this portal isn't very solid. Wait here. I'll go with Darian and come back."

Karina nodded. She wanted to see what happened, but again there was so much light that she was forced to look away. A few minutes passed, and Cayla did not return. Great. What if they had gotten stuck or something? What if Cayla couldn't teleport alone? Maybe nothing was going to happen. Karina feared that she had just let Whyland slip through her fingers. She also worried about Sian. No, Cayla would figure a way to return. They had already come so far. A phone call snapped her out of her thoughts.

It was Zoe. "What's up?"

I'm going to a parallel dimension to break a spell with a kiss. No, that sounded weird. "I'm busy," Karina said. "If by any chance my mom calls asking for me, tell her I'm with you."

"But she'll call you."

"I'll leave my phone at home."

"What are you doing?" Zoe sounded curious.

"Nothing."

"Nothing doesn't require excuses. Spill it." Zoe was giggling.

"I'll tell you tomorrow." If she found a good excuse by then.

"And what do I get for the favor?"

"I do a lot of favors for you and I never ask for anything in return."

"Uh, ok," Zoe said. "But then you should consider I'm doing a favor without asking for anything in return and do me a favor without asking for anything in return."

"Like doing the entire science project on my own?"

"We're even on that. I meant Josh."

Nightmarish. "Whatever, Zoe. If anyone contacts you, tell them you haven't seen me in years."

Karina hung up. She wasn't about to be blackmailed.

A strong light appeared in her room. Cayla.

Karina smiled. "You took forever!"

"It's hard to teleport alone. And we're doing it from a dingy, broken, old tower." Cayla looked at Karina. "I'm sorry for asking you to come and asking you to do this. And you're right; I shouldn't come here only asking for favors. I know Sian is a scumbag. And Darian might be wrong. But he insists, so it's better to give it a try."

Karina smiled. "It's fine, really. I actually like to help."

Cayla shuddered. "I wouldn't want to kiss someone… Sorry. I know it's disgusting."

Weird. As much as Karina couldn't find the exact words to describe the idea of kissing Sian, she was absolutely certain that *disgusting* wasn't among them. And Cayla said it as if she'd have to kiss an ogre or something, which was way over the top.

Cayla continued, "But it's quick, and he's petrified, so it won't be real. I can't say it in front of Darian, you know. Imagine me saying: 'oh, I'm sorry you have to kiss his sleazy brother.' But you can do it and come back, and you'll never have to see him again."

Karina just wanted her friend to shut up. "Don't worry."

Karina's phone buzzed. It had a text from Zoe: *just kidding, silly.*

"What's that?" Cayla asked.

"My communication device," Karina said as she texted: *me too. Smiley face.*

"It's different. Can't you talk in your thing?"

"We've been forgetting the ability to talk to people."

Cayla looked puzzled.

Karina laughed. "I'm kidding. We can talk. But for some weird reason, we prefer to write." She then shrugged. "Shall we go?"

Cayla nodded. Karina held her friend's hand and closed her eyes. After a few seconds, she felt through her eyelids some strong flashes of light and felt as if the ground beneath her had disappeared. The feeling didn't bother her. She knew what it was. After a while, she felt ground beneath her again. She didn't fall or lose balance, but stood straight and opened her eyes.

Cool, humid air reached her lungs and skin, chilling her. She was in a circular tall tower without a ceiling, made of very old, rugged stones. The wall was partly broken and had many holes as if it was part of some ruins. That perhaps explained why tele-porting had been hard. Darian stood at the entrance, looking outside as if guarding it. He turned when they came and had a smile of relief when he saw Cayla, whose eyes lit up when she saw him. There was something amazing in seeing these two look at each other. It was quite different from what she saw with her friends back home.

Darian seemed tense as he walked towards them. Karina realized she hadn't asked a thing about any potential danger.

"What's this place?" Karina asked.

Darian said, "Ruins of what once was Whyland's capital. Thousands of years ago. It's close to the garden of the Lost Castle, where my brother is. We'll have to walk there. It should take us about one hour or so."

Karina didn't mind the walking, but they had flying machines, which they called lifts, in Whyland. "Any reason we can't fly?"

"That castle has been abandoned for millennia," Darian said. "There shouldn't be any danger there. Still, it's better not to make a fuss of our arrival. Just in case."

Vague words for a vague fear. Cayla also seemed slightly tense. They walked out of the tower. Karina had never seen such thick fog. She put her hoodie on and zipped it up. There was nothing but whiteness.

Darian frowned. "It's not usually that bad."

Cayla put her hand on Karina's shoulder. "Don't be afraid. It's just fog."

For Karina, the fog had been just was a nuisance, but Cayla's words had the opposite effect as intended because they seemed to have been spoken both to Karina and to herself.

3

THE GARDEN

Cayla squeezed Karina's shoulder and whispered. "Nothing should happen. But if it does, you can still teleport from any place apart from the cursed garden. You don't need a tower. It's a gift you have."

Teleporting. Of course. Karina had done it twice, but more than a year before, and she wasn't sure how exactly it worked. Karina wondered why Cayla had whispered that. More and more she felt that there was more to the task than simply kissing a statue and returning home.

Darian turned. "What's that?"

"I was telling her not to be afraid," Cayla said.

He shook his head. "It's all good. Nobody will see us." He touched his chest and pulled his necklace with its bright orange stone. "And this will prevent us from getting lost."

Darian took Cayla's hand. Karina walked beside the princess. She wanted them to keep talking because that whiteness was gloomy.

"And how did you find out where Sian is?"

"One of his friends came to me," Darian replied. "They were a small group in the Lost Castle."

"Doing what?"

"He didn't say it, but I believe my brother was studying magic."

Sian hadn't struck Karina as the studious type, but she didn't know him that well. On the other hand, he'd struck her as ambitious and cunning, so perhaps studying did suit him, if it was to achieve some goal. "Are his friends still there?"

"They left after Sian was enchanted."

"Who did it to him?" How weird that only now this question came to Karina.

Darian looked down. "No one seems to know."

What a mess Karina was getting herself into. It sounded super fishy. But hey, Karina liked fish—and adventures.

"It will be quick," Cayla said. "Nobody will even see us or notice what we're doing."

So the strategy was sneaking in. Karina took a deep breath. She did like adventure, but sometimes she wondered how sane that was. She wanted to keep talking, so she asked Cayla about what happened after she left. The princess told her that Lylah had become queen and that peace had been established in Whyland, but she didn't sound super happy with it.

"Is there a catch or something I'm missing?"

"Years of infighting have made us vulnerable and we might have other kingdoms planning to attack us."

So now Whyland had other potential enemies. Perhaps things would never be calm. "And shouldn't you be in the castle?"

"I thought so. But my mother insisted that I travel. She told me to get to know the four corners of Whyland. Get to know the people."

"What about Darian?"

"He was assigned to travel with me." She then whispered, "I know he'd prefer to be involved in the leadership of the army."

"I heard that," he said. "I'm exactly where I've always wanted to be."

"And where's that?" Cayla asked.

"Holding your hand."

She looked down and smiled. "I know. But maybe we could do both. I'll talk to my mother when we get back. You can do a lot more than be my bodyguard."

"Don't worry about it," he said.

"And what about you?" Karina asked Cayla.

"I want to help with the politics, the administration. That's why I'm traveling. Of course, we stopped a little to figure out the flowing tower and get you here." She had a smile and put her hand on Karina's. "Thank you for your kindness."

Karina shrugged. "It's nothing. It'll be quick, right?"

Cayla nodded. Karina smiled, but her face was the opposite of what she felt. Somehow, the fact that it would be quick disappointed her. She was not sure of what exactly she wanted or expected. The one thing she was sure was that she was feeling cold and should have brought a thicker jacket. Despite her hands in her pockets, the tips of her fingers were getting numb. The hood didn't do much to warm her ears. Darian and Cayla's clothes didn't look that warm, though, but the couple seemed to be comfortable.

The whiteness surrounding them was oppressive. And Karina was anxious. Of course, maybe it was just that Karina had always hoped her first kiss would be more special, or romantic. Sure, a kiss to break a spell was as romantic and special as it could get, but not if there weren't any real feelings between the parties concerned, and if she would simply turn around, forget it, and go home. It would be better this way. Sian wasn't trustworthy. That was the part she needed to remember.

Darian guided their way, with some help from Cayla. Karina understood why the castle would be called "lost" amidst all that fog, but she had a hunch that it was not the castle, but the people looking for it. They walked for many minutes until they reached a point where the weather cleared. While it was still cold, the sky was blue, and sunshine reached them like a golden shower melting the fog. They were on a hill from where Karina saw a valley below, then a building on a small hill, with dark stone walls. It was probably the castle, but its shape was square, without any outer walls or towers. Below the castle, in the valley, there was a narrow river and a garden.

"He's down there," Darian said.

At least the view was pretty and the creepy fog was gone. There were flowers in many colors among hedge corridors. White and black pebbles formed shapes such as flowers, birds, stars, and some other symbols on the paths. It all had a fresh, pleasant, flowery smell.

"Who tends this garden?" Karina asked.

Darian grimaced. "Well, that's the question, isn't it?"

"It's all enchanted," Cayla said. "Apparently it's been so since the time it was abandoned."

Right. From lovely, the flowers seemed rather creepy. They approached a statue in the middle of a circle of drawings on the floor. Perhaps that was the prince or young king to whom this castle had belonged.

"Here we are," Darian said.

Here? Karina took a better look. Of course. That was not a statue, but Sian. The stone was light grey and very smooth. Perhaps it was just that she'd imagined his skin would still look like skin, not like marble. Plus, the statue didn't look like him, or maybe Karina didn't remember him that well. First, the statue wasn't smirking, and second, it looked rather handsome. She felt a cold breeze in her chest.

"What am I supposed to do?" Karina asked, her heart almost jumping out of her body. Fine. She knew—in theory—what she had to do, but knowing and really knowing are different things.

"Just kiss him," Darian said.

Karina took a deep breath, gathered all her courage and approached the statue. She tiptoed to reach him, but it was really hard, especially because the statue had its head looking up, which made reaching it difficult.

"Here," Darian said, as he put a log near the statue.

Now Karina had a place to step on. She would still need to reach up, but it made things easier. Kissing a statue. Only now the madness in all this was dawning on her. But it wasn't a statue. There was a person within it.

Karina hesitated. "Uh, on the lips?"

"You can do it quickly," Cayla replied.

That was a yes. Karina still felt uncomfortable. "How do we know he'd want this? I mean, he's not awake to give his opinion."

Darian rolled his eyes and waved his arms. "And he won't ever be awake if we don't try. Trust me, Sian wouldn't have a problem with a kiss from a girl he thinks is pretty."

Karina wouldn't want anyone to assume something like that about her.

"You need to think about it in a different way," Cayla said. "If you saved someone from drowning, and if you had to do mouth to mouth breathing, you wouldn't wonder whether they wanted it or not, would you? It's the same here."

At least Cayla understood Karina better. That made sense. Karina could hear her own heart and wondered if the others heard it too. She stepped on the log, terrified of what would happen, tiptoed, and pressed her lips against the statue. She kissed it lightly, as she sometimes kissed people's cheeks when saying hello; barely touching. She wasn't sure if she'd done it right. Nothing seemed to change.

"Is this how it's supposed to work?"

"I don't know," Darian replied. "You barely kissed him. I think it needs more feeling."

"You said my feelings don't matter."

"No, but it must be a real kiss, I think."

Cayla turned to him. "Since when you're a specialist in magic? We knew there was a chance it wouldn't work."

"It will," Darian said. "I know it. Maybe she needs to concentrate more, and more privacy." He held Cayla's hand and pointed to the other side of the hedge. "Why don't we go over there?"

Before they went anywhere, Karina had an idea. "Darian! Why don't you kiss him? You love him, don't you?"

He looked as if he'd just sucked a sour lemon.

"On the cheek," Karina added.

Darian scratched his neck and laughed. "Good luck with that. I'm not sure there's much love there. Take your time. I'm sure you can do it."

They walked away. Cayla cast a guilty look before disappearing behind the hedge with Darian.

Karina stared at the statue in front of her. What was she supposed to do? She tried to imagine the boy she had met almost a year before. She imagined him with a superiority smirk, saying that he was stealing a kiss from "a pretty girl". But hey, if that was what would bring him back, so be it. She wondered what would happen when he woke up. He would certainly tease her about it. Karina touched the lips of the statue, imagining those were the lips of the boy she had seen, and kissed them. But again nothing happened. Karina knew that this time she had really kissed the statue.

Odd. She had dreaded seeing him wake up, and now that nothing was happening, she felt disappointed. It perhaps meant that she wasn't even included in his broad definition of love. All the flirting and the book he'd sent her had meant nothing after all. Maybe he didn't even think she was pretty, and the whole thing was to get her to help him, or some joke to make her confused. Well, true that if he didn't think she was pretty enough for him, he suffered from some serious poor taste issue.

Or vision problems. Or maybe it was Karina who was on a too high horse. She was getting annoyed at statue Sian, especially because he had his chin up and a confident air, as if thinking he was too hot for her. How dare he? And he wasn't even hot.

Would he mock her? Maybe she'd never know. Whatever his story was, there was no part for her to play in it. She felt disappointed, which was silly. No reason to feel that way. Regardless of the result of the kiss, Karina knew it didn't mean anything special. She knew it. And yet... Perhaps it's just that she had been expecting something to happen, and nothing happened, and that was super disappointing. Not to mention she would no longer be able to brag that a guy's love for her, as superficial as it was, broke a spell. Of course, she wouldn't have anyone to brag to, cause they'd think she was crazy, but she could perhaps do some inner bragging. Anyway.

Karina stepped out of the log feeling silly and stupid, even though in theory the silly and stupid person was Darian, who had gone through all this trouble of bringing her for no reason. She felt a little hurt too, but she knew it was not their fault. It was nobody's fault, really. The idea had been outrageous from the start and she should have known it.

Cayla and Darian were nowhere to be seen. She considered looking for them but somehow felt afraid of getting lost in that garden. Well, she was in a magic garden surrounding a likely lost castle, where an annoying acquaintance had been enchanted. No wonder Karina felt uncomfortable. And she hated being there only near Sian's statue. Ugh, she hated that statue and didn't want to ever look at it again. She hated that whole plan and what a fool she felt.

"Cayla, Darian!" she yelled. "Come back. It didn't—"

Something caught Karina's eye. A movement on the floor. From beneath the pebbles on the paths, a few forms rose. All around her, these forms were coming out of the ground; something gray with a skin that looked thick and rough. She shivered. Cayla and Darian came running. The princess had a gun on her hand, shooting their weird fire at those forms. Nothing happened to those shapes, and they encircled them. Darian picked up an ax from the floor and cut in half the forms surrounding Cayla and Karina. They fell on the ground, but slowly started joining together again. That gave the girls and Darian time to get some distance from them, though.

Karina was horrified. "What are those?"

"No idea," Cayla yelled. "Stay close to us."

All around them, in all visible parts of the garden, forms were coming up from the ground. Most had human forms, but some seemed to have tails or wings. Others were some kind of four-legged animal. They had no eyes or mouth, but were rather shapes, like rough molds of clay that still hadn't received any details.

Darian tossed Cayla the axe. Karina kept close to them, as the shapes started moving towards them. They ran halfway to the hill, while those creatures closed in. Cayla was fast and used the ax to cut the figures that approached them. Even if they joined together after that, at least cutting them slowed them down, and Cayla, Darian, and Karina could find a path to escape.

Darian did his best with a stick and also kept some forms at bay. He must have tossed the ax to Cayla to protect her or because the girl was faster than he was. Cayla and Darian were very capable fighters and would certainly come out of that garden. Karina felt she was a burden to them, as she had no idea how to fight, and no idea how to fight against multiple enemies, especially undying enemies.

Something else knotted Karina's chest, though. She looked back. Down there, in the middle of the garden, a lonely statue was surrounded by shapeless forms. Would Sian be in danger? He was annoying, and he didn't like Karina at all, but she didn't want anything bad to happen to him.

"What about Sian?" Karina yelled.

"We'll come back later," Darian replied.

Karina didn't think they would ever return. Not when those awful shapes took over what once had been a beautiful garden. The boy would remain transformed forever. She felt something heavy inside her.

"Karina!" Cayla yelled, snapping Karina out of her thoughts.

She'd been staring down at the statue and had forgotten to keep moving with her friends. Forms were closing in on them from every direction, especially near where Sian was. They walked, though. Karina thought she could maybe outrun them. Not really outrun the forms, as she'd need to move across where they were, but maybe run fast enough that they would not touch her. She was now looking at the distance between her and the statue.

"Karina! Come!" Cayla pleaded.

Karina took a deep breath and made her decision. Teleporting. She could teleport in Whyland. That was her gift. She'd better use it for something good.

"Go," Karina said. "I'll teleport."

Cayla screamed "No," and something else, but Karina was too focused on the distance between her and the statue to make out the words. She ran as fast as she could, zigzagging amidst horrible forms, swallowing and burying her fear deep within her, heart racing as fast as it had ever raced, from the fear and the running. A couple times those figures almost touched her. Teleport. All she needed to teleport was to hold someone's hand and imagine herself somewhere else. She ran towards the statue. Of course, if by any chance she failed, that would be her end. Or something else. Who knew what those forms wanted?

Karina reached Sian's statue and held its hand. She thought about the blue tower in the main castle in Whyland, about safety, about the janky old tower amidst the fog. She kept that image in her mind. Nothing happened. Forms closed in. One started to pull her arm. It hurt, and she screamed.

All she wanted was to be back home. Karina felt as if she was falling, but she kept holding the statue's hand. She closed her eyes and felt flashes of bright light. The thing holding her arm stopped holding it, and the part of the statue she held became soft. She felt floor beneath her, opened her eyes, and saw the ruined tower, but only for a brief second, as the flashes started again together with the sensation of teleporting.

When she felt solid floor beneath her again, Karina opened her eyes and saw herself in her bedroom as the sun came down. Sian fell backward, but thank goodness that her bed was behind him. His upper body lay across the bed. Karina would have fallen over him if she hadn't let go of his hand. There was no statue, but a boy, with eyes closed on her bed. Sian, not the statue. He seemed to be sleeping, but he was human now. As much as she had hated him a few minutes before, Karina was glad that she had saved him, even though he seemed to still be enchanted. She looked around, almost fearing that those shapes would follow them, but no, it was just an impression. They remained in Whyland, and Karina was safe in her apartment.

Karina sat and put her head beneath her hands. She took deep, fast breaths, while her entire body shook. Fear, horror, dread, shock. What had those things been? Still, as her breath slowed down, she realized that she was safe at home, with nothing chasing or trying to grab her, and she was overcome by a feeling of relief. Tears came out of her eyes. But not everything was over. She looked at Sian's peaceful expression. He was still enchanted, and that was a huge problem since she had no idea how to wake him up. More than that, she had no idea how to teleport him back home. So two big problems.

4

A GUY WHERE?

Karina stared at the boy who had his back on her bed. With eyes closed, he had an innocent expression, almost sweet. Of course, his nose was a bit too big. Definitely not good looking. And still he dared not wake up when Karina kissed him when he should have been flattered at such an occasion. But it was no time to be upset at him. Who knows, it was likely all Darian's fault. Karina wished she had not been called into this, though, as she still felt like a fool. But she had to focus on the issue at hand. There was a fainted, enchanted, sleeping, or whatever guy on her bed. On her bed, in her bedroom. Karina couldn't even start to imagine what her mom would think about it. And it was not that she could hide him. Hide? That would be cruel. He should be returned to Whyland, from where he should have never left.

Oh, Karina, why did you teleport with him? Why? She had no answer to that. Well, except that maybe she feared that something bad could happen to him if she'd left him there. Sure, he had an awful taste for girls, but he didn't deserve to remain in a garden with horrid forms. And how was Karina to know she'd teleport all the way back home? Now here he was, and Karina had no idea what to do. She had to focus and think. Think. Come up with a solution. Her thoughts were interrupted by a voice. Her mom!

"Karina?"

Karina ran to the door, opened it, got out, then closed it quickly behind her so that her mom wouldn't look inside. "Hey."

"I didn't know you were home. There's dinner in the fridge." She took a close look at Karina. "Are you all right?"

"Yeeeeah. I was re-resting." That must have sounded the opposite Karina intended.

Her mom took a deep breath. "I know it's difficult for you, but me and your father, we had to move on with our lives."

Karina made an effort not to roll her eyes. Was her mom still on that?

"I'm fine, really. Just tired. Finals last week and all." Having been attacked by a horde of weird shapes was actually the big issue, but she couldn't explain that.

She held Karina's hand. "If there's anything you want to talk about, just tell me."

"Can I tell you not to worry about me?"

Her mother laughed and kissed Karina's forehead. "I'm in my bedroom if you need anything."

Karina nodded, trying to look normal. In her bedroom? Why? Why? Of all Saturdays, she had decided to stay home now? Karina was left to the beat of her own heart. She had to get rid of Sian, she had to, but she would need to wake him up and then figure out a way to get back to Whyland. She opened her bedroom's door and closed it behind her. Why didn't it have a lock?

What a sight: a guy from another world on her bed. If she had ever imagined something like that, the guy would obviously be insanely good looking and totally in love with her. But that was not the case here. Of course, Karina had never imagined such a thing, as that would be highly inappropriate.

Anyways, the guy was just a big problem. Karina's problem. It had been her choice to save him. She had teleported with him. She wanted to face-palm herself, but at the same time, she felt she had done the right thing. She wouldn't be in peace with herself if she had left him in that garden. But what now? She took a deep breath. She had to find a way to wake him up. Three knocks on the door startled her. The doorknob turned. Karina threw her covers over Sian and ran to the door. It was her mom. Again.

"I'm going—" She looked at Karina's expression. "Are you sure you're okay?"

"Perfect!"

"I just wanted to tell you I changed my mind. I'm going to the meeting. I'll be back soon. Call me if you need anything."

"I will."

Her mom narrowed her eyes and looked behind Karina, at her bedroom. Oh, no, Karina was about to be caught. Or not. Relief sight. She seemed suspicious, but said, "Goodnight," then turned around and left.

Karina closed the door and put her ear on it. When she heard the front door closing, she turned back to Sian. Still lying on her bed. Perhaps the effect of the kiss took some time or something. Cause part of the transformation had already happened. Maybe the rest would happen in time? Meanwhile, what would she do with his body? If her mom walked in…

Karina sat on the bed and looked at Sian. He was wearing a long grey overcoat in some kind of thick material. It looked nice. No wonder she'd mistaken his statue for a prince at first. With his innocent expression, he looked quite different from the last time she'd seen him. It had been so long. His brown hair had curls and looked really soft. She wanted to touch it, maybe just to check if he was no longer petrified, but she stopped, afraid that he'd know she touched his hair.

What had made her teleport with him? Hang on. That was

the key. She'd run back to him, risking who knows what, facing her fear, just so that he wouldn't be left behind. There was something there: not romantic love, and certainly not superficial attraction, or any kind of attraction for that matter. But there was something there. Karina would be mortified if she had to kiss his lips again, now that he looked human, and especially knowing that he had no feelings for her, but she could kiss his cheek.

Karina leaned over him, trying to remember the moment she was in that garden, and the moment she ran back to save him. She remembered how she felt seeing him there, left behind. She closed her eyes and kissed his cheek, trying to put all her feelings in that kiss. When she opened her eyes, Sian was still sleeping, same peaceful expression. Oh, dear, Karina was in trouble, with no more ideas on what to do. She sat up and looked at him. Perhaps trying to save him had been a huge mistake. Maybe Cayla and Darian would eventually figure out what had happened and would come to pick him up. Yes, that could work—as long as she found a place to hide him. She got up and opened her wardrobe, wondering how she would make room for a guy who was over six feet tall.

She heard a sound, however, and turned. Sian was sitting up, looking a bit confused. He saw her and his mouth dropped in surprise. *Surprise.* He was surprised to see her, and Karina didn't ignore the meaning of that. Still, as their eyes met after such a long time, Karina caught her breath.

5

———

DECISIONS

"Karina?" At least he remembered her name. He looked around. "What's happening?"

"I broke your spell."

He smiled and looked at his hands and arms. "I kind of noticed that." He got up and went to the window. "I want to know what's this place."

"It's where I live."

He widened his eyes. "Your dimension, you mean. How did you bring me here?"

"No idea. We were being attacked, and I teleported."

He raised an eyebrow. "From where?"

"A creepy garden where you were a statue."

He stared at her. "You can't teleport from the Darloom garden."

Karina smiled. "Maybe *you* can't. I can, cause I just did it."

Well, now she did recall that the last thing Cayla shouted had something to do with that. A good thing Karina had ignored her. Or a bad thing, considering now Sian was where he shouldn't be. He stared at her, still dumbfounded.

Karina shrugged. "Or else we're both imagining all this."

"Well, it is like a dream. I didn't think I'd see you again." For a moment Karina could almost think he was saying the truth. Her heart beat fast, sure he was saying the truth. He then had a sly smirk. "And I'm not gonna pretend to ignore how that kind of spell is broken."

Karina crossed her arms. "I kissed you on the cheek. Friendly kiss."

His eyes widened, then he frowned. "That's cheating!"

She shrugged. "It worked. What do you care?"

"Of course I care. You do realize this was just a convoluted plan to get you to kiss me, right?"

Karina laughed. His flirting didn't make her flustered anymore, now that she knew for sure it was all nonsense. And plus, she was glad that he would never know that she had indeed kissed his lips.

He stared at her seriously. "But what do you mean you were attacked?"

The memory made Karina shiver. "There were those things, they were grey, and had weird shapes, almost human—"

"Kyons. They can be summoned with magic."

"Do you know who did it?"

"The Darloom castle has a new master. Still, I don't know why…" He looked at her. "Weren't you scared?"

"Well, yes."

He looked down. "I'm sorry. Were there other people with you?"

"Cayla and Darian."

He thought for a moment, then said, "They can defend themselves, can't they? They must be fine."

"They were doing well. I'm pretty sure they escaped." Karina was not worried about them.

Sian sighed in relief, then smirked. "I bet Cayla's a better fighter than he is."

That actually made sense. "How do you know?"

He chuckled. "My brother's pathetic."

Quite an insensitive thing to say about the brother who had saved him, but she had to get to the part that mattered. "Do you know how to teleport back to Whyland?"

He stared at her. "You brought me here. You can take me back, can't you?"

"I don't—"

"How did you go to Whyland?"

"Cayla and Darian came here."

He smirked. "Cayla. Of course. She's got her mother's magic. Now, whenever someone teleports to a new place, they open a portal. You can use it to go back there."

"Can you go alone?"

He shrugged. "I have no idea how to teleport."

"You just said—"

"I know the theory of how it works. I can't do it myself. But you can teleport and open portals from impossible places. This should be super easy for you."

She was surprised that he knew that much about her, but that wasn't the point. "I don't have magic here."

He shook his head. "That's not right. Maybe you have less magic, but you still have it."

Karina stepped closer to him. "Do you know how magic works? How it's different from science? From normal things?"

He had a sideways smirk. "I do and it will be my pleasure to explain all about it to you."

"Well, tell me. I want to hear it."

"Ah, so that's what you like! Knowledge." He let out a laugh. "Now I know how to bribe you."

"You aren't going to explain it?"

"I just said I will. In Whyland. You do realize it might be in danger and I have to get back, don't you?"

"But I won't stay there. I'll teleport you and come back."

Sian ran his hand through his wavy brown hair and sat on

the bed. "You're kidding, right? You wake me up from a spell with a truelove kiss, and then you just send me away. Like that. Go on, rip out my heart."

She rolled her eyes. "Your heart will be fine. It was a kiss on the cheek."

Karina then heard a sound in the living room and steps approaching. Her door was opened before she had a chance to ask Sian to hide. Karina thought she was going to have a heart attack. But it was just Zoe, so no doomsday for Karina. Her friend had tears in her eyes.

Zoe noticed Sian and was surprised. "Sorry, I didn't mean to—"

"It's fine," Karina said. "What's going on?"

Sian got up and walked to the door. "I'll leave you two alone."

"No, no, no," Karina said. "Don't leave this room." She turned to Zoe. "Let's talk in the kitchen."

Zoe had a smile despite the tears in her eyes. "Ah, so that's what got you busy. Well, no wonder you don't want to go out with Josh."

Karina looked down. "He's just a friend." She tried to change the subject. "What about you? What's wrong?"

"Nothing really, it's just... Samy can be such a jerk some-times. But maybe I should know it."

"Did you break up?"

Zoe laughed and shrugged. "I don't even know."

Karina never really understood Zoe and Samy and she wasn't about to try it now. Sometimes she thought not even Zoe understood them. Karina asked something else, "How did you know I was home?"

"I didn't think you'd go out. I'd never thought you...

Who's he?"

Karina wasn't sure how to answer. "Uh, I have a, uh, cousin, her name's Cayla. Sian is her boyfriend's brother." That was kind of true.

Zoe made a face. "Fake cousin talk already, Karina?"

"Fine, she's not my cousin. She's just a friend who lives far away. But he *is* her boyfriend's brother."

"And what's your friend's boyfriend's brother doing in your bedroom?"

"Sounds cliché, but I guarantee you; it's complicated."

Zoe nodded. "I see. Be careful, Karina. Complicated usually means you're in the illusion of being in a relationship with a guy who doesn't take you as seriously as you'd like him to."

Great. Now Zoe was quoting something she read somewhere but didn't really learn. "It's nothing like that. We don't have anything."

Zoe laughed. "Right. Did you convince yourself of that?"

Karina buried her face in her hands when a voice startled her.

"Karina?" It was Sian. "I'm sorry for interrupting you."

"I asked you to stay in the room!"

Zoe got up. "Well, I was leaving anyways."

"Are you all right?" Karina asked.

"Fine. You have more important stuff to discuss." She winked and left.

Karina was actually glad her friend was gone, even if she felt a bit guilty for not comforting her.

Sian stared at Karina. "I know what the Kyons were after."

"Let's go to the bedroom." Only after she said it she realized what it sounded like. Ouch. For some miracle, he didn't say anything.

Once they were inside, Karina closed the door and asked, "What is it you think those things are after?"

"You."

That couldn't be. Maybe Sian was joking. But he didn't seem to be.

"It's your teleporting abilities," he added.

"But how would they know about my teleporting abilities? And what would they want?"

"That's something we'll need to solve. There are things in other dimensions that people want, and you could reach these other dimensions and get those things."

Other dimensions. Somehow Karina hadn't really considered that there had been anything other than her own world and Whyland's dimension. Still, she felt safe at home. "But they're not gonna come here, are they?"

"There's an open portal from Whyland to here. Why wouldn't they come?"

"Cause it's hard and not a lot of people can do it?" That was a guess, but a logical one.

He looked in her eyes. "They'll come back for you. Even here."

"Where should I go then?"

"To Whyland, with me. I can protect you."

Her heart beat faster. She knew it was being stupid, so she ignored it. "That makes total sense: go to the place where a bunch of creepy looking things are out to get me."

"I know how to defeat them. And I need to go to the Darloom Castle. I told you, it has a new master. I need to make sure Whyland is safe, and you're safe."

"Last time I saw you, you wanted to conquer Whyland for very selfish reasons. Now you want to convince me you're some kind of hero?"

He scoffed. "Nope. I'm the same. I'm transparent. I never said I was a hero, and I'm not going to do it now. All I'm saying is that I need you to come to Whyland with me. I know I can fix the Darloom castle. And you'll be safe."

Karina wondered if he was making all that up just to make

sure she came with him. But then what would be his reasons for that? She'd woken him up with her feelings only, so she assumed he didn't like her or even have any superficial attraction for her. It was hard to understand. The part of Karina who yearned for adventure would go with him without even blinking, but there was a part of Karina who was responsible and logical. She didn't trust Sian, and she wasn't about to go to a dangerous place with him like some lunatic fangirl.

Karina sighed. "I'll teleport you to Whyland and come back. I don't think they'll be able to find me here."

He stepped back. "You prefer to risk your life staying here than to come with me?"

He sounded hurt, but Karina knew he was just pretending and being overdramatic. "If they want me because of my abilities, they won't kill me."

"There are other risks."

She took a deep breath. "How long do you think I'll have to stay in Whyland?"

"Two, three weeks. One month. I don't know. Until everything is settled."

That would be impossible. Karina had her math final, her summer camp. "I can't. I trust you, though. Can't you defeat those things?"

"In Whyland. I can't teleport here. If Kyons teleport here, I won't be able to do anything." His tone was serious, almost cross.

"I doubt those stupid things can teleport."

He glared at her, with a set jaw. "Well, stay here then. Maybe you're right. I won't insist."

Karina took a step back from him, his tone surprising and scaring her at the same time. It only convinced her that she had to stay.

Sian noticed and closed his eyes, then opened them and said, "I'm sorry. I'm just worried. How do you think I'll feel if something happens to you?" He sounded sweet and she would have felt for him if she didn't know it was just his exaggerated drama.

"You'll be fine and I'll be fine. Don't worry."

Sian didn't say anything. He just crossed his arms and looked away, tugging her heart in the process. But what could she do? She had to take him back to Whyland, and she couldn't simply walk away from her own life for up to a month. She couldn't.

Karina wondered how exactly teleporting worked. She'd seen Cayla do it, and she'd done it, but she had only done it in extreme situations, and never from her own dimension. Cayla had touched a wall. Karina did the same, extending her hand. "Come," she told Sian.

Only now she realized they'd need to hold hands, and it made her nervous. Sian still looked grumpy, but he wrapped his hand around hers. It was the first time they touched each other, not counting the time he'd been enchanted. Karina trembled. Trembled. Now was that stupid or what? But she couldn't avoid it. Awkwardness had become electricity coming from his hand to her entire body. Something odd. He didn't like her, and she had to remember that. She tried to keep her hand limp like a dead fish, but the hand disobeyed and felt more like an electric eel. At least he didn't know that. Her heart was beating fast. "Close your eyes," she said.

The floor beneath her disappeared. She felt strong light through her eyelids. That was fast. And easy. Teleporting had never been so easy or so fast. When the lights stopped, she opened her eyes. They were in the janky old ruined tower, near the lost castle with the creepy garden. The sun was setting and there was no fog. Karina looked around and smiled. "I did it!" She then noticed she still held his hand and let it go.

He stared at her. "So you're just going to ignore what I just told you and go back?"

Karina wished she could stay. But she knew it would be irresponsible and brash. And something made her afraid. She had no idea what. "I didn't even bring anything."

He puffed and waved his hand. "Oh, excuses. C'mon, be real here." He put his hand on his chest and made a face as if he were in pain. "I know when I'm being turned down."

Karina didn't like it that he was making fun of that. She just stared.

He got normal again. "Oh, and what about the magic? All the things I wanted to tell you? Well, I guess you'll have to live without knowing any of that. Pity, no?"

That was a low punch. Of course Karina would throw it all away to learn more about a parallel dimension, about teleporting, about magic. He didn't have to say that. She knew what she was missing. Karina felt as if she had a knife on her heart. Sian was twisting it. But she couldn't just disappear like that. What about her mother? Her friends? School? She couldn't. And it didn't have to be forever.

"I might come back to Whyland. Cayla told me she'll invite me. Maybe you could tell me about magic then."

He snorted. "Not sure you noticed, but I don't hang out with Cayla or her boyfriend."

"The people who saved you. Neat."

"*You* saved me."

Whatever. If Sian could play the overdramatic game, so could she. She put her hand on her heart and tried her best imitation at a sad voice. "And you won't make an exception and try to see me if I come with Cayla. How cruel."

He burst out laughing. "Well played. One day you'll be as good as me. Pity you don't want to spend time and learn with the master. You don't know until when this portal will be open." He then became serious and looked at her attentively. "The kyons, if they come after you, you can't kill them, but you can paralyze them for a moment, with a bright light directly into their eyes."

Karina shuddered thinking of those things. "The things I saw didn't have eyes."

"I mean the position where the eyes would be."

Karina nodded and swallowed, hoping she wouldn't need to use this information. But nothing in those things suggested that they had the ability to teleport. Even Sian couldn't teleport, and he was smarter than those things.

He looked at her for a moment as if examining something, then said, "You're different. You used to be sweet. Now you're a cold heartbreaker."

Karina laughed. But he didn't laugh and had a serious expression.

She said, "I'm the same." Well, actually, she thought she had been too innocent and silly when they had met, but she didn't want to mention that. "We didn't really get to know each other, did we? Then maybe I'm just wiser."

He took a deep breath. "Fair enough, wise girl. If you need help, come and find me. I may be hurt but I'm fair. I know I'm the one who got you in trouble."

"How can I find you?"

He laughed. "The first step is coming back."

How helpful. "Well, goodbye," she said. Sian didn't reply.

Karina closed her eyes and thought about her bedroom, but she didn't feel any lights or the floor disappearing. She tried to think again, then think about home, safety, her friends, school, her mother. She tried to conjure all the thoughts she could, and nothing happened. Karina feared that she could not teleport alone. But it could be done. Cayla had done it, hadn't she? In theory, Karina was better at teleporting, so it should be easy for her. But it wasn't. She opened her eyes.

Sian asked, "So, is it going to take all night?"

"I'm sorry. I'm trying."

"I'm not complaining. I can stare at you all night. It's just that if you want to stay, just stay, you know? You don't need to pretend you can't teleport."

"Ha, ha. Hilarious. I've never done it alone, that's all." She looked down, then added, "And of course I'd like to stay, but I can't."

"You confuse me. But you can't be confused, or you won't go anywhere."

"I'm not confused."

"Then you'll have no problem teleporting."

Was he right? He couldn't be. She needed emotion to teleport. Emotion. She had to feel something. She opened her eyes. Sian was there. He looked quite decent in that dim light. Maybe way more than decent. Karina closed her eyes. She imagined Sian's statue sneering at her, mocking her, making a joke out of flirting with her. She felt the floor beneath her gone and saw strong flashes of light through her eyelids.

Karina got to her bedroom feeling cold and exhausted. But it was over. She had done it. She should be feeling proud of her powers, but she wanted to lie on her bed and cry. The magic, the adventure, she had just left all of that behind. A horrible feeling took over her chest. But there wasn't much to be done. She couldn't leave everything to follow a guy she barely knew. She wished she could, though, and hated herself for it.

She decided to sleep and changed into her pajamas. After she turned off the light, she remembered the scene in the garden and those ugly things after her. She almost wished she had stayed there with Sian.

She hadn't believed that those things, kyons, could teleport, but alone in her bedroom with her lights off, she felt sure they were coming to get her. She didn't want to question her decision, though. And still, she felt scared, so she went to the kitchen and got a flashlight. The light wasn't that strong, but she hoped she would not need it. She lay down with the flashlight beside her. Was it enough? Just in case, she got up and turned on the light. Perhaps that would also help. Eventually, she slept with the light on, a flashlight by her side, and a lump in her throat.

6

———————

KYONS

Darian carried the ax now, relieved that they hadn't seen any kyons for some time. The fog had dissipated, and the top of the old tower was visible against the darkening sky. He and Cayla had taken a lot longer than expected to get there, as those forms kept appearing even outside the cursed garden. To make matters worse, Cayla was upset, worried about her friend. Darian should also be worried about his brother, but somehow he wasn't.

Strangely, he was hopeful and relieved. The truth is that he had been doubtful the entire time they had planned to bring Karina. Although he had a hunch that the plan would work, it wasn't based on anything tangible. It was just an odd feeling, disconnected from reality. First, he didn't really think his brother could have feelings for anyone, even if he hoped otherwise. He didn't know his brother well but knew well enough to have gotten "love is poison" as a piece of—terrible —advice.

As much as Sian's friend had claimed that in theory superficial feelings counted, Darian hadn't been so sure. Plus, it wasn't as if the girl were remarkable in any way. Why go through the trouble of bringing a girl from another world when his brother could have found someone local to have superficial feelings for?

But when Karina ran back to Sian, Darian started to believe that there was something real there. Somehow, his brother had chosen to send a book to a girl who'd risk her life for him. The only issue with that logic was that the kiss hadn't worked. But then, maybe it had been foolish to think that any love-based counterspell would work on his heartless brother.

Still, Darian felt that something had happened back in the garden, and half expected to see his brother again, no longer trapped in stone. Perhaps indeed Sian had no feelings, but the girl sure did. Of course, he'd better not say any of this to Cayla, who seemed to think Sian was some kind of repulsive monster. Quite a disturbing thought, considering Darian didn't look that much different from him.

As they approached the tower, he hoped they'd find his brother and Karina. Seeing Cayla so worried pained Darian. They walked into the tower, but there was nobody there.

"Karina!" Cayla yelled. She looked at Darian, eyes misty with tears. "They didn't teleport. They didn't."

"We don't know it. Maybe they're around here somewhere. Maybe she teleported—"

"From that garden? How could she teleport from there? I tell you, something else happened, something bad." She sat on the floor and looked down.

He crouched and ran his fingers through her hair. "Let's not assume. Maybe she's safe in her world. You could check."

She looked up at him, and then her eyes widened in fear. Darian turned and saw many of those creatures from the garden entering the tower. With only one small exit, they would be trapped there. Darian grabbed the ax and ran to the door. Yes, Cayla was faster, but his arms could swing farther. He swung the ax horizontally and cut some five creatures who were coming towards them. He jumped over them. Cayla was close behind him, so she'd jumped as well. He tossed her the ax then. If one of them was to remain unarmed, it better be him.

As fast as they could, they ran away from the tower, towards their lift. Cayla swung the ax when any of those creatures got too close to them. When they reached their craft, Cayla and Darian entered quickly and took off. Once in the air, Cayla was quiet, looking out the window. Silence was never good news from her. She was probably still worried about her friend.

Darian considered whether he should say something and risk her wrath or let her calm down, but he couldn't stand seeing her so sad. He reached out a hand and caressed her cheek. "There was light, Cayla. There was light when your friend held Sian's hand. It means teleporting or something good; not dark magic."

She pushed his hand away. "Teleporting to a trap. What good does it make?"

Darian still didn't feel worried. "We don't know. We escaped, and my brother is a much better fighter than me, you, or both of us combined. They would have escaped."

Cayla snorted. "As a statue? He is indeed fabulous if he can fight in that state."

Darian exhaled. He still had the feeling that his brother had woken up, but couldn't prove it to Cayla. "The only thing we can do now is go to the castle and find out what's happening. We could talk to your mother."

"By then it might be too late." She shook her head. "You know what hurts the most? It's my fault. *I* asked her to come."

"*We* did."

Cayla rolled her eyes. "She wouldn't have done anything for you. Or your brother. It's all on me."

"That's not true. Your friend could have been with us now, but she decided not to. Whether you like it or not, accept it or not, she chose Sian." There. He'd said it.

She shuddered. "Yikes. The way you say it, it sounds… She's just nice, that's all."

"She chose to be nice then. Still, it was her choice. You should respect it. And don't blame yourself. It was my idea."

She looked away. "And I agreed." Her voice was a whisper, as if the words had been said to herself.

Darian tried to come up with something to tell her, something that would make her feel better, when the communication channel blinked.

Cayla touched it and stared at Darian. "Written. Unknown sender."

"Let's see it."

Cayla read the message, "Hello, little brother. It warms my heart to know that you still care about family, at least a little." It sounded bizarre in Cayla's voice. "Unlike you, I appreciate kindness, and I want to thank you for what you did. I know you don't care, but I'm happy to tell you I'm safe, although I won't say where. Karina is also safe, back in her own world. Poison in small doses can also be medicine. Who would have thought?"

Safe. His brother was safe, alive, and no longer enchanted. Relief washed over Darian. "See? They're fine."

Cayla was still serious and looked unconvinced. "Not necessarily. How do you even know it's him?"

"Oh, that's Sian all right."

Cayla bit her lip. "I wish we could see them in person. I don't know… Karina…"

"I don't think Sian would lie about it, and we can't go back to that tower now."

Cayla shook her head. "I don't trust your brother. He could be planning something."

"He doesn't have his position in the army. He's powerless, Cayla." In a way, Darian almost pitied Sian, except that he hoped the humbling lesson would bring him to his senses.

Cayla sighed. "True. I guess it's something else then, not your brother. There's something wrong here. Something very wrong."

"I kind of noticed it, you know?"

"We'll need to go home and get help," she said.

Darian nodded.

Cayla sighed, looked away, then looked back at him. "Darian. I'm glad we saved your brother. I'm sorry I was… well, I am still worried, but—"

"I understand. But I think we can believe him when he says your friend is fine. Look, he even knew we'd be worried. It's not like I get written communication from him from time to time. As to those creatures, we'll get to the castle and figure it all out. I promise. And we could try to find another way to teleport. You'll be able to check on your friend. I'll do whatever it takes—"

"I know." She smiled.

Cayla then suddenly got up. Darian felt startled, and more surprised when she sat on his lap, wrapped her arms around him, curled and rested her face on his chest. Darian wrapped his arms around her and held her tight. They remained like that for a long time, her face near his heart.

After some time, Darian ran his hands through her hair and asked, "What is it?"

She looked up. There was a hint of fear in her eyes, unseemly in Cayla. She whispered, "Darkness is coming. I don't know what it is—but I can feel it."

Next day at the small, old hardware store near her apartment, Karina asked help from the owner. "I need the strongest flashlight you have. One that flashes."

"You want a camera flash then."

That was brilliant. Literally.

Karina walked back home feeling guilty that she'd spent more than she'd planned. At least now she had a professional flash, even though she had no camera to go with it. She knew —or hoped—she wouldn't need to use it. It was just that she wanted to make sure she slept well. She also wanted so much more. And there was that tinge of regret she had. But isn't regret the worst feeling of all? It has no solution. It just gnawed her inside. She tried to think about something nicer instead. Math final. For her it was happy. She was hoping she would finish the class with a 100% grade. That would be a first. And then perhaps all the school would gather around her and tell her how bright she was. Ha, ha, not. But it would be nice to think so. Maybe her grades in History and French were not the greatest, but she was still smart, and she could prove it.

Karina walked into her apartment and had the feeling that there was something in her bedroom. She took in some breath as if sucking courage. The flash was still in the box. There would be no time to open and charge it. But it was still day. Late afternoon perhaps. Could it be a kyon? Well, her phone had a flash. She had to do something, and maybe she should be glad that they had come to visit during the day, not at night when she was asleep. She set the camera flash on her phone, ran to the bedroom and pointed it to the thing on her bed. But the thing on her bed was just a very beautiful girl: Zoe, who was lying with her tummy down reading a book.

"What are you doing?" Zoe asked.

Karina put her phone back in her pocket and shrugged.

Zoe stared. "You're weird sometimes."

"Just sometimes. That's good to know."

Zoe laughed. "So, I want to hear it. C'mon, all the details."

Karina was glad to see her friend so excited to study. "We could start with the exponential equations. There's a trick to them."

Zoe looked at Karina as if she were seriously ill. "No. Not that. Are you crazy?"

"I thought you wanted to study."

"I never want to study, although sometimes I'll force myself to. The guy, what's his face? What happened?"

"Oh. That." Karina looked down. "I'm not sure I'll see him again."

"Don't say that. You never know."

"He lives far. And he doesn't even like me." Karina was indeed feeling sad and decided to confide as much as she could her friend. "But he invited me to travel with him, and I wish I could, for the trip, but I had to say no."

"Why?"

"I had to go yesterday, and, you know, school hasn't finished yet, my parents—"

"Karina, I thought you knew percentages. I'm wondering which one of us has trouble with math."

"What?"

Zoe widened her eyes as if stating some great discovery. "The test tomorrow, it's worth twenty percent."

"I know that. And?"

"You don't need it."

The words were like a brick in her head. But then, in theory she didn't need the grade, but no way Karina would accept a B in Math for the semester. The semester only, it wouldn't be her final grade. But there were other problems.

"Well, what about summer camp, and my parents, and—"

Karina remembered Sian saying, "excuses, excuses, excuses". She knew it wasn't how he'd said it, but still.

Zoe said, "Get everyone to believe you're somewhere else, and you're good."

"Well, thank you, Zoe; I'll make sure to turn back time and plan my trip. That was lovely advice. As if it were that easy."

"I'm just saying. I can help you and tell people you're with me. I won't insist on Josh, but maybe you could be my guest on a video. How's that?"

"Not sure about the video, but thanks. And it's too late to change my mind. I lost my ride."

There wasn't much else to say. Karina then felt a big emptiness and regret. But then, should she really regret? She knew that going to adventures in places she knew little about could be dangerous. She didn't trust Sian. And still, she regretted. For someone who wanted to drink up the world, she had just refused a bottle. But hey, she could still get an A+ in Math. That would maybe cheer her up. Maybe.

Zoe sat in silence. She probably wanted to talk about her own situation with Samy. Karina knew it was more about venting than anything, but it was important for her friend. She was about to ask something when a sound of scraping caught her attention. It seemed to be coming from under the bed.

"Was that you?" Karina asked.

"What?"

Was Karina becoming paranoid? Maybe not. She yelled, "Get up, get up, get out of the bed."

Zoe got up, frowning and staring at Karina as if wondering if she was well. Karina took the flashlight from her bedside table and pointed at under the bed. There was nothing there. Definitely paranoid. Embarrassing.

Then she heard Zoe scream. Karina got up quickly and saw many different pieces coming together and forming a shape, starting to take form right in front of her door. Karina pointed the flashlight at it and started flashing it, but the light was not very strong. Because it was day, it was barely visible. Zoe was whimpering. Karina said, "Light. You need to flash lights at its head."

The head was not very well formed. It was just a shapeless lump, but it was becoming something. Karina threw her weak flashlight and took her phone. Her fingers shook and with difficulty, she turned on the camera. It had a flash, but it wouldn't flash many times in a row. She pointed at the thing and flashed it. The lump stopped forming. For how long was anyone's guess. She considered teleporting, but even if it worked and if she escaped, she could not leave that kyon in her house with her friend and her mother. She had to think fast. Zoe was paralyzed in fear.

Karina yelled. "Take your phone, point lights at its head!"

"It doesn't have a head." Her voice was shaky and low.

"At it then."

That thing had to come back from where it'd come from. There was a way to take it back, but the idea was terrifying. The thing was taking form now and had arms and a sort of head. Karina swallowed. Zoe screamed.

Karina waited for the light on her phone and flashed at it. It stopped forming. She said, "Light. Light on it. Please."

There was no other way, though. She would need her friend's help. "Zoe, I have to go. Get on my email account. Email the summer camp, cancel it. Tell my parents I'm with you. Hope they don't want to talk to me. I'll be back."

"The password?"

What? Of course. For the email. Karina cringed. "hotkarina333 all together. No caps."

Zoe got her phone and pointed to the thing. But the light was too soft. Why hadn't Karina assembled her professional photoflash? No time to think. She flashed the phone light at the thing, threw the phone to her friend, and walked to the kyon. She had to overcome her disgust and horror and hold the part where she thought its hand should be. The thing grabbed her, and it hurt. She wanted to scream, but instead, she closed her eyes, and thought about the ruins of a janky old tower, trying to forget that there could be more of those things there, that it could be immersed in fog, and that she would have no idea how to find anyone she knew. At that moment, she was focused on saving her friend. At least if in Whyland she had more magic, she could perhaps do something better than just pointing lights at it. The thing was slimy and disgusting on her hand.

She thought about Whyland, about Cayla, Darian, Sian. Maybe there was a chance that she would find him. Nothing happened in terms of teleporting. The thing was now becoming amorphous again, and Karina felt a cold, slimy paste going up her arms. Karina had never felt so much disgust in her entire life and feared being completely covered in that thing. She hoped that the lights from teleporting would slow it down. And then she would have to figure out the rest. She had to teleport. Sian, Sian, she focused on him and pictured his smirking face clearly. The floor beneath her moved. Through her eyelids, she felt flashes of light, and the thing stopped squeezing her hand. She didn't let go of it because she feared it would stay in her apartment. Regardless, part of it enveloped her arm already. Karina squeezed her eyes shut, hoping there would be no more forms waiting for her, and that maybe she could do something against that thing in Whyland.

When Karina felt floor beneath her, she heard laughter and a voice: "You got a new friend already?"

Sian! That was a lot more than she had hoped.

7

THE TOWER

Karina opened her eyes and saw Sian laughing while he stuck a huge mace in the thing and twisted it. He was calm but focused, moving his mace in an eight shape. The thing burst into pieces, including the part that had been glued to her arm, and it was like ripping a band-aid. Karina was expecting the pieces to come together again, but they started to melt as if they had been made of ice. Karina was so thankful Sian was there to help her, she would have hugged him if she didn't fear he'd tease her.

She asked, "What are you doing here?"

He looked up nonchalant. "Don't know. Taking a stroll." He stared at her. "What does it look like I'm doing?"

"Were you…" That could not be. "Waiting for me?"

He waved his hands. "No, Karina, I was just passing by. Now, I'm not going to lie and pretend I wasn't hoping you'd jump in my arms and call me your hero. A guy can hope, right? But I was expecting at least some appreciation."

Karina was so glad to see him that she didn't mind his teasing. "Thank you. I didn't expect you'd wait for me. I'm surprised, that's all."

"It's fine. I should be guarding here so that they wouldn't come to your world. What a lousy job." He smiled. "Or maybe I had it all planned so you would come back. No, I'd never think you'd teleport with it. Well played."

"Not really. If you weren't here..." Karina didn't want to think about it.

He stepped closer and stared at her. "Maybe deep down you know me better than you think you do. You knew I was going to be here."

Karina wasn't sure of that. But she had to plan what to do next. "I can't go back. Not with these things after me. You've asked me to stay before. Does the offer still hold?"

Sian rolled his eyes. "Do you think my offers *expire*? Am I not the same person?"

Karina shrugged. "You could be upset I said no before."

"Nonsense. You were afraid, that was all. We'll sort it all out together."

Karina smiled. She liked him when he wasn't trying to tease her. Maybe they could be friends and she'd be able to trust him. "Thank you."

He smirked. "And... you're not gonna throw yourself in my arms?"

Right. There he was again. Back to square zero. But it didn't need to be like that. It was better to get things right from the start. Karina took a deep breath. "Sian." His eyes widened. She continued, "Can I ask you something?"

"You say my name like that, you can ask for the Universe. Whether I can give it to you is a whole other conversation, but ask away."

"But that's it. We'll have to work together, and we'll have to trust each other. I saw what you did for me and I trust you."

"That's a good start."

"Please, stop it."

He stepped back with a puzzled expression.

Karina had started it, now she had to continue. "This joking about... I don't know... Me throwing myself in your arms, and you pretending to flirt with me. It makes me uncomfortable."

Sian stepped back and glared at her. "*Uncomfortable.*"

Karina closed her eyes. "It's not that, it's that everything becomes a joke, and I'm afraid that at any moment you're going to mock me."

"If I'm mocking anyone, it's myself. But of course I don't want to make you *uncomfortable.*" The words would have sliced the air if it had been solid.

"But you don't. Most of the time. And I like you as a friend."

"It's my turn now. Can I ask you to stop?"

Karina shrugged. "Sure."

It was probably his fake drama or something. He couldn't be actually upset at it. She hoped he would go back to normal, not the normal with a sly comment every now and then, but just the normal Sian who'd told her what to do against kyons and who had waited for her.

"We'd better get going," he said. No smirking, teasing, or drama, which was a relief.

He was quite pleasant when he was like this. Perhaps too pleasant. Karina shivered, realizing that the weather was chilly, and she was wearing just jeans and a tank top.

"Cold?" he asked.

"A little, but it's fine."

"We'll get there soon."

They walked to the door—and stopped.

The tower was surrounded by Kyons, about a hundred of them, and it wasn't as if they were getting formed or coming off the ground. They were fully formed and looked like almost-finished clay sculptures.

Karina wanted to go back to the tower and teleport away, but the only place she could teleport was home, and she didn't want to risk a creepy army following her. The creatures stood still as if waiting.

Her voice trembled. "How polite of them to wait outside."

"Waiting for you," Sian said. "Somebody wants you really badly, Karina."

"Now what?" she whispered.

Sian was calm. "These things don't talk, so there's no negotiation. We'll have to do it the hard way."

Karina no longer felt as afraid of those things as she'd felt before. "I could surrender and see where they take me."

He grimaced. "No way. I told you if you came here I'd protect you and I don't lie—to you at least."

Neat. But the issue would be how he'd defeat them all, cause she sure wouldn't be much help. And their stillness was unsettling. "What are they waiting for?"

"Us."

"You can't fight them all, and all I can do is run. Sorry."

"They can't all go through the door at the same time." He touched his mace. "And I have this. A dark weapon for dark creatures. Stay in the tower. I'll block the door."

For a second Karina wanted to think that those kyons didn't really wish them any harm, or that they'd just stay frozen in their position, and they would sneak past them. Sian raised his mace. The creatures ran to the tower. Ran. They could run now. Karina got inside, wondering how she could help. She didn't have her phone to flash some lights, she didn't have anything.

Sian blocked the door. He swung the mace enough to slow them down, then stuck it on each kyon to make them disappear. Karina felt hopeless and vulnerable. That was probably what people felt in sleep paralysis; they saw something terrifying and couldn't move. Sure, she could move, but what use was it if she didn't have any weapon? Her life—or safety—depended solely on someone else, and it felt awful. Sian held the door well, though. Perhaps that was all it would take: some time until all the kyons tried to get in, and that strange mace destroyed them. Still, the feeling of powerlessness gnawed on Karina.

Then there was a sound all around the circular wall, and it started to shake. Through the holes, Karina saw that all around them, the creatures were climbing the outer wall. If they reached the top, they would be able to either jump or climb down because the tower had no ceiling. "They are climbing! We need to get out."

Sian glanced back, for the first time with a hint of worry. "Come. Stay close to me."

Karina wished she had a weapon, anything, at least to try to slice them the way Cayla and Darian had done. It would only slow them down, but at least it was better than nothing. Nothing. She hated doing nothing. Then she remembered. She once had made a lift explode. It hadn't been intentional, though. Blow up walls. Could she do it? Could she really do it? She didn't want to be helpless and vulnerable.

"Wait. Let more of them climb, then we get out." She was almost sure her plan was going to flop, so she added. "So there'll be less in front of us."

Sian shrugged and continued barring the door.

When she felt the creatures were almost on the top of the tower, she ran to Sian. "Let's go."

It wasn't easy to leave the tower as there were enough things on the ground to swarm after them. And it wasn't like when she'd been with Cayla and Darian, who were two people and could surround her. Karina tried to run and zigzag through them, but two of the creatures pinned her to the floor. She tried to forget what was happening, clear her mind, and imagine that tower exploding. She imagined that it had always been meant to explode, that its material was combustible, that the stones were made of dynamite. The two creatures above her broke into hundreds of pieces. The large spiked head of a humongous mace swung above her. Sian was close. Karina didn't even have time to get up, as more creatures pushed her down. She imagined the tower collapsing just like the kyons who'd been above her. There was a portal there, and she thought about home, about Zoe, her mother, and about keeping those things away from them. She closed her eyes. Nothing around her mattered, only that tower being blown into millions of pieces.

A deafening boom startled her. An explosion? Really? It was hard to believe that she'd done it. Perhaps she'd just predicted it. There were three creatures around her now, becoming liquid and sticky. They soon turned into many pieces that disappeared like ice on a hot day. Karina got up and saw stone and pieces of kyons everywhere. The tower had indeed been destroyed. Not only any tower: a millennial tower. So far her only way home. But it had been those creatures' way to her home as well. Unbelievable. There were still some ten or twenty kyons around them, and Sian got rid of them soon. To Karina's horror, though, the pieces of Kyon that had been blown with the tower were joining together again, but very slowly.

"Let's go," Sian said.

He turned around and walked towards the woods.

Karina was soon beside him. "Shouldn't we run?"

Sian shook his head. "Nah. They won't reach us."

If he said so… On the other hand, Karina had a hunch that the reason he wouldn't run was that it wouldn't look cool enough for him. Anyways, he had the magic or whatever mace, so perhaps there was no need for them to run. He seemed to be going in the direction of the lost castle, but Karina wasn't sure.

After a while, he looked at her, thoughtful. "That explosion… I…"

Interesting. He had no idea she'd done it, and she didn't want to tell him it had been her because it would sound too presumptuous. To be fair, looking back, she wasn't totally sure she'd caused the explosion. Then she thought of all the pieces of stone that had been blown around them and worried about something else.

"Did anything hit you?"

Sian shook his head. "I blocked the pieces coming towards us."

"You fought well."

She shrugged dismissively, then showed his mace. "Easy when you have the right tool. I had it all under control." He stared at her, serious. "But your way back home is gone."

"I'll figure something else." Perhaps Cayla or Lylah could help her. Hopefully.

At first, Karina was still jumpy, fearing kyons would come out from the floor, or run after them. But Sian walked and seemed so calm that she stopped worrying about the creatures, and then realized she should be worrying about her near future. "Where are we going?"

"I need to find some friends. Siphoria."

"What's that?"

"You don't know it? It's the capital, right by the Queen's castle."

"Oh." She didn't know much about Whyland. Yeah, she had a book at home, but it had only images. How was Karina supposed to know the name of any place?

"Just a four-hour flight."

Flight? They were going to fly there? Karina was ecstatic. At the same time, she was surprised that they were going so far. Last time she'd been in Whyland everything had been in a walking distance—even if a few-day walking distance—or short flight radius.

"But we have to get to my lift first," Sian said. "It's just by the Darloom castle."

"Isn't it dangerous going there?"

"There's danger everywhere."

"More Kyons?"

"They are not the only dangerous thing looming over Whyland right now."

"Are you going to tell me about it?"

"We'll figure it all out. Together."

Figure it out wasn't very reassuring. Karina shivered.

Sian looked at her. "Listen, I don't want to make you…" He rolled his eyes. "*Uncomfortable.* But I'm wearing long sleeves under my coat. You have nothing on your arms. I can lend you my coat. If it doesn't offend you."

Karina noticed his long overcoat. It looked nice. And it was true that he seemed to have warm clothes underneath it. But he was so tall. "I think it's too long. I don't want to trip on it."

He looked at it, then looked at her and sighed.

They walked a few more minutes. Karina didn't see the dreaded castle with the garden. Instead, they came to the door of a different building. It was actually a door closing a rock formation, like a cave. It had a key lock, and Karina was surprised that it didn't have anything fancier like some sort of combination or crystal. Sian had a key in his pocket and opened it. Inside, there was a white oval machine with a round part on top, something like a zeppelin would be if it had been made in one piece.

"I'm going to apologize. This is not my real lift and it's not in great shape. It was just so I wouldn't be tracked."

Karina shrugged. "So?"

Sian slid a door. The lift was very small. It had four seats in two rows and some space on the back. It was much smaller than the lifts she had seen before, which had two compartments and a large area on the back that could fit a large table and even have two beds opened on it. "It's just small."

"Not that. It's old. My lift was small as well. My personal one. I don't mean the one from the army."

That made sense. Except that a teenager having the equivalent of a private helicopter was not as normal as Karina would have expected. But then, his father had been the commander of the king's army. Maybe his family had money, or whatever the equivalent of it was in their terms. Of course, everything was different now that the king had been deposed. Sian was likely the one who cared that his lift was now old.

They entered, and he closed the door. The thing had a black panel. Sian sat down and rested his head on the panel.

"Are you all right?" Karina asked.

He put his hands on his face and rubbed it. "I didn't sleep."

If it was true that he had been watching the tower, then he hadn't had any sleep. "You must be exhausted."

"I shouldn't. I trained for it. I could go for two days without sleep."

"Did you eat anything?"

"Why? Are you hungry?"

Now that he mentioned it, yes, but it wasn't why she asked. "I'm asking for you. You can't have spent an entire day without eating or sleeping."

"I trained for it," he repeated.

"Fair enough, even if you trained, your time's up."

The issue was where they'd find food, though. She didn't think there would be a grocery store or restaurant nearby.

Sian closed his eyes as if thinking, then said, "There's a village nearby. We could go there. I'm sorry, I can't go all the way to Siphoria."

"It's fine."

He passed his hands on the panel. Red, pink, and blue lights flickered. Nothing in it suggested that it was old. The lift was made of a dark material that looked like acrylic or plastic. Okay, there was also a difference in the lights. This lift didn't have bright lights on the ceiling. In fact, it had no light at all other than what was in the panel casting a red glow over Sian's face. The lift ascended. Karina feared it would hit the ceiling, but there was no ceiling, just something soft, like fake rock made of fabric, and the lift passed through it. Karina looked outside the window and saw only dark trees. There were no lights anywhere around the area they'd been.

The lift shook a little, like turbulence on a plane.

Sian grimaced. "I told you. It's old."

"As long as it doesn't crash."

"Hopefully it won't."

And here Karina was, having destroyed her way back home, flying in the dark, with no clue what was going to happen, why those creatures were chasing her, and how exactly she'd help Sian sort it all out. Somehow, she liked it.

8

THE VILLAGE

After flying for some twenty minutes, they landed on the top of a hill, with no houses around them. Karina looked around, wondering where the village would be.

Sian observed her. "We'll walk there. I didn't want them to see we flew here. Be on your guard. And don't say my name."

"Because of your father?"

"We're in the south. Apparently, things were ugly over here, and my father was the king's commander."

Karina remembered that. "That's why they rebelled, right?"

"But that's the thing, they didn't outright rebel. The rebellion came from within the army. I think my brother had an important role in it. But it doesn't matter. The King has been deposed, my father is no longer around…"

"But you supported your father."

"I supported what I thought was right. I was mostly in Siphoria." He looked away and scoffed. "It doesn't matter anymore."

"I'm sorry."

"Why sorry? There's no loss, no failure, only learning and experience."

Karina swallowed. Right. She remembered how he was confident that he was going to conquer the kingdom, and how she'd teleported and warned the people in the castle. She shivered as she wondered whether he knew her part in his defeat. Actually, thinking about his bright, intelligent eyes, he probably knew. But Karina hadn't been a major player in that conflict.

She said, "I'm assuming it was Lylah who made a difference."

He raised an eyebrow. "It was my own ignorance of magic that made a difference."

There was an edge to his voice, Karina wasn't sure of what. She asked, "And what do you want to do after all is said and done, and the master of the Darloom castle is defeated?"

"Defeated isn't the right word. I would say putting the Darloom Castle under control. One thing at a time. We'll focus on the rest later." He pointed to a direction where there were some lights. "We're getting there."

There were some small houses made of cement or something like it, painted yellow or orange. Lamps that looked like gas lamps hung in front of the houses, most of them extinguished now, just a light here and there. There were also a few pens with chickens and vegetable gardens. They walked on a stone footpath in the middle of the village.

Karina smiled. "This is a cute village."

Sian grimaced. "It's all right, I guess. My brother was raised in a village like this but in the north."

"Weren't you raised together?"

"I grew up in the castle and the military academy."

Sian sounded jealous of his brother, which was weird if he'd been the one raised in the castle.

"Why do you dislike him?"

"Dislike him? You have the wrong impression. I've risked my life for my brother, I've lied and done even worse for my brother, and I've protected him as much as I could. Now ask him what he's done for me."

"He got me here."

"He owed me one or two. It's fair. And I'm sure he did it only because it would have looked bad if he refused to help his brother." Sian changed his tone and said, "We have to find their leader's house. It should have a star or a different symbol in the front."

Karina got the cue that he wanted to change the subject and didn't ask about his brother anymore.

There was nobody outside, and Karina didn't see any different markings on any house. Finally, a woman came walking in their direction. She had long grey hair and blue eyes and wore a long gown with a coat over it.

"Are you lost?" she asked.

Sian said, "We are looking for lodgings for the night."

The woman shook her head. "There are no hostels here."

"I can pay," Sian said. "If anyone is willing to provide a meal and two beds."

"We have no use for your money. But we do help poor travelers. Beg and I'll help you."

Karina didn't know Sian that well, but she doubted she would ever beg for anything. She started to say, "He hasn't eaten for—" but Sian spoke at the same time, "My friend needs something to—" They looked at each other.

The woman laughed. "I like you. You're my guests for dinner. Come."

They sat at a wooden table on a kitchen surrounded by wooden cupboards. The old woman, Faria, worked on the stove. She had lent Karina a colorful knitted shawl. Sian said his name was Jojo, and Karina had to contain her laughter. She said her name was Zoe.

Faria sat down. "We're far from all cities in Whyland. Where were you going?"

"Traveling." Sian shrugged. "Beautiful scenery and stuff."

Faria laughed. "Not lost? Fool yourself as much as you want."

Karina noticed the woman had very light blue eyes, like a blind person, but she had shown them the way and was cooking like someone who saw well. She also looked at their direction when speaking.

Sian said, "As long as I'm getting somewhere, I can't be lost, can I?"

Faria shook her head. "Sometimes it's better not to go anywhere than to go on the wrong direction."

Karina disagreed. "But then you're not going to know it's wrong. You need the experience."

Faria laughed. "Oh, do you, now? You can't know?"

The woman's stare was uncomfortable, but Karina held hers. "Not always."

The woman laughed again, got up, poured a thick soup on three bowls, and set them on the table.

Sian pushed his bowl. "I don't need it, I'm not hungry."

Karina glared at him, but he didn't seem to notice.

Faria sat down. "Oh, you are going to quench your hunger with pride? And the girl will think you're rude. Do you want to be rude?"

Sian glanced at Karina, then answered, "I didn't mean that. I'm sorry. I appreciate your kindness."

Karina tried a spoon. It barely had any taste, and the thing sort of stuck on her throat, with a rubbery feel. She wasn't sure she would be able to eat it. She took another spoon and felt that although the taste wasn't great, it was filling. Actually, as she ate, it started to taste good. It filled something inside her that was not yearning for food, but she didn't know what it was. Sian ate slowly, as someone who was not hungry, but his spoon hand was trembling. He must have been starving. Stupid pride. But he accepted a second serving.

The woman then served them tea. It was sweet, but not sugary, it was more as if it was made of some herb that had a sweet taste. As they sat, Faria showed the paintings of a young man and a young woman on the wall.

"Boy, look at them," she said. "Aren't they beautiful?"

Sian looked. "Are they your kids?"

"They were," she replied.

"I'm sorry," he said.

Faria stared at Sian. "Are you now? Do you know who killed them?"

Sian put his tea on the table and sat back. His body was relaxed, but his eyes were alert. "I don't, but if you want to talk about it, I'll be happy to hear it."

The woman had a bitter laugh. "You'll close your eyes and ears and ignore what doesn't suit you. My kids, my babies, were murdered under General Keen's orders." She stared at Sian. "Now, I can't have my children back, but I could kill one of his children."

Sian listened and didn't move. The woman knew who he was. Karina feared that she would attack him, but he didn't seem afraid and just sat back.

Faria stared at Sian, "I could, and it would be easy. That would feed my revenge, my hate. I would think it would satisfy me, but it wouldn't. Hate doesn't solve anyone's problems."

"I appreciate it," Sian said. He didn't sound sarcastic or bitter, just honest. "You do realize I didn't choose my parents, don't you? And I didn't choose to be raised by my father. But I'm really sorry for what has happened to your family. I am."

"You show potential, boy, use it right. That's all I ask." She turned to Karina. "You, girl, you have a kind heart. Trust it."

Karina dropped her spoon. Being addressed out of the blue like that had startled her.

Faria continued, "I'm assuming you won't accept my offer for beds, after what I said."

Sian shrugged. "I wouldn't have a problem with that. Now that you made it clear you don't plan on killing me, I can lie down in peace with the certainty that I won't be murdered in my sleep." Again he sounded honest, almost sweet.

Faria shook her head. "I won't. But I can't guarantee somebody else in this village won't try. I suggest you go away from here and find another place to sleep. A few minutes flight will take you far enough. The soup will give you strength."

Sian got up. "Thank you for your kindness." He seemed sincere.

Faria laughed. "Come here, Sian, I need to tell you something."

Sian approached without any fear. Karina almost held him back, afraid that the woman would do something to him, even though she had kind eyes and seemed willing to help.

The woman whispered something on his ear. Sian glanced at Karina, surprised, then he shook his head and glared at the woman. "Thank you," he said. "We're leaving."

Faria said, "But I had something to tell her."

Sian stepped in front of Karina and extended his arms as if protecting her. "You're not telling her anything." He turned to Karina. "Let's go."

Karina was curious and met his eyes. "I want to hear it."

His face was a mixture of pain and pleading. "Please don't."

There was something about his voice, pleasant and almost soothing and she had trouble contradicting him.

"Fine, let's go," Karina said.

The woman had watched their interaction with a strange smile. Maybe it was indeed better not to hear whatever she wanted to say. As they left, Faria winked at Karina.

∾

As they walked back to the lift, Karina was curious and finally asked, "What did she say?"

Sian shrugged. "It was personal."

"You looked at me. I thought—"

"The world obviously revolves around you."

Karina didn't think that. What bothered her most is that she would have to die not knowing what the woman had said, and she hated not knowing something.

Sian looked at her and smiled. "One day I'll tell you."

His smile was actually sweet, and Karina had to remind herself that he hadn't woken up when she kissed him. There was nothing there. Karina looked down. "I was afraid. Faria seemed nice, but—"

"She just wanted to brag about how nice she was that she wasn't going to kill me. Maybe that gave her some consolation."

"You shouldn't have to answer for your father's crimes."

Sian took a deep breath and looked away. "Ruthless and violent." He snorted. "I was his right hand, though. But it shouldn't matter, should it? Now that he's gone. And yet it does."

"What do you mean gone?"

"Pride. He would rather die than be defeated."

Karina looked down. "I'm sorry."

"It was his choice."

Sian was proud as well, though. A fear crossed Karina's mind. "You're not like that, are you?"

"I don't think I've ever used violence if I could do otherwise. So I think I'm different from my father. Or I hope. But yes, I'm proud. The difference is that for me there is no failure, only strategic retreat. People go on and on about how to attack, when in fact knowing when to retreat is more important." He stared straight at her. "I never lose."

There was something fiery and fierce in those eyes, and something alarming in what he'd said. Red flags came out in

Karina's mind, but she wasn't sure what exactly they were signaling. It was just another reminder that she shouldn't fall for his charm—as if he had any. But at least he'd stopped with all the silly jokes about Karina jumping into his arms or ripping out his heart. She just hoped he wouldn't rip hers.

Sian was entering a dark cave, with damp walls. He asked her to follow him, but she was afraid of going inside, so he went in without her. Karina was left alone in a dark forest at night, her body trembling in fear. A light appeared in the distance.

It was Faria, with a lantern. "What are you doing here?"

"He left me," Karina said. "I refuse to go there. But now I'm here, and…" She was going to say that it was dangerous, but the forest had grown calm.

"Don't you understand? You should have asked him to stay."

"He stays if he wants to. It's not my job to ask."

"So you're proud as well? I guess that explains it."

"Explains what? What?" Karina asked. But she wasn't in a forest, and she wasn't near Faria. She was sitting in a very uncomfortable seat in an old flying craft in a parallel dimension, covered only by a colorful shawl. She looked out the window and noticed they were flying. There wasn't much to see, as it was night.

Sian turned back from one of the front seats. "What what?"

"Just a dream. Why are we flying?"

He laughed. "Was I in your dream? I would hope I'd hear something nicer."

Karina just stared.

He closed his eyes and shook his head fast as if waking himself up. "Right. Uncomfortable. Is it worse than sleeping on these seats? Or is it double uncomfortable? For me, it's just that I'm still tired and forgot to turn on the filter between head and mouth. Having to overthink everything I say is also uncomfort-able, you see?"

"Don't assume I'm dreaming about you, and you won't have to turn on any filter."

"I'm not assuming. I'm talking from experience."

Oh, the nerve. "Cause every girl dreams about you? How can you even know that?"

He frowned. "That's not at all what I said. Hey, I'll go back to my best behavior. Wasn't I nice last night?"

Karina smiled. "You were."

"And that's how you want me to behave around you?"

"I just—I don't want to fear that at any moment you'll turn around and say something flirty."

"Oh, no. That would be disgusting, wouldn't it?"

"Not disgusting. Just—"

"Forget it," he said as he raised his hands. "But thanks for the reminder."

She didn't like to see him upset, but at the same time, it was his own fault for being so dramatic, almost as if he wanted to make her feel bad for not wanting to be teased. The worst was that she had been indeed dreaming about him. But that was normal, wasn't it? She had spent time with him right before falling asleep. Faria was also in her dream, and that didn't mean she was in love with her.

9

SIPHORIA

Karina looked out the window. The moon illuminated some mountains far away. "You decided not to sleep?"

He kept looking ahead. "We're almost in Siphoria. I wasn't that tired."

Karina remembered vaguely getting back to the lift and passing out on the back seat. She must have slept just a couple hours, woken by her dream. This lift was different from the ones she'd seen before, because it had a lever and some switches, whereas the other lifts Karina had seen had just a panel, and the controlling was done by moving the hands over it. So many things to understand, and so many to ask. She moved to the front seat. Sian was sitting back, one hand on his lap, the other fiddling with his hair. He turned to her and smiled. A smile, not a smirk.

Karina tensed. "How does it fly?" The question popped out of her mouth.

"Hydrogen in the top container."

Yikes. "But that's highly flammable."

He considered. "Not if it's sealed tight, though. It's enveloped in many thick layers. Even if a lift caught fire, it wouldn't touch it unless it burned for hours."

Hours? Karina had seen one of those explode before, after being on fire for just a few minutes, and although she'd been told she had caused the explosion, now she started to question if she could really have that much power. She also questioned that tower exploding, but it wasn't a good idea to think about explosions while on a flying craft because she didn't want to accidentally cause one. She turned her thoughts elsewhere. "How does it move?"

"Propeller on the back."

"Oh." The technology in Whyland wasn't that different after all. "We have gas balloons," Karina said. "In my, uh, dimension. But the top is much bigger."

Sian considered for a moment. "Your balloons then must depend solely on the gas to stay afloat. We have propellers that help with the lift. It's not just the gas—if that's what you mean."

That made sense. A little different, but it made sense. Funny how he answered her questions so easily. That combustible top came back to her mind, and she almost asked how exactly it was involved in so many layers, but then again, it was better not to think about anything flammable while in the air. Karina looked out the window.

They approached what looked like a silver ribbon on the ground, which was a river reflecting the moonlight.

"Is that the Silver River?"

"Yes."

"Are all your names that literal?"

Sian laughed. "Maybe. One day they were descriptions, right? Before they were names."

Soon lights came out in the distance, in that glittery or Christmas light look cities had when seen from the air, stretching as long as the eyes could see, but only on one side of the river. They descended among those lights and came to a small landing pad where there were two other small lifts. They looked worse than Sian's, very old and patched up. There were none of the sleek army lifts Karina had seen before. Sian asked Karina to wait inside while he went out. He spoke to a man in his fifties who seemed to know him well. Sian got back and opened the door.

"Let's go."

Karina stepped down. She didn't have a purse or a backpack. The only thing she carried was the shawl wrapped around her, as the weather was still a bit cool. They walked by the riverbank towards the city.

Sian said, "I'll find some of my friends there." Sian looked away then looked back. "Listen, I don't think you've ever met people like them before." He stared at her. "Don't be afraid. And try not to judge them. You don't know their stories."

That was unfair. "I don't judge people."

He smirked. "That's certainly for the best."

Like with everything when you see it for the first time, Siphoria wasn't like she'd imagined it. It was artificially lit on the ground, by what looked like lamps beneath glass blocks, but it wasn't glass. There were no cars, horses, or any other moving vehicles other than some rails, and she wondered if streetcars ran on them. Even though it was the middle of the night, the streets weren't deserted. There were people on the street including some in the blue army uniforms here and there. Karina figured they also performed police duties. The houses were close together, near the streets, painted in bright colors. Most buildings were two or three stories high, but some had up to five floors. Karina noticed a young boy in a side street looking at them attentively, then looking away. Further down, she saw someone on a roof.

"Are we being watched or is it just an impression?"

Sian laughed. "Both. It's a correct impression."

"At this time at night?"

"That's when you keep watch."

He didn't seem too worried, so she didn't worry either. They came to an old house and went down a narrow staircase leading to a door. Sian was about to knock on it when the door opened to reveal a slender woman in her 60s, greying dark hair tied into a bun.

The woman opened her arms as if for a hug, looked at Sian, and said, "Aw, if it isn't the light of my life."

Sian grinned but didn't hug her.

The woman relaxed her arms and didn't seem upset. She glanced at Karina, then said, "Come in."

They were indoors in what looked like a deposit, with wooden and metal boxes, then they went to what looked like a large restaurant, with many tables, but empty.

The woman turned to Sian. "How dare you disappear for so long? No news, nothing."

"I sent some news," Sian protested.

"That you were alive. How precise." She looked at Karina. "And who is she?"

"This is Karina. Karina, this is Malena."

Malena looked at Karina, at Sian, then back to Karina. She pinched Karina's cheeks. "Oh, you're so adooooorable!"

That was a first. Not even Karina's grandma had ever done that to her. Karina tried to keep a neutral face and a smile.

Sian said, "Listen, we'll need rooms for tonight. And I'll meet some friends in the evening."

"Rooms? In the plural? You can't leave a girl like her alone in a place like this."

Karina didn't like where this story was going. But it was Sian who protested, "I can't—"

"Don't you worry." Malena winked at Sian. "I get you." She looked at Karina, "It's for safety only, dear. Please, I'm not suggesting you... I'll show you your room."

Thank goodness she didn't finish her sentence. They went

up a flight of wooden stairs and walked through a dark corridor. Malena opened a door to a small room with a bunk bed. Karina sighed in relief. Indeed she wouldn't want to be alone in a room in a place she didn't know, especially when she wasn't sure if some creepy creature would be coming after her.

Malena left the room and Karina was left with Sian.

He said, "She's right, actually. It's not a good idea for you to be alone."

"I know. And I'm tired."

"Yeah, we should rest."

As odd as it was, Karina had never slept on a bunk bed. "Can I go on top?"

He smiled, not his usual smug smile, but a silly, happy, stunned smile. "Whenever you like."

Someone knocked on the door.

Malena's voice came through it. "Have you eaten yet?"

Sian jumped to the door and opened it. "I thought you'd never ask."

They went back to that empty restaurant. Malena brought them something that looked like a vegetable pie. Karina was hungrier than she had realized, and the food tasted great. They later ate some kinds of cake and fruit and drank juice. That was the best meal she'd had in Whyland, and that was a lot, considering she had eaten in the castle before, with Cayla. Sian didn't have any problem eating and didn't refuse anything. He also seemed to be really hungry.

They went up to the bedroom, Karina climbed to her bed and lay down. It was uncomfortable because she didn't have any pajamas or comfortable clothes, so she lay with her jeans and tank top on.

The reality that she was in fact in another dimension, about to spend some time there, dawned on her. Perhaps she hadn't had the time to stop and consider anything while running from kyons or leaving a strange village. Here, lying down and about to sleep, her reality hit her. Below her, a guy she barely knew. Well, she had met him before—when he'd taken Cayla hostage. Not a great moment, granted. He had also been planning on attacking his own brother and taking the kingdom by force. But he ended up not attacking anyone, so maybe he wasn't so bad? It was better not to think too much.

Karina woke up and the room was bright with light coming from the ceiling. It looked like a semi-translucent ceiling from where come from, but it was just the way a lot of the illumination in Whyland worked. Still, it probably meant that it was already day. She went down the bunk bed. Sian was not there. It was good in a way because she needed a bit of privacy. There was no bathroom in the room, so she went to the hallway. There should be a bathroom there, but there were so many doors, how would she find it? Well, in theory, the door would need to be different, and maybe, hopefully, there would be two doors, one for women and one for men. Karina found four doors that looked a little thinner, at the end of the hallway. She tried one. It was locked. She tried another, and it was open. And yes, that was a bathroom, with a hole in the ground, a sink, and a bathtub.

When she was washing her hands, she heard, "Karina, Karina!" Sian was calling her.

She opened the door. "I'm here."

He exhaled as if relieved. "Don't disappear like that, or you'll kill me."

Odd. Or maybe not. That was exaggerated, dramatic Sian. A tall girl with dark skin and long blond hair in a braid was beside him. She wore pants and a jacket in some kind of leather and looked fierce and menacing, the neat kind of fierce look Karina sometimes wished she had.

Karina shrugged, "Well, I…" she pointed to the bathroom.

He nodded. "Sure. Listen, this is Alessa. She's a friend, and she's here to protect you."

There was something not so pleasant about it as if Karina was going to be watched or looked after as if she were a child. "Do I need protection here?"

Alessa smiled at Karina and extended her hand. "He said you're new in these parts. I can show you lots of things."

They shook hands. The girl had a strong, firm grip and a warm smile. Karina was ready to like her.

Sian raised his hands. "Good? I'll leave you two together. I have a few things to do." He turned around and left.

Karina thought he was a bit cold and distant, and figured it was because he was in front of his friend. Or maybe she had imagined something that was just not there. Perhaps she'd thought that his talk of protecting her was an excuse for something else. But now that he had simply assigned someone else to look after her, she realized it was really about protecting her. Well, duh. Anyways, at least she didn't have to feel bad that she'd asked him to stop acting flirty.

Karina was watching him walk through the hallway and disappear on the stairs when she noticed Alessa's eyes on her.

"You're close, then?" The girl asked.

"I barely know him." That was true.

The girls went to the bedroom. Alessa had brought clothes for Karina. No pajamas, alas. But then, she wasn't sleepy anymore. There were no dresses, probably because of the cold. Karina tried a pair of pants. They were too tight.

Alessa looked at her. "I went by his description, and I think I got it wrong."

"How did he describe me?"

"Cute and sweet."

Was the girl was teasing her? Testing her? Karina laughed.

"Well, no wonder you got the wrong size then, that says nothing about my body."

Alessa also laughed. "Lucky you. No, he said you were a little smaller than the princess. I guess that was my bad. I don't really know what she looks like. I got you my sister's clothes. I'll get you some of mine, so you'll blend in better. Let's go."

"Where?"

"My house. It's a short walk from here."

Walking in the city sounded fun. Karina got up and wrapped herself in the shawl.

Alessa frowned. "Oh. You'll freak out some people with that thing you have." She must have been referring to the shawl. Alessa took something from her bag. "Here. It's ugly, but at least you won't stand out."

It was a sort of a grey cloak, but not really grey, rather it looked like it used to be black but was now faded.

Alessa pointed to the shawl. "This is typical from the southern villagers, and some people used to think they are magic, but there's another problem. You were wearing that when you came with Sian. Many people know him. I am trained and I'm a good fighter, but I'd rather not cause a ruckus. Someone could want to attack his girl."

"I'm not—"

"I know. But they don't."

Karina sighed. Ugly faded black cloak it was then.

As it was day, she could see more of the city, and it was brighter and more colorful than she'd realized at night. Karina had been right, and the rails were indeed for streetcars, but not like old streetcars Karina had seen in pictures, as the ones in Siphoria had rather a sleeker design and were silver. The ground on the streets looked like cement, but then maybe it was just something similar.

After some twenty or thirty minutes, when Karina started wondering what the girl's definition of short walk was, they stopped in front of a red house that didn't look different from many others. Alessa opened a door leading to an indoor garden. There, she went to a stone wall, opened a door that hadn't seemed to be there before, and they descended two flights of stairs. Alessa's house was large, without windows, but with light coming from a bright ceiling. It had a huge middle area with seats and tables, and doors leading to other rooms.

They entered Alessa's room which had a walk-in closet. The girl pulled some clothes and spread on a sofa. Zoe back home would freak out if she knew Karina was letting someone else do a makeover on her. Karina looked at the options, then finally found brown pants, a green shirt, and a brown jacket.

"How do I look?" Karina asked.

Alessa smiled. "You'll blend right in."

"But… Do I look good?"

The girl laughed. "I don't think you need to worry about impressing anyone."

Was she implying not only that Karina wanted to impress Sian but also that it was useless? Karina snapped, "I don't dress for other people, it's for me."

Alessa shrugged. "Then your opinion should be enough."

No kidding.

Alessa must have noticed Karina's expression. "Did I say something wrong?"

Karina was going to leave it, but she decided to be honest. "You said I was trying to impress someone. Sian is the only someone I know here. I mean, if you think I'm trying to impress him—"

"I didn't mean that. I meant the exact opposite. I'm sorry. If you want my opinion, you do look lovely, but that doesn't depend on how you dress."

"I'm pretty sure I don't look lovely in that grey cloak you lent me."

"Lovely is quite relative, isn't it?"

Karina laughed. No point being upset about something silly. Alessa laughed as well.

Alessa then took Karina to a shop after insisting and saying it was part of her job. Karina didn't argue much because she did need some changes of clothes, especially underwear and socks. The clothes were for display in a long corridor with a counter at the end where a lady brought the right size. The socks were wool or something similar, but thin, and the panties were made of something like cotton, and shaped like shorts, but tight. The one bra she got was like a sports bra, and she also got a pair of soft pants and a shirt for sleeping. That was nice. But then a young woman came and measured Karina, which was a bit over the top.

"Is this necessary?"

Alessa shrugged. "It'll fit better. I always get mine custom, with little pockets for the things I carry."

Bizarre. "Your underwear?"

Alessa laughed. "My pants and jacket. You don't want to wear the same thing for days, do you?"

"I guess."

"Then pick a couple outfits."

Karina shrugged. "It doesn't matter." Fashion blind in her own dimension, Karina would hardly be any better here. "You can pick for me." The girl was actually quite stylish. "Whatever you'd wear."

Alessa shrugged. "As you wish."

That said, all Karina carried back was a parcel with the pajamas and underwear. Alessa was still quiet, and Karina tried to make some conversation, "Were you in the army as well?"

The girl widened her eyes as if the question had been outrageous. "Me? No."

"I thought… Cause you know how to fight, and you know Sian and all."

"I'm a hired—" She paused. "Bodyguard. It pays to protect people."

"So that's what you're doing with me?"

"I thought it was obvious."

A little, maybe. "So you're not his friend; he hired you."

"A bit of both, let's say."

"What do you think about him?"

"I'm not supposed to think anything, only keep you safe."

Karina sighed. She was hoping she would get some clue on how much she could trust Sian.

Alessa said, "I'll tell you what. I'm among the best. If he chose me to protect you, it says something, doesn't it?"

"I guess."

Sure, it said something, but what? Karina didn't insist because she didn't want to keep asking questions. Perhaps she should be wondering why she was in this city, following a girl she didn't know, on a plan she wasn't sure about, for a guy who lived in another dimension and didn't even like her.

When they got back to Karina's room, Alessa kept her company all the time, even when Karina took a bath. That explained why Sian had chosen a girl for the job. Alessa was for the most part quiet, almost as if afraid to say something wrong. Maybe they wouldn't be friends. They ate downstairs, at that place where Karina had eaten at night. It was indeed a restaurant. This time, the food was weird rice and some chicken and vegetables, not anything like what she'd had in the morning.

Later, Alessa taught Karina a board game that was similar to chess because it had pieces with different movements, but the board was round, and there were only four different types of pieces, three of each. They were called hearts, powers, minds, and matters. The movements didn't match the names much, as hearts were the most powerful pieces. As Alessa explained it,

Karina noticed that she could use the same technique she did with chess, which was to visualize her movements and her opponents', and base her actions on outcomes her adversary wouldn't predict. It worked; Karina won her second match. And her third. She started to think Alessa was a very poor player. On the fourth match, as Karina was winning again, the girl puffed and stared.

"Are you sure you'd never played this before?"

"I've played chess, but it's different."

Alessa looked down, and mumbled, "Maybe not that much."

They continued playing. Alessa's pieces were all cornered, and it was just a matter of time for Karina to win. This was getting predictable. And Sian, where was he? The sun was setting, and he was nowhere to be found. Karina wanted to ask Alessa, but she was afraid that the girl would tell him about it, and what conclusions he'd come to.

After a while, Karina got really anxious, afraid that something had happened to him, so she decided to ask, "Any idea where Sian might be?"

Alessa stared attentively at her board. "I think he's in his bedroom."

That was it? He just left her with a random girl in order to spend time alone? And he got another bedroom for himself? Karina was disappointed, but she should have known better. "Oh. Okay then."

"Do you want to talk to him?"

"No, I'm fine."

"He told me to call him if you needed him."

Karina shrugged. "I don't need him."

Alessa chuckled. "You sure don't." Her tone didn't sound sarcastic. She continued, "Listen, do you want to go down to the Junction? People are coming. It's going to be fun." She sounded excited for the first time.

"Is it a party?"

"Well, sort of. It's a party every night."

"Can I go? Isn't it dangerous?"

Alessa winked. "I'm with you. There's no danger. And if you hadn't been allowed to go, I'd refused the job."

A party! Not only any party, but a party in Whyland. That sounded fun and exciting.

10

THE JUNCTION

Alessa led them downstairs to that restaurant, but it was mostly empty. Karina feared that the party would be there, but thankfully no, as Alessa opened a metal door leading to a tunnel with what looked like grey concrete walls. Light came from a row of candelabra on one side. They were not wax candles, but metal sticks with an orange light on top. The tunnel led to a huge empty hall with wide circular columns. Because it was so huge and empty, for a moment Karina feared that she was being led to a trap, but Alessa seemed trustworthy. Well, Sian trusted her. And why did Karina trust Sian again? Maybe because he'd have no reason to keep her as a hostage or anything.

They entered a narrower tunnel, leading to a room with some tables where a few people played hearts and matters. The room led to a balcony, facing a huge u-shaped hall encircled by seven levels of balconies with tables. There were curtains on the back of the hall, covering what Karina assumed would be a stage. A few people occupied tables here and there.

Alessa seemed to notice that Karina was looking around.

"It's still early," she said. "But that way we can get a good table. You know you can order whatever you want, right?"

"I don't know the drinks here. I guess… Some juice?"

"Juice?" Alessa sounded underwhelmed.

"Maybe a really good one?"

"No alcohol?"

Karina laughed. It was funny to realize that people in other dimensions also drank. Well, to be fair they had a lot of similar food, similar furniture, similar clothes. Maybe they were not so far apart, or maybe those things were common in human societies. Anyway, she was in a strange place where she didn't know anyone, so she wouldn't want to drink even if she were older. "No. But you can have it."

Alessa sighed. "I'm working, remember?"

Karina winked and tapped her shoulder. "We can be boring together."

Alessa laughed. The girl got a big jar with a sweet, colorful drink. It had stripes with colors, like some liquids that don't mix with each other. They poured it on the glasses. Karina stirred the drink and watched the colors dance, mix, form shapes, then slowly go back to their stripes. But there was no oil. Karina thought that maybe there were different densities of food coloring or something. It was silly and childish, but fun.

People started coming in. Very few women wore pants. They had different styles of dresses, from long and puffy to tight and short skirts. Men wore pants and tunics like the ones from the army, but in different colors, some wore more elaborate suits. A guy wore a long black skirt. That was neat. Without makeup, in clothes that would have looked fierce on Alessa, Karina felt a bit odd. The girl was at ease, though.

Down in the hall, a band started to play. They had six musicians playing string instruments, which looked like harps, but varied from high to low frequencies. One of them was used for percussion. The music sounded messy or confusing at first, like some very improvisational jazz, but after a few seconds, Karina got used to it, and it sounded pleasing, dreamy, and almost hypnotic. There were groups of people dancing in front of the band with large, erratic movements, looking so free, daring, and bold. Alessa looked down at the people and their movement, eyes wide, as if eager to join them.

"You can go there," Karina said.

Alessa jerked her head. "Wanna come?"

Karina laughed. "No way." It was neat watching the people dance, but Karina herself wasn't a dancer even in her own dimension and would be too shy for those bold moves.

Alessa shrugged. "Then we stay."

Karina looked around, wondering about something else. "Any chance Sian might come here?"

Alessa smiled. Karina didn't like what the girl implied with that smile. Karina was just eager to see her friend. It was normal. She would do the same with Zoe back home. Right?

The girl said, "He'll definitely come—unless he's in the secret area."

So there was a secret area to which Karina wasn't invited. Awesome. She looked down. "I see."

"Oh, no, there's no fun there. If he's there, it's boring meetings. No girls there either. Sure, there might be girls, but friends, you know? I mean, he wouldn't—"

"Alessa, I'm just asking about Sian cause he's my only friend here. This is the second time you're implying something that's just not true. I don't even know what you're going to tell him."

"Oh, don't worry, I won't say that your eyes light up whenever I mention his name."

Karina felt her face getting hot. "Cause he's my friend. I agreed to accompany him, not a bodyguard. He never said, 'come to Whyland, I'll leave you with a random girl while I go partying on my own.'"

Alessa shook her head. "No, no. That's what I meant. The

secret rooms are not for partying, they're for meetings. If he's there, it's for boring business." She sat back and looked at Karina. "So you're not from here. I thought you dressed too weird. Where are you from?"

"I don't think I'm supposed to answer that." Not because it was some big secret, but because it was weird, and mostly because Karina was annoyed.

"Sure. And I'm not supposed to ask. It's just..." She got close to Karina and whispered in her ear. "Are you from Arlenia?"

"I don't know what that is."

"It's a neighboring kingdom. I've heard they might attack us. I thought maybe you were a princess or something. I know Sian is up to something, but I don't know what."

"There might be a war soon and people are partying?"

"One more reason to party harder. But really, not everyone knows how serious the situation is. They think it's a threat, but I know better."

"And what does this have to do with Sian?"

Alessa again whispered in her ear, "Apparently nothing, if you're not from there."

Okay, now Karina was curious, and she had information to bargain. "Do you want to know where I'm from? I can tell you everything you want if you tell me what you know."

"No. Sian might be able to hear us."

"You sound almost as if you are afraid of him."

Alessa stared at Karina as if offended. "Not afraid. But that doesn't mean I'd cross him for no reason."

"He hasn't been around for a while, has he?"

"A few months. Some people thought he was dead. But there he is, alive."

Karina looked up.

Alessa said, "I said it as an expression."

"Oh."

Alessa sighed. "I was kidding about telling you everything. I was just curious about where you were from, but it's none of my business." She looked down for a while, then turned to Karina. "Wanna play?"

"Maybe. What do I get if I do?"

Alessa had a half smile and nodded. "Let's do this: if you win, I'll answer whatever you want."

Karina scoffed. "Easy. And if I lose?"

"I'll think about it."

"That's not fair."

Alessa was already getting up. "Didn't you say it was easy? I'd much rather you won anyway."

They went to that other room with the hearts and matters tables. Alessa whispered on some people's ears. The girl was up to something, and only then Karina realized she wasn't going to play against Alessa. Karina was placed in front of a lady with a bob cut hairstyle and lace gloves.

Alessa watched them from a distance. In fact, quite a few people stood around them. It didn't matter. Karina focused only on the pieces and the board. Facing a new adversary was a challenge in any game, just because it's harder to understand their style and their plan. A good strategy was always to let them win the first match, then use the knowledge for the following ones. But Karina didn't have that advantage now. She had to focus on what was happening right there and then. And right there, the woman made a fatal mistake. Yes, she'd only see it ten moves later, but the mistake was made. Indeed, a few moments later, Karina won. That game really wasn't difficult. The woman looked as if she'd eaten something rotten. Alessa grinned. People stared at Karina with wide eyes.

Karina smiled and leaned back. "Who's next?"

A good-looking guy with blue eyes and black hair sat at the table, but Alessa pulled Karina. "We'd better go back to the main room."

"What's wrong?" Karina whispered.

"Nothing. But we want to go back, right?"

That was weird, but the girl was weird anyway. She got the impression that Alessa didn't want Karina to play against that guy.

They sat back at the table. The band had stopped playing. Karina stared at her juice while she figured what question to ask, and how to ask it without giving a wrong impression. When she looked up, she saw Alessa staring downstairs to a corner where a girl was talking to a man. They seemed to be arguing.

"Do you know them?" Karina asked.

"That's my sister. And her ex." The tension was clear in her voice.

"You want to go talk to her?"

Alessa sighed. "I'm supposed to be with you."

"I could go with you."

"Maybe."

Karina watched as the man pulled Alessa's sister through a door. He didn't seem aggressive or anything. What worried Karina was the panicked look on Alessa's face.

Karina got up. "We can follow them."

Alessa said, "I will. Stay here. I'll be right back."

Karina sat back down. There was something commanding and powerful in Alessa, and there was something dangerous to whatever was happening to her sister. In less than six seconds Alessa was downstairs, rushing through the same door from which her sister had left. Karina hoped everything would be fine while she stared at her juice. She was thinking she'd like something to eat, but she didn't know how to order or what to order. At this point, Karina could smell the alcohol coming from other tables. Downstairs, a multitude of people she had never seen, dressed in different styles.

A male voice startled her. "You don't belong here."

Karina looked back and saw the guy with dark blue eyes and black hair who'd wanted to play against her before.

Karina smiled. "I'm not a table or a bottle, so I definitely don't."

He laughed. "Can I sit?"

"My friend—" He had already sat on Alessa's place. Why ask, then? "Did anybody send you or something?"

He tilted his head. "No. But I didn't want to leave you sitting on your own."

Okay. Confession time. The guy was really good looking. Had Karina not been worried about other things she would think this was her lucky day. But she was thinking about Alessa and wondering where Sian was. She just wasn't in the mood for that kind of talk at that moment.

"Aliamos, but you can call me Liam," he said.

"I'm Karina."

At this moment, on the corner of her eye, she caught someone downstairs looking at her. Sian. When she turned, he was no longer there. Maybe she'd imagined him.

"You're distracted," Liam said.

"I'm looking for my friend."

"I can be your friend. Is this your first time in Siphoria?"

"Not really." That was sort of true.

"Even if you've been here before, I could show you around if you want. There are always new things to see." He moved his eyes down and up, back to her eyes. "And do."

Karina just shrugged. "Thank you."

He smiled. "That's a yes then?"

Of course not. She'd said it just to be polite. "No. I'm leaving soon."

Karina looked to her left side. She was sure she'd seen Sian, this time on the floor she was. Or else she was imagining things. In that multitude of people, it was easy to get confused.

"I'm sorry then," he said. "You're still distracted. Is it someone else you're waiting for?"

Perhaps he could help her. Why hadn't she considered this before? "Do you know Sian?"

The color left the young man's face. "You mean Sian Keen? The former general's son?"

Karina didn't like to remember whose son he was, but it was true. The guy's reaction was weird, though. "Yes."

His eyes widened. "You." He looked away. "I'm sorry," he said as he got up. "I thought you were someone else. My apologies."

The guy left. This place and these people were getting weirder by the minute. The odd juice should have tipped her off. She stirred it and watched its forms, wondering what was happening to Alessa, and if her sister was all right. She also thought Sian was the rudest person on Earth, assuming they were on Earth, for leaving her alone for hours, considering he was the only person she knew there. Perhaps she should return to her room, but she doubted she'd even know the way back. Plus, she would be alone, and that was what she wasn't supposed to do.

The chair beside her moved. She looked up, thinking it was Liam again. It was Sian. As annoyed as she was at him, she couldn't help but smile.

11

LIGHTS

Sian was smirking, as usual. "Enjoying your company?"

"Of course not. You left me alone."

The smirk was gone. He looked around. "Where's Alessa?"

"She had something. Her sister. Please don't be upset at her. I'm sure she'll be right back."

"Wow, what has she been telling you? Did she tip you off on the torture chamber for subordinates who disrespect me?"

"No, but she seemed concerned."

"She was probably concerned about you because I told her you were in danger. That's all. But I'm here."

"And you left me all day. That's rude."

He leaned forward, towards Karina. "Did you miss me?" He didn't sound sarcastic, smug, or playful. If anything, he sounded slightly surprised.

"Cause you're the only person I know!"

He chuckled. "Alessa's a person too, you know?" His voice then became soft again. "I just... I had things to do. Also, I didn't want to make you uncomfortable." He said this word with none of his previous sarcasm and bite.

"You don't." She met his eyes and had to look quickly away. She then smiled and added, "Most of the time."

He scoffed and leaned back. "I see."

Karina didn't want him to lean back and become distant again, but she didn't want him to look at her the way he had just looked. It was much worse than when he was being playful and joking about being interested in her.

She decided to change the subject. "You said you'd explain magic to me if I came. I've been here for almost a day and I haven't heard a word."

He looked around. "Here?"

"Fine, maybe not the best place. Tell me about your lights then. It's something I've always wanted to know. Not the ones here, but the really bright ones that look like daylight, how do they work?"

Sian looked up, thought for a moment, then said, "Come, I'll show you."

Karina followed him as he went to a hallway then upstairs to more empty hallways. Sian was wearing all black this time but had some fancier lace in the rim of his long coat and shirt. Of course, unlike her, he was dressed for the occasion. He opened a door, which led to a ladder. He climbed, and she followed. They came to the roof of the building. It was flat and had some silver spheres. From where she was, she could see some of the city and lights shining in the distance. "It's beautiful."

"Is it? I'm used to flying above here." He pointed to what looked like a high-rise building, with lights coming from its windows. "And I grew up there, in the military tower. But now that you say it, I'll never see it the same way."

The city was indeed much bigger than Karina had first imagined. Streets had a yellowish glow, coming from the ground. A tower by the river, empty, with no lights, caught her attention.

Karina pointed to it. "What's that place?"

"It's an older observatory. To watch the river. It's been abandoned for years, though. The army now does it all from the military tower. Come," he walked to one of those spheres. "See this? It captures the light and multiplies it inside it."

Karina was interested. "How?"

"It's a special crystal. It doesn't let the light fade. They reflect on each other and keep reflecting so that the light is always circulating. Then underneath the roof, there are many of these crystals reflecting the light, over a semi-transparent or transparent surface. It has to be big because the light is not concentrated. Not all places have it like that. The Darloom castle, for instance, which is older, is different. And here, they don't use it at the Junction, only at the upper floors."

Karina was surprised that he knew that, and that somehow it was something that interested him enough to explain to her.

"But how can it work at night?"

"It keeps the light reflecting. But also all of these spheres usually have a light-absorbing mineral. It then releases it slowly."

"Wouldn't it be easier to just have a lamp?"

"It depends. You need to burn something for the lamp, right? These spheres don't use any fuel."

He might have been meaning gas lamps, but it was true that electric lamps also used energy. And there was something else. "And how do these lights turn on and off?"

"There's another surface underneath, and it closes and opens. I know that in the castle, in the bedrooms, it closes when there's no movement."

That made a lot of sense. Still, crystals, continuing light, there was something different about it. "Isn't there some magic to it?"

"Some people would consider it so. I disagree."

"Why?"

He sat on a raised part near the edge of the roof, hair flowing with the wind. "Come. Sit." His eyes were bright with enthusiasm. "That's the greatest secret, and few people know it: the nature of magic."

Long lashes lined his bright brown eyes. As Karina sat beside him, for the first time she realized that Sian actually looked, uh… kind of good. Actually, way more than good. She must have been blind or crazy before. But she was too curious about magic for his looks to distract her. "And what is it?"

"Do you know what the difference between science and magic is?"

"People say magic is science we don't understand."

"Yes, yes. It can be. That's what a lot of people say. Magic has an aspect of unknown, things that can't be quite quantified or understood, and that's where the confusion comes from. I myself had no idea about it until a year ago. No idea." He looked away.

"Are you gonna tell me or not?"

He looked at her. "I am telling you. Cause you'll understand. With science, it can be replicated. It depends on the physical world, on nature, it doesn't depend on human interference. Magic needs the human element. It's unique, it's individual, and, for the most part, it can't be copied by another person, unless they have the same magic. It needs feeling, it needs the human touch."

Karina tried to picture how it would apply to lights or teleporting, and the idea was still quite vague. "Can you give me an example?"

"Science is like a recipe. A cake recipe. Certain ingredients react a certain way. Any person can do it."

"But is that true? Some people," she remembered her grandma, "they can do it in a way other people can't."

He nodded and raised his eyebrows. "And why do you think that is?"

She thought for a moment. Was that what he meant? "Magic?"

He smiled. "That's the principle of it. Once you know how to recognize it, you'll see it everywhere. It's that something special some people have. And even these people, they don't have it all the time."

Karina looked around, thinking that there was magic all over that city she saw, in the little things. But there was more than that. "And what about, I don't know, casting lights, teleporting from where you aren't supposed to, making lifts explode?"

"It's the same, but it's directed in a way that alters our physical reality. That's what most people would call magic; practices that seem to go against how we believe the world should behave. Still, the essence of it is the human feeling. It needs a person who has the feeling behind it. And yes, there's innate talent, and there's study. It's like music. Some people are born with the gift, but they'd need to study to get really good at it."

"But anyone can play a musical instrument. If they dedicate themselves, of course." It wasn't Karina's case, unfortunately.

"Anyone can play a musical instrument if they study. Not everyone can write a good song. That's the difference. Magic is composing a moving song, or else playing an instrument in a way that's unique, moving. The difference seems subtle, but once you think about it, it isn't."

Karina thought of songs or performances that sent shivers down her spine or movies that resonated with her for a long time after they had been seen. She even thought about Zoe and her beauty, how it had something unique, special, something quite unquantifiable about it. "There's magic everywhere then."

"There is. But it's not everywhere that you'll see magic that alters the physical reality. So that's the thing. Also remember that for most people, that's what they'll call magic. Like the previous king," he looked down, "and my father, when they forbade magic, they didn't forbid anyone to make great food, or to speak in a way that's uniquely inspiring, or anything like that. They looked at the study and practice of magic in terms of seeing through time and space, levitating things, altering the physical world. That's what they meant. But you need to understand the principle. So many people study the effects but don't understand the cause."

"And you learned this only last year?"

"Yes. There's a special library at the Darloom castle. I read as much as I could."

"And why did you want to learn about that?"

"To understand the world. To understand what happened. There's no loss, no failure, only experience. But it'll be useless if you don't learn with it. I learned, or at least I think so."

He smiled but he spoke with a soft voice. He was sure of himself, but he had none of the smugness of before. Sitting there with him, the rest of the world seemed to have disappeared. Karina didn't know if it was the night, the soft lights, or what, but at that moment she thought he was the best-looking guy she'd ever seen.

"And do you have any magic?" she asked.

Sian looked down and shook his head. "I haven't figured that out yet."

He became silent, and she didn't know what to say either. Their eyes met. At that moment, something clicked inside her. It was so scary she had to look away. There was no point telling herself he wasn't trustworthy or that he wasn't good looking—which was completely ridiculous. It hit her like a brick in the head; she was in love with Sian. Gasping for air, as if she were drowning in an ocean of newfound feelings, she looked at the city around them with its horizon of lights and a dark tower by the river.

"Are you disappointed?" he asked.

Karina was startled. "What?"

"That I don't have any magic."

That was a weird conclusion. "Why would I be disappointed? I don't have magic either." Her voice was shaky.

He laughed. "What do you call your teleporting from impossible places?"

"Oh. That. It's not something I do in my normal life, in my world, so I didn't count it."

"You must have something that is manifested in your world. You just haven't recognized it yet."

"Maybe you do, too. Not that it matters."

He sighed. "I guess for you it doesn't matter."

"What do you mean?"

Her eyes met his. There was something open, vulnerable, real, in them.

"Karina, I have a question for you." Her heart sped up, unsure if it felt dread, eagerness, or curiosity. He rose to his feet. "Do you want to know what Faria told me?"

That was it? Karina got up and laughed a shaky, nervous laugh. "Of course. Is that your question?"

He closed his eyes and took a deep breath. "Sort of." He then opened his eyes and looked at the city. "She told me you already love me." He turned to her. "Is that true?"

Karina felt as if the floor below her had disappeared, but that wasn't teleporting. With no idea why he was asking that, she didn't know how to answer. She feared that she had shown too much of her feelings, and feared, feared… She didn't even know what. And he was standing up, at a distance from her, as if… Her mouth opened, but no sound came. She had no idea what to say.

He looked sideways and scoffed. "No need to answer. I got it."

Was he making fun of her now? Karina's heart raced, but it was anger. "I'm sure she meant as a friend. That must be it. You can't think—"

"Well, she is blind."

"She's not blind. She cooked for us."

"Didn't you see her eyes? She must know her house well,

that's all." He then smiled again, and spoke in a normal tone of voice, as if nothing different or important had just happened. "Let's go downstairs, we have to plan for tomorrow."

Karina sat. She wanted to stay there, or rather, she wanted to dig a hole and hide. She wanted to turn back time and not have gone to the roof with him. Now she wanted to purge away all the feelings she'd felt just a while ago. Sian was stuck-up, ugly, and annoying, and Karina must have been hallucinating a few minutes before. And still, it hurt, and made it difficult for her to breathe. Oh, that's what she got for not following her own advice. She knew she shouldn't have fallen in love. She knew it. But she was smart and would fall out of it. She would remain in Whyland only long enough until everything with the Darloom castle was figured out. After that, she would be gone, leaving Sian and the painful memories behind.

Sian crouched in front of her. "Karina, I know I upset you. I'm sorry. But don't stay here on your own. You're still in danger."

Karina realized she had been frozen in her seat, shaking. Her mouth tasted something bitter. But then, she would be mortified if he guessed how bad she felt.

She smiled. "I was just looking at the city."

"We can come back another time." He smirked. "As friends, of course."

Perhaps it was true that blood could boil.

Sian continued, "But let's go and plan our trip. Tomorrow we have to go to the castle and that's when things will start to get tough."

Right. For him perhaps. Karina realized that facing Kyons was better than being in love with someone who didn't feel the same and have the humiliation of having the fact thrown in her face. But then, it was Karina's fault for being silly and reading too much into people. Either way, she wouldn't show she was upset. She wouldn't.

Karina smiled and got up. "I'm ready. Let's plan."

They went down the stairs to the upper hall where Karina had sat before. A blonde girl with long and very bushy hair saw Sian and came running towards him.

"If it isn't my sunshine!" She then frowned. "That disappeared for a long time."

He looked down. "Just some clouds. I was always here." He pointed to Karina. "This is Karina."

"Hello, I'm Raja," the girl said as she looked at Karina up and down.

"Hey," Karina replied.

The girl turned to Sian. "Don't tell me you're replacing me."

Sian took the girl's arm, pulled her to a corner, and whispered something in her ear. The girl looked at Karina, then back at him, smiled and punched him playfully on the stomach. Karina could feel her heart beating in anger, and wondered if it was noticeable that there was smoke coming out of her head. What was he doing? Telling the girl that Karina liked him? Were they making fun of her? If Karina could, she would scream and run, but she was too proud for that. She preferred to act cool and pretend nothing was happening. Maybe he would think he'd come to the wrong conclusion on the roof. Karina hated that roof, hated Sian, and hated being there.

Raja smiled at Sian and went in another direction. Sian approached Karina. "Sorry for that."

Karina had her most natural, uninterested voice. "For what?"

"No matter." They descended the stairs to the main hall and approached a table where a young couple was sitting. "This is Joel," Sian said as he pointed to the boy, who had blue eyes and blond hair. The girl next to him was very pretty and had short dark hair and brown eyes. "This is Aline."

Karina waved and smiled. "I'm Karina."

Sian sat, and Karina did the same.

Liam approached their table and addressed Sian. "Hey." He pretended not to notice Karina.

Sian put his arm around Karina's chair. What was he doing? He said, "Liam, we'll need to talk." He then gestured for him to come closer and whispered in his ear.

There was something captivating about the way Sian leaned forward. His hair fell sideways revealing smooth skin and neck. Against her better judgment, Karina couldn't avoid staring, and couldn't shut that little part of her that wished Sian would lean over and be that close to her. Terrible call. Sian turned and caught her eye. His lip curled in what seemed to be disgust. Karina wasn't completely sure, as she looked away as fast as she could. She caught a satisfied smirk in Liam's face before looking down to her juice.

"Sounds good," Liam said.

The boy left. At Karina's table, they ordered dinner. Karina had no idea what to order, so she just said she'd have whatever everyone else was having. While Aline and Joel decided what to eat, Karina saw Alessa in the distance. The girl made eye contact with Karina, nodded in acknowledgment, then her posture and shoulders relaxed. Her sister was with her. Karina felt relieved as well. Alessa winked and left. That meant Karina was left without a bodyguard. She felt a little sad because at that moment she would rather be with Alessa than with Sian because he never even talked to her or looked in her direction— not that she looked at his.

A waitress came with their food. Karina's was some sort of wrap with vegetables and meat inside. But it was weird, as much as had been hungry an hour before, she now felt as if there was a knot in her stomach preventing anything from getting in. She forced some of the food, just not to be rude, but ate very little. Sian ate in silence. After they finished, some people came by their table. Sian was all smiles and smooth talking. Sometimes he got up and had engaging conversations. Karina was careful and only caught him from the corner of her eye. He was boisterous, confident, charming. He knew how to be polite alright, just not to Karina. She ended up staring at her juice a lot. Too many faces looked at her with curious and inquisitive looks, as if she were the brand new animal in a zoo.

Sian sat down, after an engaging conversation with an old lady. Karina wanted to make it clear that she wasn't romantically interested in him, so she said, "Raja is pretty. Why isn't she sitting with you?"

Sian snorted. "Half the Junction is pretty. That doesn't mean they'll sit with me." He paused for a couple seconds, then shrugged. "If you want to know where she is, I have no idea."

"I thought you two were together," Karina said with the most neutral and even cheerful voice she could muster.

He grimaced. "No. She's a good friend, though."

Karina was thinking about what to reply when a sound distracted her. Joel and Aline were making out. That was so awkward.

Karina turned to Sian. "Don't we have to get up early? I wanted to rest." She wasn't really tired, but she didn't want to stay there.

Sian nodded, still avoiding looking at her. "It's a good idea. I'll find Raja. She'll share the bedroom with you. For safety."

"Raja? I thought Alessa—"

"It's just sleeping. Raja can do it."

Karina and Raja got to the bedroom.

Raja sat on the lower bed, looking disgruntled. "Are you sure you don't want to go back there? We could dance. You don't have to sit with those boring people. You can't be tired."

"You weren't chased by faceless forms. I was. I want to go to that castle, get it all settled, and go home." Karina held the ladder to go up to her top bunk.

"What about Sian?" Raja asked.

Karina tried to sound casual. "What about him?"

"You know what I mean."

"I don't."

Raja smiled. "You're gonna tell me you don't think he's cute?"

"Didn't notice."

"Fine, then."

Karina went up to her bed, lay down and closed her eyes. At least she had comfortable clothes but that was her only comfort. Alone at night, lying down, it was as if everything had been magnified. She'd been so stupid, falling for Sian. All she hoped now was to solve the problem with the Darloom castle soon and then go home. On the other hand, a part of her didn't want to leave Whyland. She liked to spend time with Sian, and she thought that maybe, maybe, if they spent more time together...

A voice in her head said, "Out of all the girls in the Junction, he sat with you." Then another voice replied, "Cause he had to, silly." Awesome inner arguments. She had to make that hopeful voice shut up because it was what had gotten her in trouble in the first place. She remembered his quick look of horror or disgust as she watched him whispering in his friend's ear. Humiliating. What she really wanted was to wash away her feelings, turn back time, and think of Sian only as the slightly annoying and not very good-looking mischievous brother of her friend's boyfriend. But then, when she stopped to think about it, was there a time when she hadn't been, at least a little, interested in him? Ugh. She'd been fascinated with him from the moment she first saw him. She'd told herself he was weird. Weird were her feelings. And now she'd have to deal with them.

12

NIGHTMARE

Karina was walking in a dark cave until she came to a bifurcation with many different tunnels, and she felt lost. She then heard two voices calling her: Cayla's and Sian's. They came from different tunnels. Karina had to choose and decided to go in Sian's direction. Cayla's voice faded. Sian was sitting on a throne. Below him, horrid creatures, similar to Kyons, but with wings like bat wings, and with real, red eyes. She wanted to turn around and run, but she was afraid. Sian got up and walked to her direction.

He held her hands. "I'm here. Don't be afraid."

Even in that place, among those horrid creatures, she felt safe. But his hands started to get slimy like the Kyon's. His eyes became entirely black, and some yellow goo started to seep from his skin, which was becoming rough and grey. Karina tried to pull her hands, but she couldn't. She screamed.

Karina sat up—and hit her head on the ceiling. She was in the hostel bedroom, on the top bunk bed. The room was dark. It had been just a bad dream but it felt so real she could almost still feel the slime on her hands and arms sending unpleasant chills through her body. The door of the bedroom burst open.

Sian was there. It was almost as if her dream was becoming real. She screamed again. He dashed up to her bed.

"What's happening?"

She looked at his face, and it was his normal face, and it was him, not some creature in a dream, and still, she was trembling.

He looked around. "Where is it?"

Karina finally was able to speak. "It's nothing. It was a dream. Sorry."

He closed his eyes and exhaled slowly. "You screamed when I walked in."

"The door burst open. I just—"

He looked down, seeming almost apologetic. "How was I supposed to come in?"

Karina sighed. "It's my fault. I shouldn't have screamed in the first place."

"Not your fault. You were dreaming."

Raja's voice came from the bottom bed. "What's going on?"

Sian looked down at the bottom bed. "Great job, Raja. One thing I ask you to do and you can't—"

"Maybe you should be glad I let you play the hero," Raja said.

"We'll talk later," he said. He then addressed Karina. "I bet you won't be able to sleep now, will you?"

Karina was still feeling a little scared of him, but she shook her head.

"Come," he said. "I'll get you some tea. You'll feel better."

The prospect of following him down to a dark kitchen, only the two of them, seemed terrifying because she still had the impression he would turn into a monster at any minute—or worse, make her feel stupid for having a crush on him. But then, it was true that she wouldn't be able to sleep.

Karina got up and followed him. He wore loose pants and a tunic in what looked like unbleached cotton. That looked comfortable and was a nice contrast to his dark hair. *Stop looking, Karina.*

~

Karina leaned on the counter while Sian worked on the stove. There was no fire, just a flat surface where he put what looked like a kettle with water. He then took it out and put in a metallic recipient with some herbs in it. It smelled relaxing, almost like lavender, and still, it wasn't quite lavender, but just something similar. He then poured two cups and they sat. Karina's hands were shaking.

"Could you maybe describe it?" he asked.

"What?"

"The dream. Sometimes it could have a meaning."

All Karina could remember was Sian's face turning horrible and scary. "No. It was just… pointless stuff, some monsters." She laughed. "You'll think I'm a little girl." Then she rolled her eyes. "Not that it matters."

He looked at her with concern. "What kind of monster?"

You. But she'd rather not say it. First, because she would never, not even under torture, confess that she'd dreamed about him. Second, because he would probably feel hurt, even though she hadn't scripted her dream. She decided to tell just part of it. "They were, sort of like the kyons, but they had wings like gargoyles, or bats, or dragons."

"I know bats, not the other things you said. But it makes sense you'd dream about that, after all you went through." He looked at her. "I'm here. Don't be afraid."

Shivers went up Karina's spine. He'd spoken just like in the dream. He reached out his hand and touched her shoulder. Karina shuddered, and he pulled his hand.

"Sorry," Karina said.

He closed her eyes and shook his head. "No need to say that."

"Thanks," she said. "For the tea."

He scoffed while still looking away. "It's all my fault anyways. I'm not doing you any favors."

There was an uncomfortable silence. Maybe Karina had to be more logical and stop wanting to go wherever he was. She had to.

"Sian, maybe I could stay in Siphoria. I could go to the castle and talk to Cayla. I'll need to find a way back home, you know."

He looked at her, looked away, then sighed. "I already apologized."

Ugh, bringing that up again. "No, it has nothing to do with… It's just that maybe it's not a good idea for me to go where kyons want to find me." How odd that only now she came to this brilliant conclusion. "And I'll need to go home."

He nodded, still looking away. "Of course." He turned to her. "You do know that the flowing tower in the Queen's Castle no longer works, right?"

She stared at the cup in her hand. "Yes, but…"

"There's a flowing tower in the Darloom castle." He stared at her with attention as if examining her or something. "I mean, sort of. But it's a portal. And… if we want to take control of that castle you'll need to be there. You'll be safe. I promise."

"What if you get turned to stone?"

"Those things don't happen twice, Karina. I'm ready and I'm prepared this time." He smirked, and it was a relief to see him getting back to normal. "Plus, you're my secret weapon."

Karina laughed.

Raja came downstairs. "Am I interrupting something?"

Sian got up. "You came right on time. I'll call the others and we'll leave."

Raja frowned. "It's the middle of the night."

"I'm up, Karina's up. We'll eat and leave."

Raja sat down and put her feet on the table. "Fine."

Sian pushed her feet. "Manners. Look who you're in front of. And we eat at this table."

Raja put her feet down but crossed her arms and rolled her eyes.

"Do you want to stay in Siphoria?" Sian asked Raja. "I'll get Alessa. I don't need you."

"It's fine," Karina said. "Leave her. I also put my feet on the table sometimes. And she didn't have to wake up just because I had a bad dream."

Both Sian and Raja gave her odd looks. Not even Karina understood why she was defending the girl, except that she had always thought that girls should stick together. Sian nodded and went upstairs.

Raja looked at Karina intently. "You knew he'd listen."

Karina just gave the girl a puzzled look.

Raja rolled her eyes. "You knew he'd listen to you, not to me."

"Cause he was angry at you." Karina wasn't sure what the girl was implying.

Raja had a half smirk. "Maybe. Thanks anyway. But you should be shooting dirty looks at me."

Bizarre logic. "Why would I do that?"

Raja sighed. "I'm trying to figure out why you don't do that."

"Okay, then." Karina looked at the girl. "You don't like me."

"I don't like your entitled attitude, that's all."

That was new, but Karina wasn't about to argue. "Thanks for being honest—I guess."

Raja had a smile that seemed genuine. "No problem. I am here to be honest any time you want."

"Awesome."

Karina smiled, even though she didn't feel like doing it. There was still some tea in Karina's cup. It was cold, but she sipped it. She didn't understand Raja and didn't think that asking would be helpful. Was Raja interested in Sian? Was the girl jealous? Karina wished she had Zoe or Cayla to talk to and bounce some ideas. But then, on a second thought, Cayla was quite clueless, and Zoe would just repeat something she'd read. Karina couldn't complain, as she never had any decent love advice to anyone other than smiling and nodding. Maybe she'd need to find a mirror and smile and nod to herself.

Karina was left alone for some minutes and got dressed. There were a couple knocks on the door. She opened to Sian, who was fully dressed but for once wasn't wearing a long overcoat, just a black shirt over brown pants.

"Feeling better now?" he asked.

"Sure."

"Good. There's breakfast downstairs."

She'd just had tea, but food would also be good. "Awesome."

"There's something I need to ask you. Joel and Aline, they're my friends. I trust them, and they're coming with us. Still, don't mention the kyons."

"Won't they notice when those things come out of the ground and chase them?"

Sian blinked slowly and said, "They won't."

"Those are the most oblivious friends anyone can have."

Sian had a nice, warm laugh. "I mean the Kyons. They won't chase any of us."

Hang on. What was he saying? "That doesn't make sense. Wasn't I in danger?"

"Kyons are the least of the danger, Karina. There's something happening with the Darloom castle and we have to settle it. That much my friends know. They don't know what has happened before, and they don't need to."

Fair enough. But then, maybe not. Karina looked at him. "That's not honest."

He waved a hand. "Pointless details, Karina. Let's not get bogged down in pointless details."

"How can you be so sure the Kyons won't come back?"

"When they do, we'll be prepared. I know what I'm doing."

"That's great because I have no clue exactly what you're doing. Do you plan on telling me?"

"I'm telling you. Of course, there's more to understand. That's one more reason you need to come with me. Some things we'll need to figure out together. Some things you'll need to see."

Karina was indeed curious to understand why those creatures had followed her, and hoped to get some answers. She had another question, "And if your friends want to know where I'm from?"

He raised an eyebrow. "Do you think they'll grasp it?"

Karina shrugged. "No idea. They're not my friends."

"*I* barely grasp it. But don't worry about it, they won't ask you anything."

"Did you give them orders or something?"

Sian stared at her for a while, then said, "No, they're my friends, and they respect my privacy, that's all."

Karina scoffed. "*Your* privacy."

"Yes, Karina, that's my privacy." He turned to leave. "Get a jacket. It will be chilly down there."

Karina went downstairs, found Aline and Joel at a table, and joined them. Raja also joined them some minutes later.

Through an open door, Karina saw Malena talking to Sian in a different room. She straightened the collar of a long wool overcoat he wore and looked him up and down as if to check if his clothes were all right. Karina wondered if Malena was a sort of mother figure to him, and to what extent she was responsible for Sian's sense of style, which perhaps wasn't as much vanity as Karina had thought. Raja finished quickly and got up to talk to Malena. She hugged the woman really tight.

Sian came in. "Ready?" he asked them all.

"What about Liam?" Joel asked.

"Change of plans," Sian replied. His voice was dry.

Malena came in and sat by Karina, addressing her. "Little one, I haven't forgotten you." Karina caught Sian's attentive eyes on her. The woman continued, "I don't have any gift for you just now, but you'll have to promise to stop by when you can."

Karina was about to say that she wasn't sure if she'd ever return, but she decided not to mention it. "I will. Thanks."

The women held her hands and looked in her eyes. "So young. But you have power. Remember that. Remember. You hold the power."

"I will," Karina replied, uncertain.

Malena laughed. "You have no clue what I'm talking about, do you?" Karina was about to reply something, but Malena tapped gently on Karina's face. "No matter. You'll learn."

Karina was wondering how much the woman knew when she heard Raja's voice saying, "Mom, you're going to freak her out."

Malena snorted. "I doubt it." She turned to Karina. "You're passed that stage, aren't you?"

Karina nodded but didn't laugh. Mom? Malena was Raja's mother? What did that mean? Karina didn't want to feel jealous because that was stupid, but she felt something knotting inside her.

They left the hostel and walked in the semi-empty streets of Siphoria. The sun was rising, painting the dark blue sky in streaks of orange, pink and purple, then light blue. Karina wore a jacket but she still felt cold in the early morning weather. They walked in silence, apart from Raja's yawns. A few blocks from the hostel, two more people joined them; a couple in their mid-twenties with light brown hair. They greeted Sian politely.

"Are we all flying in my lift?" Aline asked.

Sian shook his head. "I'll take mine."

Joel laughed. "Do you mean yours? Or that junk?"

Sian smirked. "If I fly it, it's no longer junk. My real lift is still detained." He made a sad face. "Poor thing." He turned to Aline. "Untraceable, right?"

"Of course. It used to belong to the—"

"I know," Sian interrupted. "I was just double checking."

Aline looked guilty as if she'd been about to say something she shouldn't.

They reached the landing pad where Sian's lift was.

"Ours is not here," Aline said. "We'll meet you in the south."

Joel asked Sian, "Are you going alone?"

That question had gotten Karina by surprise, as for some reason she'd been sure she'd fly back south with Sian, just as she'd come.

Sian glanced at Karina then at Joel. "Maybe." He turned to Karina. "Their lift is nicer."

The message was clear. Karina nodded. "I'll go with them." She turned to Aline. "If it's all right."

Aline glanced at Sian, then shrugged and opened her arms. "It fits everyone!"

There was something odd about the way she'd replied, as if she weren't happy about it. But now Karina didn't want to suggest going with Sian.

Aline looked at Karina with a warmer smile. "We're happy to have you."

"See you all later," Sian said as he turned and opened the metal gate to the pad.

For a second, Karina wanted to run after him and ask him if she could fly with him. On a pathetic scale, what would that be? 110 out of 100? *Get a grip, Karina.* They walked away from the pad.

Raja said, "Wait. Nobody's coming with Sian?"

"It's not a long flight," Joel replied. "One pilot's enough."

Raja rolled her eyes. "I'm not talking about piloting." She turned around and ran to the metal gate.

Great. Now another girl was doing exactly what Karina wished she'd done. Even if Sian had said they had nothing to do with each other, Karina couldn't forget the image of Malena hugging affectionately them both, she couldn't forget that Raja was a pretty girl, and she started trembling just forcing herself not to picture what could happen between these two alone for four hours. Was that jealousy? Ugly, nasty feeling indeed. Karina hated the way she felt. She almost wanted to turn back time and go with Sian, humiliation and all, just not to leave him and another girl alone for four hours.

A hand touched her shoulder. Aline. "You can go with him too. There's room."

Karina asked as nonchalantly as she could, "Why would I do that?"

13

TRAVEL

Sian sat down and stared at the panel in front of him. He could feel a small trace of fear creeping up in his body. Fear itself was a symptom. He had to focus and remember that there were millions of different ways to carry out a plan.

The door opened. He focused on not showing any reaction. It was Raja. A good thing he'd prepared himself.

"Cut it off, Sian. You don't need to pretend to me."

He laughed. "Oh, I'm pretending. That's new."

Raja stared at him. "You know what you look like? A cat whose fur has been washed down. It's all wet, meager, and sad, when it's usually, you know, fluffy and fabulous."

"I'm fluffy?" Sian leaned back on his chair. "What can I do? It won't look fabulous if it isn't washed from time to time, will it?"

Raja stared at him. "Just spit it out. What's wrong?"

"Everything is perfect, Raja, or at least as perfect as it can be."

She raised an eyebrow. "We'll have a long time to talk, and you're going to talk."

Being pestered all the way to the south. Just what he needed.

∼

Okay, Aline's lift was something else. It wasn't tiny like Sian's current lift, but it wasn't big with an empty center or with weapons on the sides like the lifts from the army. This one had more inner divisions, with some parts with comfortable couches and seats, and, in the middle, what looked like a fancy living room with white couches and a central table. The only comparison Karina could make would be to a private jet, not that she'd ever been in one, but from pictures she'd seen. The lift had also a huge luggage area underneath it. Karina only had a small bag, and she kept it with her.

The couple who had joined them latest were going to be the keepers of the castle. Their names were Georgia and Matheo, and they pushed some boxes to the luggage area.

Aline turned to Karina. "Hey, come with me."

She opened a door, but it was only the cockpit. That same smooth panel with no lights. Joel stepped in as well. He gave Aline a short kiss, then said, "I'll try to sleep a little. I want to be alert when we get there. Call me if you need me."

"I will," Aline replied. Joel left and closed the door. Aline turned to Karina. "Do you know how to pilot these?"

"I haven't flown much." That was kind of true.

"I know. It's all army, army, army, as if flying was made for war. It's so much more! I'll show you a little, though." She took Karina's left hand, pressed it on the panel, then pressed her hand beside it. Lights went up. She touched a couple with her right hand, and a light went on beneath Karina's.

Aline smiled. "Now you're authorized."

"I'd probably crash it or something."

Aline shrugged. "I wouldn't let you do it on your own."

"Aren't you afraid I could steal it?"

Aline had a puzzled expression. "You're Sian's friend. I doubt you're an idiot."

This was good. Karina wanted to know more about him, and it was lucky that the girl had started the topic. "Does being his friend prevent stupidity?

Aline looked up as if thinking. "Now that you say it. I don't know." She laughed. "Sometimes… Joel… I want to strangle him. Not that I'd do it. No. It's just. Yeah, you can definitely be Sian's friend and be an idiot. At least sometimes. But that doesn't mean you're going to steal from one of the most powerful, uh, merchants, in this continent."

"So you're a merchant?"

"My parents. I guess I'll become one. Perhaps I'm already one. I don't know. Getting entangled in more than just business, I think. I do like flying, and flying incognito more than anything. High risk, high rewards."

"That's nice."

Karina realized that the girl or her parents were probably involved in some shady business, but she didn't want to comment on that or ask any indelicate question. It turned out that asking wasn't needed. Aline was so talkative that she started to explain how their parents started their business by bringing some kind of plant from across the ocean. Karina wondered if it was the Atlantic Ocean and if their geography was comparable to Earth's. She'd need a world map. Sian could probably get her one. The thought somehow filled Karina with sadness because she imagined he'd be happy to discuss a world map with her, and somehow it hurt Karina that it would be as friends or acquaintances or whatever and nothing more.

Aline continued talking about avoiding paying taxes, bringing forbidden items, escaping the army. She thought it was funny. Well, it sounded very exciting, even if illegal.

After the girl had talked and talked, Karina risked a question, "Does Joel know all that?"

Aline had a puzzled expression on her face. "Well, I mean…" She narrowed her eyes. "How long have you known Sian?"

Oh, great. Karina hoped the girl wouldn't inquire much or expect her to also tell the story of her life. "A little over a year."

"Oh. Right. I've never seen you. But it's fine. It's fine. I'm not going to ask anything."

Aline shook her head. She was obviously dying to know more about Karina.

Well, a little bit of truth couldn't hurt. "I come from far away, and I didn't see him in the last year. I don't know him that well, to be honest. Maybe you could tell me about him?"

Aline looked straight ahead. "Yeah, well, I mean, what's there to know, right? Do you want to get Joel? I'm getting a little tired. Also, I think Georgia and Matheo might have some snacks."

And with that, Karina was kicked out of the cockpit. Not literally kicked out, but strongly encouraged to go to the back, which she did. She called Joel and sat down at the table where there was indeed some kind of finger food.

They landed about an hour later. Karina took her bag and descended the back ramp. The weather was chilly and humid and reminded Karina of when she'd come with Cayla and Darian, and that she hadn't worn any jacket at the time. This time she was dressed for the weather but she still felt a chill in her stomach. Sian and Raja were already there, waiting for them. Sian no longer wore his green coat and had a long black hooded overcoat instead. He watched as everyone disembarked.

The area around them was a well-tended green lawn surrounded by trees. As they crossed the trees Karina saw a valley and something that filled her with dread; the black square building on a hill above a beautiful garden. Being among a group of people eased her dread—at least a little. Sian's idea to assemble a team made a lot of sense. They were in the opposite direction from which she'd come with Cayla and Darian, on the other side of the castle.

As they walked, Karina's feelings started to change, as she realized she was a little excited at the thought of visiting and staying in a strange, mysterious place, of which they'd learn the secrets. Perhaps it was indeed as Aline had said; high risks, high rewards.

The castle was a rectangular building with smooth black walls that looked like ceramic. Up close, it was a lot bigger than what Karina had imagined, and even though it was wider than tall, it was as tall as an eight or ten-storey building. The entrance to the castle was a little underwhelming, though. It was a small door the same black color in a corner, barely visible. Sian had a key and opened it. They all entered a dark corridor. Everyone had some kind of light, except Karina, of course, but she was near Aline. At the end of the corridor, they came to a gigantic hall.

If the exterior of the castle was simple and plain, it was a stark contrast to the interior. The hall was tall, with golden columns, and a golden staircase leading to the upper floors, which had balconies overlooking the hall. The ceiling had a colorful painting with too many details to be registered all at once. There was a sun, a moon, some scenes of war, a couple, something that looked like farmers, and more. Not very clear from such a distance, which defeated the purpose of a painting on the ceiling. But hey, Karina was no artist or interior decorator. The floor was white and sparkly. A black, huge, rough stone stood in the middle of the hall.

Sian said, "Follow me."

They went up the stairs, and then up the stairs again, to the third floor, and came to a row of doors, which were bedrooms.

Sian pointed to the first one. "This is for me." He pointed to the door next to it. "This is for Raja and Karina". Then the next one, "Aline and Joel", and the next one, "Georgia and Matheo". He turned to them all. "We have to wait until they prepare our rooms."

Georgia and Matheo nodded and turned to descend the stairs, probably to pick up the stuff they'd brought.

"I'll help them," Aline said, and turned to follow them.

Joel held her hand. "Wait."

Aline slapped his hand. "I want to help, I'm going to help." She descended the stairs and joined the couple. Joel looked down.

Yeah, it would be nice to help, except that nobody else was helping and Karina thought that it would be sexist if only girls helped. Or maybe she was lazy.

Sian said, "We can wait downstairs. There's a nice sitting room."

They went to the second floor, not downstairs, really downstairs, as Karina had imagined. There was a huge room with windows overlooking the valley. That was weird since no windows were seen from the outside. The place had some couches on one corner, as well as some harp-looking instruments. The opposite side had furniture covered with dark sheets.

Sian was beside her. "We're going to clean it all up, don't worry." He turned to everyone and spoke more loudly. "The main rule here at Darloom is: don't go anywhere alone. Anywhere."

It made sense. Oh, wait, it didn't. Karina asked Sian, "Why are you sleeping alone then?"

Sian looked at her and paused as if examining her. "You're curious. Not worried, right?"

Both actually, but she wasn't going to say it. "It's just contradictory, that's all."

"I know the castle, Karina."

She whispered, "Really well. Especially the garden, since you spent so long there."

He smirked. "I don't plan to sleep outdoors."

"Awesome. And if you don't come out of your room, how long can we wait until we figure you're dead or something?"

"Just knock. I'll answer. The rooms are safe." He stared at

her. "Come. I have something to show you. I was going to wait, but…" He turned to Joel and Raja. "We'll be right back. Don't split up."

Sian led Karina up the stairs, to the fourth floor. She was making a mental effort not to feel giddy that she was alone with Sian again. She tried to remember some physics formulas and keep her mind away. But no, she had to focus on whatever secrets the castle held. Sian was keeping something—perhaps a lot—from her, and she had to pay attention. To the castle, not to Sian. The fourth floor was like the others, and they came to a door that was not in the same position as the doors to the bedrooms and the living room. Sian opened it with a large key and revealed had a dark hallway leading away from the center of the castle.

He turned to her. "It's better not to use any light here."

As if she had any. Karina hesitated. She couldn't see the end of the hall.

He said, "It's safe. I've been here many times."

Karina didn't want to be a child afraid of the dark, so she nodded. He entered the hallway and she followed. She wished she could hold his hand, and this time it wasn't silly crush girl thinking, just scared Karina. Of course, she'd rather die of fright then reach for his hand. The corridor had a soft turn and she bumped on the wall. Some purple light came from the end of it.

They came to a medium hexagonal room. It had a purple glow, but it didn't come from any particular point, it was as if it was coming from the air itself. In each wall there was a circular mirror, and Karina was greeted with infinite reflections of her and Sian. The middle of the room had what looked like a well. Karina stepped closer and looked. It was indeed a well, but she wasn't sure if there was water inside or not. She felt a pair of hands around her waist pulling her back.

Karina turned, and Sian let go of her. "Better not get close," he said.

She tried to get over the shock of their first physical contact other than holding hands for teleporting. She wondered if he realized that he'd touched her for the first time. Probably not. She forced her mind back to the topic that really mattered. "What is this place? This well?"

"This room concentrates the power of the castle. It's here that we're going to find the answers. I hope you'll help me."

Karina looked around, unsure of what kind of answers she could find in a bare room. She also had other questions that perhaps should have been asked long before. "How do you know all that? How do you have the keys? Why did you come here in the first place?"

He put a finger over his lips. "Later."

"But you'll answer, right?"

He nodded and walked towards the hall, gesturing for her to follow him. That dark hall again, then the door, then back to the middle of the castle, from where she could overlook the main hall downstairs. Karina still felt his touch on her waist. Her pathetic scale was going to explode. She had to prioritize. Prioritize; solve whatever was happening in the castle, find a way home, then get out.

14

THE CASTLE

Karina's outside impression had been correct. The castle had seven floors, each with high ceilings. They spent the day in the common room on the second floor. She played hearts and matters with Aline, while the others went somewhere. The girl was a good player, or else Karina's beginner's luck was wearing out. The pieces were spread on the board, and the game was even. Karina had no clue who would win. The girl was silent now, concentrated on the game, or else pretending to be. Karina wasn't sure how to start a conversation, but she had to start a conversation.

She tried, "How long have you and Joel been together?"

Aline lifted her eyes from the board. "Two years."

"That's a lot. For my friends, three months is an eternity."

The girl had her eyes back on the board. "I guess it's normal when you're young."

Karina sighed and looked around. They were alone. "Do you know what we're doing in this castle?"

"I came just to keep Joel company."

Karina had the feeling that the girl wasn't allowed to tell her certain things, or else she didn't know. She tried. "But this is called a lost castle, with magic and all. Aren't you afraid?"

Aline shrugged. "I never bought into the whole 'magic is evil' thing. I don't see why I'd do it now." She took one of Karina's pieces and rolled it between her fingers.

Hey, screw secret. If Karina wanted to find out anything, she'd have to give something first. "Do you know what Kyons are?"

Aline shook her head. Okay, the explanation was going to be more complicated than Karina predicted. "They're these really ugly, grey things, and they—"

Aline nudged her head sideways. Sian entered the room. Alone. Why was she so worried that he wasn't being cautious? Or was she just wondering why he wasn't being cautious? Raja and Joel stepped in a few seconds after. Fine, so he wasn't alone.

Raja said, "It's lunchtime!"

Aline grimaced. "Now? We're almost finished."

Huh? No. They were far from finished unless she was planning on some striking moves. Was Karina really going to lose?

Joel laughed. "It's not like anyone will touch the board while you're gone, you know?"

"We can wait," Sian said.

He pulled a chair and sat by their table, looking attentively at the pieces. He had no overcoat this time and wore a long-sleeved black shirt with a high collar. For sure one of the boxes Georgia and Matheo carried had to be his wardrobe.

Joel sat at a couch, and Raja sat at a table away from them, staring at the window.

Aline moved one her pieces.

With Sian watching, Karina's mind went blank. Somebody could try to do an experiment. There should be a scientific way to determine how stupid a crush could make someone. Of course, the logistics of the experiment would be hard because nobody would confess their crushes. Maybe they could try with really attractive people? Oh, well, Karina wasn't planning on becoming a social scientist, so she'd never know.

Karina stared at the board. Since she couldn't think, she made the most obvious move. Her mind was telling her it was a trap, but she couldn't see it, and it seemed logical. She didn't want to miss such an obvious opening. But it was obviously a trap. No surprise, Aline beat her in four more moves, as Karina kept making stupid mistake after stupid mistake. Awesome. Sian was going to think she was dumb. Not that it mattered. Aline got up. Sian still examined the pieces and the board.

Raja asked, "Are you coming or not?"

"We'll catch up," Sian said.

We. Karina swallowed. Up to now, she still hadn't succeeded in repressing physical symptoms at the mere idea of being alone with Sian. She crossed her arms and leaned back, afraid of what he'd glean from her. Sian raised his eyes from the board to Karina, examining her with the same intensity. She stared back, as unfazed as she could, thankful that her crossed arms prevented her trembling from being visible.

"Why did you do that?" he asked.

"What?"

He smirked. "You let her win."

Actually no. You sit near me and all logical reasoning escapes my mind would have been the honest reply, but she wasn't into honesty right then. Instead, she asked, "What makes you think that?"

"Observation."

At least he didn't think she was dumb. Maybe she should be flattered. But she had other concerns. "Are you going to tell me about the castle, or are we going to pretend this is a vacation?"

He laughed. "Both, Karina. That's what most of them think. Secrets come later when there are no ears to hear or eyes to see."

"It's been almost two days I've been in Whyland, and I'm still in the dark."

"But you're safe, aren't you? That was priority number one."

His voice was soft, and her heart started beating faster.

She got up. "We should eat, right?"

The dining room was on the first floor. The table was long and had seats for ten people. Karina's seat was at one end of the table, Sian's was at the other. It was not the first time that she noticed that she got some kind of special treatment, but she was confused as to the reason for that. Or maybe he wanted to sit far from her.

Raja was at his side, though. She was playful, light, sometimes tapped his arm. Neat for her. Karina felt close to petrified when near Sian, and she did realize it wasn't attractive at all. But then, did she want to be attractive? She would leave soon, maybe forever. Then, maybe not, if Cayla kept her promise. Even then, Cayla lived in a different world from Sian, even if it was the same kingdom and the same dimension.

Karina stared at her food getting cold. She'd better eat it. Across from her, Sian was all smiles, at ease and relaxed. He was indeed attractive, if only because of his confidence, easy smiles, and something else she couldn't quite put a finger to. Was it charisma? Karina decided to make peace with the fact, and make peace with her crush. Crushes happened, no shame in that. It would eventually pass.

They sat on the living room in the afternoon. Raja played one of the harp-looking things in a calm, soothing melody. Aline and Joel played a game, and Georgia and Matheo were probably working somewhere. That idleness made Karina anxious. She wanted answers, action, not to sit around doing nothing.

Karina sat by Sian. He'd been leaning back, relaxed on the couch, and straightened up. Karina didn't care. She whispered in his ear, "When are you going to tell me about that room, about this castle?"

"I'm waiting for the right moment."

"So that's what we're going to do here? Wait? I thought you were going to get rid of those Kyons who'd been chasing me."

Sian shrugged. "No. We need to take control of the castle."

"When?"

Sian looked away, then looked back at her. "One of the most important things in warfare is patience. Wait for the right opportunity to make a move, and then strike. Everything in its time. A jaguar can spend an entire day laying down, waiting. When the moment comes, it springs into action."

"That doesn't mean you can't tell me what you already know."

"I will."

The harp music stopped.

Raja was standing beside them and said, "Sian, I need to go to my room. Could you walk down with me?"

He stared at her, as if puzzled, thought for a while, then got up. "Sure."

They left the room. Aline and Joel were busy playing and teasing each other and weren't paying attention to anything else. Karina waited thirty seconds, got up, and went upstairs to where the rooms were. Before she reached hers and Raja's door, she heard Sian's voice coming from his room.

"And what's your suggestion then?" He sounded bitter and sarcastic.

Raja replied, "First thing, realize you're terrible! Just horrible. Your attempts at romance are pathetic."

"You think I should be more *romantic*?" He said this last word as if it were disgusting.

"No! That's boring. Just be you."

"Oh, I didn't realize I was being someone else. Would you care to inform me who that is?"

"Not who, what. A spineless slug." Raja paused, then her voice was soft and sweet, almost pleading. "Sian, I just want to see you again. The real you."

Sian snorted. They were silent for a moment. Karina wondered if they were going to hear her heart.

"Fine. You're right. I'm lost, Raja. Help me." His voice broke. "I need you." Sian with feelings. That was new.

Karina felt like her chest was turning to ice. Why hearing them hurt so much if she had proof Sian didn't like her? Karina closed her eyes and suppressed a snort. Hope, that treacherous light. That's what she'd been attaching herself to. Sian and Raja were still silent. Silent. Not talking, but doing something else.

Karina was startled when she heard steps coming out of another bedroom., She ran down before Matheo and Georgia caught her snooping. Karina entered the common room shaking.

Aline immediately turned to her. "What's wrong?"

"No-Nothing."

Joel also turned to her, eyes wide as if afraid. "Were you on your own?"

"No," Karina replied quickly. "I was here. Just stepped outside. Some air. I'm uh, tired."

Aline got up and caught Karina's arm. "Here," she said. "Let's go downstairs and get some water." She turned to Joel. "Are you coming?"

"I'll stay," he replied.

"Joel," Aline said, as in a warning.

He shrugged. "The rule is not to go anywhere alone. It doesn't say anything about staying."

Aline rolled her eyes. "Fine."

Karina felt a little silly walking arm in arm with Aline, but the girl was so nice, she didn't want to push her away. As they were getting to the stairs, they met Sian and Raja.

Sian's eyes widened. "What's wrong?" He then glanced at Raja quickly, and his worried expression was gone, replaced with a smug smile. "You don't want to stay and enjoy our company?"

"We love your company," Aline said, then laughed. "Just not all the time. And this trip is getting boring."

Raja laughed, "I know, right?" She then took Sian's arm and stared at Karina as if waiting for a reaction.

Karina pretended she didn't notice.

Sian said, "We do have exciting plans for tonight."

"What about my answers?" Karina asked.

Sian leaned over Karina and whispered in her ear. "In its own time, love." He then kissed the corner of her cheekbone, near her hairline. What the…?

That was the second time he touched her. That kiss would have been exciting and exhilarating had she received it before hearing his conversation with Raja, now it was just bizarre and unsettling.

Karina grimaced. "Are you drunk or something?"

Sian smirked. "Not drunk. Something."

Raja again took his arm, and they walked to the common room.

"Let's go?" Aline asked.

Aline didn't seem to have noticed anything unusual. At least Karina was so puzzled that she stopped shaking. She let go of the girl's arm.

"Yes. But I'm feeling better."

They sat in the kitchen. Aline decided to make tea. Karina tried to gather her thoughts. Was Sian in a relationship with Raja? Well, that was what it looked like. Then why was he flirting with Karina? Was he flirting, though, or was it just the way he was? And why had Karina been called to Whyland to kiss him? She should have kept in mind the fact that her kiss didn't wake him up, and known that there were no feelings from his side. She should have known. Well, at least now she had her confirmation. But why was he avoiding talking about the kyons or telling her more about the castle? Such a mess.

Aline sat with two cups. "Careful, it's hot."

Karina made her mind and decided to ask the question that was bugging her. She made an effort to speak in her most neutral, uninterested voice. "Are Sian and Raja a couple?"

Aline spit some of her tea. "Hot." She made a disgusted face, then laughed. "I should pay attention to my own advice. Now, Sian and Raja, definitely not a couple, I assure you."

Karina insisted, "But they're so close."

"They are, but not like that. And she's married."

"Oh. But she's so young."

"I know."

Married. But that didn't prevent them from being together, although it would force them to have a secret relationship. What Karina had heard absolutely sounded like a secret relationship. Plus, if nobody knew about him and Raja, it would explain why they didn't know any girl who could kiss him and break his spell. In fact, maybe he and Raja had come here to spend time together, and perhaps Karina was a distraction. That was why she got special treatment and all that. That made sense. It also explained why he disappeared from time to time. The fact that he didn't like Karina didn't hurt as much as being toyed with.

Aline was staring at her. "You aren't jealous, are you?"

Not jealous. More like furious. But Karina just blinked and pretended puzzlement. "Why would I be jealous?"

"Well, you asked that question!"

Karina shrugged. "Curiosity, that's all."

Aline waved her hands in the air. "You can't be *curious* about *that*."

"It was just a question."

"Then I'll answer. Raja and Sian are like siblings. Siblings. And I've known Sian for years. Years. For all the faults everyone says he has, he's honorable. He wouldn't be having a relationship behind anyone's back."

"Fine. I got it." Karina wished she could share what she'd heard and prove Aline wrong, but she didn't want to confess she'd been eavesdropping, plus the girl would claim there had been a misunderstanding or something.

Aline sighed. "Sorry. You can ask any questions you want. I'll answer as much as I can."

"Why are there things you can't tell me?"

"Ask Sian. He'll tell you."

Karina rolled her eyes. "No, he won't. He'll say he'll tell me later."

"Then he'll tell you later. He values his word."

"Seriously, Aline, you talk as if he were this honorable hero. He isn't. When I met him, he was taking his brother's girlfriend as a hostage, and he wanted to become king by force. Or worse, make his crazy father king. That's who Sian is."

Aline had a puzzled expression. "Why are you here then?"

"Sian promised he'd protect me."

"You seem fine. I'd say he's been keeping his word. Now, to what you said before, I doubt he'd hurt the princess. And why would it bother you, of all people, if he became king? He'd be amazing at it!"

Karina snorted. "You admire him so much."

Aline nodded. "Lots of people do."

Karina was tired of secrets, especially if Sian wasn't going to tell her anything. "You want to know why I'm here? In this castle? Because there were these weird creatures following me, following me to my own dimension. Yeah, I'm from another dimension. Anyway, he says he's here to make sure these creatures, kyons, don't hunt me again, but he didn't bother telling you that, did he?"

Aline showed no surprise, offense, or anything. She considered for a moment, then said, "We knew there were things about you which were secret, Karina. We knew we were coming here because of you, that we had to protect you, and we know that this castle has dangers and secrets, no wonder we're being careful. I think that's enough."

"You don't mind not being told the truth?"

"I was never lied to, and Joel and I came because we wanted to. Sometimes you have to trust people."

"Trust Sian?"

"Yes. You should trust him too."

There was no convincing Aline. Karina sighed and looked down.

Aline said, "I can see something's bothering you."

"Of course! I came here for answers, and all we do is sit around."

"We just got here today. Patience."

Karina closed her eyes. Two days of following Sian. Other than the bizarre purple room, she got nothing but promises, some weird flirting that she wasn't even sure was flirting, and she managed to fall in love. So embarrassing. Karina had to think. Think.

"Are you all right?" Aline asked.

"Yeah. Great tea." Karina took a sip.

Aline had a half smile. "Thanks."

Karina smiled back but kept thinking. So the "nobody alone" rule wasn't really taken seriously. It hit her. Of course not! It was for Karina. She was being watched. She hadn't been left alone for a single moment since she'd returned to Whyland.

Aline just confirmed they'd come to the castle for her. But why? Protection? Maybe. But then, there could be something else. There was only one time when she would be able to be alone, and that was at night when everyone slept. If anything happened, she could run. But then, Sian was so at ease, with all his guarantees that no Kyons would attack again... He probably knew something. Karina's hunch was that there would be no risk. All she needed was the key to that room.

15

DARIAN AND CAYLA

Darian descended narrow circular stairs. For over a year now, he sometimes descended them with Cayla to the former hidden library. They'd renamed it Lost Knowledge library, which was appropriate because so many of the books had unknown authors and unknown content. But since they'd come back from saving his brother, he hadn't been here, as he'd been assigned a new post in the army and had to spend the day working in Siphoria. He was now assistant to the communication tower. He had never had such a low ranking before. But then, his former privilege was due to his father—and his father was gone. A low position wouldn't really bother him if it weren't for the fact that Cayla was a princess and heir to the throne. The people of Whyland had decided as such, based on tradition and old beliefs about the need for a powerful king or queen in the castle. Well, Cayla's mother had special powers indeed and could manipulate matter and even people.

Cayla was special as well, not because of uncommon powers. She was special in a unique, sweet way that he sometimes thought he was the only one who saw. Her beauty, on the other hand, was already becoming legendary. She wasn't exactly a girl that would catch attention at first sight, but the more he looked at her, the more she became entrancing. Apparently, he wasn't the only one who thought so. Her mother was still renowned for her looks. Cayla was at least a thousand times prettier than her mother, and people had started to notice.

It hadn't bothered Darian when it was the two of them traveling together, but now that she was back at the castle and he wasn't, he was reminded that she wasn't just Cayla, but princess Cayla.

There was something else bothering him, as her mother had been thinking of sending her as a peace envoy to Arlenia. He dreaded that idea. He believed that Arlenia wanted a war, as there was suspicious activity on the border. But the worst was that Arlenia's young king, when still a prince, had spent as much time as he could visiting Whyland, going to balls and dancing with Cayla all night. It hadn't bothered Darian at the time because he knew Cayla wasn't interested in the prince. She still wasn't interested in the young king, but Darian wished he could scream to the world that she was his. But he couldn't. It wouldn't be right for Whyland's princess to get engaged to a simple officer, and they were too young for that anyway. And Darian's idea of marking Cayla as his was obnoxious as if he were a possessive idiot. To be fair, sometimes Darian did think like a possessive idiot, but at least he caught himself.

Cayla was standing near a shelf in a corner, in the dark magic section, shuffling a thick book, black hair shining even in the library's dim light.

She turned to greet him with her stunning smile, happy to see him, then became serious. "I still haven't—"

Darian kissed her. He hadn't seen her for over a day and realized how badly he'd missed her. Unlike their usual hello kisses, he kept kissing her. Cayla threw the book on the shelf, over other books, and wrapped her arms around him, holding him tight. He pushed her to the wall, pressing his body against hers, feeling her heart beating against his.

Cayla then opened her eyes and broke the kiss. Her lips were parted, in surprise, her eyes were pure fire. She spoke with difficulty, "Darian… Do you think…" She was out of breath. Darian started to kiss her neck. "This is the right place…"

Cayla closed her eyes, her body trembling. It wasn't what he'd been planning when he entered the library, and that was definitely not the right place for that, but again they were entering the "almost" zone, treading very close to that threshold they'd been so close to crossing. So many times in their trip together they'd been in that zone, but it had never been so fast, and never in such an inappropriate place. For some odd reason, the spontaneity of the moment made it harder for Darian to find the resolve to hold back.

The sound of someone clearing her throat startled him. He turned and saw Cayla's mother. His heart sped up as he fixed his stare on the floor. In fact, he wished he could blend in with the floor, the walls, or the shelves.

"I'll wait for you in the central table," she said matter-of-factly as if she hadn't seen anything special, and she left them.

Perhaps the fact that she'd left them instead of talking to them right away said something about the inappropriateness of the situation.

Cayla's cheeks and lips were red, but she didn't have any of her murderous looks. She was just startled. "Darian, we need to be careful," she whispered.

"Sorry. I didn't mean to. I saw you and—"

"I liked it," she said it with bright eyes and a smile. She then whispered, "But imagine if my mother walked in ten minutes later and caught us," she looked down, "you know," she looked at him in the eyes, "doing it." She walked past him. "I'll go first."

What? Wait, what? Doing it? Despite what had just crossed his mind, Darian wasn't sure if he'd want to have his first time on the floor or wall of an old library. It wasn't the right place. Still, he had been waiting for so long for her to be ready, to tell him she was ready, as in this big revealing moment, and yet, here she was, willing to be his in a stolen moment in a dirty and inappropriate place. Darian let the words sink in. Cayla believed that if they hadn't been interrupted, in ten minutes, they'd be....

He swallowed, trying to suppress the array of feelings coming to him. Of course, he shouldn't get too excited about this alternate reality because Cayla obviously hadn't considered the logistics of the situation. Still, the prettiest girl in the world, the heir to Whyland's throne, and, most importantly, his Cayla, was ready and willing. They'd need to talk. He recomposed himself as best as he could and walked to the central table.

Cayla was sitting across from Lylah. Darian sat by Cayla, and took her hand in his.

Lylah stared at him for a moment. He had the feeling that she could read his thoughts but hoped it was more about reading emotions and intentions because it would be extremely awkward if he caught even a small glimpse of what was going through his mind.

"We're about to go through some difficult times," Lylah said. "And I'll need your help."

Lylah was looking at both Cayla and Darian, but he couldn't think what kind of help she expected from him.

"Is it Arlenia?" Cayla asked.

Lylah sighed and nodded.

"I can go there," Cayla said.

Darian squeezed her hand. "I'll go with her."

Lylah shook her head. "Well-meaning, but young King Conrad will kill you, Darian."

Darian let go of Cayla's hand and got up. "I can't let her go alone."

Again Lylah shook her head. "Cayla's not going either."

Darian sat down and exhaled.

"What do you need us for?" Cayla asked.

"*I* am going," Lylah said.

Cayla seemed surprised. "You think they'll negotiate with you?"

"He'll try, but his terms are disgusting."

"You know the terms? What are they?" Darian asked.

Lylah looked at Cayla. "You. Either you marry the king, or he'll invade us."

Indeed Darian's dread of the Arlenia king was justified.

Cayla had a look of disgust. "He's crazy!"

"Definitely not husband material, I know." Lylah snorted. "Terrible seduction skills. So we know our answer to Arlenia's request." She looked at both Cayla and Darian. "But we need time, and we'll need to act. Somebody needs to stay on the throne while I'm gone. It's not superstition, Whyland stands in an important convergence of portals and the castle needs to be occupied by the blood of a Guardian. That's Cayla."

Darian looked at Cayla. She was as puzzled and surprised as he was.

Lylah continued, addressing Cayla, "I will explain this, but I can't do that now. Just know that you need to stay on the throne."

Cayla squinted. "But what about when you were imprisoned?"

Lylah laughed. "I was still queen—in a way. I was in the white castle, which was connected to this one. Nobody else was proclaimed queen while I was there. My brother's work, of course, as he was the king's advisor."

Darian didn't like that conversation. "You can't make Cayla interim queen when we are in the brink of a war. It's too dangerous!"

Lylah took a deep breath. "I agree. But I have no choice."

"Stay here," he pleaded. "Send someone else."

Lylah shook her head. "My powers will make a difference when I'm there. I need to go."

She couldn't be serious. "There's a nutcase who wants to… to…" Darian was shaking and couldn't even think the right words. "He wants Cayla. She needs to hide, not be put in the most obvious and prominent position in Whyland."

Lylah stared. Darian felt a hand pulling his. Cayla looked at him. "Darian. I can handle it. It's my duty."

He realized he was standing and sat down. He closed his eyes, trying to slow down his breath, trying to calm down. He opened his eyes and noticed Lylah looking at him.

She said, "But he'll want to murder you, not her. You need to be careful and have security with you at all times. The castle is somewhat safe, but security will be tightened."

"But Darian doesn't live in the castle," Cayla said. "That king could hire an assassin at any moment."

"Darian will be given a room here, in the castle. That's what I wanted to discuss next. Cayla, could you give us a moment?"

"No," Cayla replied. "If I'm going to be queen, even for a day, I need to know about your decisions. And whatever you want to tell Darian you can tell me as well."

Lylah waved a hand and Cayla closed her eyes and dropped back on her chair as if she had fainted.

Darian checked Cayla's pulse—still beating—then turned to Lylah. "What did you do?"

"She'll be fine. No time to argue, that's all."

A feeling of dread overcame Darian. If that was something Cayla couldn't hear, it couldn't be good. "What is it you want to discuss?"

"You. Her. What are your plans?"

"You could have asked us both this question."

"I want to know *your* plans, Darian."

That probably had something to do with what she'd just

seen. No matter. Darian decided to be honest. "I want to stay by her side until she gets old and we both get wrinkled—"

"Not happening."

Darian clenched his fists. "What?"

"She won't grow old. At least not fast enough for you to see it."

"So she can't be with me?"

"She can. If she wants to. I think she wants to. I'm just explaining she'll take longer to age."

Darian's head was spinning. "Are you going to explain this to her, or do you want it to be a neat surprise for her some forty years from now?"

"As I said, I'm going to explain it. Do not tell her. That's not your duty, but mine. She needs to learn it at the right moment. I'm a guardian, and she's a guardian. What you need to know is that it basically means long life, the need to remain as a ruler in Whyland, and some special powers."

"What powers?"

"I don't know. It varies from person to person. It might freak you out one day, maybe, but I don't need to know anything about the far future. Ten years from now is no concern. I just want to know now."

Darian looked down. "I like her. I want to be by her side." Of course, now he wondered if she would want to be by his side fifty years from now, but Lylah was very clear they weren't supposed to think about that far.

"See, the thing is, there's a wacko who wants to marry my daughter, and I'll have to leave her here, as you said, in the most prominent position in Whyland. Do you want to be the guy who hangs out with her? I don't have a problem with that, I just want to know."

Darian snorted. "You have no idea how much I'd like to declare to the whole kingdom that Cayla and I are a couple. Is that what you need to know? But I can't. It will look ridiculous.

How can the interim Queen be with a low-ranking officer? It doesn't make any sense."

Lylah stared, a stare that would be uncomfortable had he not been used to it. She said, "I was testing you. You passed. How would you like to lead the army? Did you notice that the post has been vacant for all this time? Never wondered why?"

Darian was taken aback. "I don't want to be given anything, not even for Cayla. I want to deserve them."

Lylah squinted. "Deserve. Merit is a strange concept for a kingdom whose rulers are chosen because of their bloodline, but I appreciate your feeling. It doesn't have anything to do with Cayla, though, but your own work. You had a key role in the uprising, you would have deposed the previous king—without my help. If I hadn't returned, there would have been some more conflict, against your brother perhaps, but your little revolution did depose the King. Mostly your job, Darian, even if you were humble enough not to vaunt it. The people in the army, they trust you, they follow you, Darian. Despite your age, you are the right person for the job."

"I'm General Keen's son. Is Whyland ready for another general Keen?"

"Since when do you use second names in the north? They know you just as Darian. You're also your mother's son. Like her, you have the talent to lead. Plus, you'll need to help Cayla. But that's the matter I was getting to. It might be rushed, it might be early, but you two need a public declaration of affection at the latest tomorrow."

Darian looked down. "Tomorrow? There's no time for an engagement party or anything."

"No need for a party, just the engagement."

"If she wants it."

"If she doesn't, convince her."

"What am I now? King Conrad?"

"There's nothing wrong with convincing," Lylah said. "The

issue is how you do it, Darian. You move to the castle tonight. Be careful. Don't walk alone. Tomorrow you'll be proclaimed supreme general. Help Cayla. But also trust her. She's tougher than she looks."

"I know."

Lylah leaned back and crossed her hands over the table. "There's something else. What about your brother?"

Darian was startled. "What about it?"

"Any news from him?"

He wondered if she knew what that had happened, or how much she knew. He decided to tell the truth, sort of. "We received written communication from him. He's alive."

Lylah narrowed her eyes. "Is that all?"

Cayla had asked Darian not to say anything about helping Sian or anything about the garden of the Lost Castle, but he felt guilty and didn't think it was right to keep certain things from Lylah. Part of the truth wouldn't be a problem. "Well, we got communication from him when we were in the south. Near the Lost Castle. We heard about some strange creatures crawling out of the ground and terrifying some villagers close by."

Lylah looked at him attentively. "What kind of creatures? Were they well formed?"

"Interesting you mention that. They said they didn't have eyes."

She snorted. "Kyons. Someone's playing with ancient, residual magic. I'll check the Darloom castle, I mean, the Lost Castle, when I return. Don't go there, and don't send anyone there. Is that clear?"

"Yes."

"There's one more danger, though." Lylah snapped her fingers. Cayla woke up. She wasn't startled, confused, or anything. It was as if her fainting had never happened. That was super creepy. Lylah looked at Cayla. "Be careful and don't eat or drink anything different, or that wasn't prepared by trusted cooks from the castle."

Cayla frowned. "You think King Conrad could poison me?"

Lylah shook her head. "Worse. Love potion."

Darian's stomach turned.

Cayla didn't seem concerned, "But they are forbidden, aren't they? No potion maker would risk their life and reputation to make one."

"Cayla, dear," Lylah replied. "There are people in this world who'll do anything for the right price."

"Fine, there are stupid people." Cayla rolled her eyes. "Still, love potions don't really work. They can't create a feeling, they can only amplify it, and it doesn't even last. Second, as far as legend goes, every single person who has attracted someone using a love potion was driven to insanity. Who would be mad to use it?"

Lylah shook her head. "There's your answer, dear. When someone is already mad with love, they'll think madness is a small price to pay. You did learn well, though."

"But a love potion from King Conrad will never affect me because there's nothing there to be amplified," Cayla said.

"You're wrong, darling. It needs very little, just a tiny spark. A small, temporary, physical attraction, for example, would be enough."

"But there's nothing!" Cayla insisted. "I've always thought he was creepy and disgusting."

Lylah shook her head. "He's a very handsome young man. Why call him disgusting? Old? Overcompensating for something?"

Cayla crossed her arms. "No. Because he's always been creepy with me."

Lylah nodded. "Definitely. But you don't need to be aware of your attraction."

Darian wished Lylah had done the hand thing with him for

this conversation because it would be very hard to live with the thought that Cayla had a tiny unconscious attraction for that king.

Lylah then asked Cayla, "Your heart was Darian's, wasn't it?"

Cayla looked down and nodded. Darian exhaled, relieved.

"There you have it," said Lylah. "You wouldn't notice any attraction. And then, maybe, there isn't any, and the potion wouldn't work. But you can't be sure." She got up. "I have to prepare my departure. You two, since your hearts belong to each other, do something about it. Well, I don't mean..." She pointed towards the area Darian and Cayla had been caught making out. "I mean—never mind. Do something."

Lylah left. Cayla looked at Darian and squinted. "What does she mean?"

Do something. Darian had to do something but it was hard when he felt that his chest was going to explode. By tomorrow. No pressure. It would be easier to get it out at once. "Cayla, would you... uh... one day... perhaps..."

"Just say it."

Darian swallowed, then spoke as fast as he could. "Do you think one day you'd want to marry me?"

Cayla stared as if his words hadn't made any sense.

Darian remembered to add, "Oh, I'm the new leader of the army. Like my father. But not like my father. Like me. But it means... I'm not just a bum low-ranking officer anymore. In case that would affect your decision."

She squinted. "Are you *proposing?*"

He froze. It was like a nightmare. Cayla wasn't happy, wasn't excited, wasn't smiling, wasn't looking at him in that special way that reverberated through his bones. She was mad and almost disgusted. He felt awful and didn't know what to say. *Do something. Congratulations, Darian, you just ruined everything.*

She continued, "Tell me. Are you asking me if *I want to marry you?*"

Silence. Cayla wanted an answer. He barely had any voice to answer. "Uh, yeah, sort of." He then added quickly, "But it's fine if you don't want to think about it now—"

"Darian," she was laughing. "It's not that I don't want to think about it, I mean, we are too young to think about it. It's just... I always thought it would be more romantic. You know, this is a once-in-a-lifetime thing."

Darian felt confused. "You're angry because my question wasn't worded in the most romantic way?"

"Not the question. The place, the occasion."

So she'd almost given him a heart attack because the occasion wasn't right. "Oh, I didn't know there were special rules to talk to you. I didn't know that."

"Darian, it's not that. You're proposing. I always thought... I always dreamed about it, and I imagined you—" She looked sweet.

"You *dreamed* about it? With me?"

Cayla rolled her eyes "Who else would that be with?" She smiled—then grimaced. "But it wasn't in an old stinky library."

"Well, sorry. A nutcase wants to start a war just because he wants to marry you, and maybe we need to tell him that you already have someone. If you say yes, of course."

Cayla squinted. "What do you think I'd say?"

Darian shrugged. "I don't know, but I sure never thought it would be: *what are you thinking? How dare you propose and not be super romantic?* So see, I'm disappointed as well."

She laughed. "Sorry. It's just. Sorry. I... You know the answer, right? I mean, it's obvious. I just wish we were somewhere nicer."

"You know, there are lots of things I dreamed about. Involving you. We almost just did one of these once-in-a-lifetime things. In this library. And you were fine."

"Ugh. No. I was just in the moment. We'd regret it even if my mother hadn't walked in. I also want a nicer place for that. I don't know what's wrong with you today."

Maybe she was right. Darian took a deep breath. "Let's start over, then. Forget everything. We can go to the private garden. Remember we went there when we were kids?"

"We weren't *kids*. But… yeah, it's special. It's no longer private, though." She seemed worried. "Someone could walk in on us."

All right. The demands were getting ridiculous. "And I can't propose in a place where someone might come by? Is it a secret or something?"

"Oh. Propose. That's perfect. Perfect. That's exactly the place I imagined you'd ask me…" She laughed. "If I'd be your girl-friend." She looked down as if embarrassed. "That was a long time ago. I thought our first kiss would be there."

At that moment she reminded him of the girl from three years before and why he'd fallen in love with her. Darian held her hand, kissed it, then they left the library and walked to the small garden where they used to come when they first met, as friends.

He still had a question. "What were you thinking? When you said you were afraid someone would walk in on us in the garden?"

"Did I say that? I think I'm confused."

"Yeah, we'll have some tough days ahead of us."

Of course, with so many serious things happening, Cayla's priority was to make sure he proposed in the most romantic way possible.

But she was right. Outside, among trees they'd climbed when they had been much younger, knowing that they were there for something special, gave the words a special meaning, a special weight. She looked at him in the eye and told him she wanted to be with him forever. This was not some random conversation, but an important decision for their lives. They made promises that would live with them forever. His chest felt heavy, though, with the thought that it wasn't a fair choice for her if she didn't know that he would age and she wouldn't. He tried to chase away the disturbing image of him as an old man with beautiful, young, Cayla, but sometimes it came to his mind. Well, nothing was yet set in stone, and Cayla would be free to change her mind once she learned about her nature. The thought filled him with dread, but the important thing was to think about the present. Lylah was very clear that her concern wasn't ten years from now. Maybe she knew something. But never mind; ten years with Cayla could be enough.

Darian and Cayla were engaged, and about to tell the kingdom and the rest of the world that their hearts belonged to each other. They still needed to have another important conversation about their relationship, but, with so many things happening at once, that was left for later.

16

THE BALL

With only seven people in the castle, someone, probably Sian, decided to have a ball. It was one of the stupidest ideas Karina had ever heard, but she avoided rolling eyes and laughing as much as possible. The bath was adjoint to the bedroom, and it was Aline who watched her this time, behind a thin curtain. It was weird to realize that such an old castle had running water, but it did. Then, the furniture didn't look old, so it couldn't have been abandoned for millenia. Perhaps other people had lived here in recent times. The lights, on the other hand, were different from other parts in Whyland. They had those sticks with the brilliant orange-yellow top, like she'd seen near the Junction.

Karina chased away thoughts of Sian and Raja spending time together while she bathed. It was not worth it. She got out and noticed she also had more clothes in the closet. They had probably been ordered at the store where Karina had been measured. Mostly pants and shirts, a couple jackets. Nice. There was a fancy blue dress on the bed, but Karina decided to dress in brown leathers.

Aline stared at her up and down. "You look good, of course. Obviously. But usually… we wear dresses for balls."

"Oh, are Sian and Joel wearing dresses?"

Aline shook her head. "No. Only women."

Karina suppressed a sneer and pretended disappointment. "That's not fair."

Aline still looked at her up and down. "Er, uh, but they have special suits."

Karina stared at herself in the mirror. Badass. Tough. Rough. Of course, it was only on the outside, but maybe dressing the part would help her become the part. Not really. She remembered her friend Zoe telling her how cute she was, Malena pinching her cheeks. With her young-looking face, she looked like a kid or preteen in a Halloween costume. Cute. For once she hated that word. Whatever. Her outfit was a start.

Aline insisted, "That dress is so beautiful."

Karina didn't want to be told what to wear. Angry, annoyed, lonely and betrayed, she snapped. "I wear whatever I want."

"Yes, your highness."

Karina blinked. "What did you just call me?"

Aline crossed her arms. "I was told to make you look like a princess. If you're not going to look the part, maybe we can pretend the part."

"Actually," Karina gestured to herself, "I think these clothes would be totally Cayla's style." She smiled. "I do look like a princess."

"Not in a ball."

Karina shrugged. Raja entered. She was wearing a beautiful burgundy velvet dress, her hair carefully curled, and she wore makeup. She grimaced when she saw Karina. "You still aren't dressed?"

Aline rolled her eyes. "She says she is ready. Well, I'm done here." She left.

Raja approached Karina, and pointed at the dress on the bed.

"Why don't you at least try it? If you don't like it, you don't have to wear it. Promise."

Karina shrugged. "What's the point? It's just us."

"But that's the point. A mini-ball is an occasion to dress up, to show everyone how beautiful you are."

"Maybe you want to impress someone. I don't."

"It's not about impressing anyone." Raja said. "It's feeling beautiful."

"I don't need a dress to feel beautiful."

"No kidding." Raja sighed. "So you're going to tell me that you don't care at all, I mean, not even just a little bit, about what any of us thinks about the way you look?"

"I don't give a crap about what Sian thinks, if that's what you're asking."

"*I don't give a crap*," Raja mimicked Karina. "Look at yourself." She made a mocking voice. "Oooooh, I'm prettier than every-one, I don't need to dress up."

That was ridiculous. But Karina just shrugged. "What can I do? I'm nice and I don't want to outshine you guys."

Raja sighed and stared at her. "You want to know some-thing? You don't deserve that dress, this castle, or any of his attention. You're rude, aloof, ungrateful, and you don't deserve any of that."

"I don't even want it. You can have it all."

Raja had a puzzled face. "What do you mean?"

Karina rolled her eyes. "Nothing, Raja, nothing. It's not like I haven't noticed you and Sian." Karina could also be honest when she wanted.

The girl frowned for a moment, then she had a satisfied smile. "Oh. Interesting, very interesting."

She left the room. Karina exhaled slowly. For once she could have some peace. This could perhaps be the opportunity to sneak out and try to discover something. No, not right now. Someone would soon return to her room. She was feeling like a prisoner. It didn't matter. She'd carry her plan in the evening, find out what she had to find out, and go home. Karina knew Sian wanted something from her, and she wasn't going to give it to him. It was her best revenge against him playing with her heart.

Karina sat on the bed, surprised at how much time had passed, and stared at the dress. It was made of dark blue velvet, with some complex embroidery, but it was subtle. The skirt was made of light fabric in asymmetric layers. Delicate, but not too much. Fine, the dress was absolutely awesome, and she'd love to wear it, but there was only one person in that castle who could have picked something so beautiful, and Karina was furious at him right now.

Someone knocked on the door. Karina opened and saw Sian. He wasn't all lacey as she'd imagined he'd be. He was wearing a thick long overcoat, of course, but it was leather and simple, over a shirt that wasn't as loose as the previous ones. Yes, that looked nice—as always.

He looked at her up and down and smiled. "You're beautiful."

Oh, he could at least pretend to be disappointed. Karina pointed to him, then to herself. "Right script, wrong costume."

He stared at her. "You're perfect."

He was amazing at pretending. But so was Karina, who wasn't going to show him any of her feelings. She pointed at him. "What's this outfit? The twentieth you've worn since I came?"

Sian frowned. "The sixth!"

Karina couldn't suppress her laughter. "Did you actually count?"

Sian shrugged. "I know what I wear." He looked around the room. "Wait. Who's with you?"

"You."

"Did they leave you alone? Alone?"

"Seriously, Sian, didn't you say no kyons would come here?"

His tone was angry. "Who left you alone?"

He would keep asking, it would get annoying, it was better to say it. "Raja."

Sian closed his eyes. "Of course."

Duh, they were together. No kidding.

He bit his lip. "I'm an idiot, idiot."

"Self-aware, though."

Sian shook his head. "I'm sorry for my… friend. She can be immature sometimes. It's my fault. I shouldn't have trusted her. But please don't let that happen again. You mustn't stay alone in this castle."

"It's me, right? Only me. And you're not going to tell me why. Plus you know what? I feel like a prisoner. What are you going to do next? Chain me to the bed?"

He glanced at the bed, then back at her, and frowned. "Would you want me to?" He shrugged. "I mean, I don't mind. Whatever you want."

Was he suggesting what Karina was actually thinking he was suggesting? She tried to pierce him with her stare. "What are you talking about?"

He scratched his neck. "Nope. Not something you'd like. Noted."

Hilarious. Karina ignored the attempt at… whatever he was attempting. "I don't want people following me all around this castle anymore. I want to go home and be free."

He snorted. "Free." He sounded bitter. "You know we have things to solve."

"How's a ball going to help?"

Sian smiled. "By lifting our spirits while we wait for the opportunity to figure it all out." He stood by her side and offered his arm.

"I'm not taking it."

He dropped his arm. "Fine." He then pretended to pick something on his flawless jacket.

Karina shrugged and smiled. "No answers, no arm."

Sian tilted his head. "That's fair."

"Of course it isn't! I was attacked and I need answers and a solution. It doesn't compare to taking your arm just to pretend something that doesn't even exist."

"Patience, Karina, that's all I'm asking. And you don't have to take my arm if you don't want to."

His voice was smooth, calming, soothing, comforting. She felt at ease and her anger faded. Not enough to take his arm, but she wasn't as anxious as before. Karina smiled. "Fine. Let's go."

They went upstairs to the sixth floor. One thing that castle needed desperately was an elevator. They were not above the bedrooms, but on the side opposite to the purple room. They approached a huge black door, which opened by itself, bringing in a beautiful melody.

Karina gasped in surprise. The ballroom was dark, except for silver sparkles on the floor and blue stars hung from the ceiling. Silver stars made of paper or some other very light material floated around the room, like in a recently shaken snow globe. Two of the walls were made of glass, from where she could see the sky outside and the woods. There was something ethereal and otherworldly about the room.

Sian grinned. "You like it?"

Karina had to concede. "It's beautiful."

Everyone was there. Raja, Aline, Joel, Georgia, Matheo. The castle caretakers danced in the center, in very elegant clothes. Raja and Aline sat on fluffy couches while Joel stood by a table, filling a glass. Karina walked to the table with Sian. There were many types of appetizers. Karina wasn't hungry, but she took a glass of juice and sat near Aline and Raja. Sian was left talking to Joel, soon joined by Georgia and Matheo. Karina enjoyed the music. Sian approached them and gestured for Raja to follow him. Karina pretended she didn't notice or care, but from the corner of her eye, they appeared to be arguing.

Sian came back and asked Karina to follow him. She joined Raja on a corner.

The girl took a deep breath, then addressed Karina. "I'm sorry. I shouldn't have left you—"

"It's fine. You don't have to apologize," Karina said.

"Ah, ah," Sian turned to Karina. "If you don't need an apology, great, but it's her duty to apologize. For me."

Karina rolled her eyes but wasn't sure anyone saw it, as it was dark.

Raja continued in a robotic voice, "As I was saying, I shouldn't have left you alone. I further apologize I was offended you didn't want to wear the dress. It was not my place to be upset or not." She turned to Sian. "Happy?"

He stared. "You think that was convincing?"

Raja sighed. "No." She turned to Karina. "I'll be honest then. Refusing a gift is a huge insult here in Whyland. But it wasn't my gift to be angry about, so please ignore me."

Karina shrugged. "Ignored."

"Also," Raja continued, "in my anger burst, I completely forgot you shouldn't be left alone. I forgot. It was an honest mistake. I won't repeat it."

"Pity," Karina muttered to herself.

Sian stared at Raja, jaw tight. "That was slightly better. Thank you."

Raja exhaled and walked away. What was the point of that? Pretending. It was all a big pretense. That gorgeous ballroom was a theater stage, and Karina was…not an actress, no; a puppet. Let them think so.

Sian turned to her. "Does that make up for today?"

"You think I wanted an insincere apology?"

Sian exhaled slowly, then stared at her. "What do you want?"

"I thought you were smart. Figure it out."

Karina turned around and walked back to the table with the food and drinks. Aline stood by her side. Her dress was tight fit with a short skirt. She pointed to some red balls on the table. "Those are really good."

"Nah, not hungry."

Aline laughed and grabbed one. "More for me, then."

Karina laughed.

Aline took a bite, swallowed it, then made a circular gesture with her free arm. "So, what do you think?"

"This place is amazing." She grabbed one of the small silver stars. "How do they float?"

Aline finished her bite quickly. "Magnets." She looked around. "Wouldn't it be fun to see this room filled with people?"

"I guess."

Aline walked to a fluffy couch where she sat by Joel. Karina sat at her other side, a little uncomfortable at being third wheel. That didn't last long, though, because Joel pulled Aline to the center and they started dancing.

Sian appeared at Karina's side and extended his hand. "Come."

"Not in the mood."

Sian sat by her. Karina noticed Aline and Joel, how they looked at each other, how he pulled her body closer and closer to his. Would anyone ever hold her like that? But she wanted it to be for real, not a performance. Georgia and Matheo were also dancing.

Raja stood by Karina and Sian. "So? You're the only ones left sitting." She stared at them both. "Are you dancing or not?"

"As you can see, I'm sitting," Karina said.

Raja tilted her head. "I do see that. I'm going to steal Sian then."

She pulled his hand and he went to the middle of the room with her.

All right. Wallflower. That was definitely Karina. She was glad she wasn't wearing that stupid dress because being alone always looked better when people thought you didn't care. Here she was, tough, blasé Karina, who absolutely didn't wish she were the one Sian liked. Nope. At least she could pretend. Karina got up and got another drink. She turned and watched the couples. Raja pulled Sian tight. They turned, and she stared straight at Karina, as if daring her or trying to see her reaction. Karina held the stare in a neutral, uninterested face. In fact, she stared at the back of the room and the door behind them. The other couples left the floor, but Raja held Sian's hands, and they started another dance.

Karina saw Georgia and Matheo approaching the table and she walked to them, asking about how they prepared it all. Matheo was happy to talk about his culinary creations, explaining with delight how he'd spent the afternoon preparing the food for the ball. They told her they were going to work for Sian for one year, and after that they were going to open a restaurant. With Sian's help, of course. Apparently Sian was very good at spotting and investing in talent. This was getting annoying. Karina had meant to talk about food and forget the jerk who had pretended to like her, and instead, she was hearing what an amazing boss and smart investor he was. But Karina kept listening because she was out of options. Who was she going to talk to? Raja; nope. Aline thought Sian was perfect. Maybe Joel was normal, but she would never know, since he never even looked in her direction. Forget normal, the dude was weird. And weirder was Karina because her horrific conclusion was that Sian was her favorite person there. That was screwed up.

Karina forced herself to ignore her wandering thoughts and focused on the couple in front of her. There was something beautiful in their bright eyes and big dreams. Georgia then told her about the decorations and explained the effects of the floating stars. She slipped some "your highness" and Karina figured that it was the way people addressed their superiors.

Whatever. Karina took another juice and was relieved to find herself alone by the food table.

Joel, Aline, Raja, and Sian sat around a small circular table. Raja whispered something on Sian's ear. He glanced at Karina. Their eyes met. She looked away then turned around to look at all the food as if she were choosing something. Raja had been obviously talking about Karina. The question was what or why. Maybe the girl was feeling scorned because she had been forced to apologize, and came up with a nasty remark or something.

"You're not eating." It was Sian, standing next to her.

Karina was startled. "Neither are you."

He raised an eyebrow. "You noticed. Impressive."

"I happen to notice stuff." She stared at him, then turned to the food.

Sian remained quiet for a while, then said, "I know what you want."

"Do you?"

"Come outside." He then whispered in her ear. "I'll tell you about the castle. What I know at least."

Finally.

17

FLOATING STARS

arina followed Sian through a curtain towards a balcony attached to the ballroom. As they approached the edge, Karina noticed what she was facing and her bones chilled: it was that cursed garden. She stepped back. The cool air made her shiver.

"It's cold. Couldn't you tell me inside?"

"You don't like the air? What about the stars?"

As they were far from any artificial light, the sky was indeed amazing. The stars were different from what she was used to seeing at home, but perhaps this was just Earth's southern hemisphere. She could indeed spend a long time looking at it if the temperature had been warmer and if they weren't facing that garden.

"It's cold. And this garden, I don't like it."

"Why do you dislike it?"

All Karina remembered was fear, but she never liked to confess fear. "Disappointment. Tell me quickly then."

He sighed. "This is a long conversation. Let's go inside."

They walked in and nobody else was there. Karina looked around. "What happened?"

"They left."

"Why?"

"I'm sure you can guess," Sian whispered in her ear.

He didn't have to whisper; they were alone. His hands were on her shoulders. Her heart pounded, as he slid his hands to her waist and pulled her closer. Karina *liked* it. She *liked* it. He moved one of his hands to her chin, pulled it up, and moved in to kiss her.

Wow, wow, wow. Stop everything. Yes, of course Karina would love to kiss him, but not in that situation, not as part of a farce. She pushed him before their lips met. "Hey, I wanted answers, not this."

He stared at her. "Of course. Kissing me would be disgusting."

"Yes, it would. You can't be doing what you're doing with Raja and then come and try to kiss me."

"The only reason I had to turn to her is that I can't figure you out."

"Oooh, I'm so complicated. I'm the one with cryptic messages and secrets."

Sian snorted. "Have you ever noticed the way you look at me? Because I have. Other people have." His voice rose. "What is that supposed to mean, if you refused to kiss me even to save my life?"

"Maybe you should have figured out why your brother called the wrong person to break your spell. I was home. I was fine. I didn't need this in my life."

"Oh, it's horrible, right? I'm horrible. Now can you stop looking at me the way you do? Because then everything will make a lot more sense and I won't go crazy."

"Stop playing games, Sian. I can't stand your lies."

"Lies? I hate, abhor lying, you have no idea how much. I never, ever, ever lied to you. Not a word I've told you was a lie, Karina. Not a single word."

"What about Raja?"

"What about her? You want to know, I'll tell you. I was completely lost. I'm completely lost. Confused."

Karina swallowed. "You're confused? Well, clear up your confusion, then come talk to me."

She turned around to leave. Oh, no. Tears were about to burst out, but she held them back. Anything but humiliation.

Sian pulled her hand. "Why didn't you kiss me to break the spell?"

Karina was so angry she yelled from the top of her lungs. "I did! I did. But it didn't work, did it? Because you need some kind of slight attraction, which you obviously didn't have. I felt like a fool, Sian, a fool. I should have known."

"Breaking the spell depended on *your* feelings only. Just a spark, that was all you needed."

He was probably making that up. "I could have stayed home. I broke your spell, didn't I? And I did more. When those things came after us, your dear brother wanted to run away and leave you there. Hopeless, defenseless. I couldn't. I teleported with you." Karina realized that the fear she had felt in the garden had been for him, not for her. Stupid. "You could at least be grateful."

"I was grateful! You wouldn't have been able to break that spell if you had no feelings. But you confuse me because when I declared my feelings for you, you turned me down."

"Was that in your dreams? Because I sure would have remembered if you had done that."

"On the roof. That night."

Was he insane? "You did not declare anything! You asked me about my feelings, then mocked me."

"I didn't *mock* you. I asked you, and you were silent. What was I supposed to think?"

"You ask a question like that out of the blue, what do you expect?"

"I don't know. I can't ask you because you won't answer. What am I expected to do?"

"Nothing. Go and find Raja."

"Right. How horrible. I'm a loser because I followed her advice. Perhaps it was wrong. Now I'm asking you."

It was unsettling to see him shaken, but then, it could be just pretending. She paused, then said, in a normal tone of voice, "I heard you two talking. You're together, aren't you?"

Sian frowned. "What? Karina, she's like a sister to me. All I did was ask her what to do with you. That was all."

"Don't lie to me."

"What did you hear? Tell me. What did you hear?"

Karina tried to remember. Something about romance. His voice cracking with feeling. *Help me.* Could she have misunderstood it? "You asked for help."

"That's what I'm saying. What would I need help with? I've got it all figured out. With you it was different. You don't study that stuff in strategy class. Who could I turn to for help?"

"Well, me."

"Right. You refused to even fly back here with me. I had to bring more people to make this a functioning castle and for security, not so you'd ignore me."

Karina raised her voice, "Maybe I wouldn't ignore you if you didn't disappear from time to time, and if you didn't spend your night dancing with Raja."

"You refused to dance with me."

"Did you have to dance that close? Did she have to stare at me?"

"Maybe it was stupid. Maybe it was silly. Maybe I should never have taken her advice. She said you were jealous. She told me to..." He looked down.

"That was stupid, Sian. What did you think would happen? I would look at you both, think you're flirting, then decide to get between you two? You think you'd be more attractive if I thought you were flirting with us both? You think I'd let you kiss me if I thought you were also kissing her? It doesn't work like that."

"Giving you undivided attention didn't work either. What was I supposed to do?"

"Invite me for a walk, maybe? Say something nice?"

Sian snorted. "Take you to the roof. Does that count?"

"Yeah, and then ignore me all night."

"*You* were the one ignoring me. After I declared my feelings."

He was impossible. "That was not a declaration!"

Hold on. Her heart beat faster. Was it? Was that what he thought he'd done that night; declared his feelings? She'd been so angry at him, it was like a black cloud covering all senses, all reason. The cloud started to drift away. *His feelings.* Karina whispered. "Was it?"

"Apparently not." He stared at her. "Karina, what are we arguing about?"

"I'm not sure." Her head was spinning with so much information that didn't quite compute.

Sian caressed her face with the back of his hand. "I'm an idiot. You can tell me I'm an idiot. It's all my fault."

"Not all your fault."

He was standing closer to her now. "The only reason you didn't let me kiss you just now was because you thought I had something with Raja?"

Karina let out a small breath. "Yes."

"Do you believe me? Believe me when I'm saying she is like a sister to me? That all I did was ask her for help? For you?"

It did make sense. When she put everything together, plus what Aline had told her, it made a lot more sense than Karina's stupid secret-relationship theory. Plus it was in his face. For once he was not cold, distant, and sarcastic. He was raw and real.

"Yes."

He had a half smile, then brushed her hair away from her face. He kissed her cheek, then pulled her close to him. Karina closed her eyes as he pressed his lips against hers. She smelled his clean hair, leather, and something sweet. A soft, pleasant buzz took over her body. She felt as if she were flying. Karina felt the luckiest girl in the world—or worlds. All the wait had been worth it.

When they pulled apart, Karina was dizzy. They sat in a puffy couch. It was a good idea because he was tall and if they kept like that her neck would kill her. She looked at the floating stars, sparkles on the floor, and how they were alone in that immense room.

"Sian, did you ask your friends to leave?"

He ran his fingers through her hair. "They respect my privacy."

Karina got the weird feeling that the whole point of that ball had been for them to spend those moments among floating stars. Karina remembered the dress. Sian was indeed a man with a plan, his only mistake was that she should have told her. Maybe it wouldn't have worked if he'd told her. But she felt bad. "I'm sorry I didn't wear the dress you gave me."

"It's fine. I wasn't offended or upset. I obviously chose the wrong style."

"No. It was perfect. I mean, I didn't try it, but it was beautiful. I was just angry."

"It's fine. You look good regardless. And I should have considered how you feel about getting gifts."

Karina stared at him, wondering what he meant.

He took one of her hands in his and circled his fingers on her palm. "Powerless. Dependent. I understand. I used to feel like that when I depended on my father." He looked up and stared in her eyes. "But it's different with you and me. You have immeasurable power. I don't. I'm the powerless one. I could give you all the fortune in the world, and it wouldn't even come close."

Karina laughed. "Less, Sian, less. Can you try not to exaggerate?"

"I'm not exaggerating. You don't want to depend on anyone, and I should have considered that."

He did touch on a second point that had been bothering her since she'd come to Whyland with nothing but her clothes and hadn't even paid for the food she ate. "That's true too. The hand that gives is always on top."

He squeezed her hand and smirked. "And that's why I always prefer to be the one giving." His face softened, and he caressed her forehead and hairline, brushing her hair away from her face. "But there'll never be any power imbalance here. If there is any, it tips towards you, not me. Nothing I give you is with the upper hand, nothing."

Karina shook her head. "I was just angry."

"Can I ask you something?"

"Yes?"

"If you get angry at me again, can you come straight to me? Maybe we can solve it. Maybe we could have solved it all a long time ago."

Karina laughed. "You mean two days ago. But that's the thing. How can we discuss that stuff? What could I say? *I think I like you. Do you like me?*"

"*A lot more than like,* I would have replied, instead of going around in circles."

Karina laughed. "At least we're even." She paused, thinking. "Were you waiting for this? To tell me the secrets of the castle?"

"I had to trust you. But we need to go outside, to a stream. We'll do it tomorrow."

"Sometimes I get the feeling you're stalling."

"Of course I'm stalling. Over one year waiting for this. Do you think I want to talk now?" He kissed her, then said, "I'm kidding. We do need to be away from these walls, and I'd rather do it during the day."

"Over one year, you said?"

Sian tilted his head. "Nobody believes in love at first sight. Until they do."

"Do you?"

"Not sure. I heard about you, and it intrigued me. Was it just because I knew there was something amiss, or was it something more? I don't know. I saw you in the yellow tower when you were a prisoner—"

"What? How come—"

"I wanted to talk to you, to understand what was happening, but they didn't let me. And then I met you, and we were on opposite sides, but you were sweet. You asked me to surrender, strike a deal. You sounded so worried. I thought it was because of your friends. Later I realized it was because of me. You cared. For no reason whatsoever. Now, I won't lie. I lost and I was upset. I couldn't be upset at you, though. I'd never in my life want to ask a favor from my brother. For you I did just that, to get that book to your hands. All I hoped was that you'd never forget me. And now you're here."

"I didn't need a book to remember you, Sian. But it was nice knowing that you cared."

"More than cared."

He wrapped his arms around her and pulled closer to him. Again they were kissing and kissing and kissing.

They descended to the third floor a couple hours later, holding hands. Karina's heart was tight. She feared saying goodbye to him and then waking up the next day and realizing it had been just a dream.

As they reached the door to his bedroom, Karina said, "I guess... Good-night."

He looked puzzled for a moment, then shook his head. "No,

no. Your things have been brought here. You're staying with me."

Advice about avoiding guy's bedrooms and all the meanings of sleeping together spun in her head and she tensed.

Sian blinked, seeming confused. "What's wrong?"

Karina didn't want to offend him, didn't want to suggest anything that perhaps he wasn't suggesting, wasn't sure how to express her worry, wasn't even sure if there was any reason to worry, or if perhaps she should make anything clear. Was there anything that needed to be clear?

While she thought, Sian looked inside, looked at her, then back inside, then laughed. "You're thinking further ahead than I was."

Karina pulled her hand. "No, I—"

"Sorry. I'm just… I was surprised, that's all. But there's no difference. We're still the same people we were upstairs. We can go up and sleep in the ballroom if you want to."

Karina wanted to change the subject. "Can Raja sleep on her own, though?"

"I think she's with Aline and Joel. Either way, you're the one who's most at risk here."

"And you'll only explain it to me tomorrow?"

He kissed her cheek. "Everything in its time."

Karina woke up as rays of light reached her face. She was over the covers and still wearing the same leather as the night before. She was going to rethink her opinion that sleeping in jeans was uncomfortable.

Wait. She'd been with Sian and it was just that they never properly got ready to sleep, but sleep caught them regardless.

Forget uncomfortable. The touch of his arms lingered on her, his presence, his smell. She turned to look at him, but he wasn't there. Her stomach knotted a little. Are things in daylight the same as at night? Would he still hold her? Kiss her? She remembered some of her friends and parties, and how kissing one night could be a fleeting moment. But that was pointless fear. What she'd seen in his face, heard in his voice, had been real. She just wished he'd be near her now, so she could be sure of that.

As she sat up, she noticed someone on an armchair in the corner. Raja. Karina felt embarrassed, and maybe a little annoyed to realize that she had no privacy, but she didn't want to say any of that. Instead, she said, "Good morning."

The girl got up and walked to the bed. "Hey. Sorry I'm here. Sian didn't want to leave you alone."

Well, why did he leave then? But it didn't matter. "Thanks."

Raja smiled. "No problem." She tilted her head and looked at Karina.

Karina was a little ashamed of having been jealous and thought she should be nice to Raja if she was Sian's almost sister or whatever, but the way the girl kept looking at her was unnerving. Karina asked, "What?"

"Just looking."

Karina got up. "You were provoking me last night. Trying to make me jealous. Why?"

Raja shrugged. "It worked, didn't it? You should be glad—if it's something you wanted."

"You just made me upset and angry."

She waved a hand. "Yeah, yeah, yeah. People get angry, get emotional, spit out stuff they'd been holding back. It works. Plus, if it weren't for me, he'd stall forever and never take an initiative." Raja shrugged. "I'm not asking you to thank me or anything."

If it had been under Raja's advice that he'd made his move, as clumsy as it had been, it was true that it had worked. Perhaps Karina should be thankful, except that there was still something odd about the girl. Karina decided to be honest. "I still feel you don't like me."

Raja sighed. "I don't know you well enough to like or dislike you, Karina, it's not that. It's about trust. I have no clue why you were picked as his chosen one." She rolled her eyes. "Maybe I do. You're otherworldly and all. And that's the thing. You might turn around and leave, and you might take these things different than us."

Karina felt a chill in her stomach at being reminded that she didn't belong in this world.

Raja continued, "So I don't know." She pointed a finger to Karina. "But I'll tell you something: you break his heart, I'll find you and gut you."

Charming. "I wouldn't call myself a heartbreaker, Raja, so I'm sure you can chill."

Raja narrowed her eyes. "I don't think you're sweet and harmless like everyone thinks."

Karina laughed. "Well, sweet and harmless sounds boring. And you get trampled on."

"Careful. Fear of being trampled makes people squash others." She looked down, then back at Karina. "I'm sorry, though. If I made you jealous. I was just testing you. But really, at first, you showed no reaction. I thought—"

"It's fine." Karina just wanted that awkward conversation to end. "I wanted to eat something, though. I guess you have to walk with me, right?"

Raja nodded, then walked to the door. She paused then turned and said, "Sian is like a brother to me."

"Why, though?" Karina then wasn't sure if the question was too personal. "I mean, if you don't mind answering."

Raja shook her head. "No problem. Sian used to come to my mother's business, and my mother took him under her wing. I mean, as much as she could, right? Because he had bigger wings over him. Before that, I had a real brother. He died. Maybe…" Raja shrugged. "Life is weird. It takes things from us but gives them back."

"I'm sorry."

Raja shook her head. "Nothing to be sorry. It's how life goes."

18

UNWRAPPING SECRETS

Karina and Raja reached the kitchen, which was big and had dark marble counters and a circular table on a corner. Aline, Georgia, and Matheo were setting the table. Karina sat, wondering if any of them would look at her differently or crack any comment. She wasn't embarrassed about having kissed Sian, but rather embarrassed about her prior behavior. The worst thing had been knowing that they all had conspired to have her and Sian together. Why hadn't they just told her that stuff? On second thought, Aline had told her not to be jealous of Raja. On a third thought, maybe taking a while to get together was normal. If they were together. She still had that odd feeling that the dream was about to dissipate. Only seeing Sian and knowing how he'd act towards her would put her at ease.

Aline sat down and passed her some kind of bread. "Try it, it's really good."

"Thanks."

There was a question she wanted to ask, but she didn't want to ask, but she had to ask. She found a way not to sound too specific. "Where are the others?"

Aline swallowed her bite then said, "Early morning training or something. They might leave the army, but the army doesn't leave them."

"Joel left it?"

"He's just taking time off. Sort of."

Karina then heard steps behind her. Before she turned, a pair of arms had wrapped her, and she was getting a kiss on the cheek. The arms squeezed her in a tight hug as all her worries melted away. Karina laughed with happiness as Sian sat by her side.

He smiled and brushed a strand of hair away from her face. "Sleep well?"

"Wonderful." She wondered if she looked silly.

But there was nothing silly about the way Sian looked at her. She reached out and touched his hair. It was thick and soft at the same time. Their eyes met, and Sian pulled her closer. Was it bad manners to make out at the breakfast table? Karina didn't care.

It turned out that Raja was leaving, so they all went outside to say goodbye to her. The day was cold and misty. Karina wore a fluffy black coat and wished she had a hat and a scarf or something. Sian wore a different black jacket. She was wondering if she could take a peek his wardrobe, but perhaps it was too soon.

A red and gold lift, very different from anything she'd seen so far in Whyland, had come to bring Raja back to Siphoria. It was Malena's. Raja would later travel back to the kingdom where she lived.

Raja said goodbye to each one. When it was Karina's turn, the girl hugged her then whispered in her ear. "Remember what I told you."

Right. Something about gutting her. Somehow it sounded sweet and hilarious now. Karina smiled. "Sure."

The girl entered the lift and soon disappeared in the sky.

They all turned back to return to the castle, but Sian pulled Karina's hand. "We're going elsewhere."

They walked for many minutes and the weather seemed to get foggier and foggier. Chills ran down Karina's spine as she remembered the day she'd arrived with Darian and Cayla. Sian had his huge mace, though, and guaranteed that there was no risk. Karina did feel safe by his side, but then, the image of him trapped in stone filled her with a lot more horror than it had ever done before.

They reached a stream. He stepped on it, his feet on the water. His were probably great boots. Karina wasn't sure about hers, though. He lifted her and placed her on a rock in the middle of the stream.

He looked at her. "This is a safe place to talk about the castle. The water blocks us."

Standing on the rock, she was as tall as Sian, which meant they'd have their conversation face-to-face.

"Blocks us from what?" Karina asked.

"The energy in the castle."

"Are you going to explain it, or should I just keep guessing?"

Sian laughed. "I'm pretty sure you can figure out a lot on your own, but if you want faster answers, you can ask."

Karina sighed. "Well, I do know that there's something in this castle you want, there's something you aren't telling me, and that this castle has some kind of magic, energy, or whatever that can be controlled. Is that correct?"

"Exactly, except for not telling you. I'm being as honest as possible, Karina. Now, that room with the mirrors, they are portals. A long time ago, people in the castle decided that the best way to keep something hidden and protected was to create a subdimension for them. So there are things there that can be brought back to us." He watched her closely.

"And there's something you want."

A half smile, like a smirk, except that his face looked sweet now. "There's a staff that has been kept away. With it, I'll have complete mastery of the Darloom castle."

A staff to control that castle. It didn't sound that good. It sounded quite dangerous, in fact. Karina's first thought was that they should tell the queen, but then she realized that Sian perhaps wanted to keep that castle for him, and in a way, that was a great improvement from wanting to take the kingdom.

She decided not to comment on her reservations, and asked instead, "How do you know all that?"

"There are records. I read them. Not only the books on ancient religions but boring records of what happened here a thousand years ago. Most of the truths can be found in the ordinary, the mundane. There it was."

"Am I wrong in thinking that there's some kind of sentient force, energy, magic, whatever, in this castle?"

"Sentient-looking, perhaps. It's just residual magic from someone from thousands of years ago."

"Is it magic, though? You said magic was personal, depending on talent, affinity, something."

He gestured around him with his arms. "For the person who created this, it was magic. Once it's all put in motion, the magic is there to be used. So yes, you no longer need the personal talent."

"You said the castle had a new master, though. Who or what can it be? What sent those things after me?"

"The castle can be commanded with powerful objects. But the staff is the most powerful."

"You didn't answer my question."

"Anyone could command the Darloom castle with one of those powerful objects, Karina. The thing is that I have one myself," he pointed to his gigantic mace. "And that will keep you safe. The staff will keep you even safer."

Karina sighed. "And you're not curious to know who it was?"

"I understand curiosity but I'm pragmatic. We get the staff, we get our answers."

Karina looked away, thinking. She knew Sian wanted that castle for himself, she understood why he wanted to control it, and yet... "Is it worth it messing with forces that are more powerful than we are?"

"Worth it is quite subjective. More powerful is quite debatable. The thing is; you can't lock away anything forever. One day it bursts out. We'll be safer if it's on our side. Plus, I want to make sure you're safe. I gave you my word, remember?"

Karina did remember. It seemed like an eternity before, when she thought he'd been flirting with her as some kind of joke, when she agreed to come with him even though she was terrified of falling in love. No, scratch that, she knew how she felt; she was terrified of having to admit it. All that fear seemed so ridiculous now. Still, all this talk about getting a magical object that had been put away on purpose... Karina felt queasy.

Sian touched her chin and pulled her face up. "Do you trust me?"

Karina hesitated. "I like you." Sian dropped his hand. Karina added, "A lot."

Sian looked away and snorted.

Karina said, "It's not that I don't trust you."

Sian shook his head. "It's fine. Fine. I'm sorry." He took her hand in his, brushed it lightly with his other hand, then pulled it to his chest. "This is what matters."

"With the staff, you'll be sure those creatures won't come after me?"

He nodded. "Yes, I'll be sure."

"And you think I can get it for you?"

"I know you can."

Karina narrowed her eyes. "What else does the staff do?"

"It controls the castle."

"Like what?" Karina laughed. "Will the kitchen cook for us or something?"

Sian also laughed. "Hum, not sure I'd trust a castle's cooking."

Karina laughed, then bit her lip. "And what about… You said it could also have a portal. For teleporting." She dreaded thinking about this next part, but she had to think about it. "Eventually I'll have to go home."

He let go of her hand, then stared at her with an unreadable expression. "Is that what you want to do?" His tone was neutral.

"Eventually. I…"

Karina had thousands of conflicting thoughts. Yes, on one hand, she wanted to go back and see her parents, go back to her life. On the other hand, she didn't want to go, but she didn't know how long she'd be allowed to stay, where she'd stay, and what would happen.

Sian still had an odd expression. "Yes, you can open it for the hidden objects, and you can also open a portal. To go *home.*" There was some bite in this last word. He stepped closer to her, brushing his fingers on her forehead and hair. "But you can also stay a little longer. If you want to."

He had spoken in his voice that was soft, calming, and comforting, that voice that touched her very soul. Karina smiled. "I do."

His face was close to hers. "Stay longer, then. You can go back to visit, but later. Let's sort everything we need to sort out first." He kept caressing her hair and forehead, looking at her as if she were some special and precious thing—person.

Well, thinking about the future was pointless. By Karina's calculations, she could still take a couple weeks, if Zoe had warned her parents, if everyone thought she was at the summer camp. She also feared going away, not being allowed to return, and losing all that she had right now. But wait. "You said 'go back to *visit*'? Meaning I would come back here?"

Sian rolled his eyes. "No Karina, just go away forever. What a horrible thing it would be for us ever to see each other again."

Karina laughed. "No, it's just… It didn't seem that easy before."

Sian pointed to the castle. "The portal there, it can be fixed. We could make it work as a permanent passage."

Karina's heart beat faster, but it was happiness because some of her worst fears were now melting away. "Really?"

"Why the surprise? You think I'd bring you here just so you'd go away? Or do you think I'd rip you from your home dimension forever?"

"It's not like you called me here."

"You came for me, didn't you?"

Karina could say that she'd come for Cayla, or for Darian. Maybe she'd come just to come back to Whyland again. But then, a big part of Karina's yearning to return had a face. The face in front of her. "I was told I'd break your spell and come back."

Sian shrugged. "It's clear that my brother wasn't properly briefed on the reason it had to be you. But he got you here, so whatever he did worked."

Karina laughed. "It wasn't that hard to convince me."

Sian wrapped his arms around her. "Stay then. We'll get the staff, and you can stay here."

"I don't have a place here, though. No family, school, job, home… What would I do?"

Sian smiled. "You can be my queen. Do you want to be my queen?"

Karina laughed. "I'm serious."

Sian smirked. "And I'm not? You got a problem with royalty?"

"No, but—"

"No problem. That's good to know." Sian kissed her lightly, then said, "Tomorrow. When the sun rises. You'll get your answers."

In the afternoon, Sian went out with Joel to check the castle grounds and contact people in Siphoria from his lift. Karina was left with Aline, and the girl was a lot more at ease and relaxed, talking about flying undetected and crossing the ocean. Karina envied her life of adventure, but then she hoped she would have her own adventures in the future. They played a different board game, but this time Karina was terrible at it.

Despite some periods apart from Sian, the day was spent between tight hugs, tighter hugs, and kisses of all sorts. It ended when Karina laid down on Sian's bed, wearing very soft pajamas, below fluffy covers. He also worse soft clothes, and they smelled like cotton. Everything so soft like sleeping amongst clouds, and there was nothing happier than falling asleep in his arms. He showed no intention of trying anything she didn't want.

Karina found herself in the purple room with the portals, and this time decided to look at the well. There was so much light that she couldn't see anything, though. She woke up with a start. Her body hurt, and she couldn't move at all, as she realized Sian still wrapped her tight. The dream was probably anxiety about going there in a couple hours. With some difficulty, in fact, a lot of difficulty because his grip was so tight, she turned and faced him.

Sian squeezed her even more. "Don't leave me," he said, eyes still closed, a groggy voice of someone still sleeping.

Karina kissed his cheek and whispered, "I won't."

His breathing steadied. The room was dark, but there was some light coming from the window and the moonlit sky. Sleeping he looked so sweet, innocent, with beautiful lips. Hard to believe that it was true, that they were so close together, and she was sleeping wrapped in his arms.

Karina closed her eyes and just let herself get drowsy in that smell of sheets, covers, soft clothes, affection, warm in that cuddle she hoped would last forever.

19

THE WELL

The sun hadn't risen when Sian woke Karina up. She wanted her answers, and she wanted to figure out the room, but...

"Does it have to be so early?" she asked.

Sian was already dressed, all in black, in one of his ten thousand overcoats. He sat on the bed and brushed her hair away from her face. "There's something special and powerful about sunrises. Maybe it's just the fact that we're reminded that no matter how dark or long the night is, the day always comes. It's positive energy."

"Technically, the sun was always there."

Sian chuckled. "You could say then that as much as we might turn away from the sun, we always turn back."

"You woke up poetic."

Sian took her hand in his, his long fingers brushing her palm. "I woke up with you." He leaned over and kissed her. "Get dressed. We have important things to do."

She pointed to her pajama-like clothes. "And I can't go like this?"

He stared at her. "You want to play the part, you need to dress the part."

Dress the part. Yeah, that explained a lot. "And are you going to tell me what part that is?"

Sian smirked. "Queen, of course."

Karina rolled her eyes, but got up, and picked a nice pair of pants and a jacket. She dressed and washed her face quickly. Doing important things without coffee didn't seem right. Oh, then she was reminded that Whyland, or at least this castle, didn't have coffee, so she'd need to go without it either way. And without food. But it should be fast, right? Grab the staff, and that's it.

They walked to the purple room, and this time it was much easier to go through that dark hallway holding Sian's hand. Well, everything was easier and nicer holding his hand. The room was eerie, and despite her jacket, Karina felt cold. She wondered if it wasn't dangerous. Well, it probably was a little dangerous, but not for her, because she could open a portal and return in case anything happened. Sian brought her to one of the mirrors.

"It's here. Go there, pick it up, and return. Don't look back and don't do anything else." He'd spoken in his special soft voice that seemed to cast an energy in the room.

"Or?"

Sian shrugged. "I don't know, but it's better to be on the safe side, right?"

"How do you know which mirror is the right one?"

"I read it."

He put a finger over his lips. Right. No talking in the castle. It was just that it was odd that it should be so simple, and that he'd waited two days to ask her to do that. Maybe there were more things he wasn't telling her, and she'd make sure to ask them later.

Karina took a deep breath and touched the mirror. "How do I cross it?"

"You're the portal opener, Karina."

"So you don't know?"

He tilted his head. "In theory, at least, you should be able to walk through it as if the glass were just fog."

Karina tapped the mirror. "Not fog."

"You have to do whatever portal opening you do. I'm not sure how it works."

Portal opening. Right. Emotion. Looking at him should be enough for an emotional spike. She remembered looking at him sleeping, and how he asked her not to leave her. The mirror was still solid.

She said, "This is very different. Usually I just teleport from where I am. I don't move through anything."

"The principle is the same, Karina. This just might be a little harder."

Karina tried to remember the times she teleported. A few times were when she was in danger. Fear somehow made it easier to teleport. And she'd teleported back home, leaving Sian, even though she didn't really want to. She'd used anger then because she was afraid he was mocking her. This time she'd need to do whatever she did to teleport—while walking at the same time. A bit harder, for sure.

A fear hit her. "Will you be disappointed if I can't do it?"

His eyes were serene. "That's an impossibility."

She had no idea what he'd meant.

Sian chuckled. "I know for a fact that you can cross this portal." He took a deep breath. "In your case it's magic, and it's different, but…it's a thing I learned. When I was young, my father tested how much I could withstand pain—"

"Your father tortured you?" She knew General Keen had been a monster, but this was a little much.

Sian rolled his eyes. "Torture is meant to break the victim. This was meant to make me stronger. Like tempering a sword."

"But you're not a sword."

He waved his hands, annoyed. "Yeah, no. That's beside the point. I can withstand pain without complaining or showing any reaction. It is useful. But it's beside the point."

"That's horrible."

"Whatever. That was not what I was getting at, and I don't want to talk about it. The thing is how I did it. Can you listen to me, or are you going to be horrified at my past?"

"I'm not horrified, I—"

"Can you listen to me?"

"Go on."

"The trick is in letting go of the perception of the real world. You need a strong focus, but at the same time, you need to relax. See, people stress into focus. You need to relax into focus. That will allow you to do it."

"I was told I needed an emotional spike."

"Emotion will make you relax into focus, Karina. But you can't count on using emotion like that. In a difficult situation, you can't let emotion guide you, or you'll be almost blind."

"You could have told me this earlier."

"It came to me just now. Like I told you, I don't have any magic, but I think the principle would be the same."

Karina wanted to ask him about his past, how exactly he was able to withstand pain, and how much pain, but this clearly wasn't the moment, and it made him uncomfortable. She touched the mirror. No, it was wrong. She was putting her hand as if waiting for it to disappear, but if she waited for it to disappear, it meant it was there. Relax into focus. She looked beyond the mirror, even though she couldn't see anything, and focused on what lay beyond. She took a step forward—and hit her foot.

"Easy, easy," Sian told her, hands on her shoulders, his voice soft and smooth. "It's coming. You know you can walk to the other side."

Karina tried to focus and relax at the same time, but instead of seeing herself walking through the mirror and getting the staff, she ignored what was in front of her, and instead visualized the moment her lips and Sian's met for the first time. She walked forward—and kept walking—until she found herself facing a glass display with a huge staff on it, mounted on two stands. Glass. That was probably not real either, just an illusion. Her hand moved across the glass and she grabbed it. Funny. Even though it was huge, it was lighter than a broom.

Beyond the now empty case, there was a huge metal door with delicate engravings, and she wondered what was there. Sian's voice telling her to come back straight away echoed in her mind. Curiosity. Karina would need to let go of it. But just a peek couldn't hurt, could it? *Pick it up and return.* His voice rang in her head.

Karina then heard a different voice. "Oh, do you really want to give him what he wants, girl?" It was a shrill, distant voice, neither male nor female. "He'll get it and leave you."

Karina looked around and didn't see anyone. It could be her own fear speaking, and it had such a clear voice because she was in this weird in-between dimension. Karina turned around to return to the purple room. A mirror faced her. That voice, that fear. They were pointless, right? If Sian didn't like her, he didn't have to kiss her or hold her tight. She would have gotten the staff regardless, just to save herself from the kyons.

The voice laughed. "And you believe his deceit? It was never about you. Give him the staff, and he'll leave you."

Her stomach tightened. That voice was definitely not Karina's own fear. "Who are you?"

"I am your fear, darling, and your hopes and wishes, and your dearest secrets in your heart. I am everything and more."

Karina knew she had to go back, but a couple questions couldn't hurt. "What is his deceit?"

"I can show you. Do you want to see it?"

Karina probably shouldn't trust a disembodied voice in a place where a dangerous object was kept, but she wasn't trusting it, she was just curious. "Well, show it."

"Come to me and I'll show you."

"You want me to go across that door? No chance."

"That's too bad. You'll never know."

"If what you're saying is right, I'll know it soon."

Karina walked to the mirror, upset at herself, upset at that voice, upset at the fear infecting her mind. But Sian liked her. He did. Nobody could fake it like that. Fake it even while sleeping.

The voice laughed again. "And who says he was sleeping?"

"Shut up."

Karina touched the mirror, the one she should walk across, and it was solid. Of course, she'd need to open the portal again. She almost dropped the staff there, and considered telling Sian she hadn't found anything, just to test his reaction. But her fear was that he would continue being sweet and loving, telling her to try again. The idea of not knowing whether his feelings were real or not was worse than prolonging her torture. She had to know. The best way to do it was by giving him the damn staff.

"Not so fast, girl," the voice told her. "You could try to win him. Leave the staff, and give him time to fall in love."

"I don't want to win anyone. If he's tricking me, I don't want him."

"You might still want the power. Have you thought that the power is yours? Why share it? Why give it away?"

"I'm not sharing anything, just giving him an object he wants."

The mirror was solid, and it was hard to focus after that voice had told her those things. As much as that voice was poisoning her mind, she wished she had Sian beside her calming her down, telling her what she needed to do. But that was stupid. The portal opener was her, she should be able to crack this.

"That's the spirit, that's the spirit, little girl. The power is yours."

Karina realized that she wouldn't be able to make that voice shut up, so it was better to get to the bottom of it. "And?" she asked.

"Keep the staff. Or better, come to me and I'll show you all you can do with it. Or even better, I'll explain what you'll gain if you give it to me."

So whatever was talking couldn't take it by force. Interesting.

"Why? I'm fine."

"No, you aren't, little girl. You're consumed with doubt and fear, and well aware that the thief beyond the portal is using you. He thinks you're weak."

"Yeah, yeah, yeah. I'll figure it out for myself. Thanks for the warning."

Karina tried to look beyond the mirror and remember it was an illusion. Her foot hit the mirror.

The voice said, "You're taking the wrong exit, girl."

Karina puffed, more than annoyed. "Who are you and what do you want?"

"I am more than you can comprehend. All I wanted was to show you your power. That's all."

"I'll tell you what. Next time you want to convince someone of something, don't show up as a disembodied voice and don't talk in that creepy tone. I mean, really."

"I'm sorry if I can't talk to you in that sweet, smooth, hypnotic voice that the thief uses. Do you think that's normal? Have you ever wondered how he convinced you to do all he wanted so easily? How easily you let him kiss you?"

"Not that mysterious, invisible dude or dudette. He's quite kissable." Karina remembered him at the Junction. "In fact, girls fawn over him."

"And he knows it, doesn't he? He knew how lonely, needy, insecure you were, he knew you'd be easily pliable. Oh, so much power, so much power and it could be all his."

Karina was trembling in anger. "I'll find you and stick this staff down your throat. If you have one."

The voice laughed again. "You know. Deep down, you know I'm telling the truth, and that's why it bothers you. But I'm your friend."

Karina took the staff and launched it against the mirror. She wanted to smash something, break it. Maybe that was how she'd open the portal. She also wanted to drown out the voice, but it kept talking while she hit the mirror as if it were inside her head.

"Have you ever wondered why nobody has ever wanted to kiss you? Have you ever wondered why your thief would choose you? You, out of so many he could have picked? You know your answer deep in your heart, little girl, you know it, and now you can see it."

The mirror cracked. That was a beginning. Hopefully. Karina kept hitting it, and it kept cracking.

"Oh, I wouldn't do that if I were you," the voice said.

More reason to keep trying to break that stupid mirror. Karina was so angry she hit it with all her might. Crack, crack, crack. It was working. And then, suddenly, the mirror disappeared, as if had indeed been made of mist.

But she didn't see Sian beyond the place where the mirror had been. There was no purple room, no other mirrors, and no well. All she saw was a desolate landscape at night. Rocks and ruins until the eye could see, some burned trees, that was all. She turned around and didn't see any door. All she saw was the same desolate landscape, but far away, there was a hill leading to a sleek silver rectangular tower by a river. Karina felt so stupid. She'd let the voice play her. She'd done exactly what the voice had wanted her to do.

Looking around her at that bare wasteland, without any distinguishable portal, her insides knotted. Maybe she should see what that voice wanted.

Karina yelled, "Yo, you! Voice without body! Where are you?"

Her voice echoed and echoed, even though there were no walls to reflect the sound, as if she'd yelled a lot louder than she had. Karina closed her eyes. That was probably the direst situation in her life. Alone, in a place she didn't know, without any clue on how to come back.

Did Sian know that picking up the staff could be dangerous? *Go there, pick it up, and return. Don't look back and don't do anything else.* He knew it. And had made her go regardless. Her heart was cracking like the mirror. But this was not a good time to think about that. She held on to the staff. If it was indeed a powerful object, it would help her, even if only using it for bargaining. At this point, she didn't give a crap whether Sian got it or not. But the most important thing was finding a way back, a way home, a way anywhere else. She decided to walk to the tower just because it was the only thing in that landscape. It would probably take some two or three hours. Karina sighed. Would Sian be worried? Did he care about her, though? Right now, it didn't matter.

Karina walked, but then stopped, as she thought she'd heard something on the ground. She looked back and didn't see anything different. Another sound, this time from her left. Oh, this was going to drive her crazy. Then she heard a screech. And another. She froze. But she had to look. Up in the sky, a black cloud. Birds—no, not birds. Some dark winged creatures. More were coming, and she had no idea from where. They encircled her, flying lower and lower. Karina looked at the tower. Tower. A tower.

She focused on being there, and nothing happened. She tried to think about all her anger at Sian, or her anger at the voice. Nothing happened. She tried to remember her first kiss, but the memory was now tainted with fears and doubts. One creature dove towards her, and Karina threw herself on the floor. It flew right past her but then turned around. It had golden eyes and bat wings, but it was several meters wide. Karina focused on the tower while relaxing. Relax into focus. Detach from emotion. She saw it as if it were a movie, as if it had nothing to do with her, as if the danger wasn't real. The screeches were deafening now, and she closed her eyes.

When she opened her eyes, she was on the bottom of a very tall circular room with a spiral staircase leading to different doors. She exhaled, relieved. That was probably the tower she'd seen from afar, even if it was rectangular from the outside. Not as good as being back in Whyland or home, but hey.

This was a tower. A tower from where she could teleport, or at least she hoped. She wondered where the owner of the voice she'd heard earlier had gone, or if it was here. But maybe it didn't matter. Teleport, that was what she needed. Karina heard distant screeches and tried to think. She needed a tower, a tower to teleport to. Other than the odd mirror crossing, her teleporting usually ended in a teleporting tower, or at least passed through one. She needed a tall, vertical room. The well in the purple room flashed in her mind. But it was a well, with no way to come up. Karina heard screeches and noises coming from the top of the tower. The creatures were trying to enter. If only she knew what to do with her staff.

But this was a tower, and she should be able to do teleport. Karina focused on the purple room, kept focusing, and soon had the familiar feeling of loss of balance. When she opened her eyes, she was back where she'd been before, in the middle of the desolate landscape, staring at the tower far away, by the river. A swarm of flying creatures left the tower and came in her direction. *Teleport.* Karina was back in the silver tower. That wasn't very good.

The well came in her mind again. Could that work as a tower? Would that be the teleporting portal in the Darloom castle? Karina focused on the well and teleported. She found herself outside, in that dreadful landscape with winged creatures very close to her. She teleported away, finding herself again in the silver tower.

If she remained in this loop, between the plain and the tower, she'd never go anywhere. Perhaps she should go up in the tower and check its doors. Maybe there would be something for her. The well again flashed in her mind. The well. That was where she had to teleport. She focused on it, but tried to calm down any strain. Water, water, she needed water. The river! The tower was by a river.

Karina wasn't sure if her idea would work or not, but it was —hopefully—worth a try. Karina turned around and opened the door on her level. It led outside, to a platform over the river. Winged creatures flew towards her, but she ran and jumped on the water. She hoped those things didn't know how to swim, as she let herself be submerged. The well in the purple room came clearly in her mind. She focused there. There was no change. Wait, the screeches were gone. Karina extended her hands to her side and felt solid wall. Hopefully she'd come to the right well.

20

THE LAKE

She wanted to swim up for air, but the staff weighed her down. Weird, because it felt light when she'd carried it. She let go of the staff, and it went up. Weird again, of course. Karina had to swim up to reach the surface, but her clothes were thick and heavy. The surface seemed to be far away. Perhaps coming to the well had been a bad idea. Up, up, she had to go up.

Karina was almost out of air when she felt a burst of water from beneath her, lifting her. When her head reached the surface, she was in the purple room with the mirrors, and the water had reached its top. The staff floated by her side. Sian faced the mirror she'd crossed, which was still intact.

Karina threw the staff on the floor outside the well.

Sian turned, saw her, and looked alarmed. He pulled her out of the well, her body dripping water. "What happened? Why are you in here?"

Karina didn't know what to say.

He looked at her and took her hand. "You're cold. You need to change." Sian hugged her. "C'mon, you have to put some dry clothes on."

As much as she had told herself that the voice was a bunch of nonsense, now she looked at his eyes for a trace of a lie. Well, he certainly didn't seem worried that she'd taken more than twenty minutes to return—dreadful, terrifying twenty minutes.

Karina pointed to the staff lying on a corner. "Aren't you worried about that?"

Sian stepped back. "Karina, I… Are you all right?"

"Do you even care?"

"Come, get some dry clothes, then we can talk."

Sian pulled her hand to get out of the room. He acted as if he didn't even care about the stupid staff, the one she'd risked her life for. Or was it just a front? Either way, that voice still ringed on Karina's head, and she didn't want to leave the staff unattended. "Bring that thing with you."

"So you'll think that's all I care about?"

"No. So no creepy creature comes out of those mirrors or that well. Do you have any idea what's out there, Sian? Do you? Did you know and forget to tell me, or did you just send me on a fool's errand you had no idea about? Did you care?"

Karina pulled her hand and walked to the dark corridor.

"Karina!" Sian was right behind her.

"Take that thing."

Sian held her hand. "I can't. You'd have to give it to me. If you want to."

Karina went back to the room, grabbed the staff, and threw it beside him. "Here. It's yours."

Sian flinched.

CRASH.

One of the mirrors shattered. There was nothing beyond it, just wall. That was the mirror Karina had crossed. A little late to crash on this side, though.

Sian crouched to grab the staff, a glimmer in his eye. Karina passed him and walked fast to the dark corridor, then downstairs to her room. Ugh, not her room, their room. As if they were married or something. Some stupidity.

"Karina!" Sian came in right after her.

She entered the bathroom and locked the door. "I need a warm bath. You can't come." She took off her clothes as she prepared the bath. She stayed there for a long time, trying to relax, trying to think, trying to go over what had voice had told her, trying to understand what that horrible place with the tower was, but she didn't understand anything. Sian. She wanted to figure him out, but it was hard. Why had he sent her on a dangerous errand? Was he pretending he liked her? But could he really be that good, to show it in his eyes, in every kiss, in every tight hug, even at night, hugging her tightly, almost squeezing her, the whole night?

The door lock clicked, and Karina tensed, furious at this breach of privacy. But the door was opened just a little, and dry clothes were tossed through the crack. Indeed she needed them. Karina got out of the bath. The water would not help her clear her thoughts.

Sian was sitting on the bed when she came out of the bathroom. He got up and walked to her, touching her face. "What happened?"

Karina moved her head away and sat on one of the chairs. "What did you know about the, uh, the place I went?"

"It's a subdimension, created to contain the staff."

"And you had no idea it could be dangerous?"

Sian sat and took one of her hands. "What happened?

Karina pulled it back. "I'm asking first. Tell me. How much did you know about the danger of going there?"

Sian shook his head as if confused. "Nothing. It's a subdimension containing just the staff. Since you can open portals, you'd be able to walk in and out. I have no idea why you turned up in the well. I didn't know it would happen."

"And you sent me there without knowing."

"I'm sorry. I didn't know you'd come back that way. I'm sorry. I'll never ask you to do anything that could put you in risk again, never. I promise. No matter the price." He did seem concerned, though, his voice pitching with urgency. "Believe me. I thought there would be no danger for you."

He stared at her right in the eyes, holding so much feeling, concern. Karina looked away.

Sian took her hand. "Please. Forgive me."

Karina sighed. "And you didn't wonder what was happening when I took long to return?"

Sian blinked. "You came back right away."

Karina exhaled. Time difference, perhaps. That explained why he was calmly looking at the mirror when she came out of the water—if he was saying the truth.

Sian tilted his head. "Why? Didn't you? Didn't you return right away?"

Karina debated how much she should tell him. The voice, no way. A little of what had happened, maybe. She sighed. "The mirror disappeared, the room disappeared, and I was left in this place outside, with some small ruins here and there, but no trees, nothing. It looked awful. There was this high tower far away, and those creatures."

Sian frowned. "*What*? And how did you return?"

"I tried teleporting. I just went back and forth from the plains to the tower. Then I had the idea to jump in the water, and it worked."

Sian wrapped his arms around her. "I'm so sorry. Not even in my nightmares I would have imagined that. I would never have asked you to go across the portal if I thought—" He loosened his grip on her and moved away to look in her eyes. "Do you believe me?"

"Why do you even want that thing? It's not for me, is it?"

"It's for us."

Karina got up. "Oh, and what a wonderful coincidence. You

read all about a staff hidden in a secret dimension, then I'm the one called to break your spell, the one who can open portals." She looked at him, and it hit her. How could she have been so dumb? So, so dumb. Karina swallowed. "Was it on purpose? To bring me here?"

"Which part?"

"*Which part?* What do you mean which part? Was this some plan?"

Sian shook his head. "I don't know. I brought you here on purpose, yes. I wanted to take control of the castle, yes, so that was on purpose. But you know it. Why are you asking?"

"For someone who risked spending his whole life turned into stone, you sure were very careless in this castle. For someone who plans things so methodically, who reads so much, and knows so much, it's odd that you'd be caught so unaware, while casually strolling in the garden."

"You're right. And you know the answer. You know the answer, Karina."

"You did it on purpose? To bring me here?"

Sian had a satisfied grin. "I knew you'd figure it out."

"For that stupid staff?"

He rolled his eyes. "Of course not. Can't you see? To bring you here."

"Because you wanted to flirt with me? Have you ever heard of asking girls out? Taking them somewhere nice?"

"Yeah, in another dimension. Not that easy, Karina, not that easy."

"You could have asked—"

"Asked my brother? More than I'd already asked? What should I tell him? 'Could you please convince your girlfriend to open a secret teleporting tower, just so her friend could come and see me?'"

Karina stared. Yes, perhaps it would have been hard to

contact her, but still. "What did you do? You transformed your-self in stone then asked a friend to go and get your brother?"

"No. I just told my, uh, he was my friend, to tell my brother. I didn't remain transformed into stone. I just did it when my brother came by. And when you came by. It's not hard to see when someone is approaching here."

"What if you were asleep?"

"They wouldn't risk coming at night."

"And how could you do it, if you had no magic?"

"My friend did it. It's a book from the castle. The castle itself has some magic. I learned how to use it."

"The truelove stuff about the kiss was just yarn, then? You do realize you forced me to kiss you, right?"

"Love can break simple spells. I had to know what you felt. It was a test of sorts."

"And did I pass it?"

Sian shrugged. "You cheated."

Karina almost laughed. That was what he'd said back then. But it wasn't funny now, especially if all that deceit was just to get the staff. "What about the kyons?"

"They clearly escaped my control."

Karina jolted. "*Your* control? You were the one who sent those things after me?"

Sian pulled a strand of hair behind his ear. "See, it shouldn't have gone like that. They should never have chased you guys when I was still not transformed."

"What about coming to my house? Crossing a dimension?"

"It wasn't easy, but I had to get you back."

"You put my friend and my family at risk."

Sian shook his head. "No, no, the kyons have no real risk. The most they'll do is immobilize you. And they wouldn't have attacked anyone else."

"They were attacking your brother and Cayla. I saw it."

"They wouldn't immobilize them, though, they were just… creating confusion."

"For what?"

"I needed a reason for you to stay with me. Yeah, look at me like that, like I'm some pathetic fool. Maybe. Desperate needs, desperate measures."

"What about when they attacked us in the tower?"

He looked away. "I thought you'd like it. I know I fight well. I thought you'd like to see it."

"Really? You scared the crap out of me to *show off?*"

"Not show off. I thought—"

"I'd jump in your arms thinking you were a hero?"

He looked away and fiddled with his hair. "Maybe."

Karina pressed her hand on her face. "Why so many lies?"

"I never, ever, ever lied to you, Karina. Ever. Every single word I said was true."

The nerve. "Really? Come with me to Whyland. The Kyons are after you. You are in danger. The Darloom castle has a new master."

"Every single word was true. Every single word."

"Yeah, just the words, not the sentences."

"Every single sentence, then. Yeah, you were in danger of not falling in love with me, Karina. The kyons were after you. And I'm not sure you noticed, in case I didn't give you enough hints already, I'm the new master of the castle."

Karina's stomach turned. "Why do you need this staff then?"

"For complete control over the castle and its power. I had just a little. Now I have it all."

"Couldn't you have told me that?"

"I sort of did."

"*Sort of* doesn't cut it, Sian. You said I had to get you the staff so I would no longer be in danger."

He waved his finger. "I said I wanted it so I'd be able to protect you, and that's true. It's absolutely true."

"Protect me from *you*. Awesome."

"No. Protect you from everything and everyone."

Karina scoffed a breath. "Did you think about protecting me when you sent me to grab the staff? Did you?"

"I had no idea it would be dangerous, no idea. It was a mistake and I'm sorry."

Karina sighed. On one hand, maybe the problem was that she heard that voice and broke the mirror. Perhaps it had been her own fault. But she didn't know how to feel about Sian's lies. Not lies, according to him. Deceit, then. A chill ran down her spine. Her stomach growled, and her head hurt.

"I still haven't eaten," she said. "Can we have breakfast?"

"Of course."

Sian stepped close to her, cupping her chin with one hand, and brushing away her hair with the other. Karina knew what was coming. She should turn her face or push him away, but she didn't.

Kissing him, as he slid his arms to pull her close to his body, it was hard to be angry. Maybe she should be happy that he had it all planned, that the fact that she lived in another dimension hadn't stopped him, that he'd gone that far just to bring her to him. It would be a wonderful thought if it weren't for that nagging feeling that he'd done it just for the staff. Karina pushed him away.

Sian looked in her eyes. "I understand you're angry."

"And hungry. Can we go downstairs?"

Karina ate in silence. Matheo and Georgia were there, and soon Aline and Joel came down, and that gave Karina the respite she needed to try to clear her thoughts. It was worse than she'd imagined. She looked at Sian now and then and tried to imagine him coming up with such a convoluted plan to bring her. But then, it wasn't that complicated. The tricky part was getting

Darian to bring her. Once here, he'd do everything to convince her to remain with him. Was it for her? Or was it for power, though?

Sian was drinking slowly from a cup, holding it in his long fingers. Karina loved his hands, and how they brushed her hair and held her, she loved his satisfied smirk, his ten thousand outfits, and the way he looked at her. She loved his smell, his voice, his laugh. Her knees wobbled and her heart sped up just by being near him. How terribly she'd failed at not falling in love.

Sian convinced her to go for a ride, and they flew away from the castle. Just the two of them in his small lift reminded her of when she went to Siphoria with him. That had been so different. She had been still trying to tell herself she didn't like him, thinking that all she was doing was to save herself from kyons, when in reality she would perhaps have flown straight to hell if he'd asked her. All she needed was a good excuse. Well, he'd given Karina an excuse to spend time with him. Was it the end of the world?

They landed by a lake surrounded by some sort of pine trees. Tall mountains cast their shadows on the water. Karina closed the long jacket she wore. Sian wore a long coat in threaded wool, as if he'd chosen something cozy on purpose, as if inviting a warm hug.

Karina was still wary and suspicious, though. "Is there a reason we came here, other than talking? I mean, did it have to be here?"

Sian smirked. "Do you remember how I told you I wanted to bring you to the most beautiful place in Whyland? This is not quite it, but I didn't want to fly too far."

She tried to remember that. Right. "You mean over one year ago, when you put me in a cell instead?"

"From where you teleported away and didn't wait for me. Yes."

"You expected me to just sit there, while you attacked the castle?"

"I sure didn't expect you to teleport away, and didn't know you'd put yourself in danger, or I'd kept you with me. My father had asked me to kill you. I wouldn't do it, of course."

"Why?"

Sian frowned. "You have to ask?" He snorted. "I may be a lot of things, but I'm not a cold-blooded murderer, you know? I mean, you've been kissing me for two days, I sure hope you knew that."

"I meant why your father asked you that. What would he want with me?

"He feared you had magic. He also wanted me to kill Cayla. And her sister."

"You didn't tell me that."

"I told you I didn't kill you."

"Did you put me and Cayla in a cell to protect us?"

Sian snorted. "Let's not go that far. Well, maybe, yes. In a way, you had to be away from my father. I also thought having Cayla as a hostage could give me an upper hand. Not sure I'd like to use that hand, though."

"What about me?"

"You? I meant it. I was going to come back to you. As a prince."

"You think that would have impressed me?"

Sian had his superior smirk. "Yeah, I do. I just needed time to win you over."

"You sure are confident."

"I'm not. It's the way you looked at me."

"Do I still look at you like that?"

"Now you don't try to pretend you don't."

That was embarrassing, to be caught ogling a guy who

confessed he wanted to take the kingdom by force. And she hadn't found him good looking at the time, just weird. Perhaps fascinating was the word, not weird. But the whole part about wanting to take the kingdom wasn't that nice. "You're different now, aren't you? You don't want to be a prince anymore."

"My father's dead, in case you didn't know. Either way, putting my father there would have been stupid. A lot of things I was doing were stupid, Karina. I didn't understand or realize the extent of magic. Now I do. So it was a good thing you convinced me to quit and strike a deal."

"I convinced you?"

"You saved me from some pointless conflict. There was no need to teleport away from me."

"If you had told me you were going to give up, I guess—"

"I was going to come back and tell you."

Karina laughed. "Were you really interested in me since then?"

"I just wanted to see you again. And that's the whole point. I kept wanting to see you again. I have a plan for everything, and that's how you're here. Is it bad? Is it bad being here, by my side?"

Karina thought for a moment, then conceded, "It isn't." She rested her head on his chest. "But I'll still need a way to go back home."

"Home?" He sounded upset, then changed his tone. "In the Queen's castle. I'm sure you can make its tower functional again."

"You said I could use the tower here."

"That was before. After what you told me, I'm not sure…"

True. It was better not to risk any more teleporting from the Darloom castle. "In the Queen's castle, then."

"It will work."

Karina still had to ask something else. "And why did you need that staff? I mean, if it wasn't because of the kyons?"

Sian was silent for a few seconds, then spoke slowly, "The Darloom castle concentrates more power than you've seen, Karina. Power like that can't be contained for long. I thought it would be safer in my hand."

She moved her head away from his chest and looked in his eyes. "What if I hadn't given you the staff?"

"It would still be ours. No difference."

No difference. *Ours*. Those words meant a lot. Karina felt calmer, but she still needed to know more. "And what is this power? What is it?"

"I'll show you. At sunrise. Powerful time for powerful deeds."

"Oh, no, I'll have to wake up early again." Karina laughed. "You know, I would never have never guessed you were a morning person."

He raised an eyebrow. "Who says I wake up early for sunrises? More like staying late."

"Why the change now?"

He brushed his fingers on her face. "You want to spend the night awake?"

Karina trembled at what the words implied. Or maybe it was just her impression. She tried to pretend she didn't notice it, and laughed. "After having woken up at five or something?"

Sian chuckled, and it was so nice to see him in a non-sarcastic laugh. "Yeah, the timing is all wrong."

He kissed her cheek and they spent a few moments like this, just feeling each other's warmth. Karina again rested her head on his chest and heard his heart beating despite the thick coat.

Karina was at peace and forgave him for the kyons in her house and the lies. Or not lies, according to him. She had to ask, "Why the insistence in saying you were saying the truth? I mean, you were deceiving me, and you know it."

"I don't think I was deceiving you, just revealing things slowly. As for not lying, it's just something with me. Words have power, and if I start telling lies, my words lose their value, and their power as well."

"Magic power?"

He laughed and shook his head. "Not that I know of. There are legends of people who could whisper suggestions and make anyone do their bidding. I'm not quite there yet."

Karina laughed. "You did pretty well with me."

"Harder than I expected."

She hit his shoulder lightly. "Oh, you thought it was going to be even easier?" She looked down, thinking. "Why do you think my kiss didn't work? When I kissed you to break your spell? If it was just a matter of a little attraction, I mean…"

"Right? You also got me confused. Maybe it's the way you did it. If you didn't know you had to put any feeling…"

"Maybe. I was so stressed and scared."

"Was it your first kiss?"

Karina felt the blood rising to her head. "What difference does it make?"

Sian closed his eyes. "I'm an idiot. I should have known it. I should—"

"Excuse me?" The nerve. As if it were obvious nobody would want to kiss her.

He laughed. "Oh, I bet you're picky, that's all. I'm sure plenty of boys wish they could have kissed you. You know you're pretty."

"I guess I needed someone with a convoluted story to convince me to kiss me, and that's how it took that long."

"You needed me."

"Sian, you're so full of yourself, sometimes I think you'll explode."

He kissed her neck and whispered in her ear, "You forget I also needed you. I'm just speaking from experience."

Karina felt calm in his embrace, then remembered something. "There's something else I wanted to know."

Sian had a fake exaggerated frown. "More questions? I thought your quota was over for today."

Karina shrugged. "I'll ask tomorrow, then."

Sian laughed and kissed her cheek. "I'm kidding. Ask anything you want, any time you want. It's always better to talk, isn't it?"

"Yeah. You never really told me what Faria said."

Sian tensed, broke their hug, and looked away. "I did."

Karina didn't want to insist because it clearly bothered him, but the fact that it bothered him made her even more curious. "Not really, Sian, or maybe I didn't understand it."

Sian sighed. "She told me you already loved me."

Karina was puzzled. "Why were you upset?"

"She also said you'd leave me."

"Oh. But she must have been wrong or wanted to worry you. I'm not sure I *loved* you at the time. Love is something that comes slowly, right?"

"I guess."

He pulled her close to him in a tight embrace.

In the evening they had a fire outside, by the woods. Even though it was chilly, Aline and Georgia managed to build a huge fire, more like a celebration bonfire than a campfire. Of course, they wouldn't have been able to do this before, when she'd been afraid they could be attacked. Now that Karina knew that it was all Sian's fault and that they were safe even outside, it felt good being there, warmed by the heat of the fire and Sian's tight hugs. Aline and Joel sang. Their voices were harmonious together.

Karina felt happy with her heart at ease, having forgiven Sian. Yes, maybe his flirting methods were quite unusual, but in the end what mattered was being beside him. She wasn't even eager to go back to the Queen's castle and reopen a portal to go home, as she wanted that time to last forever. Well, there was that little pang and fear that if she returned home, she wouldn't be able to come back to Whyland, but she didn't want to think about it just now and waste those precious moments worrying about the future.

Back to the castle, Karina no longer felt the slight panic at having to be with a guy in a bedroom. It wasn't "a guy"; it was Sian. And yeah, it was weird to realize that she had panicked before about what could happen or what he could try, but now she trusted that he'd never trespass any of her boundaries, and so she could relax.

Karina had already changed into her sleeping clothes when Sian came out of the bathroom. Loose v-neck shirt and pants, this time dark blue. Did he really have a whole collection of pajamas as well? It was a little silly because everything looked good on him. She wondered what he would look like without his shirt, though. Being so tall made him look skinnier than he actually was, but he was quite fit, and from what she felt, had an amazing body.

Sian smiled, walked towards her and kissed her, holding her tight and lifting her from the ground. She could kiss him a million times, every time it would make her weak in the knees and give her a pleasant chill down her spine and her stomach. Karina put her hands under his shirt and moved up to his back.

Sian put her down and stepped back. "Don't."

Karina was startled. Well, in truth she felt rejected. She looked away and sat on the bed. "Sorry."

He also sat and started brushing her hair out of her face.

This time it annoyed her as if it was a consolation prize. Karina jerked her head away and stared at him. "You know, I wasn't going to take off your shirt, and it definitely didn't mean I wanted to..." She looked away, unable to continue.

"I know."

She was going to ask what the problem was, but maybe he

also had the right to have boundaries. It was just that it was weird to see a guy being that much of a prude.

Sian said, "You're upset."

Karina shrugged. "No. I mean, surprised. You really have a problem with me touching your *back*?" Even Karina wouldn't mind if he touched her back.

"Don't know if you noticed; I'm weird, Karina."

Fair enough. He was a prude, but it was his right. "Hum… all right."

He looked down. "Give me some time. I need to trust you more."

Karina shrugged. "No problem. I also need some time to take off my shirt, I guess, so we're even."

Sian caught his breath, and his eyes flickered towards her chest before looking away. Karina flushed, trying not to think of where she'd taken his mind. He fiddled with his hair and looked away. It was the first time Karina saw him looking that embarrassed. "It's not that. It's not that I don't want to… Not now. Of course." He stared at her. "It's different. I… I have…" He closed his eyes. "I have reasons why nobody ever sees me without a shirt or touches my back or chest."

She shrugged. "It's fine."

"It's not fine. You're upset."

"Just surprised, that's all."

He sighed. "It's everything that I hate about myself. I don't want you looking at me in pity, horror, or both."

She tried to be playful. "Do you have scales or something?"

He snorted, even more annoyed. "Perhaps. I just want to make sure everything is settled between us. Give me some time."

Karina smiled. "We have plenty, don't we?"

"I hope so." He looked away as if thinking.

Karina's mind was spinning with curiosity. What was it? A very ugly tattoo? Well, she hadn't seen any tattoo so far in Whyland, so she assumed they didn't have them, and she wouldn't be able to feel it just by touching it. Fur? No, hair. Maybe he had a really hairy chest and back. That didn't make sense, though, because his beard was thin. His words came to her mind, about learning to resist pain. Karina looked at him. "You have scars."

He shrugged. "Maybe. I don't want to talk about it. Nobody's seen it since I was twelve."

Scarred at that age? Karina felt something unpleasant stirring inside her, and fury towards his father, but she kept her face steady because her anger would only upset him. "I don't care, Sian."

"Well, I do."

Fine, she wasn't going to push it or ask about it. Boundaries were for both of them. Still, she wondered what bothered him so much. Burning scars? She tried to imagine the ugliest red, scorched skin beneath his shirt. She'd still like him. Was it cutting scars, bumps? Maybe it was some infected gooey thing and that was the reason he always changed clothes. No, it would leak through his thin shirt. Regardless, she tried to imagine the very worst, disfigured skin on his back, and there was no horrific scenario where she would no longer like him. She had to tell him.

"Sian, you know I like you regardless, right? Whatever you have, however you look under your shirt... I don't mind. Nothing changes. I'll still like you."

He was still looking away. "Think about it. I'll understand if you change your mind."

Karina rolled her eyes. "Don't be silly." She pulled his face and lay her lips over his. His mouth relaxed for a long, passionate kiss.

After a moment he stopped and looked in her eyes. "You're just like I thought you would be."

"And what is that?"

"Sweet. Lovely."

"And how did you know that?"

Sian had a relaxed smile. "I read people well."

"And you knew I was sweet?"

"I knew you'd fall in love with me."

The nerve! But he had a point. She looked right in his eyes. "I guess you were right."

Having to wake up early the next day or not, they spent a long time alternating between kissing and looking into each other's eyes, bodies closer and closer. Their clothes were the barrier preventing them from going too far. For a few brief moments, though, Karina wished there were no barrier and she could be all his.

21

UNDERSTANDING

Karina walked down a dark hallway, towards a room with a flickering reddish light. As she entered, she noticed that a fireplace was lit and was the only source of light illuminating a chair with a small dark-haired boy around seven to ten years old. A man whose face she couldn't see took a poker from the fire and pressed against the boy's chest. She could smell burning skin. Horrified, she wanted the man to stop, wanted to do something, but couldn't move.

The man asked, "How does it feel?"

The boy smiled. "Comfortable."

The man pulled the poker away.

Karina woke up suddenly and tried to sit up, but she couldn't move, as if someone or something were tying her. She tried to shake herself free until she realized that what was tying her were Sian's arms, which tightened around her as she moved. She exhaled, realizing it was just a dream, in the pleasant sensation of being near him. A dream. Was it something she saw, or was it just that she had fallen asleep impressed with what he'd told her?

She closed her eyes and tried to relax and fall asleep again, but then memories and sensations from the previous night overcame her as she remembered his body in her hands and hers in his. As amazing as it had felt, what was left now was a weird feeling like guilt and embarrassment, as all the advice about what a girl could and couldn't do at the beginning of a relationship circled in her head. Had he tried something more, would she have stopped him? She didn't know the answer. But nothing had happened, had it? She didn't want to overthink the definition of nothing, or the answer could be complicated. Perhaps she should think about the definition of relationship. What were they? Where was this going?

Sian's sleepy voice interrupted her thoughts. "Are you awake?"

"Yeah. A dream woke me."

"Was I in it?" he asked in a teasing voice.

"Not sure."

A light, relaxed chuckle. "How can you not be sure?"

"It was a young boy."

"I see." He kissed her neck. "We might as well get up. Powerful time for powerful deeds."

Karina turned and faced him. "Right. You gotta make sure you're doing something important when you're sleepy and starving."

"We'll get something to eat."

Karina had a sense of déjà-vu as she sat on the still dark kitchen, eating cake and drinking tea. She hoped there was some caffeine in it.

Sian's overcoat today was in very thick leather. He took a long sip from his cup and asked her, "What do you know about Whyland?"

A big question. "Hum… A lot. A little. I know some secret

passages, names of rivers, I saw the maps in the book you gave me. I mean, I don't know. In terms of politics, people seem to backstab each other often, right?"

Sian chuckled. "That's good to keep in mind. There's something important: the portals. This is a hub of portals going everywhere. The castles control the portals, sort of. Or at least keep them closed just enough so that things won't get in."

The creepy voice at the other side of the mirror came into Karina's mind and she shivered.

Sian continued, "So that's one thing important to know, that when we're talking about kings and queens here, it's not just political leaders but more. It's not like in other kingdoms. But there are more portals though, to precise dimensions. My father wanted to find magical peoples living here, but I think they had their own portals, to subdimensions. He would only find the ones who chose to stay here, and there isn't much magic left. Darian came from one village considered magical, they were among the Lost People in the north, but he doesn't know a thing about magic." His voice had the sneering tone he used when referring to his brother, and Karina was reminded that they hadn't been raised together.

"And why is this important?"

"Because you can't simply put anyone on the throne. But it doesn't have to be Lylah either."

Karina was about to take a bite of her cake but she paused. "But she's fine there, isn't she? And you said you didn't want to take the throne anymore, right?"

Sian blinked as if startled. "I never said that."

Karina trembled. *Do you want to take the throne?* The question was on the tip of her tongue, but the possible answer terrified her. She asked something else, "What does it have to do with this castle? And the staff?"

"Finish and I'll show you."

Her stomach was shut. "I'm done."

"What about the tea?"

Karina had always hated tea, and this tea was the worst she'd ever tasted. She'd been drinking it just because Sian had made it for her. She pushed away her cup. "I had enough."

He looked disappointed. "Oh."

Karina shrugged. "Sorry. I should have said I didn't like it, I—"

"It's fine. Come, then."

He got up and extended his hand. Karina took it, feeling his thin long fingers wrapping hers and that pleasant sensation that came with it, now with an accompanying chill in the stomach with the memory of his touch.

They went through a door on the ground floor. Behind it, they descended stairs to a room with glass windows overlooking a huge hall with circular columns.

Sian looked at her and brushed her hair away from her face. "I fear this might be rushed, but I can't wait any longer. You'll have to trust me."

Karina stared at the hall with dread. "For what?"

"You'll see. However you feel, hang on. We'll sort it all together."

This didn't sound good. "Well, show me."

Sian took a deep breath. "All my life, Karina, all my life I learned to fight. Not only to fight one-on-one, but to fight wars. Win, conquer, be powerful. It sounds great, doesn't it? In theory, it does. But the reality is sad, pitiful, and bloody. If I'm going to have power, I'll do this in a clean way. I came to this castle, well, I took the trouble to find this castle, searching for answers, and I found a lot more than I hoped. Want to know what I found?"

Not really. She had a terrible sense of foreboding, but she had to say something, so she asked, "What?"

"A clean army. Everything I always dreamed." He let go of her hand and took the staff, which stood in a corner, and lifted it. "Rise."

The ground started moving. No, something was moving, coming out of the ground. Hundreds of kyons. More. Karina didn't fear them this time, maybe because they were beyond the glass, or maybe because she knew they were under Sian's control. Whatever Sian was planning to do with them was what caused her to fear. The creatures were becoming better and better formed, not the same amorphous, unfinished forms from before. They had eyes and faces.

Sian had a smirk. "They don't kill, they don't hurt, they just stop my enemies."

"And who are your enemies?"

He looked at her and raised an eyebrow. "Anyone who stops me."

The question came out of her lips as a whisper. "From what?"

He stepped closer to her and fiddled with her hair. "Today we march to the castle. You'll be queen."

She must have misunderstood something. "Which castle?"

He kissed her lips lightly. "Yours. Mine. Ours. Whyland will be our kingdom."

Karina stepped back. "Uh, are you planning on taking the kingdom?"

"Why are you even asking that?" Sian tilted his head, blinking slowly.

"You are?"

"When did I ever say I wasn't?"

Perhaps this was a horrible misunderstanding. "You mean you're going to Siphoria with this army? To become king by force? Is this what you mean?"

Sian waved his hand. "Clean war, Karina, clean war. No blood, no killing."

"Was this why you needed the staff? To bring war to Whyland? To depose the queen?"

"I don't understand why you're surprised."

"Why I'm surprised? Well, remind me when exactly you told me your plans. Remind me."

Sian looked confused, eyebrows drawn together. "I never said I wanted you to be my queen?"

Karina took a deep breath. "You did, but I didn't... I mean, can't you just take this castle? It's nice. We're fine here, and—"

"I want to bring peace to my kingdom, and I can do it. Not only that, now I have the power to protect it."

Karina looked at the window, at those horrid creatures. "Are you really planning on launching these things on your people?"

"You say it as if they were some killing machines. They aren't. And they'll only stop whoever opposes me. A lot of people support me, even inside the government. It's all a lot more complicated than you know, even though you know a little."

"You have support, great. I know people like you. Suggest an election then. Convince people to demand a change in the system of government. Come to power in a way that's right, if you want it so much."

"It doesn't work in Whyland, I told you."

"Just leave the current queen there, then. Why do you have to change anything?"

Sian stepped back. "I don't understand you. Why would you rather her instead of you?"

"I don't even live here!"

He stared at her, then turned his head away, in a mocking sneer. "You don't live here! What was it then? A joke for you? Was all this a joke? Tell me."

Was he talking about *them*? "Not a joke. I would come to visit, I would find a way. But that doesn't mean I want to be queen. I hate politics."

Sian exhaled and seemed to calm down. "It seems scary and overwhelming. I understand. You don't have to do anything. I have it all under control. You'll just have to be you, and everyone will love you. You'll have songs written about you."

Karina was trembling. Anger, fear, disappointment, she didn't even know. "Right. I'll just sit all day while you do everything."

"I'm not saying that. You'll do whatever you want. What do you like? Science? Discovery? We'll have it all for you. I can bring scholars from all over the world. You can do whatever you want."

"Yeah, I can. And I don't want to be a freaking queen!"

Sian stared at her. "It was a joke, then. All a joke."

"It wasn't. But you never told me what you wanted to do, never. You spent time away from me, probably planning whatever it is you're going to do, and you never said anything. You never asked what I thought of that. How was I supposed to know you wanted to take the kingdom by force, how?"

Sian raised his eyebrows. "How?" He snorted. "How? Maybe because that was the first thing I ever told you when we met. How's that?"

"You said you changed."

"For better. Not for pathetic. Tell me, Karina, who the hell do you think you've been kissing for three days? Who?"

"You."

"No. I never pretended I was anything I wasn't. Never."

"Really? Why didn't you ask me if I wanted to come to Whyland to raise an army of creepies and take the throne? Why didn't you ask me that? Did you think I was going to say no? Well, you guessed right."

"I told you slowly. We barely knew each other. Was I supposed to tell you I wanted you to be my queen? Really? Of course you'd run away scared."

"And how exactly did you pick me to be your queen if you didn't even know me? How?"

"I read people well. I know of your power, Karina. The

throne is the right place for you. Nothing less. You'll see it in time."

"No, Sian. I don't like it. If you're going to be king in a legitimate way, I'll support you, but—"

"That's the only legitimate way you can take the throne. How do you think it's done? By asking please?"

"Well, then, you don't need it. You have businesses, don't you? You already make a living. Maybe you could talk to your brother, I could talk to Cayla, you could have a good position—"

He snorted. "A good position. Like a dog. Do you really expect me to obey my brother and his spoiled girlfriend? Do you think they're better than us? That my brother is better than me?"

"No. But you can go to Siphoria then. You have things there, friends."

"What's wrong with you? Any girl in your position would be flattered. I mean, look at what I'm offering you. Isn't it enough?"

"Sian, I don't want war, and I don't want this stupid throne. I just want you."

"Not true. What you want is some stupid guy from your imagination that you think is me."

"What about you? You didn't even know me when you decided you wanted me as your queen. You didn't even bother asking me what I thought of that. You don't want me either."

"Of course I don't want you. If you're not going to be my queen, I don't want you."

Karina stepped back, startled. She had a bitter taste in her mouth and focused on holding back the tears that wanted to come out of her eyes. "Thanks for letting me know. I wish you'd told me this sooner."

His voice softened. "It's not this. Come with me, and we'll sort it out. I'll have time to explain and you'll have time to understand."

Her body felt numb. "Was it because of my power?"

"You're smart, Karina. Think. Think. Why was it? Why did I choose you? You have your answer."

Hold back the tears. Hold back the tears. "I don't want to be queen. I'm sorry."

"Well, leave then. You already gave me all I needed, in case you haven't noticed. Leave me and it's the end, and whatever happens is your fault."

Her skin felt as if it was turning to ice. Struggling not to cry, she had trouble making sense of what was happening. Her mind was spinning. She had to go to the castle, find Cayla, open a portal home. "I'll need a portal."

Sian snorted. "Really? You're leaving me. Walking away. Wonderful. I could never have guessed that. You're so surprising. Shocking, really. You want a portal? Not my problem, portal opener. Deal with it."

"I will." Karina turned around to get her stuff in her bedroom. She didn't even know what she was going to do. Maybe convince someone to fly her to Siphoria? Would they even do it, though, devoted as they were to Sian?

Sian pulled her hand. "Where do you think you're going?"

"Dealing with it, right?"

"Don't be ridiculous. Come with me to the castle. You can re-open the flowing tower and leave. More than you deserve, but I'm in a generous mood."

Humiliating. She'd walk to Siphoria if she had to. "Thanks, I'm fine."

"No. You're coming with me."

Karina pulled her hand. "Shut up, Sian, isn't it more than I deserve? I'll figure a way home. I'll deal with it, don't worry."

"You are leaving then? For real? A kingdom is not good enough for you."

"I don't want it, and you know I don't, so stop it."

"You stop. Fickle and false, that's what you are. Three days kissing me. Lies. All lies. Last night…"

Karina moved her hand to hit him on the face, but he was very fast and grabbed her wrist. She said, "You aren't going to shame me for that, you aren't."

"There's no shame if it's true, Karina. No shame."

"But it was true. I liked you, or I thought I did."

He still held her wrist, fingers gentle but firm. "You're confessing, right? It was never me. You want someone who'll kiss the current queen's shoes? Get my brother."

"That's disgusting. He's my friend's boyfriend. You can't be jealous of him."

"Jealous, me? That would be ridiculous. My heart's been locked away a long time ago, in case you haven't noticed." He smirked. "Oh, I guess you haven't. Too bad."

Karina's knees were weak, and her vision was blurry. Nothing made sense anymore. "Let me go."

He didn't move his hand wrapped around her arm. "And if I let you go, what are you going to do?"

"I don't know."

"Aren't you going to run to my brother and his obnoxious girlfriend? Aren't you?"

"You made them bring me here. They did this for love for you."

Sian sneered. "Love? You misuse that word, girl. What my brother has is just a very warped sense of duty. From my part, it adds to the victory."

He was still holding her wrist. "Let me go," she asked.

"I will, if you tell me you'll go with me to Siphoria and become my queen."

"Because of some magic you didn't bother to explain, I bet. It was never about me, was it?"

His face was hard. "What difference does it even make? Now come, be queen or terrible things might happen and it will be all your fault. Terrible, terrible things."

"Are you threatening me?"

"I'm explaining, Karina, it's very different. Come with me. After that, you can leave."

Right. More and more it was getting obvious that he never cared about her. As if it hadn't been obvious already. Perhaps she should come with him, learn his secrets, and find the right time to stop him, except that she couldn't stomach looking at his smug face, realizing she'd been fooled, feeling so, so, stupid. So stupid, Karina.

"Is that all you want?" she asked.

"I want lots of things. But that's all I'm asking."

Karina was trying to think. Releasing those things on Whyland was terrible. She had to do something about it, even if she didn't live there. Well, she had her own fault in it, so in a way it was her duty to do something. At that moment, though, it was hard to think. All she felt was anger, anger at that guy clutching her wrist in his bone-like fingers. But she wouldn't stoop as low as to remain by his side, lie and pretend. She was better than Sian. She stared in his eyes. "I'm going to stop you."

"Oooh, I'm scared. Terrified, Karina. How exactly are you going to do it? Run to the castle? Literally." He laughed. "Run."

"Hilarious. You think I'm pitiful and stupid. I'm not and I'll stop you. I don't care about anything anymore, I swear I'll defeat you or die trying."

Sian sneered. "Aren't we glad trying is not a mortal disease?"

Click. He'd put a manacle on her wrist and was closing the other on his.

Karina shook her arm. "Is this in any way acceptable?"

"More than acceptable, for an enemy. Isn't that what you just confessed you were?"

She wasn't going to ask or beg for him to let her go. "I am."

Sian smirked. "We're settled then."

"I'm going to annoy you all the way to Siphoria."

"Nah. I don't think so." He pulled a gray cloth from his pocket. "Do you remember this?"

She did. It had something that made a person faint. No way Karina would allow him to carry her like a sack of potatoes to use her for whatever selfish purposes he had. No way. Teleport. She had to teleport. She needed a tower, though. But did it have to be a fully functional teleporting tower? Or could any tower work? She remembered her moment on the roof, looking at Siphoria, realizing for the first time in her life she was in love. It was worth a try.

He laughed. "Want to take a nap?"

His voice faded away, and she felt bright flashes of light. Nothing held her wrist anymore, and she felt as if she were falling.

THE OTHER CASTLE

Karina fell on dusty ground. She looked up and saw the walls of a ruined hollow tower. She'd made it, she'd teleported to the tower by the river she'd seen that night from the Junction's roof. A tower she'd never been inside. It was a little like what she'd done in that horrible wasteland beyond the mirror in that dreadful castle. Her mouth had the bitterest taste she'd ever tasted, and her wrist still hurt, from that jerk's hand and manacle. But this was not the time to feel shame or regret, or to think of her stupidity and all the signs and red flags she had chosen to ignore. This was not the time to berate herself for having allowed him to mislead her, for having threaded her own trap. This was not the time. All that matter was to stop him. Stop him. He'd messed with the wrong girl.

She walked to the door, trying to think about her next steps. She saw the river and some boats, and far away, on the other side, the castle. There was also a tall metal fence around the tower. She hadn't predicted that.

A man's voice startled her. "Hey!"

Karina turned.

A man in the army's dark blue uniform held a gun to her. "This area is off limits!"

"Sorry. I need to go to the castle. I need to talk to—" She tried to think quickly. Cayla would be hard, since she was the princess. Maybe it would be easier to talk to someone else. "Darian. I need to see Darian."

"You mean the king?"

Karina frowned. "What?"

"Or is it someone different?"

"I mean Cayla, uh, princess Cayla's…"

"Right. Everyone wants to see the new king now."

Had she heard right? "Darian's *king*?"

The guard shook his head. "Girl, where have you been?"

Karina couldn't answer, as she was convulsing with laughter. Sian's pathetic, pitiful, stupid little brother was king. King. Everything Sian had always wanted. Pity she hadn't seen Sian's face when he'd heard the news. Tears of laughter were coming out of her eyes.

Karina stared at the wall. After some three hours alone in a cell, her cathartic laughter had died, and everything stopped being funny. The place was clean and the chair she sat on was comfortable, but waiting for her messages to Cayla or Darian to be sorted out and prioritized or for someone to come and verify what she'd been doing in an abandoned tower was unnerving. Oh, the fuss they'd made when she couldn't explain how she'd ended up there. Anyway, the issue was that Sian was probably planning his next move at that very moment, and here she was, unable to counter attack him.

Sian. That very morning she'd woken up wrapped in his arms. She'd be lying if she said that there was any feeling that compared to that. Then that very morning he revealed all his plans, and how she was a pawn in his game. Everything had been planned, and everything had been a lie. Had it, though? He seemed pretty sincere in his affection. Sure, but then when she disagreed with what he was doing, he changed his tune quickly. *I know of your power, Karina. Of course I don't want you! My heart's been locked away a long time ago, in case you haven't noticed.*

The worst was that, indeed, he'd given her lots of hints to his true intentions. Of course, so that later he could claim he hadn't lied. And as much as she wanted to believe that there had been some genuine feeling behind it all, the fact was that he had never said he loved her or even that he liked her. True, he'd said he believed in love at first sight, but he'd never specified whose love. He'd also said *more than liked*, and *more than cared*, which was ambiguous like a lot of what he said. For a guy who claimed not to lie, that was the final clue she needed.

Two guards, one old and one young, passed by, and one of them pushed a box of food through a small opening on the bars near the floor.

"Hey," Karina yelled. "Can you help me? I need to talk to Darian or Cayla."

The guards stopped. The oldest guard asked, "Have you made a request?"

"Yes, but it's urgent!"

The guard nodded. "Everyone has urgent requests, you know?"

The younger guard eyed her up and down. "What's your name?"

"Karina."

His eyes widened and he straightened as if he'd recognized the name. Karina wondered if he knew Darian or Cayla, and was relieved that someone would help her.

The older guard asked him, "Do you know her?"

"No." The younger guard shrugged. "Never heard."

Karina frowned. He glanced at her and away. Of course he knew who she was, but somehow he couldn't say it.

"Hum," the oldest guard said. "Just be patient, girl."

"Maybe you'll be lucky," the younger guard said, then winked at her.

That was what she hoped. She looked at the food. Weird looking rice, meat, and vegetables in a paper box, with a wooden flat spoon, like a cheap ice cream spoon. It tasted delicious. She'd been starving without knowing, and she should have known it because she'd risen before dawn and barely eaten. But hey, out of so many things she should have known, hunger was the least of them. Towards the end of the box, it became more like very bad airplane food. As her hunger settled, the lack of taste became noticeable. Hunger makes people misjudge things.

After about an hour, Karina figured she hadn't gotten lucky. Yeah, perhaps Sian had messed with the wrong girl, but now she was behind bars and could do little to enact her revenge. Yeah, it was revenge she wanted, and to recognize it as such was liberating.

After some time, steps echoed in the hall. A young man stood in front of her, someone she recognized. It was Liam, the guy with dark hair and blue eyes who'd sat at her table at the Junction. He was Sian's friend, and Karina shuddered.

"Can't believe my eyes," he said.

He wore the army's dark blue uniform. Great.

Karina looked away. "Well, don't."

"Easy, easy. I'm here to help."

She stared at him. "How?"

"I don't think you came to Siphoria to spend your time in a cell, but if you're comfortable… I've heard the food has greatly improved." He put a key in the lock.

"I didn't say I wanted to get out."

He held the key back. "Weird. I thought you wanted an audience with the princess."

"Are you going to take me there?"

"I said I was going to help, didn't I?" He lowered his voice. "I won't tell him I saw you."

"Why?"

He smiled. "I have my reasons."

Indeed, he walked with her in the direction of the castle by the river. Karina still feared that she was going to be taken to Sian, or imprisoned, or something, but since it was only one guy, perhaps she would have a chance to escape if any of that came to pass.

When they were halfway, he asked, "So? What happened? Royalty doesn't suit you?"

Karina had a queasy feeling and didn't trust him. "I'd rather not say it, if you don't mind."

"Hum. You're not giving me any information, but I'll give you some. Nobody knows you're here. Sian hasn't told anyone."

"How thoughtful of him." Karina rolled her eyes.

"No," Liam said. "He's hiding something, and that's the thing you don't want to tell me."

Karina shrugged. "Maybe."

"I can tell you something, though. Sian is coming with a new queen."

If that was true, that was fast. New queen. Was it possible for her to feel even worse than before? Still, Sian, Liam, or both could be playing or testing her. She tried not to show any reaction. "You think I care?"

"I thought you'd like to know, that's all. You should also know that I'm no longer his friend."

It all sounded like a bunch of yarn. "Since when?"

"You know it, don't you? That night when I met you."

"Four days ago, you mean."

He laughed. "Yes. And when you're curious, I might be able to give you some important information. I can tell you what's happening in Arlenia, for example."

The name rang a bell, but not so much. "I don't even know what that is."

"Interesting. He did keep you out of his loop, didn't he?"

Karina shrugged. "Perhaps."

He stared at her. "Listen, I know what it's like to be used and then tossed. It sucks, but you should never let other people determine your worth."

Used? Tossed? Those were some strong words and she didn't quite agree with them, but never mind. "I know my worth."

He nodded and, to Karina's surprise, didn't ask any more questions. He took something out of his pocket. It was a small silver disk, smaller than the palm of his hand. "This is a two-way radio. If you need something—"

"You'll track me with this."

"No. Ask Cayla. If this thing can be tracked, you can throw it away. As for now, you'll be in the castle, right? I mean, I don't need a tracker to know where you are."

Karina took it, thinking that she'd probably throw it away. She didn't trust him, but she didn't want to refuse the help of a potential ally. The disk had a darker part in the middle. "How do I make it work?"

"Press that." He pointed to the darker part.

"It better not be expensive, cause I'll sure throw it away if this thing can be used to track me."

"I'm your friend, Karina. You shouldn't fear me."

"Can you give me a reason for that?"

"The same person who disappointed you disappointed me. We could work together."

Maybe. And then maybe not. "It could also be some kind of test or joke planned by Sian."

"That's something he could do, yes. I understand your mistrust. Ah, and try to get to safety as soon as possible. Things might happen a lot sooner than you expect."

"What?"

"We're getting close now. Let's walk in silence. And hide it."

Her coat had pockets, where she put the disk. He obviously had teased some information just so she'd be curious and insist, or to make sure she'd contact him, so she remained silent.

As promised, he did take her to the castle, where she was received by other guards and told to wait in a room. Right. As if Karina had been planning on going anywhere, with the door locked. Well, now that she thought about it, she could leave if she wanted to. But then she'd end up again in the tower with the fence, back to square one. Not one, two, actually. One was in the Darloom castle, wrapped tightly in Sian's arms. Had that been a lie? What had those hugs and kisses been for? Those relaxed, light chuckles? Was it all because he was happy he would be king? Because he needed her? Well, he needed her, he'd said so. So, so, stupid, Karina. And now by the looks of it he didn't need her anymore. At least Karina knew the truth.

He told her he didn't like to lie. Well, not lie with his words. He could lie very well with every gesture. Ugh. She had to stop thinking about him and focus on a way to stop him. He was the one who'd been stupid, thinking she'd just follow him blindly, that she wouldn't step up against him. He would pay for under-estimating her.

The door opened, and Cayla entered. She had dark circles under her eyes and wore dark green pants and a thick tunic. Her black hair still looked shiny and spectacular, though.

She sounded worried. "What happened? How come you're here?"

"I returned home, then I came back."

Cayla had a surprised expression. "You teleported back to Whyland on your own?"

"Yeah…"

Cayla squinted. "What happened?"

"A few things. I have something important to tell you. Where's Lylah?"

Cayla shook her head. "I don't know. She went to Arlenia, and she hasn't come back. All our communications there have been blocked. I don't want to think the worst…"

"I'm sorry."

"They are threatening war, Arlenia, and the worst is that we have no news from the north. They could be marching right into Whyland at any minute."

"Oh." That was upsetting. Karina had to say her part, though. "They are not the only ones who are marching to the castle."

"What do you mean?"

"Sian has an army of kyons, those horrible things that attacked us in that garden, but now they're fully formed, and he's going to attack you using them."

Cayla shook her head. "No, no, you must be mistaken. They're tied to the Lost Castle. He can't bring them here. He might be fool enough to try it, but it won't work. Don't worry about it."

"It's different now." Karina didn't want to reveal all that she'd done, but she had to tell at least a little. "There was something in that castle, that changed them, increased their powers, and his powers."

"Sian doesn't have any magical power whatsoever. He can't do anything. He can't, Karina, don't worry about it."

"He was certain, though."

Cayla waved her hand. "He's stupid." She then seemed concerned. "And you? What have you been doing all this time?"

Karina felt ashamed of her previous feelings for Sian and for all that she'd done. "I was with him."

Cayla caught her breath. "He kept you prisoner?"

"No. He convinced me that my life was in danger and that I

shouldn't go home." Well, that was true. "I believed him, and I stayed with him in the castle."

"That horrible, creepy, dark castle? Weren't you afraid?"

What an odd question. "It's not that bad on the inside, it's like here, but prettier, without the crazy confusing corridors and with more windows."

Cayla looked skeptical. "I see. Once things are calmer, we can take you back using that old tower."

"That tower has been destroyed."

"What?"

"It... sort of exploded." How to explain it? "Some magic, something. I'm not sure."

"Magic doesn't explode things, Karina. Maybe a lift shot it."

Karina shrugged. "Maybe."

Cayla sighed. "We'll get you another tower. Let me just solve everything happening right now. I'm so scared, Karina, so scared."

"Your mother is quite powerful, I'm sure she'll—"

"I know. That's what I tell myself. Even if she had to hide or something, she'll survive. She'll come back. What scares me is not her, it's Darian."

"What's wrong?"

Cayla looked down, then back at her. "I'm interim queen, you know?"

Had the circumstances been different, Karina would have congratulated her.

Cayla shook her hands up and down. "But I guess nobody knows it because nobody listens to me. Do you know who they listen to? Darian. They listen to Darian, they call him king."

That king thing was a little odd, for sure. "Hasn't your mother been gone for a few days at most? I mean..."

"It was a precaution. The young king from Arlenia said he wanted to marry me or he'd attack us. That's why my mother went there. So Darian and I announced publicly that we are going to get married. Someday. Nothing settled. But officially, we're a couple. And everything changed because I was named interim queen for some reason. I don't even know why, I mean, it was just a visit. Anyway, I'm queen, and he decided he'd be king. He's giving all the orders. I'm being kept locked in my own castle. There are two guards following me everywhere I go, even now, right outside this door. Can you believe it?"

It didn't sound right. Darian seemed to be a nice guy. "Have you talked to him about it?"

"He claims he's afraid someone will kidnap me. Well, I'm afraid. I don't recognize him anymore, Karina. Sometimes I wonder if it was all for power."

Karina sighed. "You should be glad that you love someone who loves you back. It's a privilege, you know?" These last words left a bitter taste in Karina's mouth, as she realized what she didn't have.

Cayla shook her head. "I don't know. I don't know anything anymore."

"Talk to him."

She was thoughtful, then she seemed determined. "I will. I will right now. Come."

Karina wondered if Darian would take Sian's threat more seriously than Cayla, but if she talked directly to him, Cayla would be pissed. She'd need to convince her friend carefully, or convince them both once they settled whatever differences they had.

A young man and a young woman in uniforms were indeed outside the door.

Cayla yelled at them, "Enjoy listening? Tell him, tell him all I said. But you won't because I'll tell him first."

Maybe it was the stress because of the recent events, but now that Cayla had yelled at the guards, Karina realized that her friend seemed a little paranoid and was bursting with anger. Cayla's pace was so fast that Karina had to almost run to keep up with her as she strode through the hallways. The guards also followed. Cayla stopped before a large door, where two male guards stood. Cayla was going to open it, but a guard stood in front of her.

"Your Highness. You're not allowed here."

Cayla turned to Karina. "See? See? See what I'm telling you?"

Okay, that was pretty bad.

Cayla turned to the guard. "On what grounds, tell me, on what grounds can you prevent your queen from entering anywhere? Do you think you can give me orders?"

The guard lowered his head. "Not my orders, Your Highness. There's an important meeting, and it must not be interrupted."

"Whose orders?" Cayla asked.

"The King."

"King what? He's nothing. Since when he orders more than I do?"

"If you ordered your guards to prevent him from entering a room, they'd have to obey too."

"Right. Except I have no guards. I'll clue you in on something: he's only king as long as I say so. And I might stop saying it in five minutes. If I were you, I'd obey me."

"In five minutes, maybe."

Cayla squinted. "Maybe?"

Karina was feeling worried. She whispered, "We can wait."

"No, we can't. You see? It's everything that's wrong. How can I be kept out of a meeting?"

"Wait until it's finished and talk to him. Wait," Karina pleaded.

"No." Cayla turned to her own guards. "Come closer, please."

They looked at each other, then did as she'd told them. Cayla grabbed them both and headbutted them on the two guards by the door. She elbowed the guards behind her and kicked away the guns from the guards in front of her. "Grab them!" She yelled.

Karina realized the yell was for her and grabbed the guns on the floor while the guards contorted with pain. She wasn't sure she agreed with what her friend was doing, but the girl was in such a state of fury that she didn't dare disobey. The guns were silver but looked similar to pistols, or at least what Karina thought they looked like, since she'd never held one. In a couple seconds Cayla took the guns from Karina, pointed one of them at the guards, and opened the door. Karina followed.

They entered a room where five people sat at a table, bent over something. They turned as the door opened.

Darian got up. "Cayla! What's wrong?"

"Oh, how concerned you look. I'm touched," she said.

A guard from the door came in. "We couldn't stop her, she disarmed us, we—"

"Fine," Darian told him. "Leave." He turned to the people who'd been sitting with him. "Can you give us a moment?"

There were three men and two women, from old to young like Darian, and there was a big map on the table. They stared at each other, as if puzzled. One of them stood up as if to leave.

Darian shook his head. "No, stay. I'll be back. You can continue the discussion without me."

He walked to Cayla. "We'll go outside. What's wrong?"

His concerned voice sounded like his brother's fake concerned sweet voice and it made Karina nauseated. But it seemed to have calmed Cayla.

She said, "Let's go to the throne room. We need to talk in private."

"Let's go." They walked outside and only then he noticed Karina. "Well, hello. Do you have any news from my brother?"

"Yeah…" Karina replied as they walked.

"How is he? Is he all right?"

"Well…" Karina thought it was better not to mention anything yet. "He's his usual self."

"Does he have a place to live? Enough to eat?"

Karina laughed. "Oh, he isn't starving, don't worry."

Cayla cleared her throat. "How lovely it is to know you care more about your traitorous brother than me, Darian. Lovely."

"I care about you more than anyone in the world, Cayla, but I don't always get news from Sian."

Cayla snorted. "Right."

The two guards still followed them. They came to a huge golden door. Cayla turned to them. "Stay here."

She entered, and Darian followed her. Karina remained outside, hoping the best for their conversation, but feeling concerned. Perhaps her advice hadn't been so good after all. Cayla should have cooled her head first.

23

OUT

Darian took a deep breath. So many things worrying him at the same time. They had to find a way to know what was happening up north, and what was happening in Arlenia. He had to find Lylah, or at least learn what was happening to her, and here, in front of him, Cayla, who seemed furious at him for some reason he had yet to understand.

She sat in the throne and stared at him with the murderous look she sometimes gave him, except that it was somehow scarier now. "Now I'm forbidden to go to your meetings. Do you think it's right, Darian?"

That was what she was upset about? "You're not forbidden, Cayla."

"That's not what the guards at your door said."

"They made a mistake. And if you wanted to come to the meeting, you should have asked."

"*Asked?* Asked permission, you mean?"

Darian didn't want to get irritated at Cayla, but he was getting irritated. With so many important things happening, with the threat of a war against them, she was going to argue about semantics? "Ordered, whatever. You should have said something. It was an army meeting, Cayla. I've worked with these people for over two years, since the time your father sent me away and kept you locked in the castle."

"And it was my fault, I guess. My fault I don't know them like you do." She was getting even angrier and he was at a loss at what to do.

"I'm not saying that."

She paused and glared at him. "What are you saying then?"

"Cayla, there's a nutcase out to get you. I'm terrified. Terrified. And yeah, I know how to lead an army, but leading a kingdom is a lot more than I can handle. I'm overwhelmed!"

"Cause you're doing everything yourself!"

"I'm trying to hold it all together. Your mother disappeared. Of course you're upset. I don't expect you to be making decisions right now, and I'm trying to protect you."

"By locking me in? Do you have that right?"

"I don't. It's your protection, Cayla. If you made the decisions you'd do the same thing, wouldn't you? What do you want? Take a walk alone by the river? Is that what you want? Do you really think it's a priority right now? Do you?"

Cayla snorted. "You said it all, Darian. *If I made* the decisions. The problem is that I don't."

That was unfair. "I'm doing this for you! For us!"

"You know who you remind me of? My father. What are you going to do? Lock me in? Declare yourself king and imprison me in a tower?"

Darian shook his hands in despair. "Cayla, I don't have time for this. We have a serious situation now."

"Right. You don't have time for me. You're terrified? So am I. How can I know you weren't interested in power? Is there any way I can't know that?"

This accusation was absurd. "I didn't even know you were the princess when we met!"

"So you say. You enjoy this very much, Darian, and you keep me out of your decisions as much as you can. I have to stay in the castle. Fair enough. But maybe I could pick my own guards. Maybe they didn't have to report to you." She pointed a finger at him. "And maybe, just maybe, I could be at least consulted in the decisions concerning the kingdom I was supposed to take care of!"

Darian stepped back and took a deep breath. He had to remain calm. "Your guards report to me for your safety, that's all. And if I don't ask you for your opinion is because things are happening too fast. I need to make the decisions fast. I have to. You don't know anything about army strategy, Cayla. I'm sorry."

"Impressive. Impressive, Darian. I never thought you liked power so much."

"You think I like this? I hate it. You think I like it that you're the princess, and now interim queen? I hate it. I thought we'd be able to have a peaceful life. Me, you, our kids. Maybe go to a little house up north. Nope, will never happen. I'm taking more responsibility than I can. Do you think it's fun? Do you think I get a rise out of power? I don't, Cayla. You say I'm like your father? *You* are like your father. Paranoid that at any moment someone will take the power from you. Obsessed about keeping your position, your status, caring more about it than your own citizens. You are the one who could one day lock me up, threatened as you're feeling that your non-existent power is being lost."

"Shut up."

"You shut up. You know why people listen to me, and not to you? Because I fought with them, I planned with them, I conspired with them, while you were here going to balls and being a little girl. I can't change that."

Cayla rolled her eyes. "You say it as if I was enjoying it."

"It's the way things are. I can't change them."

"Yes, you can," she replied. "Stop giving all the orders."

"Oh, I will. I'll leave it all for you. You think it's fun? It's exciting, so much fun to lead a kingdom. I get a kick out of it, I do."

"Well, quit, then. You hate it, you don't care." She shrugged. "Quit, then."

Darian took a deep breath. He had to calm down. Maybe she had a point. Maybe having to lead the army and now the kingdom was tearing them apart. He knelt and took her hand. "Once it's over. Let's quit. We leave together, forget all this. We move far from here or to another country, get a little house. Just us."

Cayla squinted and pulled her hand. "Darian, I wasn't raised to be a peasant."

Darian trembled in anger, feeling offended, rejected. He got up. "You are the power-hungry one. You know why you're saying I want to keep the power from you? Because you're measuring me with your own stick."

"Yeah, yeah. As if you really wanted to be a peasant. You took this king thing all too well, if you ask me. Too well, Darian."

"You have a problem with that? I can quit, then."

"Finally you're saying something sensible. Go."

Go? Like that? After everything they'd been through? After everything he'd done for her? It was hard to swallow. He was at a loss for words, and just stared at her.

Cayla crossed her arms. "Well? I'm waiting."

If that was what she wanted, that was what she'd get, and screw the consequences. He had no crown, or anything identifying his position so took off the army's coat and shirt and threw them on the floor. "I don't want any of these. I don't want anything. I won't even get my stuff in my bedroom. I'll walk away the way I came. I'll just keep my pants, unless you insist."

Cayla rolled her eyes. "Not interested." She untied her necklace and threw it to him. "Take this."

He caught it. It was still shining. Odd. He threw it back to her and it landed on a corner on the floor. "Keep it. As a reminder of the love you've forsaken."

Darian left the room. "I quit. I'm out," he told the guards outside. They stared at him but didn't say anything. His brother's girl was sitting on the floor and also stared, but remained silent. He had to cool off, clear his mind.

He walked away. Away from Cayla, away from this castle, away from everything.

Karina guessed that things hadn't gone well, as Darian stormed out of the room. She didn't understand why he was shirtless, though, and wondered if it had been an unsuccessful attempt at reconciliation.

Since Cayla didn't walk out for a while, Karina entered the room and found her friend sitting down, staring at the necklace in her hand.

Cayla kept looking down. "It wasn't what I wanted. It was… as if I wasn't myself."

"You were angry. It happens."

Cayla raised her eyes to meet Karina's. "You know, the worst is he kept treating me like a useless imbecile. Even now! Even when I told him how wrong he was."

"Well, you're not useless, and not an imbecile."

"I know."

Karina could perhaps encourage Cayla to use her anger for something useful. "Show him, show everyone. There are two threats hanging over Whyland. You can protect your kingdom, I know you can."

Cayla's eyes met Karina's and opened wider, as if she was snapping out. "True. I'm not the useless imbecile like he thinks I am."

"Indeed. And you can deal with this kingdom's possible threat and Sian."

Cayla extended a hand as if telling her to wait. "I have the war room to deal with, then we'll discuss Sian and that horrible castle. Come. I'll try to make it quick."

Cayla tied the necklace on her neck again. Well, at least she could still contact Darian once heads cooled off. But Karina wasn't interested in Cayla and Darian drama right now.

They walked out the door, and Cayla turned to the guards. "Do not follow me."

She walked fast, and they came to the same room Darian had been before. There were no guards at the door and the girls entered.

Cayla addressed the people on the table. "So you are what's left of the War Council, right? I don't even know your names, but I don't think it matters now."

"Where's Darian?" a young man asked.

"He left. Quit. Now I think you had something planned here. Would you mind sharing?"

They looked at each other and hesitated.

"Well?" Cayla asked.

An older woman said, "We were planning another mission to the Arlenia border."

"Really?" Cayla asked. "Want to lose how many more lifts? Everyone we've sent hasn't come back. Maybe I'm stupid and I don't know anything about war, but I do know that when something doesn't work, you don't keep doing it."

The woman sat back. "It's different. We were planning different routes and brainstorming a way not to be intercepted."

Cayla shook her head. "If we disperse our army, we lose strength at our core. For all we know, that's exactly what they want. They could be coming by the ocean."

"They aren't, we're watching," the woman replied.

"Either way, I don't care, dispersing is not a good idea. We stay put and wait."

"Wait?" the young man asked. "That's not a plan. Our fellow soldiers are there, who knows what's happening to them—"

"And we want to send more people?" Cayla asked. "No. It doesn't make sense."

The people in the war council looked at each other. "There's another matter," the woman said. "We were planning an expedition. To locate your mother."

"Cancel it," Cayla said. "It's pointless. She's the most powerful person in Whyland. Perhaps in the world. If we haven't heard from her, it's one of three things: one, she's dead —and I sure hope she isn't; two, she's alive and has no way to communicate with us; three, she's being kept by something or someone so powerful there's nothing a bunch of regular soldiers can do about it. Sending people to find her is a useless endeavor."

"It's about investigating—and not abandoning her," the woman pleaded.

"Not now," Cayla said. "Whyland is being threatened and we need to protect Siphoria and the castle."

"See," the woman insisted, "finding your mother was our priority number two."

"Not anymore. What was priority number one?"

They again looked at each other, seeming uncomfortable. The woman said "Keeping you safe."

Cayla rolled her eyes. "Well, scratch that. Also, I don't want the same people following me. It would be too easy to target them. We have enemies within this castle and within this army, and you know it. Trust no one."

The young man said, "So your order is for us to stay put. You know, Darian always listened to us, and we voted."

Cayla squinted. "Voting in the army? Are you for real? If you were in a war and were attacked, would you stop and vote while the enemy came down on you?"

The young man rolled his eyes. "It would be different."

"Fine, then," Cayla said. "Sending more people there is pointless and will weaken us. We can't disperse. Not any more than we've already done. A person would take ten days to arrive here by foot from the Arlenia border. For all we know, Arlenia might be just destroying lifts and disrupting our communication, and maybe they'll be back in a few days."

Another man then said, "The thing is, can we really abandon our fellow soldiers? Who knows what's happening to them?"

Cayla shook her head. "If they're hostages, whoever is keeping them wants something. We'll hear from them. If they are dead, there's nothing to be done. If they are free and coming back, we'll hear from them soon."

The man insisted, "We'd need to help them in this case. There are also the people in the north. It's our duty to protect them."

"Really? The Lost People? The ones my father never found? They have hidden villages. They'll be fine. We can't disperse our forces. How do you vote?"

"We raise hands," the woman said.

"Hands up for staying put and watching out for anyone returning or any attack from any direction."

The woman and another man raised their hands.

Cayla also raised her hand. She turned to Karina. "You vote too." Karina raised her hand. Cayla said, "Four against three. Stay put." She turned to the woman. "I count on you. Plan whatever you want to plan. What's your name?"

"Armeen."

"I nominate you Whyland's Grand General. Do what you have to do."

She cleared her throat. "I already was Grand General."

Cayla shrugged. "You know I agree with the idea then."

She turned around and left the room. Karina followed.

As they were away from the room, Cayla whispered, "Protecting me priority number one! What a fool he is!"

"I think royals usually have protection, no?"

"Maybe. But the way it was said, as if I were some kind of object or child. Ugh. Also… There's something odd. I don't trust everyone who was there, but I'm not sure who is who. Darian's problem is that he believes in the best in people. I feel there's something weird in this story."

Indeed. Karina had been thinking how convenient it was that the army was dispersed right when Sian was planning on attacking, when she remembered something important. "Sian has connections in the army, and allies in Siphoria. Maybe it's all related." She then remembered Liam's offer to tell what was happening in Arlenia, but she wasn't sure she trusted him.

"Maybe. I know who to ask. Can't believe I didn't think about it before."

"Your uncle?" Karina whispered.

"He's overseas. So is Nia. It all happened so fast. Either way, my uncle doesn't know much."

They climbed regular staircases, then spiral staircases, as Karina wondered who they were going to see. They came to a room with many bookshelves. In an armchair, reading, was Ayanna, Cayla's younger sister, well, half-sister, as they only had the same father. She didn't look like a child anymore, but like a young teenager, with a pleasant round face, and big, bright eyes.

She raised her eyes from the book, noticed Karina, and beamed. "What confusion brought you this time?"

"Well…" She didn't even know from where to start.

Cayla said, "Arlenia threatening us isn't confusion enough?"

Ayanna frowned. "What? They're our allies, aren't they?"

Cayla sat by her sister. "Goodness, how long have you been in this tower reading?"

"A couple days? Uh, maybe more?"

Cayla told her sister about the threat from Arlenia, and then about Darian asking help for Sian. She turned to Karina "You broke Sian's spell, right?"

"Pretty much," Karina confirmed.

"What spell?" Ayanna asked.

Karina sighed. "He was in the garden of the Darloom castle, turned into stone."

Ayanna tilted her head. "Do you love him?"

Karina froze.

Thank goodness Cayla said something. "Of course not. It was some ridiculous story he came up with." She turned to Karina. "Right?"

"Yeah." Karina felt as if frost was coming from her stomach to her entire body. "They said I didn't need to feel anything to break his spell with a true-love kiss. I broke his spell with a kiss on the cheek, of, you know, love for humanity, compassion, something like that."

Ayanna was thoughtful. "Interesting. And you said Darloom. That name hadn't been used in years."

"Yeah," Cayla said. "I know it as the Lost Castle or Dark Castle."

"Sian calls it Darloom," Karina said. "But there's something important. That castle has kyons. Do you know what they are?"

Ayanna nodded.

Cayla stared at her sister. "I spent days trying to figure that out. How do you know that stuff?"

Ayanna gestured around her as if pointing to the books.

"Well," Karina continued. "Sian got a staff from the castle and—"

"The Darloom staff?" Ayanna frowned. "That's impossible."

"Not sure if it's *the* Darloom staff, but he got a staff from the Darloom castle, and the kyons changed. They became fully formed. He said they could leave the area of the castle then, and he was going to attack Whyland with an army of kyons and take the Queen's Castle."

Cayla asked, "He can't do that, can he? I mean, it's not possible, is it?"

Ayanna was silent for a moment, then asked, "What did the staff look like? Do you know where he got it?"

Karina didn't want to lie, but she didn't want to confess all she'd done either. "The staff had a roundish head, as if it were made of glass or resin, but it was strong. It had been locked away in a room with many mirrors and a well in the middle."

Ayanna shook her head. "It can't be. Were there more people in the castle?"

Weird question. "Some of his friends. Three girls and two guys."

"That's it, then," Ayanna said. "One of them is quite a powerful magician. We can't know from which tradition, or even if they're from Whyland, but he has someone very powerful with him, who took that staff."

Karina shuddered.

Cayla squinted. "You think it's possible then? He could come here?"

"Oh, yes," Ayanna said. "If that power is unlocked... I mean, he could raise an army of kyons, and that's not even the worst. Whoever is this powerful person with him, they could do lots of things. They could open holes to other dimensions and bring, well, anything."

Thankfully that the powerful person was no longer with Sian, not that she was going to tell Ayanna that. At least not right then. Karina had to get to the part that mattered. "Is there a way to stop him?"

"Where's Lylah?" Ayanna asked.

Cayla shook her head. "I just told you. Gone. Disappeared. We don't know if she's just in official business, unaware that the communications have gone down, or..."

"She should be fine," Ayanna said.

"How can we stop him?" Karina insisted.

Ayanna shrugged. "A regular army could stop kyons." She turned to Cayla. "I mean stop, not defeat, and there's a difference here, by shooting them. They'll regenerate, but they'll be contained. At some point, he might give up, or you can negotiate, something."

Cayla snorted. "Isn't it a shame a lot of our forces have been displaced north, though? And plus, there's the Arlenia threat."

"Perhaps there's no threat," Karina said. "Not from Arlenia. Everything is happening at the same time. Maybe he plotted it all. The idea was just to weaken you and invade here unopposed."

Cayla squinted. "It's just Sian. I mean, he can't plan that well, and he can't have that much influence to affect another kingdom."

"He's pretty good at planning, Cayla. I think he's been plotting all this for months. And he has friends. He *is* influential."

"Maybe he's just seizing the opportunity," Cayla said.

Ayanna said, "There's a treaty on the study of coincidences. We would need to position the variables—"

"Right?" Cayla rolled her eyes. "How long would it take? Hours? Days?"

Ayanna grunted. "All I'm saying is that it's stupid to ignore coincidences."

"I'm not ignoring. I'm saying he could just be seizing the opportunity. He could have waited for us to be weak to attack us, or he could even want to pose as the hero and savior of Whyland as Arlenia attacks. Maybe he knew about Arlenia's plans in advance. It makes sense. Or would he really have connections in Arlenia and in our north, be able to disrupt communications, and prepare a big sham just so most of our army is gone when he comes?"

That sounded exactly like Sian. "Not impossible."

Ayanna was serious. "He's got to be pretty good to have gotten that staff." She turned around and made her way back to her seat.

"Hey," Cayla called her sister. "I need your help. How do I defeat them? You said lifts, but that doesn't make sense. I shot them and nothing happened. They seem not to be affected by heat or energy, just by something physical. We were cutting them in pieces. It didn't help much, but it slowed them down."

Ayanna was opening up her book, then lifted her eyes. "Get lifts that shoot projectiles, and bring ground soldiers with cutting weapons."

Cayla nodded. "Fine then. Thanks for your help."

Karina then took her small disk from her pocket. "Do you know what this is?"

Cayla examined it. "Very old com. Where did you get this?"

"A friend of Sian's brought me here. He said he could tell me what's happening in Arlenia."

Cayla squinted. "Who was that? We need to know if there are Sian's friends infiltrated here."

"Liam. He got me out of jail."

"Jail?"

"It's a long story. But... do you think this can be tracked?"

Cayla took it again and examined it. "In theory no, but anything could have a sensor. Maybe inside it."

Karina puffed. "Great."

Ayanna called, "Guys, lower your volume. I'm trying to read here."

Cayla shook her head in annoyance. Ayanna didn't raise her eyes from the book. Yeah, Karina had bookaholic friends, but she didn't think any of them would go back to a book with a war threatening them.

Karina whispered, "Should I try to contact him and ask for the information?"

"Do you trust him?"

The answer was easy. "No."

"Just leave it here. If they come after you, all they'll find is Ayanna buried in books." She chuckled. "And I'll try to see who this Liam person is."

"What about Sian, what are we going to do?"

"I know where to get him. There's a bridge he'll have to cross to come from the south. I'll deploy a battalion there and hope to detain them long enough."

Long enough for her mother to arrive were the unspoken words. Karina understood. As they were about to leave, someone knocked on the door. Cayla opened it. A servant had a tray with dinner which Cayla put on a table on a corner. Ayanna glanced at it and then back at her book. Cayla walked to the door, and Karina followed. As they were almost at the door, the princess halted and gestured for Karina to stop, then walked back to the table and gestured for her sister to come closer.

She pointed at the tray, and whispered so softly she almost mouthed, "See this?"

It was just food, and smelled delicious, by the way. There was a plate with golden decorations in the border and four golden containers with lids and spoons. There was also an apple and a glass of juice.

Ayanna looked at it, frowned, and whispered, "Mina knows I'm allergic to apples. Everyone in the kitchen knows it. What do you think this means?"

"An impostor," Karina blurted.

"It could also be a poorly trained servant. Maybe," Ayanna said.

Cayla pointed to Karina as if agreeing. "They don't suddenly change servants without warning and training, not at a time when we might be attacked. Is there another exit here?"

Ayanna sighed, then nodded. She walked to a corner, pulled a bookcase, and revealed a very small door behind it.

"Wait," Cayla said. She walked to another door, which led to another room, closed it, then snapped the handle. She returned to them and whispered, "They'll think we're there. It will give us more time."

Good thinking. Cayla was quite a resourceful girl and it was indeed a shame that Darian had overprotected her. They walked through the door Ayanna had opened. She closed the door then pulled a chain tied to a pulley, probably to put the bookcase back in place. The passage led to a very narrow staircase, so narrow that it was barely enough for them to walk through.

"I don't think you need to come, Ayanna," Cayla said. "For all I know, we might be overreacting."

"You think I want to leave my books?" Ayanna said. "But in the slim chance we aren't overreacting, I'd better not stay there like easy prey."

Cayla nodded. "That makes sense."

They descended the stairs. Ayanna went ahead, with Cayla on the back. The staircase descended and had sharp ninety-degree turns.

Karina whispered, "This is hidden in the wall, right?"

"Yes." Ayanna no longer whispered.

"How do you learn about these passages?" Cayla asked.

Ayanna shrugged. "This one was by accident. Too much time up here."

"Where does it lead?"

Ayanna shrugged. "Why should I know?"

Cayla snorted. "Awesome, Ayanna."

"If you're not happy, go back and find your own exit."

"We'll figure it out," Karina said.

Darian sat down by the river near the old part of the port, in Siphoria's side, where fishermen and small merchants discharged their loads. There was something calming about watching people in their hustle of daily lives, but this time, it didn't make sense at all. The sun was still shining, and everyone was working as if everything had been normal, as if Darian's heart hadn't been shattered in millions of pieces, as if nothing had happened. He had trouble understanding how life could go on normally.

He'd taken an old cloak before leaving the castle, but it was thin, and he should be cold, except that he could no longer feel anything.

He looked down at his necklace. It still shone. Perhaps malfunctioning, or it was some stupid irony. Maybe its shine didn't mean that Cayla loved him, it just meant... whatever. Something. One of the many things he never had the time to quite understand. Darian closed his eyes and took in the smell of water, and even the smell from the ocean not so far away. Maybe this was his chance to go north, to forget everything. But then, maybe he had made a mistake—or a few. So terrified he'd been that something could happen to Cayla that he'd forgotten her own say in all this.

A lift flew past him. Not from the army, a private one. More and more merchants had those. The lift landed in the castle port, though. That was odd. He then noticed three more lifts moving towards the castle. Two were from the army, and it should be normal, except... Something was wrong.

He straightened and took in his surroundings. With the cloak, no one should have recognized him, but he hadn't checked whether he was being followed. Stupid. He sighed. He had obviously been followed. *Congratulations, Darian, you were so worried about Cayla that now that something's really happening you won't be able to do anything.*

No. There had to be a way. Darian got up and walked slowly away from the banks. From the corner of his eye, he saw a young man watching him on his right and a soldier on his left. No way to see if they were friends or foes, though. Darian got to a street and strolled casually through it. He couldn't look back directly, but he turned and looked at a shop. The two young men were on his tail. Maybe it was nothing.

He walked a little more, then turned quickly in another street and jumped in an open window. It was a restaurant, but empty, and he crawled through the tables in the direction of the kitchen. He heard someone walking through the front door, hid behind a vase and saw that it was one of his pursuers. Darian fumbled his pockets. He had nothing, nothing, not even a knife. Not that he would like to use it.

After the man walked past him, Darian went to the window and moved outside. He climbed up quickly and found himself on the roof, running as fast as he could away from that place. He heard a wheezing sound, then something was around him, like a net, and he fell. Right. Now a knife could have been useful. Stupid, stupid, stupid Darian. He saw a pair of boots in front of him and two more people approaching, and looked up to see yet another man.

"What a catch," the man said. "The self-declared king."

"We could negotiate," Darian said.

"Maybe," the man replied. "After I get my reward."

Great. Now Darian would be powerless to even defend himself. Cayla came to his mind, together with an overwhelming feeling of shame and regret, as a flask was waved in front of him and everything turned black.

24

RESIST

The girls came to a metal door at the bottom of the stairs.

Cayla turned the handle a few times. "Locked."

Ayanna stepped closer to it. "No. It's a code-lock."

Her sister squinted. "Doesn't look like it, though."

"Cause then it'd be obvious." Ayanna turned the handle as if she were opening a locker, a couple times for each side, except that it didn't turn as far as a locker code. "Got it," she said.

Karina was still unsure if escaping was really necessary, but then, if Sian planned to attack the castle, eventually he'd make his first move, and it would be a good idea to be far from there, so they could at least regroup and plan something away from it.

Cayla stepped forward, opened the door slowly, and peeked. She looked back and gestured for them to follow. They were not outdoors but in an underground tunnel. On top of them, there were metal plaques with holes in it.

Cayla put a finger in front of her mouth and pointed up. "It's the lift field."

Ayanna's room must have been a place for someone important some time before, as it had such a convenient emergency exit. Above them, there were sounds of steps and of things being dragged.

"Are these all?" A man asked from above the metal grid.

"For this round, yes. You can take them to the crate prison. We'll go over the castle to see if we find a few more guards."

"Easier than expected."

"For now. Let's see what happens when more forces come back from Arlenia. I'll believe we won when the new king and queen have been in power for a few weeks."

New queen? Liam had said it, but she'd only half believed it. Karina's insides were knotted, but she shouldn't think about it. Why should she care if there was someone in a position she didn't even want in the first place? There were more important things they had mentioned. Her eyes met Cayla's, who seemed to also have understood what was happening. The castle had indeed been taken. Her eye also had a glimmer of hope. *Come back from Arlenia.* It meant that Cayla's mother was likely coming back—and more forces as well. Karina thought she should hear what Liam had to say about the northern kingdom, but then remembered she'd left the disk in the room upstairs. This was no time for going back, though, and no time to have a possibly tracking device with her.

The other guard asked. "What about the princesses?"

"They're of no consequence."

Cayla stuck out her tongue.

The men walked away, and after a while, more sun came from the openings. A lift had probably taken off. The girls remained there for a few minutes, in silence, waiting. Above the grid, there were some steps, but nothing more. Karina gestured to the others to keep walking. Hopefully they'd find an exit, as they couldn't talk there, and they had to do something. Quick.

The tunnel got dark again and descended. They walked for a few minutes until they reached a metal door. Ayanna was about to open it when her sister gestured for her to stop.

"We need to think," Cayla whispered. "What are our next steps?"

"You mentioned a bridge Sian would have to cross, right?" Karina asked. Cayla nodded. Karina continued, "We could get a small force and block it, couldn't we? Apparently there's nothing north. All we need to do is delay him long enough until Lylah comes back."

Cayla sighed. "Where are we going to find this force if we don't even know who's on our side?"

Karina had an idea steering on her mind. "I think I know someone. The impression I got is that she's against Sian's plans. I'll try to find her. And you can fight well, right, Cayla?"

"Kind of. Not sure I can stop a horde of creatures on my own, though."

"I can fight a little," Ayanna said. "I learned how to manipulate energy."

Cayla turned to her. "Magic?"

"It's not called that in the books I read."

"I can help as well," Karina said before the sisters started arguing about terminology. "This girl I know, at least in theory, she fights well. She might know someone."

"Might? In theory?" Cayla rolled her eyes. "Sure sounds like a great plan."

"Do you have a better idea?" Karina was asking in earnest. She agreed that her own idea was super crappy, but she couldn't come up with anything better.

Cayla was thoughtful for a moment, then asked. "Do you know how to find this friend of yours?"

"Acquaintance. She's in Siphoria."

Cayla shrugged. "Let's give it a try."

Ayanna opened the metal door by turning the knob a few times. As they opened it, the tunnel extended for a couple meters, ending on a decrepit wooden door. They looked at each other, Cayla pulled the door open, peeked out, then opened it, and they stepped out. It was somewhere underground, like a cellar. There were some barrels on a corner, and a narrow staircase going up. The girls went up the stairs, Cayla in the front. They came up in a seemingly abandoned deposit with dusty wooden boxes. Cayla pulled up a hood and covered her head.

"I don't have a hood," Karina said.

"But nobody knows you." She turned to Ayanna. "Or you."

Karina remembered all the people that evening at the Junction when she'd spent most of the night sitting by Sian. Weird how only now she took in the significance of the gesture. Her chest felt hollow except for the imaginary ice forming in it. But Sian wasn't the point, just the people. They surely knew what she looked like. Would they recognize her, though? Days later, in plain daylight? Probably not.

Karina nodded. "Fair enough."

They headed to the door and walked outside to the colorful streets of Siphoria. Karina recognized the area where she was. It was sort of downtown, near the Junction, near Malena's hostel, and not far from Alessa's house. If she could find a reference point to remember in which direction to go... The towers. There was the military tower, and the tower by the river. Alessa's house had been away from both of them, in a street where there were rails. Perhaps she could find it.

"This way," she said to the others.

There didn't seem to be anything different in the streets. Maybe fewer soldiers than usual. Wouldn't they know about the castle? Or were they aligned with Sian's traitorous group? As much as possible, Karina chose streets full of people and tried to blend in with crowds.

It was hard to find a way while at the same time trying not to look lost, not being able to ask for information, and avoiding stopping too long at one point. As streets were getting quieter and the sun was going down, Karina felt the irritation of her companions behind her, but after about half an hour walking, she found Alessa's street. She was going on the vague hunch that the girl was interested in acting against Sian. Hopefully that was not a wrong hunch. At least her hunch in terms of direction had been correct, as she stood in front of Alessa's red door.

Karina knocked, and the door opened by itself a few seconds later. She looked back at her friends and stepped in. They were in that indoor garden that led to Alessa's house, and the door closed behind them.

Karina then felt someone pushing her, was thrown on the ground, and had her hands tied. She turned and saw Ayanna tied, while Cayla struggled against three masked people until they tied her as well. Karina's stomach sank as she realized she'd made a mistake.

One of the people removed their hoods. It was Alessa. "What do you want here?"

"Help," Karina said.

Alessa raised an eyebrow. "For what?"

Karina decided to be honest. "Against Sian. We can't trust anyone in the army, and we have to stop him."

Alessa laughed. "I have a policy of not displeasing customers, you know?"

"You seemed interested in figuring out what he was doing."

"Did I?" Alessa asked. "Impression maybe. I'll let you go, though. And please understand that this is not my real house. I'd never allow my enemies to find me."

"I'm not your enemy," Karina insisted. "I'm no longer with Sian, and he has a horrible army that's coming to attack the city and the castle."

"What for?" the girl asked. "He already took the city."

"The forces from Arlenia are going to return. If his army is not here, he'll be defeated. That's what we can do. We can delay his army."

"What army?"

"Kyons. Some horrible creatures from the Darloom castle."

Alessa sighed. "Sounds idealistic, but it's terrible business to go against Sian. I'm sorry."

Cayla then spoke, "Wouldn't it be good business to help the queen's daughter? And you could wear a mask. Nobody needs to know it's you."

Alessa looked at Cayla. "You. Oh." She crossed her arms. "What's the task and what's the pay?"

"We have to block the forces on the gateway bridge. The pay is my gratitude. If one day you need something—"

"You might no longer be queen," Alessa replied.

"True," Cayla replied. "That's why I'm not giving the price in money. Depending on what happens, I might not have any. Still, you never know."

"How many people are going?"

"Us three," Cayla said. "And then maybe you or your two other friends."

"Against how many?"

Cayla looked at Karina, who said, "A couple, uh, maybe a few hundred kyons. But they have no weapons."

Alessa looked back at her friends. "What do you think?"

Darian woke up in a luxurious cell, decorated very much like a regular bedroom, with a comfortable mattress and covers, a table and chairs, and a private bathroom. It had a heavy metal door, and other than that, he only knew it was a cell because he'd visited it before, or maybe because all the furniture was welded to the floor. At least he was a high-profile prisoner. Some consolation. No consolation. He'd messed up big time, and his heart ached when he thought of Cayla. The only odd thing was he knew this was a Whyland prison, and wondered what exactly was happening out there. He still had his necklace. Should he try to contact Cayla? He decided not to. Not when he felt ashamed, and when he was powerless to help her.

The door opened, and Sian's friend who'd contacted him about a month before came in.

"Surprised?" Liam asked.

For sure. Liam was part of Whyland's army. Was he overseeing a cell where Darian was being kept? "Who are you working for?"

"Nobody right now, and I want to change it soon, if you'll help me."

"Who's in charge of this prison?"

"Ah, that's what you wanted to know? Your dear brother, Darian. In a swift coup, he imprisoned the loyal guards standing in Siphoria and the castle. Wasn't that hard, when everyone's taking a vacation in Arlenia."

That didn't make sense. "Why?"

Liam laughed. "I'll leave that for you to figure out. I have a proposal, though. I know this room is nice and all, but I believe you must be eager to leave, aren't you?"

Darian was still trying to process how on earth his brother could have anything to do with this prison. Hold on. "Are you doing this to pave the way for Arlenia?"

Liam held out his hands. "I'm not doing anything. And your brother isn't doing this for someone else to step into the throne. Don't worry about it. I mean, worry about your brother, not Arlenia."

"One month ago, he was enchanted, and you came to me for help. Now you're doing this?"

"Again, I'm not doing anything. I want to get you out of here."

Darian crossed his arms. "Why?"

"I have good news for you. Maybe. But I think it's good. Cayla has escaped. She hasn't been imprisoned or found. I know you can find her. I need to find the girl who's with her."

"Why do you think I can find Cayla?"

Liam shrugged. "I just know."

"And you want to get me out so I'll lead you to Cayla? Why would I do this?"

Liam shrugged. "Thought you wouldn't want to leave her by herself. I don't know."

"I'm not leading you to Cayla. No way I'm doing this."

Liam shook his head. "You don't understand. I'm not doing this for Sian. I'm no longer his friend. It's for personal reasons. I won't lead anyone to your future wife, if that's what you fear."

Darian sat on the bed. "The answer is no."

Liam sighed. "Call me when you change your mind."

He turned around and left the room. Darian was left with his thoughts. His brother. How unfair, after all he and Cayla had done for him. And surprising.

Karina, Ayanna, and Cayla slept in Alessa's house, Alessa's alleged not-house, or something. The girl, her sister, and her sister's boyfriend, not that guy from that evening at the Junction, had agreed to help them. Well, only Alessa would fight with them, but her sister and the other guy would fly them there and pick them up. Alessa's two other friends said they couldn't do it, and it sucked because they were really good fighters. Oh, well.

From their calculations, the Kyons were unlikely to reach that bridge until the next day, and the best they could do right now was rest. On a thin mattress on the floor, Karina shivered, though. The covers were warm, but for some reason, she'd gotten so used to Sian by her side that her body felt cold. Somehow she missed being squeezed tight, which was odd. Not odd. It had felt good to have his arms around her. Everything a lie. It had been a good fantasy while it lasted, though. Ignorance had indeed been bliss.

Cayla lay by her side, with eyes closed, but she seemed to be awake. She hadn't mentioned Darian once since they'd left the castle, but she probably still thought about him. Karina wondered where he was, if he'd been caught with the others, or if he was free. Perhaps he'd be able to help them, but she wasn't sure Cayla would want to talk to him right now.

Karina tried to focus on the day ahead, in delaying the kyons. Would they be able to do it, in such a small number? It was worth the try.

Breakfast at Alessa's house was a lot simpler than at Malena's hostel or at the Darloom castle. They had just tea and some kind of bread with a weird spread. Karina ate as much as she could, thankful for their hospitality, and trying to make food go through her knotted throat, knowing she'd need her strength. They left early in the morning, while the sun was still rising, as they couldn't risk making to the bridge too late, and they weren't sure at which speed kyons moved, or even if they had to rest.

Walking through the streets of Siphoria towards a small lift field as the sun rose gave Karina a horrible sense of déjà-vu. Last time she also thought she would be fighting something dangerous, but she had no idea that the real danger was the one she was following. And yet, despite it all, she still had a tinge of regret that she hadn't flown with him. Sweet Sian would have liked that—if sweet Sian existed.

Sometimes she considered those two different people, and felt as if her beloved had died because no matter how much she hated what he was doing, she missed Sian horribly, and the only way to reconcile the feeling was to separate them both; the Sian she loved, and the Sian she hated. That way she could always tell herself that sweet Sian had never betrayed her and never meant to hurt her.

Oh, what nonsense. She should rather focus on kicking his ass on that bridge. Sweet or not, he deserved it. If ever she saw him. Maybe that was another reason for her rising nerves; the prospect of seeing him again, in such different circumstances.

Soon they reached the field. Karina took a deep breath and embarked on the lift. Sian's lift, the one he'd complained was old, was luxurious compared to this one. The girls were squeezed on the back while Alessa's sister, Diane, piloted the lift in the front, together with her boyfriend.

They got to the bridge in less than half an hour. As with everything, it was quite different than what Karina had imagined, even if she'd seen it on a map and even flown above it. They landed on a plateau, with mountains on their right. The ocean could be seen far on the left. The river was really wide. The bridge was quite wide also. It could fit two trucks crossing it at the same time. Not that Whyland had trucks, at least that Karina knew of. The issue was how long they could hold the kyons there. It wasn't like the door to the tower where Sian had held them off. Hypocrite. Fighting against creatures under his control. And Karina had been insanely oblivious.

They got out, and Cayla said, "We'll start preparing our defense here." She then looked up. "Oh, no."

There was a red lift flying very fast in their direction. "Is that Sian?"

"That's his lift," Cayla said.

Alessa turned to her sister. "Go back to your lift. Hide."

"It's too late. He saw us," her sister said.

There was nothing to be done as the lift landed right in front of them and Sian came out of it. He wore the same thick black overcoat she'd seen last time. She wondered if the constant change in outfit had been a part of his performance. He was alone, which was a relief. No way he could do anything against the six of them.

He walked towards them and smiled. "What a nice gathering!" He turned to Karina. "Come to check my kyons in person? Great initiative. Just watch out; there's a storm coming, and I'd hate for you to get wet."

Karina didn't feel like replying.

Sian walked towards Alessa. "How dedicated! You want to protect her even when you don't have to. Impressive. I'll warn you, though, I'm not paying overtime."

The girl was quiet. Sian turned to Alessa's sister and her boyfriend. "Diane, Mael, are you going to play for them?"

Alessa said, "They just gave us a ride. They have nothing to do with this."

Sian pretended to be surprised. "This what? Aren't you just taking a stroll?"

He turned to Cayla, but before he said anything, she said, "You're lucky you're Darian's brother or else I'd split your skull in half."

Sian showed his empty hands. "Of course. You'd kill someone unarmed who's posing no danger to you. I wish I could say I'm surprised by your lack of honor."

"You're a danger to my kingdom!" Cayla said.

"Not yours. And I'll tell you something; unlike you believe, you're beneath even my pathetic little brother."

Cayla spat at his direction.

Sian blocked the spit with his hand. "Good aim, at least."

Alessa held Cayla, whispering something on her ear, and the girls argued in whispers.

Sian approached Karina. He opened his mouth to say something, but then suddenly turned around and walked back to his lift.

There was something Karina had to know, though, and she

didn't care how stupid it looked for her to ask it. She followed him. "Sian!"

He turned. "Yes?"

"Is it true that Whyland has a new queen?"

He looked away, then looked at her. "Yes." His chest moved up and down, as in a deep breath. "I know I should have talked to you, but, like I told you, Whyland is special, it needs—"

"It's fine." She just wanted him to shut up. Her throat was closed, and it was surprising she could even form words. She focused on holding back the tears and not giving him the pleasure of seeing her humiliation.

"Fine?" He seemed surprised. "Are you sure you don't have a problem with it?"

Karina crossed her arms and made an effort to speak without crying. "No. Why?"

Sian shrugged. "I don't know, I thought… No problem then?"

Did he expect her to break down? Disappointing him was her only source of comfort. "No."

He had a glimmer in his eyes and his lips curved up as if ready for a genuine smile. "That's great."

His happy face made her insides knot. She blurted, "Is she pretty?"

What a blunder. Why can't people take back words? Karina regretted having asked that. Now, what kind of idiot asks such a question?

Sian seemed to be wondering the exact same thing, as he stared at her in confusion. "You want to hear it?"

She shook her head. "No. I—"

"Fine. Hear it then." He sounded angry. "My queen's so much more than pretty that her looks don't even matter. But yes, she's stunning. Every time I see her I'm awestruck. There. Happy?"

Karina struggled to find her voice, but she eventually did. "I'll be happy when I defeat you."

He looked away, then looked back at her. "See for yourself the kyons, see for yourself what's happening in Whyland. See for yourself. You might change your mind. And watch out for the storm."

Sian turned, embarked on his lift, and left. Karina felt dizzy. Somehow, getting the confirmation from his mouth made everything worse.

"What was that about?" Alessa asked.

Karina wasn't even sure she could talk and hoped nobody noticed she was shaking. She mumbled, "A storm. A new queen. Nonsense."

"He wants to get under your skin. If you let him, he wins."

"I still think we should have captured him!" Cayla said.

"He came to talk. It wouldn't have been honorable."

Cayla gesticulated her arms. "Screw honorable! He wanted to mess with us. He came out unarmed to spite us, to show he didn't care."

Diane then said, "If you want us to check how far the kyons are, we'd better do it soon, and we can't fly for too long, so if we don't see them—"

"We'll at least know they are not close," Cayla said. She turned to Karina. "Go with them, since you know what they look like."

Karina nodded. She didn't think they'd need someone to know what kyons looked like, but she was glad to sit for some time. She was still trying to come to terms with Sian with his fantastic, super-duper amazing and gorgeous queen. Tears were forming in her eyes, but he didn't deserve them. She wasn't going to cry. Not for Sian. Perhaps she should cry for having been so stupid, but her time would be better spent fighting his army.

The lift shook a little as it ascended. Karina's throat was closed, and she was happy neither Diane nor Mael wanted to have a conversation. A pity this lift didn't have weapons, or they could just shoot the kyons. Wait, no, Whyland weapons shot energy, and it didn't affect kyons. This area had plains so it would be easier to spot them from the air than if they'd been in an area with more trees. Karina stood close to the window, looking down, trying to find any sign of Sian's advancing force. Her heart pounded furiously in her chest. At least she was doing the right thing, and she and her friends would prevent those horrible creatures from reaching Siphoria and the castle. Her reverie was interrupted by Diane's boyfriend, Mael.

"What's that?"

Karina looked up. There were some birds in the distance. Quite large birds. Of course she didn't know what they were, though, without having had any Whyland zoology class. She was then thrown against the side window, as Diane was making a turn, but it was a slow turn, like an airplane.

"Karina." Diane's voice was tense. "Are those kyons supposed to fly?"

No. Wait. Karina looked back. They were dark, like dark brown or black, not grey, like kyons.

"Are they?" Diane repeated.

"No," Karina said. "Aren't these just birds?"

"They aren't!" Diane said.

Even before finishing her question Karina had realized the stupidity of it, as the "birds" were approaching and not only were they huge, they had huge bodies, like some giant-sized bats. But that didn't mean they weren't native giant bats or whatever, did it? Then Karina heard the screeches, and her mind took her back to that horrible moment, behind the mirror, when she was in that desolate place with the tower. Those were the creatures who'd attacked her then. But how could they be here?

∼

Darian didn't trust the guy in front of him, but he had no choice. "I'll take your offer."

Liam nodded. "Great. But there's a storm coming. No lifts can fly in that weather."

"I know someone who can."

25

STORM

"Diane, turn!" Mael yelled.

"I'm trying! Do you want to pilot it?"

"I'm trying to help."

Diane shook her head. "Karina." Some of Diane's panic was gone, replaced by a purposeful calm. "Do you know what those things are? Do you think they'll attack us?"

"They will. But they shouldn't be here, they're from another dimension. They were locked. I had no idea. I didn't know. But can they do anything against the lift? I mean, this is metal, right?"

Diane sighed. "We'll see. They could block the engine, or, I don't know, hit us."

Karina asked, "Could they bring us down?"

"I don't know! Flying school didn't have any lesson on freaky giant birds, you see?"

Karina didn't say anything. The girl was right to be angry.

They were almost finishing their 180-degree curve, but the things were very, very close. Sian's voice came to Karina, sounding as if it came from a different era, answering her question as to how they moved: *propeller on the back*. And if that was unprotected... The curve had also slowed them down, and Karina could no longer lie to herself, at the speed they were approaching, they'd reach them.

"Diane, land!" Karina pleaded.

Mael said, "No, we need to escape."

"They're going to reach us, though." Karina pleaded. "And I'd rather not risk crashing."

Diane shook her head. "We'll gain speed and lose them."

They finally had their back to the things pursuing them, and Karina realized it was too late. Hopefully nothing would happen. Hopefully. And then, impact. A creature reached them on the side, and the lift was jerked sideways.

Diane looked straight ahead. "We just need speed."

Another impact, on the opposite side. It was as if they were trying to destabilize them, not that those creatures knew how a lift moved. Then, on their back, a deafening sound like an explosion. The lift moved sideways and ahead like a car skidding on ice, then stopped moving forward. At least it was still floating. A fall from that height would kill them, and Karina hoped it didn't come to that.

Five or six creatures reached them, and the lift shook. Diane stared ahead as if frozen in shock.

Karina didn't want to ask, but she had to "Did they... Did they destroy the propeller?"

"Sounded like it. And feels like it." Mael replied.

Karina ignored the creature tapping on her window with huge claws, and turned to Diane. "Is there a way to land without it?"

The girl screamed and jumped backward as a creature dashed towards the windshield, which cracked.

"Is there?" Karina pleaded.

"Yes!" Diane moved to the pilot seat.

The creature was now tapping against the window. Thankfully the material wasn't glass and didn't shatter completely; it was just cracking slowly. But with four or five creatures clashing against all windows, at some point one of them would break through.

Diane took a deep breath, despite her trembling. "I'm landing. Karina, you're the only fighter here. If they come through—"

"I'll take care of them. Don't worry."

What a lie. But what was she going to say? That they were screwed, and that Karina had never fought against anything in her entire life? It wouldn't help them. She tried to think. Teleport. Her mind went back to teleporting. But then, could she teleport with two more people? Probably not, and she couldn't leave them on their own when it had been her fault they were here in the first place. Karina had no weapons whatsoever, and from the looks of it, neither of her companions had any either.

The lift was descending, but so slowly that they'd probably be torn to pieces before they got anywhere near the ground. She wondered if Mael couldn't fight, though.

Karina turned to him. "What about you?"

"We're musicians! But I'll do my best."

Karina nodded. Some luck. Up until then, she had only flown in Whyland in army lifts, or at least together with people in the army or rebellious groups. She had this weird notion that everyone there could fight, or that army was the only career in Whyland. Turns out no. And, of course, the one time she really needed help, she was with two musicians. Karina had to hold it together, one, because she'd asked them to come, two, because she was likely the one who had freed those things, and three, because they were counting on her.

The window by her cracked, and an ugly claw entered the lift. Mael looked back, broke the headrest from his the seat, and hit that claw. The creature went away, but another creature came in, putting its beak in the opening. Mael hit it, then gave the piece to Karina. He moved back and snapped another seat.

Turns out it was a good thing that the lift was old and could be broken apart.

Another hole was opened in the front, and Mael hit the thing with a piece of the seat. Karina hoped they could land before anything worse happened, but she wasn't sure how much better they'd be on the ground when there would be no place where they could run to.

"Does this lift have a radio, I mean, a communicator or something?" Karina asked. "We need to ask for help!"

"It doesn't!" Diane yelled.

Karina's stomach was sinking while she was hitting whatever came through the little hole in the side window. Another hole was about to be opened on the other side. She also heard the creatures doing something on top. Focus. Think. Explode! The answer was in exploding something. But what, though? She couldn't explode their flying craft. Not in mid-air. Would they be able to land, though? Karina's question was soon answered in the worst possible way, as the lift started to spin very fast while descending.

"Prepare for impact!" Diane yelled.

Like what? Karina sat and hugged her knees, the way she'd seen in airplane instructions. There was no time to wonder if it was the right thing to do or not. At least there were no claws coming through, since the spinning had probably thrown the creatures away.

They crashed with a thud. Karina sat up, amazed that nothing had happened to her, until she saw with dismay that part of the ceiling had collapsed in the front. On the back, it was just lower than normal. The window on her side was now completely shattered.

"Are you alright?" Karina asked.

"Physically? Yeah." Diane said.

"My leg," Mael complained. "Something hit it."

"I'm fine," Karina said. "I'll try to hold them back."

Try was the operative word here. Oh, dear. She hoped maybe someone was flying in the area, someone saw them, someone came to help. She didn't even care who it was. At this point, she'd be delighted to see Sian walking hand in hand with his gorgeous queen if he came to save them. If he knew what was happening, she didn't think he'd let her die like that. Not his style. But the fact that he'd let these creatures lose was horrible and reminded Karina why she'd walked away and was now fighting, or better, trying to fight him—and failing miserably. Loud screeches.

Karina closed her eyes. Explode. That was the only thing she knew how to do, and the only thing that could maybe help them at this point, but it had to explode out, not in.

She said, "Don't hit them. Wait. Don't go near the windows."

"I can't move," Mael said.

"Hang on," Karina insisted.

Eyes closed, she felt the creatures approaching. Part of her even felt sad because she felt no evil or malice in them. They were animals following their instinct. Well, so was Karina, following her survival instinct. Let them all come close. Close, as close as they could. This was no time to doubt herself or wonder if she could really explode anything. She knew she could. She had to find a place in her mind for quiet concentration, from where she could take the focus. Diane was yelling something, but it was lost, as Karina got immersed in her thoughts. Using emotion was bad, Sian had said, but she had no other choice. His face came in her mind, and his words: *of course I don't want you.*

Boom. The walls of the lift collapsed outwards, as well as the ceiling blocking Diane and Mael. The creatures were thrown far from them. Karina understood the explosion better, it was as if she pushed air outwards. Still, pushing the walls of the lift had been good, as some shards hit some of those creatures, who fell on the floor, hurt or dead. Karina crawled to the front, near

Mael and Diane. Perhaps Karina could do this explosion thing while they walked, and they could go back to the bridge and rejoin the others. But no, Mael couldn't walk. They'd need to wait for help.

Karina found a metal bar, Diane had a piece of a seat, and Mael, lying down, had the other. The girl looked terrified.

"I can keep them away," Karina said. "At least until help comes."

A creature approached, and Karina swung the metal bar but missed it. At least it flew back, like a fly avoiding being swatted. Diane hit its foot with her piece of the seat, but then the creature grabbed the piece and threw it away. Karina had wanted to wait for more creature to approach, but she wouldn't be able to. Explode outward. Boom. The creature was thrown far away, but this time there were no shards, no pieces of metal to hurt it. As two more creatures approached, Karina did that explosion thing and pushed them out. Her vision was starting to get blurry, and she felt tired, but she managed a few more explosions. They were very draining. Karina was reaching the limit of her strength and could barely even see anything. There was no place to hide.

Thunder roared above them, and fat drops of rain reached their heads. It was cool rain, but it was welcome, as the creatures seemed to have slowed down. Not so much, though. They were still approaching, and Karina's "explosions" were only pushing them a few meters. If they kept getting weak like that, the creatures would reach them. As one creature got really close, after a push that was like a child's push, Karina trembled, thinking about what was going to happen with the girl that had so kindly given her breakfast and a ride to come to a bridge and try to fight a stupid war. But the creature didn't reach Diane. It shrieked, as if in pain, and fell backward.

Karina looked back and saw Cayla and Alessa running towards them. Alessa had a gun in her hand, and a stick, which she threw like a lance. There were only about four creatures now, but they all moved in their direction. Cayla swung a branch. Karina wanted to go and help, but her eyes were almost closing. One thing she knew: no way she would be able to teleport in that state, alone or otherwise. If those creatures reached them, it would be her end. Could she at least be glad she had lived? That he'd loved, and fought, and tried? Maybe it had all been in vain, but at least it had been something. *Stop it.*

Karina opened her eyes. *Push them out.* A child's push again. At least it was something. She'd die pushing, not yielding. Another creature came in her direction, but it was hit by something. Cayla was beside Karina, fighting with an ax. Rain was pouring now. The good thing was that there were only three creatures. Maybe they'd be able to defeat them.

But there was something else coming on the ground. Was it the help they needed? The rain and her blurry vision didn't help much. They were many, and didn't look like people. Of course. Kyons. They were coming. Considering the kyons would immobilize them, it would be their doom, as they'd be easy prey. Karina's eyes were closing. Kyons were coming. Push out, push out. Boom. More like a tiny pop. Kyons and creatures were stopped for a couple seconds. She closed her eyes. Was this the end? Maybe, as she saw a strong light above her. Kyons were coming. Boom. Again, that was just a pop. Her eyes were closing. She'd better embrace the light. This time she heard another boom, and it wasn't hers, and two creatures fell on the floor. Someone jumped from the sky with a long cutting blade and kept the kyons at bay. Visions. Great. That was indeed the end. Somebody carried her towards the light.

26

THE LOST PEOPLE

Something cold touched Karina's lips. She woke up with a start. Resist, push, boom. She heard something falling on the floor, and a guy moaning in pain. She opened her eyes and found herself lying in the middle of a large lift, like the ones from the army.

"Karina?" Cayla's voice. The girl was crouched beside her, with a look of relief. She turned sideways, addressing someone else. "The draught worked." She squinted, still addressing the same person. "What happened to you?"

"I think the lift shook." A guy's voice.

Karina sat up and looked in the direction of the voice. She was surprised to see Sian's friend, Liam, there. He seemed to be in pain and was getting up. Had Karina just pushed him? At least she was weak, or she could have committed murder. Not to mention she could have destroyed the lift. Under the bright lift lights, the boy looked better than she remembered. It wasn't just the dark blue eyes contrasting with the dark hair, but the way his face was shaped, with a strong jaw, bright skin, and whatever it was that juice that made people beautiful. He might have been the best-looking boy she'd ever seen in her entire life.

Best-looking, not most attractive. Only one person still held the most-attractive medal in her eyes, and it was better not to think about him, or she'd feel unbearable pain in her chest, not to mention the shame at the stupidity of not hating him yet.

The door to the front opened. Darian came in and crouched beside Cayla. He addressed Karina, though.

"How are you feeling?"

"As if I died and came back. What happened?"

Cayla said, "We saw the lift falling, so Alessa and I went to check. You were being attacked by those horrible flying things. They weren't kyons. Darian and Liam came to save us. Liam gave you the draught that woke you up. Zayra's the pilot."

Had Karina woken up in some kind of bizarro universe, or was she hallucinating? Before losing consciousness, Karina knew that Liam was Sian's friend, not Darian's. Cayla and Darian had broken up. Last time she'd seen Zayra had been more than a year before. The girl had been Darian's flying partner and had betrayed Cayla by revealing their location to some people who wanted to kidnap them.

"Zayra's the only person who can fly in a storm," Darian said, perhaps sensing some of Karina's confusion.

"What happened to Diane and Mael?"

"We left them in Siphoria. He was badly injured," Darian said. "Alessa stayed with them."

"She fought brilliantly," Cayla added.

"What about Ayanna?"

"I told her to run back, find a village, and hide," Cayla said.

"Why are we flying? Where are we going?"

Cayla and Darian looked at each other, the way they had done a few times.

"We're going north," he said.

"To Arlenia?"

He shook his head. "Near there, but we'll go somewhere else

first. We're not dealing against strength here, but magic. We need answers."

Karina pointed to Liam. "What is *he* doing here?"

"Saving you," Liam said. "I also happen to know the location of the towers destabilizing communication and flight from the north." He winked. "Handy."

"He also fought brilliantly," Cayla said. "He and Alessa kept the kyons away while Darian and I carried you all inside. Mostly him, actually, since Alessa was exhausted."

Liam waved his hand. "Nah. It was nothing. I killed some fifty kyons, not nearly as many as I would have liked, and—."

"Killed?" Karina interrupted him. "You mean they didn't come back?"

Cayla shrugged. "At least we didn't see them. Maybe it's the distance to the Darloom castle."

"Did they reach Siphoria?"

"No," Darian replied, "They are stationed outside the city. Sian is probably waiting for when our forces return."

Karina looked from Liam to Darian and pointed to both. "But why…"

Darian nodded. "I was imprisoned, together with all the high-ranking military leaders. Liam got me out because he wanted to help you."

Karina looked at both boys. "Thank you."

Liam shrugged. "I told you I was your friend." He then pointed to the front. "Thank also the girl there. That was some impossible flying, and I know about flying." He shrugged. "Of course, I'm glad I was there, since you girls were tired. Darian here also has zero combat training, you know?" He laughed. "Sian used to say he can't squat a fly." Liam then changed his tone. "Well, of course, one more reason I'm no longer with him. What a nasty thing to say about your brother."

Darian nodded. "But it's true. I have no combat training. You'll always have my gratitude for saving Cayla and her friends." He wasn't bitter or sarcastic, just graceful, and didn't seem bothered in any way.

Liam again waved his hand. "I would have given my life." He looked at Karina. "For you."

She looked away. That was awkward and uncomfortable. The dude barely knew her. But then, perhaps she was so traumatized with weird, out-of-place flirting and insta-love—fake love—from Sian, that she was imagining things.

Darian watched as Zayra managed a graceful landing on a river bank.

"I can't stay," the girl said. "Or they'll notice I'm gone. Call me if you need me. I'll come or I'll find someone to pick you up."

"Thank you."

The girl nodded. "It was my duty."

The door opened, and Cayla came in and put her hand on his shoulder. Darian kissed her fingers. After fearing losing her, he relished in each and every touch. There were still things unsolved and unsaid between them, but at least they were together again. All the coldness, mistrust, and distance had been dissolved in a few mutual apologies and love declarations, interrupted only because they had to focus on treating the injured and unconscious and had to plan their next steps. And here they were.

Cayla addressed Zayra, "Thank you. I hope your talent gets recognized."

It was nice that she had forgiven Zayra and wasn't at all jealous of the girl.

Zayra winked to Cayla. "If you win, send in a good word for me."

"For sure," Cayla replied.

Darian said, "And if we lose, I'll do my best to send a good word to my dear brother."

Zayra laughed. "Nah. If you lose, just pretend you hate me. That will have a better effect."

She was probably right.

They were going to walk in the direction of the village where he'd grown up. He wasn't really sure that this was the right thing to do, and, in a way, felt guilty for dragging the others in this perhaps pointless quest. But then, he couldn't see any better action in the short term. Yes, Liam said he knew the location of the towers preventing communication from the north. If they could sabotage them, perhaps they could have some part of the army to help them.

That said, they could also be walking into a trap. Cayla had suggested they take the castle back, with a small force and using the secret passages, but Darian still thought that they were dealing with something greater and needed to be better prepared. He could be wrong, though, and maybe they wouldn't find anything, but he felt he had to try. Cayla ended up agreeing with him, having fought creatures she had never seen before. They also needed a break and some rest before deciding on any action.

He dreaded bringing Liam along. Yes, he was thankful that he'd helped them on the plains. Had Darian known in how much trouble Cayla had been, he would have brought more people, but Liam made up for that. Goodness, that boy was a good fighter. No wonder, trained since he was a kid—with his brother. But Darian didn't trust him at all, and it wasn't that he thought he was spying or working for Sian, but something else. There was nothing he could do, though, as the deal for getting him out was to allow Liam to accompany them. He claimed he wanted something with Karina, and Darian feared that he was just trying to get back at his brother. Fair enough, if he was against Sian, in theory, he would be their ally, but Darian still didn't trust him.

They walked in such a narrow path that they had to go in a single line. One of his arms was behind him, holding Cayla's hand. He wished he would never let it go, but it was this wish that had gotten them separated in the first place.

After the Lost Castle in the south, now they were after the lost cities in the north. Some very unimaginative naming happening in Whyland. Karina walked behind Cayla. Liam, behind her, sometimes held her shoulders, claiming it was to prevent her from falling. Right. The path was narrow but flat. He also asked if she was feeling well enough to walk and if she wanted him to carry her. Oh, nope. She should think his offer was sweet, kind, or whatever, but it came under such an air of arrogance, perhaps even superiority, that it was unbearable. Maybe that was just the way extremely good-looking boys acted; as if he was offering some kind of high privilege just by talking to her. She'd crawl if she had to, rather than be carried.

The vegetation here was denser than near the castle, with dark green foliage, and the weather was much nicer. For the first time since she'd come to Whyland this time, she wasn't wearing any kind of coat, hoodie or jacket, just a short-sleeved shirt and pants. That felt good. She didn't quite understand why they were looking for a village, though, and what Darian and Cayla expected to find there.

Even the air reminded Darian of his childhood, and not only his childhood, but more, as if he was finding a piece of himself. He'd left his village only a little over three years before, but it felt like a lifetime. A lifetime of memories, and a desire to come to terms with whom he really was, as he felt that there was something more to find out. As to why only now he had decided to return, he didn't know. Maybe it was the urgency, and the fear of seeing Cayla confronting the unknown. Perhaps he should have tried to come as soon as they'd been attacked by the kyons by the Lost Castle, but he hadn't thought about that then.

A familiar stone marked the entrance of his village, and what should be a few houses bordering a hill. He paused, feeling as if he was sinking like his heart. There was nothing there, not even ruins, marks, nothing that could tell that there had been dwellings in that place.

Cayla moved close to him and whispered, "What's wrong?"

"I think they moved away."

She was by his side, staring at the clearing. "It doesn't look like anyone moved from here."

"I'm certain of the location, though."

Was he? He started doubting himself.

Cayla stared again. "Well, your people are supposed to be hidden, right? I mean, it shouldn't be that easy to see them. Come."

She pulled his hand and walked towards the clearing. It was if they crossed a screen with the painting of an empty clearing, and came up to a village, with houses forming a circle around a central fountain. This time, it did look like people had moved away because the houses looked abandoned. He looked back, and Karina and Liam were advancing too, looking around as if surprised. Liam had an attentive look that bothered Darian very much.

A door opened, and a woman came out of it. It was Leena, the village leader. Darian's heart warmed at the sight of someone from his past.

The old woman beamed and walked to them. "Darian!" She

then glanced at Cayla and Karina as if recognizing them, but seemed puzzled when she saw Liam.

Darian looked at his companions. "Give us just a second." He walked with Leena away from the others. "I had to bring them, but I don't trust him. I'm sorry."

Leena shook her head. "It's fine. We can make him forget what he'll need to forget. Don't worry about him."

"What about Cayla and her friend?"

"They're both welcome in the Light Gardens."

"Light what?" Darian had no idea what she was talking about.

"Oh, boy," Leena said, "I thought you'd remember by now."

"Remember what?"

Leena turned and gestured to the others. "Come! Follow me."

She walked to the door from where she'd emerged. As they entered the house, however, they found themselves not indoors, as expected, but in a forest with trees wide apart, walking on a patch over bright stones. They looked down at a valley with bright buildings, made of tree resin and wood, standing up to eight floors high, with sharp towers. Darian should have been surprised that there was some kind of portal leading to another place, but he wasn't. Everything about that place was familiar. *That* was where he'd grown up. That was where the hidden people in the north actually lived. The villages were nothing but decoys, even if some villages were real enough and had no connection to hidden cities. Those were the cities the previous king had been trying to find, without any success.

Darian was torn. On one hand, he felt a sense of peace at finally understanding who he was and where he'd come from. On the other hand, he was disappointed that his truth had been hidden away from him.

～

Karina had been sure that nothing could surprise her anymore, but she was wrong. She'd been expecting a village, much like the one she'd come by with Sian. Instead, she found a hidden city. It was smaller than Siphoria, and the buildings were quite different, but it seemed magic, not rustic or rural, more like something from a fairytale.

Liam stared at the scenery open-mouthed. Darian must have been crazy to have dragged him along, as he'd probably babble about the secret city as soon as he could. Anyway, that was not her problem. All she wanted was some food and rest, she realized, taking in the fact that sometimes people's needs could be so simple.

Well, if she wanted food, she'd come to the right place. The woman, Leena, took them to a place by a river where there were tents and tables with food, music, and some twenty or thirty people; families with young and old. They all were light dresses, tunics, or pants, which was nice in the warm weather. Everyone took a huge interest in Darian and came to see him and Cayla. Some of them also introduced themselves and shook Karina's hands, and she had no idea why. Nobody paid Liam any notice, but he seemed fine with it, standing in a corner and eating from a plate. She ended up standing by him because she didn't know anyone else there, and Darian and Cayla were too busy.

"Impressive, isn't it?" Liam asked.

"Yes."

"I was one of those who thought these cities were just legend, superstition."

Leena stood beside them. "Legends come from somewhere. Come, I have something to show you." Karina was about to follow the woman, when she turned, "Just him."

He looked back, shrugged, and followed the woman. Weird.

"You love him, don't you?"

Karina was startled by the familiar voice. It was just Darian, standing beside her. Ugh, where did he get that idea? "No." She was probably making a disgusted face.

"Oh." He was startled, disappointed, or something, and looked down. "I thought…"

Karina pointed to the direction Liam had gone. "I don't even know him."

Darian laughed. "Him? It's obvious you don't like him. I was talking about my brother."

Karina caught her breath, stepped back, and knew at that instant that her reaction had betrayed her. There was no point lying or pretending. She took a deep breath. "I wouldn't call it love, you know? And it's over. He was tricking me, so it was fake."

"But that doesn't change the way you feel, does it?"

"Why are you asking this?"

"I fear you might be hiding something."

Karina looked at him. "Everybody hides something, don't they? And I don't want to look stupid."

Darian nodded. "There's no shame in love, you know? If he really did trick you, then the shame is only his."

Perhaps he was trying to be helpful, but the effect was the opposite. "Well, sure, but it doesn't change the fact I was an idiot."

Darian shook his head. "Never an idiot, that's not how you should think. Listen, I know Cayla has been given you a hard time. She is… difficult, or stubborn, and…"

"And you like it!" Karina laughed.

Darian smiled. "I love it. You're right." He got serious. "But how do you think I feel whenever she says my brother is disgusting, ugly, and all that stuff?"

Karina shrugged. "Well, it's his fault we almost died, so, considering everything—"

"She doesn't need to say he's repulsive, though. I don't look that different from him." He rolled his eyes. "Anyway, I'm gonna talk to her. Please share everything you remember, even details that don't seem to make a difference. We need to find out what happened with the Darloom castle and figure out other stuff as well. We need the truth from everyone."

Karina nodded, even if she considered the prospect of sharing those things quite uncomfortable. She then pointed in the direction Liam had gone. "Are we going to talk in front of him, though?"

Darian bit his lip. "Yes, in exchange for letting me out, I promised I'd bring him to you, and bring him with me if you were with us, so I have no choice. But Leena said—" He paused. "He's fine."

That was surprising. "If she says so…"

Darian then said, "I didn't remember any of this. They wiped my memory when I left. For now, as long as we come out of here with answers and knowledge, I don't care."

Maybe he was suggesting that their memories could be wiped too. But something didn't make sense. "Why would they wipe your memory? You're one of them, aren't you?"

"When I left this city, I went to the castle live with my father. I can understand the precaution."

Karina nodded. She then had something else to ask. "How come Sian wasn't—"

"Raised here? I have no idea. I didn't even know I had a brother until I went to the castle, some three years ago."

"Did you know your father tortured him?"

Darian looked down, then closed his eyes. "Yes, I mean, my brother told me about being starved, or punished if he didn't accomplish whatever his father wanted him to do."

"Yes, but he also made him withstand pain. I think he burned him with pokers. To train him to withstand pain without crying or yelling." Karina felt nauseous when remembering her dream. She had no idea why she was telling Darian that, but she thought she should.

"He told you that?"

Karina felt uncomfortable, but she had to explain it. "I saw it in a dream. I know, sounds silly and weird. But also, he wouldn't remove his shirt or let me touch his back or chest." Karina realized what she had just said and her face got hot, but Darian just looked curious and concerned, and not the least interested in knowing why she'd want to touch him or why removing his shirt had come up. "I guessed that it was because he had scars, and he confirmed it."

Darian seemed on the verge of tears. "It's unfair, right? I loved my mother, but I don't understand why she did it." He gestured around him. "Look at where I grew up. I always had everything I wanted, I always had love. Meanwhile, my brother..." He took a deep breath. "Starved. Tortured."

Karina remembered the awful things Sian had told her and those creatures attacking her, and said, "Well, that doesn't justify what he's done. What he's been doing. It's just... I thought you should know. But he's in the wrong, and I guarantee you, it was all his choice. He's been planning this for months. And he used me. So while I do pity the boy he once was, I don't pity the man he's becoming, and I don't forgive him for what he did to me."

Darian shook his head. "You shouldn't. But don't think love was a bad thing. It never is."

"You might change your mind when I tell you what I've done."

"I won't. And you're here, ready to make it right, even though it pains you. Isn't that true?"

Karina shrugged. "Maybe."

"And you had the choice to stay with him. Didn't you? I bet he didn't toss you like Liam wants us to believe. I bet you walked away."

"What was I supposed to do? Become queen and rule over an army of creepies? And plus, I hate politics."

"It takes guts to go against your heart."

"It takes brains, but they should always beat the heart."

Darian had a faint laugh. "Perhaps. Had things been different, you'd be my sister. I'll still consider you as such, for my brother's sake."

"I doubt he cares."

"We can't be sure. I want you to know that whatever happens, whatever we do, I don't want to hurt him. Maybe I know him very little, but he's still my brother. So, in a way, I love him as well, and I'll do what I can to protect him. We have that in common."

"Not really. I actually want him to suffer, and suffer slowly, for everything he did to me."

"She's right." Cayla was beside Darian and turned to him. "You weren't trying to convince her that your brother is anything better than a slimy worm, were you?"

Darian took a deep breath and told Cayla, "Come, I need a moment with you."

Karina was left alone again, but not for long, as Liam returned.

He laughed. "She was showing me a secret cave. Funny, right? That they should trust me."

He still looked insanely good looking, but it didn't annoy her or anything.

"Why? Shouldn't they?" she asked.

"I don't know. I wouldn't trust a stranger, but they trust me. Maybe they know I can be trusted."

Karina remembered what Darian had told her about wiping memories and suppressed a chuckle.

MEMORIES

Cayla and Darian headed to the trees, away from the others.

"What did she tell you?" Cayla's face was curious, almost anxious.

"She'll tell us later."

Cayla looked down. "I thought we kept no secrets."

Darian kissed her forehead. "It's not a secret, but it's not my story to tell. She'll tell us all."

Cayla moved away from him. "Fine, I guess."

She looked uncomfortable, and Darian was about to make her even more so, but he had to ask some questions. "Cayla, we need to know everything. Everything. We need to understand."

"That's why I wanted to know what Karina—"

"She'll tell us. But I don't think she's the only one who has untold stories about my brother."

"You shouldn't call him that."

Darian sighed. "Sian, then. You knew him as a child, didn't you?"

Cayla fidgeted and looked away. "Not much. I rarely saw him."

"But you did."

She rolled her eyes. "Well, yes. I guess."

"You guess. As if you weren't sure."

Cayla sighed. "I saw him very little, that's all."

"Fair enough. There's one thing that I want to understand, just one thing. Why do you dislike each other?"

"Darian, he tried to get you killed once. Maybe you forgive him, maybe you believe his lies, but I don't."

"We don't know if it was him, but I'm not talking about that. I mean before. Before everything, before you even met me, you disliked each other. There must be a reason."

Cayla shrugged. "How am I supposed to know? He hates everyone."

"That's not true and you know it. I saw him at a ball. People flock around him."

"Maybe they want to lick his boots." There was something uncertain about her voice. Darian could feel the avoidance and the lie beneath it.

"They would have flocked around my father then. But that's not the issue, Cayla. Both of you have a grudge or something. There must be a reason. Tell me. I swear I won't judge you."

"Me? I'm not the psychopath who's leading a hoard of monsters."

Darian breathed to keep his calm and continue speaking in a steady voice. "I know. And if we're going to defeat him, every piece of information can help."

"I don't think stuff that happened eight years ago makes any difference."

Darian spoke in his softest voice. "What happened?"

Cayla sighed and looked away. "You know kids. Pranks and stuff. Some silly kid stuff, that's all."

"Tell me, please."

Cayla closed her eyes and stared at him, her voice shaking. "You're not gonna like it."

"It could be important."

Cayla shook her head. "I doubt it, I doubt it. But I'll tell you, and it's just stupid and childish, and you're going to think..."

"You don't trust my love for you?"

She had a half smile, then looked down. "I was a child, Darian, I was a child. Stupid, maybe."

Darian braced himself to find out what was inside a hornet's nest.

Cayla took a deep breath. "I rarely saw him, and that's true. Some official business when he was with his father, things like that. He didn't live in the castle with us."

Darian's insides stirred. "He was sent to the military academy when he was five."

"Oh." Her face showed traces of shock and disgust. "I didn't know that. I thought it was some school or something. Anyway, I rarely saw him, until this one trip. I was nine. My father was courting Nia, and he decided we'd all travel together for a vacation. We went to an island far in the ocean. Your father took Sian. My sister stayed in the castle. At that time, I had two friends, two girls who spent time with me. Their parents were important people in my father's government, and the girls went with us, they were sisters. One of them was my age or a bit older, the other was eleven, her name was Anna. Looking back, it sounds silly, but I sort of looked up to her because she was older, and just seemed so confident, so sure of herself. I don't know. Stupid."

Cayla fidgeted. "Sian was weird. I think he was ten or eleven, but he was as tall as he is right now. Maybe just a little shorter. With the body of a ten-year-old. Try to picture that. When we were on the island, he didn't talk to us, and the girls started calling him names. Not in front of him, but among us. Walking stick or something. I don't remember well."

Darian got the sense that she remembered that very well, though.

Cayla swallowed. "Anna even put something on his food. Not poison, just something to make it bitter. He ate it all, never showed that anything was wrong. She followed the servants to the kitchen and passed her finger on his plate. It was horribly bitter, according to her. No idea how he did it. The girls started saying he was a sorcerer and wanted to prank him. Nia heard us one day, though, and pulled me aside. She wasn't angry, but disappointed. She told me to look into my heart and judge if what I was doing was right. It was a long conversation, and I agreed that I shouldn't mock a defenseless boy." Cayla snorted. "I thought he was defenseless, and I sort of pitied him. Anyway, I told my friends to stop the name-calling, and I forbid them from pranking him. I was polite to him when I saw him. I even asked what he was reading. Small conversation, you know?"

"You did a good thing."

She looked down and shook her head. "They started teasing me, saying I was in love with him. Like I told you, he was thin, weird, and not someone any girl would want to… And it wasn't true."

Her words dissipated the very awkward image of young Cayla with a childhood crush on Sian that had been forming in Darian's mind. He exhaled, relieved.

Cayla must have noticed. "Darian, please! You should have seen your brother when he was a kid. He didn't look the way he does now."

It was almost impossible to imagine Sian without his confident stance and smile. "So you agree he looks good now."

"He's a hundred times better looking than he was before. But that's still not much. Imagine how angry and humiliated I felt. I forbade them to tease me or say any of that, but they kept their looks and sniggers. They were my friends—or I thought so. I wanted to prove them wrong, so I started calling him names again, but that wasn't enough. They still had funny looks. I just wanted it to stop. I wanted to prove to them that I didn't feel anything for him, so I planned a trap. Don't look at me like that."

Darian didn't think he was looking at her any differently, but perhaps he was. "I'm just listening."

Cayla sighed. "It was childish, and it was stupid. We sent him a *love letter.*" Cayla was uncomfortable saying these last words. "Anonymously. Telling him to meet his secret admirer in an old, abandoned house."

"Weren't you like, nine, you said?"

"Anna was eleven. It was a childish love letter. And you said you weren't going to judge me."

"I'm just curious."

Cayla sighed, uncomfortable. "The house had a basement, and its floor was very old. There was a hole in the floor, which we covered. Stupid, stupid. But he didn't show up. He was indeed unfazed and aloof, or perhaps he just wasn't interested in any of us. At dinner, he acted normal, as if nothing unusual had happened, except that he glanced at us three now and then, more than usual. He was curious. He knew the letter had come from us, or at least one of us. We didn't have many days left, but I knew he would show up to the house. I knew it. For curiosity, at least. Anna was a good writer, and she wrote another letter. This time it was beautiful and poetic, and..."

"So she was the one with the crush."

Cayla seemed surprised, then she shook her head. "You're right, Darian, so right. I can't believe I never saw it. Perhaps the letter was real, and Anna was spilling her heart in it. He didn't show up on the second day. The girls got creative and found ways to make the trap worse than it was before. The idea was that the more he delayed, the worse it would get."

"Children can be cruel."

"Not all children. Well, he showed up on the third day, a lot earlier than the suggested time. The girls were outside looking for something else to put in the basement. I was the only one he saw. I was alone, and I could have told him to walk away, but I didn't. He knew it was some kind of prank and told me he was there was to make the letters stop. I asked him to come closer. He was sarcastic and told me that if I loved him so much, I'd walk to him. I did. I tricked him, by walking around an imaginary hole, while he walked just a couple steps forward—and fell. The girls had put pig excrements there, Darian. It was disgusting. I didn't know that. And the fall was higher than we imagined, as we later found out he broke his arm. But it didn't seem so at the time. He was calm and didn't say anything. He didn't seem hurt. The girls came back, and, because they were listening, I told him some things that were, uh, not nice, like how I pitied him or something. They were looking at me from a distance and egging me on. He just sat there, looking bored. Eventually, we left and locked the door. He didn't show up for dinner. I got worried and considered going back and opening the door, but I was afraid of what the girls would say, so I didn't do anything."

Cayla took a deep breath. "The next day, while we were playing outside, he showed up. His left arm was bandaged, and that's when I realized we had gone too far. I mean, he'd broken his arm. I had just humiliated and hurt an eleven-year-old boy."

"You were nine."

"That doesn't justify it, does it? Anyway, he challenged us to fight him. My friends ran away, saying it was all my fault. I stood my ground. He taunted me, but I just stood there. Still, he immobilized me, then pointed a dagger to my throat, saying he could kill me there and then. It was true, he could. But he said that he'd never sully his hands killing me, that I didn't even deserve that, then he walked away. I didn't tell anyone. Sian didn't tell anyone either."

"And that's why he doesn't like you."

Cayla closed her eyes as if in pain. "The story doesn't end there, Darian. We returned to the castle, and I started to see my friends for what they were: cruel and obnoxious. I decided I didn't want to have anything to do with them anymore. I spoke to my father, but he thought Anna was a good influence on me, so well mannered and all. I just wanted them sent away, and then… I told him. I told my father what they did to Sian, excluding my participation in it. I told him the kind of things they said, the kind of things they wanted me to do. He said they would be sent away." She took a deep breath. "They were. They never got to their destination, though. They died in a lift accident."

"Didn't that tip you off that your father was a monster?"

"It could have been your father, Darian. Maybe he learned about it. It was his son who'd been humiliated. All I know is that the girls who'd been my two best friends were dead. Because of me. Yes, they were cruel. But they were children. And they had a family. They all died. For a long time, I didn't have any friends. I've never told this story to anyone."

"It wasn't your fault, Cayla. Like you said, you were just a kid."

"At the time, I knew well what I was doing. And I knew it was wrong."

"Were you ever going to tell me this story?"

Cayla took a deep breath and looked away. "Maybe. I still don't see how it relates to any of this, though."

"Did you ever apologize?"

Cayla rolled her eyes. "He threatened to kill me. Plus, I buried this story deep in my memories, to the point it seemed to be another person who did these things. I thought he'd forgotten as well. I mean, I'm sure he'd want to forget a moment when he was humiliated."

Young, helpless, humiliated. Darian still had trouble picturing Sian like that. Although, from what she said, he was already proud. He was still proud. "Maybe he didn't forget, Cayla. Have you ever thought that? Have you ever thought that maybe this is his revenge?"

"A little overboard, isn't it?" She made a voice, "Oh, you threw me in a hole with shit when I was a kid, I'll take over the kingdom." Cayla shook her head. "And he never mentioned it. I saw him a few times after that. He was polite. Normal. He never tried to talk to me or ask me to dance before I met you, but..."

"Now I understand why he hates you, Cayla, and this matters."

"Yeah, I wonder where his hate was when I was opening the portal to bring Karina. When I was asking my mother to bring the book to her. So convenient."

"We know that getting Karina here was more important than whatever hate he has for you, and that matters." Darian looked at her, pale and shaking. "Thanks for telling me this. Including the worst parts. You could have blamed it all on your friends."

"Maybe I did."

He wrapped her in an embrace. "Is that why you insist he's so repulsive? Because you still remember the time you were teased about it?"

Cayla snorted. "That was a long time ago, Darian."

"Time doesn't erase certain things."

"Well, maybe. Maybe I'm reminded of how I was repulsed at the idea of any romantic feelings. For him or anyone. I was only nine. Maybe there's something of that."

"And how come..." He caressed her hair. This was off topic and was likely to make her upset, but he had to ask. "How come then you saw me and you, uh, became my friend, considering I look like him?"

She stepped away and faced him. "You don't remind me of him. Same eye color, maybe. Same hair color, fine. All the rest is different. The thing about you is that you didn't have a poisoned mind or heart, like everyone I grew up with, like everyone in the castle. You were different, like a breath of fresh air in a stuffed room. I needed that. I didn't care who your brother was."

Darian held her hands. "And now we have to defeat him."

"We will." Her face was determined.

28

MAGIC

While the party was still going on, Karina, Darian, Cayla, and Liam took a rowboat to a small island in the middle of the river, together with Leena. Darian wasn't sure Liam there was a good idea, but the boy did have inside information about his brother, and perhaps he'd be able to help them.

They sat around a fire that wasn't really to warm them up, as the weather was hot enough. Still, watching the flickering flames relaxed Darian, and maybe brought some memories from his childhood.

"So," Leena said. "You have questions for me. I'll do my best to answer them, but first, each of you needs to pay a tribute, by giving me some truths."

This was not just a conversation, but there was a ceremonial fire, and he hoped Cayla and her friends understood it.

Darian got up. "I'll start." He glanced at Cayla. "Lylah, Cayla's mother, told me Whyland always needs a guardian as a queen or king. She said she was a guardian, and thanks to the fact that nobody else was called queen in the years she disappeared, no problem came to Whyland. She also said Cayla is a guardian, whatever that means, and that she would inherit the throne. I'll also say one thing: in the little time I was, uh, kind of a king, I don't think I was acting fully as myself. I was scared, very scared. Scared of losing Cayla, and I," he looked down, "I was a terrible king, boyfriend, and future husband." He looked at her. "I'm sorry. I love you, but you didn't deserve what I did to you."

He sat near Cayla, who kissed his cheek and got up.

"I knew Sian as a child. Not much. Once, some friends teased me that I was in love with him. It was stupid and cruel. We teased him back. I think he hates me, and I don't like him either. That might mean something—or not. You know, he did take the kingdom from me, and I think once he tried to separate me from Darian. It also might mean nothing." She sat and glanced at Darian. He held her hand.

Liam got up. "I've known Sian since I was ten. We trained together. We were going to be part of a team of elite warriors, but the group was disbanded, perhaps because the king came to fear us. I have been friends with him ever since. He does things and plans things behind everyone's back. In the beginning, it was his father, then it was more of the army. I was his number two. He told me he wanted to bring her to Whyland." He pointed to Karina. "He asked me to lie to his brother so that he'd convince Cayla to teleport her here. I did that. He said he would take the kingdom, and he promised power and riches for his supporters. He confided to me and a couple of his closest friends that Karina was the key for him to take the power." He looked at Karina. "I'm really sorry. I regret my part in this. I met you and I saw you, and I couldn't forget you. I could no longer support Sian, and that's when I turned against him." He looked at Darian. "I know you don't trust me, perhaps because you don't understand my motivation." He pointed to Karina. "Well, she's my motivation."

Karina looked away and seemed embarrassed. She then seemed to have realized it was her turn, and got up, telling most of what she'd done in Sian's company. Darian was surprised to learn that his brother had friends and even owned businesses in Siphoria, but perhaps he shouldn't be. He got worried when she talked about going into a strange dimension, and bringing a staff, and how she teleported away from him when she realized what he was about to do. Karina was very embarrassed when she said Sian wanted her to be his queen and confessed that they might have been involved. It was actually baffling how his brother had had each detail planned, and how he'd duped them all. She finished by saying, "…so I know part of it was my fault, but I want to make it right. How can we defeat him?"

"Karina, it wasn't your fault," Liam said. "It might have been a love potion. He'd be capable of doing that."

"Love potions only amplify the feeling that's already there," Cayla said. "And they are quite dangerous."

Darian remembered something else and got up. "I forgot to say something. A long time ago, when I was still in the army, I got poisoned. My superior thought I was going to die. I ended up taken by the magic people from the south, and they healed me. While I was healing, they said I was a spell speaker. I think that's someone who can convince people of things, a good talker. I might have that power, but I believe my brother has even more. So that explains his allies." He looked at Karina. "And how he convinced you to do something quite dangerous." Darian sat down.

Liam said, "It makes sense. People love him, he really does seem to have a power like that."

"I don't think he knows about it, though," Karina said. "He once told me he didn't have any magic."

"He could be lying," Cayla said.

"He doesn't lie, though," Karina said. "Not with words, at least. He can trick you, but he'll twist his words in a way that they're not false. He says he doesn't like to lie."

Cayla shrugged. "Maybe he does it sometimes."

"Maybe," Karina replied.

"Is that it?" Leena asked.

"We might remember more, but I think we all brought something," Darian said.

Leena nodded. "Indeed. I'll start with the last thing you spoke about, and I'll have to say: Darian and Sian are both spell speakers. It's not so much that they can convince people to do anything, although in theory they can, but an ability that gives them good leadership abilities. There's something important, though; lying dampens this ability."

"So he knows!" Liam said.

"I doubt it," Leena said. "Sian has been brought up away from any magic knowledge. It's more likely that he feels it. Magic is a power that people can feel within themselves. He might feel that lying makes him weaker, and thus he dislikes it."

"Darian mustn't have any of this power then," Cayla said.

Perhaps he should feel insulted, but it was true that in the last years he had to act in both sides, and lied a lot. Even lately, with the secrets Lylah had asked him to keep, he had to speak non-truths.

She continued, "He keeps telling me I'm the most beautiful blah, blah, blah."

"But that's true!" Darian replied.

Cayla squinted. "I was joking."

Leena looked at her. "He does see you in all your magnificent beauty, Cayla, and he speaks the truth. As to other lies… It might be that he has no choice, and it might be that he also feels the magic, but he rejects it, therefore he blocks it by lying." She looked at him. "What is it, Darian?"

He shrugged. "I don't know."

Leena nodded. "But there's more. Spell-speaking is a powerful tool, if used correctly, but more than that, it is a sign of someone with strong magic abilities." She looked at Darian and Cayla. "Have you ever wondered what brings you together so strongly?"

Cayla was now sitting close to him, taking his hand, and squinted. "Am I supposed to wonder? Look at him."

He felt that he was blushing, but squeezed her hand. She traced circles in his palm, and he had to make an effort not to let his mind wander thinking about her touch and all the touches they had and were yet to have. But his mind had wandered, as he only heard the last part of what Leena had said.

"…powerful magic."

"What?" he asked.

"Powerful magic calls to powerful magic. It's no accident you and Cayla are together."

"I don't tend to think of myself as powerful," Darian said.

Karina found it funny that Darian, like his brother, didn't grasp his own magic.

Leena shook her head. "That's the fate of most people, they live never to understand their own magic." She turned to Karina. "Isn't that the case with Sian?"

"If he's saying the truth."

"He probably is, and yet he found the Darloom castle, he used the staff, he did things that most people wouldn't have been able to do. He must use the self-control he learned in the army to focus his magic, and he uses it well, even if he doesn't know that's what he's doing. So that's one thing you need to know. He's quite powerful. And being king, regardless of how he got the title, will amplify his magic."

Was it true that powerful magic called to powerful magic then? Was it what it was? Or had been?

Leena looked around. "Second thing is the Darloom castle and the Queen's castle. Whyland is in a specific convergence of dimensions, and that makes it need special security. See, depending on who comes through, they could not only conquer our dimension but other dimensions as well. The Light Gardens and the hidden cities in the south are just in pocket dimensions, and one reason we're here is to watch for the portals. So far they've been kept safe, though." She looked at Darian. "It's true that we need a guardian at the throne. Otherwise, the portals in the Queen castle would be open."

"Why aren't they open now then?" Karina asked. "Unless... Is Sian a Guardian?"

"Unlikely," Leena said. "But you can cross dimensions, can't you?"

"Yes..."

"Maybe you count as a guardian. Didn't he want you to be his queen? Perhaps he knew."

All the talk about Karina being queen made sense, and it still hurt that it was just because of some weird magic rule. Impressive that things like these still hurt. "He actually said something like that, that Whyland can't have anyone on the throne. But he has a new queen now."

"Does he?" Leena asked.

"I'm pretty certain he does," Liam said.

Karina felt her chest turning to ice.

Darian asked, "Why then the trouble of bringing Karina?"

Liam shrugged. "For the staff, maybe."

"And you don't happen to know who this new queen is?" Darian asked.

The awe-inducing super-duper more than pretty queen. Just the thought made her shiver.

Liam replied, "I told you, he started to exclude me from things, and he had his little secrets."

Leena said, "Maybe then he found another guardian. Maybe. That would be quite impressive. Perhaps he can sense people with magic."

That made sense. "I think he does," Karina said. "I mean, he says he *reads* people well. Also, apparently, from what I gathered, he knows when someone is talented enough to invest in them. He might be seeing their magic."

Leena nodded. "Possible, very possible. Like I said, he has quite focused magic, therefore he must be using it somehow. Detecting magic is quite advanced, but from what you're saying... But back to what matters, what I know is that there's a guardian in the Whyland throne right now." She turned to Karina. "And it's either you or someone else. Now, that other dimension with those creatures, that's where Darloom lives."

"It's a person?" Karina asked.

"Not a person. A thing, an energy. But those creatures aren't his. He conquered that land. That place is called Marisia, and the creatures are Maris. They suck blood. But there's nothing wrong with sucking blood in itself, except that Darloom causes aggression, war, destruction, and, without other animals, Maris are starving. They would like to come here, but the portal is sealed."

"I came through," Karina said.

"Because of your power. And you came through water, didn't you?"

"How do you know?"

"Well, Maris can't swim. That's one way to keep them out. And you only came back because of your power. Any other person would have been trapped there."

Knowing how much danger Sian had put her through was another reminder of how little he cared about her. But she had another question. "What about the ones who attacked us? How did Sian bring them here?"

Leena shook her head. "He didn't. He probably doesn't know about them. That's one issue with his plan. Every time the staff is used, it opens the portal. Just a little slit, but enough for some of them to pass through."

Karina asked, "So they attacked us because they were hungry?"

"Maybe. They also might have been controlled by Darloom. Your power is not a joke, girl."

Karina shivered.

Leena continued, "I don't think he knows about the Maris coming through, and they weren't under his orders. But there are more things he doesn't know. Darloom understands the deepest fears and desires in your heart, and it can use them against you."

Karina didn't want to interrupt, but she had to say something, "So you think it manipulated his desire to be king into something, something…" She didn't know how to finish. Immoral? Had he ever been moral? Well, he had some moral standards about not killing people. What she meant is perhaps that he'd been manipulated into doing something who'd hurt someone else so deeply, but she didn't want to talk about her pain.

Leena sighed. "If being king is his deepest desire, yes, Darloom might have manipulated him so that he would open the portal for him."

"But I don't think he will open the portal. He wouldn't do that."

"No," Leena replied. "I doubt he would want to open the portal and let anything into Whyland. Even if he's the most selfish and power-hungry person in the world, they would only threaten his power. That said, Darloom has ways to trick people. I fear that some of it has already infiltrated Whyland—and the castle. Darian, you said you were horrible as a king. You're not the first horrible king. Do you think your fear might have been amplified?"

Darian thought for a moment, then said, "Maybe."

Cayla stared at him. "Nice excuse."

He looked at her. "Do you think I'm horrible like that?"

"Sometimes you *are* overprotective."

Darian looked away.

Leena said, "But that's exactly the thing. Darloom is not going to change anyone, he'll only manipulate what's already there. Chaos, confusion, destruction, it thrives in it."

Karina had to get to the part that mattered. "Do you think it'll come through?"

"I don't know. There's something happening, and I'm not sure what it is."

Reassuring.

Cayla then asked, "What about my mother? Do you know what's happening up north?"

"Your mother's safe. She needs to stay away from this fight."

Cayla got up. "You knew that, and you're telling me that just now? I was dying with worry."

"No, you weren't. Deep down, you knew she was safe."

Cayla waved her arms. "Very, very deep down, then. She can come back and fix things, can't she?"

"No. She has been advised to stay away, and so she will."

Cayla sat down, or rather sunk in the bench. "What's your advice to defeat Sian then?"

"Did you hear any word I said? It's not Sian you have to defeat."

Karina was having an idea. "Would putting the staff back in its place help?"

"It might."

"Might?" Cayla asked. "What can we do to end this?"

"We can control Darloom and prevent it from coming through. That's all we can do. To end this, someone would need to confront Darloom itself."

"How do you kill an energy, thing, spirit, whatever, though?" Karina asked.

"You don't kill. You transform."

"So," Darian asked, "Should we go north and deactivate the

towers preventing communication? We'd like to get the kingdom back."

Leena shook her head. "You can, but it's not necessary. The forces from the north should return soon."

"What *should* we do then?" Cayla asked, a tone of irritation on her voice.

Leena replied, "Watch, pay attention, and remember you're dealing with magic."

Cayla let out a long sigh. Karina didn't blame her. Well, they did get some information at least. Perhaps it was too much to hope that Leena would hand them a key to save Whyland. That said, her words had just muddled things.

"There's one thing more," Leena said, "If worse comes to worst, and everything comes through, the solution would be to close all portals. You could do it in the Darloom castle, in the room with the mirrors and the well. You could close all the portals, and nothing will come through again."

Cayla got up. "That's the answer then!"

"Not really. First, you'd need very powerful magic, above the abilities of each of you here, second, it would push everything back to its own dimensions and isolate Whyland."

"And is it bad?" she asked.

"It depends on which side of the portal you end up. Regardless, the amount of magic necessary is more than any of you could do."

"What about my mother?"

"She can't do it either." Leena got up. "You can ask me more questions if you need. For now, I suggest you take the boat and return to the party. When you're tired, I'll show you to your rooms."

She left, and they stared at each other. Liam, who'd been quiet until then, said, "It's all neat and good what she said about magic and Darloom, but right now we should still defeat Sian. That way we can make sure the right people are on the throne and can defend Whyland. Tomorrow we can deactivate the towers and communicate with the forces up north."

Darian didn't look much convinced. "Leena says they're coming back regardless."

"She says it, but she could be wrong," Liam said. "Either way, sabotaging the towers won't hurt."

Darian said, "It could be a trap, though."

Liam pointed to himself. "Why? You don't trust me?"

"It's not that. Maybe Sian knows that's where we'll strike."

Karina had made her decision. She said, "Wait. I'm gonna talk to Sian."

Liam widened his eyes. "Talk? You've tried, haven't you?"

"I did," she said. "But now I know more. Maybe he'll come to understand what he's up against. If there's something worse that might come through, we should be joining forces, not trying to attack each other."

Liam shook his head. "Karina, for the thousandth time, he doesn't love you. I know it hurts you when I say it, and it hurts me too, but you need to know the truth."

How annoying. "I don't think he loves me, but I don't think he'll kill me on sight either, and maybe he'll listen."

"What can you do with maybe?"

"Try!"

Cayla looked at her with worry, then said, "Let's all go to the party. We need to rest. Tomorrow we'll be in better shape to make any decision."

Liam nodded. "True. It's been a long day. We should all try to relax a little."

A good thing at least Darian knew how to manage a rowboat and took them to the shore. Karina had no idea how Leena had gotten back, but it didn't matter.

As they reached the tents, there were no more tables with food, just a few tables with drinks on a corner. A band was playing. The instruments were actually quite similar to the ones she saw at the Junction. Karina looked at the musicians and remembered how annoyed she'd been at Diane and Mael, but the world would be boring without music. She still had questions, so many questions, and for her luck, she saw Leena away from everyone, among trees, and ran towards her.

"Can I ask you a different question?"

The woman smirked. "I was expecting you."

The smirk had thrown her off guard for a moment, but Karina soon recomposed herself. "What are guardians?"

"In the beginning, it was a race of creatures with powers to teleport. They moved from dimension to dimension, for the safety of the universe. Nowadays, there are two types of guardians; the traveling ones, who volunteer to see the safety of the people in various universes, and the guardians like Cayla and her mother. All they have is the power. In their case, they are needed here, so, in a way, they are fulfilling their duty."

There was something quite interesting about what Leena was telling her. "Why did you say I was a guardian?"

"You can count as a guardian, let's say. You have the power to teleport."

"How did I get that power?"

"Same way you got your brown eyes. Mother, father, who knows?"

"But they're just ordinary people."

"Like I said, most people will go through their lives without any inkling to their true power. That's how it is."

A spark had been lit in Karina's heart. "And how does one get to be the traveling type? I mean, from dimension to dimension. How do you do it?"

Leena shook her head. "It's a very hard life. You have to really, really want it. Just having the power is not enough."

It didn't sound hard, though. It sounded amazing. Adventure, discovery, but maybe she was being naive. Still, she had to ask, "I was just curious. How could someone, you know, in theory, sign up?"

"In theory, you need to get in touch with someone who has the connections. It could be me or Lylah. But it's a hard life."

Karina looked down. "And does it have to be someone in Whyland or could it be someone from a dimension that doesn't have much magic?"

"Every place has magic, dear, it's just a matter of what they call it, or how much they repress it. But the answer is yes, you could, in theory, sign up for it, if you want a life of danger and uncertainty."

Of course she did! After all the heartbreak, she found a reason to feel whole again, to hope, to dream. Her happiness could never depend on someone else. Now she was finally understanding her purpose, finding something that made sense. Her only fear was whether she'd be accepted and how she'd deal with her parents.

Leena took Karina's hand. "I know this is not in theory, but I'll ask you to think about it. Think it through. And..." She looked into her eyes. "It's not going to be now. There are other things on your path."

"Can you see the future?"

She shook her head. "Just your present."

Karina decided to be blunt. "Okay, say I deal with all I have to deal with, and I decide that I really want to live a life of danger and uncertainty. If I come talk to you—"

Leena nodded. "I'll introduce you to my connections. But try to focus now. There are some big things about to happen, and you stand at the center of them."

Karina took a deep breath. "I'm sorry for my part in all this and my mistakes."

"Everything is relative. Don't worry. Try to enjoy the party."

"I will."

29

LIGHT GARDENS

Karina walked back to the gathering when she felt a small hand pulling her. It was Cayla, who whispered in her ear, "Come, we need to talk."

The girls walked away from the tents towards the river.

Cayla took Karina's hand and pulled to her heart. "I'm so sorry!"

"For what?"

"Sian. You were suffering, and I couldn't see it. And I was saying how ugly and undesirable he was. I'm sorry. He's obviously not ugly, and I can see how he could get a girl interested in him if he put his mind into it. I'm sorry!"

Karina didn't like being reminded of all that. "It's fine, Cayla."

She shook her head. "I was all stressed about myself. About Darian. Oh, I'm so sorry." Cayla was exaggerating a bit.

"I'm fine, really." Karina was not fine, but she didn't want to talk about it. "I just want to solve all this."

Cayla looked at Karina. "Are you sure you want to talk to him? Are you sure it isn't because—"

"I think he still likes me? No. This is not about whatever we had or pretended to have, or about some petty revenge. There are bigger things than my sense of being wronged." Karina sighed. "The reason I want to talk to him is that I got to know him. Even with the falsities, I got to see a little of who he is. If anything, he's not dumb. If there's a threat he's not aware of, he'll listen."

"Darian could talk to him."

"I think Darian bothers him. I think he doesn't like or dislike me either way, so he'll at least listen." Interestingly, it didn't hurt to admit that.

"He could try to trap you, Karina, use your powers."

Karina shrugged. "If he traps me, it's more time to try to change his mind. But I don't think he'll trap me or even that he can."

Cayla sighed. "Try then. But—I know it's hard, but you need to get over him."

Karina cringed, hating being told what to do or how to feel. "I am over him!"

"No, you're not. You just received a love declaration from a guy who risked his life for you, and all you did was flinch."

Karina shrugged. "I was surprised."

"Fair enough, now let me tell you: you didn't see it, but I saw it, how Liam was worried about you, how he wouldn't leave your side. We tried everything to wake you up. He managed it, with a draught he had. And here he is saying he's doing it all for you."

Karina thought the conversation was uncomfortable. "I'm just… You know, once bitten twice shy?" Cayla had a puzzled face. "You don't. Either way, I'll go back to my dimension and I might never see him again."

"You don't have to marry him, Karina. Don't you think he looks good?"

"Look good? He's the best-looking guy I've ever seen."

Cayla had a sly smile. "Hum… Best-looking, Karina?"

"Isn't he?"

Cayla shrugged. "I'm biased. For me nobody comes close to Darian."

"How come you're upset when he says you're the most beautiful girl in the world?"

"Because he says it as if it was a fact, not as if it was his distorted love vision."

They laughed. Then Karina said, "At least you're sure he loves you."

"I've had my doubts at times and it was painful. But we're talking about you. You think Liam is the best-looking guy in the world. Either it's your distorted love vision, or he indeed is this super good-looking guy. In both cases, maybe you should give him a chance."

Karina still felt somewhat queasy. "Darian doesn't trust him, though."

"He's cautious. Also… Maybe he's being protective of his brother, for some very stupid reason."

"I know."

"But the fact that Darian doesn't trust him doesn't mean anything."

What about the fact that Karina didn't trust him? Maybe she was just afraid to be hurt again, and maybe it was just that she was still thinking about Sian.

The girls walked back to the gathering. Liam came smiling towards her. It was a nice smile, and Karina didn't feel as annoyed as she'd been feeling before. Perhaps Cayla was right.

"Do you want to check the cave they showed me?"

Karina felt alarmed for some reason. Then again, maybe it was just fear of being hurt. "Sure. No, I mean, can we just walk to the water? I'd rather not go far."

"It's not far. But let's walk."

They were a few steps away from the crowd, and he said,

"Listen, I used to love Sian too. Not romantically, but like a friend. He has a way to make you feel special, but it's a lie."

"I know!" Karina was almost turning back.

"I just meant to say that it's not your fault. You can choose your destiny, Karina. Don't let anyone determine your value. Don't let him put you down."

"I know my value."

"That's good because I see it too."

They were by the river and he pointed to a flat patch of grass. "We could just sit here, since you don't want to go far."

Karina sat. Her heart was pounding. Maybe she did feel something for Liam, even though it didn't seem like it. He laced his fingers on hers. She would have pulled her hand, except that Cayla's voice came to her mind: *give him a chance.*

He said, "We share the same grief, the same pain. And yet, we both broke free. We're stronger than Sian."

"Can we not talk about him?"

"I'm sorry. Can I talk about you?"

"Sure."

"When I saw you that night, I couldn't look away, I had to talk to you. I was so surprised to realize who you were. Very surprised, because you're so gorgeous, unlike everything I'd heard about you."

Karina kind of understood Cayla's annoyance at being exaggeratedly called pretty and she was also annoyed because Liam was still talking about Sian, even if indirectly, but she just said, "Thanks."

"You don't have to thank me." He moved close to her.

"Sure. You're good looking too."

That sounded terrible. If Karina had to depend on her seduction skills instead of weird insta-love, she'd die without having kissed. But sure, he was good looking. Beautiful bright eyes with very long eyelashes, and amazing lips. Maybe she would like to know what it was like to kiss him. He pulled up her chin and stared at her. His eyes were hungry, in a way that was scary and unsettling, so unlike Sian's sweet, loving eyes. Why was she thinking about Sian? She had to get over him.

Liam's lips were touching hers, and his tongue was… Ugh, what was it doing? Karina shut her eyes tight and thought that he was like a cat after a night out, when it swallowed all the food just to puke it a few minutes later. He put so much pressure on her lips. Was this supposed to be passionate? What was he trying to do with his tongue? And his breathing, one would think he was running a marathon or something. She was starting to think that the kiss was rather disgusting and wondered if it would really help her get over Sian. Maybe it had nothing to do with Sian. Karina turned her face and moved away.

"What?" he asked, breathless.

"I'm not sure I'm ready." She got up.

He got up after her and pulled her hand. "What did you think I was going to do?"

The question was weird. "Kiss. I'm not ready to kiss someone else."

"If you close your heart to love, he wins. Give me a chance, just give me a chance. I'm not asking you to love me, I'm just asking you to… give me a chance to make you forget him."

"How is rushing things going to help?"

Liam pulled her closer. "If you just… trust me. Leave your fears behind. Listen to what your heart tells you, listen."

"Give me some time."

"Think, Karina, think. Don't you want your revenge? He thinks you're suffering, pinning for him. Imagine he was standing here, imagine he could see you. You can prove to him that you don't care!"

"But that would only mean I'm still thinking about him!"

"But you still are. Aren't you? Together, you and I, we can get our revenge."

"Liam, I doubt it's a revenge when he has another queen and doesn't care."

"He won't have a queen and won't be calling himself king for long. We can defeat him. We will."

"For sure. We know that."

"One more kiss then. Just one. Just so you know you tried."

Karina sighed. "Fine."

More lips, saliva, and tongue. He was good looking, though. Shouldn't it make his kiss good? Technically no, since she had her eyes closed. With open eyes she could see his eyelashes, but it was that weird angle with too much nose. At least this time he wasn't acting like a starved cat. He pushed her against a tree and was much closer than she would like him to be, his body pressed against her, his mouth again pressing hard against hers. She moved her face, but he still had his arms around her.

"Stop it," Karina said.

"Isn't this what your heart wants?"

She yelled, "Let me go!"

He stepped back. "Fine, fine, no reason for a scandal."

She turned around to go back to the party. Darian was walking towards them.

"Is everything all right?" he asked.

"Yes." Karina ran past him towards the party.

She found Cayla and said, "I tried."

Cayla smiled. "And?"

"It might have been the most disgusting thing I've ever done in my life."

Cayla's smile faded. "I think I'm the worst advice giver in the world."

"No way. Remember when you told me about your problems with Darian? And I told you to talk to him?"

"At least I made my point. I had to talk to him."

Karina shrugged. "Then maybe I had to try."

Leena gave them a house with three bedrooms to pass the night. Karina was going to sleep with Cayla. She didn't really think Liam would try anything, at least not anything bad, but she feared he could perhaps come to her bedroom and want to talk or something. Cayla and Darian had no problem with the sleep arrangements other than taking like half an hour to say goodbye in the hall. Karina would have told them to get a room if it wasn't for the fact that Darian did have a room, and Karina didn't really want to sleep alone. Perhaps it was evil to split up Cayla and Darian when they were making up after a fight, but it had also been his idea, maybe because he didn't trust Liam.

Cayla came into the room flushed. For some reason Karina felt embarrassed, as if she were interrupting or witnessing an intimate moment.

Karina tried to get a conversation going. "So, did you guys talk it out?"

"Not really, no. So many things happening, and right now… We weren't into talking."

Cayla then asked more about Siphoria and the Darloom castle, and the girls ended up talking a little before going to bed. Karina focused on the parts that weren't painful and tried to keep a neutral tone. It was already hard for Karina to admit to herself that she hadn't forgotten Sian and her heart still hurt. No way she was going to tell any of that to Cayla, lest the girl think Karina was the biggest idiot in the world. Worlds.

When Darian had asked to see his mother's grave, he didn't imagine he'd find a mausoleum with a huge statue of her. So much of his past that he still didn't recall very well. He wished she hadn't died when he was still so young, and at the same time wondered how much she knew about her death and her future. What he most wondered, though, was why his brother had been left with his father. Maybe he knew. His people had a thing of "letting the storm pass", or "let the river run its course". He wasn't sure if it was the best approach, but he couldn't change anyone's mentality.

He heard steps behind him and knew who it was before even turning. Cayla wore a loose white dress and looked like a vision or a painting.

"You woke up early," she said.

He gestured to the statue. "This is my mother. I think it was about time we made the introduction."

"I sometimes think it's so unfair that your mother should be dead."

"We each have our own path to walk, right? Losing my parents was mine."

"Maybe."

He reached out and held her hand. She smiled. He asked, "Did you sleep well? How's your friend?"

"Karina's fine. She's with Leena now. Why do you worry so much?"

"I look at her and I see my brother."

Cayla winced. "Poor girl, she's not ugly. I'm not saying your brother's ugly, but he looks like a guy, and she looks like a girl. A pretty girl in fact."

"Very funny. I'm not the only one who sees him in her. Did you see how well received she was? I heard some whispers. They consider her Sian's... I don't even know what. Future wife, something. And he's my mother's son, so they'll respect her."

"They spent a lot of time together, Darian. They were actually a lot closer than I thought. So maybe, I don't know, she has his energy in her or something."

"That's possible." Darian took a deep breath.

"How do you feel? Looking at all this? Is it all strange or do you remember it?"

He thought about it. "Both. I feel it's familiar, but at the same time, I feel like I'm looking at a strange reality, as if I were looking at me in a dream or something. It hurts, you know, that they didn't trust me to keep my memories."

"I don't think it was you they mistrusted. You went to Siphoria castle. What if you were tortured or something?"

"Right. It wasn't that they didn't trust me, it was just that they sent me somewhere where they feared I might be tortured. That definitely makes everything better, Cayla."

She looked at him for a moment, as if thinking, then said, "At least you met me. Was it that horrible? And maybe you shouldn't have this information, this magic, at the time. Maybe what they did was right."

"Maybe. Still, things come back to me in flashes and I feel so strange. But it doesn't matter." He looked at her. "I have a question for you, Cayla."

"What?"

"You know, all this agreeing to marry, it was rushed, and maybe even unnecessary. The threat from the Arlenia king wasn't even real."

"We don't know."

"No. Still… It was forced, it was rushed. Would you really like to marry me?"

Cayla rolled her eyes. "What do you think?"

"No, I mean, really. Think about it. Would you live with me regardless of what happened? Would you have my children?"

"*Our* children, selfish."

"I'm serious."

"Fine, you want to debate that? It depends on how many, because I'm not having more than two or three."

"As little or as many as you want."

Cayla looked down. "I know what this is about. It's because I said I wasn't raised to be a peasant. It was rude, it was offensive, and I was angry. But part of it is true. I would have trouble adapting if I moved away from the castle. But being with you would make everything much easier."

"You were right to be angry. I was…" He still had trouble understanding what had happened. "Listen, before your mother went away, she made me promise that I would look after you, and that I would assume the title of king. I broke that promise, by the way, that day we fought, but… When I say I don't like being king, I mean it. Somehow, maybe, I thought I was doing the boring stuff for you. I was trying to help."

Cayla looked in his eyes. "I've prepared to become queen since I was a little girl. It would be odd for me not to do it. It was odd to be tossed aside. But I need to ask you then; if you hate power so much, do you still want to be with me? Because we might never have the chance to go to a little house and live a normal life."

"I know. But it doesn't matter. Home is where you are. Our little house could be a shack or a palace."

Cayla wrapped her arms around him and rested her head on his shoulder. "It's settled then."

He kissed her forehead. "It is."

"Then let's deal with your brother and that Darloom thing."

"Long day ahead."

30

LET'S TALK

Karina's heart pounded as they traveled south towards Siphoria and the Queen's castle. She'd gone over this many times, and she still thought she had to talk to Sian. Hopefully it wasn't her stupid heart tricking her just because it wanted to beat near him. But no, she didn't really want to see him, and that was part of why she was so nervous, as she had no idea what it would be like to see him again.

Zayra and her friend Jax piloted the lift. On the back were Karina, Cayla, Darian, and Liam. Liam was a little cooler and more distant than before, but she caught him staring at her sometimes. He'd insisted on coming, and then Darian and Cayla had to come as well. The plan to deactivate the towers interrupting communication had been postponed. That was part of what was bothering Karina. Perhaps her decision would cost them precious time. On the other hand, if she could get Sian to change his mind, things would be much better when the forces from the north returned. If she could get him to change his mind.

Karina still remembered the Light Gardens, that wonderful hidden city, and was glad that her memory hadn't been modified or wiped. But then, hadn't it? If she'd been made to forget something, she wouldn't know.

The lift landed on a small private field on the outskirts of the city.

Darian handed her a communicator. "Talk to him, and if anything happens, let us know."

Karina put it in her coat pocket. "I will." She had to get used to the cool weather again, after some respite in the north.

Liam said, "I still think I should walk with you. I can get you inside the castle, since I know Sian and his friends. I don't think they've caught up to the fact that I changed sides yet."

"Thank you, but I need to do this alone."

Somehow, she thought that coming to the castle with Liam would only aggravate Sian. It shouldn't, though, since he already had someone else. Still, she didn't want to take any risk.

Liam shrugged. "Good luck then. Do you think you can find the castle?"

Was that really a question? "Well, it's big. Not exactly easy to miss."

"She'll be fine," Darian said.

Cayla hugged her. "Good luck."

With a deep breath, she walked towards the castle.

The area around the castle had a fence, with a small gate and some guards in temporary wooden towers patrolling the area. Of course, the castle was illegally occupied, with a usurper claiming the throne. Nothing would be business as usual. Karina got in a line of people trying to get in the castle. It was mainly castle employees, who apparently didn't want to miss their shift, but many of them were turned down.

When Karina's turn came, she said, "My name's Karina. I need to speak to Joel or Sian." She hoped maybe Joel's name would help her and hoped first names would do.

A young man in the entrance replied, "Everybody does,

everybody does." He gestured for her to go away, as one scares a fly.

Karina sighed. "Can I at least wait? Can someone pass my message?"

The man shook his head, seeming genuinely sorry. "We're not a lot of people here to be passing messages. Try again next week."

Karina walked back to the lift annoyed. Darian and Cayla weren't there, but Liam was.

"I guess you were right," she said. "Can you get me inside the castle?"

Liam was sitting down and reclined back. "I don't know. I was relaxing here, you see?"

Karina rolled her eyes. "Whatever. I'll go there and be more persistent."

She started to turn around, but Liam then was in front of her. "I was kidding. Of course I'll go with you. On one condition."

"What condition?"

"You'll take my arm."

What the...? He couldn't be serious. "Perhaps I *could* take your arm, but I won't if I'm forced to. You know what? Never mind. I don't want any favor from you."

Karina walked away and then heard steps beside her.

Liam had joined her. "I was kidding. I'll obviously get you in the castle, even if I think it's a terrible idea."

The polite thing would have been to thank him, but she wasn't in a polite mood. He walked with her in a different way. They crossed the streets of Siphoria rather than going through the river. He seemed to be taking a long cut, but then, maybe it was just an impression.

As they approached the castle, they went to a side entrance. It also had a guard, to whom Liam spoke and gestured.

Liam walked back to Karina, "You can go in."

"Thanks," she muttered. His presence had helped indeed.

A guard took her by the arm and accompanied to the castle. She had the feeling that she was being dragged like a prisoner. Well, there was a big chance that she would be locked somewhere, as Sian's enemy. Why was she doing this then? Well, deep down, she didn't actually believe he would harm her.

Joel intercepted them. "Easy, easy," he told the guard. "She's not a prisoner."

"I thou—"

Joel gestured for the guard to be silent. "Fine. Just let her go. I'll take her from here."

The guard turned around and almost ran away. It was odd seeing Joel in such different circumstances. Well, they'd never been really friendly to each other, as he barely looked in her direction. "I'll get you to your room then get Sian. He might take a while, though, but please wait for him before going anywhere."

Karina imagined that she'd be put in a waiting room, like in the time she'd come to see Cayla, but they were walking to the residential area. Joel opened the door to a bedroom with a large double bed and a small living area with two couches and a small table. Joel left her and closed the door.

Karina waited a few seconds and checked it: unlocked. She opened the door and peeked outside. There was nobody in the hallway. She could have run away if she'd wanted to, but that would have been really stupid, since she hadn't come to the castle to run anywhere, but to talk to Sian.

Karina sat on one of the couches, trying to get comfortable since it would take a while. But she had barely sat down when the door opened. Karina was thinking it was Joel again, who'd forgotten to tell her something, but instead, she had a surprise.

Sian came in, short of breath, in a long dark red overcoat. His face lit up when he saw her. "You came back! You're all right."

This was weird. Karina had imagined this meeting, and in all her possibilities, this reaction had never occurred to her. She had always thought that he'd be angry, aloof, or the standard sarcastic Sian, but instead he looked at her the way he'd looked before she'd learned about his plans and they argued. Her heart was speeding up and was probably climbing up to come out of her mouth.

Sian sat beside her and took her hands. "I heard about your lift accident. I wasn't sure how hurt you were. I was so worried."

"I'm fine."

She could barely breathe. It wasn't just his reaction and the surprise, but feeling his touch again, feeling his thin, long, fingers, and even just looking at him and realizing that none of her feelings for him had ever subsided. There was something special about the way he moved, the way he walked, perhaps even the way he held himself, plus just hearing his voice gave her chills. That said, she had to have some self-respect.

Karina pulled her hands. "Where's your queen?"

Sian blinked, surprised—or perhaps pretending.

She insisted, "You have a new queen, don't you?"

"You know it. Why are you asking about it?"

"I'm just wondering where she is."

Sian frowned. "You're not making sense, Karina." He stared at her for a while, then said, "Do you mean…someone who's not you? Some *other* queen?"

Was he saying what she thought he was saying? But she had to explain her point. "I wasn't here and I heard you had a queen, what am I supposed to think?"

"I told you it was you, back in the Darloom castle, that I wanted you to be my queen. And I told you yesterday. You said you didn't have any problem with it."

What? It was Karina? The super-duper more than pretty? Something inside her changed at knowing that it had always been her, as if warm water melted the ice around her heart.

Sian looked incredulous. "Did you actually think I had someone else?"

Karina was still trying to recover from the surprise. "Maybe." But she couldn't let her heart fool her again, couldn't let herself get entangled in his pretense, even if his words from the bridge came back in such a force that shook her to the core. There were reasons why she was a queen. "Was it because I can teleport, and I can be considered a guardian? Do you know anything about the portals and stuff?"

"Like I told you, Whyland's different. It's not just anyone who can come to the throne."

Of course. It had always been her because of a technicality, not because… Anyway. She had to keep in mind why she was here. "Sian, I need to talk to you."

"I'm listening."

His voice and eyes were soft and sweet, so sweet. That was perhaps the main reason she'd come to like him so much, and perhaps it was just part of his powerful magic.

Karina struggled to focus back on the subject. "The Darloom castle, it's dangerous, Sian. Darloom's a creature, and it might trick you. It wants to come to Whyland."

"I know that, but the question is who is tricking who."

Oh, he was stubborn. "Remember when I retrieved the staff for you? That I told you there were these horrible plains with the creatures? Well, some of these creatures have come through. Something's about to come through, Sian."

"Hold on. Where are those creatures?"

"We killed them. A little south from that bridge."

Sian frowned. "What do you mean you killed them? How?"

"After you talked to us. Me, Cayla, Alessa—"

"No. No. This wasn't supposed to happen. I knew you were there, but I thought there was no danger. I didn't know it, I swear."

"We didn't know it either. I thought it was only the kyons.

We were caught unaware and that's why we had the lift accident. At least they didn't come here, I guess."

Sian looked away then back at her. "I felt it. I felt it and ignored it. I thought I was just…" He closed his eyes and sighed.

"You just found part of your magic. Congratulations."

Sian frowned. "It's not magic."

"It *is* magic. Apparently you're a spell speaker, and you can see people's magic, among other things."

Sian snorted. "If I were a spell speaker I'd have convinced you to stay with me, so that makes no sense."

She had to get back to the point. "Anyway, those things came through. Every time you use that stupid staff you open a little crack between dimensions and these things come through. Every time."

"I didn't know it. But I don't plan on using it anymore."

"But that's the thing. You're dealing with dangerous magic."

"I'm done with it. I got what I wanted."

"It doesn't end there, Sian. Apparently Darloom has some influence in this castle. It could manipulate you. They say it sees in your heart and manipulates your deepest desires."

"I know that, Karina, and because I know that I can block it. It's not going to be a problem."

"You can't be sure."

"I am sure."

Karina exhaled. "The thing is, while you're here, taking the throne for who knows which reasons, there's this thing that's planning to cross over. And a good part of the army is away. This is dangerous and complicated magic. Step down, Sian, step down and let Lylah handle it."

He stared at her. "You're afraid, then."

"Yes. That's why I came to talk to you."

His hands brushed her hair away from her forehead. Karina's entire body trembled.

He said, "I understand you were upset I didn't listen to you, but I don't know how I would feel if I had wasted this opportunity. I don't know how I would feel if I had given up plans for which I worked for months. I didn't want to risk blaming you."

"Are you happy with your plans?"

Sian nodded. "Yes. Everything went a lot smoother than even I expected. Plus, I'm here, and you're here."

"Well, that's great, but stop it, then. We don't know what's going to happen when the forces from the north return. There could be a conflict."

"We're letting them come slowly. So far everything has been going better than expected. I didn't even use the kyons. We're in peace, Karina. Trust me, please."

She had to worry about what mattered. "What about that staff? And the smaller staff, and whatever else you have from Darloom? See? That might be the thing that's allowing them to come through."

"Not really. I've realized that Darloom has been influencing this castle for quite a few years, and I only got the staff a few days ago. If anything, it might allow me to fight it."

"Well, but those creepy winged creatures only crossed now. Something is opening."

Sian took a deep breath, then stared at her, and asked, his voice soft, "What do you want me to do?"

"Step down."

Sian snorted. "How is that going to help?"

"You'll have a more experienced queen who knows more about magic, and a kingdom that's not in a civil war."

Sian took a deep breath and held her hands. "I'll tell you what I'll do: I'll let all the Whyland forces return, I'll let Lylah return, and then I'll speak to her and negotiate our terms. If she really needs to go back to the throne, for the wellbeing and security of Whyland, I'll step down. Does that solve your problem?"

"It's not *my* problem. Maybe you should put that staff back where it belongs."

"I'll research about it and see if it's better to keep it or not. If something's really coming through, I might need it."

"Why do you want to be king, though? Why do you have to do it?"

He stared at her for a long moment, let go of her hands, and got up. "You want me to step down regardless of what might happen, right? This isn't even about whatever is threatening us from another dimension, is it?"

Karina got up as well. "I was against your plan before even knowing about Darloom and its threat, so yes, I would like you to step down regardless, just because this is wrong."

He stared at her, then took a deep breath. "I'll consider your request, I will. Just give me some time. I disagree with your idea of wrong here, Karina, I really do, but I'll consider what you're saying."

Again, Karina was stunned. She hadn't expected it to be so easy. But then, he hadn't promised anything, he'd just said he'd consider it. Perhaps it was just one more of his verbal traps, where he says he'll consider her request knowing well what his decision was going to be. That said, he was civil, he was sweet, and he was looking at her as if they'd never broken up. Karina was wondering if it was worth being mad at him for some internal political squabble she had no hand in.

Well, she did have a hand, or rather, a friend. "What about Cayla?"

"Didn't you say I should step down? She'll go back to her privileged position."

"I mean if you don't step down."

"You're considering the possibility?" Sian shrugged. "She can come, be princess and live in the castle for all I care. My brother can go back to his post in the army as long as he doesn't conspire against me. But you said I should step down, didn't you?"

"Yes."

"Then there's nothing to worry about. It's upsetting that you think they're worthier than me, but I'll take it."

"It's not about being worthy."

"What is it about?"

"You took this by force. Small force, but it was by force. It wasn't the right way, Sian."

He rolled his eyes. "Not sure if you remember, but the current queen also took it by force."

"She took it back, though, and life in Whyland has improved a lot since she assumed."

"But it's not going to get worse with me. Do you think I'll persecute poor villagers? That was a stupid waste of time and resources. I'm not a monster."

"I know you aren't. Or I wouldn't have—" she was going to say *come talk to you,* but she didn't want to ruin the way he looked at her. "—come back to you."

"We'll sort it all out, I promise."

He hugged her, and it felt so good to lean against his chest and feel his arms around her. She hugged him back, and felt again that amazing feeling of being squeezed, as if he didn't want to let her go. He smelled a little less soapy than usual, but his smell was still inebriating.

"I missed you," he said.

How she needed to hear those words, perhaps hear any words confirming he felt something for her. Karina decided to let go of the chains she'd been used to lock her heart. "I missed you too."

One of his hand caressed her forehead and hair. She looked up. Their eyes met, and it was this amazing connection, as if she could see his soul, and there was nothing she didn't like in it. Before she knew anything, their lips were locked, and it was like a few days ago, when she felt as if she were floating, and all her body tingled.

He stopped suddenly, stepped back, and touched his lips as if he'd tasted something odd or had a hair in his mouth. He stared at, a look of disbelief in his face. "Who did you kiss?"

"What?" She couldn't believe he was asking this question.

He still touched his lips, in a concentrated face as if he were trying to figure out the answer. "You kissed someone."

Technically she had kissed someone, but it had been awful, so it didn't count. "I didn't."

Sian looked as if he'd seen a ghost. "Liam."

Karina was taken aback. Was it really possible that he could find that out? Well, there was a lot of magic she didn't understand in Whyland. Either way, she didn't think it was right for him to blame her. "What if did? Last time I saw you, you had a manacle around my wrist and told me I was your enemy. And I thought you had another queen."

He stared at her, as if frozen, then it was as if something clicked in him and he looked away and snorted. "You do move fast."

"How can you even know who I kissed? Do you go around kissing people and listing the people they kissed before you?"

Sian rolled his eyes. "Go around kissing people! I'm not you."

She pointed a finger towards him. "You have no right. You have no right to judge me."

His voice was cold, and he sneered. "Who's judging you? It's just an *observation*."

"You're acting as if I'd done something wrong."

Sian snorted. "Just curious, Karina, just curious." He shook his hands. "Did he also *handle* you?"

"You have no right to make assumptions about me or to shame me because you happened to *handle me*."

He blinked as if surprised. "You think I have a problem with what *we* did?"

"You're assuming I'm doing it with everybody."

"Not everybody, just Liam, and I'm not assuming, I'm asking. It was a question, Karina. You forget I also know Liam, I know how he is, and I'm not even assuming half of what I should assume. I was just curious about you."

Blood rose to her head. "You have no right to be curious about what I do or don't do when I'm not in a relationship with you."

"You were still my queen!"

"Because of some stupid rule! It's meaningless and you've told me so. Plus, until now, I had no idea I was queen because you didn't bother telling me."

"I told you. Not only told you, you made me spill out what I think about you on that bridge—for you to turn around and kiss someone else less than a day later."

"One, I had no idea you were talking about me. Two, before that, last time we saw each other you made it very clear it was over between us. Plus, you told me you wanted me only if I were your queen, that you didn't want me otherwise. What did you expect?"

"Well, if I was going to be king, what should I want you as? My *mistress*? My *one-week fling*? What, Karina?"

"That's not what it sounded like."

"You were leaving me." He stared at her, eyes narrowed. "You didn't come back to me, did you? You only pretended to come back to try to trick me into stepping down, didn't you?"

"Not trick you. I just came to talk to you."

He laughed. "And I listened to your every word."

"They were true! That's the thing, you have no right to say you shouldn't have listened to my words just because I happened to kiss someone when I thought we had broken up for good and you had someone else."

Sian rolled his eyes. "I had someone else! That's absurd and you know it."

"That's what I thought. And making me queen without my knowledge doesn't make me your property."

Sian stared at her, jaw set, then he raised his hands and shrugged. "You're right. You're not my property and you can kiss anyone you want. Sorry for my curiosity. Go. Go to your beloved."

"He's *not* my beloved."

"Or stay. It's also your castle."

He turned around and walked out of the room. Part of her wanted to rush to him, say she was sorry, explain, but that would mean humiliating herself. He had no right to judge her after declaring she was her enemy, after saying he didn't care about her. And why was he even angry? But then had he really been angry? He'd looked quite calm and composed when he left. His issue was probably some nonsense about her being his queen. Well, she wasn't his property. What hurt more was the way he'd come into the room, with bright eyes and looking at her almost as if he'd really missed her because he liked her.

Part of her did regret having kissed Liam, though. It wasn't as if she'd been in love with him or anything. It was ridiculous that those horrible, disgusting kisses should break her and Sian apart. But then, again, she wasn't sure if whatever Sian felt was even real. It looked real, it felt real, but then he turned around and acted as if it had been some kind of joke.

Karina realized something: for good or bad, she'd brought the staff for Sian, she had told Cayla and Darian about what he was doing, and she had even talked to Sian. Perhaps Whyland still had struggles ahead, but did she really have any part in it? As long as she was deemed queen, it wouldn't make any differ-ence where she went. Perhaps she could come later, find the Light Gardens, and ask about being a guardian. Later.

Home, her real home was calling her, and that was the only thought in her head. Her time in Whyland was over. She could probably use the tower by the river; teleport there, and from there, go home. The idea of being able to go, of not needing any help, was freeing. All she had to do was tell Cayla and Darian, and go. If truth were to be told, this time she'd caused more trouble than helped. Maybe things would sort out without her there. Maybe it would be better if she left. Maybe. Either way, she was leaving.

~

Sian looked around and realized he had no idea where he was in the castle. His head had a strange buzz and he could still feel Liam's kiss on in his lips, with the horrible feeling that a snail had been in his mouth—her mouth. He could see him kissing her, or more like furiously pressing his mouth against hers, not as someone who's enjoying the moment, but rather as if he were hungry for something more. *Shut it down, put it away.* Sian knew how to lock up his feelings, but it was odd to do it with images and taste. Plus, he couldn't understand how he could feel, see, and taste a kiss. What a horrible type of magic, if that was what it was. More like a curse. *Shut it down, put it away.*

He was actually way down, near the storage room and pantry. Where had he been going? He remembered how he'd walked away from the meeting like a fool.

Whatever. Joel would figure something out. Darloom, he had to deal with Darloom, as he'd postponed it long enough. He needed to close that door and understand if something wrong was happening. He headed back to his private room on the third floor, where he kept his staffs.

Sian walked in, closed the door and took the small staff. He banged it on the floor three times. There was nothing to see, except that the air seemed to be getting thicker, with an acrid smell. Then he heard that voice.

"I thought you were never going to contact me."

Sian sat down in the only armchair there. "I keep my word."

"So you say," said the voice. "I guess you have everything you wanted, don't you?"

"Absolutely. Your advice was precious. I am king, Karina is queen. That's pretty much what I asked, right?"

The voice laughed. It likely delighted in how poisoned his part of the deal turned out to be. "Of course. The only funny thing is that you never told me your little queen was a guardian. Funny detail you kept."

Sian shrugged. "How was I supposed to know you wanted to hear that detail? You never asked."

"True. I never asked, did I? Now tell me something; how is it that your queen goes around kissing other people?"

Put it away. Sian shrugged. "Got a problem with that? Kissing other people doesn't make anyone less king or queen in Whyland."

"Interesting customs. Whyland, the land of the cuckold kings."

"And queens. The last king married twice, and yet his first wife remained being deemed queen. What can I say? We're open-minded people."

"And what advice do you require now?"

"None. This is over."

"Is that so? I see your heart, young king, and I see its cracks."

"I'll be sure to call you if I need a doctor." He touched the floor three times with the staff and the voice disappeared.

Sian sighed. Until then he'd had a sense of control. That voice had guided him through the magic of the Darloom castle. Of course, it also wanted something. It thought Sian was going to open the portals for him. Stupid voice. Sian should perhaps destroy the staff, except that he wanted to make sure that destroying it wouldn't accidentally unleash that thing.

His com beeped in his pocket. Sian had blocked all frequencies, except for emergency from Joel. There used to be a time when Liam would also have access to that. Not anymore, though, and good riddance.

"Yes?"

"Lylah is here to see you."

Hold on. How? "Where is she?"

"Meeting room five."

Sian didn't think that having someone with such powerful magic within his doors was a good idea. "Who brought her in?"

"She showed up directly there."

"I'll be there in a minute."

Why was it that all the meetings he'd been expecting and dreading had to happen at the same time? True that contacting Darloom had been his choice. As to the other meeting, he'd carefully locked away all memories of it. He hadn't expected to see Lylah so soon, though. And what terrible timing.

31

ODD REQUEST

Sian entered meeting room five with a big smile. "To what do I owe the honor?"

Lylah had been staring at a wall and turned to see him. "Politeness. I came to greet Whyland's new king."

Sian took in her appearance, and his first feeling was of disappointment. He'd always heard that Lylah was magnificently beautiful, and yet, what he saw was an older version of Cayla, bony face and all. She didn't have an eternally sour expression plastered on her face, though, so that was an improvement. Lylah chucked.

Sian sat down. He wasn't going to stand before her. "Great. Now I know you're polite. What else would you like me to know?" She just stared at him, and Sian then realized that she was slightly transparent. "A projection? Neat trick."

"Not a trick. Old technology. This room has it." She smiled at him. "I'm glad to finally see you. Last time I saw you, I had to clean up your poop."

What? Was she trying to disconcert him? Anyways, no chance. Sian smiled and gave a short nod. "You'll be pleased to hear that I've learned to do that myself since then."

"That's exactly what I'm counting on, Sian."

Well, he had heard she was weird, so he shouldn't be surprised. "Wonderful."

"Did you know you're my spiritual son?"

"What?"

"Like a godson. That's one more reason I'm happy to finally see you."

Was she going to go around in circles like that? Sian shrugged. "Well, here I am."

"When you were born, I had a vision about you. I saw you here, as king. I've had moments when I doubted it, and I thought I was mistaken, that it was your brother. But no, it was you. Now I'm sure. I'm glad it isn't Darian."

Weird, weird, and weirder. Sian couldn't hold his puzzlement. "Why?"

"You need a hero's heart, and heroes don't live long."

Hero? The woman was completely gaga. "At least it's not boring, is it?"

"No, it's not boring, Sian. So, are you happy now? You did it just for the dare, didn't you? To know you could do it."

"What difference does my motivation make to you?"

Lylah looked at him for a while, then shook her head. "No difference. But I came to ask you something."

Right. She was about to try to negotiate or intimidate him, and he wasn't about to allow her. "I don't care what happens to Whyland, what threat looms over it, I don't care. I'm not stepping down from the throne."

He wouldn't give his brother, Cayla, and her that satisfaction.

Lylah smiled. "That's wonderful! It's exactly what I came to ask you. I need you to remain king at least until this threat is over."

Sian leaned on the seat, as if he hadn't been surprised or

puzzled. "Well, you didn't have to come and ask for that because I plan on remaining king."

"I guess I assumed incorrectly. Well, I'm sorry. It's just, you see, I thought you hated being bored, and being queen—or king—is quite boring. You know, there is paperwork, taxes, requests, requests, and oh, so many requests. But I'm glad you're interested in it, Sian, I'm truly glad."

Sian snorted. "You think you can use reverse psychology to sway me? *Me?*"

Lylah shook her head. "Not at all. There's also international politics. Good luck with Arlenia. King Conrad isn't too happy about the lies you spread about him."

"Just rumors."

"What about the fake threat that he'd invade us if Cayla didn't marry him?"

Sian was stunned. Who in their right mind, other than his brother, would want to marry her, let alone start a war because of her? "I didn't spread that lie. I mean, if you're going to make up rumors, they'd better be feasible, right?"

Lylah stared at him. "So it wasn't you. Interesting."

"No."

"Either way, all I want from you is your word that you'll remain king. That's it."

There was a technique in warfare called *confuse, distract, and strike*, and he was sure that was what she was doing because nothing made any sense. "In exchange for what?"

"So you need something in exchange for your word that you're going to do what you just told me you're going to do?" She looked incredulous.

Ha. Perhaps he was getting close to the catch. "Of course. Promises have value, and while my intention is something, my word is even more valuable."

"Very valuable, Sian. Well, I can tell the forces stranded in the north to obey you. How's that?"

Sian shrugged. "They've already been obeying me."

Lylah laughed. "And who do you think told them to do it? Who had the castle surrender so easily to you?"

"Why would you do that? Is it just for the pleasure of taking away my glory, or is it so that I'll surrender later?"

Lylah sighed. "Like I told you, taxes and requests are boring. You can remain king all your life, Sian. I just don't think it's going to happen."

"We'll see."

"True. Can you give me your word that you won't give up your throne until Darloom's attack on Whyland is stopped?"

"There's no attack on Whyland."

"So just promise me you'll remain king until such an attack stops."

There was a catch, there was a catch, there had to be one. "I can't. What if I die before such an attack happens?"

"If you're alive then, and if you're in Whyland, you'll remain king. In turn, I'll continue to tell all the forces to surrender to you peacefully. How's that?"

"No. What if I do get bored, and no attack happens in the next eighty years? What if I want to retire?"

Lylah sighed. "Let's say then that if no attack happens in one year you're free to quit if you want to. Does that work?"

Sian decided not to hide his puzzlement. She was playing a game he didn't understand. "Why would you be telling me to remain king? You should ask me to step down."

"Maybe I think waiting for you to get bored is better than risking a war."

"That'll be a long wait, then."

Lylah smiled. "I understand it sounds strange. It has to do with my vision: it was you. You were king and you defeated Darloom. That's all."

"I didn't open the portals for it, so, in a way, I defeated it already."

Lylah shook her head. "Not yet."

"What does defeat consist of, then?"

"Make it go away."

Was that the catch? "And then you'll want the kingdom back."

"Not necessarily. It doesn't matter. Right now, my only concern is Darloom."

Either she was gaga, or, again, this was a game way above his level. "I promise then, that I will continue being king from now until when Darloom is no longer in Whyland, and this promise in no way means that I'll have to step down then or in any time after. This promise also doesn't bind me to the throne until more than one year, after which I'm free to leave if I want."

Lylah seemed genuinely satisfied. "Well worded. You do have a talent. That's perfect."

Sian decided not to hide his curiosity. "What's the catch?"

"Catch?"

"Why would you be giving me something I want? And making me promise I'll do it?"

"The catch is what I told you before. What you told me. You now clean your own poo."

Gaga. Of course. "Fascinating."

"I'm serious, Sian. I won't be able to help you, and I'm counting on you. I know you can do it."

"What *is* going to happen, though?"

"I'm not sure, but I'll be in Arlenia, waiting for the storm to pass."

Perhaps she was just a coward.

"Not a coward, Sian," she said.

He stared at her. "You can see my thoughts." It wasn't a question.

"And your heart. You know, crying sometimes is fine."

"I'll keep that in mind when I feel like doing it."

"Where's your queen?"

Lock it away. He leaned back on the chair. "I happen to have no idea."

"Well, you should."

Sian didn't hide his anger. "Is that a threat?" Sometimes he actually delighted in letting out little outbursts of anger, as he knew they came out quite threatening when contrasted with his controlled self.

Lylah was calm. "Not a threat. Like I told you, I am your spiritual mother, I held you and cleaned you when you were a baby—"

"Didn't you have servants back then?"

Lylah smiled. "We took care of our children. The point is— I'd never try to hurt you or anyone you love."

Again, he let some of his anger show through. "Why are you telling me I should check where Karina is?"

"It's a warning, perhaps. But then, it might be nothing. In dangerous times, you need powerful people by your side."

Lock it away. "I can't keep anyone against their will." He'd managed to sound calm, bored even.

"No, you can't. But it's a good idea to know where they are."

"I'll keep tracking her. No worries."

Lylah nodded. "Of course. Make sure they are safe. Other than that, remain king, no matter what happens. You gave your word, Sian."

His mind was spinning, wondering if the woman had been threatening him, and what exactly she could do, but he didn't want to show any of that, and just smiled. "I always keep my word."

"I know. Whenever you need me, call me. As long as it doesn't have to do with Darloom, and if I'm within reach, I'll do what I can to help you."

"Great."

"Thank you, and goodbye for now."

She spun, and her image was swallowed by the ground. Sian

took a closer look. There was indeed a small silver disk with a crystal in the middle. Small detail, that would have looked like decoration for most people. Old technology. Right. This was northern technology, something from the magic people in the north, but it must have been in the castle for generations. He wished he could work it out how to contact Lylah because her behavior had been very suspicious, and he was sure she was planning something.

He walked to Karina's room. Empty. No surprise there. Yet he had this queasy feeling in his stomach. Was this just his stupidity, or was it something more, like yesterday, when he'd ignored it? He walked downstairs and found Joel and more of his friends.

Sian didn't have time to hear what they said before he communicated his decision. "We're not going to reintegrate the people coming back from the north yet. Put them in prison and try to question them. No torture. They cannot be trusted."

"That's what I was saying," someone said.

Sian nodded and pulled Joel to the side. "Do you know where Karina is?"

"Her bedroom?"

He shook his head. "I need everyone you have on the streets to locate her."

"Are they supposed to bring her to you?"

"No. Just double-check that she's alive and well."

"That's easy."

"Look for Liam as well. He's in Siphoria. If he's located with Karina, leave them. If he's located alone, bring him in for questioning."

"He's our friend, though. You don't think he betrayed us?"

A little worse than betrayed, actually, but Sian pushed it aside and got to the point. "He has information I want, that's all, and he's abandoned his post, so in a way, he is betraying us."

"Why then leave him if he's with Karina?"

Good question. *Why?* "It might mean he's protecting her, so..." How could he put it? "He's still kind of on our side."

"Fair enough."

Why would he just leave Liam and Karina? Well, he'd told her to go to her beloved, and he wouldn't blame her if she did. Lylah's words hinted at kidnapping, and that was a lot more serious than those disgusting kisses he could still taste. A lot more serious. He felt something that resembled fear and locked it away. Could he find her in the castle? Unlikely. She wasn't there. He was going to give his people fifteen minutes to try to find her, or else he'd have to do something he dreaded.

Karina had indeed teleported to the tower by the river, and then she felt the familiar feeling of falling. Actually, it wasn't like falling. She could now identify it very well as teleporting. When the bright lights stopped, she felt the familiar smell of home. Home. Her real home! She was about to open her eyes when a force jerked her to the side as if something had thrown a lasso around her and pulled her. She'd never felt it before. When the lights stopped, she saw herself in darkness. Something had gone wrong.

Darian turned off the communicator and looked at Cayla. "She went home."

Cayla squinted. "Home? In a time like this? She just walks away?"

True... But still. "It's not really any of her business."

Cayla sighed. "I know. But I thought she'd help us, she'd stick to the end, especially now, that Leena told us she has powerful magic." She shrugged. "Not that she knows how to use it any more than I do. Did she talk to your brother, though?"

"Yes. He said he'd think about what she told him. It's a start."

Cayla had a grimace. "A start. Great. We're moving nowhere."

"Maybe my people have a point, you know? In the idea of letting the storm pass."

"Are we going to just sit and cross our arms while your brother pretends he's king?"

"Pretty much. If you want, we can go back to my city."

It was weird not saying village anymore. Or maybe not. Weird had been his wrong memory about a tiny village when that wasn't at all what his past had been like. Cayla still looked impatient.

He held her shoulders. "C'mon, we know how to wait."

"I feel powerless."

"It won't be long. Lylah should return in a few days."

She sighed. "Fine. Maybe we do deserve a break."

He was about to kiss her when the door opened. Liam walked in. Finally, Darian would be rid of him. "She left. So I think our deal is over."

Liam looked puzzled. "What do you mean she left?"

"She went back to her dimension."

"Well, bring her back," Liam said.

Cayla asked, "Why would we do that?"

"You brought her for your brother, you can bring her to me. I know for a fact she loves me."

Darian couldn't believe what he was hearing. "You are delusional. But don't worry, if she loves you, she'll miss you, and she'll return. We have nothing to do with it."

"I don't think so."

As Liam said that, he pulled a knife and moved in Cayla's direction. She kicked it away, but he kicked her ribs, sending her to the corner of the lift. Darian rushed to her side, knowing she would want to get up and keep fighting. "Do not move. I'll get someone to check you."

Her eyes flashed in anger, but she remained where she was. Darian got up to face Liam. "You don't expect us to help you after this, do you?"

Liam was again holding his knife and pointing it to Darian. "Oh, yes, I do. There's more where this came from. Your girl can think she's tough, but she doesn't have the strength or training to face me. As to you, as we know, can't hurt a fly." Liam laughed.

Darian scratched his chin. "Actually, I just remembered something."

He moved fast, without thinking. It was muscle memory, ingrained in him, forgotten for years, but still there. He touched a specific point in Liam's elbow and made him drop the knife, then touched a few points on his back, and Liam dropped to the floor. Darian pressed his foot on the boy's chest, then pulled his arm and broke it. "That's for hurting Cayla." With a few more pressure points, the boy became unconscious.

Cayla was by his side. "What did you do that for?"

"Are you hurt?"

"Not much. But you broke his arm when he was already down."

Maybe it'd been petty, maybe it'd been evil, but he wasn't going to let the fact that he kicked Cayla slide. "He kicked you."

"And what was that technique? How come you never showed me?"

"I had forgotten it."

Her eyes were eager. "Can you teach it to me?"

He hated to disappoint her, but he had to be honest. "I need to ask Leena. You need to swear an oath in order to learn it."

"I'm pretty sure your oath doesn't allow you to break people's arms for no reason."

"The oath is more about secrecy and when to use the technique." Darian shrugged. "And as you well saw, I didn't use it to break his arm."

"Fine. He was an idiot, but he saved our lives. Plus, if we start committing violence against everyone who's an idiot…"

She had a good point against unnecessary violence, and Darian himself had always been against it. That was the kind of intimidation tool his father would use. Darian didn't care, though. "Being an idiot is fine. Hurting you is not. And it's not like I poked out his eye or something."

"Goodness, Darian, I thought remembering your past would make you all calm and spiritual, and here you're talking about poking eyes."

"It was just an example. I am calm and I am peaceful, but he hurt you. He also harassed your friend. My brother's—"

"They're nothing anymore."

Darian didn't really believe it. "Maybe."

"Fine. Frankly, I don't care about this idiot's arm. It's just weird to see you over the edge like that. And maybe… Usually you're all diplomatic. You're different."

He felt different. "I am. I am different. You don't like it?"

"Just give me some time to adjust."

"I'm also adjusting." He looked at Liam on the floor. "What do we do with him?"

"We could put him outside, leave him here, and fly away."

"Sounds good. See? I'm asking your opinion."

Cayla rolled her eyes. "Oooh, what an honor. You asked my opinion."

"I always do, you know it."

"Not always."

Darian feared she'd spend the rest of their lives reminding him how he'd been king and pushed her aside for two days. Well, maybe the thought wasn't that bad, if it meant they'd spend their lives together.

She squinted. "What are you laughing at?"

"Me, you. Together forever."

"Right. Way to change the subject." She smiled, though.

He pulled her towards him and smacked his lips on hers. Cayla loved impromptu, sudden kisses, and this time it was no different, as they kept kissing and were soon making out on the side bench. He'd better not forget Liam, though, because he'd soon wake up. Perhaps not that soon. It was hard to leave her when they were that close. Closer and closer. So close.

The door opened and two city guards pointed guns at them. Darian sat up and stepped in front of Cayla to shield her from the guards' eyes. "This is private property."

One of the guards recognized him and lowered his head. "Your majesty."

Great. He'd been recognized. In fact, he recognized the guard as well. "Hey, I know you! How come you're invading private lifts, and how come you're working for Sian?"

The guard shook his head. "No, no. We serve the city. Whatever happens in the castle, we take no part. It's part of the oath we take. It's meant to prevent chaos in Siphoria in case of a conflict."

Sure. Darian knew that, but he wasn't that used to the guards in the city. "How come you're here?"

The guard looked around. "Liam was supposed to be here."

Darian pointed to the floor. "There."

"We received orders to take him to the castle."

Cayla had recomposed herself and gotten up. "To whom?"

"Sian."

"So you *are* serving him," Cayla said.

"We're looking for a wanted criminal in the city."

Cayla looked at Darian with mischief in her eyes, then addressed the guards. "He's all yours."

Darian's fear, however, was that they'd imprison him and Cayla. They were both armed, and Darian wasn't sure he'd be fast enough. Maybe. But he wasn't sure. "What about us?"

The guard bowed. "Your majesty." He turned to Cayla. "Your majesty. I follow orders. I was told to bring Liam. Nobody told me to take you. Or even to inform them where you were. I just follow orders." He turned to his companion. "Right?"

The other guard chuckled. "Sure." They stepped down and pulled Liam, each holding him below one arm.

Cayla put her hands on Darian's shoulder. "Sian wouldn't kill him, would he?"

"My brother's not a murderer. And maybe this is for a completely different reason. We don't know."

She walked to the door and locked it from the inside. "So? Where did we stop?"

"We stopped where you were torturing me. And I think we'd better fly away. Just in case."

Her eyes were sad. "Torturing you? You mean you don't like it?"

She was upset, and he hated seeing her upset, but he had to tell her the truth. "I like it more than anything in the world. It's just… Cayla, you've been making it harder and harder for me to hold back."

She squinted. "What do you think I'm trying to do?"

"I don't know. Put me through a very extenuating test to see if I'm worthy of you?"

She chuckled. "You don't need to prove that."

"What is it then?"

Cayla rolled her eyes. "Do I have to spell it out?"

Darian sighed. "Yes, you do. I don't want you telling me later you regret it, that you were just in the moment. But this is not the time or place for this conversation."

Cayla stared at him and her face softened. "Fine. Let's fly north and try to get more answers. Hopefully they'll be useful this time."

∼

Sian walked down to the prison of the castle. They'd found Liam, and that was a good start.

Liam was sitting on a bench. His former friend looked his same usual self except for a bandaged arm.

Sian didn't open the door, just talked to him from behind bars. "Why did you leave your post?"

He pretended to have just seen Sian and turned to him. "Oh, hello. It was unnecessary. The towers are secured."

"Hum. Do you know where Karina is?"

"Why do you think I have that information?" There was malice and curiosity in the question.

"Just tell me what you know." He kept his tone casual, and it didn't take any effort. Sian's feelings had been well locked in his safe.

Liam looked down, took a deep breath, and said, "I will. I'll tell you everything."

There was something overdramatic in his gestures and his tone of voice, and Sian could sense some sort of deception, but he didn't say anything. "Go on."

"That night I met her at the Junction. That night everything changed."

Sian wasn't in the mood to waste time or to listen to him for long. "Spare the details and go straight to the point."

"We're… She's in love with me."

Liam wasn't lying. Surprising how he'd just said it matter-of-factly. Sian had always been somewhat proud that he hadn't turned like his father had wanted; hard, menacing. His father believed that the best way to control people was through fear. Sian had found his own way, and it didn't involve fear, but just now he wished perhaps that he had been different, and that he had been capable of cutting of Liam's thing, chopping it in pieces, and feeding it to the birds. Liam knew well Sian wouldn't do such a thing, as his eyes showed no fear.

Well, in truth Sian wouldn't hurt someone she loved, even if he couldn't understand why she preferred Liam. *Put it away.* "Where is she?" His voice had sounded a lot more threatening than even he expected.

"Please. Understand. I'm still your friend. I meant none of this to happen. You didn't really care about her, did you? She was only meant to be queen. I saved her life. She was unconscious, almost drowning in mud, about to be killed by your creatures. I woke her up and she was in love. And then, at night—"

"I don't care for your love story." His father also cut people's tongues. Why was it that suddenly he could understand his father? Perhaps because he could remember the feeling of Liam's tongue like a rattling snake aiming for his throat. Her throat. *Put it away.* None of it mattered. Violence like that was a result of anger, a result of pain. Pain only existed to the extent he let it affect him. "Do you know where she is or not?"

"She went home. Back to her dimension."

"Are you sure? How do you know that?"

"She told Darian. We were waiting for her, after she came talk to you, and she called him saying she would go home. Apparently she's capable of it."

He was telling the truth. Sian exhaled a breath he had no idea he'd been holding, then turned around to go.

"Hey!" Liam called. "Are you going to keep me here? I told you it wasn't my fault."

Sian didn't turn around, he just turned his face sideways. "You're here for disobedience. I can't let it slide. Sorry. If my queen comes back, and if she wants you released, then you'll be free."

"You can't keep me here forever."

"I didn't say forever."

He walked away, ears shut to any complaints from his former best friend. He felt as if he had a lead ball in his stomach.

Perhaps it was only his safe, too full of stuff that didn't matter. It didn't matter.

The feeling remained, though. At first, he'd thought it was like when she'd been in danger, and that perhaps Lylah had kidnapped her. But Liam really believed she'd gone home. Perhaps there were other things bothering Sian. Not pain, though. He was immune to pain. Any kind of pain.

And then suddenly he felt as if his entire body were receiving an electric shock. He didn't allow the pain to reach his brain, and yet, and yet… Something was wrong.

He walked to his room on the third floor. His mouth had a bitter taste. He took the staff and hit the floor three times.

"That didn't take long," the voice said. "So? What is it you wish to know?"

His throat was closing, and he had trouble speaking. "Where's my queen?"

"Oh, that. Interesting you should ask. I have her well taken care of, in Marisia."

There was a lie in his voice. Funny that Sian could detect a lie even in a disembodied voice. "Show her."

And there she was, in a tower, with some kind of brilliant material tying her hands and wrists. Sian's stomach dropped. Everything dropped. It was as if he was falling in a dark hole, as if he was being thrown into his safe, in a place where there was only darkness and nothingness and pain, as if his body had decomposed into millions of pieces. And he knew the image was real.

Sian could only gather enough strength for his voice not to shake and speak in a casual tone. "So what? If you kill her, she'll still be queen. It won't open anything for you. I don't understand why you bother."

"No, no, I have no plans to kill her. Don't worry about it. All I want to do is cause her pain."

Sian felt as if he had swollen a bottle of acid, but he kept his cool tone and demeanor. "You have absolutely nothing to gain with that."

"It's my bargaining chip. Let me show you."

The voice went quiet for a moment, and the image remained. She looked calm, composed, as if thinking, or planning something. Then the shock came. Her face contorted, and she let out a scream that could pierce his soul.

Sian would not let his guard down. He forced out a chuckle. "Nice trick. I saw it. You can stop it now. What do you want?"

"Open the portals."

"How?"

"Declare she's no longer queen."

"If I do that, you could kill her."

"Oh, what's the problem? Do you even care about her?" The voice had a mocking tone.

"I don't want any killings or pain."

"That's great. If you don't want her to feel any more pain, go to the Darloom castle and use the bigger staff to break all mirrors in the purple room. If you do that, you'll have her back."

That was probably the key to opening the portals. "I want her unharmed and alive."

"Unharmed and alive. No problem."

"I need twenty-four hours."

"No, you don't. You can get there much faster."

"Yes. But those mirrors might be hard to break. I'll need to figure out a way to do it, in case they need some magic or something."

"Very well, young king. You have one day. After that, I'll start killing her. Oh, don't worry; it will be slow."

"For one day, you must not harm her or cause her any more pain."

"I won't. But I want those mirrors broken by tomorrow."

Sian banged three times on the floor. He felt like vomiting, his vision was blurry, then he focused. More than ever in his life, he had to block the pain and focus.

He picked up both staffs, strapped them to his back, and rushed to Joel. "I'll need to leave, and you'll be in charge. I want every force from the north back in Siphoria, and I don't want any of the old military leaders detained. I want everyone back in their posts."

"Then they'll depose us."

"They won't. We might have bigger problems to deal with."

"Might?"

Sian sighed. "I'll do everything I can to stop it, but if I fail, something might come through."

Joel frowned. "What do you mean? I thought what you did was safe."

"So did I. I'll try to prevent anything from happening."

"If nothing happens, we'll look like fools," Joel said.

"Let's hope that's the case. Also, please contact Malena. Send her away. Send Aline away too. Perhaps evacuate the city."

Joel frowned. "When do you think that will happen?"

"Tomorrow at this time."

"We can't evacuate the city. There aren't enough lifts of boats to get everyone out. If we try it, they'll all be caught exposed, trying to flee."

True. How was it that Sian was getting stupid? "You're right. Don't say anything. We can't have panic. Tomorrow morning I'll contact you telling you if I won, or if there will be an attack. If there's an attack, the citizens must go back to their houses and find protection in basements or anywhere that's secure."

"Goodness, Sian. What's going to happen? I wouldn't have agreed with this if I knew—"

"Do you think I knew it? Do you think it was my plan?" His voice had risen more than he would have liked it to. "Lylah knew it. That's why she's in Arlenia. But it was bound to happen. Nothing you did caused it." Sian's actions had perhaps precipitated Darloom, but apparently it was something that would have happened anyway.

"Is Lylah coming back?"

Sian shook his head. "No. That's what she's come to tell me; that I would be on my own for that."

"Do you think it's on purpose, so she can take back the throne?"

"I have no idea." It was true. Whatever Lylah's plans were, he would not spare a single thought to try to decipher them. There were more important things. "Anyway. Everyone out of prison, everyone in their posts, everyone in Siphoria, near the castle."

"Where will the attack start?"

"If it starts, it will come from the blue tower."

Joel's eyes were wide. "Within the castle?"

"Yes. Tomorrow, I'll tell you if you have to evacuate the castle."

"What should I say?"

"Figure it out. I didn't make you my second-in-command for nothing."

"All right." Joel patted him on the shoulder. "By the way, did you find your queen?"

"Yes. No need to look for her anymore. Get everyone back in their posts."

"Shouldn't you be here, though? If this attack starts?"

"I'll be trying to prevent this attack from happening."

"At the Darloom castle."

Sian nodded.

"Won't the attack be there?"

"No. The crack is here, and it's going to be here. If it happens. I have to go. Good luck. I'm counting on you."

"Where are you going?"

"Right now? To Siphoria. I need to find my brother. If you find him or hear about him, contact me, otherwise, all that I asked you should keep you busy enough."

Joel's face was incredulous. "Are you meeting him to step down?"

"I can't step down."

Sian left his friend dumbfounded and maybe even disappointed. Joel was smart, capable, and pragmatic. He would prepare the city to fight whatever came through—again, if anything came through.

32

BROTHERS

Siphoria's lights were fading away behind Darian and Cayla as they flew north, when a communicator beeped.

"It's not mine," Cayla said.

"Or mine." Darian looked around. "It's the lift's. I wonder who found this frequency. I'll open it, but don't reply if we don't know who it is."

Darian pushed up the switch.

A voice said, "Darian, this is me; Sian. I need your help."

It sounded wrong, without his brother's usual bite and sarcasm, and wasn't at all his voice. Darian looked at Cayla, who shook her head. She didn't buy it was Sian either.

"I know you're there, Darian," the voice said. "All I had to do to find you was figure out where Liam was captured, and get the lift number. I know you're there, and I understand you're too upset to talk to me, but please make an exception."

Still too weird. Why would anyone try to impersonate his brother, though? And if someone did try to impersonate Sian, that would be the worst impersonation ever.

"Maybe it's him," Darian whispered to Cayla.

"Wait," she mouthed.

"My sweet little brother," the voice then said. "Don't you have a bit of fraternal love buried within that chest?"

"What do you want?" Darian replied.

~

Karina woke up and her first feeling was of extreme relief. She was alive! More than that, she felt no pain. Perhaps it was possible that she hadn't really been permanently hurt. There were no burns, no marks, no signs from the pain she'd felt. She exhaled in relief. She hadn't died, just fainted from the pain, her body's general anesthesia. She was alive. Alive!

But trapped.

If she made it out alive, she felt that she would be given a second chance, a chance to make things right. Strangely, she didn't regret having come to Whyland. Her only regret was her fateful decision to teleport back home. But then, perhaps she'd been under Darloom's pernicious influence in the castle. She would get out alive, though. Powerful magic, wasn't that what Leena had said? All Karina had to do was focus and use it. If everything worked out, she'd find a way to go to Darian's city in the north and try to convince Leena to tell her how to become a guardian and learn magic. If anything, teleporting and fighting, as much as it could lead to her death, made her feel alive. Of course, she had to get out first, but having a reason to live helped.

Her thoughts turned to Sian. Perhaps she'd kissed someone else, but he'd been super cold to her. She'd told the disembodied voice that keeping her would be useless. Sian would never open any portal for Karina, and it wasn't only that he didn't care about her, but that it wouldn't be right to exchange one life for many. He did have some principles, after all. If anything, that was one of the reasons why she liked him, but if she really had a second chance again, she would need to remember that part of him was power-hungry, manipulative, and cunning. He was both, and perhaps it didn't matter because she'd never see him again.

She still loved him, though, and realized it wasn't something she could erase with false thoughts or denial. No reason to feel humiliated if he didn't like her. At least she had felt something. She'd keep the memory of their good times as well as the memory of her mistakes. As much as she could learn with the experience, she didn't have to deny or hate it. She had loved him, and it had been wonderful.

She still loved him, in fact, and accepting the feeling was a step towards being ready to let it go. She'd focus on herself, her magic, and what she believed was her calling. Finding someone who loved her would come in time.

Two winged creatures came in, and one approached her. Its rugged, slimy claws cut her ties. Should she run for the door? No. Wait. She was too weak. A creature gave her a bowl with food, and they left. Living worms and water. She'd never, ever complain against any kind of food again. Karina from two weeks before would have freaked out in disgust just at the sight of the bowl. But she was different now, and she was going to survive this. It was all a matter of perspective, right? She could imagine this was a very exotic delicacy. Technically it was. Foreign food. Anyway, protein. Down it went.

Darian was headed for an island on the Silver River. His brother had promised to come alone, but it could be a trap.

He hoped to talk some sense into Cayla. "If you're so sure it's a trap, why not stay behind?"

She shrugged. "Don't know. I guess the worst he'll do is imprison us. I can take it. I don't want to leave you, Darian. If you really want to be foolish to go and meet him, then you'll have to bring me along."

Darian sighed. He had to fight against his urge to protect her because if he told her to stay behind she'd get upset. On the other hand, he didn't think Sian was out to kill them, but still, he dreaded the thought of Cayla imprisoned. And then again, all of their fights had been because she'd felt suffocated when he tried to protect her. His worst fear was to see Cayla hurt, or worse, dead, but then he also feared she'd stop loving him, so it was a balancing act.

Darian put his hand over hers. "We're in this together."

She kissed him on the cheek. Had they not been about to land, and not in such a tense situation, he'd pull her towards him, but both of them knew it was not the time. He just caressed her hand. And down they went, towards land, to meet his brother. His heart hammered in his chest, not only in anticipation for the meeting, but also because he'd have to land on a narrow beach. Cayla didn't know it, but he was a terrible pilot. Actually, he glanced at her tense face and realized she'd just figured it out. At least she didn't say anything. They landed with a bang and slipped over the sand.

They got out of the lift and found Sian sitting on a fallen trunk.

He had his arms crossed. "Impressive landing."

"So you're really alone?" Darian asked.

"That's what I said, wasn't it? I may do lots of things, but lying isn't among them."

"You just said my landing was impressive."

Sian raised an eyebrow. "Wasn't it? You almost sent your lift in the water. I had no idea you were that terrible, and wouldn't have chosen this island if I'd known it would endanger your life. I am truly sorry. And impressed."

Cayla was beside Darian, and said, "You should be sorry for

all the horrible things you've been doing, and all you did to Karina. She didn't deserve that."

Sian met Cayla's eyes. "I know. And don't assume how sorry or not I am. I need your help."

Cayla snorted. "And what do we get for helping you? Will you give up any claim to the throne?"

"I can't. I promised I wouldn't."

Cayla chuckled. "What can you do, then? Promise you'll never act against me, Darian, or my mother again? Can you promise that?"

Sian barely opened his mouth. "Yes."

"Right… What else?" Cayla had a grimace. "Would you promise you'll dress up as a chicken and walk around the streets of Siphoria?"

Sian stared at her. "Still into humiliating people?"

"I was joking."

Sian snorted. "Same sense of humor. But the answer would be yes."

This was so unlike his brother that could only mean that something terrible was happening. Darian asked, "What is it you want?"

Sian pointed to Cayla. "I'll need your help too."

Darian flinched, uneasy.

Sian continued, "I need help to open a portal at the Darloom castle. A portal to go to another dimension."

"Karina's dimension?"

Sian looked away, then looked back at them. "Not her dimension, but it has to do with her. She tried to teleport home but never made it. Darloom took her. She's in Marisia right now. It wants me to open the Whyland portals for him or he'll start killing her." His tone was level as if repeating information he'd read somewhere.

"What?" Cayla god to her knees and punched him. "You

miserable, despicable piece of shit. It was your fault all of this happened."

Darian was going to pull her back, but Sian held her wrists and said, "I know. Can you wait to punch me afterward? I understand your feeling, but I need to be in one piece to rescue her."

Darian crouched and hugged Cayla, as she was trembling in anger.

Sian continued, "I asked Darloom for twenty-four hours before opening the portals. I'll try to go and rescue her before this deadline."

Cayla said, "I don't trust you, and I don't know if I can teleport anyone to Marisia."

"I think I can figure out how to teleport there," Sian said. "I'm the one who's going. It's my life on the line, Cayla. Either way, we need to go to Darloom as soon as possible, and then we'll have time to work on it." He stared at Darian. "Cayla won't be in any danger."

"Just like Karina, right?"

Sian shook his head. "Karina was taken while teleporting to a dimension that's very hard to reach. It's very different than what I'm asking you to do. It'll be like opening a door."

Darian's mind was going somewhere else. "Sian, how do you think you'll rescue her? I know you fight well and all, but what chances do you have in an unknown land, against hundreds, maybe thousands of flying creatures?"

"I'll have secrecy and the surprise element."

"What if they find and attack you?" Darian asked. "Wasting your life without bringing her back is pointless."

"I have to try."

"Also, I know you're getting Siphoria ready for an attack. Do you think Darloom will come through? Are you planning on opening the portals if you fail?"

Sian sighed. "I don't trust Darloom. For that reason, I won't open the portals in exchange for Karina, and for that same reason I'm getting the city ready for an attack."

Right. If Sian trusted that Darloom would give him Karina back he'd probably open the portals regardless of the cost. Then maybe not. Sian was looking for an alternative after all. A very dangerous alternative.

"If you don't find Karina, you won't be able to teleport back on your own."

Sian nodded. "Perfect. My life will depend on saving her."

Darian sighed. "I don't like it."

Cayla asked, "I know you said you couldn't, but this is not the time to be playing king. Will you step down?"

"I can't. I gave your mother my word."

"*My* mother?"

Sian nodded. "She came to see me. I promised I wouldn't step down until Darloom was defeated. I had no idea what was going to happen, but I think she had."

Cayla stared in disbelief. "Great. She can't send me a message that she's alive, but she can talk to you."

"It was in the castle. A strange communication device, that's why."

"But we'll need her help."

Sian shook his head. "She said she couldn't help me, that I had to do it alone. She told me she'd wait in Arlenia."

Cayla squinted. "And she asked you *not* to step down? Aren't you making that up?"

Sian shrugged. "I also found it odd. Can we go? We could discuss everything on the way."

"Just a moment." Cayla pulled Darian to the side and whispered, "This could be the real trap. He'll get us far away and isolated."

"Cayla, just look at him. He's devastated. I'm not sure his plan is great, and I'm not sure I'll agree with it, but it's not a trap. Plus he's released everyone who'd been imprisoned and stopped blocking the forces from the north."

"It just doesn't make sense. Maybe it's another trick, and it's about something he wants. He doesn't even like her."

Darian couldn't contain the sarcasm. "True. He hates her. That's why he's willing to risk his life for her."

"No. He's lying. Look at him."

His brother was still sitting on the same trunk, arms crossed, staring straight ahead. He sat up straight, more like someone lost in thought than someone desperate, but that was Sian.

"He's not lying, Cayla. I'll go to the Darloom castle with him, and I'll try to help him solve it. You have to trust me that I know my brother, and I know he's saying the truth. I'll try to talk him out of going to Marisia, but we'll hear what he says and find a way to help him. Can you trust me?"

Cayla glanced at Sian, then back at Darian. "I brought her here because I trusted you."

"I know. So now we need to help get her back. I don't think Sian has deceit in his heart."

"Since when he's got a heart?"

"He's got an empty space in his chest, perhaps, but there's no malice or deceit there. Not now at least."

Cayla grimaced. "Let's do our best."

They flew in his brother's lift and hit the grounds near the Darloom castle in record time, in two hours.

They'd debated on the way, but since none of them could come up with a reasonable alternative, they had to agree with helping Sian cross to Marisia. Darian's chest tightened. These certainly weren't the best circumstances, but, for once in his life, he and his brother were acting like friends.

Sian was very quiet and wooden, speaking only when necessary, usually to make his case or to explain about the strategy he'd set up in Siphoria. He took his word he'd given to Lylah to heart, but other than that, he didn't seem interested in being king anymore. In fact, Sian wasn't interested in anything anymore, and perhaps he knew he was walking to his death.

Perhaps Darian should try to save his brother, prevent him from going, but the truth is that Sian had been raised as a soldier, and he deserved to choose to die fighting if that came to it.

Cayla had been quiet through most of the trip, holding down her anger. She blamed Sian for what was happening to her friend, and also blamed herself. Well, it *was* Sian's fault. But he was the person suffering the most behind his mask of calm demeanor piloting the lift.

Darian was surprised to walk into the Darloom castle. It was a castle, a real, livable castle, smaller but better illuminated than the Queen's castle in Siphoria. Sian had two castle keepers living there, who even offered them a snack, apologizing that they had no lunch.

Darian's first meal with his brother in more than two years. He wished it had been different.

Sian stood in the portal room with Darian and Cayla. He'd decided to leave the staffs with his brother. Over his thick leather, he wore armor found in the Darloom castle, in gold chain mail. He finally understood that they were made to fight Maris. He also put on a helmet. This would probably protect his face long enough to do what he had to.

His brother and his girlfriend looked at him as if he were entering his grave. He knew what Cayla had to do. He'd studied these portals for a long time. If she only touched but didn't step on the threshold, she wouldn't teleport. Darian would also hold her, in case something went wrong. They'd taken three hours to confirm how to do this teleporting and find the armor. All in all, Sian still had almost eighteen hours to do what he had to do. Not bad. "I'm ready."

Darian nodded. "Right. Wait," he told Sian. "I want you to know that I love you."

Sian looked down. Misused word. Darian lived in a different world than him, a world where people loved and loved back. His obnoxious girlfriend even looked almost pretty when she looked at him. Different world from Sian. And yet, here Sian was, depending on his brother's and his girlfriend's favors. He didn't feel humiliated because he wasn't capable of feeling anything anymore.

Sian said, "Don't talk to me as if I were dying. It's bad luck."

Darian smiled.

Sian added, "And thank you."

He'd only teleported once while conscious, with Karina. The memory was fuzzy, having been stored in a hard-to-reach place. Everything had been so different then.

Cayla touched the wall and an orange glow spread from her hands to the entire wall. It was his cue. After Sian stepped through, the floor disappeared from below him and he started falling. He felt some very bright lights and closed his eyes. When the lights stopped, he realized he was still falling and opened his eyes. There was a river below him, and his life depended on how deep it was. He spread arms and legs to try to slow down the fall, and then moved to a vertical position as he approached the water.

Soon he was submerged, but something pulled him to the surface. The armor helped him float. Screeches sounded in the distance and he swam to the shore slowly, so as not to make any noise. He was drenched, and the weather was cool. Looking around, he saw no building or tower. Could it be that he'd gotten to the wrong dimension? No. The screeches told him he was in the right place.

He took a better look. A sunlight reflection far away told him that there was some kind of building there. He'd be very exposed walking by the river. Across the plains, there was the base of a mountain range, with rocks, but there was no cover from the river to the rocks.

No. He was thinking wrong. If the armor helped him float, perhaps that would be the answer. He went back to the river and lay on it. The current was slow, but soon he was moving in the direction of the glimmer. Neat. The water was too cold, though, but not cold enough to kill him with hypothermia. If he ever did this again he'd dress differently.

Sian relaxed and let the water take him, focusing on the sky and trying to shut away all thoughts, blocking anything that could cause him any pain. The cold was enough.

33

TOWERS

Karina watched as the door opened and two Maris stepped in. She tried to peek outside to see if there were others. Her plan so far had been to wait for the door to open, try to do her exploding thing, and run for the river, but she had to think of something better. Perhaps there would be no better plan, though, and she had no idea if they'd open the door again.

Karina concentrated and pushed. The guards fell down, and Karina ran for the door. As she was about to cross it, she again felt that horrible pain, as if the door had a field. The Maris behind her were getting up, and she decided to try the explode-push again and go through the door. It hurt horribly, but she ignored the pain and went through. She was on the highest floor of the tower and noticed that the winding stairs had several chunks missing. Of course, these were ruins.

More Maris entered and flew in her direction. She waited for them to get close, then boom, and they spread apart, hitting each other in the process. Some of them hit the wall. Karina ran down, jumping sections, as more creatures flew towards her. To her horror, she realized that some of them pulled stones to the door, so as to lock her passage.

Focus. Focus. She felt exhausted, as doing her exploding thing drained her, but she had to fight until the end, as she would have no other chance. She tried to pull energy that she didn't have anymore, and made downstairs to the door. It was blocked with stones. She gathered all her strength, caused an explosion, and walked out. If she could, she'd collapse right there and then, but the river was just there. All she had to do was jump.

And then she felt it. Of course it wouldn't be so easy to escape. Her entire body shook and was taken with pain, horrible, unbearable pain. The moment she'd stopped because of the pain, a creature grabbed her and started flying up. The pain stopped, replaced by the horrific fear that her escape had failed, but then the creature released her, flying away with a screech of pain.

She fell, and her foot hurt like crazy, so she couldn't get up. Another creature dashed and went for her face. She blocked it and now blood gushed from her forearm. Boom. She did her small explosion and the creature was away.

That horrible, electric pain started again, and she collapsed on the floor. But she wouldn't, couldn't stop. How could the river be so close and so far? She couldn't quit when she was so close. She'd use her last bit of energy and strength. If she was to die, she'd do it on her terms.

She ignored the electric pain and the pain on her foot and walked towards the edge of the platform. Her walking was slow, though, because that pain causing thing held her in place, as if her foot were made out of lead. Boom, small explosion. Tiny actually, and now she had creatures attacking her, pain in her body, pain in her foot, but the edge was so close. There were little rocks falling, which distracted the creatures. She dragged herself to the water.

~

Sian floated on the river when he saw many Maris flying towards the tower. He took a chance and went to the shore and started to run. They were so focused on the tower, they'd probably not notice him.

When he reached the tower, he saw Karina trying to run to the river. There would be no time to reach her, but at least, if she reached the river, she'd be able to teleport. Something was wrong, though. She could hardly move and was convulsing. He grabbed pebbles from the shore and threw them at the creatures coming near her, while running in her direction. One of the creatures grabbed her, and he aimed for the eye.

Sian weighed his options. If he called for her and asked her to wait, she'd be torn in pieces by the creatures, and then he'd be doing the opposite of what he'd come to do. He kept running towards them, with well-placed pebble throws. She jumped into the water and he knew that he had succeeded in his mission.

The Maris now turned to him. This was Sian's worst self-preserving day. He had to run to the tower, where the creatures didn't fly so freely. His pebble throwing was getting better and better, but not fast enough now that there were some twenty creatures coming toward him. He ran to the tower as fast as he could, hiding below the platform where it met the shore. It was too narrow for the Maris. Now that the danger had passed, he tried to understand what had possessed him to come to this place. He heard screeches all around him and some creatures trying to break the platform. Let them screech. It was time for a new plan.

~

Karina collapsed in the water, then remembered she wanted to survive. She had to survive, but not much more made sense. Hands pulled her from the water.

"Karina, don't die." It was Sian's voice.

"Sian?"

He gave a sigh. Just a sigh, but with so much sadness and pain.

~

Darian's brother hadn't made it. He looked at the girl lying in front of him, noticed blood coming from her arm, and put pressure on it. With the other hand, he checked her breathing: normal.

"Cayla!" he called her.

He heard her steps running towards him. "They made it?"

Darian looked down. "Karina needs first aid."

Cayla looked at the room, as though realizing Sian wasn't there, and then knelt beside Darian. "I'm so sorry."

He just shook his head. "No, no. He'll come back, but we need to make sure she doesn't die, or he'll kill me."

"I'll get a med kit in the lift."

Darian nodded, then had a better idea. "No. Get the castle keepers. They must have something here."

His stomach was sinking with the realization and the fear of never again seeing his brother. Cayla came back with the castle keepers, and they took Karina somewhere else.

After a few minutes, Cayla returned. She sat by his side and hugged him. "Your brother is strong and smart. He'll find a way to survive. We can try to find a way to get him back."

"I know." Or hoped. Wished.

"You should eat something."

Darian shrugged. "How is she?"

"Unconscious, but her wounds are being taken care of."

Darian nodded.

Cayla said, "Let's go downstairs. You can't stay here."

"You go. I don't want to go anywhere."

"I'll stay then."

"Cayla, please. Go. Please. I need some time alone."

She kissed his cheek. "I love you."

Darian closed his eyes while she walked away. No, he didn't want to stay alone. He felt cold and empty, but he didn't want her to see him this way.

It had been his brother's decision. Then maybe she was right. Sian was smart and was a very capable fighter. If there was one person who could survive a hostile environment, that was him. The only problem would be how to bring him back. Darian would never allow Cayla to go, and he was sure Sian wouldn't want Karina to rescue him. But they'd find a way. They'd have to find a way.

A long time passed while Darian looked at the well, wondering if by any chance his brother could show up. His mind spun in circles and the only solution he could come up with was to go to the Light Gardens and ask Leena to help him find Sian. But that would take a lot of time.

He heard steps approaching the room and thought it was the male castle keeper, Matheo. As he turned, he felt a dart on his shoulder. It was Liam. Darian got up to fight the boy, but fell, his body unable to move.

Liam shook his head. "Like a fly caught in a web. Paralyzed. In a few hours, the poison will kill you."

Darian had been poisoned once before, and the only reason he was still alive was because of some strange magical cure. He wasn't sure he'd be this lucky this time. He wondered if Liam had gotten Cayla, but he didn't want to ask and alert him to her presence in the castle. He asked, "What do you want?"

"Respect, that's all, respect. For eight years, I've always done what your brother wanted. No more. He tossed me aside, forgot years of friendship, just because I spoke to the girl. Insecure much? Well, I understood his secret. Sian can cheat and get glory. Well, so can I."

Liam walked to the larger staff and picked it up. Maybe Sian was wrong in saying that nobody else could touch it.

He said, "Want to know how Sian became king? Darloom and Karina. Those are the two keys. I already have one, and now I'll have the other."

"Good luck."

Liam laughed. "You jest, right? You make fun of me. The girl is mine. There's no going back. The draught that awoke her gave me her heart."

Darian was surprised and disgusted. "A love potion?"

"Don't look at me like that. You owe your life to a love potion. And so does Cayla."

Darian rolled his eyes. "Right."

"But you do. So you see, it's a good thing. Speaking of love, I think you owe me one. You know King Conrad's threat? Want to guess who mangled his communication? So thanks to me, I guess, Lylah thought King Conrad would want to marry her daughter, and I'm assuming it's thanks to me that you got engaged. See? At least you got a taste of glory before dying."

So that was where King Conrad's fake communication had come from. Threatening Cayla had sounded over-the-top even for his brother.

Liam continued, "I hope you enjoyed your taste. It's my turn now, as I'll have Darloom, the greatest source of power in Whyland, by my side."

He took the staff and hit one of the mirrors. It didn't even crack. Darian was relieved because he knew that breaking the mirrors would open the Whyland portals and expose them. Liam kept hitting, though, and the mirror began to crack.

"Liam, stop. You don't want to do it. Darloom can't be trusted. You'll just destroy Whyland and maybe our entire dimension for nothing. You can't have power or glory over ruins."

"I disagree. In theory, I should be dead because I'm touching this staff, and look at me. Sometimes we have to ignore fear mongering and reach for glory."

The mirror was broken into thousands of pieces, leaving only white wall behind it. There were four more to go. Darian still couldn't move any part of his body. He felt powerless as Liam hit the second mirror. He wondered if he should call the others to try to stop him. Another mirror broke. Three to go.

Darian yelled. "Matheo, Cayla, help! Come armed!"

Liam laughed. "They can't hear it. But nice try."

Darian still tried to argue. "You think all it takes is Darloom to be king? It doesn't. My brother did it because he has connections in the army. He also had a great deal of luck."

"His connections allowed him to become king without violence. With an unstoppable army, you don't need any of that. Plus I have the girl."

Another mirror cracked. Two to go.

"You don't. She doesn't like you. Even if the potion takes effect, how can you live with someone and not know if they really like you?"

"You think I care? Who would want that boring thing? I kissed her, I tried, and it was like kissing a dead body. What do you think your dear brother wanted?" Another mirror broke.

Liam was on the last one. A silver thing came flying and hit his neck. Liam touched it and collapsed. Cayla ran in and put her hands over her mouth. "I killed him!"

"You saved us. He was destroying the mirrors. Cayla, I'm poisoned, I need help. I can't move."

She held his hand. "Darian?" She then picked the dart and rushed out of the room.

He lay back, thankful that she was sensible and ran to get help instead of crying by his side or something stupid.

～

Karina felt as if the floor beneath her cracked and she was falling in the gap. She sat up with a start. Georgia was beside her bed. Not her bed, Sian's, in the Darloom castle. It made sense. Karina had teleported to this castle, and Georgia must have found her. Then she remembered Sian's voice.

"Is Sian here?"

"He came in a few hours ago. How are you feeling?"

She was bandaged, and her foot still hurt, but that wasn't much. "Fine."

Cayla came running, with a dart in her hand. "Do you know poisons?" She was almost crying.

Georgia got up. "Matheo knows. In the kitchen."

Cayla disappeared as fast as she'd come.

Karina didn't understand what Cayla was doing there, though. "What's happening?"

"I don't know. He came with his brother."

Right. *No.* What were they doing together? "Why is she asking about poisons?"

"I don't know."

Karina got up. She had a horrible feeling that something dreadful was happening and she had to know what. As she left the room, Georgia didn't follow her or say anything. On the fourth floor, she entered the purple room, where she found Darian lying on the floor and Liam also lying on the floor, unconscious, among shards of broken glass. Only one mirror remained. "What's happening?"

"A lot. How are you feeling?"

"Weird. There's something—" She noticed he was lying on the floor an didn't sit up to talk to her. "Was it you who was poisoned?"

"Yes. Liam did it. He tried to break the mirrors and open the portals. It would have destroyed Whyland. I think he's dead. I'm sorry. Do you love him?"

"Who?"

"Liam."

Yuck. "No. Why are you asking me that?"

"He… He gave you a love potion."

"Are these things even real?"

Darian shrugged. "In theory, yes. They are forbidden, of course, and very dangerous. But it should have acted immediately. Maybe he was scammed."

Karina looked down, thinking. "I kissed him. Could it have been the potion?"

"Maybe. It should have amplified whatever feelings you had for him."

"But I didn't want it, though. It was horrible. I just did it because I thought it would help me forget…" She looked down, and then asked, "Where's your brother?"

Darian grimaced. Probably the poison.

Karina said, "You're poisoned. It's fine, you don't have to talk."

He closed his eyes again in pain. "I can talk. Karina, when was the last time you saw my brother?"

"At the Queen's castle, before I teleported, I mean, tried to teleport home."

Darian sighed and closed his eyes. Karina had heard that sigh.

He asked, "How did you return? From the dimension where you were kept?"

There was something wrong in his voice, though, like a knot, and plus Karina realized it had been Darian's voice she'd heard when she was taken out of the well. "Where's Sian?"

Darian paused.

"Where's your brother?" Karina insisted.

"He went to rescue you."

Karina trembled. "What?"

"He hasn't returned."

"Why? Why? He can't teleport back. He can't teleport on his own. Why did you let him go?"

"He's convincing, Karina, and he... He thought it was his duty."

She walked towards one of the walls, the one from where she'd gone retrieve the staff. "I have to get him back."

"No. Please. Don't. All he wanted was to keep you safe. We'll find a way, we'll figure out something. Don't go alone storming a dimension where you can't do much. Please. Sian would hate that."

Tears ran down her eyes. Maybe Sian didn't like her that much, maybe he'd tricked her, maybe he'd rejected her because of a kiss, but she didn't want him to die. "But every second that passes—"

"Please. He wanted you alive. That was all that mattered. It was his last wish."

Karina then remembered he last moments with those creatures, how one of them let her go, how there were pebbles falling. That was Sian. Why hadn't he yelled to her? She felt a hollowness inside.

Cayla and Matheo entered the room. He held the dart and turned to Darian. "Not your day today. This is a paralyzing poison, that's all."

"Are you sure?" There was a glimmer of hope in Darian's eyes.

"Yes," Matheo replied, and then frowned when he looked at the end of the room. "That's Liam." He walked towards him and checked his pulse. "Dead." He examined him. "It wasn't the cut, though."

Shivers ran down Karina's spine when she realized she was

near a dead body. Plus, Liam was obnoxious, but she hadn't wanted him to die.

Cayla approached him. "So the knife didn't kill him?"

"No," Matheo answered. "I'll take him away. And I'll bring an antidote. Hang on."

They were silent for some time. Fear, anguish, and the weight of death clouded Karina's thoughts.

Finally she spoke, "We can't leave Sian there."

"We won't," Darian replied. "We'll get advice in my city, and then we'll go rescue him, but we'll go with a plan."

That wasn't good enough. "We'll take a day flying back and forth, and it might not even make a difference." The mirror was no longer there, and she had no idea what to do. "How did he go? How did he teleport?"

Cayla pointed. "The wall. But don't go, Karina, please. It was his choice."

Karina approached the wall and touched it, trying to remember the way she'd teleported before, but then someone tripped her, and she fell. It was Darian, who'd crawled towards her.

"No. No way you're going." Darian was yelling in a very un-Darian way. "Yeah, my brother might die. I know it. He gave his life to save you, and I'm not going to let it be in vain."

Cayla ran towards Darian and touched his shoulder as if to calm him down. She looked at Karina and touched her shoulder as well. "He's right."

Karina sat on the floor and crossed her arms. Crying was useless, but the tears had a will of their own and dripped regardless. "What do you plan to do? I assume you want to do something, right?"

"The best we can do right now is get help and advice. In my city, they'll be interested in protecting him, since he's my moth-er's son."

Karina tried to think. Maybe simply teleporting to Marisia

would be stupid. She was indeed exhausted as if her use of magic had depleted her. Still, there had to be a way to bring Sian back, a way to save him. It wouldn't be fair to leave him there, with no means to return. She had to come up with a solution. But what?

34

SIAN

Sian lay down in the thin space between the ground and the platform. He was literally in a tight spot. The creatures were no longer trying to get to him. They had probably gotten bored, and there was no point on trying to reach him with beaks and claws, when they could just wait. Eventually he would have to come out, unless he wanted to die of starvation there. No. Not a death he'd want.

When Lylah had mentioned that heroes don't live long, he wasn't expecting his life to be *that* short. Hero. What had he done? Thrown pebbles? He'd never heard and would probably never hear any song about a hero throwing pebbles to save his beloved. *Ex-beloved.* Maybe she'd be happy with Liam—hoping he changed.

Never mind. Actually, there were tons and tons of songs about heroes being betrayed by friends and women. Disgusting. How was it that he was belonging to that genre now? *Put it away.*

Mistake after mistake after mistake, and here he was. On the upside, it wasn't boring. Plus, he had reached his goal and become king, even if for a short while. Everything had lasted such a short while. What was he doing hiding then? He, Sian Keen, King of Whyland, was soaking wet, lying down and hiding? He'd lost almost everything, was he going to lose his dignity as well? Por dignity, had been battered and tested in the last few days. Yet, it was the only thing he had.

Sian decided to come out and face the creatures. He walked from below the platform, and then to the shore of the river and raised his arms.

"Come! I'm here!"

He heard wings flapping and screeches. Six creatures made a circle around him. They had hair on their bodies, and if it wasn't for the claws, their bodies would resemble monkeys. The eyes were gold and piercing. They hadn't lunged for him straight, and this was a good sign. Could they understand him? In theory, he should be able to communicate in another dimension, but he didn't know if these creatures could even talk.

He tried. "If you want my blood, and if you want my death, I'm fine with it. But we can also work together. Darloom has taken your kingdom, hasn't it? I might be able to help. Or something different. What is it you want? Blood? In my dimension, we eat the meat and don't touch the blood. Maybe we can find common ground, cooperation. Do you have a ruler? Do you like your ruler? Maybe we can topple your ruler. Tell me what you want, and I'll help you."

The creatures screeched. He should have known. If he could understand them, he would hear words, not screeches. They probably hadn't understood him, but they were communicating with each other. The largest creature took flight, then dove and grabbed him from below his arms and took flight again. In seconds he was up in the sky, high above ground. He had no fear. The worst that could happen to him was death. *Heroes don't live long lives*. At least he was fulfilling one criterion for hero, not that he even wanted to be one.

All he wanted was his dignity. He thought about his brother

then. Well, it was easy to love dead or almost dead people, so no wonder those had been his last words.

They flew to a mountain range, and then to a huge cave, with stalagmites. There was a lake at the bottom, but they flew to an opening inside the cave. There, over pelts, sat a creature similar to the others, but larger. It was probably their leader. In front of it, over a platform, there was a sphere made of a purple semi-translucent stone. Sian was dropped on the floor and rolled so as not to get hurt. The creature screeched, and then Sian heard a voice from the stone.

"Why no fear?"

He wondered if it was Darloom, but there was something different about it. Sian smiled. "Nothing to lose."

"What about your life?" the stone asked after the creature screeched.

Was that a sort of translator? Sian didn't doubt anything anymore. He said, "It was never meant to be permanent."

"So you say you'd like to free us from Darloom. How noble. Would you like to do that, or is it just a story so that we don't devour you?"

Sian considered. As always, being honest was the best solution. "It's both. Darloom has tricked me, and I don't think being eaten alive is a comfortable death. Plus, I can't teleport, I doubt anyone would come for me, and… since I'll stick around, I'd rather do something useful." He shrugged. "And make some friends."

He had never been picky about who his friends were and wasn't about to change that, especially when he had no other choice.

The leader creature screeched, and the stone spoke. "What about topping a ruler? How do you propose to do that?"

Sian figured that it had been a poor idea to suggest that. "See, I don't think good rulers should be deposed, ever. I was just wondering. Just in case, you know, if they didn't like their ruler, I never meant offense to you, uh, your… Does your highness have a title?"

Its screeches now sounded like laughter. "I'm not the ruler of this land. And I happen to dislike our ruler. Can you fight?"

"Very well—for a human at least."

The leader creature got up. Its wings were huge and somewhat majestic. It approached Sian, and then opened its beak and gave the loudest screech ever. Sian wondered if he was being shouted at, and waited for the stone translation, which, to his disappointment, didn't come.

The creature sat back down. It screeched, and the stone said, "No fear. Interesting, very interesting. Would you like to be our champion?"

"Am I in a position to have a choice?"

"No."

Sian raised his arms and pointed to himself. "I'm your champion, then. What do I have to do?"

"Fight our king. And win."

Right. It was probably as large as that creature, with sharp claws and beak, but hey, perhaps Sian could be faster. Something else intrigued him. "What does fear have to do with it?"

"Darloom feeds on fear."

"I thought it fed on your heart's wishes." Sian was thankful he no longer had any.

"They are the same."

"What if someone is afraid to fight, how is that…"

The creature screeched, and a voice came from the stone. "At that moment, your heart's biggest desire would be to survive, and the fear would be for your life."

"I see."

Darian drank the antidote Matheo gave him. It was weird to

trust his brother's servants. Actually, now that he thought about it, the weirdest thing was the fact that his brother even had servants. He'd always imagined that Sian was hiding somewhere, alone, not that he had friends, contacts, and certainly not that he'd take the kingdom. He'd never again underestimate his brother, and he hoped he'd have tons of chances never to underestimate him. That thought put him at ease. They shouldn't underestimate his brother in Marisia either.

Cayla stared at him attentively, her eyes wide, which was unusual for her. Karina had eyes lost in the distance. Darian closed his hands, then moved his arms, and was finally able to sit up. "That worked. I guess it sped up the healing process."

Matheo was surprised, then laughed. "I think it did." He closed his fist and punched the air as if celebrating a victory. "I knew it!"

Cayla squinted. "What do you mean *you knew it*? Isn't it obvious, if it's the antidote for his poison?"

"I wasn't totally sure. I invented it."

Interesting. Darian's vision had opened, and he could see the magic in the young man. Cooking, antidotes, it was all related somehow. He was curious to something else. "Which poison was it?"

"Zelofrax." He then put his hands over his mouth.

"But that's deadly!" Cayla said.

The young man scratched his neck. "Well, yeah. Not anymore, right? I mean, it's cured. I didn't want to worry you."

So Darian had indeed received a lethal poison. "If I had only a couple hours to live, I'd like to know."

"Why?" Matheo asked. "If you'd do things much differently, then you should reconsider your life."

Whatever. Darian wasn't into philosophical ponderings. "How do you know the poison won't kill me?"

"It stopped acting. It kills you by paralyzing your muscles. You're moving, so…"

Perhaps Matheo had been right in lying to them, as he spared him and Cayla a lot of unnecessary pain. "Thank you." He turned to Cayla and Karina. "Shall we go? I don't want to waste any time."

"What if he comes back?" Karina asked. "I think I'll stay."

"No. You might have to learn some magic to help us get Sian back. You have to come with us."

She didn't look happy but nodded as if resigned.

They all got up. As they were leaving the room, a sound got their attention and they turned. The last mirror was cracking by itself, and then it shattered.

Darian tried to catch his breath. No. No. It couldn't be happening. After all they'd done. He hoped their information had been wrong, and that perhaps breaking all the mirrors wouldn't do anything. It was a stupid hope. He took his communicator. All frequencies had been changed, and he didn't even know who was in charge in the castle. His brother's lift should have the right communication channels, though.

"We need to fly back to Siphoria, and I need to contact the castle. Come."

He ran downstairs and outside, towards his brother's lift. He hoped he'd be authorized and was relieved when he could open the door and then turn it on with the palm of his hand. Cayla and Karina were not far behind him.

He turned on the communicator on the lift to the emergency channel.

"Joel speaking."

Right. Joel, sub-commander in the Siphoria division, and right now his brother's assigned general commander.

Darian skipped formalities and introductions. "There's an attack. They're going to come from within the castle."

"We know. Perimeter closed. Lifts are positioned and more are being called. Anything else?"

Darian remembered the damage that those winged creatures

could make. "Make sure the lifts are not too close. Within shooting range, but far away. And some forces on the ground."

"It's all being set up. I'm taking care of everything, like you asked. The citizens are being told to stay indoors. Malena has been sent away. Are you safe?"

Only then Darian realized that Joel thought he was speaking to Sian. "This is Darian. My brother is caught up on something else."

"Oh."

"Keep it up, though. It looks like you're well prepared. I won't keep you any longer. Just a question: is anything coming through yet?"

"In the blue tower, yes, a few creatures, but we dealt with them."

"Thank you." Darian closed his eyes. A few creatures. Maybe it wouldn't be that bad. He turned to Cayla. "Do I sound like my brother?"

Cayla grimaced and shook her head, while Karina said, "You do."

Surprising. Cayla seemed surprised as well, but didn't say anything.

Karina then said, "I can teleport you to Siphoria. One by one. Or at least one of you. It will be faster."

Darian shook his head. "No way. Until we know what's happening, you aren't teleporting anywhere. We can't take any risks."

Karina sighed. "Fine. And I guess trying to get Sian back will be postponed."

"Not really. As soon as we know that the defenses are well set up we'll work on getting him back. I promise. He's my brother."

～

Sian stared at the bowl in front of him. Moving worms. Now, he wasn't a picky eater or anything, but they could at least have cooked or seasoned them.

The master creature screeched, and then the stone translated it. "The girl liked it."

Girl? Sian was puzzled.

The creature continued. "She ate it all."

Oh, he knew who they were talking about, but wished they hadn't dug up that memory. He had been doing so well. Either way, he wasn't going to allow someone to best him at such a test. If she could be tough, so could he.

Yuck.

He missed Matheo and Malena and all the restaurants in Siphoria and perhaps he shouldn't think about it considering at least he was alive, and she was safe. Plus, he'd better get used to the local food, since he'd spend a long time here. Next time he'd try to get some fire, salt, maybe some herbs… The creatures stared at him. *Whatever, just swallow, Sian.* He smiled.

The creatures then got agitated, and a few of them flew away. Sian asked, "What's happening?"

"The tower opened," the Maris leader said, and the stone translated.

Sian nodded. He had no idea what they were talking about, and it was probably something that didn't concern him. The other creatures flew away, and only the leader remained.

The creature's golden eyes were on him, examining him, perhaps expecting something.

"Doesn't it bother you?" the creature asked.

Sian shrugged. "I don't know what it is, or what it means."

"The tower. Connecting your dimension and ours."

Sian dropped the worm he'd been holding.

"There. I finally smell your fear," the creature said.

How. *How?* He hadn't accepted Darloom's offer, he hadn't opened anything. Perhaps his had been a losing game from the start, and he had been right that he couldn't simply make a deal with that voiceless entity. And here he was, far away, powerless to do anything. He hadn't even warned Joel that the attack was indeed going to happen. They'd be completely unprepared. It was his fault in so many ways, but regret didn't help. He had to think and find a way to lessen the impact on his city.

"Aren't you going?" Sian asked.

"My place is here."

And then another thought crossed his mind. "Can't you prevent it? There will be a lot of deaths. Not only my people, your people too. We have weapons and flying machines, and there will be deaths on both sides."

"My dear fearless boy, you presume too much if you think you're the only one who has nothing to lose. And don't forget all the hate ingrained in them. Years under Darloom's influence. You shouldn't fear for us."

"I have to go there. I… I won't harm your, uh, subjects." He'd just realized he shouldn't be calling them people. "I just want to protect my city."

"You made a promise and your promise holds you. That said, before the time comes, you can go anywhere you want."

"Thank you."

The creature remained sitting. Of course, Sian could go anywhere he wanted, except that nobody would help him. Maybe it was fair. He walked to the edge of the chamber. It was a long way until the opening on the other side, with a lake on the bottom. He could jump and swim on the lake, but then he'd have a hard time coming up.

He grabbed the side of the cavern and made his way through the rocks. When outside, sunlight dazzled his vision and it took him some time to see the valley and the river far below. The Maris were flying into the tower, but not out. The passage was there, but it was too far. Sian looked down. It would be a very hard descent without equipment and would take too long. There had to be another way.

A cool breeze made him shiver, as his clothes were still damp. Sian sneezed. He hoped he wouldn't die of pneumonia because that would be pathetic. A Maris flew below him. The claws were in the front, not on the back, and the creatures were much bigger than Sian. His armor was golden, but if he removed it he'd be black. Black like those large, powerful wings. He took out his armor, then went to the ledge and waited.

As a huge creature came flying, Sian jumped. He almost missed it, but got on its back. It was slippery, though, with no place for him to hold. The creature jerked upwards, and Sian dug his fingers to hold himself in place. There was some thin hair in the middle and he held on to it. The creature started flying again. Perhaps the jerking motion had been the scare of something falling on him, but now it was hard to think that he made any difference, right above the middle of its wings.

The creature flew into the tower, and then flew up, like all the other Marisians. Sian was all in black, with his face down, and appeased with the notion that the creatures smelled fear, and its absence made him invisible. There was no ceiling on the tower, but it wasn't open to the sky either. It was bright as the sun, and the creatures were flying towards it. Lucky that he was flying because he'd never be able to cross that portal on foot.

Karina still couldn't believe she was flying away from the portal that could lead her to Sian, and away from the portal from where he might come through. But he couldn't teleport, so expecting him to come through was a bit silly. And yet, knowing that he could not teleport back was like sticking a knife on her chest.

They reached the outskirts of Siphoria much faster than all

the other times Karina had flown. This lift wasn't as huge as the ones from the army, but it was comfortable, with nice couches on the back and an open area. The important thing was that it flew faster. They had to land far away because the perimeter around the city had been closed for flight.

Even from the air, she saw that there was something happening around the castle. About forty lifts surrounded the city, at a safe distance from the castle. There was something like a blue mist around the castle and some dark clouds.

Karina ran towards the castle, ignoring whatever Darian or Cayla yelled. She still had that odd urge to face danger, fight it, and knew that she had at least some power to fight even other-worldly creatures. If she couldn't get Sian back, she'd at least help defend his city. But she had a feeling, a hunch, and if that feeling was correct, she'd better run like she'd never run before.

She reached the river on the opposite side of the castle, which was indeed surrounded by a blue energy, but where Karina expected it to come from some kind of different tech equipment, it actually came from the hands of some people standing around the castle. The creatures struggled inside the shield they formed, but it was like a balloon getting bigger, and she feared it would eventually explode.

Sian noticed that the light had dimmed, and opened his eyes. This was unlike teleporting, it was just like flying somewhere else, maybe because there was no real teleporting, since there was an opening.

He was above the Queen's castle, looking at his city from among hundreds and hundreds of Maris stuck together in what appeared to be a big bubble above the castle's blue tower. He had made it back home, but those things were also about to invade his home, and he wasn't sure how he was going to help.

There were lifts in the distance, and some kind of barrier preventing them from entering. As far as Sian knew, all barriers collapsed sooner or later. Perhaps it would give the people in the city time to hide, but on the other hand, it would cause a sudden burst of creatures, and that would be hard for the army to deal with.

Something strange happened. The creature he was on flew upwards, while the others flew down, so that he and the creature were isolated on top. This couldn't be good.

And it wasn't.

A voice boomed in the sky. "Citizens of Whyland. Here I have your king. Open this barrier or he dies."

No. He wasn't going to be used as hostage or bait, not that he thought anyone would care if he died. And he didn't care either. Sian stood on top of the creature and shouted, "No. Whyland, fight, defend yourselves!"

He then jumped and fell on another Maris, got up, and jumped from creature to creature, until he saw he was out of the tower and jumped down, towards the grass outside the castle.

35

AFTER THE FALL

Karina's heart didn't actually stop, otherwise she'd be dead, but that was what she felt like. From elation at seeing Sian alive, she was now watching with horror as his body fell. No, no, no. Explode, push. But what… What could she do? Push him up. Slow his fall. It was so far, and she couldn't see him, she couldn't know if she was doing anything right. And then it was even harder to see.

The barrier opened, and Maris flew everywhere. One of them came in her direction. She did her mini explosion but just small enough to keep herself safe. She wasn't going to exhaust her magic as she ran to the bridge and towards the castle in the opposite direction of people retreating.

Karina kept her energy just strong enough to scare away the creatures, waiting for them to get close enough before doing anything. Like that, she reached the grass around the castle to the place where Sian had fallen. She was running as fast as she could when she bumped into someone and couldn't believe her eyes. It was Sian! Standing, and looking up to the sky.

"You're alive!"

He looked at her and his eyes had a spark before looking away. "Disappointed?"

The question was so stupid that she was just going to ignore it. "You saved me. You didn't have to. You shouldn't have."

Sian shrugged. "It was my fault. I clean up my mess." He looked up. "Usually. When I can."

An idea was coming to Karina, and she was recognizing what that idea really was, and the energy with this idea. She realized some of her impulses and insights had something more to it.

"Sian, we can close all the portals. We can seal Whyland. If you come with me."

He considered her. "To the Darloom Castle?"

Karina nodded.

"How?"

Karina was about to explain, when another voice caught her attention. "Nice. But plan this elsewhere. I can't hold this for long."

It was Leena, who had a blue energy around the three of them.

Karina wanted to run and hug her, but she obviously wasn't going to interfere with her protective circle. "You saved him! You saved Sian from the fall!"

"No," she replied. "It was you. But you ruined our barrier."

Karina was surprised. "Sorry." She had to find a way to make up for that. "You said we could close the portals with powerful magic. Would that send these creatures away?"

Leena said, "It would snap everyone back to the dimensions where they belong. Our city might be isolated and lost again. But if you can manage it, you might be able to save Whyland."

Karina turned to Sian. "I know how to do it. We can teleport there. Take my hand."

"Teleport? What if they—"

"They're busy here. Trust me."

Sian held her hand and immediately she saw flashes of light and the distinct feeling of being teleported. She saw the tower by the river, then they were in the purple room, where the mirrors had been broken.

Sian seemed dizzy. He opened his eyes slowly and then looked around. "How did the mirrors break?"

"Liam broke them."

Sian frowned. "With the staff?"

"Yes, and he died right after."

"I'm sorry." He said it as if he was consoling her.

Karina felt awkward. "You don't think I liked him, do you? Not that I'm super happy with his death, but…"

Sian was startled, then stared at her as if examining her. "He was under the impression you were in love with him. Why was that?"

Karina felt embarrassed and hated having to talk about that. "Darian said Liam gave me a love potion." Sian frowned, and Karina continued, "But all it did is make me think he was good looking." Now that she thought about it, it made sense. "Cayla says those potions only amplify what's already there, so there was nothing there. I kissed him just to spite you and I knew what I was doing. I guess it did spite you." She looked down. "Not that I knew you'd feel it. It must have been horrible."

Sian looked at her, a horrified expression on his face. "It *was* horrible." He was thoughtful. "Love potion? I'm glad he's dead, then."

He then stared at her as if trying to figure out something. So he was going to reject her because of a couple kisses. What a steep price for a mistake, but then maybe there were other reasons besides that. Perhaps it was for the best, considering what they were about to do.

"If this works," she said, "we'll never see each other again."

"At least you're alive and well. That's what matters."

"You too. I was so worried."

Sian looked around. "How do you propose to seal Whyland? Do you think you have the powerful magic it takes?"

"Not me. Us. Remember when you told me about magic? It's specific, it's non-replicable, it depends on the person, it has feeling. Well, love is magic."

Sian raised an eyebrow. "One-way love?"

Karina should feel hurt or deflated, but at that point it didn't matter. "Yes. And it's selfless, it's pure feeling. There's something special about it."

He turned and looked down on the well. "So it's not weakness, it's strength." He snorted. "As with everything that causes pain."

"I won't focus on the pain, but on the good moments, and on the feeling. When I heard you had stayed behind in Marisia… I just lost it. I almost went there on my own, but your brother wouldn't let me."

"He was right. All I wanted was to see you safe. It's weird to look back and realize it," he looked at her, "but I'd have given my life for you."

Karina trembled. What? Well, he had gone alone to Marisia for her, hadn't he? But it didn't make sense. "Why, though?"

He rolled his eyes. "You're crazy. You want to use my feelings to save Whyland and now you're asking about it as if it was this big mystery."

"You said one-way love."

"Whose love were you thinking, Karina?"

Her voice barely came out. "Mine."

"But you left me."

"After you refused to listen to me. Then you walked away because I kissed someone when I was angry. And I had been given a love potion."

He looked away and back "I was upset. But I almost got you killed. How can you forgive that? After all I did."

"I also made mistakes. At least we're fixing them, Sian."

He shook his head. "You didn't do anything." He closed his eyes then looked at her. "Come here." He pulled her towards him in a tight embrace. "And now you'll have to leave again, right? For good?"

"We need to save Whyland, don't we?"

"We're king and queen, I guess our wishes come last. But you can't ask me to let you go."

Karina leaned on his chest. She didn't want to leave him either. "We have to do this, Sian. You have to do it. We're actually lucky we're king and queen, as it amplifies our magic."

He ran his hands through her hair. "I know. It's my fault. I might lose you but at least you're alive."

Karina stepped back. "Let's do it quickly." If she remained in his arms too long she would end up deciding to stay with him and let Whyland and the entire world burn down.

Sian's eyes were misty, and a tear ran on his face. "Sorry I did it all wrong. And it was so short."

"We'll save your city. It will be worth it." No, it was not worth it, it was a horrible sacrifice, but they had to make up for their mistakes. Karina held his hands. "Close your eyes and imagine these portals around us closing. See them destroyed. And put some feeling in it."

He smiled. "Feeling?"

He let her hands go, pulled her towards him. First he brushed his lips on hers, softly. He kissed her, then stepped back and gasped, as if surprised.

Perhaps it was still the fated kisses with Liam. "Do you still feel it?"

He shook his head. "Just you. That's all I feel. That's all I want to feel." He sighed.

Karina's voice was tight. The last thing she wanted to do was leave him. "Focus on the portals."

"And you."

Their lips met again. Karina wanted to melt into his being, remain like that forever, with his taste, his smell, his touch. Maybe he was a little weird and not everything he did was right, but she liked him. At the end of the day, even if he made mistakes, he was making up for them.

Karina was also giving away what she most wanted and felt as if her heart was being torn from her. But the portals would close, and Whyland would be safe.

She felt as if they were both vibrating, and then that the floor and the castle were vibrating as well, as in an earthquake, getting stronger and stronger until it ended in an explosion.

Karina fell on her bed. She looked around to see if everything was standing still. Everything looked and felt normal—except her heart.

Darian felt the city tremble and embraced Cayla. When it stopped, there was silence for a while, until he felt it was safe to come out. They walked out of their hiding place and saw destruction in the city, but the sky was clear of Maris.

He'd only understand things a few days later, when Lylah returned. She sat in front of them, explaining something about a vision with Bianca's son as king, defeating Darloom.

Cayla asked, "Why didn't you tell us?"

"I wasn't sure, and I didn't want to change the course of things. Turns out I was right."

"No," Cayla replied. "We should have prevented Sian from opening these portals."

Lylah shook her head. "It would only have delayed the inevitable."

"And why didn't you help us?" The pain was clear in her voice.

Lylah sighed. "I had another vision. It was me, dying in this attack. I always thought I'd meet my death head on, but things are different when you have people you care." She looked at

Cayla. "I wanted more time with you. And I'm not sure I would have helped. See, he had to be king."

Cayla shook her head and didn't seem satisfied. Darian asked, "Now Darloom is defeated, isn't it?"

"Hardly," Lylah replied. "But Whyland is protected. At least for now."

"Then where's my brother?"

Lylah looked at him for some time. "Darian, I could lie to you, say he was hiding, like he did before, but no. He's alive, but he has to live a hero's life."

Darian wanted straight answers, not riddles. "Where?"

"He is wherever he needs to be. Didn't you listen? He's going to defeat Darloom. It hasn't been defeated yet."

Darian closed his eyes. "And where's that?"

"I don't know."

It wasn't the answer he wanted.

"Does he need to remain king?" Cayla asked.

"No," Lylah said. "But we might not need guardians anymore. We could try something different."

Cayla looked down, disappointed. Darian held her hand.

Darian and Cayla went outside. He took her hand. "Are you sad? I know you've always wanted to be queen, you prepared for it all your life."

Cayla looked away. "I might have to reinvent myself. Or discover who I am."

"It might be good. Maybe instead of thinking you are who you were told since you're a child, you can… I don't know."

"Find myself."

Darian kissed her forehead. "We'll find it together. I didn't want to be in the army either, you know?"

"But you were good at it."

"Maybe I can be good at other things."

Cayla smiled. "I'm pretty sure you're amazing."

Darian laughed, but then his thoughts returned to his brother, his future, his and Cayla's future. So many questions.

She caressed his face. "I'm sorry you can no longer return to your city."

Indeed. And that hurt. He'd found out about his past and his identity only to lose it right after. Yes, the portals to Marisia had been shut—but so had the portals to the magical cities. "At least I'm here with you. We know that's where I belong."

Cayla smiled, then got serious and thoughtful. "You're still worried about your brother."

"A little. I mean, your mother wouldn't lie—I think. But…"

"Maybe he's also finding himself," she said.

"Maybe."

Karina ended up telling Zoe everything. Her friend already knew a bit, and the difference from a bit to a lot wasn't that much. Plus her friend had covered for her by going to the summer camp in Karina's place. The idea had indeed been perfect. And perfect for Zoe too because she'd met someone and fallen in love.

Zoe insisted, "Are you sure you won't see him again? There's no way?"

Karina shrugged. "I don't understand these things well myself, and the people who could have explained them to me are far away. Plus, who knows, maybe opening a portal there could put them at risk again."

Karina felt a hollowness in her chest, and it wasn't just Sian. She remembered those moments in the Light Gardens, when she thought maybe she could be a guardian, even not knowing well what a guardian was. She remembered the thrill at jumping straight to danger, of doing something meaningful, finding her path. Maybe she could find something similar.

Zoe was thoughtful. "You know, if there are many portals to many worlds, and people travel to them, there must be someone here, in this dimension. Maybe you could find them, maybe they could help you open the portals."

The idea made sense, and yet, what were the odds of finding anyone? Still, it was a tiny seed in her mind. She glanced at the book Sian had sent her. It hadn't been pulled back to its original dimension. Maybe… Maybe there would be a way.

The explosion pulled Sian back, away from Karina. He opened his eyes, taking in his surroundings. He should be shocked, but somehow he wasn't. That was not Whyland, but Marisia. His promise must have bound him to this word.

His lips still tasted his last kiss, and the one before last. He could taste the kiss she'd given him before, and feel all the ecstasy, elation, and so much love. The disgust and discomfort he felt when he got the glimpse of that kiss with Liam had been hers. He regretted his reaction. Perhaps all of this could have been avoided. But then, so much could have been avoided if he'd done things differently.

He remembered the last time he'd been on these plains, and with horror realized that he'd not only been willing to die, he'd been welcoming death. Guilt, emptiness, who knew? He was different now, and willing to open his safe, from where pain sprang, but also power. He'd learned he had magic, and more, he had love.

For so long he'd believed his greatest wish was to become king of Whyland, when in fact he'd gotten it all wrong. In his desire to see himself as king by Karina's side, being king wasn't the part that mattered. But he couldn't have known it when he locked parts of himself away. And it was cowardice. Planning to be king was much less scary than looking inside himself. But the path of least fear is not the path of least pain. At least he learned from his mistakes—not that it would help him much in Marisia.

Perhaps one day he'd find a way back home. Meanwhile, he'd better get used to worms and winged friends. He walked towards the mountain. If Maris hunted based on fear, he was invisible—and ready for a tough climb.

EPILOGUE

Karina followed the man in front of her through an underground tunnel. He opened a metal door and she found herself in a tall circular room with metallic walls. A teleporting tower, except that this looked a lot more high-tech than anything she'd seen, with some kind of electric panels on its walls. Not sure what the tech was for, since she'd teleported into ruins before, but whatever.

The man moved to some controls on the corner. "We have the information, we have the sketches, we tried everything, but something's missing."

Karina smiled. "You need magic."

WITHIN MAGIC

PORTALS TO WHYLAND BOOK III

1

ICE AND DREAMS

Sian had never been in such a landscape. It might have been a river one day, but now all he saw was solid ice. Ice everywhere, and the lights of a city far away. Karina called his name, she was close, but somehow she couldn't see him. He walked to her and held her gloved hand.

"Sian?" she gasped in surprise, her voice almost breaking.

"It's me."

Her face was smile and tears, soft and lovely as always, looking at him that way only she did, as if he were something more amazing and wonderful than even he thought he was. Quite a feat.

He pulled her towards him, thinking that if only he held her tight enough this time, she wouldn't disappear from between arms. Maybe there was a right way to hold her.

There wasn't. His hands were no longer solid, or she was no longer solid, as they moved through her. He'd feared kissing her, afraid that she would disappear again, but since it was inevitable, he brushed his lips on hers. Their energy blended and electrified him. Still, she disappeared—like she'd done so many times.

A strong gust of wind blew so much powdery snow that he couldn't see anything. When it stopped, he was no longer on the frozen landscape, but in a forest by a running river. He felt hot despite the shade of the trees.

A person with a silver cloak and hood walked in his direction. A woman, as she wore a dress under the cloak and had thin, delicate hands.

"I finally found you," she said.

Her voice was soft and calming while at the same time ringing in his ears like a familiar song. This was a dream. Well, of course. Any place where there were people, not Maris, had to be a dream. Every time he saw Karina it was a dream—or maybe a nightmare, reliving their parting over and over.

"Wait," the woman said. "Hold on. Stay."

"It's not like I was planning on going anywhere."

Still, he was surprised that he remained there. The realization that he was in a dream usually pulled him awake.

The woman exhaled and smiled. Her hood covered the top of her face, but he could feel her eyes piercing him. "The fight tomorrow. Don't wear shoes."

This was quite odd advice, and unnecessary. "There won't be any fight."

"Please, don't wear shoes tomorrow."

Sian blinked. "Right. I'll consider hurting my feet on the rocky, uneven, rough ground just because you said so. Who are you again?"

"Everything is energy, Sian. Negative and positive working together, making the world you see. You can connect with the energy of the ground, separate opposites, manipulate energy. That's how you'll win."

"Miss Everything-is-Energy, that's some neat philosophy."

She chuckled. "It's who you are. It's what you can do. Ground yourself and let the energy flow or—" She sighed. A sad sight. "If you fail, everything will be lost tomorrow."

"What everything?"

"More than yourself."

"I'll think about it. Any other advice?" Not that he was planning on following it, he was just curious.

"Plenty. But what is advice but words you'd better find out for yourself? This is all I can give you now."

The woman disappeared in front of him as if she had never been there in the first place.

Sian sat up, his heart racing, short of breath. Weird. It wasn't even as if he'd been scared in the dream. It had felt so real, though. He climbed out of the nook in the cave wall he'd chosen for his bed. Only now his body was getting used to the hard floor covered with leaves. He walked down to an inner, well-hidden cave with a small entrance Maris couldn't get through. It had a pond secluded from their eyes. The weather was finally getting warmer and he wouldn't almost freeze in its water.

His reflection stared at him. His hair was now below his shoulder, split ends like flowers, but what he disliked most was the overgrown beard on his face. He'd wondered if he could ask a Maris to use his sharp claws on him, but ended up deciding that the risk outweighed the nonexistent gain. He'd better get used to this new wild, rough look, and perhaps to this new wild, rough Sian.

Appearances were still important in Marisia, but it wasn't about clothes, beard, or hairstyle, but about how he held himself. What mattered most was not giving way to fear—or worse, despair.

After one last look behind him to double-check that nobody peeked, he took off his clothes slowly. His pants skid off easily from his ribs, thinner than ever. Worms and herbs were anything but a fattening diet. He'd still been exercising, walking, training, and climbing, so at least the muscle wasn't lost. He removed his shirt last, avoiding his reflection. The clothes were not yet rags, but were getting close to there. Well, in a place where everyone was naked, it was unlikely that he would be criticized for his lack of style. Plus, nobody was going to catch her breath and look at him up and down here—at least he hoped not, as female Maris were far from his type.

As his feet felt the bottom rock, the words from the dream came back to him. Clear dreams like that usually had some meaning or some relation to something that was real, but he couldn't figure out what not wearing shoes could mean. He waded in the water, feeling it all around his skin, refreshing and purifying. A part of the small pond had mud and it sort of worked as soap. Sort of. Better than nothing.

The dream came to his mind again. Energy, positive, negative, yada, yada. It sounded like some mumbo jumbo people in some villages in the North or South of Whyland would say. Mumbo jumbo—he knew it had meaning and wasn't nonsense, but didn't understand why people with magic couldn't also work on their communication skills. If someone could take the trouble to pass a message through a dream, why not take the trouble to find a way to be intelligible? And that voice, there was something familiar to it, but he had no idea what.

He wished the part of the dream with Karina had lasted longer. It wasn't the first time he'd dreamed about her, and every time what he most felt was the agony in knowing she'd disappear. And she'd been disappearing faster and faster. Perhaps he was seriously contemplating that he'd never find a way back from Marisia.

Sian took a deep breath and dove, the clear water caressing his skin and hair. He should better focus on the day ahead, when he was going to challenge the Marisia King. His chances of beating him in combat were zero.

~

The freezing wind felt like knives hitting Karina's face as she walked from the metro to the address she'd been given. Zoe walked with her, making them not one nutcase who ventures in extreme cold, but two. Well, she was curious, and who could blame her? Karina sometimes thought her friend also wished one day she'd venture in another dimension. Her friend's hood and tuque covered her now blue hair. Somehow she'd managed to make it look natural and elegant. Of course, she wasn't that elegant now under her thick coat and with a red nose.

When the windchill brought the sensation close to -40, Karina always felt as if her nose would fall off. Still, she had never heard news about fallen noses, so she was pretty sure hers was safe and still attached to her face, even if she could no longer feel it. Senses can be deceiving.

Sian had been in her dreams—again. They should be good dreams, but there was always the dread of parting. The taste of his brief kiss still lingered in her mouth, and that felt good. But something was off about his appearance, and with her fuzzy memory of the dream, she wasn't sure what it was. What she did know was that it gave her a horrible feeling, as if he were in danger, suffering, or both. Could he have been imprisoned for his crimes? Her chest tightened with the very real possibility. It was just a dream, though, and couldn't have anything to do with reality, only with her own fear. And that fear was nonsense. Darian—and Cayla, by consequence—wouldn't allow Sian to be mistreated, even if he were imprisoned. Still, her dread for him also pushed her forward, as she tried to find a solution, a way to reach him, a way to at least make sure he was all right.

Her heartbeat reverberated through her body as she approached the address. The sky was already black even though it was only five in the afternoon. She and Zoe walked in a deserted street until she reached a metal door in what looked like a deposit or old warehouse. The night, the location, and the ugly door gave her the creeps, but the cold made her want to enter whatever building it was.

"Are you sure this isn't dangerous?" Zoe dared voice one of Karina's fears.

She wasn't sure, no. "I've met Karl before at a cafe. He was all right. You don't have to come, though."

"I'm not going to turn around now." Zoe smiled. "For one thing, I'm freezing."

Karina laughed, nodded, then pressed the bell.

She had posted ads online asking for people who knew about interdimensional teleporting, and while she'd gotten quite a few trolls, this guy seemed legit. He was part of an association for teleporting, researching obscure texts about the topic. They'd come to Montreal after sensing intense activity in the city. The activity had been Karina. She now wondered if the high-rise where she lived worked as a teleporting tower, despite the floor divisions.

But she didn't want to try from her home. Well, in truth she'd tried more times than she could count, and nothing happened. Either way, this guy had built a tower, and this is what she'd come to see with her own eyes.

But trusting strangers and trusting people who didn't know much about advanced magic was quite a risk. Plus, her goal was to go to Whyland, and she did wonder whether trying to go there wouldn't open portals and make them vulnerable again. She also feared ending up in the wrong place, being locked away from home forever, or being lost, not to count the millions of things that could happen. She took a deep breath. The book Sian had given her was in her bag, and, if she was so good at opening portals as he'd claimed, why couldn't she find a way there? That if nothing went wrong. And if six months hadn't changed everything.

～

Darian had been in the north for two days. This was the warm north with deep forests and wide rivers of his childhood, for at the time he wasn't always in the Light Gardens; he also ventured in Whyland. Now that the communication with his city had been broken, some sources of trade were gone as well. The official explanation had been people moving out and natural catastrophes erasing villages from the map.

The north had rearranged itself, and Darian had been there overseeing a new trade port and a small military base, manned mostly by northern people, because it was important for them to have defenses there. Whyland was at peace—for now—and it allowed him to focus on different endeavors, but they couldn't forget that tides change. But then, maybe he'd been there in the faint hope that he could find his city again. This time there was nothing, though, and no sign of anyone from the Light Gardens.

Back in Siphoria, he was eager to see Cayla. Five days away from her was torture. He rushed to the council room, where she could be meeting with advisors or representatives from other kingdoms. He hated that part because he still hadn't forgotten Arlenia. As much as King Conrad's threat turned out not to be true, the thought of Cayla anywhere near him was unbearable. And yet they'd met a couple months before. Darian had to bury his jealousy.

Today there were no international representatives in the castle, though, and Cayla wasn't there. Darian knew where he'd find her.

Cayla was at the castle's small training yard with Alessa. Darian hadn't told her, but he'd gone to the criminal archives and researched all he could about the girl. She seemed to have been involved in a murder for self-defense many years before, when she'd been arrested, and then mysteriously released. The recent records implied she'd been working as a highly paid bodyguard, usually looking after big criminals' wives or companions. Blotchy past, no doubt, but she got along with Cayla and made her happy. And perhaps she'd been only trying to survive. Now, hired as an official defense teacher, the girl would have no need to go back to her life of crime.

Alessa showed knives and their use. Cayla wore a light dress, and she was so focused that she didn't notice his presence. Darian just stood watching her, sunlight reflected in her hair, dark eyes staring at the knives. Determined. Strong. Beautiful.

With a blunt knife, Alessa touched some points on Cayla's neck, and then Cayla did the same. Darian approached them.

"Funny," Cayla said. "I'm not sure I feel comfortable learning the right spot to kill a person."

Right. Leave girls to themselves and they start talking about girly stuff, like how to commit murder.

"You never know," Alessa replied. "Hopefully you'll never need it. In any case, you could use it to decide which points to avoid, or even to give someone a quick death."

Cayla sighed, a hint of worry on her face. Darian in fact hoped she'd never have to fight again, but he couldn't blame her for wanting to be prepared.

Cayla said, "Can we go back to the fighting stances?"

"Sure," Alessa replied. "Much more likely to be useful."

Cayla took two knives and held them. "Before, I never understood why two, if you usually only strike with one. Now I get it."

"You do?"

"Defense, right? It's not because it's sharp and pointy that it's attacking, it's just—"

Cayla noticed Darian and dropped her knives. She had a smile but also a look of surprise, and ran towards him. "Are you stalking me now?" Her tone was playful.

"Yes." He laughed. "No. I just got here."

Alessa was arranging her knives and looking in the other direction. With nobody else there, he lifted her, sat her on a low wall and kissed her. He'd missed this closeness, their physical connection, her warmth, her smell, her taste. He loved the softness of her skin in his hands.

Then, he felt a horrible pain in one of his fingers and pulled it away before she noticed it was bleeding.

She looked worried. "Did you cut yourself?"

"Just a little." That was a lie. The cut was deep. He tried to sound playful. "What's this? Some kind of trap?"

She shook her head. "No. I was learning how to hide knives… I didn't know… I'm so sorry. But you should watch your hand!"

"Shouldn't the knife be sheathed or something?"

"Not when you hide them like that. I'm so sorry. I didn't expect…"

Darian shook his head. "It's fine. But if you have more of those, you'd better tell me where they are."

She looked at him. *That* look. "Maybe you can find them."

His hands were behind him, one of them stanching the bleeding on the other, and he tried to focus away from the pain. "I guess you do want me to chop a finger off."

She chuckled. "That's the last thing I want."

He kissed her lips lightly. "I'll see you later. We—"

"No. I can stop training."

"No, no. Continue. You like it. Plus, I just got in Siphoria, I need a bath. I can see you tonight. We could have dinner in the city."

Cayla squinted. "I missed *you*. Not food."

Darian laughed. "You can have both. Later."

"Later, then."

He kissed her forehead and turned away, rushing towards the castle's medical office, hoping she didn't notice the blood dripping on the ground.

Four Maris carried a sturdy net where Sian lay, looking down. In any case, he certainly hoped it was sturdy enough for him to get to Marisia's castle. Not a very dignified way for a possible future king to arrive, but the alternative would be walking there. On the bright side, he wouldn't get tired from flying. The river, mountains, and plains passed below him as they approached a rockier and even drier area.

Sian laughed at himself remembering the day he realized that the reason the Maris from this tribe had picked Sian to be their champion. It wasn't because they thought he had some special talent, but rather because they didn't want to sacrifice one of their own. Every tribe had to send a challenger every year. It would have been their leader's son, as he was the only one at the right age. Instead, Sian was going. Smart move. Sian was smarter, though.

Still, he liked the leader's son, Komiak, or at least that was what he understood his name was. They'd spent some time practicing fighting together, which only convinced Sian of the pointlessness of even trying.

The thing was, in theory there was no point in a king making people challenge him. Wasn't that a huge risk? Apparently not, because the king always won. It was probably a display of his power, a reminder as to why he was their leader, and an appearance of fairness, so that nobody would dispute his leadership, since in theory he "earned" it against every tribe every year.

But not all tribes liked to send their own. With some coordination, Komiak had spoken to other leaders. The solution was simple: disobedience. If all tribes refused to send a champion at the same time, there wasn't much the king could do. He couldn't retaliate all his subjects. And if he tried, they could all attack him together. This was a decent plan, but prone to some risks, since it depended so much on everyone's cooperation.

Sian had a second plan. There was a plant that grew near the river with highly sedative properties. He'd studied the plant and learned that the seeds carried the active principle. It had taken him quite a few very sleepy nights to figure that out, but he did. With this, he concocted a powerful sedative, to be spilled on the king's fountain. Sian hoped it didn't come to that, but it was solid as far as a backup plan went, hoping that the super-powerful king wasn't that good a fighter when sleepy and groggy.

The one thing that didn't put Sian at ease was that Komiak never stopped training. The fact that the young Maris was still thinking he'd need to face the tyrant king the following year was far from reassuring. Another issue was that Sian hadn't negotiated with anyone directly. Cut off from his ability to talk to people—or creatures—needing a stone to translate what he spoke, he felt as powerless as he'd never felt in his entire life.

They landed at the front yard of Marisia's king's lair after about an hour of flying. It was a cave like a lot of the dwellings on this land. There were cave dweller Maris, and plains dwelling Maris, but the plains with few trees or ruins and shades were far from where Sian had been living.

At least one thing in common between the king and the tribe that took him. Sian calmed down his heart, reminding himself that the day he'd decided to come to Marisia he had forfeited his life. He should be glad that he was still alive, perhaps living on borrowed time, and should thank every second he still had a chance to breathe, a chance to fight, a chance to survive.

The cave was a lot more gigantic than even he could imagine. Its first chamber could fit the Siphoria castle. It had no lake or water in it, only stalagmites and stalactites and some water dripping from the ceiling. Hopefully the Marisia King would drink from a small personal fountain, or else Sian's failsafe plan would be doomed. No, he couldn't give into despair. There was a life for Sian, with much more than he had now, and he had to hope one day he'd find it back—or it would find him.

For some time he'd dreamed that maybe someone would come and try to rescue him, bring him back home. He'd watched the river and the areas by that fated tower, but no human had ever come. Perhaps all the teleporting paths had been blocked. Perhaps Sian's life was destined to be semi-starvation and loneliness forever. Maybe. But he wasn't going to give it away for nothing, he wasn't going to give it away for a tyrant king who had to kill his subjects just to make sure they knew who was the boss. Had he been the real boss, he'd never need this nonsense. The stupidity of forcing Maris to fight him and overusing his authority would be his downfall. It had to.

They crossed the gigantic chamber, Sian, Komiak, and three more Maris. Sian had hoped they'd come in a larger number, but the custom was for a small delegation, and it made sense not to act suspicious. Sian still sometimes didn't understand why they didn't just straight up have a mutiny and revolt against the king. But then, maybe, authority had been ingrained in their brains. When someone is born into a societal structure, it is hard to even conceive something different, and changes are scary. The alternative, however, would be to die one by one.

Like the cave Sian had been living, this one had a second chamber, but this was even bigger than the previous one, with a ceiling higher than even the highest tower in Whyland, and the shape of an arena. Down, on the bottom, stood the king. Sian reminded himself of his plan in order to quelch the small pang of fear almost forming in his chest. The creature was huge, like four times the size of any regular Maris. Each of his talons was thicker and longer than Sian's arms, and he thought he had pretty well-built arms—as far as humans went. His beak was so huge that he would be able to snatch off Sian's entire upper body.

So that explained why that king had been so confident in calling challengers. It had nothing to do with braveness, but with cowardice, fighting creatures who were so much smaller than him. Incredible how nobody had ever called him up on that. Then, maybe, whoever did call him up was no longer around to say anything. On second thought, it wasn't that incredible.

The purple stone was round and clumsy but Sian carried it as he didn't want to stay in the dark as to what was being said. He also wanted a chance to speak, if it came to it. Komiak took Sian in his claws and they flew to a nook in one of the cave walls. There were more nooks with other tribes, as if in an arena or theater for a spectacle.

Sian was at a great disadvantage not knowing how to fly. He could climb, though. The walls were rough enough that he could move on them, if it ever came to that. His climbing had improved a lot in the last few months. Where before he would see smooth rock, now he found fissures and cracks for his hands and feet. Feet. He stared at his very old boots and remembered the words in the dream. They made no sense, but then, how much of his logic applied to that world? How much of his logic had been trained away from magic, away from so many things that he was only now grasping?

That dream had either been his own mind telling him something he didn't know, or someone trying to give him a message or warning. Perhaps it was literal. Sian sat down and unlaced his boots.

Komiak looked at him. The Maris means of communication was very different from humans. They sent thoughts and images. Screeching was more for show, emphasis, or distant alerts. Komiak never screeched, but he could communicate with the purple stone.

The stone spoke, "Good idea. I don't think you'll be allowed to wear those."

Neat that nobody had told him that—except the dream lady. "Right. Anything else I didn't know?"

"We'll try to allow you to wear your clothes."

Yes. That point. Sian didn't see how wearing clothes could change the result of the fight. In fact, looking at that Maris king, Sian could wear a spiked armor, and it wouldn't change anything. Unlikely that a frayed shirt and thinning leather pants would do much. No way he'd stand naked in front of an audience. But then, in theory he wasn't even supposed to fight.

A cold chill ran through his spine. "Komiak." The creature looked at him. "Did you forget our agreement?" Sian whispered, which was stupid. That stone wouldn't whisper.

Komiak just stared at him. It would be foolish to say anything about their plan.

Sian took a better look at the place where the king stood and his heart sank. He had running water behind him instead of a small pond or drinking fountain. There went any hope for his failsafe plan. Perhaps he'd always known that it would have been useless, and yet, planning, trying, and doing something had been a better alternative than agonizing powerlessly.

He still had the crushed seeds, though. Maybe they could be useful.

More and more small groups of Maris came and placed themselves in the different nooks in the wall surrounding the cavern. Sian could almost hear his heart and realized that if Maris hunted based on fear, he was likely not invisible at that moment. Fear was stupid, though. Useful as a warning, but not much more, and pointless.

So many creatures were coming. Of course they could overpower that obnoxious king, and it was a very logical thing for them to do.

Some of the Maris stared in his direction, likely thinking that his tribe had brought their fresh snack. Lovely to think that he was in a place where hundreds of large, deadly creatures considered him food. Then again, he'd already overstayed his time in Marisia for months, and took the time to appreciate this as another shot at survival.

The Maris settled as if awaiting something. There was something oppressive, odd about that silence. Sian also knew that Komiak would give the sign and the Maris would attack the king. How many would join them and how many would try to take the opportunity to gain the favor of the king was the remaining question.

An ear-piercing screech interrupted his thoughts. The king had spoken—or something. The stone didn't translate him, though. Sian was about to ask Komiak what was happening, but couldn't because all the Maris screeched in return. Some form of salutation, probably. On a nook in the middle of the chamber, a Maris screeched, then they stood in silence. The creature was likely communicating with the others. Komiak then screeched.

The stone said, "I'm sorry. Survival comes first." It then changed its tone, as Komiak screeched. "The traitor is here, among us, and we brought him as a prize to our king."

So that was it, then? They'd decided to turn against him?

Sian turned to Komiak. "Don't do this. He'll kill you one by one. He'll kill you all."

Komiak ignored him and continued, "In return for bringing him, we ask that he be allowed to challenge you as our champion."

Noises came from all the nooks, and Sian thought that they were some kind of laughter. Sian said, "I hope they make *you* challenge him and die."

"At least my brothers will still survive," the stone said, translating Komiak's thoughts. In Sian's mind he could see a large group of Maris going to Komiak's cavern and killing everyone. So that was his fear; that if he betrayed the king, they'd kill his people. But it could be avoided if everyone worked together.

It continued, "We've been betrayed. Fight him and keep in mind what you learned. Your chance is small, but it's a chance."

The king screeched.

"He accepts it," the stone said. "Reluctantly, but he does. Good luck."

Komiak grabbed Sian with his claws and they flew towards the center. King Sarat was even huger from up close. Sian knew from training that size was not always an advantage when fighting. Smaller combatants could be faster. That said, size mattered a lot in terms of power and resistance. Calculating his odds was pointless. All that he could hope for was an honorable death.

He saw himself reflected in those golden eyes, straight and proud, despite his gaunt and shabby appearance. In his mind he could see Siphoria, Malena, his friends, his brother, Karina, the Whyland throne, the day he closed all the portals and saved his land from the creatures he faced right now. It had all been worth it. And maybe, like Lylah said, he was destined for a short life, but not anyone's life; a hero's life. At least it had never been boring.

2

CHALLENGES

Karina stood waiting, her heart accelerating, her face freezing. Months of trying and hoping beyond hope were finally coming to fruition. Hopefully.

The door opened and Karl welcomed them inside. He was a man in his forties, with greying blond hair and green eyes. The girls entered and hung their coats by the door.

Karina pointed to Zoe. "This is my friend, the one who helps me teleport." It was a lie, but it was her excuse for bringing her.

Karl smiled and extended a hand. "Ah. Nice to meet you."

Zoe shook his hand and smiled. Karina didn't see a place to put her boots, and the floor was hard, unfinished cement, probably too cold for someone to wear just socks.

Before she asked, Karl said, "You can keep your boots. Cold today, isn't it?"

Karina laughed. "I guess global warming doesn't translate into warmer winters, just wacky weather."

Karl's eyes were somber. "One more reason to go away while we can."

That was an odd thought. Perhaps humanity was indeed doomed, but she still considered it would take some two to five hundred years. Karina had never wanted to teleport away just to escape some climate catastrophe. Okay, sometimes, when it was cold like that, she wished she could teleport to the Caribbean or something, but that was different. Still, she said, "True."

Karl turned around and showed another door. "Come."

Zoe stared at her and grimaced, probably also disagreeing with the man. Karina shrugged. The door led to descending metal stairs. This place had the feeling of an old, abandoned factory or deposit and Karina could feel her friend's tension. But then, of course a teleporting tower would be well-hidden. Or at least it should be.

The clank, clank, clank of Karl's shoes on the metal steps didn't feel as loud as Karina's own heart. Hers and Zoe's rubbery boots were silent. This could be foolish, irresponsible, dangerous. And yet, there was no way to stop it now, and no way she could have stopped looking for someone with a tele-porting tower or any teleporting information, no way she could have stopped hoping.

There was that nagging feeling that Sian was in danger. True or false, she couldn't shut it off, and it overwhelmed all reason. And still, meeting Sian again was also scary in its own way. Would he have found someone else? Would he still want to conquer Whyland? Did he even remember her? She thought he did, but the heart had a funny way of influencing logic and thoughts. For all she knew she could be delusional, and perhaps all Sian had done was just because of her power. But then she always convinced herself that she had to find out the truth, and with that thought, she found her justification for what she was about to do—whatever it was.

～

Sian stared at the Marisia King, who stared back. If this had been a staring contest, he'd have very good odds. Unfortunately, it wasn't a staring contest. To make matters worse, being the first, he had no idea about the creature's fighting style. But no battle was won—or lost—until it was fought. Sian wasn't about to give up.

As he got in a combative stance, years of training kicked in, observing every muscle of his opponent, aware of every micro movement, as if time slowed down. No sound reached his ears other than King Sarat's breath, staring at him with a mix of curiosity and disdain. All of Sian's attention was focused on the creature. His entire life condensed in that moment.

The king lifted his claw and moved it to hit Sian, who waited for it to get close enough, jumped, and climbed the king's leg towards the top of his body. He ran towards the king's head, hoping to reach its eyes. The creature jerked, then rolled on the ground, and Sian jumped away before being crushed by that body. But lying down sideways, the Maris was an easy target, since his head couldn't move much. Sian jumped on top of its beak, again aiming for the eyes, but then unbearable pain shot through his entire body, and he fell.

Sian couldn't avoid the pain but he could pretend he didn't feel it in the hopes the creature would give up. He jumped on its neck, a place the king couldn't reach either with his beak, wing, or claws, and as Sian pressed his body against the creature, the pain stopped. Either the king had given up or being that close prevented him from making Sian feel pain.

So that was how this king won: by cheating, doing his weird magic to weaken his adversaries. Anyone with less tolerance to pain would have been convulsing on the ground. The creature jerked and moved to try to drop him, but he held on. If Sian had a sword or any cutting weapon, he might have won by now. But there was very little he could do with his bare hands. At that, the creature took flight and rolled so fast that Sian was thrown on the ground. The fall was short, and since Sian was used to jumping from heights, he rolled and cushioned his fall. All this because he'd lost focus for a second —no more.

Pebbles. If he could find pebbles he could aim for his eyes. But there was nothing. No, there was something; the stalagmites on the corner. He ran towards one, watching the king with the corner of his eye. As the creature lunged on him, he jumped away. Its beak cracked a pillar of rock. Sian jumped on it feet first—what a terrible time not to wear boots—and finished breaking it. Now he had a lance, a very raw, heavy, clumsy, blunt lance, but a lance nonetheless.

And then he felt it; again pain throughout his body, as if he were burning. The king eyed him, perhaps realizing that whatever he was doing had some effect. Sian let his pain show, contorting face and body and letting out the scream of pain that had been buried within—perhaps all the screams he'd buried. He focused on his pain and his rage, took his improvised lance, and threw it at the king's face. It buried itself deep in his eye. Sian had to bottle down his revulsion, as he ran towards the king, and jumped on the stalagmite, burying it even deeper.

King Sarat dropped dead. Silence overtook the cave.

Sian stared, only half believing it, only now taking in what he'd done, taking in the enormity of the obstacle he'd faced. It was almost as if another person had taken over him, commanded his reflexes, fought for him.

He knew who that person was: the son his father had always wanted. The magnificent, strong warrior; the one he'd honed, trained, and tortured Sian to become. Years and years of training, of pain and suffering, had just saved his life. His father had saved his life.

As much as Sian had always rejected what his father had taught him, had always believed that cunning beat strength, this time it was all he had. And he'd won because he'd been prepared. In fact, when thinking back about his father, he'd never yelled at him, never beat him in rage. The only pain and suffering he caused was training, believing it was for his son's own good. Perhaps a more compassionate father would have found a better way to train his son, or even wouldn't train him to face a cruel world.

General Keen gave his son what he could give. As twisted as it had been, it had been his way to love. His father's love had saved Sian. A tear formed in his eyes with the realization.

A screech pulled Sian out of his reverie. He hadn't prepared for this part because he'd never believed it would have come to this. Maris in several nooks screeched. They were communicating. Perhaps they were planning something.

"Bring me the stone!" Sian yelled.

Komiak flew, but not to bring him the stone. Instead of going towards Sian's direction, he aimed at the cave's exit. Coward.

More screeches, and hard looks at him. Well, their looks were always hard. This was the moment Sian had to establish his authority.

He didn't care if they couldn't understand him. Perhaps they'd catch a little, perhaps they'd catch images or something. He yelled, "I'm your king! And you'll obey me!"

Me, me, me, his words echoed on the cavern's walls. The Maris stood in silence. After a few seconds, they flew in his direction. He knew what they were doing. They weren't coming to greet him for his victory but to finally enact the plan Sian himself had devised. Disobedience. Mutiny. They hadn't dared to do that against King Sarat. No, they couldn't defy the king who'd oppressed them. But now that their new king was smaller than they were, they had no problems getting together to gang up on him. Cowards. Perhaps all his suffering and training would turn out to have been in vain. Cowards. Cowards.

"Cowards!" Sian yelled and stood. The ceiling was high enough that the creatures flew in circles around him. So they wouldn't even dare face him on the ground, but fly and lunge at him from above. Cowards. Sian couldn't even call them dishonorable; it had been his idea in the first place.

~

Karina stared at the tower in what looked like brushed steel walls with some wires and copper-colored circles. Maybe it was a different type of teleporting tower.

Karl turned to Karina. "So, you think I need magic, huh? I assume you believe you have that *magic*." There was an edge about that last word, almost as if he didn't believe it meant what it meant.

"Maybe, but I can't be sure."

He stared at her. "You didn't come here just to see if my tower was real, did you? You want to go somewhere."

Karina paused, then said, "Well, that's the point of a tower, isn't it? Going somewhere."

"Somewhere specific, I meant," Karl said.

Zoe replied before Karina did, "Well, of course. No mystery there. She wants to return to a place she's been before."

Karina wasn't sure if it was good to be that straightforward, but the man didn't seem bothered.

He nodded. "Of course, of course. I understand. Now, see, I also have somewhere I want to go. If you can open the portal for me, you are welcome to use this tower to go wherever you want. How's that for a deal?"

Karina nodded. "It's fair. That said, I can't guarantee I'll be able to open the portal for wherever you are going."

Karl shook his head. "Nonsense." He picked up a metal plaque from the corner and brought it to Karina. "Can you see what's in this?"

It was just a silver plaque, but, as she stared, an image formed on it. It was the top of a tower, with windows facing a darkening sky and city lights below.

Karina was curious about that plaque. "What's this?"

"Lumina. The city of light."

Indeed it looked like a beautiful place, but Karina's question was different. "I mean this plaque."

"A rare object," Karl replied. "Together with rare archives with instructions. In theory all you have to do is look at this plaque while standing in the middle of this tower. I've tried, but it didn't work. Again, perhaps you know the secret I'm missing."

The secret was magic, but the man didn't seem to grasp the concept. To be fair, neither did Karina, at least not completely. If she had never seen it in action, she wouldn't believe it either, and even having used it, she didn't quite understand how it worked.

She took a deep breath. "Maybe. So you want me to stare at this picture?"

Karl shrugged. "I want you to do whatever you can to open a portal there."

Her heart beat faster. She didn't want to teleport to a place where she didn't know anyone and wasn't sure she'd be able to return. But just looking at the picture couldn't do anything, could it? There was more than that involved in teleporting. Maybe that was what Karl was missing. "Did you try looking at the picture and imagining yourself there?"

He frowned. "Of course. That said, the instructions are different. The idea is not to teleport there, but to open a way for them to come here."

A chill ran down Karina's spine, as she imagined strangers from another dimension entering her city. "Isn't it dangerous?"

The man rolled his eyes. "It's Lumina; the city of light, they are good people. And it's not a complete dimension like this, just a city."

Perhaps like the Light Gardens. Karina missed that place too, together with the chance of being a guardian, whatever that

meant. Even then, opening a portal for strangers like that...
"Why would they want to come here?"

Karl sighed. "They left the instructions."

Karina hesitated, taken by a nauseous feeling. She decided to pretend she was trying, then lie that she couldn't do it. Maybe later she could still find a way to go to Whyland. But then, yikes, what if her only way back was through this tower? And what if she teleported back when the building was locked? So many things she hadn't considered. She was just going to pretend to open the portal, say she couldn't do it, then try to stay away from Karl.

"All right." Her voice sounded cheerful. "I'll stare at it." She smiled. "Let's hope it works."

Karina looked in the direction of the plaque and the image. The city was beautiful, seen from windows among white walls, many lights below and a setting sun on the horizon. She didn't even keep looking to get more details, but relaxed her vision as if she were looking beyond it, so that her eyes didn't focus on the image.

She felt goosebumps. Since she'd returned from Whyland she'd get those when in the presence of strong magic. Often simple magic that goes unrecognized as such, as when someone sings a song with enough emotion. But she couldn't be doing any magic. It didn't make sense. She looked up.

"Don't stare at me. Stare at the panel," Karl said.

"I'm not sure it's—" she was going to say working, but Karl pulled a pistol.

Zoe ran in her direction. Heart speeding up, Karina stood in front of her friend and tried to sound brave. "You can't kill us. People know I'm here."

Karl shrugged. "I hide my identity well. C'mon. Stare at the plaque."

"I can't do magic if I'm nervous!" Karina pleaded.

"Just stare at the plaque, girl, and nobody will get hurt."

~

As the first Maris lunged towards Sian, he ducked, but then there was another close by, and its claw hit his shoulder, cutting his shirt and the skin beneath it. More Maris came, and they encircled him, while others, flying, attacked him. Sian ran towards King Sarat's body. He tried to take back his improvised lance, but it had been buried too deep. As a creature flew towards Sian, he jumped down, placing himself close to the fallen king's body, so that any attack could come from only one direction.

All he could do was duck, but at some point there were so many claws and beaks trying to reach him that there was nowhere to run. Death was facing him, calling him away from this world. The woman from the dream came back to his mind. Energy, positive, negative. Sian was kneeling, with arms around his face, but he decided to plant his feet on the ground and give it a try. So much magic he had never understood, magic that he'd been told he had even if he'd never felt it or recognized it. And if he had any magic that could save him, this was the time to connect with it. This or never.

He felt something on the ground, something in the air, something around him. Meanwhile, he moved so as not to allow the creatures to hurt him so much with their beaks, but his arms had deep cuts, metallic smell of blood overwhelming his senses. He'd never yield. He'd never yield. If all the strength he had wasn't enough, he'd call on whatever great power, greater energy he had access to.

Sian screamed as he saw a blue light surrounding him, expanding away from him. Electricity. It was electricity that expanded from him and hit the creatures who'd been attacking him. In the confusion of that blue light and some feeling he'd never had, he heard tormented screeches and a few creatures falling dead in front of him. Sian had found his magic. He'd never heard of it, as much as he'd studied; apparently he could make electricity. But he still hadn't won. If he didn't control these creatures soon, they'd attack him again. Ignoring the blood on his arms and forehead, he jumped over one of the bodies in front of him. He didn't care whether they understood him or not. Surely they'd get the meaning.

"I defeated king Sarat, so now I'm your king, and I demand respect. If you want to obey me, I'll let you survive. If you want to challenge me, you can do it one by one, as honorable beings."

A few Maris who had been attacking him stood staring, while a couple turned around to fly away. Sian felt the energy on his arms, and directed it towards the ones who were trying to flee, and then to more Maris who were going on the direction of the exit. They all dropped dead.

"Nobody moves!" he yelled. "You are going to stay and honor me as your king, as your tradition says you should. You were brave enough to challenge me, brave enough to attack me, don't you dare run."

Show them, show them who has the power. Make them fear you, respect you. Only through fear you'll have respect.

Somehow the creatures had understood him because they either remained on their nooks or around him. *Show them.*

"Now, defy me, and this is what will happen to you."

Sian used his weird electricity magic power and directed it towards the creatures surrounding him. They were killed instantly.

On the walls, on the nooks, the Maris shifted, uneasy. *Show them.* Nobody would ever defy Sian again. He felt high on power, invincible, as he could have killed them all. Killed them all, and it would have felt good. Instead, he directed his energy towards one nook and killed a random Maris.

"I can do this to every single one of you, but I won't. Go home. Go to your tribes and tell them—tell them who is the new king. Tell them to either fear me or come here and challenge me the right way." The creatures stood still. "Go!" he yelled.

Indeed the creatures understood him because they flew away. Sian felt the power flowing through him, causing such a pleasant feeling. He almost killed some flying creatures just for fun. Just because he could. Wasn't it the point of power? Doing whatever he wanted just because he could?

He stared at the bodies in front of him, proud of himself, when he heard a woman's voice.

"This is not you, Sian."

He froze and stared again at the carnage. While he'd been forced to kill some creatures in self-defense, he'd killed others just to impose his authority, just to feel powerful. Was that who he'd become when imbued with power? Was he just like his father? Sian trembled. Killing the attacking Maris would have been enough. No, he could have just injured them, and it would have been enough. They weren't brave creatures. There was no point in what he'd done. More, he knew that controlling subjects through fear was stupid, it only made them bid their time to turn against you. What had he done? He knelt, horrified, shocked at himself.

"This is not you, Sian," the voice repeated.

Tears were running down his eyes at the realization of the monster he'd become. In a land of monsters, he'd become the worst of them. No. Wait. There was something else in Marisia, something else other than its creatures; Darloom. Horrified, Sian recognized that horrible creature's influence in the last minutes. From the moment Sian had found an upper hand, a feeling of invincibility, of being drunk on power, had taken over his mind, and he didn't fight it. So stupid.

"Don't you think you can avoid me," Darloom's shrill voice said. "You have nowhere to run, and I think I've proved we can be best pals."

Sian stared at his hands, horrified that he'd used that evil creature's energy, horrified. "You can't control me."

"Maybe not. That only proves that you are solely responsible for what you've just done."

No. Sian had allowed Darloom because he had been injured, afraid, desperate, and weak. Fear. Fear of being killed, fear of being betrayed, that was what had allowed those horrible thoughts to enter his mind. He was no longer feeling any of that. Sian remembered Whyland and this horrible creature's influence on the castle. It depended on a physical place, perhaps a place where there was some kind of portal. This cavern was his place in Marisia. Sian crossed the bottom of the chamber and climbed the wall towards the exit.

Darloom wasn't going to leave him alone. He said, "Leaving so soon? Do you want to go outside and be torn into pieces? Don't you realize that's what your beloved creatures are planning right now?"

"I'll deal with them. Don't worry."

Sian reached the exit on top, and looked down with a bitter taste in his mouth, seeing all the needless killings.

"Not needless, young king. You had to teach them to respect you," Darloom's voice said.

"Fear is not respect, dude."

Sian wasn't sure if his magic would work again, but he had to try. He pointed it towards the stalactites on the ceiling. His energy hit them—and nothing happened. No kidding, of course electricity wouldn't break stone. He had to find a way to collapse that cave, bury it.

"Really, my friend?" Darloom asked. "Are you ready to lose your power? To lose your protection? I can have you killed right now."

Sian just ignored that voice and made his way towards the second exit and stepped outside, in the sun. A creature flew in circles around him. Sian wondered whether he'd be able to use that weird electricity outside the cave, and feared that the creatures would attack him. The Maris landed by his side. It was Komiak, with the stone.

"I'm sorry," the stone said.

"I assume you had no choice," Sian replied.

"We always have a choice."

Sian shook his head. "That place is weird. It feeds into your fears. Maybe it had nothing to do with you. I'm also sorry."

"I heard what happened. You just defended yourself. It wouldn't have been necessary if maybe I had stepped up to defend you. You earned the title of king."

King. Hilarious. Sian had wanted it for so long, and now he'd finally earned it in a completely honest way. But he obviously didn't want to be the Marisia King, so the only victory that mattered was keeping his life. He was still worried about Darloom and what it could do.

Sian stared at the creature. "All right. Now, not as a king, but as your friend, I need a favor, the most important favor of all."

"What is it?"

"We need to demolish this cavern and block its entrance. This is the source of evil in your world."

"A cave?" the stone managed to sound surprised.

"Yes. There's a creature controlling it. It has done a lot of damage in my kingdom already, and has been influencing King Sarat. It has just influenced me, and made me do something horrible."

"We'll destroy it."

Komiak screeched, and after a few minutes more and more Maris came. Sian stood outside, observing the work they were doing. He was alert to any sign of danger, but the creatures were afraid enough that they avoided him. So he had gained authority with fear. His father would have been indeed proud. His father. In Siphoria's castle, under Darloom's influence for who knows how many years? Had it been his fault? And with his amplified fear, had it been such a mystery that he'd raised his son for a cruel world? Maybe he could claim that his father had chosen not to resist Darloom, but is it a choice when you don't know it?

Sian had felt and acted exactly like his father would—and would have continued like that if he hadn't received a warning. Perhaps he'd just had some better protection. He couldn't help but be overwhelmed with deep forgiveness and understanding, and even some regret at his bitterness against his father. He'd just been raising him to survive. And indeed, Sian was a survivor.

When the Maris finished their work, Sian asked Komiak to take him to the tower by the river. It was a human building, from an ancient time when people had inhabited this land. It could maybe also be a teleporting tower, and perhaps he'd figure out how to teleport away. He'd tried the river hundreds of times—no success. Perhaps someone would still come for him. He had to hope. He couldn't have survived just to die— abandoned and forgotten.

But he hadn't been forgotten. He knew he hadn't. Now, no longer bound by any promise, he felt that he had a chance of being rescued. He arranged a room in that tower from where he saw the desolate landscape below him. Pain shot through his upper body as he noticed a deep wound on his left shoulder. He'd better clean it—and hope river water would be enough to prevent infection.

3

LUMINOUS

At gunpoint, Karina looked at the plaque in her hands. Zoe was behind her. Dragging her friend into this had been an awful idea. Just staring at an image was unlikely to open a portal, and she feared what the man would do to them if nothing was opened. Those goosebumps again. Perhaps it was only fear.

Karina had to stop being afraid and anxious and try to come up with a solution. Somehow, being threatened in her own world, with a gun that she knew was real, scared her more than any experience she'd had in Whyland. She wondered if she should try to teleport with Zoe. That, if that teleporting tower worked, of course.

When Karina was about to reach out for her friend's hand, convinced to try to teleport away, she heard a sound behind her. A sound somewhere between water boiling and wind. She knew that sound, and turned to see three young people wearing white hooded robes with golden rims and embroidery. It meant she had opened something, even if it didn't seem possible. She glanced at Karl, who still held his weapon but started to relax, his face in awe and surprise. Karina pulled Zoe's hand and ran to the door, taken by pure instinct that something not-so-pleasant was about to happen. It didn't make much sense. These people didn't look evil or anything, and if they were indeed from this city of light, there shouldn't be anything to fear. Despite that, alarm bells were ringing inside her.

A girl stretched her arm towards Karl. The palm of her hand had a light. Karina wanted to scream for him to lower his weapon, but before she said anything, a ray came out of the hooded newcomer's hand. Karl fell back, dropping his gun. Karina didn't know if he was dead or alive, and wanted to run, but didn't want to turn her back to that people.

The girl now pointed her hand towards Zoe and Karina, who wasn't going to wait to see what she was going to do. There was no time to think. Push. Explode. Whatever she did. It worked. The three newcomers fell back. Karina pulled Zoe's hand and ran up the stairs. One of the hooded people yelled "stop" or something similar.

Why had her magic worked in her own dimension? Perhaps residual effect of that teleporting magic, but it didn't really matter. All they had to do was run.

When they were at the top of the stairs she heard steps from below and closed the door leading down. Thankfully it had a lock, and she hoped it would hold. The girls ran to the door. Zoe was about to run outside without her coat, but Karina took both girls' coats and threw Zoe's to her.

"You don't want to freeze outside."

There was banging on the door leading to the stairs. The girls ran outside while still putting their coats on and kept running for two blocks.

When they got to a busy street with more lights and heavy traffic, Karina slowed to a walk.

"Wait. I don't think they can follow us outside." She couldn't run anymore, not after having run up those stairs in record time.

Zoe matched Karina's fast-walking pace. "What was that, Karina?"

"No idea. I'm so sorry."

They had to get away from that place as fast as possible. Still, the cold outside, the fact that those people didn't have coats, and being in a busy street, even though there were no pedestrians, calmed her.

"And what did you do?" Zoe asked. "When you pushed those people?"

"Something I didn't know I could do here." Magic in her own world was weird even for Karina. So far there had been a clear division between Whyland and her own home, between a place where magic existed and her dimension. She knew there was magic everywhere, but had never realized that magic that affects the physical world could also exist here, and more, that she could also have it here.

They were not very far from the metro, from normality.

Maybe not. A light appeared in front of her and became the girl, one of the three hooded people. Karina turned around to run but the two young men were behind her. How could they stand that cold?

"Wait," one of the boys said. "Wait."

"They're guardians!" the hooded girl protested. She was raising her hand and stared at Karina. "You can't fight us all."

Maybe. But she knew what they could do with their hands raised, and despite her disbelief whether she could do anything outside, in her own dimension, she had to try. Karina focused on her mini explosion and indeed the girl fell back. Her light shot sideways, breaking the accumulated melted and refrozen snow on the sidewalk. Shards of ice flew everywhere. No idea how no car stopped. Karina turned to the two hooded guys, about to do the same, but one of them had what looked like a protective field.

Karina grabbed her friend's hand and ran towards the street, away from those people, dodging cars until they reached the other side. "Maybe they'll die of hypothermia if we keep them out long enough."

Zoe was shaking. "They didn't look cold."

Indeed. No red nose or shivering, despite their thin-looking cloaks. Maybe it was revolutionary material, or maybe they were something different from regular humans. And of course, one of the boys appeared in front of them. He had long blond hair and brown eyes. "Apologies for my sister. I mean no harm."

Trying to run from them wasn't working, so it was time to change strategy. "What do you want?"

"Portals, that's all," the blond boy replied. "If you can open portals, you can help us."

Karina crossed her arms. "And how would we have helped if your sister had killed us?"

He shook his head. "Again I apologize, but she wouldn't have killed you."

"Is Karl, the man who had the gun, alive?"

The boy shrugged. "He had a weapon pointed at us. Were we supposed to wait?"

Talking. Talking was good. Maybe she could come up with a plan while they talked, but her mind was blank, unable to find an easy way out when they were outnumbered by people with superior magic. The boy was glancing at Zoe quite a lot. Karina didn't blame him; she was pretty. Hopefully that would count to their advantage.

Zoe must have noticed it, as she asked, "And if we help you, how do we know you won't hurt us?" She didn't sound angry or threatening, but mild and sweet.

"We're Luminous, from the city of light. We spread light, you see?"

Karina rolled her eyes. "I saw you spreading light to Karl."

"We were scared. We didn't know who you were or what you

wanted. Let's all calm down, go back to that tower, and open some portals."

Karina was angry and about to say something snarky, but Zoe replied first.

"We're so sorry for that. We'll be happy to help you." She glanced at Karina, her eyes beseeching, then turned to the guy. "Of course we'll open whatever portal you want!"

Ugh, opening portals for people who kill first, ask questions later sounded terrible, but Zoe had a point that confronting them wouldn't help. It was better to pretend to comply. Hopefully they'd just teleport away and leave them alone.

"I'm Satwak," the blond boy said. He pointed to the girl. "That is Faizana." He pointed to the other young man. "And that is Geralm."

"Neat." Karina shrugged. "Let's open some portals, then."

"I'm Zoe," her friend said. "This is Karina."

Satwak nodded. "Again, I'm sorry this didn't start in the best terms."

Faizana and Geralm now joined Satwak, and they didn't seem as friendly. Karina wanted to run away. Instead, they walked back to the building where the tower was.

Zoe turned to Satwak. "It's freezing today. Aren't you guys cold?"

He stared down at himself. "No." He turned to his companions. "Do you feel anything?"

"No," Geralm replied.

"So interdimensional teleporting makes you invulnerable to cold?" Zoe was really into making conversation. It was nice that she managed to sound calm despite what they had just been through.

"Maybe that, maybe our magic. We can't be sure. We don't have ice like this in our city."

Weather; universal conversation starter indeed.

"What do you have in your city?" Zoe asked.

"The weather is usually mild; never too cold, never too hot."

"Sounds lovely," Zoe replied.

Satwak smiled. "It is. But there are other lovely things in the universe."

Lovely was the fact that they were being dragged back to the tower against their will. Then again, Karina couldn't face the three of them at once, and she didn't want to risk hers or her friend's life. Perhaps, like herself, they were just quite desperate to go somewhere.

They reached the building and found the metal door locked. The girl, Faizana, shot the lock with her hand light thingy and it opened. The way downstairs now felt gloomy, and Karina couldn't help dreading whatever was coming even if she kept telling herself that these were just scared people who wanted to teleport somewhere.

Zoe somehow managed to make conversation with Satwak as if nothing weird was happening. Hopefully it would help diffuse the tension, and hopefully Karina and her friend would be free and left unharmed after doing whatever they wanted them to do.

They reached the tower. Karl was lying down, eyes open.

"Is he dead?" Karina asked.

Satwak nodded. "We thought we were going to be attacked, that someone was trying to invade our city. It was a mistake."

A mistake that could have cost Karina and Zoe's life, had Karina not used her weird magic.

Satwak looked at Karina. "No, no. As I said, she wasn't going to kill you."

Was he reading her thoughts? "That's great to know." She couldn't hide her sarcasm.

"I know you don't believe it, but we meant no harm."

Their meaning wouldn't help Karl. But perhaps she shouldn't be upset about him. Pointing a gun towards a portal from where you expect people from another dimension to come should win the prize for dumb idea of the year. He shouldn't have threatened Karina and Zoe either.

Zoe touched Karina's arm. "They meant no harm."

Her eyes were pleading. Maybe she had a point. *Let's be nice to the people who can kill us without warning.* Hopefully her friend wasn't pretending, though. Karina pointed to Satwak and whispered. "You know he can read our thoughts, right?"

"Not really," Satwak said from a distance. "Just glimpses, emotions."

He shouldn't have heard Karina, but at least he confirmed what she'd just said. Zoe tensed. So she was afraid despite her relaxed demeanor and previous chit-chat.

Satwak pointed to Karina's bag. "Can I see what's in there?"

His tone was polite, but it wasn't a question. Karina smiled. "Sure."

Her mind went back to Chemistry, as she visualized the periodic table and repeated: Lithium, Sodium, Potassium, Rubidium, Cesium, Francium. Satwak definitely could read more than just glimpses, because he stared at her and grimaced. She wondered if chemistry was studied the same way everywhere. The boy took her book and his eyes widened.

Geralmis looked at the book as well. "Is that... the portal hub?"

Satwak chucked. "Looks like it. What a gift."

Fine. If they knew what it was, there was no point in chanting the first group of the periodic table.

"It's no longer a portal hub," Karina said. "It's been sealed." She shrugged, wondering if perhaps she'd made a mistake providing them information. "Not sure what you can do with a book, though."

"Open portals," Satwak said—as if it were the most obvious thing in the world.

Karina decided to be honest. "I tried. It doesn't work."

Geralmis now stared at her, eyes narrowed. "You tried. You mean you can—"

"Probably not," Satwak said. "See? She couldn't do it."

"How come she has this book, then?"

Satwak stared at his friends. "Objects sometimes travel to other dimensions. We can't know."

The girl, Faizana, was now close to them. "We'd better leave or guardians will find this portal. Let's bring them with us and see who's the opener."

"I think it was the man," Satwak said. He stared at Faizana. "Which you killed."

Karina again focused on the periodic table as if nothing else existed.

"Why were they here, then?" The girl pointed to Karina and Zoe. "We need to bring them with us and question them."

Satwak glanced at Zoe and Karina, then said, "I'll check them."

He put his hand on the top of Karina's head. "Why were you here?"

Despite Karina's effort, Sian's image flashed in her mind. She shut it off quickly, but not before Satwak noticed it. His eyes widened in what looked like a mix of surprise and joy, kind of like a kid who gets the Christmas gift they'd been wishing. Then he got serious again, and his posture straightened as if he'd become alert. Karina focused on the periodic table again, to see if it could deviate his attention, trying to shut down curiosity about his reaction.

Satwak turned to the others. "It's her. The other girl has nothing to do with it."

"Let's bring her with us, then." Geralm pointed to Zoe. "Her too, or she might talk."

Satwak approached Zoe and put his hand over her head. "No. She'll forget what happened here."

Karina wanted to do something, but she wasn't sure what.

"Where are you taking Karina?" Zoe asked.

Satwak hesitated, then said, "Our city, but she won't be harmed. I promise you."

Zoe's eyes had tears. "No."

"I'm sorry." His voice was almost a whisper.

Karina's heart beat faster. Should she try to use her magic and prevent whatever he was going to do? Would she be able to confront them? But before any smart idea could form in Karina's mind, Zoe closed her eyes and collapsed. Great.

Karina ran towards her friend. Still alive. She turned to Satwak. "What did you do?"

"Don't worry. She'll wake up soon. We have to go."

Right, Zoe had just been knocked out. Karina had seen it enough to believe it. The issue was that any escape plan was doomed, as she wouldn't be able to carry her friend. Faizana grabbed Karina's hand. Soon she felt as if she were falling or floating, and closed her eyes due to the intense brightness. When she opened her eyes, she was on the top of the tower she'd seen on the plaque. This was unlike any teleporting tower she'd been, because it wasn't at the bottom of a tall circular room, incorrectly called tower, but rather on the top of a tall building from where she could see a city below. The sun shone on triangular roofs and distant woods.

There were five more hooded people, hands in front of them, around the tower.

"Close it now." Satwak said, staring at Karina.

"What?" Was he even talking to her?

"Close the portal."

"I don't know how to do it."

"Yes, you do."

Karina closed her eyes and imagined that door closing, visualizing a cord being cut, and wasn't sure if it was right. She pictured doors shutting, a wall being erected, a light between worlds turning dark... She had no idea if this would close the portal and she was afraid of what they might do to her.

Karina opened her eyes. "Did any of this work?"

"It did."

A man with very long black hair approached them. "Who's this you brought?"

"A gift," Satwak said.

This sounded horrible, and that man gave her the creeps.

"A portal opener," Faizana added.

"She's friendly to our cause and wants to help us," Satwak said.

The man with the long dark hair raised an eyebrow. "Huh. Doesn't look like it."

"She's just afraid."

Karina started to think that Satwak was protecting her and wasn't sure if she should feel glad or worried about whatever he wanted. Hopefully this wouldn't take long and she'd be able to be back home soon. She'd told her mother she was going to sleep at Zoe's, but that would buy her a night only. And there was school and everything. Yuck. First she had to make sure she remained alive.

The man with the dark hair approached. "We need to test her. She could be a spy."

Satwak, who carried Karina's bag, took the book with the images of Whyland and tossed him. "This. Maybe she could open a portal there."

Just opening a portal, not teleporting, was something new and strange. Again, something she wasn't sure she could do. The man opened the book and his eyes brightened. Karina hated that.

He gave the book to Karina. "Stare at an image in it."

Karina shuffled the pages until she came to a picture of a misty forest, which she imagined was very far from any populated area.

"No, no, no," the man said. "Somewhere busier, like a city." He took the book from her and opened at the image of a city. Siphoria.

Her heart sank. What were her options, though? If she opened the portal, she could put her friends at risk. If she didn't open it, she could put her life at risk. She decided to unfocus her vision and just pretend to look at it.

"You're not looking at it," the man said.

"I thought that was the right way to open a portal."

Indeed, she'd been doing something similar to this back in her world, in that strange tower.

"She's too nervous," Satwak said. "Give me some time with her."

"Be brief, then," the man snorted.

"Come." Satwak's voice was again kind, and he led her out of that room, into a different corridor, then to a room with a chair.

Karina didn't sit and neither did Satwak. He just lowered his hood. He had golden wavy hair, brown eyes, and was younger than she'd thought at first, looking somewhere between sixteen and twenty-four.

"I'll be brief," he said. His voice was harsh. "That man you just met is my uncle Firis. You either help him willingly or he'll make you do it. It might hurt. And I don't mean just pain, but harm, and I'll spare you the details unless you insist. So if I were you, I'd do my best to help him—and pretend you like it."

"You promised my friend I wouldn't be harmed."

"That's why I'm asking you to cooperate. You have to help me."

"Why do you want to go to Whyland, though?"

Satwak shrugged. "Does it matter? We don't even care about that place, if that's what worries you; we just want to reach the portals."

This didn't sound good, but Karina couldn't see any way out

of this. Plus, the portals were closed. Maybe it wasn't a terrible idea.

"There's something else," he said. "Some of us can indeed see people's thoughts. Firis is very good at it. So I'd be careful."

Karina narrowed her eyes. "You can read them too."

"A little."

He was lying.

Satwak smiled. "Fine, then. More than a little. But nothing like Firis. So if you value your life and your physical integrity, pretend you want to help us. Oh, my uncle has ways to use your magic without your consent. You don't want him to do that either. So you might want to comply."

Karina had a thousand questions, including: why were they doing this? What would they do to her once she opened the portals for them? Who were those people? She swallowed.

Satwak took a deep breath. "Portal openers are rare here. As long as you're useful, and as long as you don't cross my uncle, you'll have no reason to fear."

The question in her mind was: and *what happens when I stop being useful?* But the answer was obvious: *never stop.*

Sian sat down and stared at his shoulder. Maybe it would be better to remove his shirt, but he didn't want to do it. Ragged as it was, the shirt still covered his upper body. Maybe he shouldn't care about it, now that he was alone, but he couldn't help it.

There was goo coming from the wound and his shoulder and upper chest were swollen and painful. The Maris didn't use any herb to cure their infections. Their bodies were different. He'd seen them getting hurt and healing. He had to find something… Salt. The only answer was salt. That could maybe stop the infection. There was none there, though. Sian got up and stared out the window. All rivers went to the same place. Maybe if he followed the river he could come to an ocean where he could clean his shoulder—if the ocean was clean. The river didn't have any visible end, though, and he'd traveled in that direction, to the King's cave, and had not seen any sign of ocean. Sian could die trying to reach a distant source of salt water. He'd die alone and abandoned, away from the only place where there was any hope for him to be found.

Karina followed Satwak back to that room with all the guards. Satwak covered his head with his hood again. Everything was a blur around Karina. She tried to focus her mind on *helping these really nice people*. There was movement of more hooded guards coming in. Karina took the book and looked at it. It was a picture of the Silver River, Siphoria, and the abandoned tower. This must have been an old picture, as it didn't include the military tower. But no, she shouldn't be remembering any of that. Or maybe she should? To make sure a portal was opened? Everything that had happened since she'd left her home that afternoon flashed in front of her, starting with her eagerness and anticipation as she braved the extreme cold. Speaking of cold, she still had her icky boots and coat, and was starting to get hot. At least focusing on her physical sensation allowed her mind to focus on something.

"You have to reopen that portal," Satwak said. "We'll need to go through it." He then whispered, "And don't even think about teleporting away."

Weird that the last thought hadn't even occurred to her. Maybe because fear was taking over her mind. Maybe because she wasn't even sure how to teleport, and then maybe because these people would follow her.

Comply. Perhaps Satwak was right, it would be worse if she were killed or forced away from her free will. Ignoring how much she hated what she was doing and trying to pretend she knew how to open and close portals, she thought about the tower in that building where Karl died, and about Siphoria.

"Go!" Firis, the dark-haired man, spoke.

Karina raised her eyes and saw some of those guards, soldiers, or something disappearing in front of her. So they were teleporting. There could be an invasion in Whyland, and she was allowing it. She focused on how hot she felt, trying to shut off any other feelings or thoughts.

Someone took her arm. Satwak. "I'll take her to interrogation."

Firis stared at her. "No. Put her with the others."

Karina felt Satwak shudder. "She's more useful conscious."

The dark-haired man had a grimace. "Too dangerous."

"But Lumina needs teleporters. I have an idea." Satwak's hand was on her head and then everything went dark.

4

BREACH

Cayla watched as Darian buttoned up a beige shirt, covering up his collarbone. She was still sometimes awestruck at how everything about him was perfect, from his soft hands to his amazing smile.

He stopped. "You don't like it?"

"What?" Cayla was startled.

"You're staring."

She looked away. "Sorry."

Before she looked back, he was in front of her, planting a kiss on her cheek. "No need to say sorry."

Cayla turned to him. "You mean I'm allowed to stare?"

"As much as you want." He kissed her lips.

It was a long kiss she didn't want to break away from. He pulled her close to him and she knew they'd start it all over again. Two, three, five. No point counting. Their love was infinite. And just when she was ready to get lost in his arms again, her stomach growled.

Darian stopped. "I'm horrible. I said we'd have dinner."

"We lost track of time." Just then, a memory hit her. "Oh, no."

"What?"

"Alessa. We were supposed to go out tonight." She hoped he wouldn't be upset. "I thought you would still be up north."

"There's still time, you could still go."

Cayla wasn't sure she wanted to walk away from him. "But us…"

Darian pinched her chin. "There's tomorrow. And the day after. And after. And after. You've spent your life locked in this castle."

He had a point. "True. You can come if you want."

He kissed her forehead. "Go. It's good to make time for friends."

This would actually be the first time she did that in a long time. "Are you sure?"

"You'll be disguised, right?"

"I got a brown wig." Her hair was so distinctive that covering it up was enough not to be recognized—or at least she hoped.

He smiled and ran his hands through her hair. "You'll have to show it to me one day. Well, that, and the fact that you'll be out with a very well trained bodyguard… I'm confident you'll be safe."

Cayla had been rather thinking he could be jealous, but she should have remembered that this was Darian, and he had shatterproof confidence. "Sure you don't want to come?"

Darian smiled and shook his head. Cayla kissed him and ran back to her room, hoping her friend wouldn't mind that she was late.

Darian watched Cayla run away towards her friend. Since she'd told him more about her childhood and how sheltered her life had been, he'd encouraged her to get closer to people she liked. Alessa was nice. The thought of Cayla in a place with music, drinking, and all eyes on her almost made his skin break with hives, but hopefully he'd sounded unconcerned. This was important for Cayla. He'd better swallow his immature jealousy.

Darian put on his boots and decided to make his way to the kitchen to grab something simple to eat. As he walked out, he stepped on something. One of Cayla's knives. His heart warmed remembering her giggles, as he put the object on a table and then walked outside.

In a hallway, he came across Lylah. "Where's Cayla?"

"With Alessa. Were you looking for her?"

The woman smiled. "No. I was just surprised. You're usually together. Were you going to the kitchen?"

Darian still felt a little awkward around Lylah, and would have answered whatever meant that they wouldn't need to spend unnecessary time together, but since he didn't know where she was going, he said the truth, "Yes."

"We're two, then."

It would be odd to say he changed his mind, so he had to walk with her hoping she wasn't planning on asking him any intrusive questions about her daughter or lecturing him. He wasn't sure how much she knew about his relationship with Cayla other than the fact they were betrothed and wondered if he'd feel more or less awkward if she knew everything. Maybe he'd better not think about it.

They got to the kitchen and sat at a table together. Speaking with Lylah in an official capacity was one thing, sitting together in the kitchen as if they were buddies was another, especially right after...

"Did you ever have any news about your brother?" she asked.

She'd interrupted his thoughts to turn to a subject that only made him feel even more anxious.

"Should I? I thought you knew all about him and his need to live a hero's life." He sounded more bitter than he'd meant.

"I just wasn't sure."

"Isn't there a way to find out where he is?"

Her eyes were sad, or perhaps had pity in them. "Maybe there is, but I don't know it. I'm sorry."

Darian didn't like being pitied and felt annoyed. Still, he took a deep breath and decided to ask a question that had been bothering him for a while. "Lylah?" He paused. "When the Maris invaded, and you were in Arlenia, you said it was because you had predicted your death, right?"

"Yes. I also had a vision about Bianca's boy defeating them. I thought I could ruin it if I came."

"Can all of you predict your death?"

She tilted her head. "What do you mean *you*?"

"From the Light Gardens."

Lylah shook her head. "I'm not from there, even if I have visited that city and had close friends there."

Darian sat back. "Oh."

"My family's from a different ethereal city, one that no longer stands."

"What was its name?"

There was wistfulness in her eyes. "Gleam Fortress. It's been gone for generations." She then changed her tone. "But I don't think you're interested in history, are you?"

"Well, I am. I'd like to understand where I'm from, but—"

"Your mother. You want to know why your mother didn't prevent her death, don't you?"

Darian swallowed. He'd been going in circles, but yes, that was what he meant to ask. He nodded.

Lylah stared. "Well, not everyone has visions, and not everyone can see the future. Can you?"

"How would I know?"

"Have you ever had dreams or visions that became real?"

He tried to think.

Lylah didn't wait for his reply. "You would remember if you had visions. It was probably the same with your mother. She couldn't see the future."

Darian looked down. "Yes, but..." It was hard for him to remember that, remember how he saw his mother killed by common thieves, how he hadn't been able to help. "It just doesn't make sense. They were just regular thieves. She was from the Light Gardens. I mean... Even me, I knew how to fight —defensively at least." He recalled how he was able to defeat Liam easily, using a technique he'd learned when he lived in the Light Gardens. "We should have been able to deal with three men."

Lylah stared at him and took a deep breath. "Your mother was strong, but not invincible. And her strength was not in fighting. The time comes for all of us. It was hers."

"But you didn't go when it was your time."

"It probably wasn't my time, then. Maybe that was why I had the vision."

Darian was still unconvinced and anger was bubbling in him. "Why did it have to be my mother's time?"

"I don't know. I also miss her. She was my friend, too."

There was another question bothering him, and perhaps Lylah knew the answer. "Well, tell me then, tell me why she never mentioned my brother, why I came here and had to treat him as a stranger. Why?"

Lylah stared at him and paused as if measuring her words or thinking, then said, "Sian was born here, in this castle, but your mother and father left when he was very young. I lost contact with Bianca then. General Keen came back a year later with Sian, claiming his wife had died. I didn't know *you* existed. And never had time to know. I was locked in the white tower soon after he returned."

Darian looked down. "Do you think Darloom was influencing them?"

"It's a comforting thought."

Strange reasoning. "Why *comforting*?"

Lylah shrugged. "You shift the blame."

"So you don't think it was."

"I don't know, Darian, I really don't."

Darian sighed. "Do you know if my father gave my mother a love potion?"

"Those potions are quite useful. Again, you can shift the blame for foolish choices."

"So you think it wasn't."

"I don't know. People change. Your father, at first, seemed to be a decent man. So did Cayla's father. Was it Darloom that influenced them? Was it power? Or had they always been horrible people and the potion prevented us from seeing it? I can't know."

Darian looked down. Sad, angry, disappointed, he didn't even know how he felt. "I thought you knew more."

"At one point in my life I might have thought I knew all the answers too. As the years passed, I realized that I don't."

"Love potions do exist, though. Karina was given one."

"I heard that. And why do you suppose your brother's friend came in possession of it?"

"No idea."

"It's not that hard to guess who ordered it, Darian."

"You mean my brother. Are you implying he used it?"

"No. I think he changed his mind."

"And what does it have to do with anything?"

"Do you think he'd love her any less if he'd given her a potion?"

"It'd be a pretty disturbing kind of love if you have to force someone…"

"You just enhance what's already there. Keep that in mind."

"That's still horrible. And they say you'll go crazy if you give it to someone. Maybe that's what happened to my father."

"Maybe. Then, maybe it was Darloom. Maybe it was a combination of factors."

Darian exhaled. "I just wanted to understand why my mother hid my brother from me, that's all."

"Perhaps it was to protect him."

That didn't make any sense. "When he was living in the castle, where everyone knew he existed?"

"She could be hiding him from the Light Gardens."

"They're good people."

Lylah took a deep breath. "There are tons of reasons why a child could be endangered. You don't know."

"I guess I'll die not knowing."

"Maybe. They might know the answer in the Light Gardens."

"Which I'll never reach, since the passage has been blocked."

"It won't stay blocked forever, Darian." She frowned. "Did you hear that?"

He hadn't heard anything. "No."

Lylah got up and pulled his hand. "Come. This might be your lucky—or unlucky—day."

The servant still hadn't brought their food.

"What's happening?" Darian asked.

"I'm not sure, but I need to take you to an emergency portal."

He kept walking with her. "If something's happening, I need to mobilize our defenses, I need to get Cayla. What's going on?" Even though he hadn't heard anything, the worry on the woman's face was enough to alarm him.

"You're going to the Light Gardens, and they'll explain everything to you there."

"But the portals…"

"I can open an emergency passage. It's a last resort, but at this point it might be worth it."

"At what point? I'm not going anywhere if you don't explain—"

Lylah stopped and gave him a hard stare. "Do I have to knock you out and drag you?"

He wasn't afraid of stares. "I'm not walking away with Cayla in the city, without taking care of the safety—"

Everything went black.

~

Cayla was dazzled by the lights and the multitudes in the city. It was different being in it as if she were nobody special, and perhaps different being there without Darian—and with her hair well-hidden.

"We should go straight to the Junction. My sister's playing tonight," Alessa said.

Diane had been hurt and scared the last time Cayla had seen her. It would be nice to meet her in more normal circumstances and hear her playing.

"Do they have food there?" Her stomach was still growling. "I didn't have time to eat."

"They do, and it's decent. How come you didn't have time? Evening meetings?"

"I was with Darian." That wasn't a good explanation. "Don't ask."

"I wasn't going to. He didn't want to come?"

"He was tired."

She didn't want to say that Darian wanted Cayla to spend time with friends because confessing she hadn't had friends in a long while was quite embarrassing.

Alessa stopped. "Wait."

"What?"

"I told you I'd show you Siphoria, remember? I think we can eat in a better place."

Cayla hesitated. "Are you sure? I don't want to miss your sister."

"Positive. I just remembered they're last."

Alessa led Cayla to a tiny restaurant, if that could even be called such. There was a counter at the end, some seats facing a wall, and three tables outside. The weather was good, and they sat at a table on the sidewalk.

Cayla watched the people walking on the street, a late-night rail transport passing in front of them. Everything and everyone so ordinary. She'd come to Siphoria before, usually wearing some kind of hood, but she'd never had time to just relax, sit, and watch the city live its life while ignoring her.

The woman from the restaurant brought them some sort of vegetable pie.

Alessa pointed to it. "Zafar. This is typical of Siphoria."

"I think they have it in the castle."

Her friend shook her head. "Some silly imitation. This is the real deal. You might be wondering why this place is not full, if it's so good, but it's because a lot of people buy it to take it home. They're also almost closing."

Indeed, the woman was cleaning the interior floor. Cayla felt bad. "I'm so sorry I was late."

"You weren't *that* late."

"I shouldn't have forgotten it."

Alessa shrugged, parted the pie, or zafar, and served it. It better taste good, since the service wasn't that amazing. Cayla poured water in two glasses, then took a bite of the pie. Yes, it was quite good, in a different way from the food at the castle, simpler, with less seasoning. The taste was more subtle. If anything, it was different.

Cayla smiled. "It's great."

Alessa nodded. "I told you."

As Cayla forked another bite, a sound startled her. No, it wasn't a sound, just a feeling, something. "Did you hear anything?"

Alessa looked around. "Did you?"

There weren't any guards around the restaurant and Cayla felt unsafe at that time at night, on a street where there were only a few pedestrians here and there. Maybe she was paranoid or just unused to being in the city. Maybe it was something else. She was about to suggest leaving when Alessa glanced behind Cayla.

"There's a weird group coming. Don't look. They might have nothing to do with us."

Alessa's posture was relaxed but her eyes were alert. Resisting the urge to turn, Cayla drank from her cup, ears perked for anything suspicious. The steps in the distance changed from walking to running, but then again, how likely would they be interested in Cayla and Alessa? The steps approached. Cayla tried to pull a knife from under her dress but cursed mentally when she realized she was completely unarmed.

Then, there was just a flicker of alarm in Alessa's eyes before the girl jumped over the table, pushing Cayla down, who got up and saw her friend moving fast, facing five people wearing hooded white cloaks.

Cayla reached for the water jug and broke it. Her right hand got cut, but now she could use the glass shards as weapons. Two people approached her. With a fast arm movement, she cut one of them, who stepped back. The other stepped back as well but reached out his hand.

Cayla's necklace, the one Darian had given her, the one she used to communicate with him, one of her most prized possessions in this world, was pulled from her neck. Cayla jumped and kicked the person to whom the necklace was going and he fell on the floor. So did the necklace, though. When she moved to catch it, she felt as if a strong wind wouldn't let her get near it, and another person caught it. It was a girl, satisfaction in her face.

No. No way those criminals would get her necklace. Cayla braved that odd feeling like a barrier and stepped towards the girl, but she threw the necklace to one of her friends. They seemed about to leave. So it had been about the necklace all this time? They would turn around and Cayla would take a while to catch them, and considering they could toss it between themselves, her chances of catching the necklace were very small.

Cayla did the only thing she thought she could do; she threw a glass shard towards what had been her most prized object. The orange stone shattered in hundreds of pieces, and the guy holding it fell back. Then Cayla felt again as if a strong current of wind pushed her back, fell and saw the girl with her hand up. Their attackers turned around and ran away.

Cayla got up and was about to run after them when she saw Alessa on the ground by the tables. There was blood around her. As Cayla approached, she noticed blood coming from the girl's belly, where there seemed to be a deep cut. Beside her, one of the hooded people lay down unconscious or dead. The woman from the restaurant came out and knelt with a cloth, helping to put pressure on Alessa's wounds.

Guilt consumed Cayla. "It was so fast. I didn't see it. I couldn't..."

"Hush," the woman said. "You did what you could. Hold it and I'll be right back."

She went inside as Cayla tried to stop her friend from bleeding to death. But the cut was so large! Alessa was silent and Cayla was glad that she wasn't making an effort to speak. A bell sounded in the distance. No, not distance, the restaurant. There was so much blood on Cayla's hands. The woman returned and helped her try to stop the bleeding.

Some city guards came, then soon came the medics. Cayla couldn't understand what had happened. If it had been really her necklace they were after, then it was unfortunate that Alessa should have been hurt. Cayla wasn't sure she could bear the responsibility for her friend's death. Perhaps that would not happen. Alessa was put on a stretcher waiting for a small urban lift to take her, when Lylah appeared.

She ran towards Cayla and hugged her, getting blood on her

white dress. "How are you?"

"I'm fine." She pointed to Alessa. "My friend—"

"She'll be treated. You have to come with me."

"I can't leave her."

Lylah stared at her. "Cayla, we need to sort out who these people are and what they want. If they're after you, the best thing you can do for your friend is stay away from her."

Stay away from her. Stay away from everyone. Maybe that was the only useful thing Cayla could do. "Fine. I guess I'll have to stay in the castle then."

Lylah shook her head. "Sort of. Wait just a moment."

Cayla's mother spoke to the city guards giving them instructions, then to the woman from the restaurant. She examined the body of their attacker briefly, then told them, "I'll be right back."

She approached Cayla again. "Let's go."

Cayla felt numb. Had it been her fault? And the necklace. She had no idea what to tell Darian or how he would react. She missed that necklace because until then it had been like a piece of him near her, a reminder of their closeness, their love, their connection. Now it had been shattered.

Cayla followed her mother to a smaller street. Weird. She didn't seem to be heading to the castle. Lylah stopped. "Here. We can talk." She then noticed the missing necklace and looked the most alarmed Cayla had ever seen. "Did they steal it?"

"They tried. I broke it."

Her mother frowned in confusion. "*Broke* it?"

"I threw a shard of glass and it shattered."

Lylah still seemed puzzled. "Are you sure?"

Great. Amidst everything that was happening she had to face doubt. "I saw it."

Her mother still looked at Cayla with a suspicious expression, but exhaled in relief. "Good. Listen, Cayla, there was a breach. I'd rather you stayed away from here for a while. Just in case."

"What about Darian?"

"He's away too." Lylah shook her head. "If I had known you could be in danger…"

Lamenting the past didn't help. "Who were they?"

"I'm not certain. Follow me."

Lylah entered a small building with an empty room. Before Cayla had time to wonder what it was or ask, her mother held her hand and they teleported to the castle. This was not the blue teleporting tower, but a hexagonal room with mirrors and a well in the middle, but it was very different from the other room like this she'd seen in the Darloom castle. This room was lighter and had golden details. "What's this?"

"We're deep underground, below the Queen's Castle."

Their castle. It was odd when she used the name of the castle because it was as if she were referring to herself in third person. "How come these passages haven't been used?"

"When you open a door to get out, you might allow things to come in."

"So we shouldn't open it."

Lylah raised an eyebrow. "Not if we think they've already found a way in. I'll close whatever passage they're using, but I need to see you safe first." She pointed to one of the mirrors. "I think you can cross it. It'll lead to the Light Gardens. Darian's there."

Light Gardens. The place Darian had hoped and wished to visit for the last six months, the place he'd been thinking was lost to him forever. She couldn't hide her anger. "There was a passage to the Light Gardens and he wasn't told?"

Lylah shook her head. "Emergency passage, Cayla. Go. I have things to do here."

She still thought it wasn't fair but crossed the mirror and found herself in an empty teleporting tower with white marble walls.

5

VISIONS AND GARDENS

Sian lay down shivering. Perhaps the infection would go away by itself. Perhaps he should find a way to contact other Maris. His guess was that their saliva had antiseptic properties. But the issue was that they could decide to challenge him, and he was in no state to fight anyone. Now that he'd witnessed their cowardice first hand, he thought it would be quite likely for them to attack a dying human. Dying. That word was horrible. Really? So he could defeat a gigantic beast but would be defeated by microscopic beings? Ridiculous.

"Well, it's a whole army, Sian."

He stared towards the voice. Karina was crossing the wall and entering the room. Funny he didn't remember she could cross walls. Wait. She could. At least mirrors. She lay down beside him and rested her hand on her arm.

"There's an epic battle inside you. The attackers are many, your defenses aren't ready, but there's always a way to turn the tide. No need to set everything on fire. Are you going to give up? Like that?" She shook her head. "Tsk, tsk, tsk. So unlike you."

Her tone was cold and mocking. Her eyes were still brown,

her eyes, but different. She wore the blue dress he'd picked for her a long time before and looked stunning, but an uncomfortable kind of stunning, like a beautiful statue or work of art.

Sian stared. "You're not her."

She rolled her eyes. "So perceptive. How long did it take you? A minute? Is your brain getting fried?"

"Fried brain? Really? While I'm feverish and having visions. Who would have guessed? And who are you?"

That weird not-Karina person laughed. "Me? I thought that was obvious." She changed her form and became Sian, not as he looked now, but normal, well fed, decently dressed Sian. "Don't you know me anymore?"

"It's been a long time, pal. Go back to Karina's form. You can dress as well as you want, you're still ugly."

Weird vision Sian laughed. "How dare you?" He changed his form again. This time he looked thinner, shabby, and had a long beard. "What about this?"

"Hideous. What do you want?"

The vision transformed back to normal-looking Sian. "I want you to survive."

Sian shrugged. "What for?"

The vision transformed again into Karina, but wearing the leather pants and jacket she wore the first time they kissed. Sian felt a cold shiver in his stomach, a tinge of panic with the thought that something in his life was out of his control. Her eyes were cold and all wrong, but still... goodness she was beautiful.

She smiled. "For me."

Sian sighed. "I'll never meet her again." The vision wasn't Karina and there was no point treating it like it was. "And stop pretending you're her."

Karina vision rolled her eyes again. "I'm you. It's not like you never... I'm just doing it better, see?"

"Fine. Vision whatever, since you are here and all, do you have any tips for me to survive?"

"Find Komiak."

As if Sian hadn't considered that. "I can't make it to that mountain, and if I call them, they might kill me."

"Might is the key word here. If you compare maybe to sure, and if you're talking about death, maybe is a win."

"There's a chance the infection will go away by itself."

"You know it won't."

"So you think I should call Maris to kill me?"

Karina-vision shook her head. "You forget your powers."

"The electricity thing? That was Darloom."

She grimaced. "Fried brain. Sian, think. Darloom can only affect thoughts, perception. He could only cause pain, because it relates to thoughts. He couldn't even physically hurt anyone with that magic." She had a disapproving, disgusted face. "Very different from what you did."

"Don't give me that look. I mean, maybe do, maybe I deserve this death."

"Forget the look, Sian, think. What you did there, that was not Darloom."

That made some sense. Sort of. And yet... "What was it, then?"

"You."

Sian tried to take in the information, then laughed. "Nice try, but I have no magic."

"You know you do, fried brain."

"Right. I'll assume I have electrifying magic that I have no idea how to use. Do you think I can use it in the state I'm in?"

"Maybe you can't." She winked. "But the Maris don't know it."

Could she, he, whatever it was, be right? "You have a point there."

She smirked. "One of us has to have the brains, pal."

"Your impersonation of her is still awful."

"Ooooh. As if you did so much better."

"Unrealistic, maybe. Nicer, for sure."

He felt her hand on his, and was second-guessing his impression that it was a vision. Her clothes were now the pyjamas she'd worn the last night they were together. That was a low blow. His mind took him back to that moment. He could almost feel his hands over the soft fabric, under it, touching her warm skin, soft hair. They were like two lost pieces about to snap into place. So much want and so much need for restraint—and patience—under the bitter illusion that they'd have so many more nights and days together.

His mind took him back to the present time. For once vision Karina's eyes were sweet and loving like they were supposed to be. She ran her fingers on his face, shabby beard and all. "It could be all real, Sian. It can still be real. But you have to survive."

Sian didn't care that it was just some part of himself pretending to be Karina. He wrapped his arms around her waist and pulled her towards him. But there was nothing to pull; her body disappeared and then the vision was gone. Of course. He shouldn't even be surprised.

Survive. Weird vision was right. Wasn't he a survivor?

He needed to go to the top floor and ring the bell, but wasn't sure if he could even get up, let alone go up some flights of stairs. Weird vision had a point that the Maris would probably hesitate to attack him. He had to get up, he had to go up. Why couldn't that stupid vision do that, since it had been so intent on mocking him?

Couldn't he use his weird unknown magic to ring that bell? No. He had to get up. One last shot. He had to gather his last strength, go up, and hope everything went right.

Sian made a huge effort to open the door. The stairs to the top looked interminable even if he knew there were only three more floors. A movement caught his eye. A Maris was flying towards him. Sian wondered if he should lock himself in the room again when he realized who it was; Komiak, with the stone in one of his claws.

"You look sick," the stone said.

"Infection. Do you know how to treat it?"

The huge bird approached Sian. "You should take off that dirty cloth you use over your body."

Sian shook his head. "I'm not taking that off."

"Fine, then. Come back to our cave. You kept your end of the deal, got rid of King Sarat, and you're welcome back."

"I have to stay here. It's my hope of finding a way out."

Komiak tilted his head. "You don't like being king?"

Sian didn't want to say that he wanted to find his friends and his people, lest he offend him. Well, maybe he had no choice. "I want to return to my family." There. Family didn't sound so odd. "Before that, I need to avoid dying—if possible."

Komiak opened his huge beak. Had he changed his mind and was about to chop Sian's head off? Well, no. He put his beak around Sian's shoulder. Sian felt something wet. When Komiak took off his beak, there was a dark yellow slime around his upper body.

"This is our medicine," the huge bird said. "I'm not sure it will work with that disgusting thing… But it's your choice."

Weird. This wasn't like regular saliva. "Thank you."

"I'll come back tomorrow. Please consider removing those rags and coming back home. We can be your family. At least for now."

Komiak didn't wait for a reply and flew up to the opening. Sian barely had time to enter the room again and close the door before falling asleep.

～

Leena served Darian a bowl of soup. He'd been hungry but now he was so anxious he didn't know if he could eat. And he was pissed that he'd been brought unconscious.

"Darian," the woman asked. "Do you know where your brother is?"

He shook his head. "No idea. Why? What's happening?"

Leena had a worried expression. "Lylah mentioned a breach. We're going to investigate it."

He stared at her. "So?"

"So what?"

"Are you going to investigate or watch me eat?"

"I want to make sure you're all right."

"What do you think? Something's happening in Whyland and I'm not there. Cayla's there and I'm not there. Are you sure you can't take me back?"

Leena just stared.

Darian exhaled. "Fine. You won't. I guess it doesn't matter because if I protest you'll just make me faint. Screw free will."

"For the record, I don't agree with Lylah's methods. But Cayla's coming. Even if I could take you back, wouldn't you want to wait for her?"

Darian sighed. "Can you just tell me what's happening?"

"I will. Once I know."

He looked down then took a spoon of that soup. His chest was tight. So many things bothering him. Hadn't Lylah nominated him Grand General? For what, if he would be sent away at the first sign of trouble? And not knowing was gnawing on him. The worst part was not having news from Cayla and having to wonder if she was safe.

Darian shut his eyes, trying to think, trying to calm down, trying to find a solution, anything.

A hand touched his shoulder. "Patience, little one." Leena was standing beside him.

He did his best to hide a grimace. "Little one" was rather infuriating. Especially in a time like this.

His necklace shone, like always. Perhaps he could contact Cayla. He pulled the stone close to his mouth and was about to press it, when Leena put her hand over his. "Don't. By no means should you alert anyone to Light Gardens magic. Not now."

"Will anyone tell me if she's safe?"

Leena sat at the chair beside him. "Darian, it's neither a war nor an invasion, just a breach. It means someone or something is coming or might come from another dimension, but we don't even know what it is."

"If it's nothing, why was I brought here?"

"To keep you safe. Lylah thinks it might be some enemy of the Light Gardens."

"She *thinks*. Great. And what do I have to do—"

Right then, Darian saw something that made him chill. His right hand trembled as he held the necklace stone, now black. For a second, he wanted to believe that his eyes were tricking him, that it was a shade, a trick of the light or something. No. It was black. It could only mean... He didn't know. For so long he'd looked at his necklace as a reminder of Cayla, trusting that the light meant that the two people loved each other. Cayla's love couldn't have vanished like that. They'd been fine just a couple hours before. Could she... The painful memory of his mother dying and his necklace turning black hit him. Not again, not again, not Cayla.

His voice was cracking as he showed Leena the stone. "Do you know what this means?"

Her eyes darkened. "Lylah is coming. Cayla's her daughter after all. She'll know. It might be nothing."

That last part sounded quite insincere. Here Darian stood powerless, his heart pounding. No, he wasn't going to stand here. He got up. "I have to tell her. I know where Cayla went. She's not in the castle!"

"Darian. Lylah can find her. Wait. There's no reason to assume—"

Darian shook his black stone. "Explain this."

Leena sat and took a long, deep breath. "I can't use that portal, only Lylah can. She told me she was going to get Cayla. I'm worried too, but right now, all we can do is wait. Sometimes life's like that."

Darian sat down and put his head in his hands, hoping that his stone turning black didn't mean anything serious, hoping Cayla was all right, hoping so many things. And how he regretted leaving her. If only he'd come with her. If only... But when has regret ever helped anything?

Cayla stood in the tower for a moment, surprised that she should be left alone in a place she didn't know. Venturing towards a door, she almost crashed with a girl coming in her direction. She had darker skin, brown eyes and very curly black hair.

"Are you Cayla?"

"Yes. Is Darian here?"

The girl nodded. "I'll bring you to him."

Cayla was stressed and upset, but she had to remember politeness. "And what's your name?"

"I'm Anika. I'm finishing my initiation this month."

"Nice." Perhaps Cayla should have smiled, congratulated her or asked something, but she was too worried about Alessa to care or make conversation.

Outside was a meadow. The sun was setting. Apart from some lights in the distance, there was just a small wooden house nearby and they walked towards it.

Anika opened the door to Cayla but left. Sitting at a table were Leena and Darian. He looked miserable, raised his eyes and saw her. His features were turning into a smile when he looked down at her clothes and frowned. Oh, no. The blood. He got up and stood in front of her, his face contorted in horror. "Are you hurt?" He turned to Leena, desperation clear in his voice. "She needs help."

Cayla took his hand. "I'm fine. Darian. I'm fine. The blood is not mine."

Darian exhaled then took her in a tight embrace. "I've never been so scared in my life. I thought you…"

"I'm fine." Actually, now that she thought about it, her hand hurt. The cut must have been deep.

He stepped back and stared at her. "What happened? Whose blood is it?"

Cayla was about to tell him all but she hated seeing his face in so much pain. She pulled up her hand and showed it. "I just have a cut."

"You need to stitch it." He looked down at her clothes, her hand, and her clothes, maybe trying to find a correlation.

"It's Alessa. She got a bigger cut." That was true. Cayla still debated how much she should tell him. She should tell him the truth, she should, but then she remembered the time she'd been locked in the castle by her father and even the brief time when Darian had been overprotective of her. "The table where we were sitting broke and some things fell on us. This is from the jug."

He raised an eyebrow, likely still suspicious.

"It's my fault. I got up quickly…"

Leena was standing near them and took Cayla's hand. "We'll mend it, but we should get going." She put a white paste on the wound. The bleeding and the pain stopped. "This will do for now."

Darian stared at her in silence. After a while, he asked, "What about the necklace?"

The question she'd dreaded so much. The necklace. The

necklace. The one she missed so much it was like missing a part of her. Her insides felt hollow and her heart was about to climb out of her chest. "I'm so sorry. So, so sorry. I… I don't know what happened. I…"

Darian hugged her. "At least you're here. This is what matters. Don't worry about the necklace."

Cayla was relieved. She knew how important that necklace was, what it meant, and at the same time, she'd had no choice. Still, she didn't want to talk about all that right then. His face leaned against hers. She could hear his breath, feel his heart. The words left her mouth as if by their own will: "I love you."

He whispered in her ear, "You'd better keep telling me that now that I have no ratting stone."

She wished he'd said something different. "I don't have a stone either."

"Your fault. You deserve some guessing. No. It's obvious, isn't it?"

"I guess."

He kissed her cheek. "Very funny."

Cayla didn't share his sense of humor, but she didn't say anything. At least he wasn't upset about the necklace. Leena was staring at them. Cayla stepped away from Darian and looked at the woman. "We have to go, right?"

Leena nodded.

Darian made a stop gesture with his hand and turned to the woman. "Hang on. You said I was in danger because I'm from the Light Gardens?"

"It's a possibility, yes," Leena confirmed.

"So is my brother." His voice came low, almost as in a whisper. His face was realization and pleading.

"Indeed." Leena sighed. "Do you happen to know where he is?"

He looked thoughtful. "Maybe."

6

NEW LIVES

Screeches. So many screeches. Sian opened his eyes to the darkness in his improvised bedroom. There was a faint light coming from a half-moon in the sky, but it was intermittent with shadows of Maris. Maybe they'd come to kill him. Maybe not. There was something sticky on his shoulder. Wait. He remembered his encounter with Komiak—and his vision. In theory he should have gotten better. The reality was that he couldn't even get up.

If the Maris decided to break his door and kill him, it would be his end. But then, if the Maris didn't, it would still be his end. Hero's life. What an amazing hero, killing people—or big birds—needlessly.

Well, he *was* tired of eating unseasoned worms and rodents. That was a positive in dying. He'd never given much thought to the afterlife. With so many conflicting descriptions, all he surmised was that no one had a clue. Still, he assumed the menu would be better there. If there was a menu. If there was a there. No more unseasoned worms. The thought gave Sian a smile. When had his needs gotten so simple?

There was a muffled yell from beyond the door, hard to

distinguish with all the noise those Maris were making. Maybe they were not yells, just screeches.

Then he heard it: "Sian, Sian!"

There were also sounds of banging on doors. Yay noisy vision.

Sian mumbled, "Come in. Can't you cross doors? Walls?"

The steps sounded closer to his door. This time the knocking was there. "Sian, is that you?"

The voice was familiar. His brother's? The one who never knew he existed? Not familiar. Unfamiliar. So many people to impersonate, why did the vision decide to be him?

"Come in." Sian's voice was hoarse, but it still sounded loud enough to be heard from the outside.

"Open the door, please!"

"I can't get up." The mumble was low this time. Regardless, the vision should know.

More knocks. "Sian, please, open up." Darian's voice.

Sian sat up, then leaned on the wall to stand, but collapsed. Did fever do that? How could he know it when all his training was a blur in his mind? Did he even have a mind?

He stared at the ceiling. "Just come in," he managed to say.

There were voices inside the tower, in front of his door, and screeches outside. A loud noise, like something breaking, then two people walked in.

Someone resembling his brother knelt beside him and held his hand. "Sian, we're here. We're here."

The vision felt solid and real enough for Sian to wonder if Darian had died and come to take him. Why couldn't Sian get up then? By now, he should have a strong, shiny new body—or spirit—or something. Perhaps he should close his eyes and let himself go.

~

It had taken a lot less beseeching and imploring than Darian had imagined. It was a guess, but by elimination it made sense. Thankfully nobody doubted him. Leena had taken them to another tower, and Cayla stood holding the portal open.

Relief turned to worry when he finally found Sian. Thin and sick, he lay down as if he were dying.

"We'll need to carry him," he told Leena.

Her hands were up, casting the protective barrier to prevent Maris from coming in. The huge birds were outside, probably attracted by their visit, likely ready to strike. He wondered how his brother had survived for so long.

She sighed. "We'll need to bring more people."

"He's dying!"

"If I help carry him, the barrier will break."

Darian crouched, lifted his brother's body, then put it over his shoulder. It wasn't that much weight or perhaps he didn't feel it as he rushed down the stairs. He hesitated when he came across a huge gap. Would he be able to make the jump while carrying his brother?

"Wait," Leena said.

She lowered her arms. Blue light connected the two broken edges of the stairs. "It's a bridge. Hurry."

Darian walked across it. Once he was done, he heard Leena jumping behind him. He also heard Maris entering the tower, but then saw Leena's barrier on top of them. The creatures were inside but not close enough to reach them. Anika was downstairs also casting a protective barrier.

And Cayla… they'd better be fast. He wasn't sure if holding a portal open like that required effort, but he didn't want to take any chances. His brother also required urgent assistance. If only Darian had known that there was a way to find Sian, if only he'd known that they could open emergency portals, his brother wouldn't be almost dying on his shoulders. Perhaps it had all been Darian's fault for not asking, not insisting, not trying enough. No more of that.

~

Karina opened her eyes and sat up, squinting against the strong light coming from her side. The entire wall was glass from where she could see a clear sky, as if from a great height. There were three other people in the room. Involuntarily she flinched at the idea of being helpless among strangers, but then maybe it was just a hospital. Quite a fancy hospital. Her double bed had white soft sheets and many layers of thin golden covers. The three people in the room were some awesomely good looking nurses or doctors. Perhaps she was having visions or this was a dream.

A young man with long blond hair sat on the edge of the bed. "How are you?" Apprehension, relief, and expectation were clear on his voice and expression.

He didn't sound like a hospital worker, but like a friend, a very close friend or even something more. He had small dark brown eyes, some small braids on one side of his hair, and overall was the kind of good-looking guy that didn't usually spare Karina more than two glances. Friend, definitely.

In front of the bed, there was a girl about Karina's age, with wavy dark hair and brown eyes. She observed but didn't seem as worried as the blond guy. Near her, a man in his forties or so with very long black hair. He was good looking the way actors in their forties or fifties can be good looking and had worry and concern written on his face, just not as much as the blond guy sitting on the edge of Karina's bed.

They were all well dressed, with some strange embroidery on their shirts. The older man had an overcoat. Combined with the fancy decoration in the room and the golden details here and there, Karina assumed this was a luxurious condo. Maybe something happened to her while in a very fancy party.

A few questions popped up in her head and almost came out of her mouth, like "Do I know you?", "Where am I?", or "Who are you?", but thankfully she used her brain before her mouth and found something that wouldn't sound offensive. "I... I don't remember what happened."

The older man approached her. "You went through a lot." He put his hand over her head like in a comforting caress. The gesture was intimate, as if he were a close family member. "Things will come back to you slowly."

The blond boy held her hand. Karina flinched. This was too weird. He noticed but held on tighter. "Do you remember me?"

Karina went over her mental files. Would she forget a good-looking guy? Well, considering she didn't spare many glances for guys who didn't pay attention to her, that was possible. But he sounded like a friend, someone who cared for her. Who was he? Who were those people? Perhaps she shouldn't worry so much about being rude.

"I'm sorry. I... I don't remember..." Karina looked around. "Any of you. Or this place. I don't know if should remember it."

The blond boy caressed her hand. It still felt strange, out of place, too intimate, and it wasn't like the older dark-haired man. He said, "Karina, don't worry. It will take some time. At least you're alive."

Karina flinched again. One, they'd said her name, and that she remembered. In fact, now that she was thinking, she remembered a lot of things; her family, her apartment, her best friends, Zoe and Tori. She remembered school subjects, even some memories from her childhood flashed in her mind. The only thing she didn't remember was how she'd gotten there. Also, alive?

"Was I in an accident? Did I hit my head?" Some temporary amnesia was possible, but she'd need to read more about how it worked. She wasn't sure if it was possible to forget just a period of time, and felt uneasy when she didn't know something, uneasy when she didn't have enough information to understand what was happening around her.

The blond boy turned to the man and the girl. "Could you give us some time?"

The man stared and nodded. "That's a good idea. Now that I know she's well, I can go back to my duties. Call me if you need me."

"I will, uncle."

He left the room. The girl got up after him looked back. "See you." She then also left and closed the door behind her.

The blond boy let go of her hand. "Don't strain, don't stress, don't worry. You don't remember any of this, do you?"

Karina shook her head.

"I'm Satwak, but you can call me Sat. You just saw my uncle Firis and my sister Faizana. Do you remember Lumina?"

Karina had no idea what he was talking about.

"It's our city. Where you live."

"How long have I been living here?"

"I'd say about two years."

Karina's heart sped up. That much? That much time was a void in her mind? And did it make sense to forget recent memories like a part of her life had been wiped away?

Sat sighed. "Karina, it wasn't an accident. You were attacked. With strong magic. That's why some of it might be a blur. It's almost as if… as if someone wanted you to forget us. To forget me. But you're here."

Wow, wow, wow. Hang on. "Magic?"

"Take it easy, Kah. I can show and explain everything to you again. I'm not upset you lost your memory, don't worry about it."

Kah? What the… Karina had a queasy feeling in her stomach. Memory loss. So he'd said it. Maybe she should just ask the questions burning her mind. "Can you just like, do a quick recap on how I got here? How I lost my memory? How I met you?"

"We met almost two years ago. You came to live here. We were trying to travel and the guardians ambushed us. They attacked you, but we saved you. You've been sleeping for a few days, but now you're awake. Don't be afraid to speak your mind, at least to me."

"A few days. Feels like a couple years."

"Probably."

"And what's this place?"

"It's Lumina, the City of Light."

The name meant nothing to her. She was awful in geography, but still, it was more likely she wouldn't know a city's location, not that she'd never heard of a place she should. "Does it have another name? Are we still in Canada?"

"This is an ethereal city. We aren't anywhere specific. Well, we should be tied to dimension and a geographic location, but we aren't."

This was all too weird. She wasn't even sure if she believed it. "So, is it like… floating in the air?"

"Floating in the void."

Was he joking? She decided to play along. "Is it flat? Or is it spheric like a little planet?"

"Not a planet, no."

Right. So here were some questions she'd always wanted to ask flat earthers. "What happens at the edges? Is it like a precipice into nothingness? A wall?"

He laughed. "You think I'm joking. I'm not. But yes. It's a barrier. You try to move forward and it takes you sideways. We don't go much to the edges, though."

"I'd like to see that." No kidding. What a scientific breakthrough.

"I'll take you there. I just thought you'd like to see the palace first, the city. Since you forgot it all, it will be as if it were your first time."

"Can we go now? I think I've slept enough."

Karina looked at herself. She wore what looked like a nightgown. It felt like cotton and had golden embroidery on the edges. She'd need to change and she had no idea if she had clothes there, or even what kind of clothes she wore. It all felt like a bizarre nightmare.

"Don't worry," Sat said, as if guessing her thoughts. "Your attendant will help you get dressed and then we can go. I think you're better now, and some fresh air might be good for you." He pointed to a table on the back of the room with two jugs and some glasses. "Do you want to drink something? Juice, water?"

"Some water." That was a great idea indeed. She was thirsty. And a little hungry too.

Sat poured water in a glass and brought it to her. It still felt odd, familiar, intimate. Could he be an attendant? Well, no, his uncle looked important. Karina took a long, refreshing sip.

She wanted to ask what he was in relation to her, but wasn't sure how to phrase it. "How did we become friends?"

"I saved you. A long time ago."

Something didn't add up. "And then I decided to move here?"

He looked down. "You were prevented from returning."

Home. That was a hard blow on her when she thought about her parents, her friends. Not school. That, strangely, she was glad of being away from.

"I see." Something was still strange, but the guy seemed nice. Perhaps they had been close. "And since I couldn't return you allowed me to live here? Cause you're my friend?" She took a sip.

"I'm your husband."

Karina spat her water.

7

GAP

Such a mix of emotions in Darian. Should he feel relieved that they were saving Sian? Should he feel angry that he'd been abandoned for so long when in fact there was a way to save him? Should he just be glad for this second chance to reconcile with his brother? Maybe it was everything and then more.

They'd brought Sian to a building away from the city. It was a hospital, but the rooms had earthy tones, plants, and large windows overlooking trees and flowers outside. Leena and Darian watched as two health practitioners put him on an examination table.

Darian felt strange at seeing his brother so helpless, thin, with a long beard and shabby clothes. Everything that had always denoted Sian's pride was gone. There was something strange on his right shoulder, like some widespread infection.

The male doctor took a knife and was about to cut Sian's shirt—but was stopped. Sian sat up, pushed the knife away and had his right hand around the doctor's throat.

"Calm down, it's us," Darian rushed to his brother's side.

"Easy, easy there," Leena said in her soft soothing voice.

Sian let go of the man.

Leena turned to them. "It's better if you all get out. I can take care of him."

The doctors got out, apparently glad to be getting away from Sian.

She looked at Darian. "You too."

He was going to protest, ask why, but then realized there wasn't much he could do. "I'll be outside then."

"I'll lock the door. Make sure nobody tries to come in."

She said it as if there was going to be some super secretive activity there. This time Darian couldn't contain his question. "What's happening? Is he in danger?"

"Not a lot of danger, but I think privacy will be better for him. Do stay outside, as I might need some things."

"I will."

Darian walked outside and heard the door being locked. Cayla was sitting on a bench under a tree and came running to him. "So?"

"I don't know, Leena is examining him."

She ran her hands through his hair. "He should be good in no time."

He took her right hand. They had stitched it, and now she only had a bandage over her cut. "Is it better?"

"Good as new." She smiled.

"Thank you for opening the portal for us."

"Anything for you."

For him. Of course. Not for Sian. According to Leena, they opened the portal without consulting the Guardians, or even letting them know, and they shouldn't be opening portals like that. He was glad they'd done so, as his brother could have been much worse had they waited. But something else was bothering him.

"Cayla, I have a question."

She moved her hand away from his hair. "Yes?"

"Why did you lie?"

She squinted.

"About what happened in Siphoria," he added. "You know you didn't fall over a table or whatever you said."

She sighed. "I didn't want you to worry—"

"What happened?"

Cayla was thoughtful. "Some strange people, they were wearing white cloaks and hoods, they attacked us. It was fast, and as much as Alessa and I fought back, they had some strong... magic. One of them took the necklace. I didn't want them to have it. I threw a glass shard on it and it broke."

"Broke?"

"It did. I saw it. I'm sorry, I didn't want to break it, but they were many, they were cheating with magic, and I was afraid they'd take the necklace away. What would you have done in my place?"

"I wouldn't have thought of breaking it, but I guess it was a good idea. But you should have told me." He was worried about what happened to her, but he didn't want to make a fuss out of it, lest she think she had to lie to him again.

"I was just...overwhelmed."

Darian caressed her face. "I would understand. I always do. You need to tell Leena."

"I will. Lylah also knows what happened." It was odd how sometimes Cayla referred to her mother by her name. "I think it has something to do with the breach. Whoever was there wasn't supposed to be."

That made sense. "They were after the Light Gardens. That's why they came to you. They were attracted by the magic of the necklace, the magic of this city. If you hadn't broken it, they could perhaps open a portal here." He facepalmed. "I'm so dumb. I put you in danger."

"No. How could you have known Lumina would come? Plus,

you used it to save me before, remember?" She looked down. "Not anymore."

Darian kissed her forehead. "Maybe we can find something else. It feels strange no longer being connected to you."

"We'll always be connected."

He laughed. "Always?" Darian kissed her lips softly. "I know… still, I liked carrying a reminder of you."

She had a sad smile.

"What's wrong?" he asked.

"Alessa worries me." Cayla looked down. "She had a huge cut. I hope…"

"Hush. She was being treated, wasn't she?" Darian embraced Cayla.

"*That* was my fault."

"It was the breach, Cayla, not you. Siphoria should have been safe if it wasn't for that. Don't blame yourself."

"Maybe. I hope Lylah brings news of Alessa soon."

"She will. I'm sure she will."

Darian hugged Cayla tight, hoping his love would ease some of her fears.

Karina felt numb, perhaps so overwhelmed with all this information that her senses shut down. Two girls helped her put on a dress. They were silent, and as much as Karina was burning with questions, she didn't even know where to start. Plus, since when was she so incompetent that she needed help getting dressed? Still, she played along. But the biggest question was another one: married? Satwak was certainly cute so it wasn't a huge mystery why she'd be interested in him. Still… she was so young.

These people, this place, this talk of magic, it didn't match anything she knew. Deep down there was some recognition, like when you hear a name you've heard before but can't recall. Like the name, she had no clue what any of it meant. Without two years of her life, it was as if she was being transplanted into a body that wasn't hers. It wasn't hers because she hadn't had the life experience that this married Karina had. Without the experience, she couldn't be that person. Maybe everything would come back to her mind, and then it wouldn't be weird. Maybe. For now there was a two-year gap in her life, not only two years, but very eventful ones of which she had no memory.

Even her underwear was weird, like some thinner material with a cotton feel but a shiny look, like nylon or something. Her bra didn't have wires and she hated that. At least they wore bras in this weird city. But then, perhaps this was just a prank. But who in their right mind would prank someone having a memory loss? It didn't make sense. How could she add things up, when she didn't know what to add up?

Her dress was white, with the stupid golden embroidery on the rims. Other than that the dress was simple, though, no details or anything, just some back ribbons that needed to be tied and required help. The dress was tight on top with a skirt up to her knees. Her boots were also white. Who chooses white for shoes? Maybe the attendants cleaned them.

She walked out of the room and Satwak, or Sat, was waiting for her, then he guided her to a hallway. At least he understood that she didn't remember anything and acted almost as if he were presenting the city to her, and explained a lot of things.

The palace was where they housed the government of the city and the royal family. His uncle, Firis, was the overseer, as they called their leader. Shouldn't that be mayor? And since when was an overseer family royal? Karina shut down those silly questions, when there were so many, enormous questions hanging unsaid.

They descended spiral staircases beside a glass wall overlooking a valley and houses. Karina did peek to see if she found the end of the world barrier, but she only saw horizon. In the middle of the staircase was a gap. Not a gap, as a metallic box moved up past them.

"What was that?"

"The elevator. It's for when we don't want to use the stairs."

"I know what an elevator is, but shouldn't there be cables?" Something, anything? That thing had shot up like a rocket.

"Our technology is different from yours, Karina."

"Did you explain it all for me and I forgot?"

He nodded. "A lot of it. I know you like technology. You've explained to us how your elevators use pulleys and electricity, and I've explained to you ours use magic... I don't mind repeating anything, though."

There had been something off in that interaction, but she couldn't quite put her finger where.

Sat chuckled. "You're upset I explained to you what an elevator is. I forgot you also had them. It's been a long time, and we haven't had those conversations in a while. Forgive me if I make mistakes."

Karina exhaled. That had been exactly it. He'd explained what an elevator was. They kept descending the stairs. But now the odd thing was that he was replying to her thoughts. Was he replying to her thoughts? Silence. Was he? He looked normal. Maybe she was imagining things.

"Like I told you, the top floor is our teleporting tower. We haven't used it in years, since the Guardians blocked it. Below it is the throne room, then our accommodations, and below are some government offices."

"Who are these Guardians?"

"There are other ethereal cities like this one. We used to be thirteen cities. Lumina was the most important of them. See, we have more advanced magic. But some people from those cities rebelled against us and locked us out. A city was destroyed in this confrontation."

"So you're saying they're the bad guys?" Again, Karina had a strange gut feeling telling her not to trust people who claimed someone else was a villain. Perhaps it was just common sense.

"I'm saying they isolated us. I'm pretty sure they believe what they do is wonderful."

"Is it, though?"

"They destroyed a city. They attacked you."

"Why would anyone attack me?"

"Because you were trying to get out."

"What does it matter to them? I mean," she was going to say she was worthless, but that was a strong word, "I can't harm them."

Sat shook his head. "They don't care about that."

"Are you going to tell me more about them?"

"Yes. In fact, my uncle can discuss it with you. He's very passionate about it."

"About Guardians?"

"About freeing Lumina."

Right. She'd really have to get more information about it, so that she could draw her conclusions and try to understand what was happening.

"How did I end up here?"

"A portal was opened by accident and you fell through."

She was trying to connect points a and b. "Right. But how would that make me be in touch with, uh, the royal family?"

"We hadn't had a foreigner in generations."

That would make her interesting, intriguing, and explained quite a lot. "So you called me here to compare elevator styles?"

Sat chuckled. "Sort of. Let's get to know Lumina, then we can try to retrace some of your past."

They got out of the palace. It led to a square surrounded by humongous metal statues. They had human forms, but weren't all in the same position. Some knelt, some stood, some were ready to strike, almost as if they'd been giants who had been frozen. Karina wondered if one day they had moved.

Sat pointed to the statues. "Legend says these are the real royal guards, guarding the royal family. But that's just legend, of course."

"They do look real."

"Maybe. Let's get to know more."

The square was at a hill and from there Karina had a better view of the city. It didn't look that strange. Houses had triangular roofs in many different colors. Woods surrounded the castle. They descended some stairs and came to another square, this one huge, with what looked like stores all around it. Each house had a big open door and people came in and out. Many inhabitants wore some kind of cloaks over their clothes. Many wore white, some wore light colors like light blue or yellow. When they had embroidery, it was silver.

Sat pointed to the square. "This is central Lumina. As you noticed, it's where you can buy things."

Karina nodded.

Sat added, "Only the royal family wears gold embroidery. That's why they dress differently."

"Do the colors mean anything?"

"The royal family and its protectors wear white, other people can wear whatever they want, but they prefer lighter colors."

"A whole lot of trouble to wash."

With everything that was happening, Karina shouldn't be thinking whether it was hard or not to wash lighter clothes. In fact, maybe they had some neat version of bleach and that was why they made that choice.

Sat pointed beyond the square. "That's where people live."

Karina had seen houses extending far away, then trees and fields. This was a small city. Karina guessed some three thousand people in total.

Sat nodded. "Our population is two thousand."

This wasn't the first time he was replying to her thoughts. But then, sometimes he seemed oblivious. Perhaps he was great at interpreting body language and caught her making a mental calculation face.

"Are we going to see the edge?"

Sat chuckled. "There isn't much to see, but since you insist…"

Oh yeah, she insisted. She needed to know how much of a prank it was, or if by chance she'd ended up with some brainwashed people.

Sat walked back to the castle. It didn't make much sense.

"Is it in that direction?"

"No, but it's not that close. We'd better take a capsule."

"I assume you'll explain what it is."

He stopped and sighed. "I'm so sorry. Sometimes I explain things you know as if you didn't, sometimes I just assume you understand what I say. I didn't mean—"

"That's fine."

"You'll see what it is. The edge is a bit far, and we'd take too long walking."

"But could we get there walking?" Karina was wondering about distances.

Sat shrugged. "You can get anywhere walking as long as it's in your dimension and there are no bodies of water in the way."

Dimension. Still that talk. But then, with all this weird technology, maybe she should be a bit less skeptical. Well, maybe, but the issue was convincing her rational mind.

They returned to the castle and entered that odd elevator. It didn't have buttons, just a lever, and it had no door. Karina stood back in the wall. Of course the movement of an elevator wouldn't cause anyone to move horizontally and fall, but still, being in that place, looking at the gap without any barrier made her scared.

Sat looked at her and pulled close a metal gate. "Better?"

She nodded.

He laughed. "I'm sorry, I'm just lazy."

They got off on the fifth floor and walked to what looked like a terrace or balcony. There were huge golden metal balls on it. Sat approached one of them. It had two seats and a window in the front.

Karina looked at him. "Now you're going to tell me this flies."

He had a small smile. "Maybe you're remembering things."

"Just being logical. I mean, it's not like you'd roll down the fifth floor with those things. Let me guess, it's moved by *magic*."

"Yes. Like almost everything in Lumina."

"You'll need to explain to me what magic is." It was obviously some kind of mechanics that were unknown in her world. This difference in technology was one point that almost convinced her about the theory of ethereal city. But then, who knows, this could be the future, maybe she'd been frozen in time, traveled in time. So many possibilities.

At least the capsule had doors. Karina wasn't a great fan of heights without a barrier between her and a fall, even if a fall wasn't likely.

They flew over the city. There were some large fields with plantations and some animals. Farms. Then outside, dense tree-tops in what looked like a forest. Sat landed on a clearing. It wasn't just a natural clearing, but a landing pad, with a small house beside it and markings on the floor.

"We'll have to walk to the edge."

"Of course, otherwise I suppose the capsule falls off." She still was skeptical and couldn't help the sarcasm.

"I told you it was a barrier. We would have hit it."

They walked on a man-made path with smooth stones. The trees were like trees in any temperate climate, even if she wasn't sure she knew the trees themselves.

A few minutes of silence convinced her to ask a question that had been burning in her mind.

"Satwalk." He had a face. "I mean, Sat. Can you read thoughts?"

He stopped then took a deep breath as if thinking. "A little. Sometimes, yes."

"I see." She felt a little invaded.

"I try not to, Karina. Don't worry about it."

It was just… she was among strangers in a strange land, alone, and couldn't even have the sanctuary of her own mind.

Sat took her hands. "You're not alone. I'm here with you."

All right. Weren't they a couple? She didn't even want to think what that entailed. Too much. "How long have we been together?"

"About a year and a half. We married a year ago."

Karina tried to recall the last information she had about her own age and her own life. "I was just a little less than fifteen. Married at sixteen?"

He let go of her hands and started to walk again. "Lumina is different. Marriages are also magical contracts. We protect each other. See, everyone in this city wields magic."

"Except me."

He nodded.

"So it was for my protection?"

"In a way."

"How old are you?"

He tilted his head, as if avoiding the question. "We age differently."

"How differently?"

"I'm fifty-three."

Something turned in Karina's stomach. She wondered if she'd be revulsed if he'd said one hundred or a thousand, or if it would just be the same. Then she remembered he read thoughts. "I'm sorry. It's just—"

Satwak was laughing. She didn't understand what was so funny.

"What?"

He had a weird face. "I was joking. This is not the legendary city of Gleam Fortress, where people were said to age slowly. We're normal. I'm seventeen."

Karina wanted to burn him with her stare. "Is it fun? To mess with someone who lost her memory?"

He looked down, serious. "It isn't. I'm truly sorry."

Idiot. Hopefully he'd heard that. Karina tried to think. With this talk of protection coupled with the fact he didn't seem to be the least in love with her, plus their own young age, Karina wondered something else. "Was it real? Us?"

"Try not to think about it."

"How can I not think about it, when you're making me wonder if we... you know what." There. She'd said it, and brought to her mind one of the things that spooked her out the most; the idea that she'd done something she had no memory of.

"My uncle Firis can read thoughts. Better than me. He's a good man and an excellent leader, but he fears that the Guardians might have brainwashed you. If you're in love, he'll trust that you'll be loyal to me."

Karina swallowed. "So we have to pretend?"

"I understand everything is strange to you now. Take your time. We'll get used to each other. For now, it's better not to inquire on the past, lest it bothers you."

"But I want to know..."

He raised his hands in the air, in despair. "We didn't. Happy?"

More relieved than she had expected, Karina exhaled a huge ball of discomfort from her chest. But that opened a whole lot of other questions.

He sighed. "Don't make this complicated, please. I'll teach

you how to replace thoughts, but it might take a while. Try not to think about it, but know that I'm your friend."

"So you say."

"True. But I'm the best you got."

The path stopped. Karina walked forward on it, but then when she looked back, she'd moved sideways. It wasn't like a barrier in front of her, it was as if space curved or something.

"So this is the edge."

"Yes," he confirmed.

Karina shrugged. "At least I know you're telling the truth about this ethereal city idea."

"See? You can be sure of one thing."

"Among so much uncertainty." She wouldn't have said this out loud, but it made no sense to keep her thoughts to herself just to wonder whether he'd picked up on them or not.

"I'll give you more proof when we come back. And there's something I need to ask you."

It didn't sound good. "Yes?"

"Your vows, you don't remember them."

"I don't remember anything."

"I know," Sat said. "But that makes them void."

"You mean I don't need to be married to you." She felt relieved. Who would have guessed she wouldn't want to be with the hottie in front of her? Perhaps an ethereal city made people weird and illogical. Wait, he might have heard all that. She added, "Not that I wouldn't like…"

"I understand. I'm a stranger to you and it would be super creepy to be married to me. Is that right?"

She nodded. He got the creepy part right.

He continued, "So we could each go in a different direction."

Karina couldn't read thoughts but she anticipated what he was going to say. "Except I have nowhere to go." She felt hollow inside.

"You could find a place in the city. You could go somewhere.

But I'd like to make sure you're safe. I don't want my uncle having unnecessary doubts."

His uncle, always his uncle, and it gave her an unpleasant feeling. "So what do you suggest?"

"We renew our vows. Tonight. We can pick our own words. We can make it about mutual protection and alliance, so that we don't have to lie."

"You sure won't be in any danger with mighty Karina protecting you."

He shrugged. "You never know. Don't underestimate yourself. Anyway, it will help us. Do you say yes?"

This sounded like a weird sham, and still... "Do I have another great alternative?"

"I don't want to force you."

She couldn't figure out what his motivations were. "Why do you care about protecting me?"

"You'll find out in time, as you remember things, or as I get to know you better. Why ruin things?"

"I'm anxious not knowing where I stand."

His expression was serious. "At least know you'll have an ally. Our vows are magically binding."

"What happens if you don't obey them?"

"Magic will make you obey."

"So you could make sure your partner never cheats on you? Is that fair, though?"

"It's chosen by both parties. They can also break the agreement in another ceremony."

Karina chuckled. "Like a magical divorce?"

"Yes, but it can be just different terms. You can do that once a year."

This was a difficult situation, as Karina was almost a hostage of these people. At least Sat seemed nice, but even then, who knew? And she didn't care if he heard her thoughts. "We'll make vows just to protect each other?"

"Yes, loyalty, respect, protection. It's good for you, Karina."

It sounded like a good deal, even if more and more she got the feeling Sat didn't like her. But then there was the question as to why, which he was avoiding answering. Then again, she was the one most at risk. Alone in a place she didn't know, refusing an ally would have been dumb. "Let's do it."

Karina wore an entirely golden dress. Her hair had been braided in what looked like a bird's nest. She wasn't going to argue with Lumina fashion. Well, she didn't even know fashion in her own world. The thought reminded her of Zoe, and it hurt. Anyway, if they could change this agreement or even break it, it wasn't as definitive as it had sounded. Maybe Sat was right that it would be a good idea to have someone sworn to protect her in this strange land with strange people. She just had to remember to watch her thoughts and feelings in front of Firis.

She walked in the throne room. Firis sat at a high chair. There was a circle of chairs around the middle, where she stood. Satwalk entered after her, also wearing gold. Surprisingly, he didn't look as ridiculous as she would have imagined. It was a dim gold.

Firis took their hands. Sat was going to say his words first. Of course, he loved her and she loved him, even if she didn't remember it right now.

Sat looked in her eyes as he said, "At this point and time I bound myself to my words. I'll protect, respect, and support Karina, and make sure no harm comes to her. I'll measure my words and actions to make sure she's safe, well, and provided for."

Karina then repeated the words, trying not to think about what it would mean for her to provide for him. She wasn't supposed to think about any of that, considering she didn't remember anything. Her mind was focused on partnership and loyalty.

There was no party, nothing. Quite a simple wedding. After that, Karina was sent to a dressing room where an attendant helped her change to a nightgown, and she went to hers and Sat's room. Their room.

"You did very well," he said.

Karina already felt uncomfortable wearing a nightgown, even if it was very modest, more like a long t-shirt. She looked at the room and the fact that there was only one double bed. Okay, a king bed, not a real king's bed, but a king mattress—which was likely not what they called it here. "Where should I sleep?"

Sat shrugged. "You can sleep on the floor."

What a gentleman. "Didn't you just swear to protect and respect me?"

"Sure, but the bed fits two, doesn't it? I won't touch you. Still, if you are that bothered, we can prepare a comfortable bed on the floor. That said, I don't want my uncle having any doubt about your loyalties. We're stronger if we appear united."

Fine. The bed was wide enough. It wasn't as if she'd never shared a bed with friends during sleepovers. This could be the same. Kind of. She still couldn't call Sat a friend. "Do you kick or pull covers?"

"You never complained."

That mysterious past she had no idea about.

He lay down far on his side of the bed and soon his breathing steadied.

The temporary privacy for her thoughts was a welcome relief despite the discomfort of the lack of physical privacy. Thankfully he'd told her nothing had happened between them otherwise she'd gag. Yikes. Nothing against him, it just—it didn't feel right. But then, maybe he'd said that just to put her mind at ease. But he didn't seem interested in her, so it made sense. There had to be more to this alliance than met the eye. If it was about mutual protection, she could understand why she'd need it. But what did *he* have to gain? Being nice? For what? No, there was something else. There had to be. The question was what.

His uncle. He'd given enough hints for her to fear him, so perhaps it had something to do with him. But how could she figure anything when she lacked years of information? When she didn't have her past self to guide her? How could she think and at the same time conceal her thoughts and doubts enough not to raise any suspicion? Not easy to use her mind while at the same time pretending not to use it. She'd have to manage, though, if she wanted to find her answers and her way out. There had to be one.

8

LIGHT GARDENS

Birds singing. Sian opened his eyes and sat up panting. There was a soft bed beneath him, and soft covers over him. So he was no longer in Marisia. A few hours —or, who knows, days, months—before, he'd think he was dead, but his mind was sharp now. He was alive and somewhere else. His heart warmed hoping he was back in Siphoria. The room had orange walls and a huge window facing trees.

A familiar-looking woman was sitting on an armchair. Familiar. But it had been so long, like an eternity ago, before he'd been confined to a land where he didn't belong. He took a better look at her face. Yes, he remembered; she'd cast a protective barrier over him and Karina a long time before.

The woman noticed he was looking. "How are you feeling?"

"Alive." Words weren't enough to express how much it meant. "Who are you?"

"My name's Leena."

That didn't answer much. "Are we in Siphoria?"

She took a deep breath.

Sian saved her the need to answer, and said, "No."

He chuckled. "No need for drama. Whatever this place is, it's a huge improvement. Where am I?"

"We're in the Light Gardens."

He looked at the trees he saw from the window. "I see a garden. Does it light up in the evening?"

"We're the Northern ethereal city in Whyland. I mean, we were, before the portals were blocked. This is also where your mother lived and where your brother was born and raised."

Sian took in the information. It wasn't surprising that he didn't know anything about it and had always imagined Darian to have been raised in a simple village. To be fair, he'd never asked his brother much about his upbringing. "How did I end up here?"

"We went to Marisia and brought you back. Your brother carried you."

Sian looked at his arms. "Wow. Ain't I skinny?"

He didn't want to complain, but there was something he wanted to understand. "If you could rescue me, how come it took… I don't even know how long. Months? A year?"

"Six months. We had no idea you weren't in Whyland. There was a breach in one of the ethereal cities, Lylah opened an emergency passage and brought Darian. Cayla also came. The breach meant you could be in danger. Thankfully your brother guessed you were in Marisia. That's when we found you."

Sian snorted. "*Could* be in danger? Among huge beasts?" He waved a hand. "Nah, preposterous."

Leena nodded. "You're absolutely right. We failed you and could have lost you. We almost did. It would have been tragic."

Images from his battle against the Maris king, the attack on him, and his feverish visions flashed before his mind. At least it was over. Not sure why this woman was describing losing him as tragic, but he'd take it.

"Coming late beats doing nothing. When can I go home?" He could almost feel himself back in the city, seeing Malena again, eating her food, seeing his friends, Joel, even Raja. Karina was a long-gone dream, but at least getting his life back was a good start.

"There's a breach in Lumina. While this is not sorted out, you'll need to stay here, where you're safe."

"Lumina?"

"One of the ethereal cities."

Sian couldn't connect the dots. "Why would a breach in a city I have no idea exists be a threat for me?"

Leena looked at him and hesitated.

"What?" he asked.

"Every time we open a portal we risk Lumina coming in."

"So we're locked in?"

She nodded.

"Until how long?" he asked.

"I don't know. Days, weeks, a month."

"A year maybe?"

"I doubt it. Guardians are working on it and should have it all sealed within a few days. A couple months at most."

Sian exhaled in relief. That meant he'd be home in a reasonable delay. He'd lost hope of ever seeing Siphoria again, and having it within reach was like a dream come true. He could wait—as long as they had something other than unseasoned worms to eat. He looked down at his cream cotton shirt—and noticed he'd never worn it before.

He flinched. "Who changed my clothes?"

Leena shook her head. "Don't worry. You're right to protect your secrets, but they're safe with me."

He put his hand across his chest, feeling his privacy violated, knowing that she had seen him. "I never allowed…" He was rambling. Allowed what? Saving his life?

"I had no choice. You had an infected wound and poison. I had to clean it, but I did it myself. Nobody else saw you, Sian."

He was still uncomfortable, but he couldn't argue with the

woman's logic. In a way, she did care for his privacy. "Thank you."

She nodded. "Since when have you known it?"

That didn't make sense. "Known what?"

She pointed to his chest. "That you're supposed to hide it."

Sian swallowed. Where was she going with this? He looked away. "Can you not mention it?"

Leena got up and patted him on the arm. "I'll bring you dinner in a moment. I bet you're hungry."

He *was* starving.

She continued, "Your brother is eager to see you. Can he come in?"

"Can't I go out?"

"You're still weak."

Likely. Still, it sounded boring. "Can you bring me something? A book? Maybe a book about this city, unless it's some secret I'm not supposed to know."

She smiled. "The Light Gardens keep no secrets from their own. I'll find you something."

She left Sian to wonder why he would be one of *their own*. The door opened again and Darian walked in.

"How are you?" His tone was cautious as he approached slowly.

Sian waved his arms. "Great or terrible depending on what you measure me against."

Darian looked down then back at him. "I had no idea, I had…"

Sian hated drama. He waved a hand. "You say it as if it were your duty to save me. It wasn't."

His brother bit his lip. "True, but…"

"Thanks for carrying me." Now that he'd said it, he realized it sounded kind of humiliating. Almost dying had its way of ruining someone's dignity. Sian smiled, "I'll wager you've gained some muscle since you first came to Siphoria."

"I hope so."

Darian went silent.

Sian hated those moments when conversation died and asked, "So, your hometown? I guess you'll finally introduce me to it."

His brother sighed. "I had no idea I was raised here. They wiped my memory."

That was something Sian had never heard of, but he didn't think his brother was lying. "Did it come back?"

"Yes, once I visited here. But I didn't know about it."

A thought hit Sian. "Was that why... Why you didn't know me? Why you didn't know my name when we met?"

Darian hesitated, then said, "Possibly."

"Brother, you're a terrible liar."

"Not really. I can be good when I want to. Not sure I want to lie to you, though. I..." He looked down. "Don't recall." He looked up at Sian. "Maybe I'm wrong, maybe there was something and I forgot it when my mind was..."

"Yeah, yeah," Sian interrupted. "It's fine, and I don't care. It's not your fault."

"Sian... I'm sorry..."

His brother's sad face was getting to Sian's nerves. "No issue." He smirked. "So, do you think they'll wipe my mind once I leave?"

"I don't think so. Of course we can't tell people about it, but I don't think they'd keep it from you."

Sian rolled his eyes. "Cause I'm so nice and not a threat to anyone. That's kind of sad, you know?"

Darian shrugged. "If you insist, they can wipe your memory. Maybe they will. I don't know."

"I'm just wondering because I asked Leena to bring me books about this place. Now, it would be awful if I'd spent time learning something just to forget it."

"You say it as if you'd never forgotten anything you read or studied."

"It's different when my brain chooses to discard unnecessary information."

Darian laughed, then became serious again and stared at him. "What do you plan to do once we come back?"

"Plan? Almost dying has its way of ruining any possibility of scheming."

"True. But now…"

"I just woke up."

"And what do you think? I mean, we'll have to stay here for a while, but you'll return to Whyland…" Darian was thoughtful, then added, "You're no longer king. I think you know that."

Sian rolled his eyes. "Really? While I wasn't around to defend my position, someone usurped it? How shocking. Nah, who cares about Whyland. Little brother, you're looking at the Marisia King."

Darian made a face. It was somewhere between disbelief or pity. He was silent, though.

"Not impressed?" Sian asked.

"Surprised, I guess. It's already impressive you survived for so long."

Sian closed his eyes and took a deep breath. "That what I was doing; surviving. Killing the king was part of the deal."

"What about Darloom?"

"I blocked the place where it was. Not sure if it worked."

Darian nodded, thoughtful, then, after a moment of silence, said, "I'm happy to see you alive."

Sian considered asking why, considered saying something snappy, but then he just said, "I'm happy to see you, too."

"You're different."

"Months without decent food does that to you. Speaking of which, is my dinner coming or not?"

~

Karina had a war to wage in her own mind. She had to understand the world surrounding her, and yet, had to watch her thoughts when near other people, especially Firis. Her life was coming into a routine, which should be comforting, except it wasn't.

Faizana apparently had been her friend. It didn't feel or look like it, but it was true that not all friends were people Karina clicked with, and perhaps that was the case—or maybe it was something else. Sat swore his sister couldn't inquire into Karina's mind, but still, she wasn't sure. Faizana taught Karina about Luminous customs and traditions, mostly what to dress. She was a very unglamorous version of Zoe, except that Zoe had been kind, and Faizana seemed to think Karina was an uncultured primate.

They sometimes hung out with other girls. They played a game similar to chess, called magic and matter. The similarity to chess must have made Karina pick it up quickly. Still, Karina made sure she always lost. Faizana usually had a satisfied smirk when beating Karina, and it was best if it remained this way. The girl scared her for some reason. But no, it wasn't just that, but perhaps a need to hide her strengths, act as someone meek, just to make sure nobody looked at her too closely. Not that winning a game was any impressive strength, but still… Karina wasn't sure why she was doing it, just that there was a greater game at play and she was going to be careful while learning its rules.

The best time of the day was when she was with Sat. They usually went out to the woods under the excuse that he was courting her again—as if he'd ever courted her. She didn't think he had.

What they did was something else. Something difficult and challenging. Perhaps that was why she liked it.

Today they were near a pond.

"So, what did you have for lunch?" he asked.

Answering that question was like threading a different pathway in her brain. Instead of going for her memory, she went somewhere else.

A weird image came to her. "Raw worms." She could imagine the feeling in her mouth, something slimy and tasteless. It should be disgusting, but she felt empowered instead. Maybe she was just creating a feeling of being brave and eating something so gross could be part of it.

"Hum, interesting. For a moment I was quite surprised at the diet you guys have in your world." He smiled, then got serious. "Until you were surprised at imagining something you've never eaten before. Karina, that could get you killed."

This was so frustrating. He'd been asking her to perform increasingly difficult tasks. "Your uncle will kill me if I lie about what I ate?"

"Maybe. I told you. Very soon he'll test you. Depending on what you're hiding…"

"I don't understand. You insist your uncle is good. Why then—"

"He's cautious, Karina. You saw what the Guardians did. They almost killed you. They've kept you from your family. They kept us isolated." There was anger in his voice. Like everyone here, he did hate those Guardians. He continued, "If my uncle believes Guardians have brainwashed you, I mean… I don't know… If he thinks you're hiding things, he could want to protect us."

Karina wanted to ask why Sat cared whether she lived or died, but he was as unlikely to answer this now as he'd been dozens of times before. Maybe he still didn't trust her mind to carry secrets.

"There are no secrets, Karina," Sat said, in his annoying habit of replying to her thoughts. He added, "I do that so you're aware of how much you need to watch your mind."

Karina stared at him, thinking that she could just stop talking, since he would understand everything.

Sat sighed. "For sure. You can be silent, but that's not what I want you to train. In fact, I mean, no. It's actually how you prevent someone from seeing your thoughts. You send a different thought. But it's usually in images. It can work in words."

"Is there a way to block someone from entering our mind?" Karina asked out loud because she was getting creeped out by his replies to her thoughts.

"Of course there is. But it has two problems: one, it's hard. Can you guess the second problem?"

Karina wondered what the issue would be with not allowing someone in your mind. Oh, that made sense. "It would raise suspicion. Like when you don't allow someone to get in a room or open something."

"Exactly. The person will wonder what you're hiding."

"I see." Well, she'd better learn to conceal her thoughts before Firis decided to test her. "Let's continue, then."

Asking Sat anything was pointless, and maybe the way to find answers was by first learning to dissimulate her thoughts. If he had anything he was hiding from his uncle, other than this training, he'd never tell her while she wasn't very good at it.

He ignored her thoughts or perhaps didn't catch them, and asked, "What were we doing here?"

Karina visualized them walking hand in hand while he showed her the pond and evoked a warm feeling of companionship and even love.

Sat nodded. "Nice."

The tricky thing was that whenever she pulled up those thoughts and tried to create those feelings she saw him differently, almost as if the feelings were real, and she feared falling in love, since he'd never correspond.

Sat stepped closer to her, lifted her chin and looked in her eyes. Karina shuddered, especially considering he'd just heard her thoughts. He said, "There's no danger. You need to feel in love when near my uncle. It will protect you. But there's no way you'd fall in love for real. For me. It's not in you, Karina."

Right. As if he were horrendous. "What's in me, then?"

"You'll remember it slowly."

They went back to training. Their time alone together had a lot less clarification than Karina would have wanted since they had to use all the time to practice. But it was good, she wanted to learn how to dissimulate and conceal her thoughts. That was the only way she'd be able to navigate this crazy city and maybe find her way out. If there was one. There had to be one and she'd find it, but first, she wanted to make sure nobody knew she was looking.

Karina then returned to the palace, where she had lessons about the history of Lumina. One thing was clear: they were arrogant. That wasn't the end of the world, though. In her own dimension, many countries thought they were better than everyone else, and that didn't mean they were evil. Not completely evil, at least.

Lumina was the city with the most advanced magic, the most advanced ideals, the most advanced society. They were also the only city where every citizen was capable of wielding magic. Their food production, technology, everything had some magic behind it, and, again, that made them better than everyone. She got it. As bad as she usually was with history, hearing fifty times how Lumina was the best was more than enough to remember it.

Karina didn't want to think critically about the lessons anyway because she wasn't sure what could be considered rebellious thoughts and who could pick it up. Again, in theory the teacher couldn't feel other people's thoughts, but Karina didn't want to take her chances and focused on memorizing the lessons.

Still, her mind wandered while they went through their list of overseers. Weird name, right? They should have been mayors, but, again, she wasn't about to contest the information given to her. Lumina had a royal family which had been leading it for generations. Again, she had to hear names and names and how they were wise, fair, and intelligent. The line was passed either to male or female rulers. Usually the eldest was chosen, unless one of them was born with a special talent. Which talent was a secret, of course, and Karina wondered if that could be used for younger siblings to usurp the throne. But then, there were no accounts of sibling-to-sibling disputes. But then again, the history had been written by the winners.

There were a few battles against other cities that tried to attack them or that revolted against their fair rule. Karina wished she could know what happened and why exactly they'd been isolated. More than anything, she wanted to know how she'd ended up there.

So much to learn. Her heart ached thinking about her family and friends back home. Did her parents think she was dead? Did they suffer? That was a pain she didn't think was fair. At least she had to find a way to warn them, tell them where she was, tell them she was alive. No point dwelling on pain. What she had to do was learn as much as possible and get as good as she could in concealing her thoughts, hoping she'd be good enough to fool Firis. Yet, before doing anything, she had to make sure she stayed alive.

9

IMAGES

S ian's ragged image mocked him from the mirror while he trimmed his overdue beard. He stopped, considering what it had meant to him, and then decided to leave some hair on his chin. He shaved the rest, then braided the long part and left it as a reminder.

His hair wasn't as bad now that he'd washed it properly, just dry ends. Some trimming would be good but he could wait until he got back to Siphoria. He didn't really like the clothes Leena had given him; they were cotton pants and a tunic lacking any sense of style. Fine, the pants were black and the tunic was light green, it was a nice contrast. The tunic also had some beautiful embroidery. It was just not Sian's style.

He shouldn't complain, though. This was much better than wearing the same rags for months. And it was temporary. Still, it was annoying to depend on other people's generosity as if he were a beggar. He didn't even buy his own clothes.

His thoughts turned to Karina, when she'd been in the same situation. Of course it was uncomfortable, and yet, at the time he'd never considered it. He'd imagined that she'd be happy having everything given to her. He'd been told that was what women wanted. Well, perhaps it was his father who'd told him that. He'd also told him that they only cared about power—and that he should never trust them.

Ridiculous that he somehow allowed himself to be influenced by the guy whose wife ran away. Ran away with one child only. Sian wasn't as good at cloaking the pain as he'd once been, as he felt the sting with that thought. Misguided advice and harsh parenting methods were better than nothing. His father had been better for him than his mo—no, he wasn't going to call her that.

If there was one woman who'd filled those shoes for at least some time, that was Malena. He'd met her when he was twelve, and still, she became like a mother to him. His father had sent him to her business for reasons only later he'd understand. At the time, Sian was taken to the kitchen, got cake and stories. Somehow his father was satisfied that Sian enjoyed going to Malena's and kept sending him. From a father's very warped sense of education, Sian found a mother and later a business partner. He also found a sister.

Those were the things he had to look back and remember. Still, it hurt that his father hadn't even gotten a chance to repent. One time Sian thought he was threading on his father's steps. Not all steps, but the ones he thought were good. Now he didn't know where he was going anymore. All the power in the world didn't compare to time with friends. At the same time, time with friends was sour when powerless.

He was powerless now, and had been powerless all the time he'd been in Marisia, feeling as if his identity had been torn away. Well, it didn't matter; it was temporary. The only two things he could do for now was learn as much as he could, hoping they wouldn't wipe his memory, and maybe get to know Darian a little better. If he wanted, of course. Sian wasn't going to force an oblivious brother to acknowledge him. The thought stung. No, it didn't have to sting, he could put it away.

~

This time Sat took Karina to another pond. She was glad he didn't take her to a river, or glad that there were no rivers in Lumina because it would be very strange to explain from where to where they ran when in a small circle, and her mind would have a knot. Lakes made sense, even if the whole cycle of water was weird because there were no oceans. But then, many of the rules didn't apply. She was just trying to rationalize, trying to make it fit the logic she'd known until then.

"What do you like most about Lumina?" Sat asked.

It wasn't a question like a real question, but an exercise. Karina thought about the pond and nature.

He looked at her. "Do you think it's a good answer?"

"Is it not?"

Sat shrugged. "I don't know, maybe you should include me."

It wasn't that he was vain or self-centered, but that he must have thought it would convince his uncle better. Karina wasn't sure she agreed. "Can't I like the nature? I understood the question as being about the city itself, not people in it."

"Fair enough. Do you miss your family?"

The pain and the yearning were strong, but she made sure all her anger was directed at the Guardians. "Is it okay?"

"It's great. You can miss your family and your home, it's natural. And if you understand that it's the Guardians' fault you can't go back, it means you're our ally."

Karina sighed and hid the feelings bubbling beneath the surface. "Of course I'm your ally. It's insulting that Firis should think otherwise."

"Careful there. You don't want me to repeat myself, do you?

It's not you, it's the Guardians. Firis fears they could have affected your mind."

"Do you think they did?"

"Of course not."

He sounded so sure. "How do you know?"

Sat shrugged. "Hunch. Now, I know you want to understand a lot of things, but we need to get back to training. We're shorter on time than I'd expected. Firis is going to examine you tonight."

That didn't make sense. "But I've seen him before." He'd called her to his throne room, asked how things were going, and Karina always made sure to watch her thoughts.

Sat shook his head. "It's not the same. He's going to touch your head and look inside it. It's a lot more powerful."

"And he told you that?"

"I picked it up. Which also means you have to pretend you weren't warned."

"I can do that."

"Yes, I think you can."

Karina wasn't a mind reader but a shadow of fear in Sat's eyes didn't go unnoticed. He was terrified of his uncle despite his assurances that he was a good man. Why? Perhaps one day she'd find out. Hopefully not tonight, though. She'd better be flawless and not let any stray thought escape.

They dressed Karina in a complicated dress again. It was light blue and had longer pieces of fabric wrapping around her waist. The skirt was puffy. The attendants didn't tell her anything about a special dinner or party, but it was obvious because of the dress. Well, the attendants probably didn't know anything either. As always, they entered and left in silence.

Karina wasn't supposed to talk to them, but the proximity with people while maintaining a cold distance made her feel lonely. Not a good time to think about that. Technically, mind reading was a rare skill in Lumina, but Karina didn't want to take her chances. If she wanted to spy on someone, sending an inconspicuous attendant would be the perfect way to do it.

They did her hair with some pins with glowing stars in it. Karina looked beautiful. Truly beautiful, not just cute as she'd always considered herself. Perhaps not always. Who knew what happened in the years lost in her mind? Then again, it was that odd feeling, like stepping in a stranger's body. Beautiful stranger, and still a stranger. Karina wondered if that stranger had the confidence that should come with those looks.

She stepped outside her dressing room and saw Sat, who wore a dress suit too, in light blue, with a long coat. He was sitting on a chair and got up and gawked at her.

"You look beautiful."

Time to start the show—even within her own mind.

Karina laughed. "I do, right? You look good too. What's the special occasion?"

"You won't believe it. My uncle is having a dinner in your honor."

Karina decided to be playful. "Since when do I deserve any honor?"

He laced his arm against hers. "We're honored to have you recovered and well again."

"Well, let's celebrate!"

They walked towards the throne room.

Sat opened the door for Karina and the scene surprised her. She'd thought there would be more people at the celebration, but no, it was just Firis, sitting on a round table with food on it and set for three people. Quite an intimate celebration.

Karina sat down, and even though she wasn't sure if she was

breaking protocol or not, decided to show her appreciation. "Thank you for having us here."

Firis had a warm smile and a nod. "It's my pleasure to see you recovered and my nephew so happy."

Karina focused on all the food on the table, making herself feel happy to be invited to such an occasion, glad for the favor Firis was giving them.

The old man gestured to the food. "Let's not let it get cold." He got up, stood beside Karina, and took her plate. "What would you like?'

Was he offering to serve her?

Karina smiled. "I trust your wiseness' judgement."

Firis filled her plate. As they ate, she focused on the tastes and textures of the food. They then had an aromatic tea and a sweet fruit pie for dessert. Karina didn't know the yellow berries, and she thought she'd ask Sat that later. She wondered if there were fruits from her world she was forgetting, or if she had eaten this before and had forgotten. The sugar wasn't cane sugar either, and she'd have to ask later about it. Funny that in these last days she hadn't given thought about local sugar. Well, she hadn't eaten any sugar these days, so it wasn't surprising she hadn't wondered about it. Maybe she should have wondered about the lack of sugar.

Firis stared at her. "How are you feeling?"

Sat reached out and held her hand. She said, "I'm well. It's still strange to have a part of my life missing from my mind." She looked at Sat and smiled. "But I think some things, feelings, are coming back."

Sat smiled back and caressed her hand.

Firis noticed it. "Love sweetens everything, doesn't it?"

Karina imagined a warm feeling in her heart. "It does."

"Did any memory come back?" Firis asked. "Some information about the attack, something?"

She shook her head. "I wish it had. I still don't know what happened."

Firis kind eyes rested on her. "You're not supposed to be told, you have to remember it, or we won't get pure facts when you do."

"I understand."

"Are you happy here?"

Karina looked at Sat, with his delicate face, dark brown eyes surrounded with blond lashes, giving her a loving look. She turned to Firis. "Of course. Your nephew. This place. Everything is wonderful."

Firis narrowed his eyes. "Everything? Are you sure?"

He wasn't asking as if doubting or testing her, but as if her words hadn't made sense. Well, of course. "I miss my family and I worry about them." Karina tried not to focus too much on her lost home, as she didn't want pain to spoil that moment.

Firis nodded. "You wish you could visit them. Of course. So do we. It's not fair that you should be locked here."

Karina shrugged. "It's life. I'll do the best I can."

Firis got up and walked around the table, standing by her side. Karina wondered if he was going to pour her some tea, but instead he put his hands on her head. "I'm just checking your mind. I need to see if you are recovered."

Karina's heart filled with gratitude at being so kindly treated by this great, wise man. Of course, his kindness was because she made his nephew happy, and still, it filled her with gratitude. In truth, Sat made her happy. She recalled their moments by the pond, when they walked hand in hand. She could feel his lips against hers, his arms touching her, how they ended up lying on the grass, his hands under her dress, her dress tossed aside, the comforting feeling of skin against skin...

Firis hands moved away from Karina's head while Sat's hand tensed holding hers.

"Lovebirds." Firis chucked. "I won't take any more of your time, as I'm sure you're eager to retire to your quarters."

Sat got up. "Thank you, uncle."

Karina also got up and followed him to their room. She wanted to collapse on the bed, exhausted from the mental strain of creating false memories, feelings, and images. Sat sat on the bed, rested his forehead on his hand and sighed. He looked stressed rather than relieved.

Uh-oh. That was bad. Had she failed her test? "Is there something wrong?"

Sat shook his head, still not looking at her. "You were more than perfect."

"But you're worried."

He looked up at her. "I'm just tired."

Karina wondered if it was straining for him as well. Now that she was outside Firis mind-reading range, she had to remind herself that Sat's googly eyes were as false as the images she created, even if they could feel so real. In truth, she did feel exhausted. "I'll call the attendants."

She was walking away, when Sat held her hand. "Don't."

Weird.

He added, "My uncle thinks, uh, we're tired and not going to need attendants. Turn around. I'll untie the dress. I think you can figure the rest on your own."

Yes, he did untie it, and Karina went to her dressing room and battled that thing until it was out of her body so that she could put on her nightgown. She didn't want to ask Sat to help her because he was cold, distant, and weird. Plus it would be horrible if he saw her half undressed.

She wondered if he was thinking that the feelings and images she'd conjured at dinner were real, if they were her desires, fantasies. All she'd done was pretend they were a real couple, maybe too real, but that was because she'd been eager to get Firis out of her head. Sat must have seen those thoughts. But what had he expected? Anyway, she'd better not think about it now. It was never safe.

All she wanted was to sleep. Sat spent a long time in his bathroom. When he came back, he brought a thick blanket. Karina wondered if he had a fever or something, but he made a bed on the floor. More space for her. Perhaps she should have imagined making out with Sat a long time ago if that was it took to get the bed for herself.

He fell asleep soon, and she had some respite to have her own thoughts. Was Sat disgusted? Why wasn't *she* disgusted? Had the desire been fake, or had it been real? Or had she faked so well it felt real? Regardless, that wasn't the point. What mattered was that she had been capable of concealing her thoughts from Firis, the so-called best telepath in Lumina. So-called, because she had a hunch that their overseer was only second best.

Karina's thoughts gave way to slumber and strange dreams. She walked in a dark forest trying to find someone. There was a thick fog and, even carrying a lantern, she could see no further than a meter ahead of her.

Heart racing, she sat up, recognizing her bed in the Lumina palace, then wondering where Sat was until she recalled he was on the floor. That was his problem, not hers. The dream… it had been important. Her chest ached. There was someone, something she missed. Probably home, her family, her friends. No, it wasn't any of that. It was someone else, someone important. She'd been looking for this person, but she couldn't remember who it was. So many things she couldn't remember. Still, she missed that person—and it hurt.

The nightmares had stopped. Sian wasn't sure if he should be relieved or disappointed. Only now he realized how much

Karina had been in his dreams. At first, he thought the medicine was making him sleep more deeply. Now that he was well and treated, nothing had changed. The dreams still hadn't returned. Could it be something in the Light Gardens that affected the way he slept? Maybe. Or had it been his desperation, loneliness, and pain while in Marisia that led him to these dreams?

No. The pain in Marisia had turned them into nightmares. Karina had been in his dreams way before, since after he'd just met her for a short while, knowing only that she was the girl traveling with the princess, and then later realizing she had mysterious magic. At the time, he wouldn't have imagined... Then the dreams came, like memories that wouldn't go away. Now they stopped. Something was different, and he didn't know what it was.

Sian got up and went to the kitchen. It was strange to share a house with Darian and Cayla, as if they were a family. Well, in a way, they were. The sun hadn't risen yet. Solitude was something he came to appreciate in time. He poured milk and grains on a pan, wondering if he should also make some for his brother. No. They'd wake up later and it would be cold. What he wanted to do today was find Leena. More than books, he was going to take this opportunity to learn—and convince them not to wipe his memory.

Karina couldn't wait to be alone with Sat because the idea that he was upset at her for wanting him made her feel angry, rejected, humiliated, and who knows what else.

Of course, she had to drown all those feelings under a peaceful ocean of tranquility while she had breakfast with Faizana and her friends. Well, maybe not. Karina realized she could test whether people read minds, and imagined something very inappropriate concerning the girl. No reaction. Phew.

Sat had told her over and over that the only known telepaths in the castle were him and Firis. That meant her thoughts were safe around her. Or sort of. In the castle, one could never know.

Later, when she was alone with Sat in the woods, Karina didn't wait for him to start.

"What was the problem last night?"

His eyes widened. "Problem? You were perfect. I have to say, I was quite impressed."

That didn't make sense. "You were weird after."

He shook his head. "I was tired. Don't think you're the only one who had to strain your mind."

"Is that why you slept on the floor? Because you were too tired for a soft bed?"

"You talk as if you missed me." He wasn't sarcastic or teasing, just… she wasn't sure.

"I didn't. But if I did something wrong, I'd like to be told about it, not be given subtle signs in the hopes that I'll guess what it is."

He shook his head. "No signs. I just thought we'd convinced my uncle well enough. If anyone catches me sleeping on the floor, they'll figure we argued or something. I knew it made you uncomfortable, so I stopped once it was no longer necessary."

"Oh." That made sense. And it didn't. Karina wasn't crazy, there had been something odd about him. "You're not telling the whole truth."

"Are you also a telepath now?"

"No, but I can read body language, voice tone, like most human beings."

Sat shrugged. "People misinterpret body language. It was a tense night."

"True." Still, she had to say what she'd come to say. "Sat, what I imagined when Firis touched my head… I just wanted him to stop, I just wanted—"

"Aren't we glad my uncle's not a pervert?"

"You were also in my mind. What does that make you?"

Sat raised an eyebrow. "A concerned party. But you don't have to explain yourself. You did great. For a moment even I thought it was a real memory."

"I'm glad it seemed real. It's not like I've ever kissed—at least that I remember. But that was what I was supposed to do, wasn't it? Pretend our feelings were real."

"It was, and you were better than I expected."

"Thanks." Then a thought occurred to her. She didn't bother trying to hide it, and stared at him. "You're better than your uncle."

He raised an eyebrow. "Did you also imagine making out with him?"

Karina laughed. "Yuck. I mean you're a better telepath. You don't even need to touch people's heads."

Sat's playful mood was gone in an instant. "No. No, no, no. If I were a better telepath, I would pose a risk for my uncle, wouldn't I? That means I'd be in danger. So that's not a thought you want to have."

That pretty much confirmed Karina's suspicion.

Sat frowned. "It doesn't confirm anything!"

Replying to thoughts. That was definitely not a sign of a strong telepath.

Sat shook his hands. "Whatever. Maybe. Just don't entertain that idea."

"You just said I was good at concealing what I think. Can't you trust me?"

"I just did."

"Trust me more, I mean. There's a lot you're hiding."

Sat sat on a rock and picked a blade of grass. "You too are hiding a lot. I'd rather not strain you all at once. Some truths are more dangerous than others."

Karina sighed. "You're playing a dangerous game, aren't you?

And using me." *Using me for my magic* came to her mind, but that didn't make any sense.

"Life in Lumina is always dangerous. I'm trying to protect you."

It didn't seem dangerous, but then, perhaps walking on a knife's edge with Firis wasn't the safest situation either. "You're protecting me for a reason."

Sat cocked his head. "Maybe."

Karina hated depending on Sat, hated not knowing what was happening. "I guess one day I'll find out."

"Definitely." Sat crossed his arms.

Karina wasn't imagining, he was colder and more distant. She had to finish what she'd been planning on saying. "Let me just get it out of my chest: I'm sorry if I disgusted you or made you feel invaded last night. I was just doing what you told me, and pretending we were a couple."

Sat looked down and shook his head. "No need for apologies. It was amazing."

She still wondered why he was strange.

He looked at her and added, "I'm not strange, but you're so good that we don't need to work at creating false intimacy. You can conjure it out of thin air. It's better that way, isn't it?"

"Yes." Was it, though? Did it feel better knowing that the person who was closest to her didn't want to get too close?

"I meant romantically," Sat said. "We'd never fall in love, that's all, and it can sound strange because if we imagine it well enough, somehow it can seem like a good idea. I hadn't considered that."

Why was he insisting on that? "I'm not saying it's a good idea, I just wanted to know why you have to keep such a distance."

He stared at her. "Why? Would you like to kiss me the way you imagined last night?"

"No." Her voice was dry. "And that's why you don't need to

keep reminding me that we'll never have anything with each other. It's not like I'm going to grab you in the middle of the night or jump at you and kiss you, you know?"

"I know. Sorry if I gave that impression. I'm just being normal."

Karina looked down. "You're my only friend here." That was what really bothered her, and why it hurt to feel he was so cold. She hated admitting it, but perhaps being around a telepath was teaching her—or forcing her—to open up.

He was standing in front of her in a second, put his hand under her chin and raised it softly so that they looked at each other. "I'm still your friend."

His eyes were darker than usual. He opened his mouth as if to say something else but took a deep breath instead. For a second she did wonder what it would be like to kiss him, before she turned her thoughts to what she'd eaten at breakfast.

Too late. He must have picked that up as he stepped back, his voice cold. "We won't train anymore. Soon, soon, something big is going to happen. Meanwhile, try to study about the royal line."

She was going to tell him that the brief curiosity about a kiss was all it was, curiosity, but it was better not to make a big fuss out of it and he must have read her thoughts anyways. Changing the subject was a better idea.

"I've been studying. The royal line, they have a unique magical skill, right?"

"Yes," Sat replied, not looking at her.

"Is it telepathy?"

He turned to her. "Cause my uncle has it? No. I'm a telepath, and I'm not in the royal line."

"You're in the royal family."

He shook his head. "The skill marks the royal *line*."

"Genetics don't work like that."

"It's magic, it's different."

"What other skill does Firis have?"

"Firis? No. It doesn't mean that everyone in the royal line has the skill, just that it only appears in people in the royal line. Rarely. From time to time."

"And what is it?"

"All I know is that it's been conveniently erased from our records."

10

PLANS

Leena had agreed to take Sian to the edge of the city. He wouldn't call it a city, but rather a strange area, since so much of it was forest. He sat on a boat with her.

"What happens to the river? I mean, if we're in this ethereal place…"

"We're connected to the land beneath," she replied.

"Even when we're blocked from it?"

"Yes."

The boat moved faster and faster, carving its way on slower moving water. It wasn't going with the flow of the river, and there were no sails to pick up wind. Pure magic, and he should have known it. But something else was in his mind. "What if the land were destroyed? Would this city die?"

Leena paused as if wondering why he was asking that question. Hopefully she didn't think he wanted to attack the Light Gardens. Well, who would want to attack a city that barely existed? It was just curiosity.

She finally spoke, "We could move, but it would be painful, like when you move a plant from one pot to another."

"So there is a connection."

Leena nodded. "There is."

She clearly enjoyed teaching about their city and even about magic to Sian, and he was going to take the opportunity to learn as much as he could. But then… learn for what? Last time he'd decided to learn as much as he could about magic had been for a very precise goal. Now he had no idea where his life was going.

The boat then turned, as if there were a revolving body of water beneath it.

"What's happening?"

The old woman smiled. "Try to guess."

The river went on, but they didn't.

"There's a barrier. Is this the edge of the Light Gardens?"

"It is."

Sian touched the running water. "If I were to throw something on the river, would it go on?"

"What do you think?"

Asking questions was Leena's way of teaching. He wasn't going to argue even if he thought that just giving the answer would have been a lot more efficient. Sian pictured an object from the Light Gardens, and then realized it shouldn't pass the barrier. "It wouldn't continue. How does the water continue running, then?"

"You've guessed a lot. I'm sure you know the answer."

Had he known he wouldn't have asked. But the woman enjoyed getting the answers out of him, and he wasn't going to complain. Sian considered. There was a barrier. Nothing could cross it, and yet, they were tied to the land.

"It's not the same water."

Leena smiled. "Yes, we're like a copy from the land below, but not the same."

Very freaky stuff. Karina would want a logical explanation for it, so he'd better learn what it was to tell her. A knot took the place of his heart. *Tell her.* When? Sian tried to bury the horrible feeling that came with the idea that perhaps he'd never see her again. And yet he'd known. They'd known their goodbye had been forever. But then he'd been dreaming about her during all his time in Marisia.

"Are you alright?" Leena interrupted his thoughts.

"I guess. I do want to go back to Whyland. I miss... so many things."

"You won't have to stay here long. A few days at most."

"Don't get me wrong," he said. "I'm enjoying the opportunity to learn."

"It's your city, it's past time you learned about where you are from."

Sian smiled. He didn't really agree, though. His city was Siphoria. He didn't want to say anything not to lose Leena's goodwill. There were a lot more things he wanted to learn about the Light Gardens before leaving, and the woman was kind and happy to see him so interested in their customs, magic, and tradition. It was knowledge. The more he knew, the better he could be, even if he didn't know what he was going to be better at.

Karina had some rare moments for herself, between her lessons and dinner. Nobody had told her she couldn't explore the palace, and in theory she should learn everything she could about Lumina, so she set out to explore. Nothing in it ever rang a bell or even feel remotely familiar. Very hard to believe she'd lived in this palace for the last two years. Maybe she hadn't.

She'd come to the conclusion that Sat was a mind-reading prodigy, since he was way better than his uncle. In theory Firis was the greatest mind reader in Lumina, but he had to touch a person's head to get a decent reading. Sat didn't need it, but even he couldn't read minds from behind walls, so she stopped watching her thoughts as much when she was alone.

Karina took a back door that only servants used. Again, in theory, nobody had said anything about servants' areas being forbidden. She passed by the kitchen. There were some five people preparing food. The place was calm, organized, and yet something about it was creepy. Well, yes, the silence. Every servant she'd seen so far was quiet. Was this an order, some spell, or were they mute?

Karina decided to try, and turned to a girl rolling some pastry. "Hey, I'm lost here. Do you know how to get to the bedrooms?"

The girl didn't lift her eyes and pointed to the door. That didn't go as well. All right. There was a lot more to explore. Karina had seen an external elevated area near what she thought was the second floor. She went to the third floor instead and looked for a window. There was something to see indeed. About a hundred people practiced different forms of combat, most of them using what she would describe as magic. A few colorful balls of energy attracted Karina's eyes. Faizana was shooting and controlling them. The girl seemed very powerful. Near her, another girl made a defensive shield. Sat was at a corner listening to a short woman with purple hair who seemed to be a teacher.

Further down, some forty people trained manipulating metal spheres in the air. They sometimes flew high, and even had formations, like airplanes. On another corner, a small group controlled what Karina would call drones. They were not drones, though, at least not like the drones in her world. They were probably controlled by some kind of magic. So a lot of people in Lumina used telekinesis. And they were getting prepared for some kind of battle. Perhaps they were just ready in case someone attacked. Who knew? Her history lessons mentioned wars, claiming Lumina had liberated a few cities. Karina did wonder what *liberate* meant.

Her eyes scanned the grounds until she found Satwak again,

this time dodging balls thrown in his direction. He was surprisingly good. Well, it shouldn't be surprising, as he'd probably be able to guess his opponent's next move.

His opponent's next move. That was what Firis was good at. Karina wondered... And yet, he seemed to be the legitimate overseer. Sat's mother had been his younger sister. Karina had paid careful attention to that part, wondering if there had been any foul play or maybe Firis had taken one of Sat's parents throne. Not the case. Why did she have to pay attention to the royal line, then? Why, why, why? Those were the thoughts that consumed her, and not only why watch the royal line. Why everything.

In a way, she should be glad Satwak was now cold and distant. He'd never been her friend. She was a prisoner, even if perhaps he also was. One thing that had puzzled her was why he insisted so much on them pretending, but making clear he felt nothing for her. She'd tried to brush away these thoughts, thinking maybe it was her own hurt ego wondering why he was avoiding her, but now she came to a different conclusion: she wondered about it because it didn't make any logical sense.

If he was so afraid of his uncle, and if his uncle had to think Karina and Sat were a couple, it would make a lot more sense to simply try to seduce her. Less risk. She had to admit he was good looking, so of course he had a shot if he made it seem that he liked her. Then, maybe he didn't want to pretend all the time. No, it didn't justify the risk. What was it, then? Did he have someone else? Maybe he just knew he didn't like her for real and didn't want to deceive her. That would be honorable, but didn't make sense. When people are cornered and afraid honor goes down the drain, and he was clearly afraid of Firis, who, for some reason, had to believe they were a couple.

Maybe it was something in her past. If Satwak tricked her into falling in love with him, perhaps he'd be in big trouble when her memory returned. Her past. She'd been searching in vain for an image, a sound, something from the last two years. Nothing. Nothing. Just emptiness.

Karina felt someone behind her and turned. Firis. Her husband's dear uncle.

His stare was intense. "Like what you see?"

She smiled. "They're phenomenal. So much magic, power. I can't stop falling in love with Lumina. Sorry, I know in theory I should know it already, but…"

"Your love is welcome." He looked at the window. "They are powerful. And that's why the Guardians had to isolate us; they stand no chances in a direct fight. Cowards. Afraid of power." He stared at her. "Are you afraid of power?"

"I wouldn't mind having a little more of it," she blurted.

His stare was piercing. "That can be arranged." He caressed her hair. "If you ever want someone to confide in, if you ever find my nephew is not being good to you, I'm here."

Karina looked down. "Thank you."

"Any time you need. Come to the throne room. To my personal room. My nephew doesn't need to know."

"Thank you, your wiseness." She felt deep gratitude at having the favor of such a great man.

"Call me Firis."

Karina nodded. "If you'll excuse me."

She ran away, up the stairs all the way to her bedroom, closed the door, then sat on the bed, shaking. What had that been about? Yuck. His touch still felt as if a disgusting spider had walked on her hair, and the worst is that she had to block all those feelings while he'd been doing that.

Had he been *flirting* with her? Had they ever… No, no. Maybe he was just testing her. That made sense. He had to touch her head, right? To know what she was feeling. And he had to check if she was loyal to his nephew. What better way to do it than to flirt with her? He probably thought he was hot.

Well, he could be good looking, if he didn't look like he was forty or even fifty, and if he weren't creepy.

Karina prepared her bath. She wished she could bathe in alcohol or something. It couldn't be. She was imagining things. It had been just a test, which she really hoped he never repeated.

When she came out of the bathroom, Satwak was there, worry written on his face. "What happened?"

That was surprising. "Can you pick up thoughts from that far away?"

"No. My uncle. He was feeling satisfied about something to do with you. Feeling smug, superior, and, erm… You ran from him, confused. I couldn't get more than that."

Karina wondered whether she should tell him anything, but then realized that while she was wondering, her encounter with Firis had played in her mind. "Did you see it?"

"Not clearly. Can you remember it again?"

Karina brought up the memory.

Sat's face was somber. "You're wondering if you're imagining things or getting confused. You aren't. Firis has done this to me once."

"Flirt with you?"

He had a thin, amused smile, but then his face turned sad. "I wish. He stole my love."

"Oh." Karina's mind was buzzing. So Firis was capable of that. "But he's so old."

Sat shrugged. "Being overseer has its perks, I guess."

"What happened to her?"

"Died. Accident, in case you're wondering. And no, I'm not going to talk about it."

"Is that why you hate him?"

"Of course I don't hate him. I love my uncle. All he did was show me who she was, and that was good. If anything, I'm thankful."

"Awesome. Maybe you'll be thankful now." Karina knew it wasn't truly what he thought, but couldn't hold her tongue.

Sat shook his head. "He's going to pay more attention to you now, and that's the problem. Keep thinking of him as family, and keep pretending you don't notice his advances."

Karina couldn't bite her sarcasm. "Really? I was thinking of flirting back."

Sat rolled his eyes. "Whatever. Just don't let him know you find him repulsive. You ran away from him today, but you're lucky, he thought that was cute."

"I guess he *is* a pervert."

Sat sighed. "Maybe."

Karina was thoughtful. It didn't make any sense. "Why, though? Does he get a kick out of thinking he's better than you? Is it to test me? To annoy you?"

Sat shrugged. "He wants what he wants, that's all. He doesn't care enough about me either way to bother me on purpose or to spare my feelings. Try not to worry, though. Soon something will happen, and we won't spend much time near him."

"Right. Let me guess. You aren't going to tell me what."

Sat shook his head. "Sorry."

Great. As usual. Her thoughts turned to Firis again, and she tried to clutch on a small piece of hope. "You said I had to convince him. Maybe he didn't buy it, and that's why he's testing me."

"He bought it quite well, Karina. Perhaps too well."

Cayla was glad to finally see the portal tower, the seat of the Guardians. She knew that just by being able to open portals, in theory she could count as a guardian, but these were the real deal, they went to other dimensions and met with volunteers from other ethereal cities and dimensions.

The teleporting tower was guarded, as they were still on high alert because of the breach. Anika then took her to a different room, high in another tower, with twenty chairs around a well. This was their center, where they met. Not everybody had to come in person or teleport there as the room had small blue crystals on the floor, from which members could project their images. Cayla's own castle had some of those, and now she realized that they were meant for communication with the guardians.

There were twelve ethereal cities, but only eleven kept contact. The twelfth was Lumina, which had been sealed off. Somehow, they'd found an opening, and it was most likely their people who had attacked Cayla that night. They were interested in finding and destroying the guardians, so that nobody would prevent their expansion anymore. And that was what the Guardians were trying to find right now; how exactly this breach had happened. They were also on alert and avoiding opening portals until they were sure Lumina was sealed again. Cayla didn't know how they'd do it, but she was willing to help as much as she could.

Her own mother had never told her any of that. Now Anika showed it and explained it to her. The girl had been nice, but Cayla tried to keep some distance. Being Cayla's friend was dangerous. Still no news from Alessa, nothing. Her mother couldn't send a simple message, as usual.

As they left the tower, Sian and Leena came towards them, deep in conversation. It wasn't fair. Just because he'd almost died, now he got special treatment? Yes, he was Darian's brother, and no, she didn't think he should be executed, she was very glad she'd helped save his life, but he should at least face trial. If he had suffered, it was his fault only. Actions have consequences.

Perhaps it just bugged her that Leena seemed to pay more attention to Sian than to Darian, as if he were as important or even more important than him, when he wasn't. Sian was a war criminal with no history or interest for the Light Gardens, except perhaps for his own gain.

Sian saw her and waved, the signature smug smirk on his face. "Hey, sis!"

"Hi." Cayla had a half-smile.

It reminded her of Karina. Oh, Karina, it just broke Cayla's heart that he'd manipulated her so much. True, he'd been willing to die for her. Perhaps he did have feelings. Hard to believe, but maybe.

Hopefully Karina was happy back in her own world and had been over him for a long time now. She had to be, once she came to her senses. First, he wasn't that good-looking, second, detached and sarcastic as he was, it was doubtful that he could incite any deep romantic feelings regardless of his willingness to die for anyone. It wasn't even that noble. He wouldn't need to sacrifice anything or risk his life if he hadn't put Karina in danger in the first place. And maybe that was what pissed Cayla off so much. After all he'd done, here he was, like some welcome guest, even perhaps illustrious guest, when he should be nothing but an unwelcome burden until they could return to Whyland.

Darian sat down by the lake. Rae, the young man beside him, had once been his childhood friend. One more of those forgotten memories. Their lives had moved in such different directions. Now they talked about magic, recalling his innocent years when Darian yearned for the day he'd find out what he was good at. Rae for his part wasn't exceptional with magic, but he could create protective shields and manipulate small, light objects.

Rae stared at him. "We could ask Master Siren to teach you, you know?"

Darian wasn't actually looking forward to lessons with his old master. It would be like regressing to his childhood again. "No. I wanted someone closer to my level, who still remembers how to get the basics."

"I guess. You forgot a lot, didn't you?"

"They *made* me forget." Darian had to make an effort not to sound bitter or angry, realizing then that he still carried these feelings.

"But now that your memory is back, don't you recall your training?"

"That's now how learning works, is it? If it were, nobody would need to keep studying or practicing anything."

"I see." Rae was silent, thoughtful for a moment. "And you think you're a spell speaker?"

"That's what I've been told."

"Hum. How do you do it? Do you imagine what you're going to convince someone to?"

Darian waved his arms. "That's the thing, I don't do it. I have no idea how to do anything." He added, "That's why I thought you could help me."

"Well, I'm not a spell speaker. What I do is I imagine what I'm going to create. It starts with an image. That said, you deal with words, right? It should be something sound based. But I'm guessing."

Darian scratched his head. He didn't know, he didn't want to ask any of the masters, he wasn't even sure if it would make any difference in his life. For the last three years he'd lived away from magic, and found his identity in the process. And yet, there was something stirring inside him, as if wanting to burst out.

"You know what?" Rae said. "Just stop trying to figure it out.

Let's just sit and feel the wind and the sun. If something comes, great, if it doesn't, it doesn't."

That perhaps made sense. Darian closed his eyes, focused on the moment, on the nature around him, letting his thoughts flow. If there was magic to come, it would come out of its own will.

Karina was again drawn to the yard where she'd seen people training. The encounter with Firis had been troubling but at least she knew that the area wasn't off-limits for her. Plus, perhaps it was her way to see people. This time she went to the second floor, found the door leading to the yard and walked to its edge. The worst that could happen would be somebody telling her to go away. Big deal. Then she would go back to her room or to the studies where she should be listening to more history of Lumina.

From up close, they looked even more spectacular and numerous, divided in groups here and there, many of them manipulating balls in the air, some making shields, some just wrestling. Karina was awed with so much power. As much as she disliked Lumina, she figured people born there were happy, learning so much magic. Of course a part of her wished she could go in that yard and train, move things with her mind, just... feel powerful. Karina closed her eyes and took in a deep breath. She was what she was, and all she had to do was find a way back to a world where she mattered.

"Want to try?" A woman's voice broke her out of her reverie. It was she short woman with purple hair.

"What?"

"Train. You should train as well."

The woman was cheerful but firm. There was something pleasant about her. Karina felt sorry she'd have to refuse her offer. "I don't have magic." The woman stared at her. Karina thought she hadn't been convincing, so she shrugged and added, "Sorry."

The woman cocked her head. "Fair enough. I'm here if you want to give it a try."

Karina smiled. "Sure."

Right. What would she even do? Maybe learn some self-defense. Anyway, she wasn't even sure if she was allowed to train. The idea of whether she was or wasn't allowed to do something irked her. Not even at home, as a teenager, she had to watch her step. At home her life wasn't on the line either.

The woman with the purple hair was now near a group of people wrestling. Karina didn't understand whether they were using any kind of magic. Maybe it was just regular wrestling, which was kind of stupid. If they could shoot projectiles and conjure shields, nobody was going to get close enough to anyone in order to wrestle.

Some guys wore no shirts. Nice view. Like everyone in Lumina, they looked almost too perfect. Perhaps it was just that they trained a lot.

Satwak was there. Well-toned like the others. There was something, though. Something odd about it. Perhaps it was that he should have some kind of scar. He should, if he'd been in fights. Maybe he hadn't. Still. Suddenly she closed her eyes and it was all wrong. As if in a dream, he wouldn't take off his shirt. Was it Sat, though? Karina felt a shiver. It was as if she'd caught the thread.

She walked in her mind with a vague idea where to go, holding to an end of a line, in a dark hallway. There was a memory there. As scary as the dark hallway was, she wanted to continue, even if it felt like walking through something thick and viscous instead of air. Hard to move, but the memory was there. Just there, and she held the thread.

"Hey," Sat's voice startled her.

The thread, the hall, and her memory were gone. Karina came up quickly with something to say. "Nobody told me I couldn't come here."

"Not a problem." He held her face with his two hands and kissed her forehead. "Marital love," he whispered.

A public performance? Karina thought.

Sat nodded, then laughed. "You aren't playing your part, though."

"I was staring at you bare-chested. What do you call that?"

He thought for a moment, then said, "All right. We'd better go up."

"You don't have to stop."

He shook his head, then whispered. "We have more important things to do. We're leaving as soon as we can."

More information that didn't make sense. "Leaving. Weren't we isolated?"

"I've found a way. To another ethereal city, at least."

Right. And nobody had told her anything. Something else worried her. "Won't your uncle be upset if we leave?" Not that she cared what he thought, just that she feared what he could do.

"No. He'll be quite happy."

Karina looked at her suitcase over the bed. Not really hers. Suitcases, clothes, accessories, they were all strange to her. All she knew were her nightgowns and some dresses. Very little that she could call hers in this strange body and life.

She hadn't seen Firis any more since their last encounter, which was a relief. Perhaps she had over-reacted and maybe even Sat had misread his uncle. If he truly did have some past trauma in that regard, couldn't he also mix things up, the way regular, non-telepathic people did with words and body language? It made sense. Karina avoided thinking about that in front of Satwak, though. He'd still been distant, and it was a great reminder that he wasn't her friend.

Sat came in. "Everything ready?"

"I guess. Are you going to tell me where we are going or should I figure it out once we get there?"

He took a deep breath. "We're opening a portal to an ethereal city; Forestglare. The idea is to lure some guardians there and pressure them to attend our demands."

"Oh, now you can open portals. Weren't we isolated or something?"

"We figured a way. It's new and it's going to be a game changer for us."

"Can't you go to my dimension? Or to the city where the Guardians are?"

Sat shook his head. "These passages are too well guarded. Forestglare is tiny and nobody would think we'd strike there."

Karina didn't like the idea of striking a possibly defenseless city for no reason.

Sat shrugged. "We have no choice."

Well, maybe it would be her opportunity to find a way back home, and an opportunity to stay away from Lumina—and Firis. "And how come you need my help?"

"To open the portal. We'll be five people doing it. The strength of us all will make it open."

"But I don't have magic."

"It doesn't matter."

"Fine, I guess."

They walked to the teleporting tower.

Faizana, a guy, and another girl sat in a circle. There were more warriors around them. At the opposite door, more warriors ready to enter. It wasn't as if Karina had any power to stop them.

Firis was there too, and walked towards them. "My nephew and his wife, the loveliest of them all."

Literally everyone in that room was better looking than Karina, but okay. She was happy Firis was being kind to her.

Sat gave her a plaque, with the image of a very tall room, like a hollow tower. "Just look at it and imagine opening a portal there."

Karina looked at the picture, imagining herself there, as if this tower and that could merge. She felt goosebumps and something else, as if for a moment she could float and see her own body and the circle of people there. Light surrounded her.

The warriors stepped forward and disappeared. Sat put his hand on her head. She shouldn't let him. She imagined pushing him away, and his hand didn't touch her. For a moment she felt she could destroy that place. A second hand touched her head. It was like a metal hand, heavy, and there was no way she could fight it. She didn't feel or see anything else.

11

—

CROWN

Karina woke up in a large room with tree trunks and leaves surrounding the walls. The floor had moss but she sat on a sofa with a soft fabric.

Sat removed his hand from her head. "How are you?"

Karina blinked. "You. Your uncle. Both. You made me pass out."

"You were having a reaction to the magic. It could be dangerous."

He was lying but she didn't want to waste her time trying to dig out the truth. "We're in Forestglare."

"Yes. It all went very well."

For once it was as if she could see Satwak more clearly. In fact, her mind was making more sense of things. Karina looked around. "Are we alone?"

"You can never be sure. So many trees. They say the people here can talk to them." Sat twirled his hand and a blue light encircled them. "Now we're good. What is it?"

"Wouldn't it be easier to hear my thoughts?"

"You get annoyed. And I can't be sure the trees aren't telepaths."

Karina rolled her eyes.

He added, "In any case, you can't hear mine."

"Right." Then she decided to say what she was thinking. "You want to depose your uncle, don't you?"

"Of course not. Can't you see I'm here, taking this city, to help my uncle? That I'm devoted to him?"

"Cut it off. You want to depose your uncle and you need me. I mean, that's the only explanation for this fake marriage. What I don't understand is why."

"And you think I'm going to tell you?"

"No. But I can learn a little from your reactions."

"I'll watch my reactions, then."

"Careful. It's very easy to force me to cooperate when I have no other choice. Things can change."

Sat snorted. "Considering taking my uncle's offer?"

"Ugh. Can't you read my thoughts?"

Sat sighed. "You are getting into something, fine. But the less you know, the safer we are. Please always consider me as a devoted nephew, unless you would like to see me lose my head, or worse, be put in the stasis room."

"What room?"

"A place for dangerous people. Like a prison. What matters is that a tiny hint of suspicion is all it would take for my uncle to kill or imprison me, Karina, so I'd be very careful. Same thing with you. I mean, he might not want to kill you, since, you know, you're the loveliest and all."

Karina laughed. "Are you jealous?"

"Worried."

So was she. "I'm glad I'm far from him."

His face was serious. "The passage is open. He could drop by at any time."

"What is it you fear?"

"I don't know. It wasn't clear. I thought I'd take the opportunity to be away from his range, so I'd have my freedom with my thoughts, but I forgot an important detail; he's away from my range too."

"So he could be planning anything and you wouldn't know. But don't you guys connive together? Like attacking this place? Whose idea was it?"

"Mine. As a gift to him. I think he believed it. But he might think I'm no longer necessary."

"Find a way to be useful, then."

Sat sighed and looked down. "Yeah."

"I'm not sorry for you. You are deceiving, manipulating, and using me."

"I know…"

Karina stared at him. "So you confirm it?" For once it didn't feel good to be right.

"Maybe. You're the one saying it. I understand how you feel."

Not convincing. But what bothered Karina most was something about his eyes. "You're scared."

Sat shook his head. "The usual. I just don't have to pretend I'm not."

"Right. So here we are, playing a life-and-death game for which I don't know the rules. That's so helpful."

"Not knowing the rules could save your life."

"Not *my* life. That has been lost somewhere in my past."

Sat waved his hands, as if in despair. "It could save your physical and mental well-being. Don't you dare say it doesn't matter."

Karina stared. "Were you worried about my well being when you made me aware that our marriage was a sham? Firis could have caught us."

Sat laughed and looked away. "That would be easy to explain. I'd tell him I was going slowly with you." He pointed to a corner. "There's a dress there. I'll go out and you can change. The ceremony will be soon."

"I guess they don't send attendants in an invasion."

"Not in the beginning, but that won't be a problem for long."

Karina walked towards the dress. It was dark green. "Why do I have to change in this room?"

Sat laughed. "This is our house and bedroom."

"There are no beds."

He pointed to a corner, where some fabric hung. "Hammocks. They are extended at night."

Karina looked. "More than one. Neat."

"Forestglare people don't believe in sleeping together. They're smart."

"Is that why their population is small?"

Sat laughed "Sleep. It's different from... I suppose you know."

"That was a joke."

He cleared his throat. "I did laugh. Right. I'll be outside. Knock on the door when you're ready."

That place had warmth, life, and yet it was so simple. So different from the rich gold and white of Lumina. The dress was some kind of thin velvet. Karina was going to dress up as moss, perhaps to blend in with the environment.

She still hated not knowing so much, as if she were in a chess game without being able to see all pieces. Sat should trust her. Since Firis had revealed his creepo side by flirting with her, she knew who she thought was worse.

Even then, she shouldn't assume Satwak had noble intentions. It could be just a thirst for power, perhaps desire for revenge. And how did he even intend to overthrow his uncle? If that was indeed what he was going for, it was a dangerous game he'd gotten Karina into. In theory they were here to lure the Guardians. What was Sat's plan, then? Get them to help him? But if they had no way to defeat Lumina, it couldn't work, could it?

The dress was simple, one piece with a flowing skirt. One more dress she had no say in, like everything in her recent life.

Well, if that body was strange to her, no surprise that the clothes over her body would be strange too. Karina closed her eyes. No, she had to have hope, and this place could give her that. If it was true that Lumina was isolated, and Lumina only, it meant that she could perhaps find a passage from here, a way out. Yes. She'd have to. Meanwhile, she had no other choice than to play whatever games they wanted her to.

She knocked on the door and Sat opened.

He came in and didn't look at her. "It's a crowning ceremony," he said. "Just sit, smile, and pretend you're happy, regardless of what you see."

That meant Karina wasn't going to like whatever was out there. "Who's being crowned?"

He had a face as if she'd asked a dumb question. "Us."

"How was I supposed to know?"

He shook his head. "You weren't. Sorry."

She took a second look at her dress, which seemed inappropriate for such an occasion. "*This* is for crowning?"

"We're in local fashion."

"I thought Lumina was supposed to *enlighten* the other cities. Shouldn't we bring our *civilized* ways?"

Sat snorted then rolled his eyes. "Yes, but we're peaceful, understanding, and don't impose anything."

"That's great."

"There's something else you need to know. They have a well. To communicate with other cities, and with the guardians."

"A well?"

He nodded. "Many people use water for communication. There are even portals made with water. But that's not what I'm getting at. We'll need to talk to them."

"What are we going to say? Hey, Guardians, come and get us?"

"Pretty much. But not with these words. I'll do the talking. But you need to say something."

"Like: yay, I'm so proud to bring light to this dark place?"

"If you sound sincere, it works. Don't try to say anything against Lumina or Firis. He'll be watching us. Mind your thoughts too. You need to be the perfect, obedient, loyal Lumina subject."

"I can do it—on one condition."

He raised an eyebrow. "Condition?"

"Tell me what you're planning."

He laughed. "In Lumina one must never share plans."

"Great. Then I'll just be sarcastic."

"Great. Firis will put you in the stasis room."

"Maybe I can stay silent. He's not going to punish me for that."

"Stay silent, then."

"Sat, I just need to know where you stand," she pleaded. "Do you hope to align with the guardians and depose your uncle?"

He stared at her as if she were crazy. "I never said I wanted to depose anyone."

She exhaled. "I guess we're getting nowhere."

"Nope."

Sian ran his hands through the books in the Light Gardens library. This was completely different knowledge than even what he'd found in the Darloom castle. Darloom. That had been so long ago.

Steps echoed in the room.

Leena was beside him. "Enjoying your read?"

"I'm just looking." More looking at the way things were organized. He wanted to mention something else, though. "I've been thinking… Darloom. I never defeated it."

Leena shrugged. "Defeat evil. That's a romantic and idealistic thought. How can you defeat something that can regrow at every time? You control it, and keep your eyes open for any sign of return, that's all."

"Do you think it's coming back?"

"Darloom? No. I think it will look for someplace else."

Sian exhaled. "I see. It's just… Lylah said I would defeat it. Perhaps she was wrong."

"Maybe. Maybe you're misunderstanding what she meant. Why does it bother you?"

Sian looked down. "Not bother. Just curiosity."

"You're wondering if you'll have to play hero again."

"I never played hero."

Leena nodded. "I suppose nobody does. It's other people who call them that."

Sian snorted. "I don't see anyone calling me a hero."

"No."

Her face tightened in worry as she looked at a bracelet whose red stone started to shine.

Sian was curious. "What's that?"

"Emergency meeting."

"Can I come?"

Leena looked uncertain.

Sian added, "I just wanted to learn everything."

She stared at him for a moment, then said, "Come. It's your right."

There were some three people already sitting and waiting. Sian, as not part of their assembly, got a chair in the back, behind the main circle. He wasn't sure exactly why he wanted to see it. Perhaps it was part of his idea of giving his stay a motivation, a goal; to learn as much as he could about this and other ethereal cities.

Whatever they were going to discuss would remain within the Light Gardens, since there were no transmissions from other cities. They were just waiting for everyone to come in, when Cayla came with Anika. She stared at him as if he were a hair in a soup. Stupid. As someone with no ties to the Light Gardens, she had fewer rights to be there than him. Not that he wanted to think about his ties with that city. Or that he even cared. Her disgusted look shouldn't bother him either, except… Her ties to Darian. A reminder of how unwelcome he was to his family. It didn't matter.

Some few more minutes passed until a couple people came in.

A man Sian didn't know got up. "Forestglare has fallen. It's been taken by Lumina."

Murmurs of surprise echoed through the room. They shouldn't be surprised. If there had been a breach and there had been no news for a while, it could only mean they were planning something. Here was the result of their enemy's planning. Quite obvious, frankly.

"What do they want with Forestglare?" a woman asked.

The man shook his head. "Nothing. They want the Guardians to strike. It's possibly some kind of trap. But I'll let you all watch it and see for yourselves."

The image was going to be formed on the well. Sian was far and figured he wouldn't be able to see much. A sphere came up from the well, though, as if it was some steam. Soon he was looking at the image of a couple; a young man and a young woman with crowns that looked like tree roots. The first thing he noticed was how beautiful they were.

No, how beautiful *she* was. The perfect queen of Sian's dreams.

Literally.

The one who's been in his dreams. It couldn't, couldn't. It had to be a trick, something. She'd told him she didn't want to be queen, she'd told him all she wanted was him. How could this be possible?

The young man's words didn't reach his ears. All he could hear was the loudest buzz he'd ever heard. Was this some kind of torture? Sian looked around. Why was everyone sitting normally, looking at the images? How come nobody was contorting with pain? Nobody was horrified, deafened with that sound? He raised his hands to his ears. Pain. Just pain. Nothing. He could block it. He should bock it. But the buzz was stronger than anything and took hold of his body, or came out of his body.

All this energy; pain, anger, he didn't know what else, suddenly took form and was about to explode. He fell on the floor. Everything was blue around him. So much blue, then it all faded to black.

Cayla should be feeling anxious, but she was excited and giddy instead. For the first time she'd attend a Guardian meeting, see them in action, learn what they were about. Perhaps she should feel guilty because whatever they were going to see wasn't good news. Well, but it wasn't bad either. Not knowing was worse than knowing where they had struck. With information, one could plan action. Perhaps something would finally happen and end their waiting.

As Cayla followed Anika to the meeting room, she noticed that many seats were empty and that there were no transmissions from other cities. Sian was already there, looking bored. Well, why go, then? And what was Leena thinking? You'd have to be insane to allow Sian near any type of confidential information. Darian's brother or not, he'd proved to be untrustworthy before. Again, it was not that she wanted him tortured or anything, perhaps not even imprisoned, it was just that it was so out of place... Well, she wasn't making the decisions. And it wasn't her private information to worry about. She should rather worry about the silence from her mother's end and about Alessa. It just gave her a nauseous feeling. Maybe she should focus on learning what was happening. Maybe she could even be useful.

A man spoke. So Lumina was setting up a trap? It sounded naive. But then, if they'd been isolated for hundreds and hundreds of years, perhaps they'd lost the ability to make complex plans.

The image transmission was something she'd never seen before. She'd imagined that the well would be like a portal, like the one in the Darloom castle. Well, maybe it was like it, but it was being used differently. A mist came out of the water, and on the mist, the image that had been sent to the Light Gardens.

The couple on the image didn't look anything like what she'd imagined people from Lumina would look like. They were quite young and seemed nice. Wait. The girl, it couldn't be. Karina? What was she doing there? Cayla glanced back at Sian. His eyes were fixated on the image, but his expression hadn't changed.

The young man in the image said, "We're happy to bring back a Lumina tradition to Forestglare, incorporating it to our kingdom, as had been the case for generations. The people in this city are happy and we'll proceed with local coronation traditions, since, even though we're devoted to Lumina, we're also Forestglare's king and queen."

King and queen? That sounded strange. Cayla glanced again at Sian, wondering if he'd react. Still the same. No, something was odd, it was as if he'd been stuck in the same position.

The young man continued, "As much as we're glad to bring back enlightenment to Forestglare, we also want freedom for Lumina. We beseech again the Guardians to open our portals and let us go from place to place. We can negotiate the terms, and even give up on Forestglare or any other city."

So that was what they were trying to do; free Forestglare in exchange for having their portals open. Cayla wasn't that well versed in Lumina and Guardian politics, but she could already see that it was an insane request. With Lumina free, they could conquer all cities. Why this transmission then? Was this a first warning that they were going to conquer more cities? And what was Karina doing there? Since when she'd been in Lumina? Since when she could be queen there? Something was off.

Karina said, "We thank you for considering our request…"

A sound startled Cayla, and she didn't catch the rest of her friend's words. Sian was on the floor, shaking. Leena turned quickly and created a shield around him. Cayla looked around, wondering if they were being attacked. The shield dissolved. Sian was fallen on the floor. Hopefully not dead.

Leena said, "It's fine, fine. He's been sick for a while and fainted. It's nothing."

The people in the room got back to their seats and murmurs stopped.

Cayla exhaled in relief. She couldn't even start to imagine what Darian would feel if his brother died like that.

She approached Leena. "Will he be all right?"

"Yes, yes," the woman said as she gestured for someone to help carry him.

"What was that shield for?"

The woman's eyes were pleading. "You must have imagined that. You must. Nobody else saw anything."

Cayla nodded. "I guess." So apparently the shield was a secret. She'd ask Leena when she caught the woman alone.

The woman turned to everyone. "Please continue without me."

She seemed to be in a hurry to leave. There was something odd happening.

Cayla was torn between running to tell Darian what was happening and watching the rest of the meeting. She had a queasy, uncomfortable feeling about Karina. It was so completely unlike her… With that came a fear: seeing another friend hurt. As much as in theory, Karina in Forestglare, representing Lumina had nothing to do with Cayla… Didn't it? Cayla was the one who'd brought Karina from her dimension.

She tried to pay attention to what they were saying.

The man went on and on about waiting. He continued, "…until we know what we're dealing with. If we strike now, we'll be doing exactly what they want."

"What about Karina?" Cayla blurted.

They all stared at her. She knew she wasn't supposed to say anything.

The man said, "You can talk to one of our representatives later. Would you mind leaving?"

Cayla leaned back on the chair. "Yeah, I do mind. I'm not leaving."

The man shrugged. "Stay, then."

Darian was getting close. It was odd to look for something without knowing what it was. He sat quietly by the lake, feeling the breeze on his face, the sound of rustling leaves, the movement on the water, his breath interacting with the environment around him. Beneath all that was his magic, the magic that was still unknown to him. He didn't try to latch onto preconceived notions. Yes, he'd heard he was a spell speaker, but that wasn't *his* truth.

Whatever he was, he needed to find it by himself, not be told. Sitting in silence, he felt as if something was about to emerge. Even his friend Rae had left him. Strange to realize how he appreciated solitude. And there, almost there, like an old name he was about to remember, it was coming to him.

"Darian!"

He loved that voice but was startled at the shrillness in it. Cayla ran towards him, breathless, looking distraught.

Darian got up. "What's wrong?"

She looked around him. "*That's* what you've been doing? Sitting here?"

Cayla didn't usually annoy him, but she was getting close.

"Not just sitting," he explained.

She was breathless. "We need to do something. Your brother. He collapsed. Karina. I think they're doing something to her."

"What? Karina's here?"

Cayla rolled her eyes as if he should have understood her disconnected fragments. "No. She's in Forestglare. With Lumina. They sent a message. Your brother saw it, and he collapsed. He's in the hospital now. I guess you'd like to see him, right?"

"Yes. Soon. Is he still unconscious?"

"I don't know. I ran straight here. But that's not only it. Darian, the council wants to wait, gather information, then do a sneak attack or something. Karina is there. She's not with them, I'm sure. We need to do something."

"I'll go see Sian in a few hours. Then we can talk about Karina."

Her eyes widened. "A few hours? What kind of brother are you?"

"You say it as if you cared about Sian."

"I don't, but you should."

"Well, I do, and a couple hours won't make any difference. I'm doing something important now. I guess… you don't understand, but I feel it's urgent that I connect with my magic."

She stared at him in silence for a few seconds, then said, "Your magic. Great. Once you *find your magic*, do you think you'll help me get my friend back?"

"Didn't you say the council was onto it? I'm pretty sure the guardians have a better plan than we do, not to mention more experience. I know you're anxious, but sometimes you need to wait and trust."

Cayla squinted. "So you're not going to help me?"

"I didn't say that."

She looked down then nodded. "I see. And I guess your priority now is to remain sitting there."

He took her hand. "Cayla, that's how I can help. I can't do much when I have no idea who I am. Meanwhile, trust the council. Patience. Hurry never accomplishes anything."

"Find yourself then." She turned to leave, but she was angry.

Darian held her hand. "Wait. You do know I'm going to help you, right?"

"While trusting the council and spending your day here."

Darian didn't see what the problem was. "Well, yes."

"Great. I'll talk to you later."

"You're angry."

"Wow, you're so perceptive." She then changed her tone and looked down. "I wish you were more helpful, that's all."

Darian stared at her. "If I come back running with you now, I won't accomplish anything. Let me clear my mind, find my answers, then we'll talk. I promise."

He held her hands and she didn't pull them away. Cayla sighed. "Fine, then. I guess."

She kissed him on the cheek then turned around and ran.

Darian would take some two or three hours to get back where he was. No matter. Cayla was always a priority. It saddened him to see her upset, but she would understand. He sat and closed his eyes.

Drowning. Drowning, drowning, drowning, not in water, but in a black, viscous liquid. Was that how Sian was going to die? He felt a jolt on his wrist, then sat up, panting. That hospital room again. Leena was there, staring at him with worry.

The memories came back all scrambled and out of order.

Blue energy around him. Karina, the beautiful queen he'd always imagined, but sitting by someone else. An image formed with mist. Strange memories and fragments, and something exploding.

Perhaps the woman staring at him could be of some help. "What happened?"

"Do you remember anything?"

Really? She'd make him dig the memories? He took a deep breath. "A message from Lumina. In another city. Then... I don't know."

"Do you know what happens to magic that's repressed for too long?"

It was lovely and all that she wanted to start with her teaching and rhetorical questions, but couldn't she see the state he was on? Still, he replied, "No."

"What about feelings repressed for too long?"

As self-controlled as he was, this time he'd have to forgo politeness. "What are you getting at?"

"Explode. These things explode, Sian."

"And?"

"Your magic went out of control."

"My magic?"

She looked at him for a moment. "I thought you knew. Are you going to tell me you do not know what your magic is?"

He ran his hands through his hair. "I've been told... different things." Karina telling him that he was a spell speaker came to mind. "But to be honest, I never felt I had any magic."

"That complicates things."

"Not if you tell me instead of going in circles." He then added quickly, "I don't mean to be rude."

She shook her head and patted him on the head. "Don't worry. Now, tell me, have you ever felt something like electricity in your body? Or the ability to control electricity around you?"

Sian didn't like those memories. He looked away. "It happened once. In Marisia. But that was related to Darloom, wasn't it?'

Leena shrugged. "Maybe you were being influenced by him, but the electricity is your own."

"How come I never felt it before?"

She tilted her head. "These things can take time to manifest. Or maybe they'd been repressed. Now, I don't want to alarm you. Well, maybe I do because it's serious. I saw what happened and conjured a shield around you. If I hadn't been there, your energy would have killed every person in that room."

Sian heard the words but had trouble making sense out of it. Kill? Could it really be? He snapped his fingers. "Like that? The energy would have fried everyone? But how?"

"Like an explosion."

"So I'm a walking bomb."

"Sitting-in-bed bomb."

He smiled. The joke was terrible, but he appreciated her attempt at levity. "And what does it mean? Will I have to live in isolation?"

"No, but you need to learn to control it."

That made sense. "I guess you'll assign me some super electrifier who knows what they're doing?"

She had an odd look. "Nobody else has that specific type of magic, Sian. But we can help you find your balance."

He sighed, dreading what was coming next. "Meanwhile, I guess I should be put in complete isolation lest I explode again, right?"

"Oh, you'll be of no danger for the next few days, depleted as you must be. But yes, you should learn to control it, for the future."

Sian nodded, thinking that they'd use this to delay his return home. His mind kept coming back to Karina's image despite his efforts to forget it. He had to find some distraction, purpose. Being in bed did little to help him.

Leena continued. "I'm not sure you're aware, but nobody should know about your magic."

Sian frowned. "Why?"

"It's very—unique."

"Lots of people have unique magical powers."

"Yes, and some of those powers have special meanings and need to be kept secret."

Sian stared at her. "I'm assuming you're not going to tell me why."

"I can't. I can't, Sian."

"Great."

Leena left the room and Sian's questions. After a couple minutes she was back, with something in her hand. She approached his bed and showed a glass sphere.

"I was waiting for the right moment, but waiting might only make things worse."

That was Light Gardens magic, magic he hadn't read about in the Darloom castle. "What is it?"

"Take it. It has a message."

Sian took the ball and examined it, looking for markings of some sort. Instead, an image formed in it.

A beautiful dark-haired woman spoke, "My beloved son. I hope to give you these words in person…"

Too much for one single day. He wasn't about to listen to why his mother had abandoned him. He threw it against the wall. Sian heard a crash and didn't bother looking to see what happened.

SECRETS

ayla waited in the garden outside the hospital. So much waiting. She almost understood why Darian hadn't come with her. Maybe he knew he wasn't going to see Sian and didn't want to waste his precious time. Super precious, because sitting was soooo important. Nevermind. Maybe he was still digesting all the time that had been wiped away from his mind. Sometimes she still had to come to terms with the idea that his upbringing had been very different from hers and that he was from the Light Gardens.

Leena came out when the sun was already setting, holding something in her hands. Cayla ran to her. "How's Sian? What happened?"

The woman was startled. "Fine, fine. He was malnourished for so long, he's weaker than we thought, but he's being treated."

The woman was lying, not about the fact that Sian would be fine, but about what had happened to him, but Cayla let it slide. "You were missed in the council. They want to wait, but Karina is there, and I'm afraid…"

Leena seemed puzzled. "Karina? The girl that came with you last time?"

"Yes, she's in Forestglare."

"I saw the message. She's not there."

"She is! I can show you. And the council wants to wait and do nothing. She's my friend and I think she's in danger."

Leena stared at her in pity, which was quite infuriating. "I'm still watching Sian, but I'll come with you to look at the message. Is that all right?"

"I guess." Cayla noticed that the woman held three pieces of a sphere. "What is it?"

"Nothing anymore."

Other than a brief visit by his brother, who didn't seem at all concerned, Sian was left alone. In a way perhaps it was good that nobody had paid attention to his breakdown. On the other hand, it felt... How did it even feel?

He left the hospital in the early evening, with a warning that Leena would come see him the next day. That had been all. As if almost killing a bunch of people or perhaps getting close to dying didn't matter. Maybe it didn't. And again, Darian didn't seem to know anything about it and Sian was happy not to discuss it, glad to be alone with his thoughts.

Karina's image in the transmission wouldn't leave his mind. Part of him still doubted what he'd seen, but it was likely his heart tricking him into stupid hope. So it wasn't that she had anything against being queen, her issue was with being queen beside Sian.

But anger and resentment were stupid. Who knew what had happened to her? She'd left Sian with the conviction that their parting was forever. He'd screwed up and he knew it. Time had passed. She'd moved on. And still... All this time, she'd been in his dreams. Perhaps it had been Sian's own foolishness to hold onto hope. Love was stupid. Had he really fallen so low?

And yet… Had he been in Siphoria, with his friends, with his power, he'd just shrug it off and move on. Here, alone, after half a year in starvation and suffering, he lacked even the ability to lock away this stupid pain. And it was stupid.

He knew he should never trust any girl, no matter how sweet she was, no matter her declaration of love. Maybe it had been true then. It wasn't now. But what about her morals? Had they been fake? Lumina had killed some people to invade Forestglare, and apparently she had no problem with that. When Sian had wanted to take Whyland, he wasn't going to kill a single person, and yet she ran away from him as if he were a criminal. Hypocrite.

He had to forget these things, he had to let these thoughts fade away. What did it matter? He'd soon return to Whyland, Siphoria, his life. Tons of pretty girls there. Why settle for one? Perhaps what hurt more was the realization that he'd been so dumb. Poor dignity. At least nobody had noticed.

He lay awake on his bed for a long time, perhaps afraid of what his dreams would bring him. Afraid of seeing her again, afraid of the lies his sleepy mind would make him believe.

"Hey," a girl's whisper woke him up.

He opened his eyes and sat up. So sleep had caught him. The room was dark and he couldn't see who it was other than the outline of her hair. True, he'd been thinking about finding other girls before falling asleep. That was fast. Too fast. Maybe it was a vision. He reached out to touch her hair but ended up yanking it instead.

The girl slapped his hand. "Ouch. Stop it."

The slap made him awake, which he hadn't been a few seconds before. "Sorry. Just making sure you are real."

"I'm real and it's the middle of the night."

Sian's heart beat faster. He wasn't sure who she was, what

she wanted, and if she wanted what he was thinking she wanted, which, by coincidence was exactly what he'd thought he'd wanted before falling asleep. Oh, weird difference between theory and reality, between things you think you want and the true desires, those that get buried deep. Bury deep. That's what he had to do now. He smiled, wondering if she'd see it in that darkness. "To what do I owe the pleasure of such a lovely visit?"

"I know it might sound weird, me being here, but you're the only one who can help me."

Perhaps she didn't want what he thought, and he wasn't sure if he was relieved or disappointed. Also, why wake him up in the middle of the night? "What kind of help requires whispers in the dark in my bedroom?"

"There's only one reason I'd come talk to you."

Crap. One sure-fire way of getting rid of a girl was to make an inappropriate proposal. It didn't always work, though, because there were always those who said yes. But what could he say to scare a girl already in his bedroom? Plus, she could know Leena, and he didn't want wild rumors spread about him. No, maybe wild rumors would be good. He needed to be left alone. "On my terms, then. You need to do everything I ask you."

She snorted. "Are you insane? You don't know anything about it."

Prick. He got up and came to the lamp by the window. As the light flickered, he saw who the girl was, and was taken by revulsion just at the mere thought of what he believed she wanted. Sian was frozen in shock.

She got up quickly and turned off the light. "Nobody can catch us."

Uh, catch? This was more like a nightmare. It was hard, but he found his voice again. "I think you entered the wrong room. You do realize I'm not Darian, right?"

"Well, duh. But other than the fact that he's more interested in spending his days sitting by himself and he trusts the council like a fool, he can't do what you can do."

Still weird. For a nice moment he'd been convinced with the theory of the wrong bedroom and perhaps drunk Cayla. Now… But it was something else.

"Which is?" he asked.

"You saw her in the message, didn't you? Karina."

His entire body tensed and he felt like punching somebody. Was she here to tease him? Before his body language gave him away, he leaned back on the wall. "Yeah, so?"

"So? *So?* That's what you have to say? Did you believe for a single moment that she was there by her own will? That nothing wrong is happening to her? I thought you, uh, I don't know, liked her at least a little. Weren't you willing to *die* for her a few months ago?"

Sian took a deep breath. "That time it was my fault. I had to fix my mistake. This… I mean, she's free. We weren't married or anything. And we parted ways. I'm good with her decisions."

"And you think it's her decision to invade a helpless city? Do you have anything in that mind of yours? I thought you knew her, I thought you two spent time together. I thought you… I mean, you collapsed in the meeting room."

He felt as if the girl was poking a wound. "Just tell me what you want."

"We're going to rescue her."

"She didn't look like she needed rescuing."

"Sian, of course she does! Either they are mind controlling her, or maybe it was a love potion or something. It's not her, I know it. I thought you'd know it too."

The thought had occurred to Sian, but he'd done his best to ignore it, perhaps because it would mean clinging to hope, risking getting even more hurt than he already was. Still, Cayla could be wrong. And there were other issues with the plan. "Fine, let's assume she is controlled, whatever. How do you propose to get there, how do you think you can counter her love potion, and why do you need me?"

"I can teleport better than most people here. I think I know how to get to Forestglare."

"You... *think?*"

"Uh, I'm almost pretty sure. As to countering whatever they did to her, that's why I need you."

"Me?"

"Well, yes. You know what can break most spells, don't you?"

All he knew was that all this talk about Karina gave him a horrible feeling in his stomach. "Tell me."

"Sian, you can kiss her. I, uh, I think you like her, at least a little. I..." She looked down. "Saw your reaction in the meeting. And she... poor Karina, has terrible taste, unfortunately. Despite all you did, she still... liked you."

Opposite feelings were competing in his mind. On one hand, he was ready to follow Cayla to hell, if that was what would give him at least a tiny chance to get Karina. On the other hand, so many reasons to believe she no longer wanted him. "That was months ago. A lot could have changed."

"Well," she sighed. "I mean, true. She must have come to reason, right? You manipulated her and almost got her killed. It's only obvious. That still doesn't explain why she'd side with Lumina. It doesn't, Sian. And even if she no longer likes you, which I hope, you... I saw your reaction."

Sian was wondering if she always offended people when asking them favors. Nonsense. Why wonder? This was Cayla, of course she offended people. And she had no qualms wanting Sian to risk his dignity. Again, not surprising. "So you want me to go into enemy territory, then force a kiss on its queen, illegitimate or not?"

"Well, yes, to break whatever they're doing to her. They're doing something, Sian, and you know it as well as I do. If she's there, it's our fault. My fault for first bringing her to Whyland.

Your fault for bringing her again. Now be a man, assume your mistakes, and make up for them."

Sian got up. "What are you talking about? I assume my mistakes. I went to Marisia to save her. I got separated from her to save Whyland. It cost me months living in a horrible place. I almost died. Don't you come and tell me to make up for my mistakes."

"Well, then, let's go. Let's get Karina back to normal. The worst she'll do is slap you."

"Karina's sweet. She doesn't *slap* people." Sian could imagine her looking at him with tears in her eyes, an apologetic look, but not anger.

"That's too bad," Cayla said, bringing him back to reality.

Whatever his brother saw in that girl was one of the greatest mysteries of the universe. Speaking of his brother... "Did you tell Darian?"

"Are you kidding me? Like I told you. I tried. He's all, 'let's trust the council'. And worse, he claims he didn't see Karina there. Leena says the same. It's not her. I mean, are they that amnesic? How can they forget her face? Her voice?"

How indeed? Her face had taken over Sian's thoughts and dreams ever since he'd first met her. And he hated that, especially when she was far away, beside another man. He tried to focus on the issue at hand. "Maybe there's something in that message." He tried to recall what he'd heard about projections and messages. "There's a way to disguise a person in a message so that they'll only be recognized by those who..." He stopped, suddenly aware of what he was about to confess.

"Love them?" Cayla asked, with no qualms as to how it made him feel.

His voice was tight. "Or know them well. Or something like it."

She had a smile. "See? Your kiss will work."

Yeah, yeah. It felt great to have his one-sided love thrown on his face by someone who would probably mock him and humiliate until the end of his days. "It doesn't mean much. You also saw her, didn't you? Are you going to tell me your love is romantic?"

"No, but I like her as a friend."

"Great, because I was going to tell you I'm not sure you're her type."

"Of course I'm not. I'm not a manipulative jerk."

Just a heartless prick. Of course that wasn't Karina's type. He decided to change the subject. "And when do you want to do it?"

"Tonight. They're going through Forestglare's coronation festivities. There should be a ball in a couple hours."

"You can't be sure. There could be a time difference."

She shook her head. "A time difference, yes. Time passing differently, no. And I'm basing my prediction on the time they sent the message."

Sian got up. "All right. I'll get dressed." His brother came to his mind, and he stopped. "I still think you should tell Darian."

"No. He'll try to stop us."

Sian felt uneasy. "Won't he be jealous?"

"Oh, yuck." She put her hands on her mouth. "Sorry. Sorry. I didn't mean that. It's just, you're Darian's brother."

Sian laughed. "The feeling is mutual, sis." Not only because she was almost his sister-in-law, but nevermind explaining the rest. "But I didn't mean like that, I meant... I don't know, you trusting me, not him."

"It's not like he wasn't the first person I ran to. He decided sitting was more important than me, Karina, even you. Anyways, he'll understand—once we bring Karina back."

Sian sighed, realizing his effort to bury his worry and pain was unsuccessful. "We might not bring her."

Cayla shrugged. "We'll explain what happened."

Sian nodded. "Just a moment, then."

He got dark pants and a light tunic, more than ever upset

that he didn't have access to his own clothes. He went to the bathroom and changed, then cut off his braided beard. Reminder or not, he wasn't sure if she'd like it, and he didn't want to take any risks. Risk of her not remembering him, of course. He still had dark circles under his eyes, and his cheeks were unnaturally hollow. The tips of his hair were still dull. Sian hadn't been super privileged by nature, but he did the best with what he had, except that right now he was far from his best.

Karina had walked away from him when he had a castle, power, and was looking great. Now he was nobody, thinner than before, lacking all sense of style. He closed his eyes. True that she'd told him she loved him. And yet, how firm was her love? What had happened in these last few months?

A knock on the door startled him. Cayla's voice came from the room, "Sian, we can't take forever. If she's over you, she's over you, if she still loves you, you could come in rags."

He opened the door. "You assume too much."

"I'm just saying. Plus, if she fell in love with you, it's obvious she doesn't care about looks."

For a split second he wanted to ask her how she knew, what she knew, what Karina had told her, but that would be pathetic. Plus, Cayla was obviously trying to offend him. Give and take. "Yeah. Just like my brother."

Cayla chuckled. "I know, right? Plus he's either a compulsive liar or has serious vision problems."

Sian was stunned. Her reply had been natural, as if she hadn't noticed his jab. Maybe she hadn't. He thought about Darian. "Perhaps he says it because he knows it's not obvious." Cayla had a weird look. He had to explain. "See, other than one weird time when she asked me if my queen was pretty, I never told Karina she's beautiful. It would be like telling her she has two eyes or her hair is brown. Dull conversation."

"Very dull." Her voice was tight.

Now it was Sian who'd taken a jab at her without noticing,

too busy involved in his own memories. Oh, well. Cayla deserved way worse than that. If it weren't for the fact that she cared for Karina and had helped save his life, he wouldn't even be talking to her. Hang on. If she hadn't saved his life he'd be dead, so this conversation obviously wouldn't be happening. Months of semi-starvation had indeed affected his brain. He'd better recover soon, as he'd need his wits.

But Cayla then smiled. "Yeah, your kiss will definitely work."

Sian was about to tense, but he caught himself in time, relaxed, and shrugged. "Because I didn't like to tell Karina what she looks like?" He smirked. "Interesting line of thought."

"Indeed. We were explaining how she's fallen in love with you despite your looks, which led you to your brother, who I assume you believe is in love with me, and then you voluntarily mentioned yourself. Crazy jump, right?"

Yeah, Cayla was going to rub his feelings for Karina on his face until his death. He'd better ignore her. "And it's not interesting?"

"No. Just logical."

Sian nodded. "From where are we teleporting?"

"The small tower. The one we came from."

"There might be some security there."

"Not as much as in the main tower."

They were about to do something quite dangerous, and he wasn't sure if the girl in front of him realized the extent of how dangerous it could be. "I need to get weapons."

"No kidding. Question is: where?"

Weird. "What do you mean *where*? The weapons room."

"Oh. I… You mean the guardians have a weapons room? How are we going to break into that?"

Sian walked to the chest by the wall, picked up a key, and smiled. "With this. I wouldn't call it breaking into, though."

"How come you have a key? How come you know about it?"

Sian shrugged. "I guess Leena trusts me."

Cayla snorted. "People are stupid."

"At least I got the key."

They walked outside, towards the main tower. Sian took the lead, walking among the trees bordering that part of the city.

After a while, Cayla asked, "Are you planning something, Sian?"

"Right now? Planning on doing illegal teleporting to an enemy-occupied place, to kiss someone just to make sure being queen beside a handsome king is something she chose for herself."

Cayla snorted. "You think she'd choose to be with the Luminous? Did you ever talk to her?"

"Hey, I'm just prepared for the worst." Hanging on to hope would only bring pain. "And you? Since when you're best buddies and know her so well?"

"She was ready to do the right thing when she came to Whyland."

Sian waved a hand. "Right, wrong, it's all relative. Maybe they convinced her this is the right thing."

"Exactly. Brainwashing. Which you can put an end to."

"And that's why you need me."

"For sure. And before you point out the irony of it, please remember that even enemies sometimes form strategic alliances."

"Oh, I'm your enemy now."

"Maybe not now, but a few months ago you did take armed action against my kingdom. Unlike your brother and the people in the Light Gardens, I'm not amnesiac."

"I'm not leither, Cayla. I know who you are."

"Sure do."

Sian suddenly stopped. "What's your motivation?"

"She's my friend."

He stared at her. "Doesn't cut it."

"Why? Do you know what it's like to care about people? I..."

She took a deep breath and closed her eyes. "I don't want to see any friend of mine getting hurt because of me."

"She looked anything but hurt."

"Yeah, and you think she forgot you, which she should, and now you're butthurt."

Sometimes he wished he could strangle her. "Goodness, Cayla, you're so hilarious. Nothing funnier than a guy who risks his life and spends months in hell for a girl then sees her beside another man."

"I'm sorry. It's just… it's true. You're feeling jealous, maybe wronged, and because of that you're convinced that Karina doesn't need to be rescued. It's a problem if you don't believe in it, because you might not try as hard as necessary."

He turned and pointed a finger to the annoying girl. "Hey, it's my neck and my pride on the line, but I'm not a coward. If there's even the tiniest bit of chance that I can save her from her horrible fate of having a comfortable life as a queen from Lumina, I'll do whatever it takes. That doesn't mean I have to go there under a stupid illusion."

"Suit yourself."

Leena had told him he wouldn't be a danger to anyone for a few days. He hoped she was right, because he felt very close to exploding again, and he didn't want to kill his brother's girl-friend, regardless of how she treated him.

No, Leena was definitely right, otherwise Cayla would have been fried a few times already in the last few minutes. Sian also feared what would happen if he had to kiss Karina and be rejected. Nevermind the difficulty of getting her to kiss him. Would he have to force a kiss? He didn't like the thought.

They approached the building where the weapons room was. There was nobody around it, and he gestured for Cayla to follow him. As he was about to enter, he heard a voice.

"Halt!" A young man Sian didn't know came in their direction. "Where are you going at this time?"

Sian showed his key, then pointed to the door. "What does it look like I'm doing?"

"It's… Do you have authorization to come at this time?"

Sian shrugged. "Leena told me I could come at any time. I mean, any time. How do you interpret any time other than *any* time?"

The young man narrowed his eyes. "Why do you need weapons now?"

"Sleepless. Wanted to train."

The young man nodded. "Right. And you are?"

"Sian."

"Oh. Right." He changed his tone. "Good seeing you. Let me know if you need help."

Sian shook his head. "I'm fine, thanks."

He walked in with Cayla. She said, "That was weird."

"Not really. Same thing as Darian. I guess our family… something important, whatever." He didn't want to be reminded of his mother.

"I know your mother's from here, but other than that… Do you know why you're important?"

"Me? I didn't even know this place until some time ago. Apparently they didn't know about me either. That just goes to show how super important I was."

He found a sword and strapped on his back.

Cayla made a face. "You aren't going to a ball with that thing."

Sian sighed, putting the sword back, and took some knives and a belt. The loose tunic covered it. Cayla was checking the knives.

Sian handed her a short one. "I think you can also get some. If you know how to use them."

"I can demonstrate on you. Wanna try?"

"Careful who you threaten."

Cayla made her lemon sucking face. "I was joking, Sian."

"I wasn't."

He passed by the wall with pistols, but ignored them, since they didn't work in the ethereal cities. Perhaps it was worth a try. No, where would he put them? He turned to Cayla. "Got everything?"

"Yeah, I mean, I'm hoping we won't need to use any of this."

"That's why you bring them. Cause then you'll curse saying, 'why did I have to carry this stuff?'. If you don't bring them, you'll be cursing otherwise."

"Right. Let's bring weapons as a not-need-weapons amulet."

"That's what I'm hoping."

Cayla shrugged. "Well, Luminous have very strong magic. If trouble finds us, a few knives, or even swords, won't help us."

Comforting thought. They left the room. The young man nodded, and they again walked towards the woods bordering that part of the city, going in the direction of the small tower.

"So," Sian finally decided to ask, "Do you have a plan, or is it improvise as you go?"

"No plan is perfect... But like I said, they should have a ball in a few hours."

"Why? I missed the end of the transmission, but did they send their schedule or something?"

Cayla chuckled. "Pretty much. That young king said they would proceed with the traditional Forestglare festivities."

"And you know what these festivities are."

She nodded. "Exactly. There should have been a banquet yesterday, and there will be a ball today."

"And you assume there won't be any security at this ball and we'll be able to sneak in."

"Pretty much."

That made no sense. "Did you hear what I just said?"

"Yes. There won't be any security."

"Care to elucidate why?"

"Well, Sian, it's obvious."

"In your mind, maybe."

"Think. Why do they send a transmission basically saying 'we're here, and these are our plans for the next five days'?"

Sian took it in. "It's a trap."

"Obviously."

"That just means we go in, but not out. Is that your plan?"

She stopped. "No, no, no. See, they're waiting for Guardians, which we aren't. Not really, at least not the ones who do security, who would be going there to either gather information or try to do something."

Sian saw a bunch of holes in her reasoning, but decided to listen in silence.

She continued, "How do they know? You may want to ask. Well, easy, people who often travel through dimensions will have some kind of residual energy."

Sian chuckled. "You think they'll have a sensor or something?"

"Maybe. Their magic is very advanced."

"So advanced that they won't see us."

"They might see us. I don't know. The thing is, they are expecting something big to happen, like an attack. Other than getting Karina, we won't do anything else."

"She's the freaking queen. She'll be the most well-protected person there."

"It's a ball"

Sian sighed. There was no real plan. How predictable.

Cayla looked at him. "Do you have a better idea?"

"Not yet."

He agreed with her that the fewer people, the easier it would be to sneak in. Other than that, if they were caught... "Does anyone know where we're going?"

"I left a note for Darian."

That made sense. "I guess he's your backup plan, then."

"No backup. We'll succeed."

They came to the small teleporting tower. Nobody was guarding it, which was somewhat surprising. But there was another problem. "You do realize that there are people in the main tower right now, monitoring all portals, right?"

Cayla smiled. "All *known* portals. Forestglarians have houses in hollow trees."

"So we'll bust into someone's house?"

She shook her head. "I got a map of the city. They also have a place called silent sanctuary. There shouldn't be anyone there."

"And you can create a portal where there isn't one."

"Like Karina, yeah. She's a bit stronger, though. That's why the Guardians won't find us either. They'll be looking at a portal-to-portal communication. They won't be monitoring this tower either."

It was lucky that Cayla could open portals. And despite her attitude, her initiative to save Karina was wonderful. Sian turned to her. "I'm glad you're her friend and you're doing this."

"I'm glad you're coming to help me."

Cayla extended her hand. Sian took it and closed his eyes, wondering what he'd find on the other side. The chance of getting Karina back sent thrills through him, while at the same time, he could be risking his life just to have his worst fears confirmed. Fears. He wasn't going to be paralyzed by them.

13

A FORESTGLARE BALL

Karina couldn't ignore the fear in the faces of the Forestglare residents. From overhearing conversations, she gathered that the most rebellious citizens had been locked up, and the remaining ones either were too weak or scared to be a threat or had loved ones incarcerated. That fear couldn't come from nothing. Karina realized that some people were killed and felt revulsion in her stomach for being part of this. City of Light. Yeah, right. More like City of Death. Perhaps the Guardians had a point in keeping them isolated.

The dress she was going to wear was black, for once, which was a relief. If she returned home, she'd steer clear of any white for years. She sighed. If she returned. It was ridiculous to get dressed for festivities, as if the Forestglare citizens were thrilled to have a queen and king from Lumina. But if those were the rules, those were the rules. Karina would play the game. She put on the dress. Well, *you play the part, you dress the part.*

Karina felt a sudden chill. The sentence rang in her mind, trying to connect with a faint memory. The tip of something was in her mind's hand. If only she could pull it... But there was this barrier blocking her. She knew there was something there, there was something she had to find. The question was what. And how to get there.

～

Cayla opened her eyes. They were inside a huge hollow tree. That meant the first part of her plan had worked. Hopefully they were in the right ethereal city, there would indeed be a ball, and they would be able to rescue Karina. She let go of Sian's hand. Weird to ask for his help, after all he'd done. But he seemed to truly like her friend, plus he was Darian's brother.

He looked around. "Seems like you did it, sis."

Yes, she'd done it. Realizing they'd actually teleported and now would have to sneak in a Lumina ball gave her chills. She smiled, "Of course I did it. We still have a couple hours, from my calculations. The first thing we need to do is find out where they are having the ball."

"Not *we*."

Cayla just stared at him. "Care to explain?"

"Don't you get it? You can go back. Go back now and be safe."

"Right. And how do you intend to bring Karina back?" Cayla had the horrible feeling that he still didn't believe her friend would return with them.

"You did the hardest part; opened the portal. Karina's a teleporter too."

"We don't know. They could have done something with her magic, for example. We don't know, it Sian. Plus, if something happens, what are you going to do? Start living in Forestglare?"

"You say it as if you'd miss me. Plus, this is a huge improvement from the last place I got stuck trying to save Karina."

"You had it coming." Yep, she said it. She almost felt sorry when she saw him almost dying, but it didn't change the fact that he was simply facing the consequences of his actions. And just because they were working together didn't mean she was going to be a hypocrite.

Sian nodded. "Absolutely. Have you considered that maybe I have more stuff coming? It's my life. Not your life. If something happens to you, how am I going to look my brother in the eye?"

How dramatic. Cayla rolled her eyes. "The same way you spent your entire life: not looking."

"I had no choice in that, sis. Here we have a choice. You also studied military strategy, didn't you?"

"Of course."

Sian had a half-smirk. "Which is hilarious because your mother made Darian grand general, with his grand total of zero classes on the topic."

"Your point?"

Sian got serious again. "I was getting there. Strategically, it makes sense for you to return. You can bring reinforcements if something goes wrong."

"They can't fight Luminous."

"Not fight. Sneak in, I don't know."

"And how am I going to know that something went wrong? Plus, we need a quick retreat. Just for a second imagine you get Karina back and she has difficulty teleporting for some reason. The delay could cost your escape."

Sian paused as if trying to come up with a retort, but he couldn't. He thought for a moment, then turned to her. "Stay here, then. Wait for us."

"She's *my* friend."

"We need to be ready for a quick retreat. That's your part, getting us out. Plus, if we're going to sneak in, the fewer people, the less attention we'll attract."

Something clicked in her. His reasoning suddenly made total sense. She didn't even understand how she'd disagreed with his idea before. She said, "Fine."

"If I don't get back by sunrise, you should return without me."

No freaking way she'd do that. Still, she didn't owe him explanations—or truths. She nodded. "Sure."

He stared at her. "It's serious."

"I'm serious. I'm gonna be here. Long, boring, night."

Sian shrugged. "Doesn't Darian spend hours sitting in nature? Maybe it's your chance to learn what the fuss is about."

"Yeah, I'll be here with eyes closed and meditating. That will definitely help us with a quick retreat."

"Just wait. Wait here."

There was something about his voice. Hang on. "Hey, are you trying to do your spell speaking thing on me?"

"I'm trying to convince you. As far as I know, I have no ma..." For a brief second he looked troubled. He continued, "No... magic spell speaking thing."

She wondered if his hesitation was because he had some other magic. Hopefully yes, if that would help get Karina back to normal. He'd better get going. "Good luck."

He nodded in acknowledgement, then turned and disappeared in the mist. One guy in a Lumina-occupied territory. She didn't want to think about his odds.

From the top of a tall tree, Sian observed its surroundings. It was a unique type of tree, with a very thick trunk, and branches only on its top, so it was very hard to climb. The months of practice in the Marisia cliffs and mountains paid off.

A clearing had been decorated for the ball, which was going to happen outdoors. Some people arrived. Wearing masks. They were half hoods with holes for the eyes, with drawings portraying animals. At first he thought only the Forestglare citizens would wear it, but he noticed someone who was giving orders to a group of people also wearing a mask.

Perhaps it was a local tradition and they wanted to keep it. Still, what was odd was how this arrangement would make Forestglare and Lumina citizens indistinguishable. He'd already thought about his chances of getting in, and considered that people from Lumina could think he was from Forestglare and vice-versa. Very easy for a stranger to walk in. With masks, it was a piece of cake. This was too easy.

Of course, many of the Lumina attendants were likely highly trained warriors ready to step into action if anything happened. So that was how they were setting up the trap. Maybe there was something else Sian was missing, but if not, they mostly counted on their numbers and perhaps their alleged magical superiority. A tight bet. A lot of things could go wrong.

A group of some ten people came in. They didn't wear uniforms, but Sian could tell by the way they walked that they were guards. A couple came behind them, without masks. A blond young man and… the air left his lungs.

She wore her hair loose, a black dress, and no mask. In her head, a tiara, matching a necklace. Karina had never looked so beautiful. Sian closed his eyes, feeling his stomach turning to ice. Radiant and healthy, what were the odds she needed any type of rescue? The young man beside her wore a crown and no mask. He'd seen him in the projection, and yet, it was unnerving to see how good he looked. King. Karina was queen. There was no question what they were to each other. Not only that, she and the young man exchanged glances in a way that conveyed ease, trust, intimacy even. Was there any more to see? Anything to try?

Perhaps it was time to turn around and go back, leaving her to her beautiful dress and conquered throne. Both things she'd refused when it was Sian who offered. When blond pretty-face offered her, she had no issue.

Sian took a deep breath. Anger clouded judgement, and he needed his mind if he was going to give this a try. Did he even want to give it a try? To hear it from her lips? He had to do it, just in case, in the tiny chance things were not what they looked like. Plus he'd given his word to Cayla. Not that Cayla mattered, but his word did.

Karina and that stupid king sat on a dais. Sian thought the guards would stand around or behind them but no, they spread around the clearing. Fine, maybe they wanted to be on the lookout for any suspicious activity, but shouldn't someone guard their royalty?

A couple came in, and they greeted Karina and blond pretty-face. They were from Forestglare. Sian had thought that the two populations would be indistinguishable, but it wasn't true. The local citizens had defeat and perhaps even despair in the way they carried themselves. As much as perhaps they tried to pretend to be cheerful, it was a thin layer over a broken interior. Sad.

Lumina people stood tall and proud, feeling superior. This was another factor Sian would need to consider when his turn to sneak in came. But what struck Sian about the couple was how close they got to Karina, when there were no guards near them.

Sian scanned the trees to check if there were guards ready to jump into action or shoot anyone who tried anything, but no.

What kind of idiot leaves their queen in such a vulnerable position when they were hosting a party attended by their enemies? As much as there were guards around them, it was just a matter of one fast movement, and Karina could be dead. Their head of security needed a serious lecture.

Maybe it was something else, though. Were she and the stupid king bait? Sian fought the urge to go down there that instant and do something. If he wanted to rescue her, he needed to watch and plan, and now he was very much convinced that she needed rescuing, despite whatever she thought. If she wanted to be conqueror queen, fine, but please do so with competent security.

Look beyond. As with any situation that doesn't make sense, there was probably more to be seen. Sian fought his revulsion and took a closer look at the silly king, who smiled and seemed relaxed as he greeted people.

Then, it was just a brief second, but it looked as if he was examining the guests, checking them for something. How, though, in a brief hello? He also looked around a couple times.

Blond pretty-face expected something all right. Why he had no security around him was the question. Maybe he was super powerful and thought he could deal with any possible threat. Still, that left Karina in a quite vulnerable position. She for her part looked… hard to say. Calm and serene were perhaps the words. The perfect queen—as Sian had known for a long time.

Put it away. Better not think about the past and focus on getting to her. From the way things looked, that part wouldn't be hard at all. The issue was how to kiss her, and how to escape after that. He'd figure it out later. Sian took a deep breath and started his descent, the cool wind agitating his tunic.

The houses in Forestglare were in the middle of the forest, not like a village surrounded by woods, but instead they were part of the forest. Since most of them were hollow trees, an unaware visitor could even miss them. This made it easier to walk in it without being seen, moving from tree to tree.

He wondered how the Luminous had conquered this place. As much as the citizens were peaceful, all these trees should have made it a challenging territory. Perhaps they'd threatened the Florestglarians into submission and cooperation. That wasn't too hard to do. Imprison and threaten somebody impor-tant and well-loved. That could be the case. He still felt uneasy, afraid of what a desperate citizen could try and what it could mean for Karina.

Far away from the clearing, he found what he wanted; a couple leaving a house. He had two sleeper pouches on his pockets. In a swift movement, he ran to the two people and pressed them on their noses and mouths. They fainted, and Sian pulled them inside. So far so good.

Since they were home, the odds that someone would find them were slim. Still, Sian had better hurry and get finished soon. He took the man's mask. It looked like an eagle or some kind of bird. A Maris? How interesting. He took the woman's mask too, just in case, checked if there was anyone outside, and then left and closed the door.

He hid his belt with weapons under a bush. It would be foolish to attempt to enter the ball with that. Hopefully he'd have time to come and get it back, otherwise, well, too bad. Climbing on another tree, he examined the area. There was only one entrance, and Lumina guards dressed as partygoers all around the clearing. But they blocked people from entering only, not from leaving, as he watched a couple walking towards the trees.

In the clearing, a band played. Sian didn't know those instruments. People danced in groups, in slow movements. Hang on. Everybody did everything slowly. Something was odd.

He stared at the entrance again. Right. They were handing wooden cups with a blue drink inside. It was probably the drink that made them slow. Interesting. Was that what Lumina was counting on? That their enemies would drink the blue thing and get too slow? A little risky as far as strategy went.

Still, how to avoid that drink? In other circumstances, it would be super easy. His father had trained him to force himself to vomit. Almost killed him in the process, but thankfully Sian had been a fast learner and didn't die from poisoning. So it could be super easy; drink it, go to a quiet place, and get rid of it.

The hiccup was on how he was supposed to try to get Karina back. He suspected that she wasn't into puke-flavored kisses. To just pretend to drink and spit it out wouldn't work either. The guards were watching the guests carefully. Sian took a better look at the middle of the clearing and how the guests were behaving. He noticed that even some Lumina people were also intoxicated with that drink—or perhaps pretending. Slow movements. Right.

The guard handed him the cup with the sky water, as they called it. Sian lifted it slowly to his mouth, but poured it on his chin, as if he was having trouble with his coordination.

"Oops. Can I have one more?" he said slowly, with a drunk voice.

The guard poured it again. Sian took the cup and looked at it. "Pretty." The cup then slipped from his hand and rolled away. "Sorry." Sian smiled apologetically. "Another cup?"

The guard gave him an annoyed look.

"Please?" Sian pleaded.

Another guard stepped close to the first one. "Just go in. And don't cause trouble."

Sian smiled. "No trouble. This is wonderful."

He staggered into the clearing.

There were already about a hundred people there. The band played cheerful music, but he couldn't help but notice their sad, resigned faces, even beneath the colorful hoods covering half their faces.

The people danced in groups, some alone, a little like people danced in Siphoria at the Junction. The only issue was that the people here had no sense of rhythm and their slow movements didn't match the beats of the music. The drink, maybe? What kind of drink makes people off beat? Anyway. Not everyone danced, and this was his chance to walk, or rather, stagger, and observe. He found a place where he could see Karina from afar. She was whispering in blond pretty-face's ear, then turned. Her eyes immediately found Sian's.

What an awful position, to have a celebration where the attendees had to be drugged so they would look cheerful, plus who knows what threats were used against the citizens so that they would come.

Satwak had told her the drink was a Forestglare tradition, but still, she saw the way it was being forced on them. It was all wrong. Hopefully no one would attempt to kill Sat or Karina. Drugged or not, all it would take was one wacko. Plus there could be some Guardians coming, and who knows what they would do or what they would try. That was what she thought this whole celebration was about: luring them in.

Karina leaned over to Sat. "I know you're good." She meant a good telepath, but she didn't want to say it out loud, not even whispering. She continued, "But it's a lot of people. You couldn't possibly, you know, get a sense of them all."

"Of course not, but when someone is not in the same syntony as the others, it's striking and noticeable. Even non-telepaths can detect suspicious behavior in a crowd; it's like raising a red flag."

"Guardians would be smarter, wouldn't they?"

Sat shrugged. "Being smart doesn't mean you can change the way you think."

Just then, something made her turn. On the far corner, leaning against a tree, was a tall guy, looking at her. She caught her breath, unsure if it was the intensity of his stare, his brown curls coming out from under the half-hood mask, or his lips.

Damn it, Sat was just beside her, probably hearing her every thought. He'd certainly understand that she'd find a guy hot, though. Right? And she and Sat were not romantically involved anyway.

Sat leaned over. "Hey, this looks like so much fun. I'm going dancing. You should go too." He got up and joined the crowd.

This was so strange. Karina had been expecting that he'd reply to her earlier thought, maybe tease her or something, not that he'd ignore her and plus walk away. But it wasn't as if he were jealous or upset, just truly interested in the party. Perhaps he'd seen something and wanted to check. She still felt uneasy sitting there alone, when she knew most of the people there considered her an enemy. But then, Sat was so calm, and he'd sworn an oath to protect her. Maybe she should trust his judgement.

She looked again towards the brown-haired guy, but he was no longer there. Had she imagined him? No. She looked at the crowd. There he was, in its middle, moving with them. Again he looked at her. Who was he? What was odd was how he stared at her directly, something nobody in Forestglare had yet done. And she was staring back.

Karina caught herself and looked way. She was almost out of air, though. Well, no wonder, who wouldn't be breathless when a super hot guy looked at her that way? All right, she couldn't see his entire face, just his eyes, lips, and jaw, but still, something about him…

She scanned the crowd for Sat and found him dancing among a group of people, as if he were just as intoxicated as them. A walking—or dancing—target, though, because, like Karina, he wore no mask. That was some trust in his mental abilities.

Her eyes met the brown-haired guy's in the crowd again. Karina felt awkward because she didn't know how to flirt. Zoe always told her to look at a guy, count three seconds, then look away, but Karina always feared she'd make a fool of herself. This guy, though, she had trouble looking away. She had to know who he was. Sat was dancing, and he'd told her to do the same. Maybe he had a point.

Karina got up, descended from the dais, and walked towards the middle of the clearing. From this position, it was hard to find the guy, because she no longer had the advantage of the high platform, and she wasn't tall. The people were having fun and ignored her. She just moved with the music, while trying to get closer to the position where he was.

Never in her life—at least in the life she remembered—she'd wanted so much to get close to anyone. She wondered if that strong wanting wouldn't send flares that Sat should be picking up from a distance. Well, he'd told her to dance. Maybe he was too busy paying attention to something else.

Not very comforting to know he could be ignoring her, when he'd said he would watch for any threats or intruders. Still, at least he was leaving her alone, and perhaps finding the brown-haired guy was worth risking her life. She felt lost in that crowd, though, and also wondered if he'd really looked at her or if she was imagining it. Plus, she couldn't find him. Again she wondered if he'd been a vision or something. Did she still have her sanity, with her memory loss and all?

Walking and looking around could look suspicious. There was a circle of people dancing and she joined them, so as to look more natural. Did she look natural, though? Their dance didn't make much sense.

She felt something over her head. Before she screamed, she realized it was one of those hood-masks. Somebody held her waist and turned her, swiftly throwing a shawl over her. Karina was face-to-face with the brown-haired guy.

14

UNMASKING

He leaned over and whispered in her ear. "Let's go outside slowly. I don't think they'll notice us."

Karina's heart beat faster. He was quite direct, as if it were obvious Karina wanted something with him. Well, it *was* probably obvious. Too late to play hard-to-get and she didn't even know how to play anyway. He took her hand. Her heart was going to explode. They walked towards the woods outside the clearing. She feared someone would stop them, but perhaps Sat or the guards would only notice something if she felt threatened. Maybe the fact that she wore a mask and had a shawl over her dress meant people didn't recognize her. Still, shouldn't someone be wondering where their queen was? Well, not her problem.

The music faded behind them. As she felt there was nobody around them, she voiced the question that had taken over her mind, "Who are you?"

He stopped as if surprised, looked around, then said, "Let's go a little farther."

So there was something important he was going to tell her.

They walked a few more minutes, then he pointed to a thick fallen branch and said, "Let's sit."

He sat beside her and pulled out his mask. His face was quite striking, but what she liked the most was his eyes and the way he looked at her. He brushed his fingers against her mask. "So you don't know who I am?"

She almost apologized, explained she remembered nothing from the previous two years, then thought it was better to be cautious even if perhaps he was someone from her past. "Should I?"

"That's a good question."

His hand moved to the bottom of her hood-mask and he pulled it up. He caressed her forehead and brushed her hair away from her face. It felt natural, comforting. More than anything, she wanted to kiss him. Her eyes closed.

His forehead leaned against hers, then his nose touched her face. Was she really going to kiss a complete stranger whose name she didn't know? His lips were touching hers, and she parted them, inviting him in.

There was so much feeling in that kiss, and if felt so good, familiar. Images then passed through her mind. Her and the brown-haired guy, in another kiss, beside a well. A place with giant birds and pain. A girl with shiny black hair. Silver shoes. A woman with black hair. Flying machines. His name came to her mind; Sian. He was not a stranger. Realization hit her.

Karina gasped, pushed him away, and stared at him. "Me and you. We are..." She paused. Her memory was still blurry and she wasn't sure exactly how to explain what they were to each other.

"In love," He said. "Me at least. Do you remember me now?"

Sian felt like an ass having thought that she had forgotten him, that she had willingly chosen blond pretty-face. Karina had tears in her eyes, exactly like in all his dreams. Everything about her was like in his dreams. He wondered how she'd ended up as a Lumina representative, but he'd have time to ask that later.

She looked down as if thinking. "It's all mixed up. They brought me to Lumina. They made me forget, forget everything."

He kissed her cheekbone. "It's fine. Can you come with me now? I'll take you away from here."

She nodded.

He caressed her hair and kissed her forehead. "Let's go."

"Sian, I think there's a trap, they're planning something."

Sian kissed her hairline. "I know. But we'll leave soon." He kissed her face twice more, then got up and reached his hand towards her.

She looked so lovely he wanted to just sit there and keep kissing her, but they had to leave as soon as possible. Well, two seconds wouldn't make a difference. He pulled her closer and kissed her lips again, and perhaps it was a terrible idea because it took a lot of effort to stop it.

Karina smiled. "We need to go."

"Exactly what I was thinking." He promised himself no more kisses until she was safe in the Light Gardens. "Come."

One more wouldn't hurt. He kissed the corner of her face before turning in the direction of the sanctuary and their portal, walking at a fast pace.

They were walking hand-in-hand as if nothing had ever come between them. For now at least. Once they were back, he'd certainly have to talk to her. Marisia had given Sian plenty of time to go over his actions, and he wasn't proud of them. He'd need to find a way to explain, a way to apologize. Still, for now, she held his hand as if nothing mattered. Not surprising considering her memory was probably still damaged.

What bothered him most was how easy it all had been. Sian

kept his ears perked for anything unusual. He picked up his belt with the knives, then put back his mask and Karina's, sorry to hide half her face.

Flashes of Karina's life were playing in her mind like movie trailers without dramatic music and narration. Images and images, plus some disconnected sounds, so much that they were overwhelming. Her memory was snapping into place, but it was odd to acquire two years of memories in such a short time. Plus, she was a completely different person from what she'd been thinking in the last few days. Helpless and without magic were not descriptions that applied to her.

He wants you for your magic. That thought had been with her all this time, but it didn't match the reality she saw. Now she understood; teleporting. They'd wanted her teleporting. With horror, she realized that she'd been the one to open the portal to Forestglare. How many deaths on her hands? Her hands. Now holding the other person who once had wanted her for her magic. Had he changed, though? At this point it didn't matter much. If he got her out of Forestglare, afterwards she could try to figure him out. For now, her heart was leaping with the knowledge that the super hot guy she'd seen five minutes before was actually her—something.

This time she would be smarter. Right, coming from the girl who had been playing into her captors' plans until five minutes before. But that was because they'd taken her memories. She'd been right to feel that her mind had been transplanted into a different body, because, without her last two years, her mind was the mind of a fourteen-year-old.

Holding Sian's hand, she felt safe, which was a little ridiculous because last time he'd been the one to put her in danger.

Still, what mattered was getting away from the Luminous. She was curious about one thing. "How did you get here?"

"We'll talk later."

True. Masked and walking, they would be unnoticed by any onlookers, but if there were anyone around them, their talk about teleporting and who knows what else would probably catch attention. There wasn't anyone in that area, though.

Well, there wasn't—until there was. A faint woosh in the distance alarmed her. "We need to run." She realized she had no idea where they were going. "Are we going far?"

Sian obeyed right away striding forward and pulling her hand. "No."

But it was too late. A golden flying capsule passed them and landed on their way.

Sian kissed her face and whispered, "I'll hold them back. Run towards the silent sanctuary, that tall tree, there, yell for Cayla, and go without me."

What a ludicrous idea. "I'm not leaving you."

"Karina." He was almost growling. "Run. Save yourself."

She wasn't afraid of angry voices. "We'll sort it out together."

"Karina," he insisted, his voice dangerous.

Again a warning. Against what? What was he going to do to her?

She turned to him. "No!"

Then she saw who was coming out of the capsule: Satwak, blond curls flowing in the wind.

The blond boy walked towards them with his hands raised. "My name's Satwak. I come in peace. I need your help."

Before Karina had time to process the situation or even say anything, Sian had rushed towards Satwak, dropped him on the floor, punched his face, and had a knife on his neck. "Give me one reason not to kill you."

Aggressive Sian was new and somewhat terrifying. Karina

had always thought about him as calm, cool, and collected. She ran towards them. "Sian, no."

Satwak spat blood. "You're scaring her."

Sian glanced towards Karina then back to him.

Sat added, "And you're not a murderer."

"You're wrong," Sian replied.

With all her memory coming back so suddenly, Karina's mind wasn't the sharpest, but she suddenly realized why Sian was beyond himself. She knelt beside him and put her hand on his shoulder. "He never touched me, Sian. We never had anything."

"Why are you queen, then?"

"We pretended to be married. He said it was to protect me." Karina wasn't sure about the protecting part, but she had to calm him down.

"It was," Satwak grunted. "I had to protect her from my uncle. That's why I did all I did. I knew she loved you, though, and I respected that."

Sian glanced at Karina and then stopped pressing his knife on Satwak's neck. "What do you want?"

"I need your help."

"Right. Capture and enchant someone's love, that will certainly get them in a cooperative mode. You win points for creativity, but fail in basic logic."

Sat shook his head. "I didn't capture her, I mean, I did, but I had no choice. She opened a portal to our dimension, the first person in years. My uncle would want the teleporter who did it, so I had to bring her. He would have put her in the stasis room, from where he'd suck her magic. I prevented it by telling my uncle I wanted her for a wife. Lumina hasn't had teleporters in generations, it would be to our advantage if I had children with her. And plus, she'd help us conquer other cities. Forestglare was just a sample of what Karina can do. I did this so that he'd keep her conscious. Firis agreed and he thinks we're in love."

Sian turned to Karina. "Is that true?"

"The pretending part, yes, but this is the first time I'm hearing his reasons."

Sat again spit some blood. "My uncle is a strong telepath. I had to keep her mind safe from him. I also needed to convince him she'd cooperate with us. I couldn't tell her any of this or let her know about her past. She was learning to block her mind, though. Once I knew she was strong enough, I'd let her have her memories back and help me. I had to get to you."

"Me?" Sian sounded incredulous. "What can you want with me?"

"I have to depose Firis."

Karina knew that part, she just didn't understand how Sat planned on doing that.

Sian shrugged. "Yeah. Why should I care?"

"Because you should be in his place."

He rolled his eyes. "Yeah, yeah, yeah. Been there, done that. I'm not deposing any king for anyone anymore. I know I did it once, but that doesn't mean I wanted to become a professional usurper. Do your own dirty work."

What was he talking about?

Satwak shook his head. "It's different. Firis is too strong, and we can't organize any counter movement or he'd find out. The stasis room, it's horrible, he keeps most of the strong magicians there and sucks their magic. Of course, he only gets part of the original magic, but it's enough to make him quite invincible. My sister is in that room!"

He glanced at Karina. "My youngest sister, not Faizana. There's more. Once Lumina killed all the teenagers who didn't manifest any magic. That's how everyone in the city is so strong. Nowadays everyone has at least a little bit, but the weaker ones are silenced and taken as slaves."

He turned to Karina. "Like the attendants who helped you get dressed. You thought they were creepy. A little worse than creepy. I need to do something, but I can't. If I were to try to talk to anyone about what to do against Firis, they'd be caught the next day—and so would I. What am I to do?"

Karina felt pity for the city, for Sat's sister, but she still didn't understand what Satwak hoped to accomplish and why, of all people, he was singling out Sian, whose magic wouldn't do much against Luminous.

Karina crouched. "We could get the Guardians to help you, Sat." Sian gave her a horrified glance, probably annoyed at the use of the nickname. Karina pretended she didn't notice. "We can do that for you. Just tell us what you need."

"I saw Sian in your mind, Karina, I saw him, and then I knew all my prayers had been answered. Firis is not the real royal line, I told you so."

He had *sort of* told her so.

Sat turned to Sian. "You have a spiral on your chest, don't you?"

Sian tensed, glared at Karina, then shrugged. "Not sure. I have a bunch of scars."

That didn't make sense. "You couldn't have seen it in my mind. I never saw his chest." She had to make it clear before Sian started to think she'd peeked while he slept or something.

Satwak closed his eyes for a moment, then said, "No. I saw the scar in a dream, then I saw Sian in your mind. I connected the dots. You're the royal line, Sian, and should be our overseer."

He raised an eyebrow. "Because of a scar you don't even know if I have?"

"It's a birthmark, and it means you can manipulate electricity. Can't you?"

Sian was surprised, or perhaps even shook, but for a second only. "I bet lots of people can."

Sat shook his head. "It's unique, and it can defeat Firis."

"Great. I'll think about your city and your needs. Right now, if you don't mind, I'm taking Karina back. Try to stop us and you'll find out whether I can be a murderer or not."

"I'm alone here. If I wanted to stop you I could have called more people. Just give me your word you'll help me."

Karina didn't like that. "Lumina is invincible, Satwak. I saw you guys training. We'll talk to the guardians, but still… Even if Sian is your lost royal, and if he has special magical powers, what can he do?"

"His power, if he uses it, he could defeat the entire Lumina army."

"How?" Sian asked.

"I didn't find out that part."

Sian snorted. "Awesome."

Karina was quite relieved at seeing no signs of greedy Sian. He wasn't the least interested in an opportunity to be king, or overseer, of the most powerful ethereal city. Perhaps he had changed, or perhaps it had always been Whyland that he wanted.

And he was right that they had to leave. Karina turned to Sat. "We'll do our best to help you. It's in our interest too. Now we need to go."

"Right. After all I risked for you, you'll just take off, without even a word that you'll help me."

Sian turned Sat's face to him. "Hey, hey. You said you wanted *my* help. Now leave her out of it. I'll do my best. That's my word and I don't lie. I'm not going to promise the impossible and I'm not going to die for your dysfunctional city."

Sat shrugged. "Fine. Go. I won't stop you."

Sian got up and released Satwak, who got up as well. Karina wondered if he was going to try anything, but he seemed resigned. As far as she knew, other than his impressive mental abilities, all he could do was cast shields, so he wouldn't overpower them with magic. Sian took her hand.

"Wait," Satwak said. "How did you get here?"

Sian glared at him. "What does it matter to you?"

"It's just... some guards caught an intruder. A girl. Black hair."

"Cayla?" Karina was surprised, but she shouldn't. Sian needed help to teleport.

Sian walked towards Sat. "It's to your best interest to get her out."

Sat raised his hands. "It is. It is. But I'll need to break her out. I need help."

Sian sighed, then whispered to Karina, "The tallest tree in the sanctuary, it's our portal. Go there and teleport to the Light Gardens."

Whispering was stupid because Sat was a telepath, but this was not the time to explain that. Karina nodded.

Sat sighed "Yeah, go. Save yourself." He then put his hand on his head. "No. Wait. Firis is coming. He should be here at any second."

"And?" Sian asked.

"He can feel a strong teleporter. If Karina isn't here, he'll know where your friend, Cayla, where she is. If Karina gets back to the ball... it will confuse him. He'll be near a strong teleporter, so he won't feel your friend, who's further away. Karina can get out later at night. Otherwise you won't have a chance to get out with your friend."

"I'll go back," Karina volunteered. "Sian, get away, get Cayla away. I can teleport later. I could even use the main tower. It's easy now that I know I can do it."

"Not if he wipes your mind."

"You know where Karina is, and you know you can save her. She's been safe for days. A couple more hours won't hurt."

Sian's expression was pained.

"Sian, please," Karina pleaded, "She's my friend."

"I know. She's also my brother's love."

"I'll go back," Karina added. "Sat's right. I've been safe for days. I just need to give you time to escape."

Sian sighed. "Fine. Where do we rescue Cayla?"

"That direction." Sat pointed away from the ball. "The prison."

Sian hugged Karina and leaned his forehead against hers. "Be safe. Be careful."

"I will."

He kissed her briefly on the lips, then turned to Sat. "Let's go."

Karina walked back towards the ball, so many confusing emotions. She hoped Cayla would be all right. As for Karina herself, it would be easy to teleport away after the ball. Her only danger was if Firis inquired into her mind. But Sat didn't seem worried, so there was probably a good reason for that.

This was torture. For a brief second, Sian almost considered leaving Cayla and taking Karina to safety. But of course, then he'd never be able to face Darian or Karina, so he had to save her, even if the price was way too high. True, Karina had been safe all this time, but every second she remained was a second something horrible could happen.

"Is the prison far?'

"A couple more minutes," blond pretty-face replied.

"Can't we take your flying ball?"

"It only sits one." He sighed. "Listen. I'm sorry. I'm sorry if I had to deceive Karina, but I swear, I do, I always treated her well, and always made it very clear that there was nothing between us. And she loves you."

Dude was trying to get on his good side. "I just want to see her safe."

"I'm protecting her. I'm doing everything I can."

"It better be good enough. For your sake."

"I know. Listen, you should think better about what I told you. Lumina, we're rich. You'd be happy as its overseer. Karina will accept if she knows it's for a good cause."

"Trying to guess my thoughts?"

"Not guess. I'm a telepath."

If that was true, he could be a dangerous opponent. "So you say. Can you prove it?"

"You considered cutting my thing in pieces and feeding it to the birds. Not really, but the thought crossed your mind."

Sian shrugged. "It's a normal reaction, right?"

"Maybe. Not with those details, though. The girl we're going to rescue, Cayla, you don't like her much. You're some kind of childhood enemies or something."

"Point proven. Now leave my thoughts alone."

"But I can't, I need your help. All you want is to go back to your city, but you also want Karina. You need to think about your future. What are you going to offer her?"

"Want another punch? If you were so good at reading my thoughts, or her thoughts, you'd know that offering a usurped kingdom is the last thing she wants."

"But it won't be usurped, that's the thing. And I spent a lot of time reading her mind, Sian."

Sian grabbed pretty-face's throat. "Will you shut up or do I have to make you?"

"Fine. It's weird. You're usually against violence, aren't you?"

This time he took a knife and pointed at the annoying boy. "I'm beyond myself with worry, okay? So don't push me. I'll talk to you once Karina's safe."

"I'm sorry."

Sian released his knife and they kept walking. He hated wasting time with pointless conversation, and blond pretty-face's leaps in logic.

But Satwak didn't seem to want to be quiet. "She thinks you're hotter than me."

Again trying to flatter him. "Well, she's not blind."

Satwak shrugged. "I thought you'd like to know."

Right. So stupid. Since the dude wanted to talk, they'd better talk about something useful. "You know what I want to know? Your plan. You said I could use my magic to defeat Firis. How?"

"I… I'm not sure."

"You're not sure, and you expect me to help you?"

"Hey, I'm desperate. I'm hanging to foolish hope. But from everything I read, if you have the special royal magical skill you'll be invincible in Lumina. That means you can take it, and then free my sister. That's what I'm trying to do. Wouldn't you do that for your brother? Even if you don't get along?"

"I would come up with a decent plan."

"I'm trying my best! Do you believe in destiny?"

"Not really." He then remembered Lylah telling him that she'd had a vision. "But it's true that some people have glimpses of the future."

"Right, but think about it. Destiny brought Karina here, brought you here. What were the odds?"

"Very slim." Which led to the other part that bothered Sian. "What were you going to do if I hadn't shown up? Would you just keep her forever?"

"I was teaching her to block her mind. Once she was strong enough, she could find you. When I saw you in her mind, I knew something had been set in motion."

"A lot of maybes."

"Things have worked out so far, isn't that a sign?"

"You must be delusional to think that Cayla being caught and Karina staying behind means things are working out."

"They'll be safe."

"They'd better. Or you might have to say goodbye to more than your foolish plan."

15

COMPLICATIONS

Karina walked back to the clearing trying to look natural, as if she'd just walked out to take some air. She tried to keep her mind blank, afraid of Firis. Her bubbling emotions had to quiet down for now. She sat back at the dais. Not much had changed. Some people still danced. Perhaps less. Some were fallen, asleep on the edges of the main clearing. Fantastic. She scanned the crowd. No sign of Firis.

Then she heard steps behind her and her stomach dropped. She focused her mind on the music, on the people dancing.

Firis was beside her. "No idea how glad I am to see you alone."

Karina smiled. "Far from alone. Look at our lovely guests." She gestured to the dancing grounds.

He sat on the chair by her. "True. Where's Satwak?"

Karina scanned the crowd. "He was dancing just now. I don't know. Must be around here somewhere."

"Silly boy, if you ask me." Firis took her hand and caressed it. "Now, this is a lot better, isn't it?"

"What's better?"

He got up. "Let's dance."

"I think they dance in groups."

"Silly apes, these ones. They don't deserve you."

Karina got up, focusing on the music, on the moment.

Firis kept holding one of her hands but put the other around her waist. "I've given a lot of thought to what you asked me."

Karina truly had no idea. "What?"

"You wanted more power. Tell me, beautiful," he whispered in her ear, "how would you like to be the overseer's wife?"

Karina bottled down her feelings. "Why would you want Sat to replace you?"

He laughed and pinched her chin. "Are you a silly girl or a smart girl?"

Her fear was unlikely to go unnoticed. She'd better run with it. "I'm afraid of hoping for more than I can have."

"There's nothing you can't have. You know what you have to do."

"Perhaps I'm silly. I'm not quite following."

Firis smiled. "Be mine."

That was quite direct. "I swore an oath. To Sat."

"You care about your oath? That's not a problem. It was only for one year or until death. I can arrange it."

Karina gulped, shutting her thoughts away. "I don't want him to die."

"Are you telling me you prefer him?"

"No. I just don't want him to die." This was getting creepy and facing him was hard. She looked down. "I'm so afraid, so afraid. And so ashamed of my feelings. What kind of person am I?"

"A smart one."

"Everyone is seeing us. What will they think?"

"They'll think that they'll have to respect you twice as much from now on."

"What if Sat comes back?"

"He'll respect your choice. And mine."

Karina had a nauseous feeling. "I can't help feeling I'm being a bad person."

"Nonsense." He let go of her waist and pulled her hand. "Come. Let's make it official."

"Where are we going?"

"My house."

Panic was taking over Karina. "I'm still sworn to Sat."

"I told you it doesn't matter. And he won't mind. If it bothers you that much, I can do something about it."

Firis could probably feel her pulse pounding. And she had to keep him busy.

Karina stopped and pulled her hand. "No."

Firis' mouth twitched.

She continued, "Romance me, seduce me. Of course I want to be your equal. But you'd better treat me as one."

He smiled. "Forgive my overexcitement. And you misunderstand me. I mean to take it as slowly as you want."

"Tonight, then. I'll come to your room. After Sat is asleep."

He shook his head. "I don't mean to share you with my nephew anymore. Unless you're lying to me. Are you cruel enough to fool me?"

"No. I'm just—overwhelmed."

"Is that it? Or are you stalling? See? I need to be sure. There's only one way to be sure."

"I just need some time."

"I'll give you plenty."

He walked pulling her by the hand. Karina shut her thoughts away. Eventually she'd have to use her mind, though. They came to a tree and Firis opened the door. It was one of those one-room houses.

An idea hit her. She whined, "Here, though? These are not for people, but for animals. I deserve something better, don't I? Can't we go back to Lumina?"

He walked towards her and caressed her hair. "Oh, dear, you

deserve all the best in the world. And you have a good point. This is not a place for civilized people. But I'm tired of being civilized, aren't you?"

She was aware of his hand on her head, and her mind went blank. "What do you mean?"

"You know what I mean." He cupped her head and leaned in to kiss her.

Karina turned her head, focusing on the time she swore her oaths to Satwak.

"Still thinking of Satwak? If you're too worried about him, I'll order my men to deal with him right now."

Time to change strategy. "I don't even like him, Firis. I just didn't want you to think poorly of me."

He smiled. "Interesting."

Karina focused on food, imagining a nice plate of sushi, sad they didn't have sushi in Lumina, but still feeling hungry. "I'm starving. Can I eat something first?"

"You could. If I didn't get the feeling you're stalling. Kiss me. Or else, if that's not what you want, just say the word."

Karina pushed him away. "Well, I don't want it. Not like this. Like I said, either you treat me well or no deal."

"No deal, then." He walked towards her, about to put his hand on her head again. He'd probably make her unconscious or try harder to get her thoughts.

Karina stepped back and used her magic, directing an explosion towards him. Firis blocked it with a shield.

"Since when can you do magic?"

"Always." She was going to gag if she had to pretend for another second. "And you're the most disgusting man in the universe."

Perhaps it hadn't been a good idea to offend him. He lifted his other hand, about to shoot some ray. Karina made her explosion and collapsed the tree on them.

~

Sian and blond pretty-face approached a metal building, which looked like a temporary structure.

"I'll go there and check. Wait here."

"No." Sian realized something. "You are lying." How could he have been so stupid not to notice it before? "Cayla's not here."

Satwak stared at him. "Why? I mean, I can't be sure, but I'm not lying. Do you want to look at the prison?"

"I know when people lie."

Satwak raised his hands. "Fine. But it's true that Firis can sense strong teleporters. He'd also wonder where Karina is. If you want to escape, that's your chance."

"I came here to take Karina back, and that's what I'm doing."

"She can return at any time. You, on the other hand, need someone to teleport you. You'll be a dead man if you walk on that ball now. Go to the Light Gardens, plan something, then come back. Your special power works in Lumina, not here."

Sian moved to punch him, but the prick blocked him. Sian said, "I'll do what you're saying. You'd better hope Karina teleports soon. If anything happens to her, I'll personally make sure your sister never leaves that stasis room. Got it?"

Blond pretty-face nodded. "Perfectly. Now, rush before someone does find out that there are intruders in Forestglare. I'll go back to make sure everything is going well with Karina."

Sian hated that plan, but he also hated rushing senselessly onto something.

A red flare shone in the sky above the clearing.

"Oh, no," Satwak said. "I swear, it's not my fault. You'd better get away fast."

Right. That flare was likely a signal to the Lumina's forces. Sian's chest tightened. "Karina's there."

"She's not an intruder! How many times do I have to tell you she's safe! They'll send sentries. I need you alive. Please teleport away as fast as you can."

The only reason Sian didn't run back to the ball was because he feared for Cayla. Why hadn't she teleported back like he asked? He ran towards the sanctuary.

Karina's entire body hurt. She felt exhausted, with her magic depleted, but she had to escape. All she needed to do was run to a teleporting tower, and there was one not far from there. First she had to get all the wood and rubble away from her. She heard the sound of wood being moved and knew Firis was doing something. If he got to her, he could read her thoughts and maybe erase her memory again. Who knows what else he could do? And now, with his talk of *kiss me* and *be mine*, she was more scared than ever.

Depleted as she was, she had to give it one more try. *Boom.* The rubble was pushed away. No sign of Firis. She had to reach the main tree, where their teleporting tower was. She'd run three steps when somebody tackled her. Firis. She could recognize his smell. Ugh. Disgusting.

He put his hand on her head. Karina thought she was going to faint. Instead, images came to her mind as if someone else controlled it. Her meeting with Sian, the conversation with him and Sat. Karina focused on the periodic table, but it was too late. No, no, no, Firis shouldn't be getting that information.

Sian was just a few meters from the tree from where they would teleport away when he heard something coming fast in their direction.

"Behind you!" Cayla yelled.

Sian turned. And saw four huge felines, some kind of jaguar, running towards him. They had black fur and were bigger than the animals in Whyland. He had a split second to think. Outrunning them wouldn't be possible. If only he had his magic… He tried doing whatever he'd done in Marisia, but he didn't feel anything. No electricity, no weird magic, nothing. He'd have to fight his way out of this mess.

He yelled, "Teleport away! I'll hold them."

Cayla yelled something that sounded like *my ass*, but he was too focused on the big cats coming towards him.

What a lovely time not to have a sword, a lance, or a pistol. On the floor, he saw something; a long branch. He caught it just in time to swing it against his first attacker. Two more were coming from the sides. He swung the branch and hit one, but as a jaw came to him from the other side, he lunged forward and fell. A feline jumped on him and got stabbed in the neck. First one killed. No time to feel bad for creatures who were likely not aware of what they were doing.

Sian pushed the animal from above him—and saw the three others coming for him. He'd accepted and welcomed death before, but not now when he was leaving Karina in that place. Getting up fast, he picked up the branch, but and a jaguar caught it with its teeth. Sian let it go.

A jaguar came from behind and dropped him face down on the ground, pushing him with his claw. Sian scanned his mind for a solution, an escape. With his back to the animal, he couldn't stab him or try to defend himself in any way. So this was it. He wished he left this world in a more dignified manner. He trusted Cayla to try to save Karina. Perhaps she'd be much happier without Sian. He wished he'd said some kind of goodbye to Malena, Joel, Raja, even Darian.

A hand grabbed his. He no longer felt the weight of the paw on his back, but heard a scream. Crap. Cayla's.

"Get up," she pulled him.

They were in the teleporting tree. Jaguars were entering. Then they were in a completely black place. It felt as if walls were closing in on them, about to suffocate them.

"I can't," she said.

Can't? Teleport to the Light Gardens. Well duh. How could he have been so stupid? "Go somewhere else. Anywhere."

Strong flashes of light forced Cayla to close her eyes. When they stopped, she looked—and recognized the tower in Marisia. Other than that, horrible pain on her right arm—and a lot of blood: one of those cats had taken a huge bite of it. What a price to save Darian's stupid brother.

Screeches sounded in the distance. This time there was nobody to shield them. "Will the creatures attack us?"

"They won't." Sian was calm. He'd lived there, so he probably knew something. His forehead was bleeding.

"You're hurt," she said.

"You're worse."

"Did you find Karina?"

He just stared at her as if he wanted to murder her or something. Right. She'd keep that in mind next time she saw him about to become cat food.

Sian looked down and shook his head. "Why didn't you teleport away like I asked you?"

What. The. Freak. "Excuse-me? Sorry but you'd be dead by now if I hadn't stayed."

Sian looked down and shook his head. "No. I turned back because I thought they'd captured you. I wouldn't leave you there. That's what cost Karina's escape."

"But did you get to kiss her?"

He nodded. "I did, and yes, you were right. They'd wiped her memory." He shook his head. "We'd never make it back to the Light Gardens. The portals are being watched, aren't they?"

"I didn't think… that portal. But it makes sense they'd isolate Forestglare."

"It means Karina's stuck there."

Cayla wasn't sure, but a glimmer on his face looked like a tear.

"Quite interesting things in this mind of yours," Firis said, then removed his hand.

Karina was still immobilized, trying to come up with an escape plan, now that she realized Firis couldn't read much of her mind when he wasn't touching her head.

"Uncle." Satwak's voice. "I have a gift for you. I had to be sure, I didn't want to raise false hopes. Now I'm sure. I've found the lost royal."

What was he doing? It was probably too late to try to pretend to be on his uncle's side.

"Is that so?" Firis asked. "Why isn't he here, then?"

"Our magic pumas were sent to kill him. He won't make it out of Forestglare."

"Stupid boy. Who told you to kill him? I'd have more use for him alive."

"But he's too dangerous, isn't he?"

"Stupid legends."

Firis had been immobilizing Karina on the floor but then got up. She sat and was about to get up when the man turned, pointed his hand towards her and shot some kind of blue energy. Too late to block it. But she didn't feel any pain or get hurt. Instead, her body couldn't move. She'd been frozen in place, like some kind of sleep paralysis.

"Well, if he escapes," Sat pointed to Karina, "he'll be back.

She's our bait."

"And you're going to tell me that was why you wanted to keep her conscious?'

"Yes. I thought I saw something in her mind, but I wasn't sure. Now I am. And if he brings the guardians with them, even better. We can get rid of them in one swift move."

Firis took out a knife and pressed against Karina's face. "Do you think this… Sian, do you think he'll mind if she has one eye missing?"

"Why take any chances? She's already ugly with two eyes."

"I disagree. She'd make a lovely addition to my collection." He turned to Karina. "Perhaps you'll change your mind." Firis walked to Sat and put a hand on his shoulder. "My beloved, trustworthy nephew, who turned in his sister, sometimes I wonder…" He made a swift movement with his arm, then it sounded like something ripping. Sat fell forward. Firis continued, "Just wondering, I guess, if you'd predict my move. Perhaps I'm wrong. I'll get someone to patch you up—if you survive."

Firis walked away, leaving Karina paralyzed and Sat on the ground bleeding from a wound on his lower back.

She made an effort to speak. "Sat?"

"Alive," he grunted.

She didn't think Sat had been working for Firis, and she didn't think Firis bought it either. "You should have run away."

"Save. You."

Karina didn't see how Sat had saved her, but perhaps he got points for trying. There was a lot of blood and she couldn't do anything for him. "Don't speak, it's a lot of effort. I just wanted you to know that Firis, earlier, he was trying to, uh, kiss me. He threatened to kill you. He said, 'if Sat worries you so much, I'll kill him'. And maybe that's what happened in your past. Maybe she had no choice."

Sat grunted.

"Don't try to speak. I'm just saying."

Karina made an effort to move. No. It was wrong. She was trying with her body. She'd need to try with her mind. Two people came running towards them. Great. Faizana knelt beside Satwak. The other man watched Karina.

"Sat, Sat, wake up," the girl said.

Sat grunted.

Faizana turned to the man. "Go. Get help. Now."

The man said, "I have to—"

"Now!" Faizana roared.

The men ran. The girl turned to Karina and slapped her face. "You. It's your fault. If my brother dies, I'm going to kill you, and I'll do it slowly."

Sat grunted something.

"Firis stabbed him, not me."

"I saw you two dancing. I know what you want."

Karina rolled her eyes, surprised that she could do that much movement. "Yeah, yeah, he's so sexy."

The girl moved to punch her. Karina blocked her—with her mind. It wasn't her body she had to use, but her mind. She focused, and with another mini explosion, got rid of the magic paralysis. She got up and bolted to the nearest hollow tree, hoping to make an improvised teleporting tower and hoping the girl didn't shoot her. Better not hope. Karina turned and saw the girl with her arm raised, palm facing her. "Don't kill me. I'm bait. Ask Sat."

The girl frowned and looked at her brother. Karina turned and got in a tree. She focused on the Light Gardens. But that wasn't easy, because she'd never used a teleporting tower there. Did they even have those? Whyland. No. All the towers she knew were either destroyed or blocked. Her own home. She tried, and felt as if a dark cloud was suffocating her. She couldn't make it. There was only one choice. Karina closed her eyes. When she opened them, she was in the Lumina tower. About twenty guards encircled her.

She moved as if to walk through them, but two guards blocked her.

Karina stared at them in what she hoped was disgust. "Excuse me? Is there a reason you're blocking your representative queen in Forestglare?"

"We block all unauthorized entry."

"From unknown citizens. Simple soldiers. I'm Forestglare's Queen. Now let me go."

The guards spread out and she walked away from the tower. What an impact that saying something with confidence made. She couldn't believe she'd managed it, shook with worry about Sian, worry about Sat, not to mention that since she'd learned what had happened to her she realized her parents must be dying with worry and suffering. So unfair. Perhaps she should have tried to teleport home. Duh. From the Lumina tower, it might have been possible. She was about to return when she heard rushed steps and decided to run and hide. Stupid, stupid, why didn't she block that passage?

Maybe she shouldn't be that harsh on herself. It had only been less than an hour since she regained knowledge about her magic. With all that was happening, it was too much to expect her to know how to use it and to make all the right decisions, and plus she felt depleted. Karina ran downstairs and got in a room, hoping they wouldn't find her.

No. She had to start doing things right. Her chances of escaping these crazy people unscathed were slim already without stupid mistakes. She'd have to get things right from now on. That said, she was probably still too weak to teleport back home. And if Sian's magic was strongest in Lumina, closing the passage wouldn't have been smart. She closed her eyes. If Sian was alive. The thought of losing him right after finding him again was too much. No, she wasn't going to entertain that thought. He was smart, Cayla was smart. Sat wanted him alive. Of course they'd escape.

16

NEW PLANS

Cayla listened as Sian told her what had happened in Forestglare while wrapping her arm in a piece of cloth. They'd entered a chamber in that tower and closed the door. So far, no Maris had come, but she was still afraid.

"There," he said as he finished tying her arm. "If you don't get proper medical attention in a few hours, you'll lose your arm. Darian will kill me."

He'd said it about ten times now, as if Darian were some kind of murderer. Cayla was sick of replying to that so she just ignored him, thinking about what he'd told her instead. "But if you're the royal line, let's assume it's true, if you died, there would still be Darian."

"Exactly. One reason not to lose an arm to keep me alive."

Ignoring wasn't working and she was losing her patience. "Will you shut up! Of course Darian wants to see you alive and he'll be glad I saved you. Where do you get these freaky ideas?"

"My freaky head."

"Karina, too. I told you she's my friend. How would she feel if you died?"

Sian shrugged. "Didn't you say she should forget me? Perhaps it would be best for her."

"Fine. If I ever see you almost dying again, I won't interfere. Now it's too late to go back, so don't piss me off."

"Well, had you teleported back like I asked you, none of this would be happening."

"Yeah, yeah, yeah. Your thankfulness is touching, Sian."

He crossed his arms and looked away.

Perhaps she should be quiet, but she didn't want to. "And you're being stupid. Didn't you say the guy lied? He could have lied anyway. If it's true he can see your thoughts, he would know what to tell you so that you wouldn't teleport Karina away. Plus, he couldn't claim I had been captured if I'd been with you!"

Sian glared at her, looked away, then looked back. "That's a valid point."

Cayla stared for some time, waiting for the rest of the sentence and some retort, but it didn't come. Being attacked had really affected Sian.

"So… back to our thoughts. The royal line would continue, but there's a special skill only you have, is that right?"

"That's what the guy said. Again, we can't take it for truth. But… Leena also told me not to mention what I can do, so there might be something there."

"I'm assuming Darian doesn't have it, so even if he were to be in the line, he wouldn't be able to take Lumina."

"Well, I'm not taking that stupid city, especially after what Satwak did."

"We just need to get Karina."

Sian nodded. "If we ever get out of here."

Cayla wasn't that worried. "Darian will wake up, he'll see my note, and he'll look for us. They'll find us."

"How are they going to guess we're here?"

"By elimination? I don't know. He'll find me." True that they no longer had the twin necklaces, and more than ever she missed hers, but she trusted Darian. She regretted not having trusted him more, not having talked to him, not having listened to him. Perhaps they could have come up with a better plan than the one that got them stuck in Marisia without rescuing Karina. Too late now.

~

Karina's heart was pounding so hard that she feared it would give her away. There were steps in the hallway and doors being opened. She'd be caught—and have nowhere to run to. Perhaps she should just surrender. They weren't going to kill her —yet.

She opened the door and raised her hands. "I'm here."

Her hope was that they'd try to take her back to Forestglare, and, in the teleporting tower, she'd have her chance to escape.

Five guards approached her, and two of them held her. This was not her day. No. She'd kissed Sian. It would never be a terrible day. She was dragged not to the teleporting tower, but to the throne room. Firis was there. Karina panicked, and in the moment the guards let her go, she used her magic to cast an explosion and ran away to the elevator. When she got out on the first floor, metal balls were circling her. Karina pushed them away and ran outside. All she had to do was hide long enough not to be caught, and hope that the Guardians or Sian would come and save her. Now, hoping Sian would come to the very place where people wanted to kill him was a terrible hope. Karina ran down the stairs, turning and pushing away some flying capsules. Most of the security was around the teleporting tower, so she'd been correct to run away from it.

Even when Karina was exhausted from running, she kept running, until she reached the woods. With the impression they'd quit, she climbed a tree and waited.

After many minutes, she heard someone calling her, "Karina!"

The voice was familiar, and she was glad when she recognized it. Sat. He was alive! But she shouldn't trust him. If he needed Sian to defeat Firis, he'd obviously want Karina caught. That was the truth she should have seen when he faced her and Sian on their way out. Too late, now.

He stopped below her tree. "I know you're there."

You can pick up my thoughts and find me? She thought.

"Pretty much."

How come you can walk and you aren't dead?

"This is Lumina we're talking about. We don't die from silly wounds."

Good for you.

"Come down. I need to talk to you."

Isn't your medicine super advanced? Climb.

"Kah, don't be silly. You know they are going to find you soon. Who do you prefer? Me or Firis?"

Karina jumped down. "What do you want?"

"I want to apologize. Truly. But you see, I don't even care about my life. I just want the freedom of my people. My sister's freedom. If you're such a good person as you think you are, you'd help me. You'd understand."

"I told you I'll help you."

He was acting weird and Karina had better escape.

"Im sorry," he said as he raised a hand and shot a yellow flare in the sky.

Karina ran, but it was no good, as soon she was surrounded. Someone paralyzed her, the same way Firis had done. Sat walked towards her and put his hand on her head.

Asshole, she managed to think before it all turned black.

~

Sian's head was going to explode if Cayla continued trying to ask him about what blond pretty-face had said, about his powers, about some unfeasible plan, as if they had any way out of that dump. Fine, he also thought someone would figure out where they were, but his estimates weren't nearly as optimistic as hers. And her voice was grating. She had saved his life, though. He would have felt thankful if she stopped annoying him.

He decided it was best to tell her the truth. "Fine. Want to know my power? I can control electricity. No idea how I can do it, no idea how it's done, no idea how to control it. I've only used it twice. Once, when I killed a bunch of Maris like a coward. Twice, in the meeting room, when I collapsed. According to Leena, I would have killed everyone in that room if she hadn't shielded me. How this freaky magic I have no control over can make any difference, I don't know."

She covered her mouth with her hand, as in surprise. "Sian, don't blame yourself. When people can't control their magic, accidents happen."

"In Marisia it wasn't an accident."

"Wasn't it self defense?"

Sian shrugged. "Maybe."

She thought for a moment. "Lumina probably has something that can be affected by your type of magic, or, I don't know, has some affinity. The issue is what. We can research when we get back."

Right. In about a month. What good would it do? But he didn't want to argue. "That's an idea."

He fell silent, hating himself for having been so stupid, incompetent.

"Stop blaming yourself," Cayla said.

"Thinking you're a telepath too?"

She shrugged. "It's in your face."

"I didn't ask you to look."

"I'm not gonna close my eyes just so you can mope without interruption."

Sian got up. "There's a window, you know? You could look outside."

He took a look at the valley. Amidst so much disappointment, one thing lifted his spirits; the vegetation was growing back. Sian would have smiled if he didn't feel he was about to drown in an ocean of sadness.

So far no Maris had come to the tower. Perhaps they were both invisible, unafraid. Not true, though. Sian was terrified about what could happen to Karina. Powerlessness was one of the worst feelings in the world. No wonder his father, and so many more people, coveted power over all things. As much as it had a dark side, it could also mean being able to do something for the people he loved.

Cayla stood beside him. "You still hate me, don't you?"

Seriously? She thought he had any room in his mind for her? He tried not to be rude, though, for Darian's sake. "Of course not. I'm just worried."

"Sian, maybe there's a reason we're here."

"There is. We rushed into Forestglare with a lame plan and I was an idiot. So?"

"Not that." She looked down, bit her lip, then looked back at him. "I want to apologize for how I treated you. When we were kids. It was horrible and I have no excuses."

He waved his hand. "Oh, please. You think I care about some stupid stuff from years ago?"

"Maybe you don't. I do. If it helps, the whole plan to shame you—"

"I don't want to hear about it." Trying to be polite with Cayla didn't work.

"It wasn't my idea. The girls, it was them, which doesn't excuse me—"

"I asked you to stop. I'm not interested in helping you feel better about yourself. You did it, own it."

"I am owning it. And I was wrong. It was cruel, it was stupid, and I hate the person I was. I know it doesn't change anything, but I really wanted to say I'm sorry. I've always been sorry."

"You're delusional. I'd rather you hate me than feel sorry for me."

"Sorry for me. For *my* actions. People died because of a stupid game."

That didn't make any sense. "What do you mean?"

Cayla was startled. "You don't know? Anna and her sister, and their family. They were sent away—and had an accident."

Was she accusing him of what he thought? "I never told this to anyone. Not a single person knows about what you did. I wasn't aware they died in an accident. I think it's sad, but I have nothing to do with it."

She had tears in her eyes. "I do. I told my father."

He snorted. "You know who to blame, then."

Cayla started bawling, and it was awkward because Sian wanted it to stop but didn't know what to do.

She spoke between sobs. "I know I'm a horrible person. Nobody should be my friend."

What? "I didn't mean you. I meant your father."

She shook her head. "Karina's in danger. Alessa's hurt. I don't even know if she's alive or not."

"Alessa? The same Alessa?"

Cayla nodded. "We almost died together." She dried her eyes with the back of her left hand. The right arm looked terrible and that worried Sian more than anything. But worry wouldn't fix it.

"Blaming yourself is not going to help anyone," he said.

She still wept.

Sian added, "And for the record, I never had any resentment against you. I just thought you were a little snob and self-centered, that's why I wasn't very friendly, but no resentment. And I might have been wrong."

"When I met Darian, you tried to separate us."

Now she was getting to a real reason he didn't like her, and hoped she didn't push it because it wasn't proper to upset someone already crying. He had to be honest, though. "Well, of course. I wanted my brother alive. Unlike you." He shouldn't have added this last part, but then, he wasn't in a very hypocrite mood.

"How could I have known my father would want to kill him if he saw us together?" At least she stopped crying.

"Oh, really? Why didn't you present him to your father, then? Why meet in secret?"

"We were just starting. We were just friends."

"I'll take it. You had no idea he could have died. Fine. I warned you, though. I warned you and you didn't listen."

"I didn't think it was true."

"You could have checked."

"I was fourteen. I was in love."

"Selfish love, Cayla, because Darian almost died because of that."

"Right. You're going to tell me you weren't the one who betrayed us?"

"Are you out of your mind? I was fifteen. I had to duel and kill a man. You think it's easy? You think it's fun? You think I didn't have nightmares about it for years? How do you think I felt, learning that I was about to lose the brother that I had just found? The only decent family I had? The brother I'd been trying to protect?"

"It didn't look like you cared about him."

"Well, because *he* didn't care. What was I supposed to do? It takes two to be friends. That didn't mean I couldn't watch his back."

Cayla watched him for a moment, then said, "You two need

to talk. Darian loves you, Sian, despite everything."

Sian snorted. "Despite everything. Cause I'm obviously not worthy of my virtuous brother's love."

"That's not what I said. Plus, I saved you. I teleported you from outside a tower. It's not normal magic. You know how I did it? Love. Love for your brother, because I knew he would be devastated if something happened to you."

"He'll be upset about your arm."

"Well, I'm pretty sure he thinks your life is worth more than my arm. And so does Karina. That's two people already, even if you disagree."

"Fine. Fine. I don't hate you, I don't hate my brother, I don't hate anyone. You do have good reasons to dislike me, though, after you almost died and saw your friend almost dying— because of me. I accept that."

"True. But still, you're Darian's brother. We can't hate each other."

"Hate is a waste of time and energy. I don't entertain such stupid notions."

"Great. I also think you like Karina, and she likes you. I just hope you find better ways to show your feelings than deceiving and manipulating."

"Yeah, I was totally planning on doing that, since it worked so well last time." Again Cayla was poking his wounds.

"You can't say it didn't, though."

"Yeah, I almost destroyed Whyland, almost got her killed, almost got you killed, plus I ended up in this place for months, and almost got killed. I kind of noticed I made some mistakes, you know?"

Cayla shrugged. "Perhaps that was the only way you knew how to love."

"Yeah, sure." Again he looked at her arm, and more than feeling worried, he welcomed the opportunity to leave that conversation. "Listen, the Maris have a type of medicine. It could help your arm. It might be scary, though."

Cayla rolled her eyes. "Right. I'm going to be terrified of a medicine."

Sian smirked. Just because of her attitude he decided not to explain to her what he was going to do. He opened the door, went to the middle of the tower, climbed the steps to the top and rang the bell.

A few minutes passed when he heard a familiar set of wings. Komiak. Sian realized that it hadn't all been awful when he lived in the mountain with that tribe. The terrible days had been when he'd come to this tower, hurt, guilty, and alone.

Sian walked towards the giant bird and hugged his chest. "Thank you for being my friend."

Komiak had brought the stone. "Are you back to assume the throne?"

"No. I'm leaving. I might never come back. You have many tribes, though, you don't need a king, do you?"

"There's already a lot of infighting."

This wasn't Sian's problem. "Hopefully things will settle down. Is there an official way for me to quit?" He was wondering if he'd have to sign something, which was ridiculous, as they didn't have paper.

"No," the stone replied. "If you're not here to claim it, you'll lose it."

Sian nodded. That was good. "What happened to the others? No Maris tried to attack us since we got here."

"We have rain, plants, more animals. Less hungry. Less desperate. Humans taste horrible."

Sian chuckled, wondering if they would be half as bad as those terrible worms. "That was fast."

"Three moon cycles."

That was a lot more than the time he'd passed in the Light

Gardens. Perhaps there was a time difference. There was something Sian had to say.

"I'm sorry. For the killings."

"They were cowards to attack you like that and deserved to die."

Maris had a more brutal view of the world. Perhaps living among them for so long had affected him. He still felt bad. Sian got to the part that mattered. "I need a favor. My sister is here. She's hurt."

They opened the door to the room where Cayla was sitting. She saw Komiak and opened her mouth as if to scream, but perhaps decided against it. "What, what, what's this, Sian?"

She was terrified, and Sian was a terrible person because he had to suppress his laughter. "A friend. He'll help your arm heal."

Komiak approached Cayla while she let out a deafening scream.

Karina woke up in Forestglare, tied to a chair with some brilliant rope. She was by their well, a transparent blue energy ball around her. Her muscles were still paralyzed. Sat watched her. He'd been responsible for bringing her in. Instead of upset, she felt relieved, as she realized she still had her memories. Memories she didn't want to access right now, otherwise she'd be giving them to Satwak.

He had a pleading look.

Are you sorry or something? She thought.

He looked away and called someone, "She's awake."

Karina heard steps approaching her chair. Firis, with a relief sigh. "Finally we can get this over with." He turned to Karina.

"So sad. You'd have made a lovely consort. Alas. You chose otherwise."

"We'd better do the transmission soon," Satwak said.

Firis stepped in the bubble and stood beside her chair running his fingers through her hair, but she couldn't move away. A light shone in front of her.

The old man said, "This is a message not for the Guardians, but for those of you who dare defy us. Here we are, in Forestglare, where the population received us gladly and has participated enthusiastically in all the festivities. We came in peace and mean to harm nobody.

"Still, there are some of you who have threatened our appointed queen; my betrothed. We plead with you not to disturb our peace and happiness nor our upcoming nuptials. As you can see, she's very scared and very shaken. She hasn't been hurt, hasn't been tortured, and we plead that it may continue so. As a peaceful city, we ask for understanding, for a truce, at least until all the nuptials are completed."

The light faded. It wasn't hard to understand the man's twisted words; he was basically saying, "Come and get her or else..."

Karina still couldn't talk. She didn't think the man really wanted to marry her or anything similar, not after what she'd told him, but he could hurt her.

"He'll come, uncle, and he'll be so upset he'll be an easy prey. You'll never have to worry about anyone defying your true claim or disrupting the peace in Lumina."

"I still wish we had caught him when you first lured him here. Your secrecy had a high price, Satwak."

"I didn't want to raise false hopes." He lowered his head. "But I was wrong."

Karina would need to escape before anyone else risked their lives for her. But she couldn't try to come up with an escape plan with Satwak beside her. She wasn't even sure what he wanted anymore.

"Uncle, I still think you should have caused her some pain."

"Right. And alert all the Guardians. My message was for one person only, and only that person should react to it."

"He might bring reinforcements."

Firis' smile could only be described as evil. "Let's hope he does."

17

A NOTE

The sun still hadn't risen when Darian opened his eyes. Cayla wasn't in his room. Well, she also had her room, not that she used it much. He closed his eyes again. No. She wouldn't be there. There was something else happening. Their last encounter flashed through his mind. True, he'd been very close to connecting with his magic, but that should never have been at the price of ignoring her.

He checked her bedroom. Empty. No, there was something; a note on the bed. Only after reading it three times the meaning dawned on him.

Gone to Forestglare with Sian to rescue Karina. He hadn't seen Cayla's friend in the transmission, and neither had Leena. But Cayla had certainly seen something—and so had Sian. His brother's indisposition gained another meaning. How could Darian have been so dumb? So focused on himself, on waking up his magic, when the people closest to him were suffering. He crumpled the paper, the proof of his shame.

The sun was rising when Darian knocked on Leena's door. She took a couple minutes and came out wearing a dress, eyes half closed. "What's wrong?"

"I don't want to disturb you. I mean, of course I'm disturbing you. I have a question. Is it possible to teleport to the Light Gardens using a different, unknown portal?"

"Everything's possible. From where do you think people are going to teleport?"

"Forestglare."

She shook her head. "It's the second most isolated ethereal city, right after Lumina, and it's obvious why."

"True, but, could one *go* to Forestglare?"

The woman thought for a moment. "Well, yes. All the efforts are into blocking people from going out." She frowned. "You didn't wake me up at this time for a theoretical conversation, did you?"

"No. I—"

"Come in."

Darian entered and she closed the door after him. "Just tell me what's happening."

Should he tell her? Well, he'd need as much help as possible. "Cayla and Sian went to Forestglare."

"Sian?" She had a horrified expression.

"Well, yes. Cayla says the queen she saw was Karina. If my brother went with her, and if he collapsed when he saw the transmission, he probably saw the same thing."

She put her hand on her forehead and shook her head. "Not him, not him."

Neat how she just ignored Cayla, but it didn't matter. "I think they'll be stuck there. Or they already are."

She touched his chin and lifted his face. "You're different."

"Yeah, I spent three days meditating."

Her eyes pierced him. "Well, use it, then."

"Use what?"

"What you've awoken."

Darian sucked in a breath.

~

Would they just leave Karina sitting there, in the blue bubble? Satwak was still sitting near her, and it was super annoying because she'd never be able to escape if someone were to predict her movements.

He seemed lost in thought.

Karina wanted to bring him back to reality. She tried to speak but she couldn't. What a horrible feeling. She wondered if that was what they did to the attendants in the Lumina castle. She decided to project a thought. *Hey, I'm hungry. Is that how you treat your prisoners?*

Satwak looked at her. "Count yourself lucky. The treatment our prisoners get is usually ten times worse."

Yay, thanks for the unusual hospitality.

He just shrugged.

How could Satwak be so dumb? Yeah, dumb, and she hoped he heard it. Firis had almost killed him and didn't look like he was too interested in his nephew's survival.

"Can you hear me?" Sat asked. She looked at him, but he was looking away, his mouth closed. "I'm projecting my thoughts," he added. This time she knew he wasn't speaking. Not out loud, at least. Quite weird.

Yeah, I can hear you, she thought.

"This has been my life; not knowing if I'll survive until the next day."

You could have hidden, you could have let me escape.

"They would have found you. By catching you, I got a little goodwill from my uncle. That's my game, to stay alive and free for as long as possible, until my work is done."

But how can you do your work? If Sian comes here, what chances does he have against all these people?

"He's smart, isn't he? That's what I saw in your mind; someone who plans things well. Let's count on that."

That's a huge risk. What about me? You swore an oath to protect me, Sat.

"I haven't broken it." He looked elsewhere and it was quite creepy to hear his voice like that. "You're still safe and unharmed."

Not thanks to you, who suggested your uncle torture me.

"Suspicious of my motives as he is, he did the opposite I suggested. You should thank me. Anyway, projecting thoughts like this is tiring. I'll stop it now, but please be on the watch. I might do it again, when the need comes."

This mental talk left Karina with a nauseous feeling in her stomach. "Hoping for the best" was a recipe for disaster as far as a plan went.

Sian was upset at himself, feeling the time passing by while he remained in this place, unable to do anything.

"I'm getting hungry," Cayla said.

"Well, trust me on this one, you'll want to be the hungriest hungry before tasting the local food."

Cayla shrugged. "I guess I'll trust you."

She was quiet for a while, then said, "You're still upset."

"Me? Upset? You think? Outrageous. Why would that be?"

She sighed. "I gave it some thought. The guy, Satwak, he won't let them hurt Karina. If he has a sister that he wants to protect, he'll make sure Karina's safe."

"Not really. Do I look like someone who'd leave an inno-cent... Fine. Scratch that. I might *look* like someone who'd leave an innocent person vegetating forever. But that guy saw my mind. He knows I'm not like that. I'm no hero, though. I'm not going to risk my life to fix a problem that's not mine."

"He'll want to make sure you care about their problems, then."

Sian waved a finger. "And that's the issue, he won't want us to rescue Karina until his city is free, and he doesn't understand we have no clue how to do it and perhaps no power to do it. And there's another possibility. Maybe he was lying. Maybe he wanted to lure me there, to kill the royal line, whatever they think I am."

"Didn't he go talk to you alone, though? He would have gotten you killed or imprisoned, not allowed you to escape."

"I almost got killed, didn't I? That's the thing. Plus, regardless of what exactly he wants, we have no reason to believe anyone there cares about her well-being."

"He does. If he expects you to go back there."

"Maybe. But I bet he has no idea I'm stranded in another dimension."

"I told you. We'll get back soon."

Her optimism was unnerving. But then, Sian took another look at her arm and felt bad for getting annoyed at her cheerfulness. He'd seen people with a lot less serious injuries lying down, moaning, crying, and thinking they were dying. If he hadn't seen it with his own eyes, he'd think she wasn't hurt at all, and only his knowledge of anatomy allowed him to realize that his sister-in-law was probably in horrible pain. One more reason to worry.

Cayla smiled and got up. "Hear that?"

Sian had a pretty good ear, but he heard nothing. "What?"

"Darian!"

Cayla ran out of the chamber to the main hall. There were no Maris around, but still Sian didn't think it was a good idea. Plus, perhaps the girl was hallucinating. He got up and followed her.

He'd never been so happy to see his brother. Not that he could see his face, which was about to blend into Cayla's in a kiss that should have been left for a more private moment. Sian looked away, and saw a blond woman. Slightly familiar. His brother was still almost crushing Cayla's bones—which was not a good idea.

"Darian," Sian yelled. "She's hurt."

Darian stepped away from Cayla and said, "We'll take care of it."

Sian looked down. Regret and shame were stupid, and yet, he barely had words to apologize or explain. Then he felt Darian in front of him, and his brother's arms around him. "I'm sorry," Darian said. "I shouldn't have ignored you."

The hug felt awkward. Sian pushed Darian's arms. "Nothing to be sorry. Take care of Cayla." He then whispered. "It's serious."

Darian nodded, not half as worried as he should. Had it been Karina hurt like that, Sian would be freaking out. Maybe worse, maybe he'd be killing everyone around him with his bizarre magic. A great thing Darian wasn't like him.

Cayla approached Darian. "How did you find us?"

"I can always find you."

"I thought it was the necklace."

"So did I. We were wrong."

Sian looked away and recognized the blond woman; she had been the previous king's wife. Sian bowed. "Nia. Good to see you."

"Same here," she said, then added. "I'll teleport you one by one."

"I can teleport," Cayla said.

Nia shook her head. "Not where we're going, and you're too hurt to try anything."

The woman held Sian's hand. He saw flashes of light, then opened his eyes and found himself in a tall circular structure, a teleporting tower, with white sparkly stone. The woman disappeared, then brought Darian, then Cayla. She was quite a fast teleporter, and it was odd, because Sian had never known she could do any magic.

"Where are we?" Cayla asked.

"Brighteria," the woman replied.

That was the ethereal city with a portal leading to South Whyland.

She continued, "We didn't want to take risks and open a passage to the Light Gardens, since they're being so closely watched. You'll have to stay here for a while."

No way Sian would sit idly while Karina was in danger. "I have things to do."

"I've heard," Nia said. "And you'll be able to do them."

They walked outside the tower to a hallway with the same kind of material on its walls which soon gave way to windows on both sides from where Sian saw the depths of a cliff they were crossing.

"I thought you were overseas," Cayla said.

Nia shook her head. "My mother was from here. I came to visit—and stayed."

"Is my little brother here?" she asked.

True, Nia had been pregnant before she disappeared. That would have been Cayla's half sibling.

Nia smiled. "He is."

"I want to see him."

"Sure." She pointed to Cayla's arm. "After we fix this."

Finally. A sensible person. The girl had her arm half-chewed and here they were talking pleasantries. Perhaps better than Sian, who hadn't bitten back his tongue when they were in Marisia. But he'd been a pile of nerves. Silly excuse.

They came to a patio, then Nia took a side door and went down narrow stairs. "We don't want a lot of people knowing you're here," she said with an apologetic look.

The stairs led to a door, then to a valley, where they walked for a few minutes. Sian was reconsidering his opinion that they were sensible, if they were going to spend so much time walking. He took a look back. It was a large castle, its white walls glistening in the moonlight, with high towers. This city looked more like a kingdom, like Whyland, than just a city.

Eventually they reached a small stone house.

Nia opened its door. "Just Cayla. You two can't go in."

"For what?" Cayla protested.

"They'll heal you. Come."

Darian kissed the top of her head. "Go. Brighteria healers are among the best."

Nia took her inside and came out alone a few seconds later. "She'll heal. Don't worry." Her words were directed to Sian.

"I'm sorry," he muttered to Darian.

"It's fine. Come. We have a lot to discuss."

They walked away from the house, but not back to the castle, and then came to another house. Not a house, as it consisted of one single room with a large table. It was more like a meeting room. Leena was sitting there. Nia left.

Sian took a deep breath. This was the part where he had to tell them what had happened. Now, if it was hard for himself to accept how stupid he'd been, it was horrible to have to admit it. Twice. Plus he'd have to explain how he'd agreed to help Cayla without telling Darian and how she'd gotten hurt saving him. But he needed the help and didn't know who else to ask.

Darian didn't take it half as badly as Sian expected, though. He listened in silence, without any protest.

After Sian finished, Darian was silent for a while, then said, "Sian, anyone in your place would have done the same."

Sian snorted. "Really? Like believing in some nonsense the guy told me? Letting Karina go back?"

Darian shook his head. "You're looking at it the wrong way. Aren't you the strategist? From an intel-collecting perspective, there was no failure. With information, you can take the right action, which you couldn't before."

Sian stared at his brother, wondering if he was all right.

Darian turned to Leena. "Do you know more? About Sian's magic and the possibility he's some kind of lost royal?"

"Well, yes," the woman sounded cautious. "I'm one of the only people who knew Sian's secret." She turned to Sian. "I thought you knew it too, and that was why you were so worried that I saw the symbol on your chest."

Sian hated that talk, and hated that she'd seen him. "No. I had no idea. Just… for some odd reason I feel uncomfortable when people see me without my shirt, so I don't like it." Perhaps because of the dozens of scars bringing back lovely childhood memories, but he didn't want to talk about them.

"It's possible your mother told you not to show it. She was a powerful spell speaker, and if she's given you a suggestion when you were still a small child, it would stick in your mind."

Sian wanted to change the subject. "Can the Guardians or people from the ethereal cities help us?"

"That's what's tricky," the woman said. "And dangerous. Nobody can know about you, Sian. There was a time when Lumina conquered every single ethereal city. People were killed, enslaved. The memory is still raw even if that hasn't happened for generations. Some of the guardians could want to kill you."

That made no sense. "Aren't the guardians the good guys?"

The woman tilted her head. "Good is relative. They'd be doing it to get rid of a bigger evil."

Quite ridiculous. Sian wasn't the nicest person in the world, but he certainly wasn't worse than those people who killed teenagers.

Before Sian could point that out, Darian spoke, "They believe Lumina will go back to its full power if their royal line is reestablished."

Leena nodded. "Exactly. And that was why Sian had to be hidden as a child."

That made no sense. "In the castle? In plain sight?"

"Ethereal people aren't too concerned with what happens elsewhere. If Bianca said her son was dead, they wouldn't go and investigate it. They had no reason to suspect anything. Nobody had any reason, in fact. The Lumina special skill hasn't shown up for years, and we have no idea from where it comes in your lineage, just that it's there. Now that you're old enough, you can hide your powers."

"Like when they exploded in that room?"

Leena shook her head. "I had no idea you were so unstable. I was going to talk to you and suggest you stay away from the Light Gardens, I just didn't have the time."

Sian shrugged. "I'm not even interested in your ethereal city. I was forced to stay there, remember?"

"What would you do in my place? You hear about a breach in Lumina, and that they came to Whyland. Who do you suspect they are looking for?"

Whatever. Those things didn't matter. "Fair enough. What I want to know is what I can do, how my magic manifests in Lumina."

"Nobody knows. I searched for it. It's been erased from all archives."

"Excellent. And the good guys could have killed me just because in theory I have a power they have no clue what it is."

"People fear the unknown," Darian said. He had gotten weird in these last few days. Too calm and philosophical.

Sian sighed. "I just want to get Karina back. I feel pity for Lumina, but it's not for me to fix it."

Leena fixed her eyes on Sian. "You'll need to go to Lumina, find your magic, overpower their army, and then you'll be able to get her back."

"Just that?"

"Exactly," the woman agreed.

Sian didn't understand how she could say all that with a straight face.

Darian reached out his arm and touched Sian's shoulder. "I'll help you."

"Wow, thanks, that multiplies my odds for two. Now let's see… zero times two…"

"You're forgetting your magic," Darian insisted.

"Right. The magic I have no clue how to control and nobody has any idea how it works in Lumina. Now, really. I do accept your help, but I'm not overpowering an army on my own. That's just absurd." He turned to Leena. "Maybe, if the Guardians loosen the hold on the portals, maybe Karina can teleport away."

Leena shook her head. "Too risky. She could be mind-controlled or brainwashed again and bring the Lumina forces with her."

"I thought I could overpower them. Have no fear. Super me will be around."

"You need to go to Lumina for your power."

Sian sighed.

Darian then said, "I'll tell you what I propose to do: we can open a passage to Lumina from here. We can get old diagrams and maps from the city and find a way in, an improvised tower. You go there, try to find your magic, see if you can do something. If you can, you teleport to Forestglare with your new power and get Karina back. If you can't, you come back and we try something else."

Sian would hate to return empty-handed again. Everything about this plan sounded even worse than Cayla's plan, and look where it had gotten them into. And there was another problem.

He turned to Leena. "Isn't my magic depleted, though?"

"I don't know. How do you feel?"

"I sure don't feel magical."

"It's been a day, and you recovered well," Leena said. "While you might not be able to explode and kill everyone around you, you should be able to do something."

Should. Maybe. I don't know. This wasn't a way to plan things. Sian closed his eyes. He recalled his fight against the Maris, and how his magic had saved him. If he could connect to that power again, he had good odds. He didn't know if he had to go to Lumina, though. But maybe it would be good to find out about that place.

"So the suggestion is just to get to Lumina, check it out, see if I find my magic, and then go to Forestglare?"

"Pretty much," Darian confirmed.

Sian tapped his fingers on the table. "Right. So, meanwhile, aren't these Guardians supposed to take care of interdimensional stuff? What are they doing?"

Leena shook her head. "Caught in some debate. Lumina got Forestglare to sign as if the occupation hadn't been an invasion, so the Guardians have no legal grounds for a retaliation. The other issue is that they fear Lumina, so most of them are strengthening their own city protections."

"Why is Brighteria helping?" Sian asked.

"Not all of Brighteria," Darian replied. "We got Nia to help because she likes Cayla. We'll be doing some illegal portals. But it helps that Brighteria doesn't get along with the Guardians much, so they won't be paying attention here."

Leena got up. "Come. You'll have to regain your strength."

Sian kind of agreed with that despite his anxiety. They went to another house, close by, this time. It was a family house, with a young man with dark brown hair and a blond toddler. The young man was setting the table. "Welcome. Nia and Cayla should join us soon."

His voice was familiar. "Do I know you?" Sian asked.

He reached out his hand. "My name's Talon. I'm Lylah's brother."

Another hidden brother. Interesting. "What are you doing in Brighteria?"

He smiled. "Came to visit and stayed."

Sian still felt he knew the man, but he didn't know from where, which was odd, since he was good at remembering people's faces and names—a great trick to get more allies.

There was a thrill going through Darian. He still hadn't told anyone about the magic he'd found. He'd been upset that connecting with it had led him to neglect Cayla and his brother, but now he felt that it had been the right decision.

Someone knocked at the door. Nia opened it and entered with Cayla, who had changed into a light blue dress. Other than a bandage on her arm, she seemed fine. Darian glanced at his brother's funny expression then rushed to hug her.

"How are you?"

Cayla smiled. "Much better." She then whispered, "Can we come outside for a moment?"

They left the house. Darian looked at her arm. "Once I had an accident and Brighteria healers also gave me a miracle recovery. We have that in common now."

She smiled. "Yeah… I'm glad it's fixed."

"You were very brave. Thank you for saving my brother."

Cayla squinted. "Have you told him that? Because he annoyed me to no end, complaining you'd prefer my arm to his life."

Darian just closed his eyes. "That's Sian." He was going to make some other joke when it suddenly hit him that it was exactly like his brother to think Darian valued so little his life. The thought stung, not that he felt offended, but rather sorry— or guilty.

"What?" Cayla asked.

Darian shrugged. "Maybe I failed to show him how much I value him."

She rolled her eyes. "Oh, my. Could it be because he disappeared and conspired against you? He never reached out to you other than when he needed, Darian. I'm not saying he's a horrible person, I'm just saying that it goes both ways."

"Both ways. And perhaps I should consider mine."

"You're here. You're helping him. That's what matters." She sighed. "There's something I wanted to tell you."

"Yes?"

"The Luminous sent another transmission. It's a veiled threat against Karina. She's in Forestglare, and the Lumina overseer wants Sian there before the end of the day. He's threatening to hurt her or… other stuff."

"How long do we have?"

It was Nia who spoke, "A couple hours."

It felt weird to realize their conversation was being overheard, but that wasn't the worst.

Darian rested his forehead on his palm. "We lost so much time…" He then looked at Nia. "We need to show Sian the transmission."

"No." Cayla held his wrist. "I thought about it. I don't think it's a good idea. He's… he's not well, Darian. If he sees that, he'll do something stupid."

"Should we just lie to him?'

"You say it as if you didn't enjoy lying."

More than she knew, and than even he had known until recently. Darian nodded. "Fine. Cayla, I just need you to teleport Sian to Lumina. Can you do that?"

"Of course."

"Wait a second," Nia said. "I agreed to help, but I'm not helping with a suicide mission. This is just insane."

"But it's not—" Cayla started to protest.

Darian cut her. "No, no, Nia might have a point. Come

inside and we'll discuss this. We won't do anything you don't agree with, Nia."

Cayla squinted at him. She was so lovely when she was angry, Darian wanted to kiss her, but instead he just whispered in her ear, "Trust me."

18

ILLUSIONS

Sian noticed that there was something slightly off about Darian when he came back with Nia and Cayla. And there was something definitely off with her arm. He wasn't crazy; he knew about injuries. That recovery was impossible. Great news, though. One less worry in Sian's mind.

Cayla embraced the little boy and Lylah's brother. So this was Nia's house. Some shared looks between Nia and Talon revealed a little more. Sian felt as if he was invading something quite intimate. A happy home. This was something he'd never seen before. Perhaps with Malena and Raja, but that had been after the woman had been through so much pain. Here, there was something almost sacred about the quietness and peace, the love that was palpable in the air. It just gave Sian sadness and longing, since he didn't know if he'd ever have any of that.

Darian came to him and whispered, "I'll need you to convince Nia to help us."

Strange. "Why me?"

"I think you're the real spell speaker between the two of us."

Great. "How many magical powers I don't know how to use am I going to have to try today?"

"Forget magic, just try to convince her the way you convince people when you want to. She says she won't help with a suicide mission."

Sian sighed. "Well, that's a tricky one. You know I hate to lie. How am I going to tell her it's anything but what she's thinking?"

Darian shrugged. "Don't know. You're the spell speaker, Sian."

Right. Sian was everything.

Darian added, "I have to do something with Cayla, I'll be right back."

Cayla didn't understand why Darian had to watch the transmission so many times.

"Trying to come up with a plan?"

Darian stroked his chin as if thinking. "I think I *have* a plan."

"Care to share?"

"It's what I told you. Just teleport Sian to Lumina. From there, the passage is open to Forestglare and he'll be able to teleport without help."

"And if he isn't?"

"You're the backup."

That still sounded like a very lame plan. "Fine, but he made me promise I'd not save his ass again."

"I don't think you'll have to do anything, Cayla. I'd never make you risk your life. I'm sorry it came to it earlier. It was my fault. Maybe if I had helped…"

Cayla disagreed. "I should have insisted. Talked to you more."

Darian shook his head. "You tried." He embraced her in a tight hug. Tugged in his arms, there was no place for fear or worry. He then whispered, "And you're the bravest person I know. That's only one of the million reasons why I love you."

She broke the hug to look him in the eyes. "Really?"

He ran his hand through her face, ending at her lips. "More than I can put into words, and when I do they sound all wrong. 'I love you' doesn't quite convey what you mean to me. But I guess it's the closest I have, and I should have said it more often."

Cayla's heart was beating fast and she was at a loss for words. She closed her eyes, enjoying the sensation, his touch, then his lips against hers, as they dissolved into a kiss.

Karina was starving and was almost glad for it because at least she wasn't focusing on her fear. She'd spent so long wondering what would be like to see Sian again. It had been better than in her dreams—but so short, and now she risked never seeing him again. Not only him, her family, her friends, everything. She had no idea what was going to happen to her but she doubted Firis would just allow her to live normally in Lumina after what had happened. She took a deep breath. The fault had been hers, trusting the wrong people, trying to open a teleporting tower where there shouldn't be any. A tear ran down her eyes. Was ignorance a decent excuse for anything?

Satwak hadn't moved from his chair. He was probably starving too. He hadn't tried to communicate since earlier, and neither had Karina. There were guards all over the clearing with the well. Funny that Forestglare should have everything outdoors like that. Didn't it rain? It should rain if it was a forest.

A flash of lightning, then a low rumbling came as a response. Right. Because nothing could get worse. Well, rain would affect their visibility, so perhaps it wasn't so bad. Thick droplets hit the ground, but Karina didn't feel wet. The water was running on the circular ball shield around her, and she was dry. After a couple minutes, a girl was brought to the clearing and cast a shield, protecting all the area from the water. So that was Karina's answer.

With dark clouds in the sky, the day was turning into night. The wind was shaking the trees. A lightning bolt illuminated the area. When it was gone, Karina couldn't believe her eyes, and couldn't drown her horror.

Sian was there, on the opposite side of the well. He glanced at her. There was something wrong about his glance, though. It lacked Sian's intensity. This was more like a curious glance. He walked forward and raised his bare hands.

"I come in peace. Let her go, and you can have me."

This was unlike Sian. Couldn't he see all the guards among the trees? Couldn't he see that if he was giving himself away there would be nothing left to negotiate? No. Sian was smarter than that.

"Kill him!" Firis voice came from beside Karina.

Satwak got up. "Uncle, no! This is your chance to prove that you're the true ruler of Lumina. They're all watching."

Sian pointed to Firis. "That is not your true overseer. It's me. Here's your chance to lay down your arms. You have a prophecy, don't you? The Royal line keeps the prosperity in Lumina. Well, that's me."

"I'm going to repeat once." Firis' voice was fierce and certain. "Whoever dares defy me will pay the price. Kill him."

Metal balls and energy rays were directed at Sian. They hit a shield. Karina's heart was thumping on her chest. She wanted to scream and yell so many things. Sian was not casting the shield, though, because he had a look of surprise.

"Keep firing!" Firis yelled. "Whoever is shielding him won't be able to hold for long."

Thunder roared in the sky. Karina glanced at Sat. He looked elsewhere, but seemed focused. Was he the one shielding Sian?

Firis walked towards his nephew. This wasn't good. He was about to put his hand on Sat's head when the young man got up, turned, and tried to stab his uncle. With a wave of a hand, Firis sent Satwak far from where he was. The shield around Sian disappeared, and all the rays and balls hit him at once. This was like sleep paralysis. Karina was unable to move, unable to scream, as her worst nightmare took form in front of her.

Sian took a deep breath as he stood in the Brighteria teleporting tower. He'd gotten his brother's promise that he would rescue Karina if Sian failed, and that made it easy to walk into what could be certain death.

It felt odd to repeat his failed experience and teleport with Cayla again, but it was different with Darian having encouraged them. Nia had taken some convincing. Sian still wasn't sure about his so-called spell-speaker ability, but he knew how to charm when he wanted to. Of course, he had to tell his secret, but she didn't strike him as the murderous type. Hopefully she wouldn't babble, but he wasn't thinking far ahead anyway. His goal now was to get Karina and make up for his previous mistake. Hopefully he'd never set foot in an ethereal city again.

Cayla held his hand and soon he had to close his eyes due to the strong flashes of light. He opened his eyes when he felt his body submerged. They were in a tall tower all right, but it was a water reservoir. Sian swam up until his head emerged and he caught a long breath.

Cayla emerged a few seconds after him. "I guess it's wetter than we thought."

"Aren't we glad it's water, not grains?"

Cayla chuckled, then got serious. "Sure you want to go alone?"

"It's my destiny, isn't it?"

She nodded. "Good luck." Then she swam down and disappeared.

He felt a lot more at ease without having to worry about an additional person.

The tube was open on top and he swam to the edge. It wasn't simple, because the tower ended in an opening, like a funnel. Made with smooth metal, it was a hard climb. Sian removed his shoes, and only then, with the grip of his feet, he was able to make it to the border. Bare feet. Perhaps it could make a difference.

From the edge, he saw a glistening city under the dawning sun. Far away, on the top of a hill, a high tower, which was the main castle. From the top of it he should be able to get to the portal to Forestglare. Before that, he'd need to figure out how to get down from that water reservoir. He had an inkling that his special skill didn't allow him to fly. The tower was too tall for him to jump, and he was far from its outer wall to find a way to climb down.

He went to the edge, lay belly down and turned his body to see what was below. The outside of the tower wasn't smooth metal as he'd imagined. He dangled from the edge of the opening, then jumped in the direction of the reservoir—and slipped —until he found a groove for his feet, then hands, slowing his descent.

No alarm, no pursuers. It meant Lumina didn't have a system against intruders, or else he'd come up in such a weird place that whatever system they had didn't catch him.

Now all he had to do was walk to the main tower... and what? Declare himself the new king or whatever they called it? Sit somewhere and wait for his magical abilities to manifest? Well, at least he wasn't feeling weak, and if he had to fry some people, he'd hate it but he'd be able to do it. Hopefully that would be enough against the legendary Lumina might.

Her heart tight, Karina dared look at the place where Sian had been. Instead of his body, she found empty ground. But they didn't have time to remove his body. Her thoughts weren't making sense. Were her eyes betraying her?

"Find him!" Firis roared.

So Sian had disappeared. She didn't understand how, but cherished the idea that he'd be alive, hidden somewhere. Karina still couldn't move, though, and it was a problem.

Firis ran to her. "Show up or I'll cut her hands off."

He was about to touch her hand when she decided to make one last effort. *Push. Explode.*

"Don't." It was Sat's voice, inside her head. Karina gave up, but she wasn't sure she should listen to him. He added, "I released the magic binding you, but he'd better not know it yet. Use it when he's distracted."

That made sense. At the same time, if she didn't move away, the man's threat would make Sian show himself.

"He escaped once, he'll escape again." Sat's voice echoed in her head.

And she took too long to think because at this point her hand was being raised.

Sian's voice came from behind her. "I'm here."

Firis turned and shot a ray from his hand. Sian disappeared before the ray got him. Was he teleporting? This was Karina's chance. *Boom.* Firis fell down and she ran away.

"Take her," Firis yelled.

At this point the guards had dispersed, looking for Sian, who appeared somewhere else, because Firis yelled another set of instructions, which allowed Karina to run and find a tree to climb. She knew that staying close to Firis was dangerous, but she doubted she'd be able to run very far. She needed to get to the teleporting portal, but that was the place with the most security in Forestglare.

Firis then dragged Satwak to the middle.

"Karina," he called in a singsong voice. "If you don't show yourself I'll kill him."

Satwak wasn't really her friend. His goal was honorable, though, and he'd tried to help her. Karina felt torn.

Sian walked unopposed and reached the heart of the city, in front of the main tower. His feet hurt from the prickling of rocks and sticks. That said, being barefoot had worked once, and he wasn't sure what he was going to face.

He found himself in a square with strange metal statues surrounding it. The tower stood above it, just a few steps away. Of course walking in the city would be completely different from entering a type of government building, though. He wondered if he should climb it. No, he'd be an easy target if someone spotted him from the outside. He closed his eyes. Did he feel different? Any special magic? Not that he knew.

"Halt!" a man yelled behind him.

Of course. Sian turned. The man had no visible weapons, but that shouldn't fool anyone, since at least in theory, everyone in Lumina had strong magic.

Sian raised his hands.

"Who are you?" the man asked.

A couple different answers went through Sian's head, like saying he was taking a stroll, just walking, whatever, but the man probably knew he didn't belong there.

"My name's Sian Keen. I'm your true overseer." He still thought the word was funny. "I'm here to take back what's mine." Just take. He wasn't planning on keeping it.

The man stared at him for a moment, then asked. "Can you prove it?"

That was interesting. Sian had expected a laugh or something else. Could he prove it, though? "If you know the symbol of the Royal line, I could—"

"Nobody knows it, and it could be forged. Regardless, if you are the lost royal, your powers should be unmatched. Show me."

The man didn't move, but some whooshing in the air attracted Sian's attention. Some ten metal balls were flying towards him, from all directions. With no idea how to fight against inanimate objects, Sian waited for them to get close and jumped down, dodging them. It didn't work, though, as the balls fell over him then floated again. Think, Sian. No, not think. If it was about magic, what he had to do was feel and react. Sian sent a current of electricity to the man, but it met a shield and dissipated. This wasn't good. If people from Lumina could cast shields against him, there was no way he could do anything with his power. The man sent an orange flair from his arm.

Sian took the opportunity to run away from the square, but before he could get far he was surrounded by about eight people.

"State your purpose and surrender!" a woman yelled.

Sian raised his hands again. "Firis is not very nice, is he? I'm here to depose him."

This time he did get some laughs. Perhaps he was attuning his sense of humor. Should Sian try again to use his magic against all these people? Would they block him? Before he made his mind, something hit him from behind and he collapsed. This wasn't going well.

19

EMBRACING MAGIC

Karina pondered if she should try to help Sat, when she heard his voice, "Leave me. Firis is going to kill me anyway. Just try to save my sister."

No. This wasn't going to end this way. One smart argument to save Satwak was that he could see in people's minds, and therefore was a good ally.

Karina jumped down and walked towards the clearing. "I'm here."

Firis stabbed Satwalk's shoulder then grabbed Karina's hair. "Now it's time to hurt you."

"Impostor!" Firis yelled from the other side of the clearing. "Arrest him and protect the Forestglare queen!"

How could there be two Firis?

The guards were confused. Well, of course. While Karina had no doubts that the real Firis was the one holding her by the hair, Karina had been crowned in that place, and it wasn't logical that Firis would be threatening her so.

A couple guards approached the real Firis. He turned to attack them, and it was Karina's chance to run away.

While the two Firis had a shouting match, Karina came to Satwak. "Can you walk?"

"He paralyzed me," came his voice.

She grabbed him from beneath his arms and dragged him, meaning to hide them both. Satwak was bleeding too much, though. As she was away from Firis, she crossed Faizana. In silence, the girl put Satwak on her shoulder and carried him away. Hopefully what he had was just a silly wound for Lumina standards.

Karina came to the tree they'd been using to teleport. There was indeed confusion, as all that was left were two guards.

Before they could do anything, Karina pushed them away with her magic. She got in, hoping to teleport somewhere else, but it was like trying to go through a wall—unless...

Karina opened her eyes and recognized Lumina. That wasn't a lot of progress, but she just wanted to be away from Firis. Plus, if Sian's powers were bigger in Lumina, this was better. Sian. The more she thought about it, the less convinced she was that it was Sian who'd shown up in Forestglare a few minutes before.

Whoever had done it was the same person as the fake Firis, either casting illusions, teleporting fast, or both. Hopefully he'd be safe, whoever he was, and Satwak too. As much as she disliked "shoot first, ask questions later" Faizana, the girl cared about her brother.

There were about five guards around the tower.

Karina nodded and walked through them, trying to exude the confidence that wouldn't make them suspicious.

"Where are you going?" one of them asked just as she was about to cross the door.

She frowned. "Excuse-me? Since when do I answer to you? I'm under Firis orders. Now let me pass before he comes here and unleashes his fury."

She kept walking, aware of her steps reverberating in the hall. Despite everything that had happened, she still had her black dress and tiara. *Dress the part and act the part.* The castle was less guarded, probably because so many people had been sent to Forestglare. For some reason, she went to the window overlooking the square.

There she saw him. Unconscious and being carried inside. Sian. This time she knew it was him, even if he was unable to pierce her with his intense stare. Four people surrounded him. Karina rushed to the elevator and went downstairs. She was about to meet the group head on, perhaps talk them into releasing Sian, but then she got the feeling it wouldn't work, and if it didn't, the price would be too high.

Karina hid and observed where they were going, following from a distance. They took the elevator to the second floor. Karina went up the stairs. Those people didn't try to muffle their steps, so she knew in which direction they had gone. The issue was that they weren't coming back.

Karina came to a poorly illuminated hallway and heard voices from its end, where there was a double door. She waited. Eventually, two of them passed by, and Karina saw her chance of going in. The place had innumerable horizontal glass containers where people lay suspended in a pink liquid. Sian lay at a table.

"We don't know if that's what we need to do with him," a young man said.

"No, but that way Firis can decide. Remember we're on high alert for an overseer impostor," the woman replied.

"What if he's telling the truth?"

She chuckled. "He'd be a tad bit more powerful, don't you think? It's not as if he gave us any fight. Disappointing."

Karina knelt behind a table, considering her options. She could fight them, perhaps by exploding some of those containers. No. She'd better wait.

∼

Sian walked beside a river, with no memory of how he'd gotten there. A woman with half her face hooded approached him.

When she removed her hood, Sian recognized that face. The face in the glass ball he'd broken, the face whose words he didn't want to hear. He turned and ran, but his legs were short and he couldn't run far. The woman scooped him up with one arm. His body was a child's.

"My love," she said. "Stay close."

Her other arm held a little bundle. No. A baby.

"Can you walk?" she asked.

Sian had to walk. Since the baby had come, he was always second. He was struggling behind when someone else scooped him up. His father. His mother turned back but instead of smiling she turned around and ran. Was she running from him? From his father? He yelled for his mother to return, and yelled, and yelled, and yelled, as she disappeared.

"Sian." Bianca's voice came from behind him.

Sian was alone, and turned. "I wasn't worth saving, was I?"

She shook her head. "It was the hardest decision in my life. Every day I remembered you, every day I thought about you, but I figured you were safe with your father. The Light Gardens protected me, but not you."

Sian snorted. "Very safe with my father."

"I did my best. I had people watching you. All I heard was that you were growing up to be a very strong and capable young man, happy, good-looking, popular. How was I to know?"

Sian was crying and he hated it. She didn't deserve his tears. "Yeah, I mean, it's not like people miss their mothers or anything."

"It was a mistake and I'm sorry."

She moved in to hug him and somehow he lacked the

strength to push her away. It didn't feel good, it didn't feel bad. It just felt odd. She ran her fingers through his hair.

Sian then was on Malena's establishment, eating cake for the first time in his life. It wasn't that the castle didn't have cake, just that his father didn't let him eat it. And yet, his father had sent him there.

Even though he suspected that he hadn't been sent to eat cake, he pretended to believe it. For the first time, he heard what a good boy he was. Was he? Even though he failed and failed and failed? But Malena didn't care if Sian won or lost his fights, if Sian did or didn't do the tasks he was assigned. Somehow, just existing was enough for her. Despite no blood ties, she treated him well just because he was good. And Sian almost believed it, until he came back to the academy just to hear what a failure he was.

He was back by the river. Bianca said, "I always loved you, Sian. You were my firstborn and the light of my life."

"But duty was more important."

She shook her head. "Protecting you was more important."

Protecting him. Sian then found himself in the castle, where, by accident, he overheard his father. "Sian is the brightest jewel in Whyland."

It turned out that General Keen, far from hating Sian, was quite proud of his son's achievements. Achievements. Fighting. Sian's real achievements were in Siphoria, with Malena, when he learned as much as he could about handling a business, when he started to invest, when he realized he could change lives. All of this so far away.

Sian was then in the Light Gardens, outside his room. His mother walked to him. "Keeping you alive was more important than keeping you happy. I thought if you were away from the ethereal cities, you'd be able to lead a normal life, that destiny wouldn't catch up with you. But I was wrong. Now you have to find your magic. There's no escape, Sian, you'll have to face who you are."

Someone touched his face, held his neck. He felt lips on his. Strange. Children shouldn't kiss. But he wasn't one. He jolted awake and saw a familiar face in front of him. More than familiar, it was the face that washed away all the pain. "Karina?"

She smiled although her face had tears.

He felt as if he'd been unconscious for days. "How long has it been?"

"A few minutes."

He remembered then. They were in Lumina. How was Karina there? But the most important was being with her. "Can you teleport us away?"

"Look around you."

Sian realized his body was submersed in a weird glass tub. At least they hadn't undressed him. He looked around. Those people were undressed. Hundreds of them, in tubs like Sian's. "This is the stasis room."

Karina nodded.

"We could set them free," Sian said.

"I wouldn't know how to, uh, get them back to normal. You've just been put here and I already had a lot of trouble." She choked a sob. "I thought you were gone."

He reached out his hand and caressed her face. "I'm here. There's something I need to ask. Do you forgive me?"

"For your stupid decisions last time I came to Whyland?"

Sian nodded.

"Well," Karina started. "My decisions are not brilliant either. It's my fault Lumina had a portal to Forestglare."

He smiled. "I'm not going to complain. I was stranded in Marisia. They rescued me because of the Lumina breach. So I guess I have to thank you."

Karina looked horrified. "Marisia? How did you survive?"

"Lots of raw worms. But you saved me."

"I was having nightmares about you."

"Oh, c' mon, I'm not that ugly."

She laughed. "I thought you didn't lie. You know you're good looking."

"That was a joke, it didn't count." He took a deep breath. "I also dreamed about you." He looked around. "So, what should we do?"

"I used to think I didn't care about Lumina, but this…"

"I know. And I do have to wonder why life has brought me here, if it wasn't to do something. But I haven't found any special magic. My magic can't defeat them. Maybe they're wrong."

"I don't want you to get hurt."

Her eyes were so kind and calming. He realized she'd always look at him like that, regardless of what he did—within certain limits of course. Limits he almost crossed. He looked at her. "Do you love me?"

She was startled, then laughed. "Sian, usually people first declare their love, then wait to see if the other person says the same."

"Is there like a rule book or something? What's wrong with asking?"

"Loving is putting your heart out there, knowing it might be torn to pieces."

He sat up and straightened. "And willing to have your whole body torn to pieces? Does that count? Because I've done it for you. And I'd do it again if I had to."

"And yet you won't tell me what you feel."

"Do I have to? To the girl who won't answer my question?"

Karina laughed and shook her head. "Sian." He perked up his ears, glad she'd finally decided to give him an answer. "Someone was pretending to be you. In Forestglare. Who was it?"

That wasn't what he'd been expecting, and it was surprising. "I have no idea. What did they do?"

"It was good, created a distraction. That's how I escaped and ended up here. They also pretended to be Firis. I thought you were working together."

Sian was puzzled, confused, surprised. "No." He sighed. "They are probably distracting Firis so that I…" He looked down, then chuckled. "Do whatever magic I don't know how to do."

"It's fine. We can teleport away. This is not your responsibility."

By this she meant Lumina and that horrible room. Because she probably thought Sian wasn't this lost royal after all. Perhaps he should feel relieved that someone finally agreed with him, but he felt just a bit disappointed that she didn't trust him.

"I don't know. I don't know Karina. You know what the problem is? I lived an entire life away from magic. As much as I tried to learn about it, can reading for one year replace a lifetime?"

She touched his shirt, over the place where his heart was. "You don't need to know it. You feel it."

"Do you think I'm this Lumina person they think I am?"

"You are you, Sian, and whoever you are, you're here to find out. And we'll find a way regardless."

This was better. It wasn't that she didn't think he was in the royal line, it was that she just didn't care. Not because she didn't care about him, but because whatever role he had didn't matter.

He held her hand. "This time, promise, whatever happens, let's not break apart. Let's find another way. There's always another way."

He almost added *don't leave me*, but then decided it was perhaps too much.

Karina smiled. "We'll stick together."

Just then she turned. The door opened. Two people were thrown backward and fell on the floor. Karina had done it, with a burst of energy coming from nowhere. Sian was surprised. He knew she was powerful. He'd always known it, but he thought it was just teleporting. Dressed like a queen, with her mighty magic, Karina looked like a born ruler.

She pulled his hand. "Stop staring and let's run."

They went out of the room. The hall was empty other than the two people unconscious on the floor. "You have magic."

"No kidding."

He stopped. "No. It's serious. *You* can defeat them."

"I can't. This is nothing. The only reason I got these two was because they were caught by surprise. Had they fought, I'd have no chance."

She started running again and Sian followed. It felt weird not to have a plan. "Where are you going?"

"To the portal. We can go to Forestglare and then from there, teleport away."

"It's not that easy, Karina."

"It's our only shot."

Was it? Or could Sian try to do whatever he was supposed to do? His mind was getting clearer. It was as if being by Karina cast away all the shadows in his mind, the anguish, the pain, the anxiety. Such a powerful magician that she was, she looked at him as if he was so special. Special just for existing.

He had to ask again. "Karina, do you love me?"

"What's with the stupid questions?" Her voice had raised an octave to the point of being shrill. She was upset. But it was unfair. This was the most serious question he'd ever asked anyone. She stopped and turned, still looking annoyed. "Of course I do. I mean, within my understanding of—"

He silenced her with a kiss, which wasn't as well received as his kisses normally were, either because she was upset or because she was worried about escaping, but after a few seconds she softened, but just for a short while, as she eventually pushed him away.

"We can't do this here. We're in enemy territory, Sian."

He smirked. "Are we?"

Images flashed through his mind. The square. The statues. The balls. The walls. Once he stopped feeling like an intruder, once he stopped seeing everything as separated from him, the truth opened up to him. The floor rumbled.

Karina was startled.

"Don't worry. That's me." He kissed her forehead. "Just trust me. And stay close. Ah, I might get a little weird. Try not to worry, all right?"

Karina wasn't sure if she should feel glad or worried that Sian was finally finding some magic. She'd thought that they'd have a much better chance of survival by simply escaping. The floor kept rumbling beneath her, and now the walls shook. Sian had his eyes closed. Karina didn't ask what was happening from fear of disturbing his concentration.

Sian opened his eyes. "Good. Let's go to Forestglare. We have an army."

Was he all right? Again, she didn't want to say anything because he sounded so confident. If his army idea didn't work, they could try to teleport away. They came to the main hall with the elevators. No. The main hall. The elevators were broken on the bottom.

Sian looked. "Oops, that wasn't on purpose." His face then got serious, focused, almost distant.

The floor kept rumbling.

She was about to ask, "What..." Then Karina saw. The metal statues from the square, and more statues, moving up the stairs at incredible speeds, three or five steps at a time.

Sian was calm, focused. That probably meant those things

weren't going to attack them. One of the giant statues grabbed Karina and then went back to the stairs, where it climbed.

They came across guards who were too shocked to do anything. One or two tried to shoot something towards the statues, but they paralyzed whoever tried to stop them.

At the portal, the thing dropped Karina on the floor. A hand pulled her. Sian's. But he didn't look at her, eyes focused on something in the distance. Would these things work outside Lumina, though? This was an open portal and anyone—or anything—could go through it.

Soon light consumed them and they were in Forestglare, followed by the moving metal statues. They came to the clearing by the well. Someone sat in the chair Karina had occupied. Darian.

And about ten guards charged towards them. That's when she understood what the statues could do; they reflected the person's magic. Some guards were immobilized, some were hit. Firis was soon pinned on the ground

Sian walked towards him. There was none of the sweet Sian, or even the sarcastic Sian. His face showed only ruthless determination. If she weren't on his side, she'd be scared. Oh, to be fair, right now, he was scary regardless.

Firis laughed. "Make one move, and your brother dies."

"Tell them all, tell them you accept me as your true overseer, and I'll give you a quick death."

"I'm not afraid of pain."

Sian crouched near him. "Aren't you? I guess we'll find out."

Karina then heard a shaky voice, "Kill him. Fast." Satwak.

She yelled, "He's dangerous and powerful!"

The statue holding Firis in place burst into many pieces. He got up and directed a ball of energy at Sian. It stopped midway.

"Pathetic effort," Sian sneered. "I could do this all day. But it's boring."

The ball returned to Firis, who shielded it. "I can say the

same. You can't kill me. I have the magic of more than a hundred people flowing through me."

"Boring. You're not mine to kill, though."

Satwak came behind Firis and stabbed his back. The man turned and sent Sat flying away with a ray of energy. A stronger ray hit Firis. Faizana's.

"Leave my brother! And for my sister" she yelled.

Firis fell. His eyes were open, glassy, staring nowhere. Dead.

Sian blinked as if coming out of a trance, but just for a second. His angry face returned and he yelled, "I'm your new overseer. If anyone disagrees, please step forward and pledge your cause."

Of course nobody did.

"Karina, Karina." A desperate plea. Satwak.

Karina ran to where he lay. His head was bleeding.

He opened his eyes and spoke with difficulty. "Please. Please promise you'll free my sister, you'll restore order in Lumina. Promise."

A hand touched her shoulder. Sian's. "A deathbed promise is binding, Karina." His voice was soft.

"Promise," Sat insisted.

She turned to Sian. "We can't leave those people there, can we?"

"It's a hard decision, Karina, but if you want to help Lumina, I'll back you up."

She turned to Sat. "I promise."

Sat exhaled.

SETTLING DOWN

Karina went through her clothes, trying to figure out what to bring and what to leave, but nothing seemed appropriate. Clash of styles. Karina got up and put them back in her wardrobe.

Zoe stood by her. "Yeah, I bet they're not the latest style over there, are they?"

Karina laughed. "No."

"Take just a couple, just so that when you come to visit you don't look like an alien."

"They don't dress like aliens."

Zoe shrugged, then sat on the bed. "You know what part I find most impressive?"

"The moving statues?"

"No. You playing femme-fatale with sexy evil uncle."

Ugh. "Trust me, he was not sexy."

She had a teasing face. "Aaaah. But you do agree you were being a femme fatale."

"Oh, no. I don't think he ever liked me. It was just weird."

Zoe looked up as if thinking. "Hum, didn't you say you had to project a thought about sexy times?"

Karina was regretting having told Zoe so much. "Yeah, so?"

"So?" She rolled her eyes. "Isn't it obvious, Karina? I bet even Satwak got a little different, didn't he?"

Karina shrugged. "He was always weird and distant. No wonder, he had to gain my trust but didn't want me to fall for him or anything."

"You didn't tell me how he survived."

Karina also sat. "I have no clue. Those people have some impressive doctors."

Zoe was thoughtful. "If only we could learn from them..."

"Yeah, but I've heard that was how it started. Lumina went to other places to spread their superiority and ended up taking over the other cities."

"Still, it's a shame. And they're still going to be isolated?"

Karina nodded. "Yes. The Guardians don't know who the new overseer is. For Sian's safety."

Zoe was twisting a lock of hair on her finger. "Do you think it would make any difference if they knew it was Sian? I mean, would they say: 'all right, Lumina is being led by the guy who took over a kingdom less than a year ago. Nah. What are the chances he'll go after any ethereal city?'"

"Very funny, Zoe. Anyway, Lumina is still isolated, other than a special portal to Brighteria. Another portal was made from Brighteria to Siphoria. There's one from there to the Light Gardens."

Her friend stared at her. "And you really want to be a guardian? The jerks who could kill Sian and didn't lift a finger to save you?"

Yeah, it didn't make sense, but at the same time... "I'll get magical training. And teleporters like me are rare."

"Maybe there are a bunch of teleporters in our dimension."

That made sense. "Maybe. But teleporting is not in their destiny."

Zoe sighed. "I guess. I wish I could figure out *my* destiny."

"You will. It can take some time. You could come visit one day, you know? I think Sat finds you cute."

Zoe rolled her eyes. "Sounds tempting. A guy who can read your mind. What's the fun in that? And you know I'm already taken. Plus, I saw that magic, and… I won't lie and say I'm not afraid."

"I'll still come and visit."

"How often?'

"I don't know."

Zoe pointed a finger towards Karina. "Well, figure out something. If you guys are that advanced, find a way to email or text me."

"It's magic, not technology, Zoe."

She shrugged. "Doesn't sound that different to me." Zoe then looked up again. "I'm thinking something. How did Darian pretend to be his brother?"

"I'm not sure exactly how. Cayla told me. Darian's magic is the magic of illusion. He found it I think sitting down and waiting for it to hit him. Incredible, right? I wish inspiration would hit me like that when I had to write essays."

Zoe rolled her eyes. "You have to meditate, not browse the internet."

Karina nodded. "True. Now back to Darian, his illusion clashes with his spell-speaking. He had to choose one."

"He chose the lies."

Karina shrugged. "Well, it is more useful."

Zoe looked at Karina. "And how does Sian disguise himself? Because you said he's talking to the other cities."

"Just a cloak, plus some manipulation in the message."

"Um, cloak. Sounds sexy."

Her friend was into teasing her, but Karina decided to play along and smiled. "He's always sexy."

"True. I bet you prefer him without a cloak. Speaking of which, did you ever see him without his shirt?"

Oh, this was getting worse. "Yeah…"

"What does he look like?"

Desire, sunshine, perfection, tenderness, openness, vulnerability, strength, love. "Uh… Someone who's exercised all his life."

"You can say hot, Karina."

"You asked what he looks like, not what I think about him. I'd think he was hot even if he had a flabby belly."

"But flabby bellies are super hot." They laughed. Zoe then got serious. "And did you guys… already…"

Karina got an empty feeling in her stomach. She knew what her friend was asking but decided to steer the conversation away. "Pacify Lumina? It's a long process."

Zoe nodded. "Long process. I see. And how did you convince your mother to let you go?"

"I brought Sian to talk to them."

Zoe chuckled. "Since when he's an ideal son-in-law?"

"Spell speaker."

"Lucky for you." She then hugged Karina. "I'm going to miss you, my nerdy, kind, supersmart, reading-challenged friend."

"I'll miss you too."

Not only her friend. It was an entire life she was walking away from. It wasn't for a guy. It wasn't for curiosity. It was just that she'd finally found where to make a difference.

Tears ran down Sian's face as he hugged Malena. He'd been to Siphoria to make sure things were settled down and to say goodbye to his friends. Leaving that city was like ripping out a piece of him, especially now, when he finally understood what Malena had been for him.

"Thank you," he said, "for loving me like a mother. Like my mother never did."

"Sian, darling." She broke his hug and took his hand. "There's one thing you need to understand. People don't love like you want them to, or like sometimes you even need them to. They love the way they can. Our lives are screwed up and we love in screwed up ways. Your father loved you. Your mother loved you. I'm sure your brother loves you. Don't shun his love just because it's not the way you think it should be."

"But yours is perfect. Karina's is perfect."

"It might not always be. But don't judge them. Your love is not perfect either."

He remembered everything he'd done to Karina. "Far from perfect. But I'm trying to be better."

"I'm sure you'll do whatever you have to do wonderfully. I've always known you were a good boy."

Tears ran down his face again. She could never know where he was going, what he was going to do. It felt lonely and strange. "I'll come and visit."

"You better!"

Cayla had to come to terms with quite a few things. She should have noticed that Leena had been too eager to show everything to Sian and Darian. Well, she wanted to retire. The Light Gardens also had a lineage system of leadership, and it was quite silly that she hadn't realized what it meant.

Leena's role was temporary. Darian decided to take the seat. Cayla could have decided to stay between Whyland and the Light Gardens, but in the end, she knew that Whyland was changing. Plus, she'd always dreamed of being queen just because she had no idea what else was out there in the world.

Now she wanted to improve her magic. Cayla, like her mother, was a descendent of Gleam Fortress. That meant she would probably take longer to age, and she'd be more powerful than most, but it also meant her magic bloomed later.

Cayla had yet another dream. The Guardians had proven to be the most incompetent interdimensional force. The world needed something better. She thought that perhaps with Nia, Darian, Karina, and a few more, she could start something new. She hadn't told anyone yet, but that was her plan.

The most shocking thing was that Darian had proposed and she'd said yes. But for real, not in some unspecified future. Well, she figured that getting married wouldn't change her life much, and since he insisted...

But the butterflies in her belly told another story. The image staring at her in the mirror had a very complex hairdo with a crown of braids. Her eyes had been lined with dark blue ink. She thought it was weird at first, but now, looking at her image, she liked it.

If they were to do this right, they should be getting married in the Light Gardens, but Sian had been avoiding the ethereal cities, so they did it in Whyland, in the castle, in their garden.

She walked in and saw Darian wearing a red suit, just like he'd done in the first ball they had together. Tears ran down her eyes, and she hoped that the ink was truly waterproof. Her loved ones sat in a circle on the grass. Her mother smiled when she saw Cayla, even if she'd been against this wedding claiming Cayla was too young. Nia held an unwilling Leo, and Talon—it was weird to get used to his new name—tried to distract the boy.

Ayanna was near them. Alessa was there too, looking fierce and amazing as always. Leena looked more emotional than Cayla would have expected. Sian held Karina tight, whispering something in her ear. Karina gestured for him to turn and look, but he kissed her cheek instead.

∼

Karina whispered, "You have to look at the bride!"

"I'm trying to make a point."

Cayla and Darian sat in the middle of the circle. This was similar to Lumina that the couple chose their words.

Cayla said, "I promise to love you, respect you, cherish you, and look at you, at the real you, today, and to renew this promise and this intent with each sunrise."

Darian then repeated that. Those were beautiful words.

"This is nonsense," Sian whispered.

"I think it's beautiful."

"They're promising just for today. I mean, why get married?"

"I think the idea is that every day they have to start again and bring their best."

He had a face. "What if you wake up in a bad mood?"

"You try to remember your vows and treat the other person well, despite the bad mood."

Sian shook his head. "I don't know how it's like where you're from, but in Whyland we promise to love each other forever."

"It doesn't make a difference. People break up all the time." She thought about her parents and tons of other parents. That wasn't a good thought at a wedding.

"Maybe. But when you promise, you mean it." He held her hand. "We'll do it Whyland style."

Uh? And when had he proposed that she didn't remember? When had she ever said yes? She could have asked these questions, she could have teased him, but the truth is that he'd just given her a love declaration.

She smiled. "Whyland style, then."

"Sooner rather than later. Think about it. I'm taking care of that dysfunctional city where more than half the people want to kill me, and I'm doing it for a promise you made for a dude that ended up not dying."

"Hasn't Sat been helpful?"

"Satwak. Say his full name." He was frowning, and she wasn't sure how much of it was teasing.

"It's a complicated name."

Sian widened his eyes. "It's two syllables. You don't call me See."

"Is that what you want?"

"Of course not." He had a playful smirk. "I'm more into Dearest Eternal Love of my Life, Light of the Universe, Owner of My Heart."

"Can I shorten it to Sian?"

Sian waved a hand. "Yeah, ignore my wishes."

She rolled her eyes.

He pointed his finger at her. "But you are. You had no issues marrying him."

How many times would she have to explain it? "I was being threatened."

"Right." He made a high-pitched voice. "Oh, no, you could have upset the Lumina overseer." He stared at her, his voice back to normal. "Well, you are upsetting the Lumina overseer."

Karina scrunched her face. She'd been between there and the Light Gardens, and Sian didn't like it. Too bad, she had her life too.

Darian and Cayla were hugging everybody and it came to Sian and Karina's turn, so they got up. Cayla stopped in front of Sian and extended her hand. "Friends?"

"No way."

Cayla stepped back.

But then, Sian hugged her. "You're my sister now."

"You're my new brother," she replied.

From Cayla's previous dislike of Sian, this was a huge step. Heartwarming. Just not as heartwarming as hugging her friend.

"We'll see each other," Cayla said.

"For sure."

Karina looked at Sian and Darian. They shared a strong embrace.

Sian said, "I love you, little brother. You're one of the best things that happened in my life, and the best brother anyone could ever ask for. Sorry I never told you that before."

Karina looked away because she got the feeling Darian was crying. Maybe Sian was too. Her eyes met Cayla's and they shared a smile.

Karina didn't regret splitting her time between the Light Gardens and Lumina, even if it was uncomfortable having to keep her mouth shut about Sian and her teleporting into the city of light. After one month of training with Anika, she felt that her magic was getting stronger.

In Lumina, things were getting better. The people who'd been in the stasis room were getting medical treatment. Some of them had lost their memories and it had been so long that they were having trouble getting them back.

The attendants were no longer mute, even if it was hard to notice, since most of them were still afraid of speaking. Everyone was terrified of Sian, which made him quite uncomfortable. Slowly he was making friends, but his role was a burden. But if he hadn't been meant to take it, why had he been born with the Lumina affinity magic?

Karina went to the training grounds. Even if Lumina wouldn't take any military action against anyone, Sian didn't want to get rid of their training. It was part of their traditions.

They were still powerful and magnificent. The woman with short purple hair approached Karina. "Want to give it a try?"

Karina felt embarrassed, since her magic was so inferior to everyone there. She was even more embarrassed about her lack of manners. "What's your name?"

"Gia."

"I'm—"

The woman had a half bow. "I know who you are."

Of course. Everyone did. Karina smiled. "Nice to meet you."

"Come give it a try. There's always something to improve."

A lot to improve, in Karina's case, and plus she was already training… But then… why not?

Karina stepped in the grounds. "What do you want me to do?"

She'd been doing a lot of physical preparation with Anika. The girl said that the body had to be ready for the mind. Karina imagined Gia would give her an exercise like that.

But instead of instructions, the woman sent a gigantic metal ball flying in Karina's direction. By pure reflex, she pushed it away. That had been close. Had the woman meant to attack her?

"See?" Gia pointed. "You're doing it wrong."

Well, no kidding, genius. She hadn't even warned Karina. But she decided to be polite. "Why?"

"The problem is that you think you have to use your energy to push the ball. That will get you tired in no time, you could even faint."

Well, yeah, Karina always felt depleted after using her magic. But it was normal, wasn't it? "What energy should I use?"

"Don't feel that it's coming from you, feel as if you were just manipulating the energy around you. Can we try again?"

"All right." Another gigantic ball in her direction, and Karina tried to do what the woman had told her. It was like ten times easier.

"That's a little better. There are a few tricks you still need to learn. You're using less than one percent of your magic, girl."

"How do you know?"

"I can see it."

"Can you tell me some tricks?"

"Sure thing, but it won't do you no good if you don't practice correctly. You need to come here every day if you want to reach even one-third of your potential."

Karina didn't like hyperbolical math statements. If you want to exaggerate, use something less specific than math. "You said I'm using only one percent of my potential. If I were to be thirty-three times stronger, I'd be more powerful than Sian."

"He, he. Sure thing. But he can harness the power of the city. That's a tough one to counter." She laughed. "Like that, eh? Come in the morning. From nine to ten. You need consistency, not long hours."

This was so, so much better than the crappy training Karina had been getting. Of course Anika—and sometimes Leena—did their best. But still, this was a whole different kind of best. She turned around, thoughtful.

"We start tomorrow!" Gia said—or ordered—because she was the scary teacher type. The kind that pushed you to your best.

This was the day Karina decided to move to Lumina and stop her here-and-there nonsense.

Sian still sometimes had troubled dreams. He now understood what Lylah had meant when she'd told him she didn't enjoy being queen. Having power was also responsibility, selflessness.

At least he started to enjoy the city. Slowly they were getting more arts, music, and Sian was getting a hint of normality—if it weren't for the fact that everyone was scared of him. They should be scared of Karina, but she trained alone in the morning so they probably hadn't seen what she could do. He hoped she'd never need any of that. Hoped, but at the same time kept talks with his brother about a new type of Guardians.

The issue was that Lumina had better not get involved in

any of that. They were too powerful. He'd listened to the historical records. Lumina conquering and domination had started hundreds of years before with good intentions. They had the best magicians, the best teachers, the best doctors. Perhaps they'd failed because they considered the other cities inferior.

Sian didn't know what to do. Sharing wisdom with the world was a noble goal, unless it became imposing. If they were to get involved in a society for interdimensional security... Darian said it would be just Karina and him, and still, they had no idea what they were becoming. He and Karina could take an army if they wanted. It was good but at the same time scary.

His other bothersome thoughts were about all the unhappy upper-class citizens now that the attendants had to receive fair wages. The working class now was free, and there was talk about resistance. The only good thing was that he could threaten to unleash the city on them and then they'd all shut up. But this wasn't the right way to do politics. He wasn't sure what the right way was. It was a process. Sian's strategy had always been to make as many allies as possible, but he was just beginning to understand the Luminous, so it was hard. He didn't regret having become Lumina overseer. To refuse it would have been to run from his destiny and from who he was. Plus he was lucky that he had Karina with him, helping him take care of the city.

She rested her head on his bare chest, her presence so calming. His scars no longer made him uncomfortable. They were part of who he was. A sign he'd gone through pain and suffering and had healed. Not that anyone other than Karina ever saw them.

But then, other issues sometimes haunted him. He'd never told anyone, but there was something quite dark and dangerous about his magic. He suspected Karina had felt it, but she, more than anyone, understood he had to use it. If Sian could, he'd never use it again.

Then there was Darloom. It had left Marisia. Perhaps blocking the cave had worked, perhaps no longer having a king serving it made it go away. Who knew? Still, it had gone somewhere. Sian couldn't forget that he'd made a deal with Darloom once; to be king beside Karina. Fine, he was now overseer, but it was pretty much the same. And he got it.

A chill ran down his spine; a reminder that peace was something he'd need to fight constantly to maintain. At least it wasn't boring.

ABOUT THE AUTHOR

Day Leitao lets her characters take her to new, incredible places, and she hopes to bring readers with her too.

She's originally from Brazil and lives in Montreal, Canada.

To learn more about her books, visit her at dayleitao.com

Don't forget to sign up for news, updates, and a free novella at dayleitao.com You'll get *The Spell Speakers*, a prequel novella where you'll learn more about Darian, Cayla, and Sian's past.